MW01165790

Spaced Out

Three Novels of Tomorrow

Judith Merril & C. M. Kornbluth

Edited by Elisabeth Carey and Rick Katze

NESFA Press

Post Office Box 809
Framingham, MA 01701
www.nesfa.org/press
2008

Publication History

Gunner Cade by Cyril Judd (Judith Merril and C. M. Kornbluth) first appeared in *Astounding Science Fiction*, March-May, 1952; Simon and Schuster, 1952.

Outpost Mars by Cyril Judd (Judith Merril and C. M. Kornbluth) first appeared in Galaxy *Science Fiction*, May-July, 1951; Abelard Press, Inc. 1952.

Shadow on the Hearth by Judith Merril, Doubleday and Company, 1950.

"Judith Merril's Novels" by Elisabeth Carey is original to this volume.

Contents

Spaced Out

JUDITH MERRIL'S NOVELS

From the late 1940s to the early 1970s, Judith Merril was a strong formative influence on the development of modern science fiction, as both a writer and as an editor. As an editor, her *Year's Best* series and other anthologies helped to raise literary standards in science fiction and create the "New Wave." As a writer, she gave us "That Only A Mother," "Daughters of Earth," and other thoughtful, provocative, or just plain fun stories.

As a writer who was a;lso a strong womam livng, in the 1940s and 1950s, a life that in the 1960s would be described as 'libeated,' she also gave us many strong characters. They were as often background characters as protagonists, and were there just because Judy Merril assumed that they would be there—not stuck in to make a point, however important. And so "Daughters of Earth" is about strong women because it's about human colonization of space through the lives of one family of women. But Mimi Jnathan, a minor character in *Outpost Mars,* is a strong woman simply because Merril takes it for granted that that's how women are. Or rather, that's how people are—weakness or strenth is just not a function of gender. We take that for granted now; it was less commonplace then. It's part of what makes her stories still readable and enjoyable today, even when the outward trappings of the societies clearly reflect the 1950s. Gladys Mitchell, in *Shadow on the Hearth,* is a 1950s housewife, with the attitudes and assumptions of her time, but she also has both backbone and brains, and quickly learns to cope when she has to step outside her accustomed role.

In *Homecalling and Other Stories*, we collected her short fiction. Now, we bring you three novels—one solo novel, and two collaborations with another giant of early sf, C. M. Kornbluth, under the pen name, "Cyril Judd."

Shadow on the Hearth. This was Judith Merril's first novel, the story of a middle class suburban family struggling to survive a nuclear war. Gladys struggles to keep her family together, safe, and fed, while waiting for word of her husband, and fending off the almost-subtle advances of a neighbor who is the neighborhood's civil defense officer. She's a conventional 1950s suburban, middle-class wife, smart and competent and very respectable, and of all the challenges she faces, realizing that she can't pretend not to take charge or completely shield her sixteen-year-old daughter from the frightening things happening around them are the most alarming. It's a story that's been told many times since, including *Testament*, *The Day After*, and most recently *Jericho*. This is one of the earliest, and remarkably gentle.

Outpost Mars. Sun Lake Colony on Mars is working to break their dependence on Earth and become truly Martian. Unfortunately, they stand in the way of the expansion plans of an especially ruthless businessman and a disgraced politician's hopes of political redemption. Add to the mix a muckraking reporter, a major drug theft, and a new mother who claims her baby was stolen by the planet's mythical bogeymen, the "Martian dwarves," and Tony Hellman, the handsome young doctor who also serves on the Sun Lake Colony's governing council has more stress and excitement than he cares to deal with.

Gunner Cade. This one is an utter romp. Cade is a loyal soldier of the Empire of Man, in the service of the Star of France, until he's left for dead on a battlefield, gets picked up by subversives, and starts getting an education about how things *really* work. Secret cults, mysterious ladies, kind-hearted brothel madams, sexual impurity in high places, corruption in the very *highest* place…It's all a terrible shock, and Cade is struggling to remain alive long enough to have a chance at regaining his mental balance. Becoming involved in rebellion against the Empire of Man is almost an afterthought.

Elisabeth Carey
April, 2008

Gunner Cade

CHAPTER ONE

FAR BELOW the sleeping loft, in ancient cellars of reinforced concrete, a relay closed in perfect silent automaton adjustment; up through the Chapter House, the tiny noises multiplied and increased. The soft whir of machinery in the walls; the gurgle of condensing fluid in conditioners; the thumping of cookers where giant ladles stirred the breakfast mash; the beat of pistons pumping water to the top.

Gunner Cade, consecrate Brother in the Order of Armsmen, compliant student of the Klin Philosophy, and loyal citizen of the Realm of Man, stirred in his sleepbag on the scrubbed plastic floor. He half-heard the rising sounds of the machinery of the House, and recognized the almost imperceptible change in the rhythm of the air blowers. Not quite awake, he listened for the final sound of morning, the scraping noise of the bars at windows and gates, as they drew back reluctantly into the stone walls.

> It is fitting that the Emperor rules.
> It is fitting that the Armsmen serve the Emperor through
> the Power Master and our particular Stars.
> While this is so all will be well, to the end of time.

The words came to his mind without effort, before he opened his eyes. He had not fumbled for them since his sixth year when, between his parents and himself, it had been somehow settled that he would become a Brother of the Order. For at least the six-thousandth time, his day began with the conscious affirmation of Klin.

The bars grated in their grooves, and at the instant, the first light struck through the slits of windows overhead. Cade shivered inside the scanty insulation of his bag and came fully awake, at once aware of the meaning of the chill. This was a Battle Morn.

The air blew steadily stronger and colder from the conditioners, tingling against his skin as Cade slipped from his sleepbag and folded it, deflated, into the precise small package that would fit the pocket of his cloak. Timing each action by the habits of thirteen years, he unbuckled his gunbelt, removed the gun, and closed away the belt and sleepbag in the locker that held his neatly folded uniform. It was by now reflexive action to open the gun and check the charge, then close the waterproof seal.

Battle Morn! With mounting elation, Cade performed each meticulous detail of the morning routine, his body operating like the smooth machine it was, while his mind woke gradually to the new day. He thought vaguely of commoners lolling late in bed, mumbling a morning thought of the Emperor and breaking their fast at a grossly laden table. He thought vaguely of Klin teachers waking with subtle and elaborate propositions that proved what any Gunner feels in his bones. He thought vaguely of his own Star of France, doubtless haggard this morning after a night vigil of meditation on the fitting course.

He thought, too, of the Emperor—the Given Healer; the Given Teacher; the Given Ruler—but, like a gun's blast came the thought: *this is not fitting.*

Guiltily he brought his attention back to the bare room, and saw with dismay that Gunner Harrow still lay in his bag, yawning and stretching.

The indecent gaping was infectious; Cade's mouth opened first with amazement, then to say sharply: "Battle Morn, Brother!"

"How does it find you?" Harrow replied, courteously, unashamed.

"Awake," Cade answered coolly, "and ready for a good death if that is fitting—or a *decorous* life if I am spared today."

The Marsman seemed to miss the reprimand entirely, but he climbed out of his bag, and began to deflate it. What kind of Chapter House did they have on Mars?

"How long till shower?" he asked, unconcerned.

"Seconds," was Cade's contemptuous answer. "Perhaps twenty or thirty."

The Marsman sprang to life with a speed that would have done him credit under other circumstances. Cade watched with disgust as the other Gunner rushed for the wall cabinet and stuffed away his sleepbag, still unfolded not yet fully drained of last night's air. The gunbelt was thrown in on top, and the cabinet door slammed shut, with only an instant left to seal the waterclosures of the gun. Then the ceiling vents opened, and the needle spray showered down and around the room. A cool invigorating stream of water splattered against the naked bodies of the men, cascaded down the three walls of the room, and drained out through the floor vent, leaving just enough dampness for the scouring by novices when the Gunners had left the room.

Cade took his eyes from the Marsman, and tried to tear away his thoughts as well. He watched devoutly while the swirling waters struck each wall in turn, touching his gun to his lips, *For the Teacher,* at the first impact; to his chest, *For the Healer,* at the next; and at the last, the long wall, to his brow, with awe, *For the Ruler, the Emperor.*

He tried not to think of Harrow in the room beside him, saluting the cleansing waters with an unchecked charge in his gun. It was true then, what they said about conditions on Mars. Laxity at any time was bad enough, but to let the peril of sloth pass from the previous day through the purifying waters of a Battle Morn was more than Cade could understand. A novice might meet the shower unprepared; an Armiger might fail to check his charge beforehand; but how did Harrow ever rise to the rank of Gunner? And why was such a one sent to Cade on the eve of battle? Even now, his own Battle Morn meditations were disturbed.

Anger is a peril at all times. And anger is acutely unfitting on Battle Morn before the Klin teacher's lesson. Cade refused to think of it further. The water vents closed and he dressed without regard for the Marsman.

Each garment had its thought, soothing and enfolding: they brought peace.

UNDERSUIT: *like this the Order embraces the Realm.*

SHIRT: *the Order protects the Power Master, slave of the brain, loyal heart of the Realm.*

HOSE: *Armsmen are sturdy pillars; without them the Realm cannot stand, but without the Realm the Order cannot live.*

BOOTS: *Gunners march where the Emperor wills; that is their glory.*

HELMET: *the Order protects the Emperor—the Given Teacher, the Given Healer, the Given Ruler—the brain and life of the Realm.*

CLOAK: *like this the Order wraps the Realm and shields it:*

Again he touched his gun to his lips: *for the Teacher;* to his chest: *for the Healer;* to his brow, with awe: *for the Ruler, the Emperor.*

Briskly, he released the waterclosures, and dropped the gun into the belt on his hip. A gong sounded in the wall, and Cade went to a cabinet for two steaming bowls of concentrate, freshly prepared in the giant mash cookers far below.

"Brother?" Harrow called across the open door.

Silence at this time was customary but not mandatory, Cade reminded himself—and Harrow was new to this Chapter.

"Yes, Brother," he said.

"Are there other Marsmen among us?"

"I know no others," Cade said, and congratulated himself on that fact. "How would it concern you?"

"It would please me," Harrow said formally. "A man likes to be among his own people in time of battle."

Cade could not answer him at first. What sort of talk was this? One didn't call himself a man in the Order. There were novices, Armigers, Gunners, the Gunners Superior, and Arle himself, the Gunner Supreme. They were your brothers, elder or younger.

"You are among your own people," he said gently, refusing to allow himself to be tempted into the peril of anger. "We are your brothers all."

"But I am new among you," the other said. "My brothers here are strangers to me."

That was more reasonable. Cade could still remember his first battle for the Star of France, after he left the Denver Chapter where he spent his youth. "Your brothers will soon be beside you in battle," he reminded the newcomer. "An Armsman who has fought by your side is no stranger."

"That will be tomorrow," Harrow smiled. "And if I live through today, I shall not be here long after."

"Where, then?"

"Back to Mars!"

"How can that be?" Cade demanded. "Mars-born Gunners fight for Earthly Stars. Earth-born Gunners fight for the Star of Mars. That's fitting."

"Perhaps so, Brother; perhaps so. But a letter from my father at home says our Star has petitioned the Emperor to allow him all Mars-born Armsmen, and I would be one of them."

"Your Star is the Star of France," said Cade sharply. He himself had received Harrow's assignment yesterday, sealed by the Power Master, and counter-sealed by the Gunner Supreme. He was silent a moment, then could contain himself no longer. "By all that's fitting," he asked. "What sort of talk *is* this? Why does an Armsman speak of himself as a *man*? And how can you think of your 'own people,' other than your brothers in arms?"

The Mars-born Gunner hesitated. "It's newer on Mars. Six hundred years isn't a long time. We have a proverb—'Earth is changeless but Mars is young.' Families—I am descended from Erik Hogness and Mary Lara who mapped the northern hemisphere long ago. I know my cousins because of that. We all are descended from Erik Hogness and Mary Lara who mapped the northern hemisphere. I don't suppose *you* know anything about your eight-times great-grandfather or what he may have done?"

"I presume," said Cade stiffly, "that he did what was fitting to his station as I will do what is fitting to mine."

"Exactly," said Harrow, and fell silent—disconcertingly resembling a man who had wrung an admission from an opponent and won an argument by it.

Cade went stiffly to the door and opened it, leaving the empty bowls for Harrow to return. The line of Armsmen came in sight down the corridor, and they waited at attention to take their place among the Gunners, marching in silence and with downcast eyes along the route of procession to the lectory.

Seated on the front row of benches, with twenty rows apiece of Armigers and novices behind, Cade was grateful that the Klin Teacher had not yet arrived. It left time for him to dispel the perilous mood of irritation and suspicion. By the time the man did appear, Cade's troubled spirits had resolved into the proper quiet glow of appreciation.

It was fitting to be a Gunner; it was fitting to be a Klin Teacher; they were almost brothers in their dedication. The glow nearly vanished when the man began to speak.

Cade had heard many teachers who'd been worse; it made not a particle of difference in the Klin Philosophy whether it was expounded by a subtle, able teacher or a half-trained younger son of a Star, as this fellow appeared to be; what was fitting was fitting and would be until the end of time. But on a Battle Morn, Cade thought, a senior teacher might have been a reasonable tribute. *The peril of pride,* came as a thought like a gun's blast, and he recoiled. In contrition he listened carefully, marking the youngster's words.

"Since the creation of the worlds ten thousand years ago the Order of Armsmen has existed and served the Emperor through the Power Master and the Stars. Klin says of armed men: 'They must be poor, because riches make men fear to lose them and fear is unfitting in an Armsman. They must be chaste because love of woman makes men love their rulers—the word *rulers* here means, as always, with Klin, the Emperor—less. They must be obedient because the consequence of disobedience is to make men refuse even the most gloriously profitable death.' These are the words of Klin, set down ten thousand years ago at the creation of the worlds."

It was wonderful, thought Cade, wonderful how it had all occurred together: the creation of the worlds, the Emperor to rule them, the Order to serve him and the Klin Philosophy to teach them how to serve. The fitness and beautiful economy of it never failed to awe him. He wondered if this creation was somehow THE Fitness, the original of which all others were reflections.

The Teacher leaned forward, speaking directly to those in the front row. "You Gunners are envied, but you do not envy. Klin says of you Gunners: 'They must be always occupied with fiddling details'—I should perhaps explain that a *fiddle* was a musical instrument; *fiddling* hence means *harmonious,* or *proper.* Another possibility is that *fiddling* is an error for *fitting,* but our earliest copies fail to bear this out—'with fiddling details so they will have no time to think. Let armed men think and the fat's in the fire.'"

Good old Klin! thought Cade affectionately. He liked the occasional earthy metaphors met with in the *Reflections on Government.* Stars and their courts sometimes diverted themselves for a day or two by playing at commoners' life; the same playfulness appeared in Klin when he took an image from the kitchen or the factory. The Teacher was explaining the way Klin's usage of *think* as applied to anybody below the rank of a Star was equated with the peril of pride, and how the homely kitchen-metaphor meant nothing less than universal ruin. "For Klin, as usual, softens the blow."

Irresistibly Cade's thoughts wandered to a subject he loved. As the young Teacher earnestly expounded, the Gunner thought of the grandeur of the Klin Philosophy: how copies of the *Reflections* were cherished in all the Chapter Houses of the Order, in all the cities of all the Stars of

Earth, on sparsely settled Venus, the cold moons of the monster outer planets, on three man-made planetoids, and on Mars. *What* could be wrong with Harrow? How *could* he have gone awry with the Klin Philosophy to guide him? Was it possible that the Teachers on Mars failed to explain Klin adequately? Even commoners on Earth heard Teachers expound the suitable portion of the Philosophy. But Cade was warmly aware that the Armsmen's study of Klin was more profound and pure than the commoners.

"—so I come to a subject which causes me some pain." Cade brought his mind back sharply to the words of the Teacher. This was the crucial part, the thing he had been waiting to hear. "It is not easy to contemplate willful wickedness, but I must tell you that unfit deeds fill the heart of the Star of Muscovy. Through certain sources our Star of France has learned that pride and greed possess his brother to the North. With sorrow he discovered that the Star of Muscovy intends to occupy Alsace-Lorraine with his Gunners. With sorrow he ordered your Superior to make ready for whatever counter-measures may be fit, and it has been done. As you know, this is Battle Morn."

Cade's heart thumped with rage at the proud and greedy Star of Muscovy.

"Klin says of such as the Star of Muscovy: 'The wicked you have always with you. Make them your governors.' *Governors* is used metaphorically, in the obsolete sense of a device to regulate the speed of a heat engine—hence, the passage means that when a wicked person is bent on unfit deeds, you should increase your efforts towards fit and glorious deeds to counter him. There are many interesting images in the *Reflections* drawn from the world of pre-electronic—but that is by the way. I was saying that this is Battle Morn, and that before the sun has set many of you may have died. So I say to all of you, not knowing which will have the fortune: go on your fitting and glorious task without the peril of pride, and remember that there is nobody in the Realm of Man who would not eagerly change places with you."

He stepped down and Cade bowed his head for the thought: *The Klin Philosophy in a Gunner is like the charge in his gun.* It was a favorite of his, saying so much in so little if you had only a moment, but if you had more time it went on and on, drawing beautifully precise parallels for every circuit and element of the gun. But there was no time for that; the Superior, the Gunner Superior to the Star of France, had appeared. He cast a worried little glance at a window, through which the sun could be seen, and began at once:

"Brothers, our intelligence is that one hundred gunners, more or less, are now flying from an unknown Muscovite base to occupy the Forbach-Sarralbe triangle on the border of our Star's realm. Time of arrival—I can only say 'this afternoon or evening' and hope I am correct. The importance of the area is incalculable. It was a top secret until the information evidently got to Muscovy. *There is iron ore in the district.*"

A murmur swept the lectory, and Cade murmured with the rest in astonishment. Iron ore on Earth! Power metal still to be found on the ten-thousand-year-old planet after ten thousand years of mining for the stuff that drove engines and charged guns! All reserves were supposed to have been exhausted four hundred years ago; that was why rust-red Mars had been colonized, and from rust-red Mars for four hundred years had come Earth's iron.

"Enough, Brothers! Enough! Our plan will be roughly the same as that employed in our raid last month on Aachen—two divisions to the front, one in reserve. The first company under me will be based at Dieuze, about forty kilometers south of the triangle. The second company under Gunner Cade will be based at Metz, fifty kilometers west of the triangle. The third company will be in reserve, based at Nancy, seventy kilometers southwest of the triangle. The companies will proceed to their bases in two-man fliers immediately after this briefing.

"After arrival and the establishment of communication, my company and Gunner Cade's will send out air scouts to reconnoiter the triangle. If no enemy action is discovered from the air, scouts will parachute for recon on foot. The orders I will issue from that point on will depend on their reports. Man your fliers and take off at once, Brothers. May your deeds today be fitting and glorious."

Chapter Two

CADE, ICILY CALM, ran from the Chapter House two hundred meters to the flying field. He was not panting when he swung himself easily into his little craft. His fingers flew over the unlabeled switches and dials of the control panel. It had been many years since he'd relied on mnemonic jingles to recall the order and setting of the more than two hundred controls. As the red electronic warmup fog misted from the tail of the flier, his passenger, Armiger Kemble, vaulted in and was immediately slammed back against his uncushioned seat by a 3.25-G take-off .

Paris was a blur beneath them, the Paris that Cade, Denver-born, had seen only from the air and the windows of the Chapter House. Minutes later Reims flashed past to their left. The braking and landing in the square at Metz were as cruel as the take-off. Cade had never spared himself or anybody else on service, though he did not know that he was famous for it.

"Brother," he said to the battered Armiger, "line up the command set on Dieuze and Nancy." To his disgust Kemble juggled with the map, the compass and the verniers of the aiming circle for two minutes until he had laid beams on the fields at the reserve base and the other front-line command post. *The peril of pride,* he guiltily thought, choking down his annoyance. The twelve other ships of his company had landed by then.

"Brother Cade," said the voice of the Superior. "Scouts out!"

"Scouts out, Brother," he said, and waved two flyers aloft. From them a monotonous drone of "No enemy action" began over the command set.

The tune changed after five minutes: "Rendezvous with first company scouts over Forbach. No enemy action."

"Brother Cade," said the Superior, "order your scouts to jump. My fliers will provide cover."

Cade ordered: "Second company scouts—Gunner Arris, take over Gunner Meynall's flier on slave circuit. Brother Meynall, parachute into Forbach for recon on foot. Armiger Raymond, recon Sarreguemines. Armiger Bonfils, recon Sarralbe."

Brothers Meynall, Raymond, and Bonfils reported successful landings. The Gunner in Forbach said, "No commoners about at all. As usual. I'm in the village square headed for the 'phone exchange. No en—" There was the sound of a gun and no further report.

Cade opened the Raymond-Bonfils circuit to the Superior and reserve company and snapped: "Take cover. Forbach is occupied. Gunner Arris return to base with fliers immediately."

The Superior's voice said: "First company fliers return to base immediately. Brothers Raymond and Bonfils, report!"

Armiger Raymond's voice said: "Sarreguemines is empty of commoners. I've taken cover in the basement of a bakery whose windows command the square. I see movement at the windows of a building across the square—the town hall, 'phone exchange, water department and I don't know what else. It's just a village."

"Brother Bonfils, report!"

There was no answer.

"Brother Raymond, stand fast. We shall mount an attack. Hold your fire until the enemy is engaged and then select targets of opportunity. You will regard yourself as expendable."

"Yes, Brother."

"Third Company at Nancy, you are alerted. Second Company and Third Company, rendezvous with First Company in ten minutes, at 10:36 hours, two kilometers south of the Sarralbe town square. Align your fliers for unloading to fight on foot; we shall conduct a frontal assault on Sarralbe and clear it of the enemy. The third company will be on the left wing, the second company will be our center, and the first company will be in the right wing. Gunner Cade, you will detail one flier to amuse the enemy with a parachute attack on the town hall as our skirmishers reach the square. Into action, Brothers!"

"Load!" yelled Cade to his company and they tumbled into their craft. On the slave circuit he took the fliers up in dress-parade style, hurled them to the rendezvous and released the ships for individual landings. The first company was aligned straight as a string to his right, and moments later the third company touched down.

His Armiger Kemble had done a most unsatisfactory job lining up the communications, Cade reflected, but it was not fitting in a Gunner to hold a grievance. "Brother," he said, "I've chosen you to conduct the diversion our Superior ordered."

The youngster straightened proudly. "Yes, Brother," he said, repressing a pleased grin.

Cade spoke into his command set: "Gunner Orris. You will remain here in your flier during the attack, with Armiger Kemble as a passenger. On my signal you will take off and fly over the Sarralbe Town Hall, dropping Brother Kemble by parachute to create a diversion. After dropping him, return your flier to its present position and dismount to join the attack on foot."

The Armiger climbed out of Cade's flier to head for Orris' craft, but hesitated on the ground and turned to brag: "I'll bet I get a dozen of them before they get me."

"Well, perhaps, Brother," said Cade, and this time the grin did break out as the Armiger marched down the line. Cade hadn't wanted to discourage him but the only Muscovite gunman he had a chance of killing before he was picked off in mid-air was their roof spotter. But how could he be expected to understand? Thirty seconds of confusion among the enemy could be vastly more important than killing thirty of their best Gunners.

The clock said 1036; men boiled out of the fliers and formed a skirmish line carefully ragged. The raised right arm of the Superior, far on the right of the line, went down and the brothers began to trudge forward, all with the same solid, deliberate stride...

Cade's eyes were on anywhere but his boots; they were scanning bushes for untoward movements, the ground for new dirt cast up in the digging of a foxhole, trees for unnatural man-sized clumps of foliage among the branches. But somehow he felt his feet in his boots, not painfully but happily. *Gunners march where the Emperor wills; that is their glory.*

Off to the right a gun blasted. The Superior's voice said in his helmet: "Enemy observation post, one novice. We got him but now they're alerted in town."

He told the men flanking him: "Enemy O.P. spotted us. Pass the word, brothers." It murmured down the line. Brothers who had absently let themselves drift into a dress-parade rank noticed it and lagged or heel-and-toed until the line was properly irregular again.

It was done none too soon. Some thirty meters to the left of Cade the excellently-camouflaged lid of a firing pit flipped up as the line passed.

The Muscovite blasted two Armigers with a single shot before he was killed. Defilading fire into a straight rank would have netted him twenty. The wood grew thicker and direct flank contact was lost. "Scouts out," said the Superior's voice, and Cade waved two Gunners forward.

Their eloquent arms were the eyes of the company. One upraised and the company saw possible danger; it halted. The upraised arm down and forward and the company saw safety; it trudged on. Both arms moved forward in a gesture like clasping a great bundle of straw and the company was alarmed by something inexplicable; it inched forward with guns drawn, faces tingling. Both arms beating down like vultures' wings and the company was face-to-face with grinning death; it hurled its fifty bodies to the ground to dodge the whistling scythe.

Grinding himself into the ground while his eyes methodically scanned before him for the well-concealed Muscovite combat patrol that had been harassing them, Cade thought: *It is fitting that we Gunmen serve.* He saw the unnatural movement of a bush and incinerated it. In the heart of the blaze was a black thing that capered and gibbered like a large ape: one more of the enemy charred to nonexistence. His blast had given away his position; automatically he snap-rolled two meters and saw flame blaze from a tree's lower branches to the spot he'd fired from. Before the blast from the tree expired he had answered it.

He thought: *While this is so, all will be well to the end of time.*

The surviving scout's arm went up with an air of finality. The company halted and the scout trotted back to Cade. "Ten meters of scrub and underbrush and then the town. Three rows of four-story stone houses and then the square, as I recall. The underbrush is clear. But those windows looking down on it—!"

"Plunging fire," Cade muttered, and he heard a sharp intake of breath from beside him. He turned to look sternly on the young Armiger with the stricken face, but before he could reprove the lad, he heard Harrow, the Marsman, intervene.

"I hate it too," the Gunner said, and the unexpected note of sympathy broke the youngster completely.

"I can't stand it," he babbled, hysterically. "That feeling you get when it's coming at you from above and all the ground cover in the world won't help—all you can do is run! I can't stand it!"

"Quiet him," Cade said with disgust, and someone led the Armiger away, but not before Cade noted his name. He would deal with it later.

"Brother," Harrow spoke in his ear, earnestly.

"What is it?" Cade snapped.

"Brother, I have an idea." He hesitated, but as Cade turned impatiently away, he rushed on: "Brother, let's give them plunging fire. No one would have to know."

"What are you talking about?" Cade asked blankly. "There aren't any trees high enough or near enough."

The Marsman said wildly: "Cade, don't pretend to me. I can't be the only Gunner who ever thought of it! Who's going to know the difference? I mean—" His throat sealed; he couldn't get the words out.

"I'm glad to see you have some shame left," Cade said disgustedly. "I *know* what you mean." He turned aside and called out: "Bring back the coward Armiger! Now," he went on as soon as the youngster was with them, "I want you to learn for yourself the consequences of submitting to the peril of fear. Your outburst made *Gunner* Harrow propose that we—we fire on the houses from our *fliers.*"

The Armiger looked down at his feet for a long moment and then faced his commander. He said hoarsely, "I didn't know there were people like that, sir. Sir, I should like to request the honor of being permitted to draw fire for our men."

"You have earned no honors," Cade snapped. "Nor does your rank entitle you to privileged requests." He looked meaningfully at the Mars-born Gunner.

Harrow wiped sweat from his face. "I would have got back to Mars," he said bitterly, "back with my own people, if I'd lived through this one."

"You deserve less than this *Gunner* Harrow," Cade pronounced sternly into a sudden listening silence. The firing was momentarily stilled; the enemy was awaiting their action. All the Armsmen of France within hearing distance of the episode had edged closer to be in on the final outcome. Cade seized the moment to impress an unforgettable lesson on his men. He said loudly:

"Klin wrote: 'Always assume mankind is essentially merciful; nothing else explains why crooks are regularly returned to office.' If you know as little of the Philosophy as you do of decency, Brother, I should explain that a *crook* is an implement formerly used by good shepherds and in this case stands, by a figure of speech, for the good shepherd himself. I shall obey Klin's precept of mercy. We need a Gunner to draw fire from the house windows so we can spot those which are—are you listening to me?"

The Mars-born Gunner was mumbling to himself; he looked up and said clearly, "Yes, Brother, I'm listening." But his lips kept moving as Cade went on: "We have to draw fire from the house windows so we can see which are manned, blast them with a volley and take the house in a rush."

"Yes, Brother, I'll draw their fire," said Harrow.

Cade wheeled suddenly, and confronted the rest of his company. "Are you Armsmen," he demanded fiercely, "or commoner kitchen gossips? Back to your posts before the enemy discovers your weakness! And may the fighting scourge your minds of this memory. Such things are better forgotten."

He called the first and third companies on his helmet 'phone and filled them in—saying nothing of the disgraceful episode.

"Well done," the superior told him. "Rush the first row of houses immediately; we have your coordinates and will follow behind after you have secured a house or two."

Harrow's muttering had started again and become loud enough during the conversation to be a nuisance. He was repeating to himself:

"It is fitting that the Emperor rules.
"It is fitting that the Power Master serves him.
"It is fitting that we Gunmen serve the Emperor through
the Power Master and our particular Stars.
"While this is so, all will be well until the end of time."

Cade could not very well rebuke him.

Harrow distinguished himself in drawing fire from the house windows. In such an operation there is the risk that—well, call him the "target"—that the target will walk out in a state of exaltation, thinking more of the supreme service he is rendering than the actual job of rendering it. Cade was pleased and surprised at the desperate speed with which Harrow broke from the end of the wood and sped through the brush, his cloak flaring out behind him, displaying the two wide Gunner's bands at the hem: a new brown one above for France; an old red one below for Mars.

A bolt from one window missed him.

"Mark," snapped the first in a row of picked shots.

A bolt from another window blasted Harrow's left arm, and he kept running and even began to dodge.

"Mark," said the second of the sharp-shooters.

A third window spat fire at the dodging Gunner and hit the same burned arm.

"Mark."

Another bolt from another window smashed his legs from under him.

"Mark."

There was a little surge forward in the line of waiting stormers. Cade threw his arm up, hard and fast. "He's crawling," he said. "They'll finish him off."

From a small and innocent-looking stairwell window fire jetted.

"Mark."

"He's done," said Cade. *"While this is so all will be well…*Marksmen ready; stormers ready. Marksmen, fire. Stormers, charge." He led the way, crashing through the brush, with a torrent of flame gushing over his head: his marksmen, with the initiative of fire, pinning down the Muscovites at their windows—almost all of them. From two unsuspected windows fire blazed, chopping down two of the storming party. They were met with immediate counter-fire from waiting marksmen in the wood. And by then there were ten Gunners in the dead ground against the house wall. With Cade in the lead, the Armsmen of France swarmed down a narrow alley that separated house from house and blasted down a side door.

Like coursing hounds they flowed through the house, burning down five Muscovite Armsmen already wounded by the neutralizing fire from the woods, finding two others dead at their windows. They lost one Armiger of France, to the desperate dying fire of a wounded Muscovite. The house was theirs.

The rest of the company, except for a pair of guards, trudged across the brush and entered.

Cade stationed men at the vital upper windows and sat, panting, on the floor of a bare second-story room. All the rooms were more or less bare. It was probably so through all three villages. He had seen commoners migrating.

Clots of them, oozing slowly along the roads. Their chief people in ground cars, cursing at the foot-sloggers who wouldn't get aside. The carts, piled high with household goods. The sniveling, shrieking children. And yet—and yet—there was a puzzle in it. Not always, but almost always, they knew in advance. The Muscovites, in possession of the great secret of the iron ore, had arrived to find that at least part of the secret was known to the lowliest commoner—enough at least to send him out on the road.

They were into the afternoon now, with nothing to do but wait for the first and third companies. This would last a week, easily: three villages to clear. Perhaps the feint at the city hall—if it came off today—would crumple the Muscovites. And when they got to Sarreguemines there would be Brother Raymond in the cellar—

He sat up with a guilty start. Nobody had checked the cellar in this very house, if it had one, probably because cellars didn't have windows. He got wearily to his feet and limped downstairs to the first floor. There seemed to be no further steps down—and then he saw a gap between the wall and an immense cherry-wood cabinet bare of its dishes and mementos. It creaked open when he tried it and there were his cellar steps with a guttering light at the bottom.

An old, old face, brown and wrinkled and ugly, was peering at him by the flickering light.

"Come up, commoner," he said. "I wish to look at you."

"No, sir," the wrinkled face squeaked in the voice of a woman. "No, sir, I cannot, sir, to my shame. My daughter, the lazy slut, put me and my dear brother down here when the armed men were about to come, for she said she and her great fat husband couldn't be bothered with us. I cannot come up, sir, because my legs won't go, to my shame."

"Then send up your brother, commoner."

"No, sir," the hag squeaked. "My dear brother cannot come up, to my shame. My lazy slut of a daughter and her great fat husband did not leave the right food for him—he suffers from the wasting sickness and he must have the livers of animals every day—and so he died. Are you an armed man, sir?"

"I am a Gunner of the Order of Armsmen, commoner. Did you say you had food down there?" Cade suddenly realized he was ravenous.

"I did, sir, but not the right kind for my dear brother. I have the bottled foods and the foods in boxes and sweet cakes; will you come down, armed man, sir?"

Cade prudently swung the great cherry-wood chest wide open and descended the stairs. The woman lighted his way to a corner with the candle; he expected to find a table or larder, but the light to his disgust flickered on the wasted body of a tall man propped against the cellar wall.

"That's no concern of mine, commoner," he said. "Where is the food? I'll take it and eat it upstairs."

"Armed man, sir, I must unlock three locks on this chest—" she gestured with the candle—"to get you that and my hands are old and slow, sir. Let me pour you a bit for your thirst first, sir. You are truly an armed man, sir?"

He ignored her babble as she poured him cider from a jug. "So that on your hip is a gun, sir? Is it true, sir, that you only have to point it at a person and he is shriveled and black at once?"

Cade nodded, suppressing his irritation with effort. She was old and foolish—but she was feeding him.

"And is it true, sir," she asked eagerly, "that a shriveled and black commoner cannot be told from a shriveled and black armed man?"

That it was impossible to let pass. He struck her mouth, wishing furiously that she would get the food and be done with it. And truly enough she did begin to fumble with the clanking old locks in the dark, but kept up her muttering: "I see it is true. I see it is true. That is what happens when something is true. I call my daughter a lazy slut and she strikes me on the mouth. I call her husband a greedy hog and he strikes me on the mouth. That is what happens—"

Rage is a peril, he told himself furiously. Rage is a peril. He gulped down the cider and repressed an impulse to throw the mug at the old fool's head or smash it on the old fool's floor while she fumbled endlessly with the clanking locks. He bent over to put it precisely on the floor, and toppled like a felled oak.

At once he knew what had happened and was appalled by the stupidity of it. He, a Gunner, was dying, poisoned by a babbling idiot of a commoner. Cade dragged feebly at his gun, and found the squeaking old woman had taken it first. Better to die that way, he thought in agony, though still a shameful horror. He hoped desperately as he felt consciousness slipping away that it would never become known. Some things were better forgotten.

The old woman was standing in front of him, making a sign, a detestable sign he half-remembered, like a parody of something you were dedicated to. And she skipped nimbly up and down the stairs with shrill, bat-like laughter. "I tricked you!" she squealed. "I tricked them all! I tricked my slut of a daughter and her greedy fat husband. I didn't want to go with them!" She stopped at last, grunting with animal effort as she tugged the body of her brother, an inch or less at a time, to the foot of the stairs. Cade's gun was in the waistband of her skirt.

As the last light glimmered out, he thought he saw the deep-etched leather lines of her face close to his. "I wanted an armed man, sir, that's what I wanted. And I have one!"

CHAPTER THREE

PERIL…PERIL…rage is a peril, and vanity, and love of ease… This death was fraught with perils. Cade groaned in the endless dark, and the still-living flesh shrank with revulsion as the evil vision persisted and his limbs were logs of stone.

To come to this end, this useless end! He who had lived decorously, who had served fittingly, he, a sturdy pillar of the Emperor, Gunner Cade! *This end is not fitting!* He would have cried out bitterly, but his lips were icy barriers, frozen shut. He could not breathe a word of protest or command.

And still his heart beat pitilessly, pumping gall and fury through his veins.

Rage is a peril. Cade turned his anger inward, seeking to bludgeon his spirit into a fit frame of mind before death came. *Armsmen march where the Emperor wills. Peril flees in the face of fitting service.*

Two visions filled his inner eye. He turned from the ancient ugly face of evil to the fair countenance of service and found at last the fitness that he sought. This death was proper. If She appeared, then all was well and would be till the end of time, for She came only at the last to the Armsman who marched where the Emperor willed and died in the service of his Star.

Then this was a fitting end, and the perils of rage and vanity had been only a trial. He looked again upon the ugly grinning face and found it had lost all power over him. The pure features of The Lady floated above and behind it and exaltation coursed through him as his heart beat on.

The heart beat on, and it was fitting, but it was not the end. The serene countenance of The Lady bent over him, and yet he lived. All

Armsmen knew She came only at the last, and only to those who were fitted, yet...

He lived. He was not dead. The frozen lips moved as he muttered, "Vanity is a peril." He was alive, and the lined old leather face was only a hag he had seen before; the lady was a flower-faced commoner girl, beautiful to look on, but soullessly mortal.

"Very well," the crimson lips said clearly, not to him, but across his recumbent body to the hag. "Leave us now. They will be waiting for you in the chamber."

"The armed man lives," the old voice rasped in reply. "I served the armed man well and he still lives. My slut of a daughter would never believe I could do it. She left me behind for dead, she and her greedy..."

"Leave us now!" The younger woman was dressed in the gaudy rough cloth of a commoner, but her voice betrayed her habit of command. "Go to the chamber, and go quickly, or they may forget to wait."

Cade shuddered as the pincer fingers of the hag creased the flesh of his forearm. "He lives," she said again, and chuckled. "The armed man lives and his skin is warm." Her touch was a horror. Not as the touch of woman, for there was nothing womanish about her; she was past the age of peril. But his skin crawled as with vermin at the unclean fingering. He lashed out to strike her arm away, and discovered his hands were bound. The old woman shuffled slowly away toward a door, and while the young one watched her go, he pulled against the bonds, testing his strength.

Then the hag was gone, and he was alone with the young female commoner, who looked most unfittingly like a vision of glory, and spoke most presumptuously like a man of power.

The bonds were not too tight. He stopped pulling before she could discover that he might free himself.

She was watching him, and perversely he refused to look at her. His eyes took in every detail of the featureless room: the unbroken elliptical curve of the ceiling and walls; the curved door, fitting into the shape of the wall, and almost indistinguishable from it; the bed on which he lay; a table beside him where the girl's long clean fingers played with a vial of colored fluid.

He watched, while she idly turned the cork in the vial to expose the needle end. He watched while she plucked a swab of cotton from a bowl, and doused it in colorless fluid from the only other object in the room, a small bottle on the table. He kept watching, even when the girl began to speak, his gaze obstinately fastened on her hands, away from the perilous beauty of her face.

"Cade," she said urgently. "Can you hear me? Can you understand what I tell you?" There was no command in her voice now; it was low-pitched and melodious. It teased his memory, tugged at him till he stiffened with the remembrance. Only once before had a woman called him by his Armsman's given name. That was the day he entered the Order, before he took his vows. His mother had kissed him, he remembered now, kissed him, and whispered the new name softly, as this girl was saying it. Since that day, his eleventh birthday, no woman had dared to tempt him to peril with a familiar address.

He lay still, thrusting aside the memory, refusing to reply.

"Cade," she said again. "There's not much time. They'll be coming soon. Can you understand me?"

The hands on the table moved, put down the needle and the swab, and floated toward him. She placed her palms on his cheeks, and turned his face up toward hers. Cade could not remember, even from childhood, the touch of hands like these. They were silken, but smooth—soft, resilient, unbelievably good to feel. They felt, he thought—and blushed as he thought—like the billowing stuff of the Emperor's ceremonial robe, when it brushed his face as he knelt at devotions on Audience Day.

This was no Audience Day. The hands of a commoner were on him and contact with any female was forbidden. The blood receded from his face, and he shook his head violently, releasing himself from the perilous touch.

"I'm sorry," she said, "I'm sorry, Armsman, sir." Then, incredibly, she laughed. "I'm sorry I failed to address you properly, Sir, and profaned your chastity with my touch. Has it occurred to you that you are in trouble? What do you place first? The ritual of your Order, or your loyalty to the Emperor?"

"Armsmen march where the Emperor wills," he intoned. "That is their glory. Armsmen are sturdy pillars; without them the Realm cannot stand, but without the Realm the Order cannot…"

Boots, he thought. *Hose.* They were gone. He lifted his head a little, and pain stabbed at the back of his neck as he did so, but before he dropped back, he saw it all: garish crimson-patterned pajamas of a commoner; soft-sole sandals of a city-worker. *No boots, no hose, no cloak, no gun!*

"What unfit place is this?" he exploded. "In the name of the Order of which I am a member, I demand that I be released and my gun returned before…"

"Quiet, you fool!" There was something in the command that stopped him. "You'll have them all here if you shout. Now listen quickly, if there's still time. You are the captive of a group that plots against the Emperor. I cannot tell you more now, but I am instructed to inject you with a substance which will…"

She stopped suddenly, and he too heard the steady footsteps coming nearer from—where? A corridor outside?

Something pressed against his lips, something smooth and slippery.

"Open your mouth, you idiot! Swallow it, quick! It will…"

The door opened smoothly from the wall, and the footsteps never lost a beat. They advanced to the center of the room, and stopped precisely, while their maker stared about him with an odd bemusement.

"I seek my cousin," he announced, to no one in particular.

"Your cousin is not here," the girl answered smoothly. "I am the helper of your cousin, and I will take you to him." Three steps took her to the rigidly erect figure, and she touched him lightly on the nape of the neck. "Follow me," she commanded.

With no change of expression on his pale face, the man turned and went after her, his uncannily steady footsteps marking time toward the door. But before they got there, it opened again, and a sharp-featured, worried face peered in. The newcomer was small and wiry, dressed in the grey uniform of the Klin Service, tunic belted properly over the creased trousers; domed hat set squarely on his head, boot-wraps neatly wound around his calves, he was breathing hard, and he closed the door hastily behind him, leaning against it till he regained composure.

"Here is your cousin," the girl said coldly. "He will take you in charge now."

Lying still on the bed, Cade instinctively stopped struggling with the bonds on his wrists, and let his eyelids drop closed, just as the man in grey looked toward him and asked:

"How is he? Any trouble?"

"He's no trouble," the girl's tone was contemptuous. "He's just coming to."

"Good." Cade heard the sharp intake of breath, and then the nervous edginess went out of the man's voice. "I am your cousin," he said evenly. "You will come with me."

"You are my cousin," answered the toneless voice of the sleepwalker. "I am to report that my mission is accomplished. I have succeeded in killing…"

"Come with me now. You will make your report in…"

"…killing the Deskman In Charge of…"

"…in another room. You will report to me priv…"

"…of the third district of Klin Serv…"

"…privately. In another room."

Cade let his eyelids flicker open enough to observe the agitation of the man in grey as the droning report went on unmindful of the efforts at control.

"…Service. Am I to destroy myself now? The mission is successfully accomplished." It stopped at last.

And not a moment too soon. Cade's hands, now free, were safely at rest again when the man in grey turned back to look at him.

"Seems to be all right still," Cousin said stiffly, surveying him, Deliberately, Cade let his eyelids flutter. "He's coming out of it though. I better get this fellow out of the way."

"Perhaps you'd better." The girl's voice now expressed infinite disgust. "Is he one of yours?"

"No, I'm just taking his report. Larter put him under."

"Larter's new," she admitted, and fell silent.

"Well…" There was a moment's embarrassed silence, and Cade let his eyes open all the way, to find Cousin standing, hesitant, in the doorway. "Maybe I better stay around. He's a Gunman, you know. He might…"

"I said I can handle him," she replied. "Suppose you take care of your man before he gets…*watch out!*"

The sleepwalker's eyes were large and brilliant, fascinated by the needle on the table. He saw Cade, stretched out on the bed, and sudden animation flooded his face.

"Don't let them do it to you!" he screamed. "Don't let them touch you! They'll make you like me."

While the other man stood ashenfaced and horrified, the girl acted so swiftly that Cade might almost have admired her, if it were possible to use the word in connection with a female commoner. She was across the small room, and back again with the needle in her hand even as the man screamed his warning to Cade. Before the commoner could lift his arm to brush it aside, she drove the needle home, and the plunger after it.

"S-s-s-s-t!"

The man in grey was ready when she hissed at him.

"You will come with me," he intoned. "You will come with me now. You will come with me."

Cade had seen hypnotists at work before, but never with the aid of a drug so swift as this. He felt the capsule the girl had given him getting warm and moist between his lips. Horror seized him, but he waited as he knew he must till the door was closed behind those inhumanly even footsteps.

He knew exactly how fast the girl could move. *Gunners are sturdy pillars. It is fitting that we serve.* His timing was perfection itself as he spat the dangerous pill from his mouth and leaped from the bed. She had hardly time to turn from the door before his fist caught her a round blow on the side of the head, and she crumpled silently to the floor.

Chapter Four

He had to get out of here.

He had to get back to the Chapter House. He looked at the girl, sprawled on her face on the floor, and was uncomfortably aware of the feel of the rough commoner clothes against his own skin, and then acutely conscious of a blank feeling on his right hip, where his gun should be.

The Klin Philosophy in a Gunner is like the charge in his gun.

He remembered, and shuddered as he remembered, the awful calmness with which she had admitted plotting against the Emperor. *It is fitting that the Emperor rules. While this is so, all will be well till the end of time.*

Cade took his eyes from the crumpled figure of the girl and examined the strangely featureless room once more. There was nothing new to be seen. He approached the inconspicuous door. Beyond it, there was a way out. This place of horrors, whatever and wherever it was, would have to be burned from the face of the earth, and the sooner he escaped the sooner it would happen. Without pride but with solid thankfulness he was glad that he, a full Gunner, was here instead of a novice or an Armiger.

Beyond the door was an empty corridor whose only purpose seemed to be the connection of the featureless room with other rooms fifty meters away. He was suddenly sure that he was underground. There were six doors at the end of the fifty-meter corridor, and he heard voices when he listened at five of them. Calmly he opened the sixth and walked into an empty room about ten by twenty meters, well-lit, equipped with simple benches and a little elevated platform at one end. Along one wall were three curtained booths whose purpose he could not fathom. But he dived into one with desperate speed at the sound of approaching voices.

The booth was in two sections separated by a thin curtain. In the rear section, against the wall, you could look out and not be looked in on. It was an arrangement apparently as insane as the grey, egg-shaped room, but it was a perfect observation post. Through the gauze-like inside curtain and the half-drawn, heavier outside curtain, he saw half a dozen commoners enter the place, chatting in low voices. Their clothes were of the usual cut, but a uniform drab brown instead of the ordinary gaudy particolor.

The drab-clad commoners fell silent and seated themselves on a front bench as others in more customary clothing began to straggle in. There were about fifty of them. One of the front-benchers rose and, standing in front of the little stage, did something that Cade recognized; he made the same detestable sign with which the old poisoner had mocked him. Watching carefully, the Gunner saw that it was an X overlaid with a P. The right hand touched the left shoulder, right hipbone, right shoulder, left hipbone, and then traced a line up from the navel to end in a curlicue over the face. It was manifestly a mockery of the Gunner's ten-thousand-year-old ritual when donning his gun. Cade coldly thought: *they'll pay for that.*

All the seated commoners repeated the sign, and the standing man began to speak, in a resonant, well-trained voice: "The first of the first of the good Cairo." He began making intricate signs involving much arm-waving. It went on for minutes, and Cade quickly lost interest, though the seated commoners were, as far as he could make out, following raptly. At last the commoner said: "That is how you shall be known. The first of the first."

Idiotically, twenty commoners from the back benches got up and filed out. Cade was astonished to see that some of them were silently weeping.

The speaker said when they had left: "The first of the first of the good Cairo in the second degree," and the lights went out, except for a blue spot on the platform. The speaker, standing a little to one side, went through the same signs as before, but much more slowly. The signs were coordinated with a playlet enacted on the stage by the other drab-clad commoners. It started with the speaker spreading his palms on his chest and an "actor" standing along in the center of the platform. Both speaker and actor then made a sweeping gesture with the right hand waist-high and palm down, and a second actor crawled onto the platform…and so on until the first actor, who had never moved, laid his hand successively on the heads of six persons, two of them women, who seemed pleased by the gesture.

About midway through the rigmarole Cade suddenly realized where he was and what it was all about. He was in a Place of Mystery! He knew little about the Mystery Cults. There were, he recalled, four or five of them, all making ridiculous pretensions to antiquity. Above all, they were ridiculous when you thought of them: commoners' institutions where fools paid to learn the "esoteric meaning" of gibberish phrases, mystic gestures and symbolic dramas. Presumably a few clever souls had made a good thing of it. They were always raiding each other for converts, and often with success. Frequenters of Mysteries were failures, stupid even for commoners, simply unable to grasp the propositions of the Klin Philosophy.

There were—let's see—the Joosh Mystery, which had invented a whole language called something like Hibber; the Scientific Mystery, which despised science and sometimes made a little trouble at the opening of new hospitals; and there were others, but he couldn't recall anything called the Cairo Mystery.

But it was frightening. If they could swallow the Mysteries, these weak-minded commoners could accept *anything* else—even a plot against the Realm of Man.

The lights were on again and the ridiculous proceedings outside apparently were drawing to a close when two more commoners entered. One of them was the man in grey—"Cousin."

He murmured something to the drab-clad speaker—Cade could guess what. The Gunner burst from the booth toward the door at a dead run.

"Stop him!"

"Sacrilege!"

"A spy!"

"Get him! Get him!"

But of course they didn't. They just milled and babbled while Cade plowed through them, made the door—and found it locked.

"Cousin" announced loudly as Cade turned his back to the wall, "Seize him, beloved. It is a spy trying to steal our most secret rituals."

"He's lying," yelled Cade. "I am Gunner Cade of the Order of Armsmen. My Star is the Star of France. Commoners, I command you to open the door and make way for me."

"A ridiculous pose, spy," said Cousin smoothly. "If you are a Gunner, where is your gun? If you are of the Star of France *what are you doing here in Baltimore?*"

The commoners were impressed. Cade was confused. *In Baltimore?*

"Bear him down, my beloved!" shouted Cousin. "Bear down the spy and bring him to me!" The commoners muttered and surged and Cade was buried beneath their numbers. He saw the keen face of "Cousin" close to him, felt the stab of a needle in his arm. For the first time, he wondered how long he had been drugged. *Baltimore!* Of course, the Mysteries were world-wide. He could as easily have been in Zanzibar by now, or his native Denver, instead of France…or Baltimore.

There was no doubt about it; the Mysteries would have to be suppressed. Up to now they had been tolerated, for every Mystery solemnly claimed it was merely a minor auxiliary of the Klin Philosophy and that all adherents were primarily followers of Klin. Nobody had ever been fooled—until now.

"He'll be all right now," said Cousin. "Two of you pick him up and carry him. He won't struggle any more."

Gunners march where the Emperor wills; that is their glory. Cade struck out violently with arms and legs at once, as the commoners attempted to lift him from the floor. Nothing happened—nothing except that they lifted him easily and carried him out of the big room. *Vanity is a peril.* An emotion flooded Cade, an unfamiliar feeling that identified itself with nothing since earliest childhood. He was frog-marched down the corridor, ignominiously helpless in the hands of two commoners, and understood that what he felt was shame.

They carried him into the featureless room again, and strapped him to the bed on which he had awakened—how long?—before. He heard "Cousin" say: "Thank you my beloved, in the name of the good Cairo," and the door closed. Rage drove out shame and vanity both as a woman's voice said clearly: "You bloody fool!"

"He is, my dear," said "Cousin" unctuously. "But quite clever enough for us. Or he will be shortly, when he understands how to use the limited intelligence his Order has left him." Gleeful satisfaction trickled through the man's voice. "He is quite clever enough—he knows how to kill. And he is strong—strong enough to kill. Let me see the bruise he gave you…"

"Take your busy little hands off me, Cousin. I'm all right. Where will you start him from?"

"He can come to in any park; it doesn't matter."

"If he fell off a bench he might be arrested. Someplace with a table for him to lean on—?"

"You're right. We could dump him at Mistress Cannon's! How's that? A chaste Gunner at Mistress Cannon's!"

The girl's laughter was silvery. "I must go now," she said.

"Very well. Thank you, my beloved, in the name of the good Cairo." The door closed.

Cade felt his shoulders being adjusted on the table where he lay. He looked at grey nothingness. There was a click and he was looking at a black spot.

"Cousin's" voice said: "You notice that this room has little to distract the attention. It has no proper corners, no angles, nothing in the range of your sight for your eye to wander to. Either you look at that black dot or you close your eyes. It doesn't matter which to me. As you look at the black dot you will notice after a while that it seems to swing toward you and away from you, toward you and away from you. This is no mechanical trickery; it is simply your eye-muscles at work making the dot seem to swing toward you and away, first toward you and then away. You may close your eyes, but you will find it difficult to visualize anything but the dot swinging toward you and away, first toward you and then away. You can see nothing but the dot swinging toward you and away…"

It was true; it was true. Whether Cade's eyes were open or closed, the black dot swung and melted at the edges, and seemed to grow and swallow the greyness and then melt again. He tried to cling to what was fitting—*like this the Order wraps the Realm and shields it*—but the diabolical hypnotist seemed to be reading his thoughts.

"Why fight me, master Cade? You have no boots. You have no hose. You have no shirt. You have no cloak. You have no gun. Only the dot swinging toward you and away; why fight me; why fight the dot swinging toward you and away? Why fight me? I'm your friend. I'll tell you what to do. You have no boots. You have no hose. You have no cloak. You have no gun. Why fight your friend? You only have the dot swinging toward you and away. Why fight me? I'll tell you what to do. Watch the dot swinging towards you and away…"

He had no boots. He had no hose. He had no cloak. He had no gun. Why fight his friend? That girl, that evil girl had brought him to this. He hated her for making him, a Gunner—but he was not a gunner, he had no gun, he had nothing, he had nothing.

"You don't know. You don't know. You don't know. You don't know. You don't know. You don't know. You don't know."

The self-awareness of Cade was no longer a burning fire that freed him from his scalp to his toes. It was fading at his extremities, the lights going out in his toes and fingers and skin, retreating, retreating.

"You will go to the palace and kill the Power Master with your hands. You will go to the palace and kill the Power Master with your hands."

He would go... his self-awareness, a dim light in his mind watched it happen and cried out too feebly. He would go to the palace and kill the Power Master with his hands. Who was he? He didn't know. He would go to the palace and kill the Power Master with his hands. Why would he? He didn't know. He would go to the palace and kill the Power Master with his hands. He didn't know. The spark of ego left to him. watched it happen and was powerless to prevent it.

Chapter Five

Blackness and a bumping...rest and a sensation of acceleration...a passage of time and the emergence of sounds...a motor, and wind noise, and voices.

Laughter.

"Will he make it, do you think?"

"Who knows?"

"He's a Gunner. They can break your back in a second."

"I don't believe that stuff."

"Well, look at him! Muscles like iron."

"They pick 'em that way."

"Naw, it's the training they get. A Gunner can do it if anybody can."

"I don't know."

"Well, if he doesn't, the next one will. Or the next. Now we know we can do it. We'll take as many as we need."

"It's risky. It's too dangerous."

"Not the way we did it. The old lady came along with him."

A jolt.

"You've got to walk him to Cannon's."

"Two blocks! And he must weigh—"

"I know, but you've got to. I'm in my greys. What would a Klin Service officer be doing in Cannon's?"

"But—oh, all *right*. I wonder if he'll make it?"

Lurching progress down a dark street, kept from falling by a panting, cursing blur. A dim place with clinking noises and bright-colored blurs moving in it.

"E-e-easy, boy. Steady there—here's a nice corner table. You like this one? All righty, into the chair. Fold, curse you. *Fold.*" A dull blow in the stomach. "Tha-a-at's better. Two whiskies, dear."

"What's the matter witcha friend?"

"A little drunkie. I'm gonna leave him here after I have my shot. He always straightens up after a little nap."

"Yeah?"

"Yeah. I don't wanta see any change out of this, dear."

"Thass different."

"Back so quick, dear?"

"Here's ya whiskey."

"Righto. Mud in your eye and dribbling down your left cheek, dear. You hear me, fella? I'm going bye-bye now. I'll see you on the front page. Haw! I'll see you on the front page!" The talking blur went away and another, brighter-colored one came.

"Buy me a drink? You're pretty stiff, ain't you? Mind if I have yours? You look like you got enough. I'm Arlene. I'm from the south. You like girls from the south? What's the matter with you, anyway? If you're asleep why don't you close your eyes, big fella? Is this some kind of funny, funny joke? Oh, fall down dead. Comic!"

Another bright-colored blur: "Hello; you want company? I noticed you chased away Arlene and for that I don't blame you. All she knows is 'buy-me-a-drink'; I ain't like that. I like a nice, quiet talk myself once in a while. What do you do for fun, big fella—follow the horses? Play cards? Follow the wars? I'm a fighting fan myself. I go for Zanzibar. That Gunner Golos—man! This year already he's got seventeen raids and nine kills. That's what you call a Gunner. Hey, big fella, wanna buy me a drink while we talk? Hey, what's the matter with you anyway? Oh, cripe. Out with his eyes open."

The blur went away. Vitality began to steal through sodden limbs, and urgent clarity flashed through the mind. *Go to the Palace and kill the Power Master.* The hands on the table stirred faintly and the mind inside whirred into motion, tabulating knowledge with easy familiarity.

You killed people with your hands by smashing them on the side of the neck with the side of the hand below the little finger—sudden but not positive. If you had time to work for thirty seconds without interruption you took them by the throat and smashed the tracheal cartilage with your thumbs.

Go to the Palace and kill the Power Master with your hands.

One hand crawled around the emptied whiskey glass and crushed it to fragments and powder. If you come up from behind you can break a back by locking one foot around the instep, putting your knee in the right place, and falling forward as you grasp the shoulders.

A gaudily dressed girl stood across the table. "I'm going to buy you a little drink, big fella. I won't take no for an answer. I got it right here."

His throat made a noise which was not yet speech, and his hands lifted off the table as she stood beside him with a small bottle. His arms would not lift more than an inch from the table. The drink in his mouth burned like fire.

"Listen to me, Cade," said the girl into his ear. "No scenes. No noise. No trouble. As you come to just sit still and listen to me."

Like waking up. Automatically the morning thought began to go through his mind. *It is fitting that the Emperor rules. It is fitting that the Power Master—*

"The Power Master!" he said hoarsely.

"It's all right," said the girl. "I gave you an antidote. You're not going to—do anything you don't want to."

Cade tried to stand but couldn't.

"You'll be all right in a couple of minutes," she said.

He saw her more clearly now. She was heavily made up, and the thick waves of her hair reflected the bright purple of her gossamer-sheer pajamas. That didn't make sense. Only the starborne wore sheer; commoners' clothes were of heavy stuffs. But only commoner females wore pajamas; starborne ladies dressed in gowns and robes. He shook his head, trying to clear it, and tore his eyes from the perfection of her body, clearly visible through the bizarre clothing.

Following his eyes, she flushed a little. "That's part of the act," she said. "I'm not."

Cade didn't try to understand what she was talking about. Her face was incredibly beautiful. "You're the same one," he said. "You're the commoner from that place."

"Lower your voice," she said coolly. "And this time, *listen* to me."

"You were with them before," he accused her. His speech was almost clear. His arms worked all right now.

"Not really. Don't you understand? If you'd swallowed the capsule I gave you in the hypnosis room, you'd never have gone under. But you had to bash me and make it on your own. See how far you got?"

She was right about that. He hadn't succeeded in getting out of the place.

"All right," she went on, when he didn't reply. "Maybe you're going to be reasonable after all. You're feeling better, aren't you? The—compulsion is gone? Try to remember that I came after you to give you the release drug."

Cade found he could move his legs. "Thank you for your assistance," he said stiffly. "I'm all right now. I have to get to—to the nearest Chapter House, I suppose, and make my report. I…" It went against all training and was perhaps even disobedient, but she *had* helped him. "I will neglect to include your description in my report."

"Still spouting high-and-mighty?" she said wearily. "Cade, you still don't understand it all. There are things you don't know. You can't…"

"Give me any further information you may have," he interrupted. "After that may it please the Ruler we two shall never meet again."

The words surprised him, even as he spoke them. Why should he be willing to protect this—creature—from her just punishment? Very well, she had helped him; that was only her duty as a common citizen of the Realm. He was a sworn Armsman. There was no reason to sit here listening to her insolence; the City Watch would deal with her.

"Cade…" She was giggling. That was intolerable. "Cade, have you ever had a drink before?"

"A drink? Certainly I have quenched my thirst many times." She was unfitting, upsetting, and insolent as well.

"No, I mean a drink—a strong alcoholic beverage."

"It is forbidden…" He stopped, appalled. *Forbidden!…for love of woman makes men love their rulers less…*

"See here, commoner!" he began in a rage.

"Oh, *Cade!* Now you've done it. We've got to get out of here." Her voice changed to a nasal wheedle. "Let's get out of this place, honey, and come on home with me. I'll show you a real good time—"

She was cut off by the arrival of a massive woman. "I'm Mistress Cannon," said the newcomer. "What're you doing here, girlie? You ain't one of mine."

"We was just leaving, honest—wasn't we, big fella?"

"*I* was," said Cade; he swayed as he rose to his feet. The girl followed, sticking close to him.

Mistress Cannon saw them grimly to the door. "If you come back, girlie," she said, "I may wrap a bar stool around your neck."

Outside, Cade peered curiously down the narrow darkness of the city street. How did commoners get places? There was no way even to orient himself. How had they expected him to get to the Palace?

He turned abruptly to the girl. "What city is this?" he demanded.

"Aberdeen."

That made sense. The ancient Proving Grounds where he himself and all the Armsmen for ten thousands of years had won their guns in trial and combat. The city of the Palace, the awesome Capitol of the Emperor himself. And in the Palace, the High Office of the Power Master, the grim executive.

"There is a Chapter House," he remembered. "How do I get there?"

"Gunner, understand me. You aren't going to any Chapter House. That's the best and quickest way to get yourself killed."

A typical commoner's reaction, he thought, and found himself saddened to have had it from her. She had, after all, incurred some risk in defying the plotters.

"I assure you," he said kindly, "that the prospect of my eventual death in battle does not frighten me. You commoners don't understand it, but it is so. All I want to do is get this information into the proper hands and resume my fitting task as Gunner."

She made a puzzling, strangled noise and said after a long pause: "That's not what I meant. I'll speak more plainly. You had an alcoholic drink tonight—two of them, in fact. You're not accustomed to them. You are what is known, among us commoners—" She paused again, swallowing what seemed inexplicably like laughter. "—among us commoners as blasted, birdy, polluted, or drunk. I'll be merciful and assume that your being blasted, birdy, polluted, or drunk accounts for your pompous stupidity. But you are not going anywhere by yourself. You're going to come with me, because that's the only safe place for you. Now please stop being foolish." Her face was turned up to his, pleading, and in the wandering rays of light from a distant streetlamp, even under the thick coating of cosmetics she seemed more than ever the perfect likeness of The Lady, the perfection of womanhood that could never be achieved by mortal females. Her hand slipped easily around his arm, and she clung to him, tugging at him, urging him to follow her.

Cade didn't strike her. He had every reason to, and yet, for some reason he could not bring himself to shake her off as he should have done, to throw her to the ground, and leave her and be rid of her peril forever. Instead he stood there, and the flesh of his arm crawled at the soft touch of her hand through the commoner's cloth he wore.

"If you have nothing more to tell me," he said coldly, "I'll leave you now." They were at a corner; he turned up the side street and noticed that there were brighter lights and taller buildings ahead.

The girl didn't let go. She ran along at his side, holding on, and talking in a furious undertone, "I'm trying to save your life, you bloody idiot. *Will* you stop this nonsense? You don't know what you're getting into!"

There was a watchman standing across the street, on the opposite corner, a symbol of familiar security in immaculate Service grey. Cade hesitated only an instant, remembering where he had last seen that uniform desecrated. But surely, surely, that was not cause enough to lose all faith.

He turned to the girl at his side. The touch of her hand was like fire against his arm. "Leave me now," he told her, "or I cannot promise for your safety."

"Cade, you *mustn't!*"

That was intolerable. *Love of woman*, he thought again, and shook off her arm as he would have brushed away an insect.

He strode out into the street. "Watchman!"

The man in Greys lolled idly on his corner.

"Watchman!" Cade called again. "I desire to be directed to the Chapter House of the Order of Armsmen."

"Your desires are no concern of mine, citizen."

Cade remembered his commoner's clothing, and swallowed his ire. "Can you direct me …sir?"

"If I see fit. And if your purpose is more fitting than your manner. What business have you there?"

"That is no concern…" He stopped himself. "I cannot tell you…sir. It is an affair of utmost privacy."

"Very well, then, citizen," the Serviceman laughed tolerantly. "Find your own way…privately." He was looking past Cade, over the Gunner's shoulder. *"She* with you?" he asked with alerted interest.

Cade turned to find the girl right behind him again.

"No," he said sharply.

"OK, girlie," the watchman demanded. "What're you doing out of the district?"

"The district…" For the first time, Cade saw the girl fumble and falter. "What do you…?"

"You know what I mean. You're not wearing that garter for jewelry, are you, girlie. You know you can't solicit outside the district. If you was with this citizen, now…" He looked meaningfully at Cade.

"She is *not* with me," the Gunner said firmly. "She followed me here, but…"

"That's a dirty lie," the girl whined, suddenly voluble. "This fella picks me up in a bar, we was in Cannon's place, you can ask anybody there, and he kicks up such a rumpus, they tossed us out, and then he says we're goin' to his place, and then we get out here to the corner and all of a sudden he remembers something else he wants to do, and leaves me flat. These guys that come in and get loaded and then don't know *what* they want…!" She wound up with a note of disgust.

"How about it, citizen? Was she with you?"

"She was not," Cade said emphatically. He was staring at the garter the Serviceman seemed so concerned about. It was a slender chain of silver links fastened high on the girl's thigh, pulling the thin folds of her pajamas tight against her flesh.

"Sorry, girlie," the Watchman said, firmly but not unkindly. "You know the rules. We're going to the Watch House."

"There, you see?" She turned on Cade in a fury. "See what you did? Now they'll cage me for soliciting, and I can't pay, so it means sitting it out in a cell, all on account of you don't know what you want. Come on, now, admit it how you made me come with you. Just tell him, that's all I ask."

Cade shook her off with disgust, "You were following me," he said. "I told you I'd keep you out of trouble if I could, but if you're going to insist on…"

"All right now," the Serviceman said, suddenly decisive. "That'll be enough out of both of you. You both come along and you can get it straightened out in the Watch House."

"I see no reason…" Cade began, and stopped even before the Watch-man began to reach for the light club in his belt. He did see a reason, a good one: at a Watch House, he would be able to get transportation to the Chapter House. "Very well," he said coldly. "I shall be glad to come along."

"You *bloody* idiot," said the girl.

CHAPTER SIX

"WELL, WHICH ONE of you is making the complaint?" The bored officer behind the desk looked from the girl to Cade and back again.

Neither replied.

"She was out of her district," the other Watchman explained, "and they couldn't get together on whether she was with him or not, so I took 'em both along in case you wanted to hear it all."

"Official infringement on the girl, huh?" the Deskman muttered. "If she don't want to make a complaint we got nothing against the man. All right. Matron!" A stout, clean-looking woman in grey got off a bench along the wall and approached the desk. "Take her along and get her name and registration. Fine is ten greens…"

"Ten greens!" the girl broke in miserably. "I haven't even got a blue on me. He was the first one tonight…"

"Ten greens," he said implacably, "or five days detention. Tell your troubles to the matron. Take her away. Now…" He turned to Cade as the stout woman led the girl away. "We'll take your name and address for the record and you can go. Those girls are getting out of hand. They'd be all over town if we let 'em get away with it."

It was too much to attempt to unravel now. Cade dismissed the puzzle from his mind, and said, in a low voice: "May I speak to you alone?"

"You out of your head, man? Speak up, what do you want?"

The Gunner looked around. No one was too close. He kept his voice low. "It would be well if you speak more respectfully, Watchman. I am *not* a commoner."

Comprehension came over the man's face. He stood up promptly, and led the Gunner into a small side room. "I'm sorry, Sir," he said hast-ily. "I had no idea. The gentlemen usually identify to the Watchman on street duty when such incidents occur. You're a young gentleman, Sir, and perhaps this is your first… little visit to the other half? You under-stand, Sir, you needn't have been bothered by coming here at all. Next time, Sir, if you'll just identify to…"

"I don't believe you quite understand," Cade stopped the meaningless flow. "I desired to come here. There is a service you can do for me and for the Realm."

"Yes, Sir. I know my duty, Sir, and I'll be glad to assist you in any way you deem fitting. If you'll just identify first, Sir, you understand I have to ask it, we can't chance ordinary citizens passing themselves off as …"

"Identify? How do I do that?"

"Your badge of rank, Sir." He hesitated, and saw confusion still on Cade's face. "Surely, Sir, you didn't come out without it?"

The Gunner understood at last. "You misunderstand, Watchman," he said indignantly. "And you presume too much. I have heard of the degenerates among our nobility who indulge in the kind of escapade you seem to have in mind. I am not one of them. I am a Gunner in the Order of Armsmen, and I require your immediate assistance to reach the nearest Chapter House."

"You have no badge of rank?" the Watchman said grimly.

"Armsmen carry no prideful badges."

"Armsmen carry guns."

Cade kept his temper. "All you have to do is get in touch with the Chapter House. They can check my fingerprints, or there might be a Gunner there who can identify me personally."

The Deskman made no answer; he walked to the door and pushed it open.

"Hey, Bruge!" The Watchman of the street got to his feet, and came toward them. "You want to put a drunk-and-disorderly on this fella? He's either cockeyed drunk, or out of his head. Was he acting up outside?"

"The *girl* said he was drinking," the other man remembered.

"Well, you're the one'll have to register the complaint. I'm not letting him out of here tonight. He's been telling me in deepest confidence that he's really a Gunner in the Order…"

"Say, that's how the whole thing started," Bruge remembered. "He came up to me asking where was the Chapter House. I figured he was just a little crocked, and I wouldn't of pulled him in at all except for the argument with the girl. You think he's off his rocker?"

"I don't know." The Deskman was silent for a moment, then made up his mind. "I'll tell you what, you sign a d-and-d, and we'll see how he talks in the morning."

Cade could endure no more of it. He strode angrily between the two men. "I tell you," he announced loudly, "that I am Gunner Cade of the Order of Armsmen, and my Star is the Star of France. If you do not do what is necessary to identify me immediately, you will pay dearly for it later."

"Say, now…" Another Watchman, who had listened idly from the bench, stood up and joined them. "I'm a fighting fan myself. It's a real privilege to meet up with a real Gunner, first-hand." He was short and stout, and there was an idiotic smile on his beaming moon-face, but at least he seemed more alert than the others. "I hate to bother you, Sir, at a time like this, but I was having a little argument just yesterday with Bruge here and you could settle it for us. Could you tell me, sir, for instance, how many times you've been in action this year? Or, say, your five-year total?"

"I really don't remember," said Cade impatiently. "This is hardly a fitting time for talk of past actions. I must report immediately to the nearest Chapter House. If your superior sees fit to do his duty now and call the House for identification, I shall endeavor to forget the inconvenience I have suffered so far."

"How about it, Chief?" the moon-faced one appealed to the Deskman, turning his face away from Cade. "Why don't you let Bruge here make a call for the Gunner? It's only sporting, isn't it?"

There was an unexpected smile on the Deskman's face when he replied. "OK—go on, Bruge, you go call up." He winked in a friendly fashion.

"All right," said Bruge, disappointedly, and left the room.

"I wonder, Gunner Cade," Moon-face said easily, "how many men you've killed since you became Armiger? Say in offensive actions compared with defensive actions?"

"Eh? Oh, I've never kept count, Watchman. No Gunner would." This fellow at least was civil. There was no harm in answering the man's questions while he waited. "Numbers killed don't mean everything in war. I've been in engagements where we'd have given half of our men to get control of a swell in the ground so unnoticeable that you or you probably wouldn't see it if you were looking at it."

"Think of that!" marvelled one of the watchmen. "Did you hear that? Just for a little swell in the ground that slobs like us wouldn't even notice. Hello, Jardin…" He hailed another man in grey who had just entered. "Here's the man you want," he told Moon-face, "Jardin can give you facts and figures on the Gunner."

"You mean Cade?" the new man said unhappily. "Yeah, I sure can. It's only eight kills for the second quarter. He would have hit twelve, sure, only…"

"Yeah, it's a shame all right," Moon-face broke in. "Jardin, I've got a real treat for you. A France fan like you and Gunner Cade is your favorite too. Well, here's the thrill of a lifetime, man. Gunner Cade, himself, in person. Jardin, meet the Gunner. Gunner Cade, Sir, this is a long-standing fan of yours."

Two more men had come in, and another was at the door. They were all standing around listening. Cade regretted his earlier impulse to answer the man's question. A distasteful familiarity was developing in Moon-face's attitude.

"Quit your kidding," Jardin was saying, almost angrily. "I don't see what's so funny when a good Gunner dies."

"I tell you the man says he's Gunner Cade. Isn't that true?" Moon-face appealed to the Gunner.

"I am Gunner Cade," he replied, with what dignity he could muster.

"Why, you…!"

The outburst from Jardin was stopped abruptly by the Deskman.

"All right, that's enough now," he said sharply. "This farce is no longer fitting to our honored dead. Jardin is right. Fellow," he said to Cade, "you picked the wrong Gunner and the wrong Watchman. Gunner Cade is dead. I know because Jardin here lost twenty greens to me on him. He was silly enough to bet on Cade for a better second-quarter total of kills than Golos of Zanzibar. Golos topped him with—but never mind that. Who are you, and what do you think you're doing impersonating a Gunner?"

"But I *am* Gunner Cade," he said, stupefied.

"Gunner Cade," said the officer patiently, "was killed last week in the kitchen of a house in some French town his company was attacking. They found his body. Now, fellow, who are you? Impersonating a Gunner is a serious offense."

For the first time, Cade realized that Bruge had left, not to call the Chapter House, but to collect the crowd of Watchmen who had assembled while they talked. There were eleven of them in the room now—too many to overpower. He remained silent; insisting on the truth seemed hopeless.

"That's no d-and-d," the Deskman said in the silence. "We'll hold him for psych."

"Want me to sign the complaint?" It was Bruge, grinning like an ape.

"Yeah. Put him in a cage until morning and then to the psych."

"Watchman," said Cade steadily. "Will I be able to convince the psych, or is he just another commoner like you?"

"Hold him," somebody said. Two of them expertly caught Cade's arms. The questioner flicked a rubber truncheon across Cade's face. "Maybe you're crazy," he said, "but you'll show respect to officers of the Klin Service."

Cade stood there, the side of his jaw growing numb. He knew he could break loose from the Watchman holding him, or disable the man with the truncheon by one well-placed kick. But what would be the good of it. There were too many of them there. *It is fitting that we Gunmen serve*—but the thought trailed off into apathy.

"All right," said the man with the truncheon. "Put him in with Fledwick."

The Gunner let himself be led to a cell and locked in. He ignored his cellmate until the man said nervously: "Hello. What are you in for?"

"Never mind."

"Oh. Oh. I'm in here by mistake. My name is Fledwick Zisz. I'm a Klin Teacher…attached to the lectory at the Glory of the Realm ground car works. There was some mix-up in the collections, and in the confusion they concluded I was responsible. I should be out of here in a day or two."

Cade glanced uninterestedly at the man. "Thief" was written all over him. So Klin Teachers could be thieves.

"What does a silver garter on a girl mean?" he suddenly demanded.

"Oh," said Fledwick. "I wouldn't know personally, of course." He told him.

Curse her, thought Cade. He wondered what had happened to her. She'd said she couldn't pay the fine. Probably she was locked up with a real prostitute. Curse them, you'd think they could tell the difference!

"My real vocation, of course, was military," said Fledwick.

"What?" said Cade.

Fledwick hastily changed his story. "I should have said, 'the military teachership.' I was never really happy at the Glory shop. I'd rather serve humbly as a Teacher in an obscure Chapter House of the Order." He raptly misquoted: "It is fitting for the Emperor to rule. It is fitting for the Power Master to serve the Emperor."

"Interested in the Order, eh? Do you know Gunner Cade?"

"Oh, *everybody* knows Gunner Cade. There wasn't a smile in the Glory shop the day we heard the news. The factory pool drew Cade in the 'stakes and it's play or pay. Not that I know much about gambling, but I—uh—happened to have organized the pool. It was so good for the employee morale. When I get out of here, though, I think I'll stick to dog bets. You get nice odds in a play-or-pay deal, but there's a perfectly human tendency to think you've been swindled when your Gunner is—so to speak—scratched and you don't get your money back. I've always thought—"

"Shut up," said Cade. You'd think the fools could tell the difference between her and—oh, *curse* her. He had worries of his own. For one thing, he seemed to be dead. He grinned without mirth. He had to get to the Chapter House and report on the Cairo Mystery, but he was in effect a commoner without even a name. A Gunner had no wife or family; no one to notify, no one to identify him except his Brothers in the Order—and the watchmen were not going to bother the Order. They *knew* Cade was dead.

He wondered if this were happening for the first time in the ten thousand years since creation.

Everything was all wrong; he couldn't think straight. He stretched out on the jail cot and longed for his harder, narrower sleepbag. *It is fitting that the Emperor rules—* He hoped she wouldn't antagonize them with her disrespectful way of talking. Curse her! Why hadn't she stayed in her own district? But that went to prove that she didn't really know anything about the trade, didn't it?

"You!" he growled at Fledwick. "Did you ever hear of a prostitute wandering out of her district by mistake?"

"Oh. Oh, no. Certainly not. Everybody knows where to go when he wants one. Or so I'm told."

A crazy thought came to Cade that if he were dead, he was released from his vows. That was nonsense. He wished he could talk to a real Klin Teacher, not this snivelling thief. A good Klin Teacher could always explain your perplexities, or find you one who could. He wanted to know how it happened that he had done all the right things and everything had turned out all wrong.

"You," he said. "What's the penalty for impersonating a Gunner?"

Fledwick scratched his nose and mused: "You picked a bad one, sir. It's twenty years!" He was jolted out of his apathy. "I'm sorry to be the one to tell you, but—"

"Shut up. I've got to think."

He thought—and realized with twisted amusement that one week ago he would have been equally horrified, but for another reason. He would have thought the penalty all too light.

Fledwick turned his face to the wall and sighed comfortably. Going to sleep, was he?

"You," said Cade. "Do you know who I am?"

"You didn't say, sir," yawned the Klin Teacher.

"I'm Gunner Cade, of the Order of Gunmen; my Star is the Star of France."

"But—" The teacher sat up on the bed and looked worriedly into Cade's angry face, "Oh. Of course," he said. "Of course you are, sir. I'm sorry I didn't recognize you." Thereafter he sat on the edge of his bed, stealing an occasional nervous glance at his cellmate. It made Cade feel a little better, but not much.

It is fitting that the Emperor rules—he hoped that leaving the "district" was not too serious an offence.

CHAPTER SEVEN

CADE OPENED his eyes.

Dingy walls, locked door, and the little Klin Teacher still sitting on the side of his bunk across the cage, fast asleep. At the thought of the man's futile determination to hold an all-night vigil over the maniac who had claimed to be a dead Gunner, Cade grinned—and realized abruptly that a grin was no way for a Gunner of the Order to start his day. He hastily began his Morning Thoughts of the Order, but somewhere, far down inside him, there was a small wish that the Thoughts were not quite so long. He had a plan.

Seconds after completing the familiar meditation he was leaning over the other bunk, shaking the Klin Teacher's shoulder. Fledwick almost toppled to the floor and then sprang to his feet in a terrified awakening. He was about to shriek when the Gunner's big hand sealed his mouth.

"No noise," Cade told him. "Listen to me." He sat on Fledwick's bunk and urged the little crook down beside him. "I'm going to get out of here and I'll need your help to do it. Are you going to make trouble?"

"Oh, *no* sir," the Teacher answered too promptly and too heartily. "I'll be glad to help, sir."

"Good." Cade glanced at the lock on the cage door—an ordinary two-way guarded radionic. "I'll set the lock to open fifteen seconds after it is next opened from the outside. You'll have to raise some sort of noise to get a Watchman in here."

"You can set the lock?" Fledwick broke in. "Where did you learn—?"

"I told you. I am a Gunner of the Order. I expect your full cooperation because of that. I have a message of great importance which must be delivered to the Chapter House at once. Your service to me, by the way, should win you a pardon."

Cade read on the little man's face the collapse of a brief hope. Fledwick said brightly: "The pardon is immaterial. Whatever I can do to serve the Realm, I will do."

"Very well, you don't believe me. Then I will expect your full cooperation on the grounds that I must be a dangerous maniac who might tear you limb from limb for disobedience. Is *that* clear—and believable?"

"Yes," said Fledwick miserably.

"Excellent. Now listen: you will attract a guard's attention. Say you're ill or that I'm trying to murder you—anything to get him inside. He will come in, close the door and look at you. I will overpower him, the door will open and I will leave."

"May I ask what I am to do then? The City Watch has been known to mistreat prisoners who aided in escapes."

"Save your wit and call me 'sir!' You may come along if you like. You would be useful because I know nothing of the city, of course."

He got up and went over to the lock.

Fledwick was next to him, peering over his shoulder. "You mean you're *really* going to try it? Sir?" There was awe in his voice.

"Of course, fool. That's what I've been saying." Under the Teacher's dubious stare he got to work on the lock. The cage-side half of its casing was off in less than a minute. It took no longer for his trained eye to analyze the circuits inside. Fledwick nervously sucked in his breath as the Gunner's sure fingers probed at tubes, relays and printed "wires." But it was child's play to avoid the temper-triggers that would have set alarms ringing, and the more sinister contacts designed to send lethal charges of electricity through meddlers—child's play for anybody who could re-wire a flier's control panel in a drizzly dawn.

Cade snapped the cover back on and told Fledwick: "Begin!"

The little man was near tears. "Sir, couldn't we wait until after breakfast?"

"What would they give us?"

"Bread and fried sausage today," said the Teacher hopefully.

Cade pretended to consider, and decided: "No. I don't eat meat until nightfall. Did you forget that I am a Gunner of the Realm?"

The little man pulled himself together and said evenly: "I *am* beginning to wonder. I had been thinking of warning the Watchman when he came in."

"Don't! I can silence both of you, if I must."

"Yes, of course. But you needn't worry about me. Your work with the lock— If we get out I know of a clothing warehouse and a certain person who's interested in its contents—and to be frank, perhaps I was overoptimistic when I said the misunderstanding that brought me here was a minor one. There are certain complications."

"Such as being guilty?" suggested Cade. "Never mind. You should have a pardon from the Gunner Supreme for this morning's work. Meanwhile, think me burglar, lunatic, or what you please, but start howling. It will be daylight soon."

Fledwick practiced with a couple of embarrassed groans and then cut loose with a hundred-decibel shriek for help on the grounds that he was dying in agony.

Two watchmen appeared, looking just-waked-up and annoyed. To Fledwick, writhing on his bunk, one demanded: "What's wrong with you now?"

"Cramps!" yelled Fledwick. "Unendurable pain! My belly is on fire; my limbs are breaking!"

"Yes, yes," said the Watchman. He addressed Cade with exquisite politeness. "Oh starborne one, go sit on your bunk and put your hands on your knees. My mate's going to be watching you. One move and sleep-gas fills the block. We'll all have a little nap, but when *you* wake up the desk chief will pound you like a Gunner never was pounded before, oh starborne one."

He nodded to the other Watchman, who took his stand by a handle that obviously controlled the gas. Cade rejoiced behind an impassive face; the outside Watchman was a slow-moving, doltish-looking fellow.

Fingers played a clicking code on the lock's outside buttons and the door sprang open in a satisfactorily lively manner. The Watchman bent over Fledwick, now moaning faintly, as Cade counted seconds. As the door sprang open again, Cade was on his feet; before it had completed its arc the Gunner's fist was tingling and the inside Watchman lay crumpled half on Fledwick and half on the floor. Cade was through the open door and on the too-solid fellow outside after the man realized there was something badly wrong, but before he could do anything about it.

Fledwick was in the corridor by then. "Follow me," Cade ordered. It was odd, he fleetingly thought, to have somebody under your command who couldn't half-read your mind through endless training, somebody whose skills were a guess and whose fighting heart was a gamble. They passed empty cells on their way to the guard room. Its door was stout, equipped with a peep-hole and firmly locked in case of just such an emergency as this.

Through the peep-hole Cade saw three drowsy Watchmen. The liveliest was at a facsimile machine reading the early-morning edition of a newssheet as it oozed out.

"Boyer," called the newshound. "Grey Dasher won the last at Baltimore. That's one green you owe—where's Boyer?"

"Cell-block. Fledwick was yelling again."

"How long ago?"

"Keep calm. Just a second before you came in. He went with Marshal; they haven't been more than a minute."

Cade ducked as the newshound strode to the door and put his own eye to the peep-hole. "A minute's too long," he heard him say. "Marshal's the biggest fool in the Klin Service and that big maniac's in there with Fledwick...Put on your gas guns."

There were groans of protest. "Ah, can't we flood the block?"

"If we did, *I'd* have to fill out fifty pages of reports. Move, curse you!"

"Can you fire a gas gun?" whispered Cade. The Klin Teacher, trembling, shook his head.

"Then stay out of the way," Cade ordered. He was excited himself, by the novelty and his unarmed state. They say we don't know fear, he thought, but they're wrong. *Arle, Gunner Supreme, safely dwelling in a fearful place, I pledge that you'll have no shame for me in this action.* Tuned to battle pitch he thought of the good old man, the Gunner of Gunners, who would accept even the coming scuffle as another fit deed by another of his fit sons in the Order.

The stout door unlocked and the newshound came through first. Like a machine that couldn't help itself Cade smashed him paralyzingly with his right arm where the ribs and sternum meet and a great ganglion is unguarded. Cade's left hand took the Watchman's gun and fired two gas pellets through the half-opened door. One of the Watchmen outside had time to shoot before he went down, but his pellet burst harmlessly against a wall.

Fledwick muttered something despairing about "up to our necks," but Cade waved him along into the guard room. The Gunner reconnoitered the street, found it empty and returned for the Teacher.

"Come along," he said, pitching the gas gun onto the chest of a prostrate Watchman.

Fledwick promptly picked it up. "What did you do that for?" he demanded. Cade glared at him and he hastily added: "Sir."

"Put it back," said Cade. "It's no fit weapon for a Gunner. I used it only because I had to."

There was a look on Fledwick's face that the Gunner had seen before. It was partly puzzled resignation, partly kindliness and affection and—something else that was suspiciously like condescension. Cade had seen it from the starbornes of the Courts, and especially the ladies. He had seen it often and was puzzled as always.

"Don't you think, sir," said the Klin Teacher carefully, "that we might take the gas gun along in case another emergency arises? I can carry it for you if you find it too distasteful."

"Suit yourself," said Cade shortly, "but hurry." Fledwick dropped the weapon inside his blouse, securing it underneath the waistband.

"Sir," said the Klin Teacher again, "don't you think we should do something about these Watchmen? Roll them behind a door and lock it?"

Cade shrugged irritably. "Nonsense," he said. "We'll be at the Chapter House with everything well again before they're discovered." Fledwick sighed and followed him down the steps and along the empty streets. There was a light mist and a hint of dawn in the sky; the two green lights of the Watch House cast the shadows of the Gunner and the Klin Teacher before them on the pavement, long and thin.

"How far is the Chapter House?"

"Past the outskirts of Aberdeen, to the north. Five kilometers, say, on the Realm Highway—wide street two blocks west of here."

"I'll need a ground car."

"Car theft too!"

"Requisition in the service of the Realm," said Cade austerely. "You need have no part in it." Theft—requisition. Requisition—theft. How odd things were outside the Order! And sometimes how oddly interesting! He felt a little shame at the thought, and hastily reminded himself: *Gunners march where the Emperor wills—that is their glory.* Yes; march in soft-soled commoners' shoes, in a requisitioned ground car.

It would be easy—a pang went through him. How easy had it been for the girl? He would investigate with the greatest care. She might suffer from her association with him now that he had broken out. The Klin Servicemen would undoubtedly mistreat her unless they were made aware that his eye was on them. He had seen last night that they were

not above petty personal vengeance. Not Teachers, they were neverthe-
less supposed to be the Arm of Klin; as the Teachers kept order in men's
minds, the Watchmen kept order in the body politic. But what, after all,
could you expect from commoners? He would have to let them know
that his eye was on them in the matter of the girl.

"Here's a good one," said Fledwick. "From my own shop." Cade surveyed a Glory of the Realm ground car, parked and empty. Fledwick was
peering through the window and announced with satisfaction: "Gauge
says full-charged. It will get us there."

"Locked?" asked Cade. "I'll take care of—"

Fledwick waved him back calmly. "I happen to be able to handle
this myself, because of my, well, familiarity with the model." The little
man took off his belt, a regulation Klin uniform belt, to all appearances,
until, surprisingly, it turned out to be of very thin leather, folded triple.
From within the folds he took a flat metal object and applied it to the
Glory car's lock. There were clicks and the door swung open.

Cade stared at the Klin Teacher as he carefully replaced the object in
his belt. Fledwick cleared his throat and explained: "I was planning to
get one of the Glories out of savings from my meager stipend. There's a
clever fellow in the lock shop who makes these, uh, door openers and I
thought how convenient it would be to have one if I should ever mislay
my combination."

"For the car you hadn't bought yet," said Cade.

"Oh. Oh, yes. Prudence, eh, sir? Prudence."

"That may be. I shall leave you now; there is no need for you to
accompany me further and you know, I suppose, that Gunners may
consort with those outside the Order only if it is unavoidable. I thank
you for your services. You may find pleasure in the knowledge that you
have been of service to the Realm." Cade prepared to enter the car.

"Sir," said Fledwick urgently, "I'd find more pleasure in accompany-
ing you. That pardon you mentioned…"

"It will be sent to you."

"Sir, I ask you to think that it might be a little difficult to find me. All
I desire is to see my humble lectory again, to serve fittingly in expound-
ing the truth of Klin to the simple, honest workingfolk of the Glory
shop, but until I get the pardon I'll be—perforce inaccessible."

"Get in," said Cade. "No, I'll drive. You might absentmindedly
pocket the steering panel." He started the car and gunned it down the
street toward the Realm Highway.

"Hold it at fifteen per," Fledwick warned. "The radar meters kick up
a barrier ahead if you speed."

Cade kept the car at fifteen with his eyes peeled for trouble—and
open as well to a host of curious sights. The broad highway was lined
with merchandising shops. Shops and shops selling foodstuffs in small
quantities to individuals. Shops and shops selling commoners' garb,

each only slightly different from the next. Shops and shops selling furniture for homes. It seemed such folly!

Fledwick turned on the ground car's radio; through the corner of his eye Cade saw him tuning carefully to a particular frequency not automatically served by the tap plates.

Why, Cade wondered, couldn't they all be sensible like the Order? A single garb—not, he hastily told himself, resembling in any way the uniform of the Armsmen. Why not refectories where a thousand of them at a time could eat simple, standardized foods? His mental stereotype of a commoner returned to him: lax, flabby, gorging himself morning, noon and night.

How good it would be to get into the Chapter House in time for a plain breakfast, and to let the beloved routine flow over him. He knew it would quench the disturbing thoughts he had suffered during the last days. It was all a wonderful proof that the Rule of the Order was wise. *Nor shall any Brother be exposed to the perils of what lies without his Chapter House or the Field of Battle. Let Brothers be transported, by ground if need be, by air if possible, swiftly from Chapter House to Chapter House and swiftly from Chapter House to the Field of Battle.*

How right and fitting it was! The perils were many. Uncounted times he had let his mind be swayed from the Order and his duty in it. When he woke today he had almost willfully chafed at the morning meditation. He could feel the warmth of the Order that would soon enfold him—

"Cade!" shrilled Fledwick. "Listen!"

The radio was saying on what must be the official band: "—claiming to be the late Gunner Cade of France and the unbooked Klin Teacher Fledwick Zisz. Use medium-range gas guns. The Cade-impostor is known to be armed with a gas gun, and has the strength of a maniac. Zisz is unarmed and not dangerous. Repeat, all-Watch alert: bring in two men escaped this morning from Seventh District Watch House. They are an unidentified man claiming to be the late Gunner Cade of France—" It droned through a repeat and fell silent.

"They haven't missed the car yet," said Cade.

"They will," Fledwick assured him mournfully. "Or they have missed it and haven't connected it with us yet." He was gloomily silent for three blocks and then muttered angrily: "Unarmed and not dangerous!" He fingered the gas gun through his blouse. "Unarmed indeed! Sir, a little way more and we're out of the city. If they haven't got the noose tight yet—"

"Noose?"

"Blocking of exits from the city by Watchers. They'll have every gate covered soon enough, but if they don't know about the car they'll cover the public transports first. We do have a chance." It was the first faint note of hope Fledwick had permitted himself.

Cade drove on at a steady fifteen per. The sun was up and traffic moving in the opposite direction, towards the city, grew heavier by the minute. Once they passed a city-bound car trapped by speed bars that had risen, cagelike, from the paving to hold the speeder for the Watch.

"They stop at the city gates," said Fledwick. "After that, you can speed up. The Watchers have nothing faster than this."

The noose was not yet tight. They rolled easily past a sleepy Watchman at the gate. Either he hadn't received the alert, or he assumed District Seven was no worry of his. Gunner's instinct kept Cade from taking Fledwick's advice and speeding. He rolled the car on at an inconspicuous twenty per, and the decision was sound. A green-topped Watch car from the city passed them and Fledwick shriveled where he sat. But it kept going on its way, never noticing the fugitives.

The highway was now dotted with cars. Just ahead, and off to the left, was a grey crag. "Chapter House," said Fledwick, pointing, and Cade sighed. The whole insanely unfitting episode at last was drawing to a close.

The radio spoke again: "To all Armsmen and Watchmen." The voice was vibrant and commanding. "To all Watchmen *and* Armsmen," said the voice again, slowly. "This command supersedes the previous all-Watch alert concerning the Cade-impostor and the unbooked Klin Teacher Fledwick Zisz. Both these men are heavily armed and both are dangerous. They are to be shot on sight. Armsmen: shoot to kill. Watchmen: use long-range gas guns. New orders for Watchmen and Armsmen both are: *shoot on sight!* These men are both dangerous. There is to be no parleying; no calls to surrender; no offer or granting of quarter. Your orders are to shoot on sight. No explanation of any Armsman or Watchman who fails to shoot on sight will be accepted.

"Description and records follow…"

Cade, in frozen shock, had slowed the car to a crawl, not daring to make a conspicuous stop. He listened to fair physical descriptions of both of them. His "record" was criminal insanity, homicidal mania. Fledwick's was an interminable list of petty and not-so-petty offenses of the something-for-nothing kind. He too was described as a homicidal maniac.

"You're armed and are dangerous now," Cade said stupidly.

His answer was a volley of wild curses. "You got me into this!" raved the little man. "What a fool I was! I could have done my five years standing on one foot! I had friends who could have raised my fine. And you had to bully me into making a break!"

Cade shook his head dazedly. Fledwick's flood of rage poured over him and drained away, powerless to affect him after the impact of the radio announcement.

"But I *am* Gunner Cade," he said quietly, aloud, as much to himself as to the unbooked Teacher.

CHAPTER EIGHT

"IT'S A MISTAKE—that's all," Cade said numbly.

"Very well." The little man's voice was acid. "Before we are killed because of this curious mistake will you decide on a course of action? We're still approaching your Brothers' House, and I want none of their hospitality."

"You're right," said Cade. "The Brothers," he said, feeling an unwarranted note of apology creeping into his voice, "the Brothers would obey the official-frequency command. It's their duty. I would myself, though the command was most—unusual. I don't think I've ever heard its like, not even for the worst criminal."

Fledwick was past his first fury. He studied Cade's bewilderment and said slowly: "Back in the cage, when I saw you fix the lock, I thought you were either a Gunner or a master burglar—the greatest master I ever heard of. And when you laid out five Watchers without working up a sweat I thought you were either a Gunner or a master burglar *and* the greatest strongarm bucko I ever saw. But when you tossed away that gas gun because it wasn't fitting, I *knew* you were a Gunner. Cade or not, you're a Gunner. So it's a mistake, but what can we do and where can we go?"

Cade suddenly laughed. The Order was perfect after all; the answer was so easy. He sent the car swinging in a bumpy U-turn over the parkway strips. "To the Gunner Supreme!" he said.

"The Gunner Supreme," echoed Fledwick blankly. "The chief of all the Gunners. Wouldn't he shoot us twice as fast as an ordinary Gunner? I don't understand."

"No, you don't," said Cade. He tried to think of some way to make the wonderful presence clear, knowing he would fail. Of all things in the Order, the meaning and being of the Gunner Supreme had most of all to be *felt*. "We in the Order are Brothers," he carefully began. "He is the father. The Power Master disposes of us to the several Stars, but the assignment is without force until it has been sealed with the seal that is in the gun-hilt of the Gunner Supreme.

"He touches his gun to ours before we first put them on as Armigers. If he didn't touch them we wouldn't be actual members of the Order. The memory of him touching our guns steadies our hands and makes our eyes keen and our wits quick in battle."

And there was more he could never tell to anybody. Those in the Order knew it without telling; those outside would never know. There were the times you didn't like to remember, times when your knees trembled and you sweated advancing into fire. Then you thought of *him,* watching you with concern clouding his brow, and you stopped trembling and sweating. You felt warm and sure advancing into fire to play your fitting part.

"This paragon of Gunners—" began Fledwick ironically.

"Silence, thief! I will not tolerate disrespect."

"I'm sorry…may I speak?"

"With decorum."

"You were right to rebuke me." His voice didn't sound quite sincere, but he had, Cade reflected, been through a lot. And, being what he was, he didn't realize that the problem was *solved*—that the Gunner Supreme would understand and everything would be all right again. "Where," Fledwick asked, "does the Gunner Supreme live?"

From beloved ritual Cade quoted the answer: *"Nearby to the Caves of Washington, across the River Potomac to the south, in a mighty Cave that is not a Cave; it is called Alexandria."*

"The Caves of Washington!" squalled Fledwick. "I'll take my chances with the Watchers. Let me out! Stop the car and let me out!"

"Be still!" Cade yelled at him. "You ought to be ashamed. An educated man like you mouthing the follies of ignorant commoners. You *were* a Teacher of Klin, weren't you?"

Fledwick shuddered and subsided for a moment. Then he muttered: "I'm not such a fool. You know yourself it's dangerous. And don't forget, I was born 'an ignorant commoner.' You sprang it at me before I had time to think, that's all. I felt as if I were a child again, with my mother telling me: 'You be good or I'll take you to the Caves.' I can remember her very words." He shuddered. "How could I forget them?"

" 'I'll take you to the Caves.

" 'And the Beetu-Nine will come and tear your fingers and toes off with white-hot knives of metal.

" 'And the Beetu-Five will come and pepper you with white-hot balls of metal.

" 'And the Beefai-voh will come and *grate* your arms and legs with white-hot metal graters.

" 'And last, if you are not a good boy, the Beethrie-Six will come in the dark and will hunt you out though you run from Cave to Cave in the darkness, screaming. The Beethrie-Six, which lumbers and grumbles, will breathe on you with its poison breath and that is the most horrible of all for your bones will turn to water *and you will burn forever.' "*

Fledwick shuddered and said feebly: "The old bitch. I should have kicked her in the belly." He was sweating greasily from his forehead. "I'm not a fool," he said belligerently, "but you don't deny there's *something* about the Caves, do you?"

Cade said shortly: "I wouldn't care to spend a night there, but we're not going to." Fledwick's reminiscence of his mother's threat had shocked him. No wonder, he thought, commoners were what they were.

There was nothing *in* the Caves—he supposed. One simply, as a matter of course, calmly and rationally avoided the horrible things.

"Alert, all Armsmen and Watchmen!" said the radio. It wasn't the same vibrant, commanding voice that had issued the "Shoot on sight" order, but it was bad news—the bad news Cade had been expecting since then. "The Cade-impostor and the unbooked Klin Teacher Fledwick Zisz are now known to have stolen Glory of the Realm ground car AB-779. That is Glory of the Realm ground car AB-779. Watchmen are to shoot the occupants of this car on sight with long-range gas guns. When the occupants are paralyzed Watchmen are to take them with all possible speed to the nearest Chapter House of the Order for immediate execution by Armsmen. Armsmen's orders are unchanged. Shoot to kill; destroy the ground car on sight; kill the occupants if seen outside the car. That is Glory of the Realm ground car AB-779."

The broadcast cut off and the only sound in Glory of the Realm ground car AB-779 was the soft whimpering of Fledwick.

"Keep your nerve, man," Cade urged. "We'll be out of here in a moment." He stopped the car and rummaged through its map case for the Washington Area sheet. Then he stepped out of the car and yanked Fledwick out bodily, after him. Finally, Cade set the car's panel on self-steering at twenty per and opaqued the windows before he started it cityward on the highway.

Standing in the roadside scrub, the little thief followed the vanishing car with his eyes. "Now what are we going to do?" he asked lymphatically.

"Walk," said Cade grimly. "That way we may live to reach the Supreme. And stop snivelling. There's a good chance that an Armsman will spot the car and burn it without knowing it's empty. And then they won't have any easy time deciding that we got away."

The little man wouldn't stop sobbing.

"See here," said Cade. "If you're going to be like this all the way, it'll be better for both of us if you dig in somewhere and take care of yourself for a few days while I make it alone."

The unbooked teacher gave a last tremendous sniff and declared shakily: "No cursed chance of that, Gunner. Lead the way."

Cade led the way across a stubbly field for a starter.

For the Gunner the five days of overland march were refreshing and reassuring. Here at last was something familiar, something his years of training had fitted him for, something he understood completely. And to his surprise, Fledwick was no burden.

On the first day, for instance, they crawled on their bellies up to the chicken yard of a food factory through its great outlying vegetable fields. Cade was suddenly chagrined to discover that he didn't know what to do next. In action, if there was food you demanded it or took it; if there was none you went without. Here there was food—and it would be self-destruction to seize it in his usual fashion. But Fledwick's unusual belt gave up another instrument that sheared easily through the aluminum wire. Fledwick's pockets gave up peas he had picked and shelled along the way, and he scattered a few through the gap in the wire. A few repetitions and there were clucking chickens on their side of the barrier. The little man pounced silently four times and they crawled back through the vegetable field with a brace of fowl each at their belts.

After that Cade left the commissary to Fledwick, only reminding him that he did not eat meat before sundown and warning him that he wouldn't look kindly on Fledwick devouring a chicken while he chewed carrots.

Once they thought they were in danger of discovery. At an isolated paper mill on the second day they saw Watchmen, a dozen of them, drive up and fan out to beat a field—the wrong one. If they had picked the right one, Cade could have slipped through them with laughable ease, and so perhaps could Fledwick. Cade guessed he would be expert enough at slipping across an unfamiliar room in the dark without betraying himself by squeaks and bumps. From that to a polished job of scouting and patrolling was not as far a cry as he would have thought a few days earlier.

After the incident at the paper mill Cade surrendered to the ex-Teacher's pleading that he be taught the use of the gas gun. Disdainfully, for he still disliked handling the weapon, Cade stripped it a few times, showed Fledwick the correct sight-picture and told him that the rest was practice—necessarily dry-runs, since the number of pellets was limited. Fledwick practiced faithfully for a day, which was enough for the ignoble weapon in Cade's eyes. He went to some pains to explain to the ex-Teacher that gas gun and Gun were two entirely different things—that there was a complex symbolism and ceremony about the Gun of the Order which the gas gun, weapon of commoners, could not claim.

Cade learned as well as taught. In five days, it seemed to him, the cheerful conversation of the little man told him more about the world outside the Order than he had learned in the past thirteen years. He knew it was none of his affair to listen as Fledwick told of the life in shops and factories or the uses of restaurants, theaters, entertainment, radio, and dives. He consoled himself with occasional self-reminders that he didn't ask—he just listened. And there was a good half that he didn't understand because of linguistic difficulty. Fledwick had a twinned vocabulary. Half of it was respectable and the other half was a lively argot, richly anatomical, whose roots were in a shady world Cade had never known. Here and there a word was inescapably clear because of context.

Less articulate himself, Cade still tried to interpret to the ex-Teacher the meaning that the Order and its life had for him, a Gunner. But he found that although Fledwick sincerely admired the Order, he did so for all the wrong reasons. He seemed incapable of understanding the interior life—the rich complexity of ritual, the appropriateness of each formal thought, the way each Armsman moulded his life to Klin. Cade sadly suspected that the ex-Teacher saw the Gunner Supreme as a sort of glorified Klin Service Deskman. He could not seem to realize that, merely by *being himself,* the Gunner Supreme made the interior life of the Order tangible, that he was the personification of fitness and decorum. But Cade decided he could forgive Fledwick a lot after he had snared a plump turkey without a single gobble an hour before sundown.

The third afternoon Cade spent a full hour over his maps trying to avoid an inevitable decision. That night he insisted on a march of five kilometers by starlight alone. They woke at dawn, and Fledwick gasped at what he saw to the south.

"Is it—?" he asked hoarsely.

"It's the Caves of Washington. Skirting them fairly closely—three kilometers or so—is the only way we can avoid a huge detour around thickly-populated areas. I was afraid you'd balk if you saw them first by daylight." Cade did not add that he had feared he would have balked himself. He cheerily asked: "Did you ever think you'd spend a night this close to the Caves?"

"No," Fledwick shuddered.

They breakfasted on stolen—or requisitioned—fruit while Cade, less calm than he appeared, studied the battered skyline to the south. It was a horrible thing: a rambling mound of grey stone, with black gapings in it like eyes and mouths. Toward the peak there was a thing like the vertebrae of a man's backbone outlined against the morning sky. It was as though some great, square shaft had toppled and shattered where it struck. It was a horrible thing, and Arle, the Gunner Supreme, lived in a mighty Cave that was not a Cave. In the shadow of Washington, not even the negative was reassuring. Washington was a horror. It made him think of obscenities like firing from a flier. Or the women at Mistress Cannon's.

Cade found himself unable to swallow the fruit pulp. "Let's march," he growled at Fledwick, and the little man scrambled to his feet fast. They skirted the Caves with a generous margin and Fledwick kept up a running stream of nervous chatter—about places like Mistress Cannon's, it happened.

For once, in his nervousness, Cade asked a direct question. Had Fledwick ever heard of a woman wearing the garter who spoke unlike a commoner and had such-and-such eyes, hair and manner? The ex-Teacher badly misunderstood. He assured Cade that after this mess was cleared up, any time the Gunner was in Aberdeen he could fix him up with the nicest little piece who ever wore the garter and he would personally guarantee that Cade would never notice if she spoke like a commoner or a starborne—

Cade thundered at him and there was total silence until they reached the shining Potomac.

Fledwick couldn't swim. Cade made him water wings by tying his trouser cuffs, whipping them through the air until they ballooned and drawing the belt tight. He had to push the half-naked little thief into the river and toss the wings to him before he'd believe that the elementary field expedient, trusted by Armsmen for ten thousand years, would work. Cade towed him across and they dried out on the south bank as the Gunner oriented his map.

"That's it," he said, pointing to the East. And he felt covered with dirt for having given a thought to the commoner girl while he was this close to the Gunner Supreme.

Fledwick only grunted doubtfully. But when ten minutes of brisk walking brought them to a clearer view of the pile he stopped and said flatly: "It's more Caves."

"Oh, you fool!" snapped Cade. *"A mighty Cave that is no Cave* are the words. And you used to be a Klin Teacher! It obviously means that it looks like a Cave but isn't to be feared like one."

"Obvious to you, perhaps," Fledwick retorted. "But then so many things are perfectly clear to you."

"This is not one of them," the Gunner answered stiffly. "I intend to walk around it at a reasonable distance. Are you coming or aren't you?" Fledwick sat down obstinately and Cade started off to circumnavigate the gloomy, dome-shaped mound that should be the residence of Arle. It looked like Caves, right enough…he heard Fledwick pattering after him and declined to notice the little man when he caught up.

They marched around the crumbling dome, about three hundred meters from its rim—and it began to assume a shape on its western front that exactly justified the traditional description. The Cave that was no Cave was a gigantic building from one side and a mouldering ruin from the other.

"Fives," murmured Cade abstractedly studying it.

"Eh?" asked Fledwick, and the Gunner forgave him for the sake of someone to tell his puzzling discovery to.

"Fives—five floors, five sides, a regular pentagon if it were not half cave, and I think five rings of construction of which we see only the outermost."

"Drop!" snapped Fledwick, and Cade dropped. "Guards," muttered the ex-Teacher. "Armsmen? Watchmen?"

Cade studied the insignificantly small figures against the huge facade.

"Armsmen," he said, heavy-hearted. "We must assume they have received the order to kill us. We will have to wait until night to slip in and bring this before the Gunner Supreme himself. I would trust no one below him."

CHAPTER NINE

THEY SETTLED THEMSELVES in good cover on a grassy mound half a kilometer from the Building of Fives. Fledwick turned face-down and dozed off. The five days had taken a lot out of the city-bred man, Cade thought, but he'd been a good companion through it all: clever and quick, though no Armsman, useless only when his sharp mind raced ahead of his courage and petrified him with expected terrors.

For Cade there was no sleep. With his eyes trained steadily on the Building of Fives one part of his mind accumulated and stored the information he needed—the pattern of patrol, the number of guards, time between meetings at sentry posts, the structure of the building and the flesh and bones of the terrain around it. And all the while he pondered the deeper problem he had to solve.

Their chances of getting in were good. Without pride—*pride is a peril*—Cade knew he was among the best of the Emperor's Armsmen, but the necessary feat savored of the impossible. It was too much to expect that he, practically alone, could outwit or overcome a company of sentries. If he failed to pass them and so did not come into the presence of Arle, the Supreme, there had to be a way of getting him the word, whether Cade lived or died.

He ripped off a square of his ragged shirt for writing paper—and there was a flexible little knife Fledwick had casually extracted from his belt and lent him to eat with. A tiny puncture in the middle of each fingertip of his left hand. Then carefully, painfully, one finger at a time, he squeezed the drops of blood out until the friction pads were smeared with red. He pressed each finger to a once-white diamond in the patterned fabric of the shirt.

With a few more drops on the knife point he could write, one letter to a diamond:

CADE DID NOT DIE
AT SARRALBE
CAIRO
MYSTERY
BALTIMORE

That was enough. They could identify the prints, and perhaps even the blood. They could go to the house of the hag who had poisoned him, raid the Mystery with its underground corridors, check on the Watch House's "impostor," piece together the story—a thing he might not live to do.

Cade wiped the blade and his fingers to leave no signs that would puzzle or frighten Fledwick. The ragged cloth from his shirt he knotted about a small stone and dropped in his pocket.

With the last light of the sun the guard was changed at the House of Fives. Cade breathed easier when he saw that the night guard was no heavier than the day. It was a guard of honor, nothing more. All around the side that was not ruins paced single sentries on lonely fifty-meter posts, meeting under arc lights, turning to march through the dark until they met at the light marking the other end of the patrol. It was understandable. The staring cave mouths were fearsome enough to need little guarding.

Cade nudged his partner awake with his bare toes, broken through the ruins of commoners' sandals.

"Is it time?" Fledwick asked.

The Gunner nodded and explained. In two more hours the first alertness of the guards would have worn off and the lassitude of a ceremonial guard mount would be creeping on…not yet strong enough for them to fight against it. Every commander knew that time of night, the time to take green or lazy troops by surprise and teach them a lesson in alertness those who lived would never forget.

They would use their two hours until then to make the approach to the building. Fledwick chewed on a stolen turnip and finally asked: "And then? When we're there?"

Cade pointed to one particular arc light. Behind it, to the right, gaped the black emptiness of a cave mouth, barely distinguishable from shadows the arc lights cast of jagged rock on smoother rock. As they watched, two Gunners came in view, approaching with metrical precision from opposite sides to meet exactly under the light, saluted—gun to brow—and wheeled and marched off like synchronized puppets.

"Watch *him,*" Cade pointed. "The one with the red stripe." Together they watched while the Gunner disappeared again into the blackness and waited until he emerged again, thirty meters beyond, in the brightness of the next sentry post. Here the arc lights showed not gaping ruins but the smooth surface of the building proper. Somewhere in between, invisible, was the junction of ruins and building.

"He's our man," said Cade simply.

"A friend of yours, sir?" asked Fledwick, over-politely.

"He's a Marsman," said Cade, ignoring the flippancy. "The Marsman has not been born who can meet an Earth Gunner in combat and win. Their training is lax and their devotion is lacking. We will take him in the dark, halfway between posts, silently. If we work swiftly and all goes well I will have time to take his cloak, boots and helmet and make his next round to the sentry post. If there is no time for that, I am afraid we will have to use the—gas gun—to stun the approaching sentry. Then," he concluded with a shrug, "we have the full pacing time to make our entrance."

Fledwick spat out a fibrous bit of turnip and stared across the field at the sputtering lights. At last he looked up at the Gunner.

"The *full* pacing time? Almost a *whole* minute?"

"Fifty-three seconds. Even you can move that fast," Cade said scornfully.

"You noticed there were bars on the gates—sir?"

Cade was losing his temper. "I noticed," he growled. "I'm not a fool of a commoner."

"No, sir. I'm very much aware of that. Would you tell a fool of a commoner how we'll get through the barred gates in fifty-three seconds?"

"Serve you right if I didn't. But I can't expect you to show the courage of a Brother. We won't enter the barred gates at all. We'll go through the unbarred cave. It's got to lead into the Building." Cade's impassive face betrayed nothing—not that he was sure he lied; not that he knew death was minutes away for both of them. "We're starting now." He began to work his way down the hillock, ignoring frantic whispers from behind. At last rustling grass and heavy breathing told him that Fledwick was following. He smiled. The noise, he suspected, was to worry him and make him angry. But he knew that when silent sneaking was needed, Fledwick would deliver.

Ten meters down he paused. "You may stay behind if you like," he whispered. "I shall not think ill of you."

He waited in the dark and grinned at a sound between a curse and a sob, followed by more of the rustling and heavy breathing.

"Quiet!" he whispered sternly, and they began the passage.

A full two hours later they crept up to the very edge of the patrol posts and separated. Cade, crouching, thrilled to the awareness of all his muscles tensing for the spring. It was almost disappointingly easy when the split-second came and the Marsman fell silently, perhaps forever, on the concrete path. The neck blow was never certain—either way. Cade had tried not to hit too hard. To kill a Brother in combat was fit and glorious, but never had he heard of any precedent for what he did.

He stripped the silent figure with desperate haste and threw the garments onto himself. Cloak and *the Order, wraps the Realm;* Helmet and *protects the Emperor;* Boots and *march where the Emperor wills.*

But the cursed boots wouldn't fit. He looked up and saw in the distance the opposite sentry approaching, almost in the circle of light. With infinite relief he heard the small hiss of the gas gun and saw the sentry drop, with only one arm in the pool of light beneath the arc. Now Cade no longer needed boots. He buckled on the Marsman's gunbelt and felt sudden wild optimism come with the familiar weight on his hip. He flipped the message-wrapped stone from the pocket of his commoner's shirt under the cloak and dropped it by the felled Marsman. From somewhere Fledwick crept up beside him and together they raced for the yawning black hole in the ragged, moldering wall.

Cade leaped clear of the cave-mouth's jagged edge and found sure footing on the rubble inside. Fledwick couldn't make it. Cade hauled him in, shaking violently and gasping for breath. But Fledwick picked himself up and stumbled after Cade into the deepening darkness of the interior.

They heard voices and tramping boots, and a clear shout: "In here— loose rock—they went *inside!*"

There was anger in the voice, but something else too: awe.

Cade had not let himself think until now of the enormity of this campaign. He had attacked a Brother off the Field of Battle, and perhaps killed him. He had assisted a commoner, and worse, an unbooked Teacher, into classified ground. If successful, he would invade without request or warning the private dwelling of the Supreme. But somehow overshadowing all this was the realization: *you are in a cave, and you are none the worse for it.*

A blast of hot air rolled through the cave, followed by pungent ozone. "They're shooting into the—the cave," he told Fledwick. "Stay down and nothing will happen."

For minutes afterwards the air crackled above them and Cade lay motionless, waiting and hoping to be spared to complete his mission. He thought again of the terrible roster of his crimes, but they had been the only possible answer to crimes worse than he knew could exist. That men should plot against the Emperor...

The firing stopped. The two or three bends they had rounded were ample protection from the direct effects of the fire, it appeared. Voices echoed down the cave again, and Cade had a mind's eye picture of Gunners peering in cautiously, but never considering pursuit.

"—wasting fire. Get torches—"

"—we'll smoke them out—gone inside—"

Cade groped along the floor with one hand and then pulled himself cautiously over to Fledwick. "Get up," he whispered. "We can't stay here."

"I can't move," a broken voice whimpered too noisily. "You go ahead."

Wounded, Cade realized—or hurt when they hit the ground. He scooped up the little man and tossed him over his shoulder. He did not groan, Cade noted with surprise and respect. The Gunner started forward.

First, get away from the light. They had food in their pockets, a full-charged gun, a dozen gas-gun pellets and a knife apiece. If they could find a spring for water, a place to put their backs against, they could hold out for a long time; and a flood of new energy came with the mounting excitement of the thought that they might yet come out of this alive!

They turned a corner of some sort that cut off the last light from the entrance. Cade's eyes adjusted to the gloom; he could make out a little of the shape and structure of the cave. And his eyes confirmed what his feet and groping hands had told him...what he had known before, and told to Fledwick, but had not dared believe: the cave was artificial, a disused corridor in a decayed old building.

Cave and Building were one!

What was Washington?

He wished he could tell Fledwick, and examine the idea in the light of his quick, acquisitive intelligence. But the little thief was taking his injury nobly; this was no time for explanations.

The cave—he couldn't think of it as anything else yet—seemed endless; doors were on either side. Any one of the dust-choked rooms might do for a stand, but there was no need to choose one until the sounds of pursuit were heard.

On his shoulder the limp bundle wriggled and came alive.

"You can put me down now."

"Can you walk?"

"I think so."

Cade lowered the man to the ground and waited while Fledwick found his footing.

"You mean," the Gunner demanded with as much outrage as he could pack into a whisper, "you're not hurt?"

"I don't *think* so." Fledwick was unashamed. "No, not a scratch."

Cade kept a contemptuous silence.

"Where do we go?" asked Fledwick.

"I think," he said, slowly, "if we keep on going we'll find our way to the other part of the Building."

"The *other* part? You really meant it?" The little man darted from one side of the corridor to the other, feeling the regularity of the walls, clutching the door jamb. "It is part of the Building! But it was a Cave?"

"I told you—*a Cave that is not a Cave.* But you chose to believe in your beasts and horrors and other commoner's tales. Keep moving!" His brusqueness covered a churning confusion in his mind. If the Cave was simply a disused part of a building, why weren't they being followed by the sentries?

They rounded an angle in the corridor—an angle of Fives—and saw at the end of the new corridor, far ahead, a dim, luminous rectangle, like the light around the edges of a closed door.

CHAPTER TEN

FLEDWICK redeemed himself.

There was no radionic lock in existence, Cade was certain, that he could not open. But this door was locked in a manner the Gunner had never seen before with an ancient mechanical device no longer in use anywhere—except among commoners.

The ex-Teacher seemed perfectly familiar with it. He removed from inside his surprising belt a bit of metal that he twisted in an opening in the lock.

Cade stepped up first, as was his due. The door opened easily an inch or two, and then, before the Gunner could adjust his eyes to the light, there was a voice.

"Who is it? Who's there?"

Cade almost laughed aloud. He had been ready for a challenge, the blast of a gun, conquest or defeat or even emptiness. He had been ready for almost anything except a startled question in a feminine voice. He pushed the door open and Fledwick followed him into the room.

Only two things were certain about her: she was starborne, a Lady of the Court; and she was just as surprised as he.

She stood erect beside a couch on which, he guessed, she had been resting when the door opened. Her eyes were wide with surprise, fast turning to anger, and their brilliance was intensified by the color of her hair, expertly tinted to a subtly matching blue-green shade. Only the starborne would or could wear that elaborate coif: soft coils of hair piled high on the crown of her head and scattered with seemingly random drifts of golden dust. As her anger grew, her eyes, too, seemed to flash with cold metallic glints.

The headdress marked her rank and her clothes confirmed it. She wore the privileged sheer of the nobility, not fashioned into obscene pajamas as he had seen it once before, but a fluid draping of cobweb-stuff whose color echoed just a trace of hair and eyes...as seafoam carries the faintest vestige of the ocean hue. The same golden specks that dusted her hair were looped in fairy patterns through the fabric of the gown, and here and there, where the designer's scheme planned to attract the eye, the flowing robe was caught and held by artful incrustations of the dust.

Cade stood speechless. He had seen Ladies of the Court in such attire before, though not so close or so informally. But the vision itself was responsible for only part of his consternation. It was her presence here, in the private dwelling of the Gunner Supreme, that took his breath away.

The woman raised a delicately fashioned tube of gold to her lips and sucked on it. In a small bowl at the other end a coal seemed to glow and when she dropped her hand again a cloud of pale blue smoke came from her lips and drifted lazily across the room to where Cade stood. Its heavy fragrance dizzied him.

"*Well?*" demanded the woman.

The Gunner formally began: "We come in Klin's service—" and could think of nothing more to say. Something was terribly wrong. Was it possible that he had mistaken the ritual description of the place? Had the slow afternoon of planning and the violence of the night gone for nothing? It seemed, from the furnishings and the woman, to be the palace of a foreign Star. And what could he tell the lady of such a one?

Fledwick leaped into the breach. Words began to pour from him with practiced ease: "Oh, starborne Lady, if you have mercy to match even the smallest part of your beauty, hear me before you condemn us out of hand! We are your lowly servants! We throw ourselves at your feet—"

"Silence, fool!" the Gunner growled. "Lady! This commoner speaks only for himself. I am the servant of no woman but of my Emperor and my Star. Tell me who is the master of this house?"

She scanned him coldly, her eyes lingering on the discrepancies of his gear. "It is enough for you to know that I am its mistress," she said. "I see you wear stolen garments while you speak of loyalty."

There was no possibility at all that she would believe him, but Cade was suddenly and unspeakably weary of subterfuge. "I am no usurper," he said quietly. "I am Gunner Cade of the Order of Armsmen; my Star is the Star of France. They say I died in battle for my Star at Sarralbe, but I did not. I came here for audience with my father in the Order, Gunner Supreme Arle; if you are the mistress here I must have come wrongly. Whatever place this is, I demand assistance in the name of the Order. You will earn the thanks of the Supreme himself if—"

She was laughing a low, throaty chuckle of honest mirth. "So," she said at last, her voice catching to the tag ends of her laughter, "you are Gunner Cade. Then you—" She turned to the little thief. "*You* must be the unbooked Klin Teacher. And to think that you two sorry creatures are the…the *dangerous* homicidal maniacs the whole world is searching for! How did you find your way in here? And *where* did you get those uniforms?" She was a Lady with commoners; unthinkable that they would not obey if her voice had the proper whip-crack in it.

"The cloak and helmet that I wear are stolen," Cade told her flatly. "I got them less than an hour ago from a sentry at your gate. I also stole—"

"Starborne, have mercy!" shrieked Fledwick suddenly. "I am frightened. I am only a poor thief, but they are right about *him*. Call your master! Quickly! Give us in his power, starborne Lady, before he—oh, Lady, *he has a gun!*"

"Stupid!" she chided him, still smiling. "If he has, he can't use it. Do you suppose that an Armsman's gun is such a simple affair that any madman can fire it?" She took a step backward.

"I don't know," Fledwick shrieked with fear. "I don't *know!* But I beg you, Starborne, call your Lord! Call him now, before *he* kills us both!"

Cade listened to it all, incredulous and immobile: that this miserable, snivelling little creature, whose life he had saved more than once, should turn against him now…betray him *after* the danger was over! It was unbelievable.

The woman was watching him, he realized, out of the corner of her eye. She stepped back once more. Well; let her call her Lord, then, Cade thought angrily. That would serve his purpose; that was what he wanted…

The Lady took another backward step, as Fledwick went on pouring out his gibberish fright, and at last Cade understood what the little man was really up to.

He reached beneath his stolen cloak, and drew the Marsman's gun. He did not aim it at the woman, but pointed it instead at Fledwick's quivering head. "Traitor!" he shouted. "For this you die!"

The woman's nerve broke at last. She hurled herself across the room to a silk-hung wall and stabbed frantically at a rosette.

"Don't shoot!" wailed Fledwick, finally permitting himself a broad wink. "Please don't shoot! I'm only a poor thief—"

While he babbled, Cade made a menacing grimace or two and wondered who would turn up. Any Star at all would do. He'd have his gun on him, Fledwick could barricade the place and a message would be sent at last to the Gunner Supreme, with the life of the Star, or whoever was this Lady's master, as hostage for its delivery.

The woman took a hand. "Stop this brawling!" she screamed. Fledwick stopped. Her face was white but proud. "Hear me," she said. "I've summoned—help. If there is bloodshed in my chambers, your death is certain. It will not be a pleasant one. But I have a powerful protector." Good; good; thought Cade. The more powerful the better. We'll soon get this farce over with.

"If you surrender now," the woman went on, fighting for calm, "you will get justice, whatever that may be in your case." She stood composedly, waiting for a gunblast or a plea for mercy.

There was no need to continue play-acting. Cade holstered the gun, confident that he could out-draw whatever retainers the master of the place might appear with. Out of admiration for her he swallowed a smile of triumph before he said: "Thank you, Lady. And thank you, Fledwick. You know strategies that I have never been forced to practice."

Mopping his brow, the little thief said from the soul: "I suppose you think I wasn't afraid of that gun?"

"What nonsense is this—?" the woman began indignantly, but she went no further. The door opened and someone strode into the room.

"Moia!" the man called, seeing only the woman against the silk-hung wall. "What is it? You called—"

He followed her eyes to the two strangers, and they stared back, Fledwick with curiosity and apprehension and Cade with astonishment and veneration. He had automatically drawn the gun. Just as automatically, when he saw the proud, straight head, the gold band on the swirling cloak, the gun with a great seal on its hilt, he performed the Grand Salute of the Order, which is rendered only to the Gunner Supreme.

Abased on the floor, Cade heard the sonorous voice ask with concern: "You are unharmed?"

"Up to now." The Lady's shaky reassurance ended with a forced laugh.

"Good. You may rise, Gunner. Show me your face."

"He's no Gunner!" the woman cried. "He's the commoner posing as Cade! And he has a gun!"

Calmly, the Supreme said: "Do not fear…He is a Gunner, though the cloak he wears is not his own. Speak, Brother. What brings you here in this unseemly manner?"

Cade rose and holstered the gun he had proffered in the salute. With downcast eyes he said: "Sir, I am Gunner Cade of France. I come with an urgent message—"

"I have already received it. A most dramatic message, most effectively delivered. I was studying it when the Lady Moia's signal reached me. It *was* your work?"

"Yes, sir. I was not sure I could reach your person alive. Sir, I must warn you that there is a conspiracy, perhaps a dangerously powerful one, against—"

"You will tell me of it shortly. Your—the cloak you wear. It seems familiar. Or have you become a Marsman?"

"It was the property of a Brother in your service, sir. I hope I did not kill him. I knew no other way to come to you."

"He is dead. I owe you thanks for that. He guarded an important post and guarded it badly. I shall see to it that a better man replaces him, before others less friendly than you find their way to this room." He turned from Cade and addressed the Lady Moia: "We shall leave you now to rest and recover from this upsetting incident. I promise you the guards will be taught an unforgettable lesson. I will be back when I have heard this Brother's story." Their eyes met and Cade saw them smile as no Armsman should smile at a woman, and no woman should smile at an Armsman.

"Your story will be better told in my own quarters," Arle spoke, without self-consciousness, to Cade. "The Lady Moia's apartment is no place for gory tales." He looked absently about the room until his eyes fell on the open corridor door. "Yes," he muttered. "We must change that lock. You." For the first time he seemed to notice Fledwick. "Close the door and bolt it. There will be a new lock tomorrow, my dear," he added to the Lady Moia. "Meanwhile the bolt will serve. Will you be all right by yourself for a while?" His fingers dipped into a carved gold box on the table and took out a golden smoking pipe, like the one she herself held, and placed it absently between his lips.

"I'm all right now," she assured him with sudden nervousness. "You needn't worry, and the lock may be replaced whenever it's convenient.

The pipe, sir!" The Gunner Supreme started. "It's a new plaything of mine," she said, with self-deprecating humor. "I doubt that you would care for it."

Arle took the tube from his lips and studied it as though he had never seen it before. "A strange plaything," he said disapprovingly. "Come along, Gunner. And you too, I suppose." That was for Fledwick.

The room he took them to was the first reassuring thing Cade had seen in the place. It was a lesson room like those you could find in any Chapter House. The walls were bare, with standard storage space, there was a table in the center and Order benches all around. Cade sat down on Arle's permissive signal; Fledwick remained standing.

"Now," said the Supreme, "let me hear your story."

Cade started. The mad business had gone through his mind so often that it was like a verbatim recitation: doping and capture by a hag in Sarralbe; resurrection in Baltimore; the Cairo Mystery. He had waited so long to tell it and gone through so much for the opportunity that somehow now the whole business was a disappointment. And there was one final lunatic touch: the Gunner Supreme appeared little more interested in hearing the tale than Cade was in telling it. From time to time Arle asked a question or made a comment: "How many were there? Did they seem to be local people or from overseas? A wicked business, Brother! No recognizable Armsmen, of course?" But his eyes were glazed with boredom.

Could he lie to the incarnate Order? He stumbled in his story; the question burned in his mind, and then the fire went out. He was lying to Arle by omission. He was leaving out the girl of the Cairo Mystery, who had twice tried, the second time with success, to save him from hypnosis. He let the Gunner Supreme understand that he had automatically come to his senses on the street and then gone on to his arrest—"with some wearer of the garter who was following me"—for impersonating an Armsman. The rest was straightforward, including the attack on the guard and the long trip through the corridor. He told how Fledwick had forced the lock, and the Supreme examined the ex-Teacher's curious key with more interest than he had shown up to that point.

"Very well," he said finally, tossing the key to the table. "And then?"

"Then we entered the—the Lady Moia's apartment." Cade choked on the words.

The Lady Moia's apartment. I am its mistress. The Lady Moia rang—and the Gunner Supreme, the incarnation of the Order of Armsmen, answered her call. And quickly! Cade raised his eyes to the fine, proud old face.

"You're troubled, Brother," said the Supreme. "If it will ease your mind, I should tell you that the Lady Moia is one of the graces of this place. Visiting Stars and their Courts are not exposed to the rigors of an Armsman's life in Chapter House. It is the Lady Moia's task to prepare fitting apartments for them and to treat them with the ceremony that I, of course, cannot extend."

To be sure. It was so sensible. But the smile he had seen was unexplained, and it was unexplained why the Lady Moia, hostess and social aide, could summon the personification of the Order by a push on a concealed button.

His mind a dazed whirl, Cade said hoarsely: "I thank you, sir. There is no more to tell. You know the rest." Then, at a nervous cough from Fledwick, he hastened to emphasize his virtual promise to the little man of a pardon on grounds of service to the Realm.

"Quite right," said the Supreme, and Fledwick relaxed with a sigh.

Three Gunners entered on a summons from Arle. He told them: "This is the former Klin Teacher, Fledwick Zisz. You recall that there is an order out to kill him on sight as a homicidal maniac. I find that order was a gross error. He is a worthy member of the Realm who appears to have committed some trifling indiscretions. Bring me materials for writing him a pardon on grounds of Service."

Cade stole a look at the unbooked Teacher and felt inexplicable shame as Fledwick avoided his eyes. He could not forget Lady Moia's apartment himself; how could Fledwick? He wished he could take the little man aside to tell him earnestly that it was still all right, that the Supreme's outward forms didn't count; that his inner life must be in complete harmony with Klin, that the relationship between the Supreme and the Lady Moia wasn't—what it obviously was.

Cade sat silently as the Supreme wrote the pardon and signed it in the flowing script that had been on all his own assignments. One of the Gunners dripped a blob of clear thermoplastic on the signature and Arle rapped it smartly with the hilt of his gun. The Seal.

The same seal Cade had sometimes, in secret excess of sentimental zeal, pressed ritually to his chest, mouth and brow because it had been touched by the Gun of the Supreme. He felt himself flushing scarlet, and turned his eyes away. Abruptly he rose, without a permissive sign, and went to Fledwick. "You're out of it," he said. "I've kept my promise. You weren't a bad companion."

The little man managed to look directly at him. "It's good of you to say so. And it's been worth it. How I wish I could have a picture of your face when I got us those chickens!" It was insolence, but Cade didn't mind. And Fledwick said gently, with that puzzling look Cade had got used to, but could never understand: "I'm sorry."

That was all. The Supreme handed him the pardon and waited impatiently through the little man's lavish protestations of gratitude. "My Gunners here," he said, "will take you in a ground car to Aberdeen. I think you'll have no trouble with *them* for an escort. There you should present your pardon to the Watch House and that absurd order will be withdrawn. Doubtless you wish to leave at once."

"And you, Gunner," Arle continued, "it's long since you've been in a sleeping loft." He summoned a novice and ordered: "Take this Brother to the night guard's sleeping loft. He will need a complete uniform in the morning."

Cade performed the abject Grand Salute before he left; the Gunner Supreme acknowledged it with an absent-minded nod.

CHAPTER ELEVEN

THE EMPTY SLEEPING loft at least was real and fitting. Cade took a sleep-bag from the wall, undressed, belted on his gun and inflated the bag. For weeks he had been thinking that this was the night he would sleep well. Now he knew it would not be so. What had he said to Fledwick? "You're out of it." A puzzling thing for him to say. Cade paced to the window. Five floors below was a courtyard formed by the outer ring of the Building of Fives, the next ring and two connecting spokes. All the many windows on the court were dark, but a thin sliver of new moon showed white concrete down below. It seemed to be an isolated wing. Cade stared down into the moonlit courtyard as though he could hypnotize himself into numbness.

All right, he told himself angrily. Think about it. Think about the look they exchanged. The bare pretense of interest on the Supreme's face. The absent-minded, habitual air with which he picked up the smoking tube. What do you know about it? What do you know except that you're a Gunner, and how to be one?

Maybe *that's* the way a Gunner Supreme is supposed to be. Maybe they tell you the things they do for your own good, because you're too much of a fool to understand that it's got to be this way because—because of good reasons. Maybe there's a time when they do tell you in secret and show you how it all fits in the Klin Philosophy, like everything else. Maybe the whole thing, from the poisoned cider on down to this sleeping loft, was a great secret test of your conduct. What do you know about it?

It was too frightening. He recoiled from the brink of such thoughts. They had no business in his head, curse them! He was a Gunner and he knew how to be a Gunner. He tried to think shop-talk, the best kind of talk there is. What kind of duty you had here, how long a tour they gave you, whether there was ever a chance of action or whether it was all ceremony and errands.

Think about the Cave that is not a Cave—a curious place. It made you nervous to think that you had *been* in a Cave and that it had just been a corridor, without lumbering, grumbling beasts prowling its dark lengths. This Building of Fives—had it been created ten thousand years ago like the Caves of Washington, building-half and all? Or had there first been the Caves and then the building constructed against it? A filthy thought crept into his mind. Half-formed, it said to him that if there was such a building and you were up in a flier and—*no!* What was wrong with him? He'd have to go to a corrective Teacher if this went on! Was this churning confusion what lunacy was like? He crawled into his sleepbag. That at least was good. Some six thousand daily repetitions had formed a powerful habit-pattern. Gratefully he let some of the brief meditations drift soothingly into his mind and across it, ironing out the perplexities. And tomorrow he'd have a proper uniform again. undersuit, shirt, hose, boots—where the Emperor wills—cape, helmet…Cade was alseep in the empty loft.

He dreamed of the Gunner Supreme threatening the Lady Moia with a gun, and the Lady Moia turned into the girl of the Cairo Mystery. He tried to explain respectfully to the Supreme that it wasn't the Lady Moia any more and that he had no business shooting her. "Cade!" the girl called faintly. "Cade! Cade!"

The Gunner sat up abruptly. That call was no dream. He ripped open the quick release of his sleepbag and peered through the window into the courtyard. Four figures were dark against the concrete, one of them smaller than the others.

There was some sort of flurry down there and he saw the smaller figure in full, no longer foreshortened. Somebody had fallen or been knocked down. Now he got up, expostulating and waving something white, and was knocked down again. He struggled to his feet and held out the white thing with a desperate, pleading gesture, not only in the arm but in every curve of his small, expressive body.

Fledwick!

Cade needed no more interpretation of the scene below. It was all there in the little thief's offer of the paper. Cade knew the white scrap was the pardon, written and sealed by the Gunner Supreme. And he saw one of the three other men snatch it impatiently from Fledwick and tear it across.

As if he were remembering the scene instead of seeing it enacted, Cade stood helplessly at his window, waiting. He saw Fledwick shoved against a blank wall and saw the other three draw guns. He saw the partner of his five-day march burned down by three guns of the Order, fired simultaneously at low aperture. And last he saw the three remaining figures separate, two to a door in the inner ring, one through a door directly below, into the building where he himself stood watching.

He was sick, then and there, and after the spasm passed he realized that he had seen murder: murder with guns of the Order, wielded by Armsmen at the command of the Gunner Supreme, after Arle himself had lyingly granted and sealed a pardon.

This was no secret into which he would someday be initiated; this was no test of courage or belief. This was no less than lies, treachery and murder at the command of the Order, incarnate, the Gunner Supreme!

The door to the loft opened silently and a figure slipped without noise across the floor to Cade's inflated sleepbag.

"Were you looking for me, Brother?"

The assassin spun to face the harsh whisper, gun in hand. He was burned down before he fully realized that his intended victim was not helplessly asleep.

Cade's thoughts were crystal-clear and cold. His burned body had been found once before in Sarralbe; it would now be found again, to buy him precious time until the assassin-Armsman was found missing. He rolled the charred body into the sleepbag he had occupied and slowly burned the flimsy fabric to a cinder with a noiseless discharge at minimum aperture. Presumably anybody within earshot had been alerted for the crash of one lethal blast, but not two.

Cade donned his medley of commoner's garb and ill-fitting uniform and slipped out along the way he had been led, through empty corridors, down empty ramps. He knew only one way out. The wing seemed to be deserted, and he wondered if it was because it held the apartment of the Lady Moia or because it was where murder was done.

The lock on the inner door to the Lady's apartment was radionic. Cade solved it quickly and slipped through to the cushioned outer chamber. The room was dimly night-lit, still fragrant with the smoke of the golden pipes and the subtler scent that the Lady wore herself. He saw the glitter of golden trinkets on the table—boxes, pipes, things whose use he couldn't guess at—and realized that he had not yet plumbed the depths of the impossible. He was about to become a thief.

He did not know where he was going or how he would get there, but clearly the Houses of the Order were barred to him. For the first time in his life he would need money. Gold, he remembered from childhood, could be exchanged for money, or directly for goods. He reached for the glittering display and filled all the big pockets of the commoner's cloak. The sum of trifling metal objects made a surprising weight.

There was a third door to the room, and it stood ajar. He tiptoed across the floor and peered through to the Lady Moia's bedroom. She was asleep, alone, and Cade felt somehow relieved. The beautiful dark head stirred on the white pillow, and he drew back. Unskillfully, he worked the mechanical latch of the door to the Cave, nervous at each scratching clicking sound it made. But in the room beyond the Lady slept on, and at last the door swung open.

When he had come in with Fledwick, fleeing through dark corridors at midnight, his terrain-wise eyes had automatically measured and his brain recorded every turn and distance. He was able to retrace his steps and find the Cave opening in a matter of minutes.

The ceremonious patrol was not yet changed. He saw, crossing the Cave-mouth at intervals, a new man instead of the Mars-born gunner whose cloak was now on Cade's back, but Arle's promise to the frightened Lady had otherwise not been acted on. Clearly, the Gunner Supreme had every confidence in his assassins. Cade stood within the shadow of the Cave-mouth and watched the Gunners on their sentry go, silhouetted by starlight and arc light as they met and marched and met again.

The fools! he thought, and then remembered what a prince of fools he was himself, and had been since the day of his decision in his sixth year—until less than an hour ago.

Leaving the Cave-mouth was infinitely easier than entering. This time he knew what waited on the other side: nothing but acres of high grass in which a man could hide forever. *A man.* The thought had come that way, unbidden: *a man.* Not *a Gunner.*

Cade was only one more shadow between the sputtering lights, a streak of darkness that the routine-fuddled minds of the sentries never saw. Safe in the tall grass, he lay still for long minutes, until he was certain there had been no alarm. Then, cautiously, he began to inch along. At last, over a fair-sized rise of ground, he rose and walked, heading for the river.

Soon, very soon, he would have to decide where he was going and what he would do. For now, he knew that Aberdeen and Baltimore were to the north. He was at the Potomac river again in a matter of minutes, but he could not cross by swimming, or even with the aid of waterwings like the pair he had made for Fledwick only yesterday. The gold would have weighed him down, and he was stubbornly determined not to abandon it.

He trudged on along the southern bank of the river looking for a log big enough to float him and small enough to steer, or for an unguarded bridge. The first dawn light was creeping into the sky when he heard angry voices over the brow of a knoll. Cade dropped and crawled through the rank grass to listen.

"Easy with it, curse you!"

"You can do better? Do it and shut your mouth!"

"You shut your own mouth. Yell like that and we'll both wind up in the crock on a sump tap."

"I can do a sump tap standing on one foot."

"I hope you have to some day, curse you, if I'm not in on it. I got better things to do with my time than standing on one foot in the crock for two years."

"Just go easy on the smokers is all I asked—"

Phrases were familiar. "Standing on one foot through a tap in a crock" meant "serving a short prison term with ease." That much he had learned from Fledwick. The talkers were criminals—like him. Cade stood up and saw two commoners in the hollow below, loading a small raft with flat boxes.

It was a moment before they realized that they were not alone. They saw him on the knoll and stood paralyzed, while he strode down on them.

"What're you up to?" he demanded.

"Sir, we're—we're—" stammered one. The other had. sharper eyes. "Hey!" he said coldly, after studying Cade for a moment. "What is this—the shake? You're no Armsman."

"It's not the shake," Cade said. Another phrase from Fledwick.

"Well, what is it? A man doesn't take a chance on twenty years for nothing. You're in half a uniform and even that doesn't fit. And the gun's a fake if ever I saw one," the commoner pronounced proudly.

The other was disgusted. "Me falling for a phony uniform and a fake gun! On your way, big fellow. I don't want to know you before you get crocked for twenty."

"I want a ride on your raft. I can pay." Cade took a gold smoking-pipe box from a pocket. He was about to ask: "Is that enough?" but he saw from their faces that it was, and more. "I also want some commoner's clothes," he added, and then cursed himself silently for the betraying "commoner's"—but they didn't notice.

"Sure," said the man who couldn't be taken in by a fake gun. "We can take you across. But I don't know about clothes."

"I can fix that," the other man said hastily. "You're about my size. I'll be glad to sell what I'm wearing. Of course I ought to get something extra for selling you the blouse off my back—?"

Cade hefted the box. There seemed to be a lot of gold in it, but how much gold was a suit of clothes?

The man took his silence as refusal. "All right," he said. "I tried," and stripped down to his undersuit. He wasn't nearly as big as Cade, but his clothes were baggy enough to cover him. As Cade methodically transferred his plunder from one set of garments to the other, their eyes bulged.

"You'd better bury your toy," one of them warned. "A fake gun's the same as impersonating."

"I'll keep it," said Cade, dropping the skirt of his tunic over the gun. "Now get me across."

Watching the last gold ornament disappear, the unbluffable commoner said tentatively: "We have some more transportation."

"Hey," said the other.

"Oh, shut your mouth. Can't you tell when a gaff's on the scramble?"

So, Cade reflected, he was a gaff on the scramble, who needed transportation. "What have you got?" he asked.

"Well, my rog, we're on the distribution end for a smoker works. To a gaff that won't sound like much, but a sump tap is a tap same as for gaffing. We get them from—from the manufacturer and put them across the river. A ground car picks them up there. The driver could—"

"For two gawdies like that last one," his partner interrupted determinedly, "we'll take you to the driver, vouch for you and tell him to drop you off anywhere along his route."

"One gawdy," Cade offered cautiously, wondering what a smoker was.

"Done," the friendlier one said promptly. Cade fished for and handed over a box about like the last one. The commoner caressed it and said: "Let's have a smoker on the bargain. They'll never miss 'em." Without waiting for an answer he opened one of the flat boxes on the raft and took three pellets from it. The two commoners dropped theirs into aluminum tubes, lit up and puffed, and Cade realized at last that "smokers" went into smoking pipes like those fancied by the Lady Moia.

"Thanks," he said, dropping his pellet into a pocket. "I'll save mine." They gave him a disgusted look and didn't answer. He realized he had made a more-or-less serious blunder. There were fit and unfit things among commoners too, and he didn't know how many more unfit things he could get away with.

The pellets lasted only a minute or so, leaving the men relaxed and gently talkative while Cade strained his ears and wits for usable information.

"I smoke too much," one of the men said regretfully. "I suppose it's the temptation from handling the stuff."

"It doesn't do you any harm."

"I don't feel right about it. Shoving the stuff's a living, but if the Emperor says we shouldn't, we shouldn't."

"What's the Emperor got to do with it?"

"Well, the first Emperor must have made the sump tables about what you can do and what you can't do."

"Oh, no. The first Emperor and the sump tables were made at the same time. Ask any Teacher."

"You better ask a Teacher yourself...but even if the first Emperor and the sump tables did get made at the same time, I wouldn't feel right about it."

"That's what I told my girl. With her it's buy me this and buy me that, and now she wants a sheer dress from a sump shop and I told her even if she got it she couldn't wear it where anybody would see her and even if she wore it in private she wouldn't feel right about it."

"Women," said the other one, shaking his head. "The sump tables are a fine thing for them. Otherwise they'd all be going around like starbornes and you wouldn't have a green in your nick—there's the car. Let's get across."

Cade had seen the blink of lights across the bank. The raft shoved off with Cade sitting on the cases, one man poling and the other, in his underwear, hanging onto the edge. The car, on a highway that paralleled the river bank for a kilometer, was a large passenger car of nondescript color and peculiarly dirty identification numbers.

"Who's that?" demanded the driver, joining them. He was a big man run to fat, and had a section of three centimeter bronze pipe in his fist.

"Gaff on the scramble. A real rog. We said you might drop him along the route."

"*Would*, not *might*," Cade said.

"Got troubles enough," said the driver. "Scramble on, duff." Duff was obviously a ripe insult. The driver hefted his bronze pipe hopefully. Cade sighed and flattened him with a medium-hard left into his belly. To the others he said: "Look, you—you duffs. Give me back one of those boxes. And if you make any trouble I'll take them both back."

They conferred by glances and handed one of the boxes over. Cade showed it to the driver, who was sitting up and shaking his head dazedly. "This is for you if you drop me off where I want."

"Sure, rog," the driver said agreeably. "But I can't go off my route, you understand. I can't lose my job for a little extra clink."

"I'm going to Aberdeen," said Cade, with abrupt decision.

"Sure thing. Now if you'll wait while we load—"

The flat boxes of smokers went into a surprising variety of places in the car—under the seats, inside the cushions, behind removable panels.

Cade watched, and wondered why he had chosen Aberdeen. After a minute he stopped trying. He had to begin somewhere, and it might as well be with the girl. She knew something—more than he did anyhow. And with Fledwick murdered, she remained the only person who had not betrayed him at any time since he plunged into the month-long nightmare of conspiracy and disillusion. Besides, he assured himself, it was sound doctrine. The last place they would expect him to go would be the one place he'd been caught before.

Still musing, he sat beside the driver. "Where in Aberdeen?" the man asked when they were on the road.

"You know Mistress Cannon's?"

"Yuh. I deliver there," said the driver, obviously disapproving.

Cade risked asking: "What's the matter with the place?" It might be a nest of spies.

"Nothing. The old woman's all right. I don't care what kind of a dive you go to. I said I'd take you and I will."

Thirteen years of conditioning do not vanish overnight. Cade was guilty and defensive: "I'm looking for somebody. A girl."

"What else? You don't have to tell me about it. I'll take you there, I said. Myself; I'm a family man. I don't go to lectory every day like some people, but I know what's fitting and what isn't."

"You're running smokers," Cade said indignantly.

"I don't have to feel good about it and maybe I don't. I don't smoke myself. It's not my fault if a lot of ignorant duffs that got born common can't rest without smoking like a Star and his court. Say 'The Emperor wouldn't like it' and they pull a long face and say 'Oh, it can't matter much and I'll give twice as much to the lectory and the Emperor'll like *that,* won't he?' Fools!"

Cade feebly agreed and the conversation died. As the moralistic evader of the sumptuary laws covered his route, Cade let himself doze off. He knew a man who would keep a bargain once it was made.

Chapter Twelve

AT EACH START and stop Cade half-opened an eye and went back to sleep again. But finally the driver shook his shoulder.

Cade woke with a start. Through the window, across three feet of sun-splashed, dirty paving he could see stone steps leading down to a heavy door. Ahead, another set of steps apparently led up to another door that remained out of his vision.

They were in a narrow alley, barely wide enough for the slightly over-sized car. On either side, continuous walls of soot-dusted cement rose to a height of three or four stories above the ground. There were no windows, no clearly marked building lines, nothing to mark the one spot from another but dirt and scars on the aging concrete, and the indentations of steps at regular intervals along both sides.

The driver took three neatly packaged bundles from inside the arm-rest of the front seat, closed it and held them expectantly.

"Well?" he demanded. "Sitting there all day? Open it."

Cade stiffened, and then made himself relax. He was among commoners now and would be treated as one himself. It was a lesson he would have to learn as thoroughly as any back in Novice School. His life depended on these lessons too. "Sorry," he mumbled. "Cannon's?"

"Don't you know it?"

Cade opened the door and muttered: "Looks different by daylight." He followed the driver down the stone steps. The man knocked rhythmically, and the door opened a little. Cade knew the beefy face at once.

Elaborately ignoring the driver, Mistress Cannon said hoarsely: "The drinking room doesn't open until nightfall, stranger. Glad to see you then."

The driver said, with interest: "I thought he was a friend of yours. Gaff on the scramble. Some people I know said he's a rog."

Her faded blue eyes swung slowly from Cade's face down his multi-striped clothes to the ragged scandals he still wore, and returned as slowly to his face.

"Might have seen him before," she admitted at last, grudgingly.

"Me, and my—clinks, too," Cade said quickly. The rest was inspired: "Last time I was here one of your girls took everything you left."

The woman placed him at last. "She was no girl of mine," she insisted defensively.

The driver had had enough. "That'll do," he said. "Fix it up any way you want to between you. I'm behind time now."

The door creaked farther open.

"You wait here," the woman told Cade, and led the driver out of the room. It was the kitchen of the establishment. Cade wandered about, touching nothing, but examining with intense curiosity the unfamiliar miscellany of supplies and equipment.

The big food rooms of Chapter Houses where Cade had spent hundreds of hours as a Novice were no more like this place than—than an Armsman's sleep bag was like the Lady Moia's couch. The single thing he could identify was a giant infrabroiler in one wall; it was identical with those used in the preparation of the evening meat meal in the Houses. But there the similarity ended. Through the transparent doors of the cooler he saw not an orderly procession of joints and roasts but a wild assortment of poultry, fish, meat, and sea food, jammed in helter-skelter. Along the opposite wall were more fruits and vegetables than he had known existed—pulpy luxuries, he thought, for degenerate tastes.

There was to be recognized, at last, a cooker designed to mix and warm in one operation the nutritious basic mash on which Armsmen mainly subsisted. But here, instead of being a gleaming, giant structure it was a battered old machine perched on a high shelf almost out of reach. For some reason, Cade concluded, mash wasn't popular at Cannon's.

On other shelves around the room there were hundreds of bright-faced packages, containing unknown ingredients for use in a dozen or more specialized mixers and heaters whose equal Cade had never seen before. Over it all was an air of cheerful disorder, jumbled but purposeful comfort that struck for Cade a haunting note of reminiscence.

So many things these last few days had stirred old memories: memories of a childhood he had dismissed forever when he took his vows. Already, he realized, he was unfitted for the Order. The ritual and routine that had been as much a part of life as breathing had proved itself dispensable. At times it had even seemed like folly. A corrective Teacher, he thought—and then wondered whether he wanted to be corrected. Of course he wanted to get back into the Order. But the Gunner Supreme...

He coldly dismissed his personal tangle of loyalties. The first thing he needed was information, and that meant the girl.

"No girl of mine," Mistress Cannon had said. And long ago: "If you come back, girlie, I may wrap a bar stool around your neck." That didn't matter. He needed a starting point; one well down into the criminal half-world in which the girl had moved with such assurance. You went from one person to the next in that world: from the smugglers to the driver to Mistress Cannon's. A smile spread over his face. What would he have said not long ago if someone had told him he'd need the good will of a minor crook to gain admission to a—what did he call it—a dive? He, a Gunner among the best?

"Man," said the hoarse voice, "don't smile like that: I'm not as young as I used to be and my figure ain't all it once was, but I'm not so old either I don't get butterflies in the belly once in a while." Mistress Cannon stood in the doorway, eying him with an absurd mixture of good-fellowship and flirtatiousness. "And by the Power!" she chortled, "he can blush too! Big as a house, and built like an armed man, and a smile to give you goose-bumps, and he can blush yet! Well, we got some girls that like 'em that way. Me, I like 'em loaded." There was an abrupt change in her manner. "Lazar says you're on the scramble. What're you carrying?"

He opened his mouth to answer, but didn't have a chance.

"Big fellow, there's plenty rogs before you who spent a day or a month upstairs and no questions asked or answered. No safer place in Eastcoast until—trouble—blows over. But I can't do it cheap. Lazar brought you in and I like your face myself or I wouldn't do it for all the clink in Aberdeen. Protection comes high any place. Here you get it with a nice room, three meals and all the—"

The woman liked to talk, Cade thought weakly, and let her go on. What she was saying amounted to good luck. He could stay here—and the driver had assumed that this was just what he'd wanted.

The woman stopped for breath, wheezing a little, and Cade seized the chance: "You don't have to worry about money. I'm—I'm loaded. I can pay whatever you ask." In all the colorful flow of words, that much had been clear.

"What with?"

He pulled out the first thing his fingers touched in an outer pocket. It was a tiny, glittering piece of jeweled uselessness, five tiny bells hung on a thin wire loop. It tinkled distantly with almost inaudible music as he put it on a table. The woman's eyes were glued on the golden bauble.

"Practically valueless," she said composedly when she looked up. "Too hard to get rid of."

"I didn't know," Cade said apologetically, reaching for it. "Maybe something else—"

"All right!" she exploded, shaken again by heaves of flabby laughter. "Outbluffed on the first try. You have the other one, of course?" Cade, searching his pockets for a mate to the bauble, realized vaguely that he was supposed to have done something clever. He turned out on the table all he had and poked through it.

"I'm sorry," he said at last. "It doesn't seem to be here."

The woman looked up dazedly from the array. "You're sorry," she echoed. "It doesn't seem to be here." She looked at him again, searchingly and for a long minute. "What made you come here?" she asked quietly.

"First place I thought of," he said. Something was wrong. What commoner notion of fitness and unfitness had he violated now?

"Or the only place," she said, musingly. "And don't tell me it was liquor you were out on that other night. Maybe the tart you were with couldn't tell the difference, but I've been around for a lot of years. I know drunk when I see it and I know dope, too. A youngster like you...well, now I know you're good for your room. But wandering around loaded with gawdies you don't half know the value of—didn't anybody ever tell you not to jab up until the job was *through?* And that means selling it after the pick, too."

Cade could make nothing of it. "If you have a room for me," he said patiently, "you'll be well paid. That's all I'm asking of you."

For some reason, she was angry. "Then that's all you'll get! And when you start to yell for the stuff don't expect me to run it for you. Come on!" She jerked open a door and led the way up dark stairs. To herself she was grumbling: "You can't make a man talk if he doesn't want to, not even to somebody who wants to help. Think they'd have more sense!"

At the stair head she produced a ring of keys like the one Fledwick had used. She opened a door with one and handed it to Cade.

"That's the only one there is," she said. "You're safe up here. If you get hungry or if you get off your darby perch and want some fun, you can try the drinking room."

He closed the door on her and studied his quarters. The room was not light or clean. The shelves in the storage wall were stuck. It didn't matter; there was nothing to store. The bed was an ancient foldable such as he had seen only in commoners' houses entered during action.

It was hard to remember: he was in a commoner's house now, and living as one. He turned the key, locking himself in. Then he dumped his treasure trove on the cot, fingering the pieces thoughtfully. He hadn't made much of her talk, but her face had shown she was immensely excited over the—the gawdies. Or did that just mean boxes? *Why* had she been excited? They could be exchanged for money, or food. Money could be exchanged for clothes, food, shelter, entertainment. Fledwick, too, had been that way about money, if he had understood correctly. The little man had habitually run great risk of imprisonment and shame for its sake. And the men on the raft—they had tried to get extra gawdies from him. It all meant that he had something commoners wanted badly, and a lot of it.

He lay down on the bed and found its pulpy lumps unbearable. The floor was better than the mattress. To find the girl he would have to face the drinking room. Recalling the night he had been there, he remembered the noise, the smells, the drink he had been given, the close air, the foolish women. But the bar was his reason for being there. The girl of the Cairo Mystery had found him there before; there he might find her now. He thought about clothes—he would need some. And boots—slippers, rather. As a commoner he could not wear boots. And clean clothes. Even a commoner would not wear the same things all the time, he supposed.

Mistress Cannon had anticipated him. She was waiting in the drinking room below with news.

"Wish you'd come down a little sooner. I had old man Carlin hanging around, then he said he had to hit. But he'll be around first thing in the morning. I would've sent him up, only I figured you were sleeping the jab off."

Was he supposed to know who old man Carlin was? He asked.

"Carlin? He runs the sump shop around here: sells court clothes on the side. Why those tramps are willing to pay such crazy prices for it I never knew. To give the boy friends a thrill behind locked doors, I guess. Back when I had it I would've beat a man's ears off if he couldn't get a thrill out of me without fancy-pantsy court sheers on. *You aren't from the District, are you?*"

He hesitated, startled by the gunblast suddenness of the question.

"That's what I figured," she said soberly, lowering her voice. "Listen." She bent across the table toward him, and a too-musky, too-strong scent issued from the deep cleft between her breasts. "You want some good advice, I can give it to you. Even if you don't want it. You're on the scramble and you jab—a bad combination—and you don't want to get pumped, not by me or any other old bat. All right, that's smart enough, and you got sense enough not to try to lie when you're jabbed up. But you don't have to get up on the darby perch either, like you did with me. Listen—"

She stopped to wheeze, and went on earnestly: "I come into my kitchen this afternoon, and found you standing there grinning at yourself, and you could of had the whole house with a gold ribbon tied around it. Ten minutes later, you're giving me your high-and-mighty starborne act, and you come damn near not having any room here at all. A fella with a face like yours, and that build, he's a fool not to make some use of it. You don't want to talk man…smile!" She straightened up and waved to a newcomer farther down the bar. "I got to tend to customers," she said. "You got a handle I can call you by, in case they ask?"

Cade smiled inwardly at the absurd advice—and at the question that came fast after it. For the first time since he'd met the Mistress, he looked her fully in the eye. She was hardly a perilous female, after all, in spite of her loose talk. He remained silent, but slowly and deliberately he let the inner smile spread on his face.

"That's it!" she crowed, delightedly. "You're no fool! Hey, Jana!"

A willowy brunette detached herself from a group of girls talking in a corner while they waited for the place to fill. She walked with studied languor toward them; the silvery garter on her thigh pulled the flimsy stuff of her trousers tight against her at each step.

"Jana, I want you to meet a friend of mine," Mistress Cannon said. "Nothing's too good for my friend, Smiley!" She winked at him, a lewd and terrifying wink as massive as a shrug, and bustled off.

"That's some send-off you got, Smiley," said the girl. Her voice was husky and, quite automatically, she assumed the same position Mistress Cannon had, leaning far forward and compressing her shoulders. Some commoner notion, he thought uneasily, as he observed that it exposed quite a lot of her to a table-mate.

"Yes," he said stiffly. "She's been very good to me."

"Say, I remember you!" Jana said abruptly. "You were in here last week. And were you troubled, brother! Were you troubled!"

Suddenly she frowned: "What's the matter, Smiley?"

He couldn't help it. The shock of being addressed as *brother* in this place by this woman showed on him.

"Nothing," he said.

"Nothing?" she asked wisely. "Listen, I see you're not drinking—" Cade followed her glance and noticed there was a small glass of vile-smelling stuff on the table. He pushed it away. "—and I've been arguing with Arlene about it ever since—you remember her? The little blonde over there in the corner?" Hope flared wildly, and vanished as he saw the girl she meant. "Anyhow, she says it wasn't liquor and I say I never saw a man your size and age out where he sat like you were. Not on liquor. You don't have to tell me if you don't want to, but—?"

She let it linger on a questioning note.

Cade, profiting by instruction, smiled directly at her, and held the smile until he felt foolish.

The results were unexpected and dramatic. She whistled, a long, low whistle that made half a dozen heads turn their way inquiringly. And she looked at him with such adoration as he had seen only a few times before, from new Armigers on the Field of Battle.

"Bro-*ther*!" she sighed.

"Excuse me," said Cade in a strangled voice. He ran from the enemy, leaving her in complete and bewildered possession of the field.

Chapter Thirteen

Cade learned fast at Cannon's. He had to. His eyes and ears, trained for life-or-death differences in action, picked up words, glances and gestures; his battle-sharpened wits evaluated them. He survived.

And Cannon's learned about Cade, as much as was necessary. He was Smiley, and Cannon's etiquette permitted no further prying into his name or rank. He was talked about. Some said he was starborne, but no one asked. His full pockets and Jana's wagging tongue gave him the introduction and reputation he needed.

His build? He was obviously a strong-arm bucko. His rumored golden trinkets? He was obviously a master gaff—a burglar. His occasional lapses of memory and manners? He was obviously addicted to the most powerful narcotics. That too explained his otherwise inexplicable lack of interest in alcohol and women.

As a bucko and gaff he outranked most other habitués of the place: the ratty little pickpockets, the jumpy gamblers, the thoroughly detestable pimps. As a jabber of unknown drugs he even outranked the friendly, interesting, neatly dressed confidence men who occasionally passed through. Drugs were a romantic, desperate slap in the face of things as they were. Mistress Cannon disapproved—there had been a man of hers; she wouldn't talk about it. But to her hostesses it was the ultimate attraction.

Nightly, Cade sat in the barroom at a corner table near the stairs with an untasted drink before him. Carlin, who dressed commoner girls and tramps secretly in court gowns, had taken his measure and provided him with blues and greens for as much of his plunder as he had chosen to display. The old man had dickered endlessly over each item, but with Mistress Cannon loudly supervising the transaction Cade emerged with two full sets of clothes made to order for him, two weeks of exorbitant "board" paid, and a surplus of clink. In his room, behind one of the storage shelves, he had found a hiding place for his remaining gawdies: one last golden box containing half a dozen smaller trifles.

With this much security—a place to live, new clothes, good food, clink in his pocket, an enviable reputation and a hidden reserve—he could turn his full attention to his quest for the girl of the Cairo Mystery. He asked few questions, but he listened always for a word that might lead to her. Every night he sat at his table, his chair turned to the door, watching every new arrival, buying drink for anyone who would talk—and that was everyone.

First there were Mistress Cannon and her girls. Then he could ask openly after he learned that it was not strange to seek renewal of acquaintance with a girl who had struck one's fancy. But none of them knew her, none remembered seeing her except that night when he had met her there.

It was a setback, but there was no other place to look except Baltimore—and they'd had no trouble handling him there once. If nothing at Cannon's led him to the girl he would act without her, and gradually an alternative plan formed. While it was growing, over the course of his two weeks' stay, he drank in everything he heard from the endless procession of people willing to talk while Smiley bought.

There was a Martian who had jumped ship, and taken to liquor and petty thievery. For two nights Cade listened to him curse the misstep: he babbled monotonously about his family and their little iron refinery; how there had been a girl back home and how he might have married and had children to grow up with the planet. The Marsman didn't come back the third night, or ever.

He wasted one night. This was on a quiet, well-spoken, grey-haired man, himself a former gaff who had retired on his "earnings." He came for the first time on Smiley's fourth night in the bar and for almost a week. He came again every night. He was a mine of information on criminal ways and means, nicknames, jargon, Watch corruption, organized prostitution, disposal of gaffed goods. On the last night, the wasted night, after chatting and drinking for an hour, he confided without warning that he was in possession of a secret truth unknown to other men. Leaning across the table in excitement he whispered clearly: "Things have not always been as they are now!"

Cade remembered the rites of the Mystery and leaned forward himself to listen. But the hope was illusory; the gentle old man was a lunatic.

He'd found a book, he said, while still gaffing years ago. It was called "Sixth Grade Reader." He thought it was incredibly old, and whispered, almost in Cade's ear: "More than ten thousand years!"

Cade leaned back in disgust while the madman rattled on. The book was full of stories, verses, anecdotes, many of them supposed to be based on fact and not fiction. But one thing they had in common: not one of them mentioned the Emperor, Klin, the Order, or the Realm of Man. "Don't you see what that means? Can't you see it for yourself? There was a time once when *There was no Emperor.*"

In the face of Smiley's bored disinterest he lost his caution and spoke loudly enough for Mistress Cannon, at the bar, to catch a few words. She stormed to the table in a loyal rage and threw him out. She later regretted it. Word got around and the incident brought on the only Watch raid during Smiley's stay at Cannon's.

The whole district was minutely sifted and Cade too had to submit to questioning. But the Watchers were looking for just one man, and Smiley's origins did not concern them. Later, word got to Cannon's that they had found the madman in the very act of airing his mania to jeering children on the street. He did not survive his first night in the Watch House. Those rubber truncheons, Cade remembered, and wondered whether it had been necessary to cope with the poor fool so drastically.

There were others who came to the table and talked. There was a pastel-clad young man who misunderstood Cade's lack of interest in the girls and immediately had the matter made crystal-clear to him. Mistress Cannon pitched him limply out with the usual hoarse injunction: "And don't you *ever* come back in here again!" But he probably didn't hear her.

One night there was a fat-faced, sententious fellow, a con man who had hit the skids because of liquor. Smiley bought many drinks for him because he had been in the Cairo Mystery—and several others. He explained that the Mysteries were a good place to meet your johns, and was otherwise defensive. Cade dared to question him closely after the con man had poured down enough liquor to blur his brain and probably leave the incident a blank next morning. But he knew little enough. He'd never heard of hypnosis in connection with a Mystery. A featureless, egg-shaped room had nothing to do with the Cairo rites. Mysteries were strictly for the johns; the revenue from them was strictly for the blades, like him and Smiley. He proposed vaguely that they start a new Mystery with a new twist and take over all the other blades' johns. With his experience and Smiley's looks it'd be easy. Then he fell asleep across the table.

There were many others; but *she* never came and he never heard a word about her or anyone like her.

When the two weeks he allowed himself were past he knew vastly more than he had known before, but none of it led to the girl. It was time for the other plan.

Mistress Cannon protested hoarsely when he told her he was leaving. "I never saw a man go through a load like that so fast," she complained. "You didn't have to buy for everybody that said he was a rog. Listen—I made enough on that liquor to cover another week easy. You don't tell anybody about it and I'll let you stay. Two weeks won't do it in this town, but three weeks might. What about it?"

"It's not the money," he tried to explain. She was right about his blues and greens being gone, but she didn't know about the box of loot he still had in his room. "There's a job I've got to do. Something I promised before I came here."

"A promise doesn't count when you're hot!" she shouted. "What good will it do to try and keep your promise if you get picked up by the Watchers as soon as you step out of the door?"

He wasn't worried about that one. The Cannon grapevine was efficient and he knew the search for the "impostor" Cade had bogged down, at least locally. Two pedestrians had been incinerated by a young Armiger ten days ago. Though a strong order had been put out that identification of the two as the Cade-impostor and ex-Teacher Zisz was not confirmed as yet, the local Watch had naturally slacked off its effort almost to zero. If Arle was making any search, it was undercover.

All Cade wanted was a place to leave everything he had except his gawdies and the better suit of commoners' garb. Reluctantly Mistress Cannon provided him with one of a pile of metal boxes in her kitchen: private vaults with self-set radionic locks, hidden under layers of food-stuffs.

Cade dressed in his room for the last time in the sober, dignified suit he had specified. Old Carlin had grumbled at the requirements: "Think you're going to Audience?" and Cade had smiled...but that, as a matter of fact, was exactly it: the alternative. The only one.

He could have tried to plunge into the Cairo Mystery and been hyp-notized again for his troubles. He could have gone to a Chapter House and been burned down. But there was still, and always, the Emperor. This was the morning of the monthly Audience Day; he had timed it so.

Even here at Cannon's this much remained sure: the rogs and blades, the whores and hostesses were unfit people, but they were loyal to the Emperor, every one. There had been no trace of the conspiracy he sought. The insane burglar with his imaginary book had been an object of horror to them all.

The Realm is wide, thought Cade, *but not so wide that the Emperor will turn a deaf ear to any plea.*

His only fear was that he would not be believed when he told his complex and terrible story. The Emperor's benevolence would be sorely tried to comprehend a plot against him in an innocent Mystery; and to add to that the defection from fitness of the Gunner Supreme. Cade wondered what he himself would have thought of such a tale a few weeks ago.

But it would get to persons less full of loving-kindness than the Emperor. He had seen the iron-faced Power Master at ceremonies—a grim tower of a man; the gentle Emperor's mailed fist. Which was as it always had been, which was as it should be. It wasn't hard to visualize the Power Master believing enough of the story to investigate, and that was all that would be needed.

Cade had in his pockets as he left only half the remaining smaller gawdies and a handful of clink: three blues and a few greens. The gold box and the Gun of the Order were in the kitchen behind hardened bronze under a layer of meal. There was something like a tear in Mis-tress Cannon's bloodshot eye when she said: "Don't forget you're coming back. There's always a place for you here."

He promised to remember, and the promise was true. He hoped he would never have to see the place again; but he knew he wouldn't forget it to his dying day. Such—*irregularity!* No order in their lives or thoughts, no proportion, no object, no fitness. And yet there was a curious warmth, an unexpected sense of comradeship strangely like that he had felt for his Brothers in the Order, but somehow stronger. He wondered if all commoners had it or if it was the property of only the criminals and near-criminals.

When he closed the door behind him and started down the street he felt strangely alone. It was the same street down which he had walked in the lamplight with the elusive girl following behind. He rounded the corner, where another Watchman now stood, and trudged to the Palace in bitter solitude. What would happen would happen: he gloomily thought, and cursed himself for his gloom. He should have been full of honorable pride and exultation over the service he was about to render to the Emperor, but he was not. Instead he was worried about the commoner girl.

The girl, the girl, the *girl!* He had lied to the Gunner Supreme by not mentioning her—but only after he already had suspected that the Supreme was an unfit voluptuary, false to the Order. Hopefully he tried to persuade himself that she would come to no harm; realistically he knew that, harm or not, he could not lie to the Emperor and that she might well be caught and crushed in the wheels of justice he was about to set in motion.

CHAPTER FOURTEEN

As a respectable-looking commoner of the middle class, Cade was admitted without questioning through the Audience Gate, a towering arch in the great wall that enclosed the nerve-center of the Realm. The Palace proper, a graciously proportioned rose marble building, lay a hundred meters inside. A Klin Serviceman—the gold braid on his grey meant Palace Detail—led the newcomer to a crowd already waiting patiently in the plaza.

"Wait here," he said brusquely, and strode off.

Cade waited as further commoners arrived and the crowd began to fill the open square. He noticed, however, that from time to time one of the throng—usually well-dressed—would approach a loitering guard for a few words. Something would seem to change hands and the man or woman would be led off toward the Palace itself.

The Gunner managed to be nearby next time it happened; he smiled bitterly as his suspicions were confirmed. Even here in the Palace, under the very eyes of the Emperor, there was corruption almost in the open.

The next Serviceman to approach the crowd with a newcomer took him inside for the modest price of one green. And he gave Cade what the

Gunner took to be complete instructions: "When you enter the Audience Hall, wait for the appearance of the Emperor. After he appears, face
him at all times, standing. Keep silent until you're announced. Then,
with your eyes lowered, not stepping over the white line, state your case
in ten words or so."

"Ten words!"

"Have you no brief, commoner?" The guard was amazed.

A brief would be a written version of his case. Cade shook his head.
"It doesn't matter," he said. "Ten words will be ample."

He turned down the Serviceman's friendly offer to locate a briefsman
who would, of course, require something extra for a rush job. Ten words
would be ample; the ones he had in mind would create enough furor to
give him all the time he'd need to state his case.

The guard left him finally outside the ornate door of the hall with a
last stem order: "Stand right here until they let you in."

"And when is that supposed to be?" a fussily dressed man at Cade's
elbow asked as the Serviceman walked away. "How long a wait *this*
time?"

Before Cade could say he didn't know, a white-haired granny scolded:
"It doesn't make any difference. It's a real treat, every minute of it. I've
been promising myself this trip—I live in Northumberland, that's in
England—for many a year and it's a fine thing I finally got the greens
for it saved, because I surely won't be here next year!"

"Perhaps not," said the man distantly. And then curiously: "What's
your complaint for the Emperor?"

"Complaint? Complaint? Dear me, I have no complaint! I just want
to see his kind face close up and say 'Greetings and love from a loyal old
lady of Northumberland, England.' Don't you think he'll be pleased?"

Cade melted at her innocence. "I'm sure he will," he said warmly,
and she beamed with pleasure.

"I dare say," said the fussily dressed man. "What *I* have to lay before
the Emperor's justice and wisdom is a sound grievance—" He whipped
out and began to unfold a manuscript of many pages. "—a sound grievance against my cursed neighbor Flyte, his slatternly wife and their four
destructive brats. I've asked them politely, I've demanded firmly, I've—"

"Pardon." Cade shouldered past the man and seized the old lady
from Northumberland by the arm. He had been watching again the
ones who got beyond the Gate, and how they did it. To an expectant
Serviceman he said: "Sir, my old mother here is worn from travel. We've
been waiting since sun-up. When can we get into the Hall?"

"Why, it might be arranged very soon," the Serviceman said non-
committally.

Cade abandoned the effort; apparently there was nothing to do but
pay. Bitterly he pulled another green from his pocket. He had just one
more after that, and a few blues.

"It's only your old mother you want admitted?" the guard asked kindly. "You yourself wish to wait outside for her?"

Cade understood, wavered a moment and then handed him the last green he owned. It didn't matter. Once in the Hall, in the Emperor's own presence, there could be no more of this.

And he was in the Hall, with the puzzled, grateful old lady from Northumberland beside him, her arm tucked under his.

"Over there," the guard pointed. "And keep your voices low if you must speak."

There were two groups waiting, clearly distinguished from each other. One was composed of commoners, about fifty of them, nervously congregated behind a white-marble line in the oval hall's mosaic flooring. There were perhaps as many persons of rank chatting and strolling relaxedly at a little distance from the commoners. At the end of the hall was a raised dais where, he supposed, the Emperor would sit in state. By the dais was a thick pedestal a meter high. Klin guards stood stiffly here and there, with gas guns at their belts. The nearest of them gestured abruptly at Cade, and he hastily moved into the commoners' enclosure.

Granny was clutching his arm and pouring out twittery thanks. But Cade, already regretting the impulse, turned his back on her and worked his way through to the other side of the group. He was joined a minute later by the overdressed fellow who had talked to him outside the Hall.

"I saw you couldn't persuade the guard," the man said, "so I paid without quibbling. I wonder how many more times the Greys will expect us to pay?"

"That had better be the last," Cade said grimly.

"Such a pity!" someone said from his other side.

"Eh?" Cade turned to see a sour-looking middle-aged woman, staring with pursed lips across the Hall at a space near the dais that had been empty only a few minutes ago. It was filling now with starbornes—Ladies, high dignitaries in the Klin Service and a few Brothers of the Order, their cloaks banded with the Silver of Superiors below colored stripes that designated their Stars. Cade silently studied the stripes: Congo, Pacificisles, California, and of course Eastcoast. He had served under none of them; they would not be able to identify him on the spot. But at the same time they would not half-recognize him, assume he was the Cade-impostor and blast him where he stood.

"*Such* a trial to the Court!" the woman insisted, again pursuing her lips and shaking her head with enjoyment.

"What?" asked Cade. She pointed and he realized he had asked the wrong question. "Who?" he amended it, and then he saw—

"*Who's that?*" he demanded, clutching the sleeve of the man next to him.

"What'd you say? Would you mind—this cloth crushes." He picked Cade's hand from his sleeve indignantly, but the Gunner never noticed. It was *she:* he was certain of it. Her back was turned to him and her hair was a brilliant, foolish shade of orange-red to match her gown, but somehow he was certain.

He turned to the woman beside him: "What about her? Who is she?"

"Don't you know?" She eyed him significantly. "The Lady *Jocelyn,*" she whispered. "The peculiar one. You'd never think to look at her that she's a niece of the Emperor himself—"

The fussily dressed man interrupted with a snickering question to show that he was up on the latest Palace gossip: "The one that writes poems?"

"Yes. And I have a friend who works in the kitchens, not a cook but a dietician, of course, and she says the Lady Jocelyn reads them to *everybody*—whether they want to listen or not. Once she even began reciting to some commoners waiting just like us—"

But Cade was not listening. The Lady Jocelyn had turned to face them and her resemblance to the girl of the Mystery collapsed. The bright red hair, of course, was dyed. But even Cade, as little competent to judge women's clothes as any man alive, could see that it was a bad match to a wretchedly cut gown. She was round-shouldered and evidently near-sighted, for she stood with her head thrust forward like a crane. When she walked off a moment later after surveying the commoners indifferently, her gait was a foolish shamble. The only resemblance between this awkward misfit of the Court and the vivid, commanding creature who had saved his life was in the nature of a caricature.

All around him there was a sighing and a straightening. The Emperor had entered, and was seating himself on the dais. Two Klin guards moved to the commoners' area and there was a subdued jockeying for position. Before Cade understood what was going on, one of the guards had relieved him of his last few blues, examined the small sum with disgust and stationed him well to the end of the line. Curse it, how much more was he supposed to know that he didn't? He realized that the guard's instructions had not been instructions at all but a last-minute warning which hit only the things he wasn't supposed to do: not talk, not turn his back, not overstep the line, not be long-winded—a mere recapitulation of things he was supposed to know. What else was involved? The commoners he had known at Cannon's were loyal, but shied from the idea of an Audience. He saw plainly from the people he was with that it was a middle-class affair. What else was involved? He was glad he wasn't at the head of the line—and hastily fell into step as the line moved off to stop at the enigmatic pedestal before the dais. Cade saw the fussily dressed man at the head of the line; he dropped currency—*greens!*—on it and murmured to one of the guards.

Thank offering, love offering, something like that, he vaguely remembered now, much too late to do anything about it. He glowered at the white-haired granny halfway down the line and berated himself for the impulse that had made him pay her way in. She, canny, middleclass, had saved her money for the offering.

"Commoner Bolwen," the guard was saying, and the fussily dressed man said to the Emperor, with his eyes lowered: "I present a complaint against a rude and unfit person to my Emperor." He handed his bulky brief to the guard and backed away from the dais.

Not a blue on him, Cade thought, and the line was shortening with amazing efficiency. "Offering," they called it. Did that mean it was voluntary? Nobody was omitting it.

"I ask my Emperor to consider my brilliant son for the Klin Service."

"Loyal greetings to our Emperor from the city of Buena Vista."

"I ask my Emperor's intercession in the bankruptcy case of my husband."

Cade looked up fleetingly at the Emperor's face for possible inspiration, and lost more time. The face was arrestingly different from what he had expected. It was not rapt and unworldly but thoughtful, keen, penetrating—the face of a Senior Teacher, a scholar.

There was a guard at Cade's side, muttering: "Offering in your left hand."

Cade opened his mouth to speak, and the guard said: "Silence."

"But—" said Cade. Instantly the guard's gas gun was out, ready to fire. The guard jerked his head at the door. He was no moon-faced, sluggish, run-of-the-mill Watchman, Cade saw, but a picked member of the Service: no fighting man, but a most efficient guard who could drop him at the hint of a false move. And there were other guards looking their way...Cade silently stepped out of the line and backed to the great door, with the guard's eyes never leaving him.

Outside the Hall the guard delivered a short, withering lecture on commoners who didn't know their duties and would consume the Emperor's invaluable time as though it were the time of a shop-attendant. Cade gathered that the offering was another of the commoners' inviolable laws—even stronger than the one that made you use a smoker pellet when it was offered to you. Something as trivial as that, and it had barred him for a month from bringing his case to the Emperor!

The ridiculous injustice of it was suddenly more than he could take. Like an untested Brother suddenly thrust into battle, Cade choked on panic and despair. But for him, now, there was no faith in the Gunner Supreme to carry him through the moment of ordeal. There was no one, no reason for him to carry this burden at all. He who had dedicated his life and every deed in it to the Emperor was turned away because he didn't have greens to drop into a platter!

The guard was snarling that he had showed disgusting disrespect for the Emperor—

"Respect for the Emperor?" he burst out wildly. "What do you know about it, grey-suited fool? I'm risking my life to be here. There's a conspiracy against the Emperor! I was trying to warn—" His self-pity was cooled by a dash of cold fear. Next he'd be telling his name. Next the gas gun would go off in his face. And then there would be no awakening.

But the grey-clad guard had backed away, his weapon firmly trained on Cade's face and his finger white on the trigger. "Conspiracy, is it?" said the guard. "You're mad. Or…whatever you are, this is a matter for Armsmen. *Walk.*"

Cade trudged emptily down the corridor. He had said it and he would pay for it. There was an Auxiliary Chapter House in the Palace, and every Gunner worthy of his Gun would have a description of the Cade-impostor firmly planted in his memory.

"In there." It was an elevator that soared to the top of the Palace and let them out at an anteroom where an Armiger stood guard.

"Sir," said the Serviceman, "please call the Gunner of the Day." The Armiger stared at Cade, and there was no recognition in the stare; he spoke into a wall panel, and the door opened. They marched through the Ready Room into the Charge Room, where the Gunner of the Day waited. Cade stared downward at the familiar plastic flooring of a Chapter House, as he approached the desk. He could brace himself against the inevitable tearing blast of flame; he could not bring himself to look his executioner in the eye.

There was no blast. Instead there came a voice—dry, precise, familiar, and astonished: "Why, we thought you were—!"

"Silence!" said Cade swiftly. The Gunner was Kendall of Denver, a companion for years before his assignment to France. After the first show of surprise, Kendall's long face was impassive. Cade knew his former Brother's mind: form a theory and act on it. By now he would have decided that Cade had been on one of the Order's infrequent secret assignments. And he would never mistake Cade for the hunted Cade-impostor.

"Guard, is there a charge?" Gunner Kendall asked.

"Sir, this cursed fellow failed to make the voluntary offering in Audience, he talked in the Emperor's presence, and when I pulled him out of line he yelled about a conspiracy. I suppose he's mad, but if there's anything to it I—"

"Quite right. I'll take charge. Return to your post."

When they were alone, Kendall grinned hugely. "We all thought you were dead, Brother. There's even an order out to kill someone impersonating you. You took a fine chance coming here. We have Brothers Rosso and Banker in the Palace detail besides me; they'll be glad to hear the news. How may I help you?"

Escort to the Emperor? No; now the Emperor need not be troubled with it. The Emperor's right arm would set this crazy muddle right. "Take me to the Power Master, Brother. At once."

Kendall led the way without question. Through corridors, down ramps, through antechambers, Cade saw doors open and salutes snap to the trim uniform of the Gunner.

They passed through a great apartment at last that was far from ornate. There was an antechamber where men and women sat and waited. There was a brightly lit, vast communications room in back, where hundreds of youngsters tended solid banks of sending and receiving signal units. There was a great room behind that, where men at long tables elaborated outgoing messages and briefed incoming ones. There were many, many smaller rooms further behind, where older men could be seen talking into dictating machines or writing, and consulting lists and folders as they worked. Endlessly, messengers went to and fro. It was Cade's first glimpse of the complex machinery of administration.

In a final anteroom, alone, they sat and waited. Cade felt the eerie sensation of being spy-rayed, but the orifice was too cunningly concealed for him to spot it.

"Gunner Kendall, come in and bring the commoner," said a voice at length—and Cade stiffened. It was the vibrant, commanding voice he could never forget; the voice that had broadcast the "kill-on-sight" command.

He followed Kendall from the anteroom into a place whose like he had never seen before. It had every comfort of the Lady Moia's bedchamber, but was sternly masculine in its simplicity. The whole room pointed to a table where the iron-visaged Power Master sat, and Cade rejoiced. This was the man who would crush the conspiracy and root out the decadent Gunner Supreme. . .

"Sir," said Kendall in his precise way, "this is Gunner Cade, mistakenly supposed dead. He asked me to bring him to you."

"My spy ray showed me that he is unarmed," said the Power Master. "See to it that he does not seize your weapon." He got up from the table as Kendall backed away from Cade, with confusion on his face. Cade saw that the Power Master wore a gun of the Order—a gun he deliberately unbuckled and flung on the table with a crash. Slowly he approached Cade.

The man was fully as tall as Cade, and heavier. His muscles were rock-hard knots where Cade's were sliding steel bands. Cade was a boxer, the Power Master—a strangler. With his face half a meter from Cade's, he said, in the voice that once had ordered his death: "Are you going to kill me, Gunner? This is your chance."

Cade told him steadily: "I am not here to kill you, sir. I'm here to give you information vital to the Realm."

The Power Master stared into his eyes for a long, silent minute, and then suddenly grinned. He returned to the table to buckle on his gun. "You're sure he's Cade?" he asked, with his back turned.

"No possible doubt, sir," said Kendall. "We were novices together."

"Cade, who else knows about this?"

"Nobody, sir. Only Brother Kendall."

"Good." The Power Master swung around with the gun in his hand. A stab of flame from it blasted the life out of Gunner Kendall. Cade saw the muzzle of the gun turn to train steadily on him as Kendall toppled to the floor.

CHAPTER FIFTEEN

"SIT DOWN," said the Power Master. He laid his gun on the polished table as Cade collapsed into a capacious chair. Numbly he thought: it wasn't murder like Fledwick; Kendall is—was—a Gunner under arms. He could have drawn…but why?

"I can use you," said the Power Master. "I can always use a first-rate Armsman who's had a look below the surface and kept his head. You could be especially useful to me because, as far as the world knows, you are dead—now that Kendall has been silenced. Also you seem to have an unusual, useful immunity to hypnosis."

"You know about it," said Cade stupidly.

The Power Master grinned and said, rolling the words: "The Great Conspiracy. Yes; I have my representatives in the Great Conspiracy. I was alarmed when they advised me that a most able Gunner had been turned loose with a compulsion to take my life—and even more alarmed when I found you had slipped through the fingers of the fools of the City Watch."

The girl—was she his spy in the Mystery?

"Now," said the Power Master briskly, "tell me about your recovery from their hypnosis."

"I was left in a drinking room to come to my senses," Cade said slowly, uncertain of what to tell. If she was his spy—but he risked it. He might be shot down like Kendall, but he would know. "I felt the compulsion mounting," he said evenly, "and then it went away for no apparent reason. It has not returned. I left the place looking for a Chapter House. One of the women followed me, and we were both arrested by the Watch."

The Power Master looked up sharply, and Cade was certain that there was surprise in the glance. "You don't know who the woman was?"

"No," said Cade. That much, at least, was true.

"You're sure?"

"I've been trying to find out," he admitted, shamelessly, and the Power Master did not bother to repress a cynical smile. Cade didn't care: the girl was no spy of the Power Master's. His claim that the hypnotic compulsion had vanished by itself stood unchallenged. In spite of his bullying show of omniscience, the man did not really know everything.

"Tell me the rest," said the Power Master. "What happened to your partner in criminal insanity—the unbooked Teacher?"

Cade told him of their cross-country journey, the shattering discoveries at the Building of Fives that climaxed in the treacherous murder of Fledwick. The Power Master smiled again at the involuntary pain in Cade's voice as he mentioned the presence of the Lady Moia. And he nodded approvingly as Cade told him of his two weeks at Cannon's—"waiting for the hue-and-cry to die down"—and of his failure to reach the Emperor.

"You've done well," he pronounced judiciously at last. "Now I want to know whether you've profited by it all.

"Since your novitiate, Cade, you've been filled full of brotherhood and misinformation. You've been doing all the right things, but for the wrong reasons. If you can learn the right reasons...Tell me first: why did you Gunners of France fight the Gunners of Muscovy?"

"Because they tried to seize an iron deposit belonging to our Star," Cade said simply. Where was the man leading?

"*There was no iron deposit.* One of my people faked a geological survey report for the Star of France and seeded a little Mars iron at the site. I held it in reserve as a bone of contention. When the French Star was making overtures to the Muscovite Star concerning a combination of forces, I let the news of the 'iron deposit' leak to Muscovy, with the results that you know. There will be no combination between France and Muscovy now, or for many years to come."

It was an elaborate joke, Cade decided, and in very bad taste.

"All your wars are like that," said the Power Master, grimly. "They are useful things to keep the Stars diverted and divided. That is the purpose of the Great Conspiracy as well—though the Stars who think they are behind it do not know this. It requires immense funds to keep a vast underground organization going; the half-dozen or so Stars now supporting the Cairo Mystery conspiracy will soon be bled white and drop off, while others take their place. My agents will keep anything serious from ever coming of the Cairo affair, of course. I confess it almost got out of hand, but that is a risk one must run."

This was no joke, Cade numbly realized. It was the end of his world. "What do the Stars who...think...they are behind the conspiracy want?" he asked, fighting for calm.

"They want to kill me, of course, and go their own wild way. They want more, and more, and more Armsmen. They want to fight bigger and bigger wars, and destroy more and more villages...You've been taught that the Stars are loyal to the Realm, the way commoners are loyal to the Stars. The truth is that the Stars are the worst enemy the Realm has. Without a Power Master to keep them out of harm they'd have the Realm a wreck in one man's lifetime.

"And your precious Gunner Supreme? Cade, I suppose you think he's the first one like that in ten thousand years and will be the last one like that until the end of time?"

"That was my hope," Cade said wearily.

"Disabuse yourself. Most of them have been like that; most of them *will* be...must be, if you can understand. Arle is plotting, if you please, to supplant me, merging the two offices. It is only to be expected. A Gunner such as yourself may survive years of combat because he has brains. He becomes a Gunner Superior, in intimate contact with a Star. He figures in the Star's plottings. The women of the Court, fascinated by the novelty of a man they can't have, bend every effort to seducing him and usually succeed. His vows are broken, he misses the active life of battle, he intrigues for election to the office of the Supreme. By the time he wins it he is a very ordinary voluptuary with a taste for power, like our friend Arle.

"But Cade, this is the key; don't forget it: *there must be a Gunner Supreme.* As a fighting man you know that. Many a time the fact that the Supreme lived somewhere and embodied your notion of the Order has saved your life or saved the day for your command. The fact that the Supreme in the flesh is not what you think doesn't matter at all."

Cade leaned forward. The abominable thing he was about to say was a ball in his throat, choking him so he had to get rid of it: "The Emperor?" he asked. "The Emperor? Why does he allow it? Why?"

"The Emperor is another lie," the Power Master said calmly. "The Emperor can't stop it. He's just a man—an ordinary one. If he attempted to make suggestions about my task of running the Realm, I would very properly ignore them. Emperors who have offered too many such suggestions in the past, Cade, have died young. Their Power Masters killed them. It will happen again.

"And that's as it should be. As you know, the line of the Power Master descends by adoption and the line of the Emperor by male primogeniture. The Power Master chooses a tried man to succeed himself. The Emperor gets what chance sends him. Of course the line of the Power Master is stronger, so of course it must rule."

His voice rose almost to a roar. *"But there must be an Emperor.* The Power Master is unloved: he sends people to death; he collects taxes; he sets speed limits. The Emperor does none of this; he simply exists and is loved because everybody is told to love him. People do it—again, the right thing for the wrong reason. If they didn't love him, what would happen to the Realm? Think of such a thing as all the commoners becoming criminals. What would we do when the Watch Houses were all filled? What would we do if they kept attacking the Watch Houses until all the gas-gun charges were used up? But they don't all become criminals. They love the Emperor and don't want to sadden him with unfit deeds."

The Power Master rose, holstering his gun, and began to pace the room restlessly. "I am asking you to think, Cade," he said with blazing intensity. "I don't want to throw away a fine tool like you. I am asking you to think. Things are not what they seem, not what you thought they were.

"For many years you did your best work because you didn't know the right reasons. Now it's different. There are other jobs for you, and you won't be able to do them if you're blinded by the lies you used to believe. Remember always that the Realm as it is *works*. It's been kept working for ten thousand years by things being as they are and not as they seem. It can be kept working to the end of time as long as there are resolute men to shove the structure back into balance when it shows signs of toppling."

Stopping for a moment at the feet of the slain Gunner Kendall, he said simply: "That was for the happiness of millions. They are happy, almost all of them. Gunners are contented, the Klin Service is contented, the Courts are contented, the commoners are contented. Let things change, let the structure crash and where would they be? Give each commoner the power I hold and what would he make of it? Would he be contented or would he run amuck?

"Cade, I don't want to...lose you. Think straight. Is there anything really unfit about the work I do, the work I want you to do for me? You made a trade of killing because the trade was called the Order of Armsmen. My trade is conserving the stability and contentment of order of every subject of the Realm of Man."

The passionately sincere voice pounded on, battering at Cade's will. The Power Master spoke of the vows Cade had taken, and he destroyed their logic completely. Cade had dedicated himself to the service of the Emperor—who was no more than the powerless, ceremonial excuse for the Power Master. With ruthless obscenity of detail he told Cade what he had given up in life in exchange for a sterile athleticism.

He spoke of food and drunkenness and drugs; of dancing and music and love: the whole sensual world Cade had thought well lost. He wooed the Gunner with two intermingling siren songs—the fitness of his new service under the Power Master and the indulgence of himself that was possible in it.

It would have been easy to tumble into the trap. Cade had been drained empty of the certainties of a lifetime. The Power Master said there was only one other set of certainties, and that if Cade would only let himself be filled with them there would be the most wonderful consequences any powerful man of normal appetites would want.

It was easy to listen, it would have been easy to accept, but…Cade knew there was even more than he'd been told. There was one thing that did not fit in the new world, and that was the girl. The girl who had not wanted the Power Master killed, or the Gunner either. The girl who had warned Cade—rightly—that he would be going to his death if he tried to reaffiliate with the Order.

There was no all-powerful, all-loving Emperor any more; there were no loyal Stars; there was only the Power Master—and the girl. So, thought Cade, treachery is the order of the day and has been for ten thousand years. He knew what answer he would give the Power Master, the answer he had to give to stay alive, but he was not ready to give it yet. A lifetime of training in strategy made him sharply aware that a quick surrender would be wrong.

"I must ask for time, sir," he said painfully. "You realize this is…very new to me. My vows have been part of me for many years, and it's less than a month since I…died…in battle. May I have leave to spend a day in meditation?"

The Power Master's lips quirked with inner amusement. "One day? You may have it, and welcome. And you may spend it in my own apartment. I have a room you should find comfortable."

CHAPTER SIXTEEN

THE ROOM WAS COMFORTABLE by any standards Cade had known; it was second in luxury only to the smothering softness of the Lady Moia's apartment. Compared to Mistress Cannon's mean quarters or the sleeping lofts of a Chapter House it offered every comfort a dog-tired man could ask. And it was also, unmistakably, a prison.

There were no bars to guard the windows and presumably the "shoot-on-sight" order had lost its force. Yet Cade was certain he could not leave the place alive without the express permission of its master. If there had been any doubt about the answer he must give tomorrow, this room would have resolved it.

And it went deeper. If he'd had any tendency to give that answer in good faith, or any hesitation at the thought of falsely declaring his allegiance, the room dispelled it. Given freedom, he might have found it hard to return and commit himself to treachery and deceit with a lying promise to the Power Master. As a prisoner he owed no honesty to anyone but himself. And perhaps to the girl—if he could find her.

The Gunner slept well that night. After breakfast had been brought him his host appeared.

Cade did not wait to be asked. Saluting, he said: "My decision is made; it was not a hard one. I am in your service. What is my first assignment?"

The Power Master smiled. "One that has been awaiting you. The Realm is threatened—has been threatened increasingly—by the unbounded egotism and shortsightedness of one Star against whom I cannot operate in the usual way. Until now...until now I have been searching for a man who could do what was necessary. You are the man."

He paused, and the silence in the room was explosive.

"You will go to Mars," he said finally, "and arrange the death of the Star of Mars. You will return alive. The details are your own concern. I can supply you with a flier and with money—whether to buy men or machines I do not care."

Cade's mind accepted the job as a tactical problem, putting off for the time being the vital decision as to whether the commission would be fulfilled. For now, it would be necessary to act...even to think...in terms of fulfillment.

"I will need an identity."

"Choose it. I said the details were your own concern. I can offer, merely as a suggestion, that you would do well to adopt the identity of a lapsed Armiger—you have known such cases—who took to the district. You might as well put the time you spent in that brothel to some use. And I can assure you that under such an identity you'll find yourself welcome in the Court of Mars. Yes," he said in answer to Cade's look of shocked inquiry, "things are that bad. Did you suppose I'd send you to kill a Star for anything less serious? Now, when you've decided on your course of action and prepared a list of your needs, call me—" He indicated a red button on the wall communicator. "Either I or a trusted servant will be there."

As he pointed, the set chimed. The Power Master depressed the button.

"Here."

"Message, sir. Shall I bring it?"

"To the outer room." And to Cade: "Call when you're ready."

The Gunner lost no time. He seated himself at a desk at one end of the room, and was already listing the funds, transport, and identification he would need when the door opened again.

"You are going to have a visitor," the Power Master said coldly. "I am very interested in knowing just how she discovered—"

"She? *Who?*" Cade was on his feet, the list forgotten.

"Whom do you suppose? How many Ladies of the Palace do you know?"

It was the Lady Moia, then. And the memory of her still hurt. It would take time to recover from the shocks of that night. "One, sir, as I told you," he said formally. "And I would prefer not to see her if that is possible."

"It is not possible. She knows you are here and I have no grounds for refusing her admission without revealing your identity. *How did she know you were here?*" the vibrant voice demanded.

"Sir, I don't know. I haven't seen her since the Building of Fives—"

"The Building of Fives? You spoke only of the Lady Moia there." He peered closely into Cade's puzzled face and suddenly burst into a wide, wolfish grin. "You *don't* know!" he exploded. "My virtuous Gunner, this is the girl for whom you waited two weeks at Cannon's—I had a report from there last night, an hour after you went to sleep—a mysterious girl, a girl whom you had met just once." He was dragging it out, enjoying himself hugely. "Oh, Cade, you were so *upright* yesterday; so true to your vows. How could you have…neglected…a little thing like telling your master about the girl?"

Cade felt the blood rush to his face, but it was not the reflex of shame. It was she; she had found him after his futile, stupid hunt for her. And she was no commoner or wearer of the garter, but a Lady of the Court!

"No," laughed the Power Master. "I won't spoil the joke. You'll learn who she is shortly from her own—shall I say, delicate?—lips." The facade of grimness relaxed; the Power Master sat comfortably on the couch, chuckling. "If it's any satisfaction to you, Cade, I will admit that my respect for you, my hopes for you, have risen. I can use a man who knows how to keep his mouth shut. So she Saw Life after all?" His intonation was heavily satirical, amused. "Proof again that the simplest answer may sometimes be right. The whole Palace has been buzzing about it for three weeks, and I thought I knew better!"

Cade tried to concentrate on what he was hearing and make sense of it. "The whole Palace?" he asked uncertainly. "You mean you knew about her? The whole Palace knew?" Then why, he wondered, all the secrecy now? Why was he a prisoner here? None of it fitted with the Power Master's attitude of yesterday.

"Yes, of course. But *they* all thought it was the daring impostor-Cade she met…and only I knew it was the real Gunner, chaste and pure. Or so I thought. Now it seems I had the right information; but they have the right interpretation of it all. And, to think of the horror on your face yesterday when I talked of these wicked matters! Cade, you impress me; you'll be a good man to have in my service." He broke out chuckling again. "I keep wondering…she must have made a peculiar-looking tart. What did she look like? She's so—you know."

"So beautiful?" asked Cade.

The Power Master stared at him wonderingly. "We'd better get you off to Mars," he said dryly, and glanced at a paper he held in his hand. "She says she recognized you yesterday in Court but didn't want to 'betray you.' Now that I've 'captured' you she wants to see you before you die."

Abruptly he ceased to be a man enjoying himself. "Cade," he said grimly, "I can understand and excuse your lie by omission of yesterday *if* it was prompted by mistaken loyalty to your little friend. You are, after all, unsophisticated. But if I find there's anything more to it, your little friend's visit will be quite literally the last you will enjoy before you die."

The door closed behind him and Cade sank into a chair, burying his face in his hands. Had he gone mad? Had everybody?

"Traitor, face me! They said you lied and I did not believe them, but I know now. Look me in the eye if you dare!"

Cade jumped up. He hadn't heard the door open; the first thing to reach his ears was the unpleasant whine of her voice, contrasting ludicrously with the melodramatic words. He looked at her, heartsick as he realized the monstrous joke somebody was perpetrating. It was the Lady Jocelyn. He had noticed the resemblance himself yesterday—*but who else could know about it?*

"Traitor," she said, *"look on my face* and see how you erred when you thought to victimize a foolish and ignorant commoner girl. *Look on my face."*

He looked, and something impossible was happening.

The Lady Jocelyn's squint-stooped head moved back to sit proudly on her slim throat. Her round-shouldered stance straightened for a moment and settled to a supple, erect figure. The near-sighted, peering eyes flashed with humor and arrogance. She still wore an ill-fitting robe of lurid orange and her stringy hair still missed matching the color of her robe, but none of these things mattered. It was she.

"Have you nothing to say for yourself in your shame?" she demanded, in a voice that was also a caricature.

"A thousand pardons, Lady," he said hoarsely, his heart thudding. "If I had known, if you had permitted some word of your rank to cross your lips I could not have lied to you." *If Fledwick could hear me now!* The girl winked and nodded "go on."

"Surely your warm heart will understand and forgive when I say that only your beauty drove me to my crime." The story seemed to be that the Lady Jocelyn, the Palace butt, had gone out on the town incognito and been arrested, to the hilarity of the Palace wits. She was pretending to assume that he was under death sentence for daring to insult her by taking her at her face value.

"Forgive?" she declaimed. "Forgive? Justice will be done; there is nothing to forgive. A life for an insult to the blood imperial. I have come to console you, fellow. Bring a chair for me. You may sit at my feet."

Cade did as he was told, by now far beyond any effort to take control of the situation. He knelt as she sat down and pulled a sheaf of manuscript from a sagging pocket in her voluminous robe.

"I shall console you for an hour by reading from my works." She launched into what he supposed was a poem:

> *"There is no whisper uttered in the Realm*
> *That goes unheard. By night, by day, no voice*
> *Is raised involuntarily or by choice*
> *Unheard by him who holds the Palace helm."*

She cleared her throat and Cade nodded, jerking his head a little at the wall communicator. He understood.

> *"The doors are many in the Realm at Man;*
> *This door unguarded, that door triply sealed;*
> *Each loyal subject wearing like a shield*
> *The key: to live as fitly as he can."*

Her knee pressed sharply against Cade's shoulder during the three words "this door unguarded." He managed to concentrate on the message.

> *"Starborne or common, we must take and use*
> *The lives that we are handed for our lot.*
> *Great Klin can tell us what to do or not;*
> *Not now or ever is it ours to choose."*

The words were *take and use—now.*

She rattled her sheaf of manuscript, and from its bulky folds a flat case slid; he caught it before it struck the floor. *Take and use—now.* It was the smallest size of 'caster. He had it open in an instant and saw a half-hour reel of recorded tape ready to roll. All dials were at zero.

> *"My voice is small; I do not know the way*
> *To reach all at the willing hands that serve,*
> *Setting at ease the flesh and bone and nerve.*
> *But if I spoke like thunder, I would say:*
> *Good people, follow Klin by night and day."*

My voice—I do not know—setting. Swiftly he mixed bass and treble volumes to match her voice—and hoped the spy-mike system was anything but high-fidelity. He started the tape on a quick nod from the girl and was relieved to find that he'd done well. In a very fair approximation of her adenoidal whine the 'caster immediately began to drone out:

> "
> *What beauty lies in loyalty! What joy!*
> *Is there a heart that throbs with lesser thrill—*"

He placed the box carefully on her chair as she rose and followed her silently from the room. The Power Master, on the other end of the mike, was welcome to his share of the Lady Jocelyn's verses.

Chapter Seventeen

SHE LED CADE through endless twisting dark passageways and stairs. Doors opened at a touch from her hand where no doors seemed to be, and never once did they encounter another person in their flight. There was more to the Palace than met the eye, Cade realized...

When they emerged at last it was into a narrow alley like those of the district where Cade had spent two weeks. A ground car whisked them away from the alley door. Cade never saw who was driving. He followed the girl into the back seat and turned to her promptly with the thanks and questions uppermost in his mind, but she put one finger to her crookedly painted mouth and shook her head.

Cade sat back, forcing his body to relax, but his mind was busy, fascinated by the puzzle of her constantly shifting personality. She had been a commoner at their first meeting, but one with an air of command, an important person in the Cairo Mystery. Then she had been a wearer of the garter, openly seductive—and vulgar. And now a Lady of the Court, a niece of the Emperor himself!

He knew now that the first time she had been a spy; he did not know for whom.

The second time she was in masquerade. The Palace thought it was on holiday—he knew it was not.

This time he could not doubt her true identity; but the awkward, graceless, shambling fool of the Audience Hall was not the same Lady Jocelyn who sat beside him now, erect and confident.

All he had learned so far was what she was not—except two things: that she was still, and always, even under the make-up of her Palace role, exquisitely beautiful, and that she had rescued him again...for what?

The car came to a discreet stop at the edge of a field and the girl gestured him to open the door. She led him briskly across the field to an ancient, unpainted structure; Cade had no chance to look at the vanishing car.

"Open it," she said, at the door of the building, and her voice was the commanding voice of the egg-shaped room. Cade heaved a wooden bar out of double sockets and pushed the double door open.

There was a space flier inside—twelve meters of polished alloy.

"You can fly this, Gunner," she said. It was a statement, not a question.

"I've taken fliers to the Moon and back," he told her.

She looked worried. "Not Mars?"

"I can take it to Mars," he said—and he or any Gunner could.

"I hope so. This flier is loaded and fueled, with food aboard." She pressed a folded paper into his hands. "These are the coordinates of your landing-point on Mars. There will be friends waiting there, or they will arrive shortly after your landing. If you take off immediately you will probably be out of radar range before they can pursue.

"They?" he demanded. "The Power Master's fliers?" As far as he knew, the Power Master disposed only of freighters and ferries, without a ram in his space fleet.

"Cade," she said steadily, "we have no time. I've helped you before, against your will. Now I ask you to take off immediately—without questions or argument. First you must strike me—knock me unconscious."

"What?"

"You've done it before," she said angrily. "I must have a cover story to delay them with while you get clear."

Cade looked down at her, at the brilliant eyes and lovely face beneath the grotesque make-up. It was strangely pleasant, this warmth he felt… strangely unlike the peril he had been taught to expect from such nearness to a woman. It felt much as the touch of the Gunner Supreme's seal to his lips had felt in another life. Even as the thought came his lips tingled.

"Cade!" she said furiously. "I tell you, there's no time to waste. The tape gave us a half-hour at the most, even if they didn't get suspicious before then. Do as I say!"

A Palace ground car roared down the highway across the field, braked screechingly and began to back up.

"They're here," she said bitterly.

With only a momentary hesitation Cade struck her as she had said he must—but he did not leave her lying there to cover his escape. He picked her up and raced into the building and up the ramp to the control compartment lock standing open and waiting. He buckled her limp body into an acceleration couch and clanged the lock shut as a shouted challenge to surrender echoed in the building.

He slipped into the pilot's seat and reflex took over. Straps, buckles, neck brace, grid one temperature and voltage, grid two temperature and voltage, first stage discharge buildup and fire.

His blackout lasted only a few seconds. He turned in his straps, craning his neck to see the couch. She was still unconscious. Indicators flashed on the panel and his hands worked efficiently, as if with a life of their own, even though he had not flown out of atmosphere for three years. For ten minutes he was necessarily a part of the ship, his nerve system joined with its circuits by his swift-moving fingers on the controls. Last of all he cut in the flier's radars and unbuckled himself.

He kicked himself over to the couch, frightened, to feel the girl's neck. She shouldn't be out that long, he worried. But she was and there was nothing he could do about it.

Distractedly he began to search the ship for medical equipment. He braced himself in toe-holds, spun open the air port of the control compartment and floated into a cargo room perhaps three meters deep. In there, except for the space filled by an oversized loading lock, the bulkheads were lined with locked cabinets. Floating free in the compartment were four sealed crates. It was cargo not medicine, here.

Aft of the cargo compartment was a bunk-lined cabin with a tiny galley and a vapor cabinet—the living quarters. She would want water. He filled a valve bag from the tap and gummed it to his thigh with a scoop of paste from one of the ship's omnipresent pots. When he kicked his way back into the control compartment, he found that the girl had freed herself from the couch and was swaying against a bulkhead with an uncertain hold on a grabiron.

"You fool," she said in a deadly voice.

"You told me to take the ship to Mars," he said flatly. "That's what I'm doing."

"Give me that water," she said, and drank inexpertly from the valve. "Cade," she said at last, "I suppose you meant well but this means death for us both. Did you suppose they'd let you chase off into space with a member of the Emperor's family on board? They'll destroy us and I will be reported killed—'unfortunately'—in the action. If you'd listened to me, I could have given you time for a safe escape."

Cade pointed to the stern-chase radar. "Look," he said. "There's nothing in sight—one pip."

"*Where?*" She pushed off from the grabiron and landed, clutching, by the screen.

"See?" he showed her. "A meteorite, most likely. Or even another ship. But not after us. They couldn't get into the air in less than two hours. Not unless they have fliers fueled and ready to go. By then we'll—"

"Suppose they have?" she blazed. "Wasn't *this* ship ready to go? Have you learned nothing? Do you still think the Realm's what it seems to be? This ship has been waiting six years for a Gunner to fly it and now it's to be destroyed because of your folly!"

Cade floated before the screen, watching the green point on the grey ground. It was just becoming recognizable as three bunched points. Each second that passed made them more distinct. "Fliers," he said: "What are they—cargoes, ferries, recons, rams?"

"I don't know," she said venomously. "I'm no Gunner. Rams, most likely."

"With you on board?" Rams were designed for annihilative action. They matched velocities with their quarry and crushed it with their armored prows. It meant death to all aboard the victim.

"I see you're still living in your ethical dream-world," she said. "I'm just a good excuse for the attack, Cade. If only you'd listened to me. What are you going to do now?"

"Outrun them if I can." He floated into his seat again. "I can try an evasive course and accelerate all the ship will take." It wouldn't be enough, and he knew it. "If the other pilots are inferior—"

"They won't be!" she snapped. He wondered whether she knew that rams had relays of pilots; always fresh, always solving for the difference while the quarry took evasive action, always waiting for the moment when the victim's single pilot tired after hours of dodging and began to repeat his tactics.

He reset the stem radar for maximum magnification and got a silhouette of three ugly fliers, smaller than his own, with anvil-like beaks. They were rams.

"Cade, listen to me." Her voice compelled attention. It was more than a tone of command, more than the urgency of the words. It carried a desperate seriousness that made him pause.

"I'm listening."

"You'll have to fight them, Cade. There's no other way."

He looked at her unbelievingly.

"There are guns aboard," she said, not meeting his eye.

"What are you talking about?"

"You know what." She looked squarely at him, with out shame. "Fire on them!" she said.

CHAPTER EIGHTEEN

IT HAD BEEN A ROTTEN THING to hear from the lips of the lax and dissolute Mars-born gunner who had died in France. To hear *her* speak the unspeakable tore his heart.

"It's for our lives, Cade!" she pleaded, shamelessly.

"Our lives!" he was passionately scornful. "What kind of lives would they be with a memory like that?"

"For the Realm of Man, then! The mission we are on!"

"What mission?" He laughed bitterly. "For a lie, a farce, a bad joke on the lips of the Power Master? What is the Realm of Man to me? A weakling Emperor, a murderous Power Master, a lying lecher of a Gunner Supreme! I have nothing left, Lady, except determination not to soil myself."

"Jetters and bombles!" she exploded, pleading no longer. "That's the way you're thinking—precisely like a commoner's brat terrified of the Beetu-five and the Beefai-voh!"

"I have no fear of the Beefai-voh and I don't believe in bombles," he said coldly. "I believe there are things one knows are wrong, detestably wrong, and I refuse to do them. I wish—I wish you hadn't said it."

She was fighting for calm. "I see I'll have to tell you some things. I won't try to pledge you to secrecy; your promise would be meaningless. But I hope that if the time comes, you'll let them torture you to death without revealing what I say, or that it was I who said it."

He kept silence.

"You've never heard the word 'history,' Cade."

He looked up in surprise. He had—used by the mad little burglar who'd been beaten to death in the Watch House.

She went on, frowning with concentration: "History is the true story of changes in man's social organization over periods of time."

"But—" he began, with an incredulous laugh.

"Never mind! You'll say it's meaningless. That 'changes' and 'social organization' are words that just can't be used together—that 'changed social organization' is a senseless noise. But you're wrong.

"I cannot tell you my sources, but I assure you that there have been many forms of social organization—and that the world was *not* created ten thousand years ago."

Her burning conviction amazed him. Was she mad, too? As mad as the little burglar?

"Try to understand this: thousands of years ago there was a social organization without Emperor or Stars. It was destroyed by *people firing from fliers*. That was a terrible way to fight. It killed the innocent—mother and child, armed man and unarmed. It poisoned food so that people died in agony. It destroyed sewer and water systems so that homes became stinking places of corruption.

"The social organization was destroyed. Homes and cities were abandoned—yes these people had cities; ours still bear their names. They lived like talking, suffering animals who only knew that things had once been better. Every year they forgot more of what that something better had been like, but they never forgot the supreme horror of death from the skies. Every year the details of it grew more cloudy and the thing itself grew more terrible."

Cade nodded involuntarily. Like a night attack, he thought; the less you saw the worse it was.

"There were centers of recovery—but that's no part of my story. You said you didn't believe in jetters and bombles? Cade, the jetters and bombles were *real*. The Beefai-voh and the rest of them are the names of the fliers that brought the supreme horror to that social organization."

"The Caves!" said Cade. The place called Washington, the rumbled ruinous blocks of stone with staring black eyes in them, haunted by the bombles—

"Yes, the Caves! The Caves everybody is afraid of and nobody can explain." She paused, almost breathless, then went on, tensely: "Cade, you must fight. If you don't, you're throwing our lives away on folly."

Cade didn't believe it. The vague appeal to sketchy evidence—it was as if a patrol leader came back and reported: "Sir, I didn't see it but I think there's a two-company enemy group somewhere up there in some direction or other." He gripped a grabiron in his fist until his knuckles went white. Ten thousand years of Emperor, Klin, Power Master, the Order and the Stars and the commoners...*that* was the world.

"They're coming up fast," she said emotionlessly, staring at the screen.

"Where are the guns?" he said hoarsely, not meeting her eye. And he knew he was only pretending to believe her story, pretending it was true so he could save her and himself at any cost in self-loathing.

"In the chart locker. Ten, I believe."

Ten guns. He would be able to fire at unheard-of aperture until coils fused and toss one aside for another. Ten guns—like that. As though a gun were not an individual thing, one to an Armsman, touched by the Gunner Supreme...

"We must get space suits on," he said. He opened the locker and began to select his own units. Even after three years, he remembered his sizes. He dogged a pair of Number Seven legs against the bulkhead and tugged himself into them, donned Number Five arm pieces and sealed a torso unit around his body and to the limb units. He selected units for the girl and helped her into them; she didn't know how.

"Helmets now?" she asked calmly.

"Better carry the—the guns to the cargo room first." They made two arm-loads. Cade wiped a palmful of paste against a cargo-room bulkhead and stuck his load to it in a near row. The girl ranged hers beside them.

"Helmets now," he said. "Then you go back to the control room. I'll airtight this section and open the cargo lock. You watch the screens—do you know the alarms?" She shook her head. "The proximity alarm is a loud buzzer. I won't hear it in vacuum; you call me on the suit intercom when it goes off. Just talk into the helmet. If I succeed in driving them off you'll have to bleed air out of the control room until pressure is low enough for me to open the door against it. You hold down the switch on the upper left of the control array that's labeled 'Space Cock.' Can you do that?"

She nodded; they clamped on the plastic domes and sealed them. "Testing intercom. Do you hear me?"

"I hear you," sounded tinnily inside his helmet. "Can you turn your volume down?"

He did. "Is that better?"

"Thank you." That was all. A casual thanks for lowering his volume and not a word about his decision. Didn't she realize what he was doing for her? Was she fool enough to think he believed her wild "history"?

He sealed the fore and aft doors and plucked one of the guns from the bulkhead. Full-charged. No number. What did a gun without a number mean? A gun without an Armsman matching it was unthinkable—but here were ten of them. Cade set each gun for maximum aperture and tight band, bled the air out of the compartment by a manual valve and spun open the big cargo lock.

After that there was nothing to do. He floated and waited and tried not to think. But in that he failed.

What did he know—and how did he know it?

He knew Armsmen were Armsmen: fighters, masters of the Gun's complexity, masters of fighting, the only masters of fighting there were. That was an essential datum. He knew they were in the service of the Emperor—but that datum had crumbled under the ruthless words of the Power Master. He had known the Gunner Supreme was the embodied perfections of the Order, and that datum was a lie. He had known that it was abomination to fire from a flier—and found himself about to commit the abomination. He had known that for Armsmen there was only one woman, and not a woman of flesh: She who came fleetingly to those who died in battle, and in her fleeting passage rewarded Armsmen for their lives of abstinence. But he knew that for him there was another woman now—sometime mystagogue, traitress, whore, weakminded noblewoman, expounder of insane 'history.' What did he know and how did he know it? He knew that, false to the Order and to She who came, he wanted this woman and did not know her secret.

"Proximity alarm," said the voice in his helmet.

"Message received," he said automatically in Armsman style and smiled bitterly at himself.

Cade kicked his way to the array of guns. Two he gummed to his thighs and two he clasped in his gauntlets. It was a grotesque situation. One man, one gun, it was supposed to be. But why? he demanded. Why not one man, two guns; one man, four guns; one man, as many guns as he needs and can lay his hands on? He shoved off to a port and began a hand-over-hand, spiderlike crawl from one quartz disk to the next, peering into the star-powdered blackness. The sun was astern of the flier; it would throw the rams into glaring relief. They wouldn't be able to stalk the victim in its own shadow.

There was a triple wink of light that became a blaze ripping past the ports. The rams had overshot in their first try at becoming part of the same physical system as their prey. They would return…

Cade wondered whether there could be peace in the Mysteries from the confusions that plagued him, and recoiled from the thought. He knew them, at least, for what they were: traps for the johns and clink for the blades. Peace? Perhaps there was peace at Mistress Cannon's, where a man could wallow deep until not one ray of sunlight found him. At Cannon's you could drink and drug and couple while you had the greens, and then it was a simple matter to haunt dark streets until you found your nervous, late-going commoner. And then you could drink and drug and couple again where no ray of sunlight could find you. If firing from a flier was right, could a life at Cannon's be wrong?

The rams appeared ahead again and the flier seemed to gain and overtake them. Cade knew it was an illusory triumph; he was being bracketed. They were far astern now.

What did he know and how did he know it? He knew the Order and the Klin Philosophy and the Realm of Man had been created ten thousand years ago. He knew it because he had been told it by everyone. How did they know it? Because they had been told it by everyone. Cade's mind floated, anchorless, like his body. He didn't believe in jetters and bombles. That was for children. But he did believe in not firing from fliers. That was for Armsmen. Children and Armsmen had been told all about it…

"I'll take you to the Caves.

"And the Beetu-nine will come to tear your fingers and toes off with white-hot knives of metal.

"And the Beetu-five will come to pepper you with white-hot balls of metal.

"And the Beefai-voh will come and grate your arms and legs with white-hot metal graters.

"And last, if you are not a good boy, the Beethrie-six will come in the dark and will hunt you out though you run from Cave to Cave, screaming in the darkness. The Beethrie-six, which lumbers and grumbles, will breathe on you with its poison breath and that is the most horrible at all, for your bones will turn to water and you will burn forever."

The three rams blazed past the open port again and seemed to hang in space far ahead of the flier. Their next "short" might do it.

"Clennie's filthy. He told me he made a nail-hole in the wall and peeks at his sister every morning when she gets dressed. Anybody who'd do that would fire from a flier."

"—embarrassing but necessary questions have to be put by the entrance board. Candidate Cade, with love of the Emperor in your heart, can you truthfully say that at night you have only normal and healthy dreams, free from such degrading fantasies as demonstrations of affection for other boys and firing a gun while flying?"

"—but oh, my pupils, there is worse yet to tell. This unfortunate young man who began by neglecting his Klin lessons did not end merely as a coward

and thief. On reconnaisance flight he lost altitude and came under the fire
of ground troops. I need not name the Thing he did; you can guess. Smitten
by remorse after his unspeakable deed he properly took his life, but conceive
if you can the shame of his Brothers—"

"*—heartbroken, but it had to be done. I never knew he had a rotten*
spot in him, but I saw the paper myself, He 'solved' Tactics VII, if you please,
with a smokescreen—sending a flier over the enemy left flank and having the
Gunner set fire to the trees with a low-aperture blast of his gun, uh...from
the, uh, from the air: It just shows you can't be too careful—"

"*I receive this gun to use in such a way that my Emperor, my Gunner*
Supreme and my Brothers in the Order will never have cause to sorrow—"

"*They're bunched in the square; we'll have to blast them out with a fron-*
tal smash. Cade, take your flier over for an estimate of their strength. Leave
your gun here; we know they're low on charges and it wouldn't do to have
yours fall into their hands if you're shot down."

The flier seemed to shoot past the rams again. The next time, velocities would match...

No; it would never do for him to take his gun. He remembered soar-
ing over the plaza, tacking and veering as flame squirted from the densely
massed troops below, busy with his counting. He dropped an imaginary
grid over them, counted the number of men in one imaginary square
and multiplied by the total number of imaginary squares as he shot back
to the command post on the outskirts of the Rhineland village with his
estimate and joined in the costly advance on foot.

He had been told and he believed. How much else, he thought—as
though a harsh light had suddenly been turned on—had he been told
and believed against all common sense and reason?

Bring on your rams!

This time it was neither a short nor an over. Suddenly the three rams
stood, less than a kilometer off, as though frozen in space.

They were smaller than Cade's freighter and boasted a wealth of
propulsion units, as against the freighter's central main thrust tube and
concentric ring of smaller steering tubes. He rejoiced as he saw conning
bubbles rise simultaneously on the three craft just behind their ugly,
solid anvil-beaks.

A propulsion unit came into play on the outermost of the rams—the
reserve. Red haze jetted from a midships tube precisely perpendicular
to the main thrust and the ram drifted outward to double its distance
from the flier. Its forward component remained unchanged; it neither
fell behind nor drifted ahead.

Aboard the two rams in action there must be relief at the flier's failure
to take evasive action; they would now be plotting the simplest of sym-
metrical double-collision courses. Presently one of the rams would jet
"over" or "under" its quarry to stand out on the other side the same distance as its mate; simultaneously the rams would add equal and opposite

lateral thrust in amount proportional to their distance from the flier, and the victim would be crushed between the two ugly anvil-beaks.

Cade didn't know what standard doctrine was for ramming distance, but he was content to improvise.

Both rams showed red exhaust-mist. One was standing in closer; the other was moving "up" to hem the quarry in. Cade anchored himself at the lip of the open cargo lock; the conning bubble of the oncoming ram was sunbright in his sights.

The gun gushed energy for three seconds before it failed. Cade hurled it through the lock into space and snatched another from his right thigh. It was not needed. The conning blister was still there, but blackened and discolored. He couldn't tell whether it had been pierced, but the ram issued uncertain gushes of red mist from one tube and. then another, tacking and veering, and then flashed off at full thrust in what seemed to be the start of a turnaround curve.

The other ram was still working itself painstakingly around the flier with conservative jets of exhaust. Cade, half-through the lock, emptied the full charge of the second gun and a third at his hull, and saw sun-lit diamond flashes spraying through space—debris from exploding ports! The ram didn't wait for more, and when Cade looked for the reserve craft it was gone.

A good engagement, thought Cade. Presumably they wore space suits aboard the rams in action, so he could claim no kills. The conning blister hadn't shattered like the ports—perhaps because it had been extruded into space-cold for only a few seconds and the gun hadn't tickled it hard enough to set up destructive strain. And the psychology of it was important, too. The terrifying novelty of a ship-to-ship firefight, of a gun being used from a flier—Cade laughed thunderously inside the helmet at himself, at Clennie, at the embarrassed entrance board examiner, at the Klin Teacher with his moral lesson, at Novice Lorca's smoke screen, at the Oath of the Gun, at the Gunner Superior of France and his frontal smash.

A small, tinny voice in his ears yelled: "Turn your volume down! Turn it down!"

"I'm sorry, Lady," he said chuckling. "Did you see how I routed them? Now if you can find the space-cock. I'll be able to open the door."

She found it and bled control-compartment air into space until he could shove the door open, airtight it again and start the control-compartment pressure building.

CHAPTER NINETEEN

HE HELPED HER take her helmet off, and then she helped him. They stood looking at each other, waiting for adequate words. Her eyes dropped first, and Cade momentarily felt she was ashamed of the thing she had made him do, the faith she had shaken and then destroyed.

But it made no difference now; the faith was destroyed—and for what? Cade stared long and hard at the Lady Jocelyn and a fresh torrent of laughter burst from him, the sound echoing and re-echoing in the vaulted compartment.

It was so ludicrous. There she stood, feet hooked under a toe-hold, a squat and misshapen figure no more womanly than the radars or the hulking compression pump. On top of the bulky mass of padding and metal and fabric the flaming, orange-red hair of the Lady of the Court was tangled and matted. Her face paint, never designed for beauty, was smudged and rubbed until she seemed a mocking distortion of the woman to whose beauty he had awakened a month ago in an under-ground center of intrigue.

He did not answer the mute question in her eyes and she did not choose to put it into words. Instead she said quietly: "Help me with my suit, please."

Cade, suddenly sobered, showed her how to unseal the members and stow them in the locker. And then, though he had thought himself past being shocked by the woman, she took him by surprise again. As though she were a commoner domestic she said: "I'll fix us something to eat. Is the pressure up in the cargo room?"

He checked the gauge and spun the door open for her. "Don't come in for a few minutes," she said. "I'll be changing my clothes and wash-ing up."

How many was a *few?* Cade spent half an hour getting out of his own suit, minutely inspecting it and stowing it away, and performed as many other jobs as he could find. There were not many. At last, cautiously, he hauled himself through the cargo room to the third compartment aft, the living quarters. Its door stood open and he went in.

"Oh, there you are. I was going to call you." She was at the tiny cooker, and two valved bottles of mash were beginning to gush steam. "There's a table and benches," she said, and he clicked them out of the wall, staring.

She had washed up. The soiled Court mask was scrubbed away and the perfection of her face was a renewed surprise. Her hair was bound with a cloth as if it were still damp from washing—he hoped the hair-dye had washed out. And instead of her sagging orange robe she wore a fresh set of mechanic's coveralls. The sleeves and legs were rolled and the belt pulled tight to her waist. She looked trim…and tempting. How did a man—a man not in the Order—go about telling a woman that she was beautiful?

"You've time to wash," she said pointedly.

"Of course, thanks," he said, and kicked over to the vapor chamber and thrust his head and hands in to be scrubbed by the swirling, warm mist and dried by the air blast. Turning to the table he realized with sudden alarm that he was expected to sit across it from her.

"Excuse me," he said, found a coverall for himself, and fled to the control room to change and pull himself together. To sit across the table from her and look at her while he ate! He told himself it was a first step. The sooner he unlearned his role of Gunner the simpler life would be. The mash would help. There was no sundown in space, but his stomach knew the time—mid-afternoon—and he was sure it wouldn't accept meat food for two hours. The coveralls helped too. He was glad to rid himself at last of the commoner's-best-suit he had bought at Cannon's with stolen money. Coveralls were a far cry from boots and cloak, but he had worn them in his Novice years.

Eating was easier than he had expected. There were thigh-straps on the benches and the table had a gummy top. It was an illusion of gravity at a time when the digestive system could use such assistance. The girl didn't speak as they solemnly chewed their mash, sucked water from their bottles and fished carefully through the trap of the jar for chunks of fruit that had carefully dehydrated crusts but were juicy inside.

At last Cade said: "Tell me more."

"More about what?" she asked coolly. He knew she understood what he meant.

"You know what. 'History,' for instance. Or, more to the point, what cargo we are carrying and to whom?" He had not forgotten, even while fighting off the rams, the locked cabinets and sealed crates.

"There's nothing more to tell."

"You said before take-off that the ship had been waiting six years."

"It was nothing. Forget about it."

"So you're a liar too?" he asked hotly. *Anger is a peril.* The thought came unsummoned and he pushed it away; the direful warnings of Armsmen's training no longer bound him. "What other accomplishments does the Emperor's niece have?" he demanded. "I've seen you as traitor, whore, and spy. Thief too? Is the flier yours? Or is it just something you decided to make use of—like me?"

"*Get out of here!*" Her face was white and tense with rage. "Get—out—of—here," she repeated through clenched teeth.

Cade unbuckled the thigh straps and rose slowly, holding the table. He had been used long enough, by Stars and the Order and by her, at the risk of his life. Things were going to go his way for a change. "Do you really think you can get out of answering like this?" he said coldly. Coldly he looked down at the girl's trembling shoulders and, thinking of Mistress Cannon who had taught him how, he forced a smile.

She was silent, lips compressed to choke back the words she might regret, eyes flashing the fury she was trying to control.

"It's not that easy," he said. "Even a Gunner can learn the facts of life, eventually. You've done everything you could to destroy the meaning of my vows. What makes you think you can still count on the behavior they imposed?" She was rigidly holding onto herself, but he knew she couldn't keep it up.

"Have you forgotten that I spent three weeks out in the world without you—learning things you never taught me? I saw another woman like you, too. You don't imagine you're the only one being used by an ambitious traitor? I don't know who your master is, but I know hers. The Lady Moia…"

"Get out of here!" she screamed. *"Get out! Now!"* Tears streamed down her face as she freed herself and stood but she was not sobbing.

"No." He pulled himself one "step" toward her around the small table. "Not until you answer me. You may be content to serve your own master, but I tell you that *I* am tired of being used. For thirteen years the Order used me as it pleased, and I was willing. Then I 'died,' and the Cairo people tried to use me as their murderer. Their chosen victim, your friend the Power Master, tried to use me the same way against the Star of Mars. By the Realm!, even a drunken con man at Cannon's thought he could use me for *his* ends. I've had enough! Do you understand that?"

He stopped, realizing that his tirade had given her a chance to gather her own control. "You saved me twice," he added more quietly, "when others tried to use me. Why? Why, to use me yourself, of course. To fly this ship. *What for? For whom?* This time I'm going to know!"

He let the last words ring a moment in the air, and then he snapped at her: "Whose cargo are we carrying? What's in it? *Whose woman are you?*"

"My own!"

He hadn't been watching for it; he had looked for collapse.

Her hand stung as it whipped across his cheek. He seized her arms as she floundered from the floor; they drifted together against a bulkhead. "Answer me!" he said sharply. She was crying now, sobbing in an agony of frustration and defeat. He felt her tense body relax, helpless and beaten.

She would fight no more. He knew he could release her and she would tell him what he wanted to know. He meant to release her; he started to. But in some way he did not understand, his hands refused to obey him. Her body was close to his and her face turned up, suddenly startled and questioning.

He had never done it before; he didn't know how to do it. But his face bent down and for a long time, a timeless moment, his lips were on hers.

She pulled away at last, and he held fast to a grab-iron, oblivious to everything except the surging new sensations in him. This was how a man, an ordinary man felt about a woman. This was what had been denied him all his life. This was what the Power Master had ruthlessly described in words. This was what brought the Gunner Supreme scurrying from planetary and Realm affairs to the side of the Lady Moia. This was what Jana had offered him at Cannon's. And none of them had quite understood that it was a thing without meaning to him—until now.

He looked up at her, standing across the room from him now, and made another discovery. She was quite helpless against him; he could take her when he liked. And that wasn't what he wanted.

He had kissed her, but that was not all. She had kissed him, and a whole new world had been in it.

"Jocelyn," he said quietly. He could taste the word in his mouth. It was a plea and a caress.

She said coldly; "I thought that this at least I would be spared from you. I will tell you as much as I can and then ask you to leave me alone."

"Jocelyn," he said again. She ignored it.

"I served as spy in the Cairo Mystery, yes. You should be glad I did. And you may believe me or not as you like, but I am neither whore nor thief. I serve the Realm of Man. As for the cargo, it does not concern you, and I would be a traitor for the first time if I told you more than that. Now will you go?"

"If you wish." There was nothing more to learn, and much that he had learned unsought needed thinking over.

He left the room without looking at her again, and did not try to speak to her again that day. She slept in the cabin aft and he tried to sleep on the acceleration couch in the control room, while thoughts tormented him.

Thinking was no help. He was bound to her, whatever she was, whoever's game she played. But no matter how he turned and twisted each new fact, he saw nothing but a reasonless and chaotic conflict. She served the Realm of Man? So claimed the Power Master, off-hand killer and father of lies that he was. So doubtless claimed the weakling Emperor, the rebellious Stars, and the treacherous Gunner Supreme.

He had no reason to suppose there was sense to it at all. Always before things had had meaning: each ritual gesture, each emphasis of wording, each studied maneuver in battle had had a meaning and a place in the fitting world of Klin. But now it seemed instead that there was just a world of random forces, clashing because of this man's lust or that man's pride. How could he demand more of her than the world offered?

In the morning he was hungry and it was not unreasonable to go to the galley for food. She was distant and polite and for the better part of a week she remained so. Then he tried once more to question her.

He asked again about History. She bit her lip and told him she never should have spoken as she did and never would have told what she had except to save their lives. "You would do best to forget you ever heard the word."

"Can I forget that I have fired from a flier?" he asked gravely and she looked away.

About the cargo she would not speak at all, and his bitterness grew daily at the galling thought that he was expected to be a pawn in some game and be content with the role he who had led companies and would surely have risen to the rank of Superior.

There were four days left to the voyage when he decided to force the cargo. He could have done it openly; she was powerless to prevent him. But he insured his privacy by noisily rattling the handle of the door to the cabin at midnight by the chronometer. She must have been sleeping lightly. In less time than it would have taken him to actually open the door he heard the dogs on the other side thud to. He rattled again, noisily, and then went off, grumbling as loudly as was reasonable. He smiled grimly, wondering when she would find the courage to come out—and more grimly still when he recalled that all the flier's food was on the other side of the dogged-down door. Well, he had fasted for three days before. And now he would find out who was playing with his life.

The metal sheathing on the free-floating crates yielded easily to the lowest aperture of a gun. The contents of the crate nearest the break-through point were also metallic, but were undamaged by the blast of the gun. It was guns that were in the crate—at least a thousand of them. Guns of the Order, or replicas, full-charged and without numbers. He was not really surprised.

Methodically, Cade opened the three other crates—all the same. And the lockers? The locks were radionic and not simple, but he solved them, each quicker than the last, and sampled the contents.

At the end he went back to the control room making no effort to cover up his work.

Ten thousand guns of the Order, bound for Mars. He knew now for whom the Lady Jocelyn worked.

He slept, and in the morning tried the cabin door. It was still dogged down, and he called on the ship's interphone.

"What do you want?" she asked coldly.

"First, to apologize for disturbing your sleep."

"Very well."

"And something to eat."

"I can't see how to get it to you," she said indifferently.

"You can't afford to starve me. I still have to land the ship, you know."

"I have no intention of starving you." There was a hint of humor in her voice. "I was thinking it might be a good idea to *weaken* you a little."

"I've weakened already," he said. "I did some hard work last night, and I need food."

"What kind of work?"

"I'll show you when you come out." He didn't have to wait long. There was a scant ten minutes of silence, before she called back:

"If I bring you some food, will you give me your word not to make a fool of yourself?"

"Certainly," he said cheerfully, "if you feel there is any value in the word of a lapsed Armsman. By what shall I swear?"

Silence.

Then, almost timidly: "By yourself."

And it was thoughtfully he answered: "By myself, I swear that I will do nothing to distress you."

"All right. Five minutes," she said, and cut off.

Cade waited. He heard the dogs thud back and the door open. Silence then, and he made himself sit still and wait. Ludicrously, a valved bottle of mash floated through the open door from the cargo room. It must have drifted from her hand when she saw the ripped-open cargo. Cade watched the bottle bump to a gentle stop, and rebound from the bulkhead to drift within his reach. He was hungry; he wanted the food; but he let it go slowly past him. Jocelyn floated in a moment later, pale but self-possessed.

"All right," she said. "Now you know. Don't ask me to explain, because I won't. I can't. Not if you tried to get it out of me by torture. I have some loyalties I do not violate."

"I have not," he said briefly. "What was left of them you violated for me. And I'm not going to ask you to explain. You keep forgetting that I've talked to others besides you these last few weeks. The Power Master, for instance. And a miserable little Marsman who came to Cannon's to forget his loneliness. And—" He thought of the Mars-born Gunner, Harrow, who had died for a terrible sin, "—and others," he finished shortly.

Cade picked the bottle of mash from the air and tasted it.

"All right," she said and dropped all pretense of indifference. "Just what is it that you imagine you understand?" He let the bottle go; the mash was cold and he was no longer hungry.

"To start with, I know what loyalty you hold."

He waited, but she said nothing. "I won't pretend to understand why an Imperial Lady should serve as spy for the Star of Mars, but—" He paused with satisfaction. Her face was impassive, but one sharp indrawn breath had given her away. "Do you deny it?"

"No. No, I don't deny it."

"Then perhaps you will want to explain it?"

She was thoughtful and she spoke reluctantly: "No. I can't. What else do you know?"

"Why should I tell you?" He was bargaining forthrightly now. "Why should I answer your questions?"

"Because I know more than you do. Because there are some things it's dangerous to know. Besides," she added, "I can't possibly tell you more until I find out just how much you *do* know."

"All right." He had nothing to lose…and he wanted to talk about it. "I'll tell you what I know and what I think:

"First, I have known for some time that the Star of Mars is petitioning the Emperor for the assignment of Mars-born Armsmen to his Court. 'Till now, of course, they have always been dispersed among the Earth Stars. But a month or more ago, requests were being made for the return of seasoned Mars-born Gunners, and for the retention of native novices on Mars when they reached the rank of Armiger.

"Second, I know the Power Master is determined that this petition shall not be granted. I *think* I know why—"

She leaned forward just a little, eager for what he might say next.

He went on, deliberately shifting his ground.

"—why Mars wants its Armsmen at home, and why the Power Master will not allow it. The reason is so obvious it would never occur to anyone outside the little clique of schemers and tricksters and—History students in which you live! It's Mars iron, nothing more."

She sat back again and seemed almost bored; this was nothing new to her. Then he was on the right track.

"All of Earth's machinery needs Mars iron. If the Star of Mars had an Order of his own, composed entirely of Marsmen, with their peculiar devotion to their homes and families—I've talked with them, and I know how they feel—then he would hold more real power than the Emper…than the Power Master himself."

He laughed out loud, remembering the waking formula that had prepared him for the day each morning for six thousand days of his life.

"It is fitting that Armsmen serve the Emperor through the Power Master and our particular Stars. While this is so, all will be well to the end of time," he quoted aloud. "I said that many times each day for many years," he told her.

"I think the Star of Mars knows his request will never be granted, and I think he is now preparing to train an outlaw Order of his own to serve the same purpose."

A fleeting smile crossed her lips; in spite of everything, Cade realized, she still thought of him as a Gunner, with a Gunner's attitudes, She could not possibly have realized how much she was revealing with that small smile of satisfaction.

He had half-guessed before, but he was certain now, that the training of outlaw Armsmen had already begun. It took three years of novitiate drill before a Brother was given a practice gun in the Order proper. How many of them were there? How many half-trained, whole-hearted Marsmen waiting right now for the guns he was bringing on this ship?

For the first time in ten thousand years, guns would be fired that had never been touched by the Gunner Supreme. Then he remembered: not in ten thousand years. In History...how long was that?

"What purpose?" she asked.

Cade snapped to attention.

"Oh, a private armed force of his own. A force powerful enough to make a stand against the Earth-born Armsmen. It wouldn't have to equal the combined strength of all Earth forces. Nothing near that. He must know the Power Master will never let Earth Stars combine to that extent. These guns, the guns you would have had me carry unawares if you could, will make him strong enough to become Power Master—or Emperor in your uncle's place."

He stopped talking and waited. She said nothing.

"Well," he asked impatiently. "Can you deny it? Any of it?"

"No," she said slowly. "None of it. Except one thing. I am—you *must* understand, Cade—I am no man's paid spy!" She said the words with such unmistakable contempt that for the moment Cade found them hard to disbelieve.

"Then, *why?*" he asked intently. "What are you working for?"

She smiled. "I told you once: for the Realm of Man." And her earnestness lost all meaning because once more she had refused an answer. But she went on: "Cade, you found me first in the Cairo Mystery. You didn't trust me then, and you discovered later that you *should* have trusted. Do you know what I was doing there?"

"The Great Conspiracy!" he sneered. "Every Star a Power Master! Add chaos and confusion to cruelty and unreason! Yes, I know what you were doing there!"

"If you'd think with your brain instead of your anger," she snapped, "you'd realize how wrong *that* is. No, *wait* a minute," she said quickly as he opened his mouth to protest, and went on, talking fast: "I wasn't working for the Conspiracy; you must know that by now. Why should I have tried to save you from the drug? I have no special fondness for the Power Master." She paused for breath; and Cade had to admit that that made sense. It was the single paradox that kept the rest of what he knew from forming a clear picture.

She resolved it. "Cade," she said steadily, "much of what you've said today is true—*most* of it. There are some facts you still don't know, facts I don't dare tell you. They're dangerous even for me to know; for you, they would be fatal. The lives of other people are involved, and of one more important than you or—that doesn't matter now. But you can surely see, with what you do know, why I was working in the Conspiracy?"

"Why yes, of course—because your master ordered it!"

Her hands balled into furious fists, shaking in impotent anger at his refusal to be swayed. "Because—I—needed—*you!*" She spaced the words evenly in a last effort at control. "You or any Armsman I could get; someone to fly this ship. I *told* you it's been waiting for six years. Waiting for a pilot, nothing more. And I got the pilot. Now do you see? I couldn't let you kill the Power Master. I couldn't let him kill you either. I needed you for this."

Well, he thought bitterly, now it fitted. It all hung together. She'd had a job to do, and she had done it, calmly betraying one group after another, to accomplish it. And he himself....he was a pilot for the Star of Mars. And nothing more.

She took stunned silence for surrender. "You *do* understand?" she asked more quietly. "Cade, later perhaps, I can tell you more, but now—"

"Now you've said enough. Unless, of course, you want to tell me—*being no man's paid spy*—just why you chose to act against the Great Conspiracy in favor of another one just like it? What makes you favor Mars' conspiracy?"

"Not conspiracy! Healing!" The dam broke at last; words and dreams held back too long began to flow out now in passionate floods. "Healing the life of man," she said proudly. "Saving it from the dead grip of the Power Master and the Klin Philosophy! How *can* I make you understand?" Her face passed from earnest pleading to the raptness of a visionary. "I've told you about History, but it's still just a word to you. You haven't studied—

"You don't know what 'science' means, do you? Of course not; the word is half forbidden and half forgotten because science means change and change means threat, to the Klin stasis and to the Power Master.

"Mankind is dying, Cade, because men are chained to their machines and forbidden to make new ones. Don't you see that one by one the machines will wear out and—"

"No," he said warily. "I don't see. The Brothers of the Order build new machines. When old ones are gone, new ones are always ready. Klin Teachers study and build machines."

"But no new ones," she said. "Science means *new* things, Cade; searching for the truth with no roads closed, no directions forbidden. Cade, there was a time—I know from History—when men powered their machines with the metal uranium. It's gone now. Thorium was used next, and now it's gone too. And now the iron. Earth's iron is gone. When the Mars iron is gone too, what next? There should be ten million men working day and night to find a new power source, but there are none.

"There are other ways to destroy civilization besides firing from fliers! They'll have to stop making fliers and ground cars. The cities will become great sewers when the pumps stop turning. Inlanders will get sick, with ugly lumps of wild tissue growing from their necks, because there won't be anybody to bring them fish and salt from the oceans. Babies will grow up crooked because there won't be power for the milking machines in the food factories, or for the boats that catch the cod and shark. Animals will overrun the growing food because there won't be wire for fences or power to charge them. Diseases will rot mankind because there won't be power for the biodrug factories." She stopped, worn out with her own intensity, and watched him silently. "Does it mean anything to you?" she asked with a touch of bitterness.

"I don't know," he said bemused. He was thinking of what the Power Master had said to him that day, with Kendall dead on the floor. It made this much sense at least: that here were two honestly opposing forces. The Power Master's view of the world made more sense, from what he had seen of it, than Jocelyn's, but...if he could believe her instead, a man could have something to fight for again.

"All that," she said quietly, "can be cured by science. And there are other things—'art' is one. Another word, Cade. It means exploring this universe and making new universes with language and sound and light. It makes you laugh and weep and wonder; no man alive today can understand the joy of making and giving art, or the joy of receiving it from the maker.

"You don't know what 'freedom' is. But perhaps you'll learn—soon. I hope—" She hesitated and looked up at him defiantly. "I hope when we reach Mars you will accept service under the Star of Mars. He is the man to follow at this time. But for now, *I cannot tell you more.*"

"Then I won't ask," he said. There was too much to think about already. And he knew all he really needed: he had learned the meaning of at least one new word, and that was "love."

Chapter Twenty

THEY HAD THREE DAYS more of space: days in which Cade found it less and less difficult to remember that the Order was behind him. The old life was finished; the old certainties gone. There was just one certainty now—a woman. The only possible woman for Cade in the new life, just as the Lady of the Order had been the only possible woman for Cade the Armsman. Until they landed he could share a growing friendship and...something more. What might come later he did not know, except for one thing: if they lived through the landing on Mars he would find some way to stay at her side. The Star of Mars could be no worse a master than the Star of France. Surely he was a worthier one than the Power Master.

Knowing this much and no more, Cade used the time he had to win the liking and strengthen the confidence of the Lady Jocelyn. Never had he known himself capable of such fluent conversation or such avid listening.

Too quickly, Mars filled the heavens and Jocelyn's gentle friendliness disappeared behind a barrage of preparations and crisp instructions.

The coordinates she designated took them to a craggy basin in the southern hemisphere, less than a hundred kilometers from the capital city of Mars.

The spot had obviously been chosen to afford a combination of convenience and secrecy. From the air it was one of those blank patches that showed neither red nor green, but only featureless grey. No red meant no iron: none of the characteristic family-operated strip mine refinery complexes of Mars. No green meant no water: no farms and farm-families raising vegetables and goat meat for the miners and city-dwellers of the planet. Featureless grey meant unobserved isolation.

Cade braked the big flier to a stop on level ground as though it were a ground car. He unbuckled himself from the control seat and looked out of a port at a desolate valley surrounded by gnarled old hills as high as any on sandstorm-lashed Mars. Jocelyn at his side surveyed the emptiness impatiently. She was already swathed in bulky synthetic furs.

Cade found a suit for himself and donned it. He came back to find her pacing the small area of cabin floor.

"Can your lungs take Mars air?" she demanded.

He nodded. "I've fought in the Alps and the Taurus." With Brothers crumpling about him, he remembered—brave men, tireless men who happened to lack the body machinery for battle on half-rations of air. "How about you? There's a respirator in the locker."

"I've been here before." She stopped him with a nervous gesture at the air lock.

Cade set the mechanism in motion and there was an equalizing outrush of air. Momentarily his sight dimmed and he had to cling to an iron for support. The girl, lighter and with bigger lungs, recovered before he did and was through the lock before he could walk certainly. Her eyes swept the horizon anxiously. "Your butcher-work on the crates isn't going to make things easier," she said. "We'd better start unloading and have the—the cargo ready to go."

"To go to the Star of Mars?"

"Yes."

He followed her back into the ship and opened the cargo port amidships. While she emptied locker after locker, Cade moved the bulkier crates outside. Fifty meters from the flier the pile of guns grew tall. But at every trip the girl's impatient scanning of the horizon was repeated.

"I assume your friends are late?" he asked uneasily.

"The less you assume, the better," she said. And then she uttered a gasp of relief. There was a black dot topping a hill and then another—dozens, hundreds at last.

"The Armsmen of Mars?" He was torn between surprise at their unexpected numbers and contempt for their ragged approach.

"Far from Armsmen, Cade. The word is 'patriots.' You've heard it before." There was an unreadable quality in her voice. Cade could not tell whether she despised these people or admired them. "It means that they love their homeland. They are devoted more to Mars and its ruler than to the Emperor."

He couldn't help it; a shudder went through him at the thought—and a moment later he was smiling at the shudder.

"They're just porters then."

She started to shake her head and then said: "In effect, yes. Just porters."

The crowd was drawing nearer. Patriots or porters, whatever they were, Cade saw clearly that there were no Armsmen among them. They were farmers, miners, clerks from the city. They walked easily as you'd expect Mars-born people to, and clearly had no difficulty with Mars air. Their clothes were lighter than the furs he and Jocelyn wore against the chill. And they all carried uncouth sacks over their shoulders. Cade thought of the guns jostled and scraping together in the sacks and set his teeth obstinately: a gun now was just a killing-tool, the way a saw was just a cutting-tool.

There were boys in their teens and not a few women among the mob; it numbered some nine hundred, to carry about fifty thousand guns.

How, he wondered, could this rabble keep a secret? And then he thought of Harrow, the dead Gunner: "...a man likes to be among his own people...it's newer on Mars...I don't suppose you know anything about your eight-times great-grandfather..." If all these people shared that feeling!

With the crowd came noise, the undisciplined chatter of nine hundred excited people. A tall, lean-faced fellow in his middle years turned to the rest and yelled sharply through the thin air: "Just shut up, all of you! Shut up and stand where you are!" A few lieutenants repeated the crude command. After a minute the shipward drift of the crowd halted and there was silence.

The man said to Cade: "I'm Tucker. There wasn't anything said about a woman. Who's she?"

The Lady Jocelyn said dramatically: "A daughter of Mars." If there was the faintest tinge of mockery in her voice, only Cade thought he heard it.

The lean-faced man said, feelingly: "Mars blesses you, sister."

"Mars blesses us all from the highest to the lowest." It seemed to be password and countersign.

Tucker said: "We're glad to have a high-born Lady among us, sister. I was told the flier of the ship wouldn't be a brother?"

"Not yet. He will be. He is an Earth-born Gunner who will train Marsmen for the day of liberty."

"It's growing," said Tucker rapturously. "Nothing can stop it!" It was beginning to sound more like the mystic nonsense of the Cairo gang than businesslike military identification procedure.

The mob was getting noisy again and military procedure took another body-blow. Tucker turned and bawled at them: "You all shut up now! Get into some kind of a line and get your sacks open. And don't take all day!" Cade watched them milling and groaned at the thought of turning such a mob into Armsmen. But he swallowed his disgust; what she wanted of him, he would do.

They did get whipped into line eventually by roaring non-coms. Cade couldn't make out whether these were merely temporary, self-appointed leaders, or whether there was any organization in this gang. But somehow a dozen Marsmen got busy sorting out sixty-gun piles from the heap and dumping them into waiting sacks. The guns couldn't have been carried under Earth gravity, but their weight on Mars consti-tuted no more than a good working load. Cade was very glad that guns of the Order had two centimeters of six-kilogram trigger pull before you hit a five-gram pull and firing contact. There were no accidents.

Jocelyn told him busily: "We won't need the ship and I don't want to leave it here for a monument. Shoot it off to somewhere on automatic take-off."

It was sound doctrine. By the time the empty flier roared, off, its ultimate destination an aimless orbit in space, the tail-end of the line of porters was snaking past a melting pile of guns. Tucker, the lean-faced "patriot" leader, was yelling again, trying to make himself heard over the combined noise of rockets and rabble, to get them to form a new line of march heading out of the valley.

As the noise of the vanishing flier was lost in the distant sky, the man's shouts were drowned out again by the terrifying crescendo of jets. Not one ship this time, but a fleet. An instant later a hundred or more space-recon fliers roared low over the hill-rimmed basin.

They fanned out beautifully; to land beyond the crags in a perfectly executed envelopment on the largest scale Cade had ever seen. He won-dered numbly whether the brilliant maneuver had been performed on individual piloting or slave-circuit control.

The Martian rabble broke its uneven ranks. Nine hundred of them milled pointlessly about asking each other frightened, stupid questions; the total effect was a thought-shattering roar. The Lady Jocelyn's hand

gripped Cade's arm through the wadded sleeve of his furs. Her face was
deathly pale. He must have radar stations on Deimos and Phobos, Cade
thought, to pin-point us like that…

Then there was a voice, the kind of voice nine-year-old Cade, Gun-
ner-to-be, had thought the Emperor spoke with. It roared like thunder
through the basin of rock, breaking against the rim and rebounding in
echoes—the voice of the Power Master, the voice Cade would never fail
to know whether it spoke cynically across a room, commandingly over
the radio or majestically into the thin air of Mars.

"Marsmen, my Gunners are taking up positions surrounding you.
You will drop your bags of weapons and walk to the foot of the hills to
surrender. I want only the two persons who landed by flier. They must
be held but the rest of you will be released after a search. You have fifteen
minutes to do this. If you do not, my Gunners will advance, firing."

Silence from the hills and a growing mutter from the crowd.

"Who are they?"

"Who's the man from the flier?"

"They said he's no brother!"

"Get rid of the guns!"

"They'll burn us down where we stand."

"What will we do?"

"What will we do?"

Cade shook his head dazedly; Tucker was glaring at him.

"He's lying!" shrilled a clear voice—Jocelyn's. "He's lying! Do you
think he'll let you go when you're helpless? He'll kill you all!"

Her warning was lost in the roar, except to Tucker and Cade. The
lean-faced Marsman said to her slowly: *"When* we're helpless? We're
helpless now. We've drilled some, but we don't know guns."

With the brutal mob-noise for a background, Jocelyn spoke again,
softly and almost to herself. "Two hundred years," she said emotionlessly. "Two hundred years of planning, two hundred years of waiting,
two hundred years of terror: waiting for a traitor or a fool to talk, but
nobody did. One gun, two guns, a dozen guns a year at last, waiting—"

She was swaying as she stood; Cade braced her with his arm.

"What a dream it was…and we came so close. Mars in rebellion, the
Klin Philosophy shaken, Armsmen split, the Power Master defied. Men
on Mars—men everywhere—thinking for themselves, challenging the
traditions that tied them down. Thinking and challenging!" A blaze that
had kindled briefly in her eyes seemed to die.

"We underestimated," she said flatly. Now she was talking to Cade.
"We didn't allow for the dead weight of things as they are. Two hundred
years…I hope my uncle will not suffer when he dies."

Her uncle. Cade hung on to that and comprehension came at last.
"The Emperor," he said slowly, "your uncle—the Emperor; he knows
of this?"

"Yes, of course." There were tears behind her voice. Cade marveled at his blindness, not to have understood before. It was so obvious; this way it all made sense.

"The Emperor—the last five Emperors, powerless in everything except knowledge. They and a few others in the family, a handful of men and women. Three generations ago the reigning Emperor saw that Mars was the key, that the rulers of Mars would rebel and the Mars populace would be with them. The Emperor-Mars pact was concluded fifty-five years ago. My uncle wrote the petition for Mars-born Armsmen. What a great dream it was! But what difference does it make now?"

I hope my uncle will not suffer when he dies. But he would; the Emperor would suffer and so would she. The Power Master would not let them die until he had wrung from them every bit of information that they held.

Abruptly the voice of thunder said: "Eight minutes!" and the Mars rabble flowed around them, scared, angry and confused, demanding to be told what to do and what it meant.

Tucker had been listening, dazed. "If we could fight," he said hoarsely, working his hands. "If we could only fight!"

"Thinking and challenging," echoed Cade. "Thinking and challenging." Five years to make a novice. Ten for an Armiger. Fifteen for a Gunner. To face Gunners with anything less than Gunners was like opposing guns of the Order with wooden clubs. Tucker knew that, and still dared to think: *if we could fight.*

They were patriots, Cade thought; now he knew what it meant. They were frightened now, with reason, but still they held their sacks of guns. They weren't ready to give in.

Cade said the impossible: *"We can fight them."*

"Armsmen?" said the girl.

But there was wild hope on Tucker's lean face.

"They're trained," he said foolishly. "They've had three years."

"There's no other way," Cade said to Jocelyn, ignoring the Marsman. "It's a cleaner death, and—*you* taught me to challenge the rules."

He fired his own gun straight up in a three-second burst at full aperture and a stunned silence fell on the crowd.

"I am Gunner Cade of the Order of Armsmen," he shouted into the thin air. "You have guns—more guns than the Armsmen in the hills. I will show you how to use them."

CHAPTER TWENTY-ONE

THOUGHTS BLAZED through his mind. The complex gun; the thing no commoner could master: First Study of the Primary Circuits of the Gun, Ceremonial of the Gun, Order of Recharging, After-charging Checklist, Malfunctions of the Booster Circuit, the Sighting Picture, The Gun's Inner Meaning in Klin, Aperture and Band Settings for Various Actions. In studied sequence they flashed across his mind, and one by one he threw them out.

"The way to use your gun," he shouted, "is to point it and pull the trigger. If it stops firing, throw it away and grab another." To Tucker he said swiftly: "Have you a dozen men the others will listen to?"

The lean-faced man nodded. "Get them here," Cade said. While the names were being shouted he turned to scan the encircling hills. Against the sky he could see the slender rods of radionic grids faintly discernable—ten or so, spaced around the rim of hills. What contempt they must hold him in to expose command posts like that!

Where to attack with his rabble? Straight ahead there was a nice little pass in the hills. Standard doctrine was for the defenders to command such a pass by plunging fire. Standard doctrine in the attack was to draw fire from the defenders, pin down the defenders exposed by their fire and storm the pass. The Marsmen had no training to prepare themselves for such an encounter. But off to the right was an ugly little cliff—a cliff nobody in his right mind would bother to attack or defend. It would be covered by a Gunner or so, no matter how unlikely it was. But was it so unlikely to be scaled by Marsmen to whom the air and gravity were normal—?

"Here are the men." Cade looked over the dozen lieutenants Tucker had called up and proceeded to instruct them. A long line of his teachers would have cringed at his instruction. He showed them only the triggers, the band and aperture sets, and the charge gauges. They didn't need to know how to recharge; there were guns to spare. They didn't need to know the care of guns, the circuits, the ritual, the inner meanings—all they needed was to know how to shoot. As he showed them, his wonder almost equaled theirs at the simplicity of it all.

"We will head for that cliff," he said, pointing. "Try to show your men what I showed you before we get there. Don't try to keep order on the march. The worse it looks, the better. That's all."

He gave them a minute and then stepped off for the rim of hills. He yelled a command which he dimly realized was more ancient than the Order itself and exactly as old as history:

"Follow me!"

"For Mars! For the Star of Mars!" someone shrieked insanely, and others took up the howl. Cade didn't look behind him. If he had them all, good If he didn't, there was nothing to be done about it. Perhaps some would start with him and others hesitate and then follow—so much the better. To the ring of steady-eyed Armsmen watching from the hills, this charge across the plain would seem a panic flight. Even if they had picked up the gist of his orders to the mob with a three-meter directional mike trained on him, or seen the scattered efforts of lieutenants to instruct their groups, it would seem inconceivable to them that commoners would fight.

Not that they would; Cade knew it well enough. They'd balk at the first blast of well-aimed fire. They'd shriek and run like—commoners. Mars or Earth, a commoner's a commoner; sluggish, overstuffed, stupid, soft. *Point your guns and pull the trigger.* Fine words, he mocked himself, fine words! They were supposed to have had three years of "training"— form-fours on the village square, no doubt, an hour a week. Even that didn't show. None of them had *seen* a gun before.

Thinking and challenging, he mocked. Thinking indeed, that challenged the one bedrock truth he knew: that Armsmen were Armsmen, fighters, gun-handlers, the only fighters there were.

It was insanity; *that* truth he knew, and the other truth that made insanity his only course. If the fight was lost, he was already dead, and so was *she.*

She was running alongside, keeping pace with his strides. "Do you think—?" she asked wildly. "Cade, it's the *Power Master's Guard!* They can defeat any force of Armsmen in the Realm."

"We're not Armsmen," he growled. "We're a rabble of crazy *patriots.* We don't know how to fight, but we seem to have something to fight *for.* Now fall back. Get into the middle of this gang and leave yourself room to run when they stampede."

"I won't!"

"You—will!"

Meekly she fell back and Cade strode on. Admit it, fool! he raged. Admit it! You're playing a game, a child's farce—the way you used to play Superior and Novice back in Denver. They've forged a ring of fire around you and you're charging into death: solitary death, because that mob will break and run and well you know it.

A farce? Very well; play it out as best you can, he told himself, *Gunner* Cade, trained Armsman, master of fighting that you are—*fight!*

He swung on grimly and the worn, ancient cliffs loomed ahead, grotesque engravings of wind and sand and centuries on deathless stone. If the Armsmen opened fire now, he was lost with his half-trained rabble. They'd never know enough to spread; they'd bunch like sheep—and die in a crushed mob. If they reached the dead area under the cliff there might be a momentary postponement of the butchery.

The Armsmen would have fired before now, if they expected trouble. They must be looking for a desperate attempt to push through the nice little pass and escape.

The attack of the Marsmen would have to be swift and deadly. They might take the hill! It was a thing that would rock the foundation of the Order.

"For the Star! For the Star of Mars!" he heard them howling behind him, and grinned coldly. *Patriots!* Perhaps patriots were what you needed for a murderous, suicidal assault.

His feet slipped once on rubble and the shadow of a crag was on his face. "Give me two of your guns, brother," he said to a boy with bulging eyes and a fixed grin on his face. "Up the cliff!" he shouted over his shoulder at the rabble. *"Follow me—charge!"* He broke into a run and noted coldly that the thin air roughly canceled the advantage of the lesser Mars gravity. The youth at his side, still breathing easily, pushed ahead—and fell a moment later with the fixed grin still on his face and both legs charred away by a long-range blast.

Automatically Cade blasted the crag from which the fire had come. The fire-fight had been joined.

Make it or break it now, he thought. Face your death, fire a counter-blast or two to let them know you were there, to make them pause a bit and wonder a bit and perhaps fear a bit before your commoners broke and ran.

"Follow me! Up!"

The lean-faced Tucker raced past Cade screaming: "For the Star of Mars!" His sack of guns flapped and bobbed as he began to scrabble up the cliff. There were others—wild-eyed men, a panting youth, a leathery woman—who passed Cade.

Behind him there were yells and the blast of guns. He hoped he wouldn't be burned in the back by one of the Marsmen's ill-aimed guns after coming this far...

The fire-fight grew severe as he pantingly climbed the cliff. From the hills it was rapid and deadly. From the Marsmen it was a torrent whose effect he couldn't guess at. The noise the guns made was a senseless blend of small-aperture buzz and wide-aperture roar. Cade scrambled grimly up and hoisted himself over the jagged cliff-edge into the racket of a first-class battle. A rudimentary squad of Marsmen was blasting Armsmen across a windrow of fallen comrades. They had learned about aperture by now, Cade saw with bleak satisfaction, and they were learning how to rush from crag to crag, to take isolated Armsmen in pockets of the eroded rock by flanking fire. Incredibly, in spite of the numbers of their dead, they were gaining ground. Armsmen were falling.

They didn't need his gun. Cade turned from the shooting and stationed himself at the cliff head, splitting the steady stream of Marsmen as they gained the peak, sending half to the right and half into the fighting to the left.

"Tucker!" he yelled.

The lean-faced Marsman who had led the assault up the cliff was still alive. "Tucker, take this gang on the right and work them through the hills. Keep them moving, keep them firing, keep them yelling. I'll work the rest around the left. If you see any sign of the Armsmen's withdrawing to regroup, keep your men moving, but come and check with me. That's all."

"Yes, brother." Like old times, thought Cade—except that he was fighting now to overthrow all he had once fought for…and for Jocelyn.

He dared not think of that. He had not seen her once since the beginning. Now he had a job to do and was doing it well. It occurred to him at last that they might win.

The cliff-top fighters; insanely extravagant fire had done its work. This immediate arc of the hills was cleared of Armsmen. He saw that the Marsmen were sorted out in to elementary squads and platoons—a lesson of battle, or fruit of their crude training? Whichever it was, it gave him leaders.

"Follow me!"

And they followed eagerly as he led them left, well down on the reverse slope of the hills. They worked the ragged terrain with style, arranging themselves into units of three—the useful skirmishers' triangle, from which any fighter can rush to take ground under the covering fire of the other two. Was this, Cade wondered wearily, what he had given his life to? This bag of tricks that a crowd of fanatical farmers discovered for themselves at the cost of a few lives? He dropped beneath the blast of an Armsman from a shadowing crag, and did no more philosophizing. When the crag had been undercut and toppled on the Brother, there was a new blast to face, and another, and still another.

Then they were back on the ridge of the hills and found they had taken a command post and its equipment. Some of the Marsmen paused to marvel at the radionic mast and mappers and communicator.

"Keep moving, blast you!" Cade raved at them. "Keep moving and keep firing!"

He lashed them on over the mound of dead Armsmen and into a blazing linked fire from a dozen wind-carved pockets in the rock. They had learned well. The Marsmen rushed from one eroded spire to the next…at the cost of a dozen lives they secured flanking positions and withering enfilade fire wiped out the defending Armsmen in seconds.

He cursed them forward, and the next fire they met was scattered, rear-guard stuff—three men trying to fire like thirty. It was the retreat he had, half-crazily, hoped for: not a flight but a consolidation of forces. The Armsmen would be grouped soon in one mass capable of putting out an interlaced ring of fire. In spite of his green troops' astonishing performance so far, Cade bitterly knew he could not pit them against any such formation.

The mast of another command post was in their newly won territory by the time they had mopped up the rear guard. He shouted a cease-fire and led his men straight over the rim of the hills instead of working along the reverse slope for cover. He wanted to waste no precious time while there were Armsmen to be killed. They shot down a communications man, still sending; otherwise the command post had been abandoned. Cade eagerly took his binoculars and studied the work of Tucker's men, to the right. They were strung out more than they ought to be, but one post had fallen to them and another was under attack. Signs of retreat were clear on Tucker's front also.

A sudden ferocious flurry of blasts ten meters from him sent Cade sprawling to the ground.

"What kind of cursed scouts do you call your cursed selves?" he raved at his men. "When I said kill them, I meant kill them! Let's clean up this cursed ground!"

They grinned at him like wolves, and followed in a wild surge that broke through the thin rear-guard screen and clawed with fire into a regrouped main guard. "Feint at *us*, will they?" he yelled, only half-hearing himself in the roar of blasters at full aperture. Before the butchery was over his Marsmen had lost heavily and still another command post was in their hands. The Armsmen's retreat this time was no feint...

He sent scouts forward to harry the Armsmen. From the captured post, he studied neatly ranked recon fliers, two hundred meters from the reverse slopes of the circling hills. And something incredible was happening. The ant-like figures of Armsmen were making for the fliers. They weren't going to stand and fight. They were racing for their fliers, doubling back and swerving, boiling out in panic from behind the rocks.

"Fire on them!" yelled Cade. "Pass the word to fire!" There would be no hits except an occasional accident, but it would let the Armsmen know *he* was there...

A few of the ant-like figures knelt and returned blasts, fearing a rush.

Tucker was there. "You told me," the lean-faced man panted, "you told me to report, but I couldn't get away—"

Cade didn't rebuke him, and Tucker ventured a note of triumph: "Gunner, we got their headquarters! That stopped them, didn't it?"

"It shouldn't," Cade said—and then realized the full extent of what had happened. Laughter burst from his lips. "Yes," he said, "that stopped them." Even with his words they heard the first of the fliers blast off at maximum. A moment later there was another.

Cade followed his second in command across the now-secure inner plain to inspect the headquarters post for himself. The roar of his snipers' guns, mingled with jets on take-off, was sweet to his ears.

Eagerly he examined the remains of the command post the Marsman had taken; and there was no mistake possible. It was a well-selected position, as good a headquarters as the terrain could offer. It commanded a good escape route down the reverse slope to the fliers and a good 360-degree field of fire and observation. But the fury of five hundred Marsmen had overwhelmed the strategic knowledge of ten thousand years. The place was a shambles of ruined radios and maps, telescopes, bull-horns, all the heavy equipment of command. And over the rubble were strewn the bodies of Armsmen.

Cade let out a long halloo: *"Hold your fire! Pass along the word!"* The command rang victoriously along the hills.

He walked to the central control panel of the communicator set and looked down at the crooked corpse that lay over it, a corpse half-charred and without a cloak. He rolled the body over and stared into the granite countenance of the Power Master.

Dead! Dead because he would not give his power to a subordinate. Because he had to witness the victory himself. He hadn't expected battle; none of them had.

The cease-fire had been luckily timed. Earlier it might not have been obeyed. Later it might have occurred without an order. Even so there were irreconcilables who could not bear the helpless retreat of Armsmen by the hundreds to their fliers. Several continued to fire for a minute, and one woman ran shrieking down the rocks until she was picked off.

Cade watched the cloaked and helmeted figures swarming into the slender space ships, blasting off northward, lifting on slave-control the empty crafts whose complements would never fly again. They would take news of this day with them and spread it through the Realm of Man.

It was incredible that they should have won, thought Cade—but no more incredible than that commoners should have fought at all.

Patriotism?

Wearily, he studied the Marsmen sprawled on the ground nearby. One little knot was singing some song or other about Mars. Others were talking loudly, with exaggerated laughter. One man was sobbing hysterically; he seemed to be unwounded. Many sat in silence with furrowed brows, or in near-silence, exchanging halting words.

"Yes," Cade heard, "but what if more of them come back?"

"There will be more of us. I have five brothers—"

"Yes! My boys are big for their age—yes—"

"They killed Manley, I don't know what I'll say to his wife."

"They'll take care of us. Her too."

"They *better* take care of us—"

Cade walked restlessly along the ridge, looking for something he dared not think about, through the territory that had been held until minutes ago by Power Master and Order and all the other trappings of the past.

Patriotism! The Brothers would be more wary the next time they were sent to fight against it. It was easy to imagine the bored confidence with which the five-hundred-odd Armsmen had left their fliers and climbed the hills. They had thought themselves out on an elaborate policing job; they had found themselves well-placed observation posts with good fields of fire out of sheer habit. Then, they had found their line broken by an impossible frontal assault and one command post destroyed in a matter of minutes. The loss of two or more posts had made it necessary to regroup, *to retreat from commoners.* And when the headquarters post was lost…

Ordinarily it wouldn't matter. Next-in-command-takes-over, quite automatically, in less time than it takes to say. But to these stunned Armsmen, it must have been a last straw in a nightmarish overload of their capacity to adjust.

It was the very impossibility of the attack, the inability of trained men, tradition-steeped, to believe it could happen, that had done it. When the Marsmen had scaled that cliff, the Brothers of the Order had lost their initiative of fire, and that was fatal.

They had all lost their initiative of fire now—Stars, Klin Teachers, The Order, the next Power Master. They would never win it back as long as battle-worn Marsmen could sit on a hilltop saying: "I have five brothers…my boys are big for their age…"

What had the Power Master said? "If they kept attacking the Watch Houses until all the gas guns were used up…We must have an Emperor for the commoners to love."

But there was no Power Master now, and the Emperor—The Emperor himself had made this battle possible. The Emperor and…

Until this moment he had not let himself think about her; not in the battle, for fear of doing less than his utmost; not afterwards, for fear of what he might learn. But now it was all right.

She came stumbling across the scarred rock, her face sober, her body drooping with fatigue but her head held regally high.

"Thank you, Gunner Cade, for my uncle and for me." She spoke formally, but he understood. There were no words with which he could have voiced his own joy. She was alive, unharmed. His arms could have told her, and his lips, but not with words.

"You owe no thanks to me," he said, "but to yourself and to our brothers here."

Then their eyes met and even ceremonious language was impossible.

"Ho, Gunner!" It was Tucker, coming from below. "I'm getting them together down below. Should we leave a guard here?"

"What for—?" With difficulty, Cade brought himself back to the moment and its realities. "Can your men carry more? Some of the equipment is worth salvaging."

Tucker turned over some of the headquarters rubble with his toe. "Any of this?"

"I'll look it over," he said, and turned to Jocelyn. "May I see you first? A few words—"

"Of course." She took his arm and he helped her down eroded steps to a sheltered place.

"What now?" he asked simply.

"Now? To the Star of Mars, to the Court. Then—well, perhaps we could go back. The Power Master had no heir designated; it might be safe to return to Earth. There will be endless confusion there and probably safety. But the Star of Mars would surely give you command of all fighting."

The words hung in the air.

"And you?" Cade asked.

"I don't know. There will be things to do. I'm not used to being idle."

"I wouldn't like to be his Gunner Superior," Cade said slowly. "I think I might like to marry someday."

"Oh, Cade!" There was laughter in her eyes. "This isn't Earth. It wouldn't be the Order again. Most of your Armsmen, if you call them that, would be married."

"That's true," he said. "I didn't think of that. The old habits—Jocelyn, I—" How could he say it? "You're the blood of the Emperor!" he cried out.

"The Emperor," she said softly, "is a man, too. A wise man. And married."

Now he knew there was no way to say it; words were not enough. As once before in anger, but now with tenderness, he seized her in his arms and pulled her to him. As once before in surprise, but now with full knowledge, she kissed him back.

For minutes they sat together, until a shadow began to lengthen across them. Cade stood and pulled her to her feet.

"There's work to do," he said.

"Work for both of us, my darling."

"My darling." He said the new word wonderingly, and then smiled. He had so much to learn.

Outpost Mars

Chapter One

Jᴉᴍ Kᴀɴᴅʀᴏ couldn't pace the corridors, because there weren't any. The Colony's hospital was simply an extra room built onto the doctor's rammed-earth house. They still called it "earth," though it was the rust-reddened soil of Mars.

The narrow space between bed and wall cramped his legs; the monotonous motion wearied his arm. But Jim stayed on, doggedly determined to see the thing through, rubbing his wife's back and whispering reassurances, as much to himself as to her.

"Why don't you let me take over for a while?" the doctor suggested. Jim's usefulness was over now; the man was only communicating his own panic to his wife. "Go in the other room and lie down. Nothing's going to happen for a while yet."

"Doc—" The man's voice was rough with anxiety, but he held back the frantic questions. "Please, Tony," he said simply, "I'd rather stick around." He fixed a smile to his face as he bent over Polly again.

Anna came in before Tony had quite decided to call her. It was a talent she seemed to have, one of the reasons why he had chosen her for his assistant.

"I think Jim needs a cup of coffee," he told her firmly.

Kandro straightened up awkwardly. "All right, Doc." He was trying hard to be matter-of-fact. "You'll call me if anything—when there's news?"

"Of course he will." Anna's quick assurance forestalled Tony's exasperated retort. She put her hand on Kandro's arm, and smiled down at the woman on the bed. "Not much longer now, Polly," she said with quiet certainty. "Come on, Jim."

As the door closed behind them, Tony turned to his patient, and surprised a brief smile on her lips. "You mustn't mind," she explained, almost apologetically. "He's so worried."

She had no breath for more. She twisted suddenly on the narrow bed and clutched at the air till Tony gave her his hand to squeeze. Every other form of physical labor, he reflected unhappily, was made easier by the light gravity of Mars; but the labor of childbirth was eternally the same. And there was nothing he could do right now, except to offer her the reassurance of his presence. He stood and waited, goose flesh cascading from the nape of his neck down his spine as she ground her teeth against the pain.

139

When it was gone and she released his hand, he turned to the sterilizer for a fresh glove. One more examination, he decided. Something should be happening by now.

He heard her deep inhalation behind him.

"Anna's so nice," she sighed.

He heard the difference before he turned and saw it. Polly was lying back, completely relaxed, making the most of the time before the pain returned.

"Yes, she is," Tony said. He dropped the glove on the table; another examination wasn't going to do any good, for her or for him. *Quit the damned fiddling,* he told himself. *Sit and wait. You let that poor son-of-a-gun get you down. If she can wait, you can too. Be the doctor you would have been in Pittsburgh or Springfield—any Springfield on Earth. So you're on Mars. So what? Sit and wait.*

On the other side of the door, Jim raised his "coffee" cup for the fourth time to his lips, and for the fourth time put it down untasted.

"But what do you *think*, Anna?" he burst out. "How does it look to you? You'd know if there was anything—*wrong.*"

"It looks all right to me," she said again, gently. "It looks like a normal delivery."

"But she's been—she started at six o'clock this morning! Why should it take so long?"

"Sometimes it does. That doesn't mean there's anything wrong. It's hard work, that's all. It takes time." It was useless to tell him not to worry. She went over to the work counter that ran the length of the rectangular room. "I don't think it'll be much longer now, Jim. Do you want to try and get some sleep while you wait? Or if you're going to stay up, could you give me a hand here?" She pulled out materials quickly and gave him an alky torch.

"Look," he said desperately, "you would tell me, wouldn't you, if it wasn't going right? He—Tony wouldn't want to keep me from knowing, would he? She never got this far before, you know."

Even Anna's patience could wear thin. Deftly she removed the torch from his hand before the down-turned flame could do any damage.

Kandro wanted to yell: *You don't know, none of you know. Twelve years we've been married and a man and a woman want kids, and none of you know how we want kids and all she does is get so sick you think she's dying and she never got this far before and you just don't know...*

He saw in Anna's eyes that he didn't have to say it, that she did understand. Her arms went out a little, and the big, rawboned man flopped on his knees before the plain little woman and sobbed with his head awkwardly pillowed against her...

At 3:37 a.m., Dr. Tony Hellman adjusted a tiny oxygen mask over the red button nose of a newborn infant, wiped it and wrapped it, and returned his attention to the mother.

When he had finished, he overrode Polly's plan to stay awake and stare at her baby. He gave her a stiff shot of sedative to make certain, then decided to give her her OxEn pill for the next day as well, hoping she would sleep through till late morning.

Only since the development of the magic pink pellets, containing the so-called "oxygen enzyme," had it been possible for most human beings to live a normal life on Mars. Before that, anyone who did not have the rare good luck to possess naturally Marsworthy lungs lived permanently in an oxygen mask. Now masks were needed only for babies too small to tolerate the pill.

The miracle enzyme made the air of Mars useful to human lungs as the native atmosphere of Earth—always provided the human in question took his pill religiously every day. Let thirty hours go by without renewing the treatment, and he would be dying, within minutes, of anoxemia.

Tony took a last look at the baby, made sure the tiny mask was properly adjusted, and checked the oxy tank for proper flow. Polly was already half asleep. He went quietly past her bed and opened the door to his living room.

"Sh!" Anna turned from her workbench, her face warm and cheerful. She pointed to the bunk where Jim, fully dressed in tunic and sand-boots, lay fast asleep.

"Everything all right?"

Tony nodded: "Damn sight better than I expected." After the glaring light of the hospital room, the quiet dark in here was good. More than that, Anna's untroubled presence served to dissolve all the nervous tension of the hours before. Suddenly too fatigued even to talk, he finished briefly: "Boy—five pounds, two ounces, Earth-weight—good color—strong too."

"Good. I'll finish this and then go sit with her. I'll call you if she needs anything."

"What about him?"

Anna glanced at Jim's sprawled figure. "He'll be all right." She smiled. "He can wait a few hours to meet his son."

For just a moment more the doctor stood there, watching her, fascinated as always by her delicate art. A puff on the tube, a twist as it reddened in the flame, a spin against an iron tool, another puff. All of it casual, seemingly random, and then, somehow, there was a finished piece of work—part of the intricate glass tubing always needed at the Lab, a fragile-looking piece of stemware for some new colonist's household, a precise hypodermic syringe for himself.

He watched till his weary eyes refused the bright spot of light where the pale flame washed over the glowing glass. Then he stumbled into the adjoining bedroom and slept.

Chapter Two

The Lab was the cash crop of Sun Lake. Mars had a slight case of radio-activity, nothing you couldn't live with, but enough to enable Sun Lake City Colony to concentrate and isolate radioisotopes and radioactive organics for sale on Earth at better than competitive prices, even after the stiff tariff for transport.

The materials handled were only mildly dangerous, but it was the doctor's job to render them effectively not dangerous at all. Twice a day, before work started in the morning and again before quitting time, Tony geigered the whole place. On this precaution the whole community depended, not only for safeguarding their sole source of income, but for their very lives. Every adult member of the Colony did work at least indirectly connected with the Lab; all of them spent some time there.

Among other things, it was the only building with a large enough room to serve for social functions. And it offered the only possible change from mud-colored walls, from isomorphic rooms, all just 15 x 15, from cement floors and wall bunks. The Lab had everything the other buildings lacked—steel framework and alumalloy wall sheathing; copper tubing and running hot water; built-in power outlets, Earthmade furniture; even the blessings of an Earth-import air filtering system.

The one kilometer walk out to the Lab in the early morning always infused the doctor with a glowing sense of confidence and well-being. In a year on Mars, he had lost little of his first pleasure in the buoyancy afforded by the low gravity. Walking was effortless; and, in the thin air, an hour's sunlight was enough to clear the night's chill from the open spaces. At noon, the sun would be too bright; in the evening, the cold would return as suddenly as it had departed. Now, in the first part of the morning, it was like a perfect autumn day on Earth.

Behind him, in the houses that lined both sides of the colony's single curved street, people were dressing hurriedly, eating, making plans, getting ready for the day's work. Ahead, the shining blue walls of the Lab were set off against the magnificent backdrop of *Lacus Solis* itself. The ancient sea bed was alive again with color as the early sun's rays glinted off millions of tiny particles, the salts and minerals of Mars deposited by long-dried waters in millennia past. The clean lines of the new building against that sparkling expanse constituted at once a challenge and a reassurance—this is what man can do; here is everything he needs to do it with.

If we can...a second chance for man, if we can learn how to use it...

Tony unlocked the storage cabinet built into the massive lead-lined door of the Lab. He took out his suit of protective armor—probably the only Earth-import wearing apparel ever bought and paid for by the Colony—but before he got into it, he turned to look back just once at the little huddle of houses where, a few hours ago, Polly Kandro had affirmed her faith in Sun Lake's future in the most emphatic personal manner.

The solidity of the Lab was a disagreeable symbol of the Colony's present status; it was still the only decent structure Sun Lake had to show. Halfway up the almost imperceptible three kilometer slope from "canal" bed at his left to "sea" level at his right sat the Colony, lumpishly. Every building, like Tony's own home-and-hospital, was tamped native dirt. The arc of dull rust-brown huts squatting close to the ground and close to each other presented to Tony a monotonous row of identical plastic-windowed backsides.

Behind them, fields A, B, C, and D showed, even from the Lab, the work of Sun Lake's "mudkickers"—the agronomists who, using tools as ancient as the mutation-creating particles that stream from a cyclotron, were changing Mars plants into things that could nourish an Earth animal, and changing Earth plants into things that could draw nourishment from the grudging Martian soil.

Mutated bean plants whose ancestors had been a button-bearing Mars cactus dotted field A. Mutated cauliflowers—the size of apples, dark brown and still manufacturing in themselves too much potassium cyanide to be edible—darkened field B; another few plant-generations and they would be food for the Colony table, though tasting somewhat of the neutralized cyanide bitter almonds.

Ten kilometers beyond the fields of bastard Earth-Mars vegetation, there had been beauty only recently—the fantastically eroded Rimrock Hills. Five months ago, however, the first pre-fab shacks had gone up in the camp on the other side of the hills. Three months ago the first furnace had been fired at Pittco Three: Pittsburgh Coal, Coke, and Iron Company's Mars Metal Refining Plant Number Three. Now a dirty shroud of yellow-stained smoke draped the peaks from dawn to dark.

With a feeling of intense distaste, Tony started climbing into his suit of armor. *A second chance for man…*

His own high-flown thoughts mocked him. Another chance to do exactly as they had done on Earth. Already the clean air of Mars was thickening with the eructations of Earth's commerce. Nor was the camp beyond the hill a lone offender. Even Sun Lake, to survive at all, had to maintain a cash crop economy—and the Lab was the potentially deadly crop.

Tony made sure that every flap on his suit was zippered and closed, and the last adjustments made on the helmet. He picked up the hand counter from the bottom of the compartment and worked the screw around to calibrate out Mars' naturally heavy background "noise." The needle eased to zero on the dial. Only then did he open the heavy door of the Lab itself and begin his slow trip of inspection through the building.

All areas were well under the threshold of danger, as usual, except for a hot patch in the isotope room. Tony chalked a yellow line around the spot and marked the door of the room with a bright yellow cross. Finished, he headed straight for the clean-up room and checked the condition of the exterior of his suit against the bigger stationary radiation counter that was kept there.

Not until he was sure he hadn't picked up anything on gloves or boots did he remove his suit and dump it down the chute for routine de-radiation. He hated to take time for the rest of the procedure today: he had to check with the men who were working in the hot spot; he had to get back to the hospital to see Polly; he had a patient, Joan Radcliff, who worried him badly.

He stripped and dumped his clothes down another chute, sand-scrubbed himself, and, holding his breath, walked through the stinking alcohol spray. Methyl alcohol, cheaper and easier to produce in the Lab than water, and sand for soap made bathing an ordeal instead of the pleasant ritual it had been on Earth.

Tony moved fast, but by the time he had put on a fresh tunic and boots and emerged into the central hall, the Lab was already full of people getting set for the day's work. He edged past a knot of busy conversationalists in the corridor.

"Hey, Doc—"

He paused, and that was his undoing.

"How's Polly? Tony, hold on—how's the baby? Are they all right?—Doc, wait a minute. Did everything go all right?—Where are they?—What is it…?"

He answered the same questions a dozen times. It seemed that half the population of Sun Lake was in the corridor with him, and they all wanted to know the same thing. Finally, despairing of getting through until he had satisfied them all, Tony climbed up on a chair and addressed the crowd.

"Five pounds, two ounces, Earth-weight—a boy—wrigglingest baby I ever saw. Plenty lively, and he looks just like his old man. What else do you want to know?"

"How's Polly?"

"Fine. So's Jim." The hoary joke got its inevitable laugh.

Then one of the chemists said, "I make a motion for a birthday present. Let's build that other room onto the Kandro house right now."

It was an offer that had been made months before, and that Polly, hesitant and slightly superstitious, had refused. "There'll be time enough after the baby's born," she had told them, and stuck to it.

Tony knew why; knew about the first time, eleven years before, when she had carried a child for seven months, and then had to pack away all the things she had lovingly collected for its birth. They had stayed in their cartons for four more years, and two more miscarriages, before she gave them tearfully to a luckier woman.

"When is she going home, Doc?" one of the electronics men asked. "How much time have we got?"

"I don't know. Maybe tomorrow morning," Tony told them. "She's in pretty good shape. It's just a matter of where she'll be most comfortable. I don't imagine she'll want to stay in the hospital very long...After all, it's not exactly designed for luxurious convalescence." They were all familiar with the crowded little room; he waited for a dutiful laugh to die down, and added, "I think tomorrow will be about right—not later than the day after."

"We better get started then," Mimi Jonathan, the pert black-haired Lab administrator, spoke up. "Suppose I make up some work parties, and we get things going?"

She produced a pencil and paper and began taking down the names and abilities of everyone whose Lab work was not too pressing. Two groups of volunteers left promptly, to collect soil from the old "canal" bottom, and to set up the frames for ramming. Others would have to stay in the Lab to set up the machinery for work on the synthetics that would paint the new room, build the new furniture, and clothe the new baby. While Mimi plunged into the complexities of reassigning work space and job time, the doctor managed to get away from the enthusiastic crowd.

He made his way to the isotopes room, and was happy to find Sam Flexner, the chemist in charge, waiting for him at the yellow-chalked door.

Tony opened the door and pointed out the ragged chalked circle on the floor. "Any idea what it is?"

"We were running some radiophosphorus," Sam said doubtfully. "But there was no trouble on the run. Must be spillage." The chemist had a young open face, and Tony liked him. He began to fill in the necessary report.

"What reason?" Spillage was unusual.

"It's a bigger order than we usually handle—must have been a hundred kilograms." Sam looked up sharply. "It was all right yesterday, wasn't it? The afternoon checkup?"

Tony nodded.

"Then it must have been at closing. I—well, I left a few minutes early yesterday. Figured the boys could close up all right, but I guess one of them took a lazy man's load in his tote box—filled it up too high to save himself a trip. I'll check on it and tell them in a nice way, all right?"

"That should do it. But I better have a look at the checkout tubes."

Sam brought over a tray of tubes resting in numbered grooves. He was wearing one like them pinned to his own lapel. The contents of the tubes was its normal dirty white. Purple would have meant "too close to hot stuff too long."

"Okay," said Tony, checking his form. "That hot spot there, I think you'd better chisel it out and get one of the suppliers to take it way out and dump it."

"Old Learoyd was here with a load of vanadium dirt. He'll do it when he leaves for Pittco."

"Fine. Get it done. And tell Learoyd to put the stuff in the *back* of his rig. I don't think you could kill any of those old boys with anything subtler than a meat ax, but I wouldn't want him to sit next to it for a ten-hour trip." He dated and timed off the form. "That's that. Only you better stick around till close-up after this." He smiled and put a stop to the young chemist's attempt at explanation. "How's Verna, anyhow? Something better happen soon, if it's going to make all this trouble."

Sam grinned back. "You may hear something soon," he admitted. "But please don't—uh—"

"Doctors don't gossip," Tony said. "One thing about this place," he added, "we can't help making history every time we turn around. Have a baby, and it's the first baby; have another baby, and it's the first girl born; slice out an appendix, and it's the first abdominal surgery. Let's see—you and Verna will be the first marriage between a drop-in chemical engineer and a share-holding agronomist—if she'll have you."

"Sounds like one of those weather records," complained Sam. "The coldest three p.m. reading at the corner of Spruce and Juice on a January 16th since 2107."

"It's your place in history," Tony assured him. "We'll all be footnotes. I'll see you this afternoon."

Chapter Three

TONY STEPPED OUT with springs in his knees, and, feeling the waxing heat of the morning, threw back the hood of his parka. The marvelous clear air of an hour earlier was fast disappearing, as the mineral trash that covered Mars' surface began to heat and roil the atmosphere. He looked off toward the Rimrock Hills, mourning their vanished beauty; then he stopped in surprise, squinting at the enigmatic black bugs crawling back and forth within the shadow of the hills.

He stood there, watching, as the seemingly random pattern of motion trended gradually in the direction of the Colony.

Who would be out on the desert afoot? He stopped and shielded his eyes. There were about twenty of them, and they were humped with— carbines and oxy masks.

The military!

But why? There'd never been a visit from Commissioner Bell's little intercolony police force before; never been any occasion for it. Each colony handled its own internal policing.

It was a year now since Bell's boys had been out for anything except routine administrative work, such as guard mount over the rocket; the last time was when an ace foundryman for Mars Machine Tool was rightly suspected of committing mayhem on a Marsport shopkeeper. Mars Machine Tool's colony administration insisted on being unimpressed by the evidence and refused to surrender him to Marsport. Bell's boys had simply walked in and taken him away for his trial and conviction.

But Sun Lakers weren't given to mayhem.

Tony headed back for the Lab as the crooked trail of the soldiers straightened out into a beeline for the same place. He had his patients, but he was also a member of the Colony Council and this looked like Council business.

In the Lab he went straight to the front office and asked Mimi, "Did Harve ever get that recorder put together?"

"Last week," she said. "It's been a blessing too. Why?"

"I think Bell's boys are paying us a call." He told her what he'd seen outside. "It might be useful to have a record of it."

Mimi nodded thoughtfully, and flipped a lever at the side of her desk. "That'll register anywhere in the office," she explained. "I'm a pacer—Harve set it up so I could walk all over the office while I talk, and still have it recorded."

Sam Flexner was also there. He put down a completed report form on the spillage in his department to ask, "What do they want?"

"I don't know," Tony told him. "But I think we'd better put in an intercom call for Joe Gracey to come on out here. He ought to be tending his seedling in C Area. Phone the South End to send a runner and get him out here on the double."

Gracey was the senior agronomist, and, like Mimi and Tony, a member of the Colony Council. The fourth member, and most recent addition, was Nick Cantrella; in only six months' time since his arrival at Sun Lake, Nick had risen from junior setup man to bossing all maintenance and procurement for the Lab. At the moment he was home with a nasty chemical burn on his arm. It wasn't really so bad that he couldn't be called in for an emergency, but Tony hesitated to do so, and he noticed that Mimi didn't suggest it either. Nick had a red-hot temper and practically no inhibitions.

"No," the doctor said to the questioners that began to press around him, "I don't think we ought to go out and meet them. Better just go ahead and work and get the new room for the Kandros put together. Flexner? will you stick around? It may be some damn thing or other about our atomics—some technical precaution we may have missed."

"*No*, sir," said another man emphatically. It was O'Donnell, who had ditched a law career to become a sweeper and then a maintenance man and then a good jury-rig physicist. It was his job to see that no daylight showed between the Colony's atomics practice and the law.

"Hmp," said the doctor. "You stick around too."

There was a thudding on the door and a self-conscious calling of an archaic formula: "Open in the name of the law!"

The delegation was a half-platoon of soldiers with their carbines and cumbersome oxygen masks and tanks—a choice bit of military conservatism, since a pocketful of OxEn pills weighed a hundredth as much and could keep them alive a hundred times longer. There were two civilians and an officer—Lieutenant Ed Nealey.

Tony was relieved to see him; they were fellow members of the subscription club that split the heavy postage on Earthside scientific periodicals, and Tony knew Nealey to be a conscientious and level-headed young career officer.

The doctor was extending his hand to Nealey when he remembered his protocol. One of the civilians was unknown to him, but the other was Hamilton Bell, Commissioner of Interplanetary Affairs.

"I'm Tony Hellman, Commissioner," he said. "I don't know if you remember me. I'm the doctor here and a member of our Colony's Council."

The commissioner was a small man, tending somewhat to pompous frailty. He looked like the kind of person rumor made him out to be: a never very important functionary who got the dreary Mars post when a very ordinary graft ring of which he was a prominent member was "exposed."

"Can you speak for the Colony?" he asked abruptly, ignoring Tony's hand.

The doctor cast a bewildered look at Lieutenant Nealey, whose eyes were front and whose face was set. Tony noticed he carried in a canvas scabbard the disassembled dipole and handle of an electronic "Bloodhound."

"I'm a council member," Tony said. "So is Miss Jonathan here. Another council member's ill and the third is on his way. The two of us can speak for the Colony. Now, what can we do for you?"

"It's a police matter. Do you care to make a statement before I have to drag the situation out into the open?"

"Let me take it," muttered O'Donnell. Tony nodded. The lawyer-turned-physicist firmly told the commissioner, "I want to remind you that we are a chartered colony, and, under the charter, are entitled to police ourselves. And I also want to say that we are not going to respond to any fishing expeditions until we hear what the complaint is."

"Suit yourself," grunted the commissioner. "But you're not self-policing when you steal from another colony. Mr. Brenner, tell your story."

Eyes swiveled to the other civilian, Brenner of Brenner Pharmaceuticals. *So that,* thought Tony, *is what a trillionaire looks like.* Younger than anyone could reasonably expect, and looking comfortably conservative even in a parka of orange-red mutation mink.

Brenner shrugged and smiled a little uncomfortably. "I had no choice, Doctor," he said. "A hundred kilos of my marcaine—bulk micron dust, you understand—was stolen yesterday."

Somebody gasped. A hundred kilograms of marcaine, principal product of Brenner's works, was a small fortune on Mars—and a large fortune on Earth, if it could be diverted from medical use and channeled into one of the innumerable pipelines to addicts.

"Naturally I reported it," Brenner explained. "And of course Commissioner Bell had to order a Bloodhound search. It brought us here."

"Ed," Tony appealed to the grim-faced lieutenant, "did you operate the Bloodhound? Will you give me your personal word that it led to the Colony?"

"Answer him, Lieutenant," Bell ordered.

"I'm sorry to—Dr. Hellman," Nealey said stiffly. "I checked the machine three times, myself. Strong scent from Brenner's storeroom to the Rimrocks, then some confusion in the Rimrock caves, and a weakening scent from the Rimrocks to here. It doesn't actually stand up to all the way here, but it doesn't go anywhere else. That's definite."

"Please, Dr. Hellman," said Brenner kindly. "You needn't look so stricken. All it means is that there's a rotten apple in your barrel. That happens."

Gracey hurried in, a spindle-shanked ex-professor of low-temperature agronomy from Nome University. He addressed himself directly to Brenner: "What are *you* doing here?"

"Mr. Brenner has sworn out an intercolony complaint of grand theft," said the commissioner. "You're Gracey? You needn't waste your breath trying to blacken Mr. Brenner's character. He's already informed me that there was a disagreement between you which you've taken to heart.'" His meager smile showed that what he meant was "become a little cracked over."

"He hasn't got any character to blacken," growled the agronomist. "He tried to get me to breed marcaine weeds for higher production of his hell-dust and I wanted to know why. Wasn't that naive of me? I checked on Earth and I found out that maybe ten per cent of his marcaine goes into medical hands and the rest—"

The commissioner shut him up with a decisive: "That's enough. I will *not* listen to random accusations based on newspaper gossip. I don't doubt that after marcaine arrives on Earth some of it is diverted. The world has its weak-willed people. But Mr. Brenner is a responsible manufacturer and you people— I respect your ideals but I'm afraid I can't say much for your performance. The business of Mars is business. And a major theft from one of our leading industrial colonies is very serious indeed."

"Gentlemen," said Brenner, "I *can't* ignore it. I'd like to, simply to spare the unpleasantness, but the amount involved is too important financially. And there's always the danger that some quantity might get into illegal channels."

Gracey snarled, looked as though he wanted to spit on the immaculate floor of the Lab.

"What exactly do you intend to do?" Tony asked hastily, anxious to forestall an eruption from the irritable agronomist.

"It should be quite clear by now," Bell replied, "that it is my duty to conduct a search of these premises."

"You'll keep your grabbing little hands off our equipment!" Unexpectedly, it was Flexner who exploded. "It's all nonsense, and you know it. What would we steal from that *drug peddler?*"

Brenner's quiet laugh rasped into the appalled silence that followed. Flexner, enraged, took just one belligerent step toward the trillionaire and the commissioner.

"Sergeant!" barked Lieutenant Nealey, and a noncom, unslinging his carbine like an automaton, aimed from the hip at the chemist. Flexner stopped in his tracks, red-faced with anger, and said bitterly, "So he can make the damned stuff and welcome, but all hell breaks loose if somebody hooks it."

"For the last time—" began Bell, exasperatedly, and then interrupted himself. He drew a paper from his parka and handed it to Tony. "The warrant," he said shortly.

Tony passed it to O'Donnell and there was a long, foot-tapping minute while the ex-lawyer studied the document.

At last O'Donnell said, "According to this, you plan to open our shipping crates and break into our process ovens. Is that correct?" He was pale with anger and worry.

"Correct," said the commissioner, while Brenner shrugged helplessly. "Marcaine could, of course, be concealed from the Bloodhound in lead-insulated containers."

"Then you *are* aware," said Tony, "that we manufacture radioactive materials?"

"I am."

"And you realize that there are certain procedures required by law for the handling of such materials?"

"*Doctor* Hellman! Has it slipped your mind that I represent the law you're speaking of?"

"Not at all." Tony was determined not to lose his temper. "But I could hardly expect you to carry in your mind all the time the innumerable petty details that must come under your administration. And it happens that *I* represent, here in the Colony, the observance of the laws under which our radioactives license was granted. I think that as chief radiological monitor for the Colony, I should be permitted to accompany your men in any search."

"That's out of the question." The commissioner dismissed the request impatiently. "The license you spoke of is, as we both know, a grade-B atomics license, permitting you to handle only materials well below the safety level, so I see no reason for any unnecessary fuss. Lieutenant—"

"Just a minute, please, Commissioner," Tony interrupted frantically. It was perfectly true that as the direct representative on Mars of the Panamerican World Federation, Bell was judge, jury, and corner cop, all rolled into one. Redress was as far away as Earth, and the road to Earth was the rocket from which Bell had the power to bar them.

"Don't you realize," Tony pleaded, "that our materials stay below the safety level only because we have a well-established monitoring procedure? If you insist on breaking into the process ovens and opening crates without my supervision, Sun Lake cannot assume responsibility for any dangerous radioactivity."

"I understand that, Doctor," Bell answered crisply. "Any handling of radioactives in my presence is obviously done on *my* responsibility, not yours. The commission, oddly enough, is supplied with its own monitors. I do not believe we will require your assistance. Carry on, Lieutenant."

Nealey took a reluctant step forward. Choking back his anger, Tony said flatly, "In my opinion you are exceeding your authority. Your men will interfere with our processing and break open our shipment crates. Our machinery is so delicately adjusted that any kind of handling by untrained people could easily destroy it. And we've spent the last month packing our outgoing shipments for the next rocket. You know what the law is for packing radioactives. If you broke open our shipments, the rocket would be here and gone before we had the stuff decontaminated and repacked. It would be ruinous for the Colony."

He saw out of the corner of his eye that O'Donnell was unwillingly shaking his head. Bell was the law on Mars. And Bell wasn't even bothering to answer.

"At least give us a chance to look into it," urged the doctor. "Maybe we have got a bad apple. We'll find him if we do. You can't wreck us just on suspicion!"

"More than suspicion is involved here," said Bell. "The findings of the Ground Tracing Device, M-27, known as the Bloodhound, when operated by a qualified commissioned officer, are accepted as completely legal evidence in all authorized world courts."

They watched bleakly as the lieutenant began to assemble the dipole, handle, power pack, and meters of the Bloodhound.

"I have a suggestion," said Brenner. "Under Title Fifteen of the Interplanetary Affairs Act—"

"No," said O'Donnell. "We don't want it."

Brenner said persuasively, "If you're clean, there's nothing to worry about."

"Title Fifteen was never meant to be applicable to a case like this," O'Donnell crossfired. "It's one of those shotgun laws, like a conspiracy count—"

"That's enough," said the commissioner. "You can't have it both ways. Since Mr. Brenner's willing, this is your notice; I'll confirm it in writing. Under Title Fifteen of the Interplanetary Affairs Act, I advise the Sun Lake Colony that you have until the next Shipment Day to produce the marcaine thief and the stolen marcaine or evidence of its disposal. If you fail to do so, I will instruct the military to seal off Sun Lake Colony and a suitable surrounding area for a period of six months so that a thorough search can be conducted. Lieutenant, move your men out of here."

Nealey snapped the half-platoon to attention and marched them through the Lab door. The unmilitary figures of the commissioner and the tall angular drug maker followed them.

O'Donnell's face was grim. "It was written in the old days of one ship a year and never revised," he said. " 'Sealed off' means just that—nothing and nobody in, nothing and nobody out."

"But we're geared for four ships a year," said Flexner complainingly. "Shipment Day's only three weeks off. Rocket's due in ten days, two days unloading, one week overhaul, and off she goes. We'd miss the next two rockets!"

"We'd miss the next two rockets!" Tony repeated, dazed.

"Half a year without shipments coming in, half a year without goods going out!"

"He's trying to strangle us."

"It can't be legal," objected Flexner.

"It is. By the time it could be changed, the Colony'd be dead anyway."

"Even if we pulled through, we'd be poison to Earthside buyers—shipments arriving there half a year late."

"He's trying to strangle us," O'Donnell insisted doggedly.

"How many OxEn pills have we got?"

"What's Bell's angle? What's Brenner out for?"

"Bell's crooked. Everybody knows that."

"That's why they sent him to Mars."

"But what's his angle?"

Tony was still a doctor. To no one in particular he muttered, "I've got to check on the baby," and started out on the road from the Lab to the huts with the spring gone from his knees.

CHAPTER FOUR

TONY WOULDN'T TALK to the women about the commissioner and his trap. He'd try not to think about it; he'd tell himself it would work out somehow in the three weeks of grace they had—

The door to the hospital was open, but no sounds came from the other side. Polly was asleep then, and Anna had gone out.

Tony drew a cup of water from the tap on the plastic keg and set it to boil on the stove with a pinch of "coffee" makings—the ground, dried husks of a cactuslike plant that grew in some abundance on the desert. At its best the stuff had approximately the flavor of a five-day-old brew of Earth-import brick coffee, made double strength to start with and many times reheated. It did contain a substance resembling caffeine, but to Tony it often seemed the greatest single drawback to human life on Mars.

Before he put any food on to cook, he stepped into the hospital half of his hut for a look at Polly. "Well!"

"Hello, Tony." Anna had moved the baby's basket next to Polly's bed and was bending over, peering into it.

"We were watching the baby," she unnecessarily told him, and promptly returned to that fascinating occupation.

"Just what is there to watch so hard?" the doctor demanded.

"He's—" Anna finally transferred her attention; she made a helpless little gesture and smiled with an irritating air of mystery. "He's very interesting," she said finally.

"Women!" Tony exploded. "Sit for hours watching a baby sleep!"

"But he's not sleeping," Anna protested.

"He's hardly slept all morning," Polly added proudly. "I've never seen such a lively baby!"

"And how would *you* know what he's been doing 'all morning'? When I left here you were asleep yourself, and Anna was all ready to go home and do likewise. Where's Jim?"

"He wanted to go to work," Anna explained. "He was embarrassed, I guess, about staying out. I told him I'd stay. I wasn't really sleepy anyhow."

"You weren't sleepy? After twenty-six hours awake?" He tried to be stern. "So you sent Jim off to work to give him a chance to brag about his baby. You weren't sleepy, and neither was Polly, and strangely enough, neither was the newcomer here! Well, as of now, all three of you are just too sleepy to stay awake, you understand?"

Purposefully he moved the basket to the far side of the room. What they said was true, he noticed; young Kandro was wide awake and kicking, apparently perfectly content. Not even crying. Strange behavior for a newborn.

"Come on, Anna, clear out." He put the baby down and turned to Polly. "I'll give you ten minutes to get to sleep before I stuff some more sedative into you," he informed her. "Didn't anybody ever tell you you're supposed to be tired now?"

"All right." Polly refused to be ruffled. "He's an awfully nice baby, Tony." She settled herself more comfortably under the thin cover and was asleep almost before they left the room.

"Now go on home," Tony told Anna. "I'm going to make myself some breakfast. Wait a minute. Did you eat anything?"

"I did, thanks." Abruptly she turned toward him, and made a conscious effort at concentration. The abstracted look left her eyes and she was brisk and alert as usual.

"What about Polly? Don't you have to go out again? Somebody should be here."

"I'll get hold of Gladys when I leave. Don't worry about it."

"All right." She smiled at his impatient tone. "You don't have to push me. I'll go. You're still coming over for dinner tomorrow night?"

"You couldn't keep me away," he assured her.

She came back into the room and took a ration slip from the drawer where Tony kept them. "You pay in advance, you see," she added, smiling.

"And well worth it." Tony held the door for her, a habit he never quite lost even in the atmosphere of determined sexual equality that pervaded the Colony. Not until she was gone did he remember the coffee he'd started.

It was ruined, of course, and now he'd have to do without it. Water was too scarce, still, to waste because of carelessness. But coffee or no, he was hungry. He found a dish of barley gruel, left over from a lunch he'd cooked for himself two days ago, heated it, and spooned it down hastily. Then, with a final check to make sure Polly was really asleep, he set out for the Poroskys' house to find Gladys.

At fourteen, Gladys was the oldest child in the Colony—none of the adult members was over thirty-five years—and her status was halfway between that of a full working member and the errand-girl position her younger sister occupied. She was old enough to assist almost anybody at anything, still too young to take full responsibility for a job. Now, Tony found, she was over at the Radcliffs', sitting with Joan. It was his next stop anyhow.

If they did have to leave Mars, it would have at least one good effect: the life of Joan Radcliff would be saved. But, the doctor reflected, she'd die of a broken heart as surely as she was dying on Mars of—whatever it was. His star patient, the thin, intense girl lived only for the success of the colony on Mars. And life on Mars was killing her.

When he knew what she had, maybe Tony would know how to cure it. Meanwhile, all he could do was make a faithful record of its symptoms and try out treatments till he found one that would work. Or until he was sure none of them worked.

It was like an allergy and it was like heart disease and it was like fungus infection where you couldn't put your finger on the parasite. Tony didn't even have a name to tag it by.

Joan came down with it two days after she and her husband, Hank, arrived on the shuttle rocket. If the doctor didn't find some relief for her soon, it looked as though she would have to go back on the next one.

Tony bit hard on the stem of his empty pipe, slipped it into a pocket, and walked into the bedroom of the Radcliff house.

"How's it going?" He put his bag on the table and sat down on the edge of Joan's bunk.

"Not so good." She had to work for a smile; a good colonist is always cheerful. "I just can't seem to get settled. It's as if the bed were full of stale cracker crumbs and broken shells—"

She began to cough, short dry barks that rattled her thin body, feather-light on Mars, against the bed.

Cracker crumbs and sea shells!

Sometimes it seemed that the damned condition reached her mind too. It was hard to distinguish between the delirium of fever, the depression of fatigue and confinement, the distortions of mental disease.

The spasm had passed. She battled the itch to cough again and counter-irritate her raw, constricted throat. Tony, watching, knew the guts it took. She was fighting: a good colonist guarded her health; it was a colony asset.

Everything for the Colony. And for Henry, her husband. Joan was one of those thin, intense young people who give their lunch money to Causes. It had taken a lot of skipped lunches to get her and Henry to Mars as shareholders, Tony realized. But she could never have been satisfied with less—the non-voting position of "drop-in," for instance. She had to identify herself with a heroic unpopular abstraction, or life wasn't worth living.

Tony had more than a touch of it himself. All of them in the Colony did. But the doctor doubted that he had enough of it to fight against the brief, delusive relief of a coughing fit in order to get well imperceptibly sooner and go back to work for the Colony. *If* she got well.

Joan whispered, "Got some magic in your bag for me?" A good colonist is always cheerful; the great days are ahead.

"Middling magic, anyhow." He put the thermometer in her dry mouth and peeled back the blanket. There were new red bumps on her arms and legs; that was one phase of it he could treat. He smoothed on ointment and changed the dressings on the old puffy sore spots.

"That's good," she whispered gratefully as he took the thermometer from her mouth. "So cool!" Her temperature was up another two-tenths over yesterday's 101.3. And the thermometer was not even moist.

Another injection, then. He hated to use them, as long as he wasn't sure of the nature of the disease, but one of his precious store of anti-histamines seemed to give a little relief. It was temporary, of course, and he ardently hoped it was doing no permanent damage—but it did shrink the inflamed watery bladder that her throat lining had become under the action of killer-enzymes. She would be able to breathe more easily now, and to sleep. It might last as long as twenty-four hours.

One more day, and by that time Hank would be back with a little of the latest Earth-developed hormone fraction. Tony had heard that Benoway, over at Mars Machine Tool, was using it with startlingly good results for serious burns and infections.

Joan's eyes closed and the doctor sat there staring at the parchment-like lids, her chapped and wrinkled lips. Tony grimaced; she was obviously being a fool.

He rose noiselessly and crossed the room to the water jug. When he came back he spoke her name softly: "Joan?"

Her eyes opened and he held out the glass.

"Here's some water."

"Oh, thank you!" She sighed dreamily, reaching out—but she snatched her hand back. "No, I don't need any." She was wide awake now and she looked frightened. "I don't really want it," she pleaded, but her eyes never left the glass.

"Take it, drink it, and don't be silly!" he snapped at her. Then, gently, he propped up her shoulders with his arm and held the glass to her lips. She sipped hesitantly at first, then drank with noisy gulps.

"What are you trying to do to yourself? Didn't I order extra water rations for you?"

She nodded, shamefaced.

"I'm going to have some words with Hank when he comes back, to make sure you drink enough."

"It's not his fault," she said quickly. "I didn't tell him. Water's so precious and the rest of you are working and I'm just lying here. I don't *deserve* any extra water."

He handed her the glass, refilled, and propped her up again.

"Shut up and drink this."

She did, with a combination of guilt and delight plain on her face.

"That's better. Hank ought to be back tomorrow with the medication from Mars Machine Tool. I'll tell him about the water myself this time, and I don't want any nonsense from you about not drinking it. *You're* a lot more valuable to the Colony than a few quarts of water."

"All right, Doctor." Her voice was very small. "Do you really think he'll be back tomorrow?"

Tony shrugged with calculated indecision. Mars Machine Tool was almost a thousand miles away, and allowing time for food and rest, Radcliff should be back before midday tomorrow. But Joan's question was so pathetically eager, he didn't dare sound too sure. It was even harder when she opened her eyes again, while he was closing his bag, to ask, "Doctor, will it do any good, do you think? You never told me the name of it."

"Oh," he answered vaguely, "it's just something new." Just as he knew about Hank, he knew perfectly well the sixteen-syllable name of the hormone fraction. But he was afraid that Joan would know it, too, from sensational press stories, and that she would expect a miracle. The doctor was expecting only another disappointment, another possibility ruled out, another step toward the day when he'd have to break the girl's heart by ordering her back to Earth.

"I won't be able to leave anyone with you for a while," he told her as he left. "I need Gladys to stay with Polly Kandro. But remember, if you need anything, or want anything, *use the intercom. Call somebody to do it for you.* Your heart isn't in any shape for exercise."

The sun was beating down more strongly when he stepped outside. It was past mid-morning already, and he had to get over to Nick Cantrella's, give him official clearance on the burned arm, and talk to him about Bell's threat. But there were other patients, and they needed treatment more urgently than Nick. Better to get through with them first. Then when he got to Cantrella, they'd be able to buckle down to the quarantine problem.

CHAPTER FIVE

A YOUNG GIRL'S HEAD was splitting with the agony of an infected supraorbital sinus, but she was no whiner and even managed a smile.

"I've got a present for you, Dorothy," he said. "It's from a girl who was your age a couple of centuries ago. Her name was Tracy. I don't know whether it was her last or first name, but she gave it to this stuff." He held up a hypo filled with golden fluid. "It's called bacitracin. They found out that this Tracy's body fought off some infections, so they discovered how it did the trick and wrapped it up in this stuff—a good, effective antibiotic."

She hardly noticed the needle. *Misdirection is as useful to a doctor as it is to a stage magician,* he thought wryly.

A middle-aged man who should have known better was recovering nicely from his hernia operation.

"I still say, Oscar, that you shouldn't have let me fix it up. You would have been a medical marvel—The Man Who Got Ruptured On Mars. I could have had you stuffed, got you a grand glass case right next to the door at some medical museum on Earth. Maybe a neon sign! You got a nice repair job, though I say it myself, but you're throwing away world-wide medical fame. The Man Who Tried to Lift a Lead Shipping Crate Barehanded! I can see it now in all the textbooks. You sure you don't want me to undo you again?"

"All right, Doc," grinned Oscar, red-faced. "You made your point. If I see anybody even looking as though he's going to lift a gut-buster, I'll throw him down and sit on him until the crane arrives. Satisfy you?"

A not-quite-young woman suffered from headaches, lower back pains, sleeplessness, and depression. Pokerfaced, the doctor told her, "Mrs. Beyles, you're the most difficult medical problem—a maladjusted person. I wouldn't be that direct if we were on Earth, but this is Sun Lake. We can't have you drinking our water and eating our food if you don't pay for it in work. What you want, whether or not you admit it to yourself, is to get off Mars, and I'm going to oblige you. If you knew what Joan Radcliff is going through to stay— Never mind. No, I will not give you any sleeping pills. If you want to sleep, go out and work until you're too tired to do anything else."

Was he right? he wondered. He knew the woman would never believe him and would hate him forever, but it was another kind of surgery that had to be done—fortunately, not often. The woman would either change her attitude, thereby losing her ills and becoming the asset to the Colony that her strapping frame and muscles should make her, or out she would go. It was brutal, it was profit-and-loss, it was utterly necessary.

And so to Nick Cantrella at last, thank heaven. Heaven had often been thanked in the Colony for Nick's arrival. He was the born leader, the inspired and unorthodox electronics man who hadn't garnered the sheaf of degrees needed for a halfway decent job on an Earth cluttered with bargain-counter Ph.D.s.

In the Colony he had signed up as a maintenance and setup man, but spent so much of his time troubleshooting that he was finally relieved of the routine part of his work. Just recently he had been promoted to chief of maintenance, purchasing, and repairs of all Lab equipment. His new dignity hadn't kept him out of trouble. He was home with a nasty chemical burn in his arm acquired far outside the line of duty.

Tony didn't know whether he was glad or sorry Nick had missed the session with Bell and Brenner. Nick could think on his feet, but it was an even chance that Brenner's oily sympathy and Bell's open contempt of the Colony would have goaded him into thinking with his fists.

"Tony!" Nick yelled as he came in the door. "Gracey was here with the news. It's the biggest thing that ever hit Sun Lake! It'll be the making of us!"

"Let's see the arm, Combustible," said Tony dryly. "Medicine first, politics later."

Nick fumed as the doctor removed the dressing and examined the site of the burn—now just a good scar, painless, non-disabling, and uncomplicated, due to quick poulticing and a heavy coat of eschar.

Tony slapped Nick on the back. "Okay, Fearless," he said. "You can go back to work. Inhale chlorine. Drop pigs of osmium on your toes. Sit on a crateful of radiophosphorus and get a buttful of geigers. Stir nitric acid with your forefinger. There's *lots* of things you haven't tried yet; maybe you'll like them—who knows?"

"So it splashed," Nick grinned, flexing his arm. "Damn good thing I wasn't there this morning. I would've thrown those bums out. Do you realize that this is the biggest break we've ever had? Why, man, we should have been praying for something just like this to happen. We *never* would have cut the Earth tie on our own and given up luxuries like Earthside medicine. I'm glad Bell's kicking us into it. All we have to do is retool for OxEn." His face glowed. "What a beautiful job that's going to be! Those boys in the Lab can do anything—with my machinery, of course," he added.

"You can't do it, Nick." Tony shook his head ruefully. "Ask any of the biochem boys. I went on the guided tour through the Kelsey plant in Louisville while I was thinking of joining the Colony. It left me footsore and limping because that plant is ten stories high and covers four city blocks. They operate more than 500 stages of concentration and refinement to roll those little pink pills out of the protoculture. And the first couple of hundred stages have to be remote-control sterile. There isn't as much glass on all of Mars as the Kelsey people had just in their protoculture tanks. It's out, boy. *Out.*"

"Hell, we'll rig up something. With all the crooks on Mars, we can make something they want and swap it for OxEn across Bell's search cordon. Don't worry about it, Tony. This should have happened a long time ago. On our own!"

"You're missing something. What if we *do* catch a marcaine thief and the hoard and turn them over to Bell?"

Nick was thunderstruck. "You mean you think it wasn't a frame-up? One of our guys?"

"We can't rule it out until we've looked."

"Yeah, it *could* happen. Well, if you'll kindly write out my medical discharge, I'll get a majority together and put it in the form of a motion that we hold a shakedown inspection of the Colony."

"There's an easier way, maybe," Tony said. "Anybody who toted that much marcaine got gowed up on the stuff, whether he knows it or not.

It's micron dust—fused ampoules are about the only thing that hold it without leakage, and this was in bulk. Also, the thief might be a regular marcaine addict as well as wanting the stuff to sell."

"So," Nick grinned, "we line everybody up and just see which one does this." He went into a comedy routine of tics and twitches and strange yapping noises. "You know that won't work," he wound up soberly. "There isn't any way to smell out a markie."

"Practically no way," Tony corrected him. "That's why Brenner's a trillionaire and that's why marcaine gives stiff competition to Earthside narcotics in spite of the extra cost. The damned stuff doesn't affect you so people notice. You become an addict, you take your belt as often as you please, and you can live in your own private sweet-dream world without anybody the wiser until—blooie!—you drop dead from failure of the cardiac node to keep your heart pumping."

"You said *practically* no way," Nick reminded him. "What's the catch? Have you got an angle?"

"I get my electroencephalograph out and read up on the character-istic brainwave patterns of marcaine users. Then I run the e.e.g. over everybody who could possibly have carried the stuff from Brenner to here. You want to line that up for me?"

Nick nodded glumly. "Sure," he said, "but you won't find any mar-kies here. It's a frame-up, I tell you…Hello, honey! What are you doing home at this hour of the day? What's all that junk for?"

Tony turned to see Marian Cantrella, Nick's blond and beautiful wife, pushing her way through the door, her arms full of soft white cloth, scissors, heat-sealer, and paper patterns.

"You'll be witness, won't you, Tony, when I testify that I only left home because he didn't want me here?" Marian turned large violet eyes from the doctor to her husband and back again. "On second thought," she concluded, "you're no better than he is. *Could* either one of you big, *strong* men stop gaping and give me a hand with this stuff?"

Nick jumped up and relieved her of some of her bundles. "What's it all about?" He fingered the fine cloth curiously.

"Baby shirts, nightgowns, and diapers," Marian said composedly. "Are you all through pawing it?"

"Oh, for the Kandro kid." But he didn't relinquish the material. "Where'd the cloth come from?"

"I think they just ran it off." Marian took the heat sealer from him and plugged it into the house battery to warm up. She cleared a space on the table and laid out the patterns to study. "What's the matter?" she asked. "Something wrong with it?"

"No, it's a nice job." He brought the bolt of cloth over to the table and spread it out, then carefully pulled a thread loose. "But they should have replaced the extrusion nozzle. See that line there—there on the side—where it looks irregular?"

Tony went over to look at the thread Nick was holding up to the light. He couldn't see anything wrong with it, and Marian confessed she couldn't either.

"It's there," Nick told them. "It means a worn nozzle. But it's not a bad job. Who did the setup?"

"For heaven's sake!" Marian exploded. "I don't know who did it! They handed it to me and said go home and make tiny garments, so I went!"

"Okay, baby," Nick soothed her. "I just thought you might know." He turned to Tony as Marian began cutting off squares from the bolt for diapers. "I don't see how they had a machine free for it," he fretted. "Every piece of equipment in the shop was scheduled for full time until Shipment— Well," he stopped himself, "I guess it doesn't matter anyhow. From here on out we can pretty much stop worrying every time we need to use a piece of the Lab for Colony goods. The days of plenty have arrived—extra underwear and new dinner plates all around."

"Sure," the doctor agreed sourly. "All the pajamas you want—and no OxEn. Tell me, Marian, what are the women saying about this marcaine business?"

"Same as the men, I guess." She tested the heat-sealer on a corner of the first diaper, and turned the dial for more heat. "It'll blow over. Even if this shipment does get held up, it'll straighten out. Kind of a shame if we're cordoned while the rocket's in, though."

She tried the sealer again then began running it deftly along the cut edges, leaving a smooth perfect selvage behind.

"I was hoping we'd get a look at Douglas Graham," she added. "I think he's *wonderful!*"

"Hah?" demanded Nick, starting. "Oh, the *This Is* man. My rival. He should be honored to be my rival."

"What's going on?" asked Tony. "Is it a family joke?"

"Douglas Graham's a national joke," said Nick. "Now that he's going to do an Inside-Mars, that makes him an interplanetary joke."

"Oh, the writer," Tony remembered. The rocket doctor had told him last trip that Graham would be aboard the next.

"He's wonderful," said Marian. "I just loved *This Is Eurasia.* All those dictators, and the Cham of Tartary and the history, he made it sound so exciting—just like a story—"

"*This Is Mars,*" said Nick sonorously. "Chapter One, Page One, The Story of the Sun Lake Colony, or, A Milestone in the History of Mankind."

"Do you think he really will write us up?" asked Marian. "I mean if that silly marcaine business doesn't keep him away?"

"No, pet. We'll be ignored or maybe he'll take a few digs at us. His books run first as serials in *World Welfare,* and *World Welfare* isn't interested in co-op colonists. It is interested in Pittco No. 3 over the hill, I'll bet you, by the way Pittco advertises. He'll probably play up all the industrial colonies as big smash-hits for free enterprise and not mention things like the Pittco red-light house."

Marian's lips tightened. "I don't think it's decent," she said.

"Right," agreed Nick soberly. "I'll tell Madame Rose tonight. Haven't been over for days. I'll tell her my wife doesn't think her girls are decent. Want to come and make a night of it, Tony?"

"Ump," said Tony. If he was any judge, Marian's sense of humor didn't go that far.

"That's not what I meant!" she cried indignantly. "I meant it wasn't decent for him to hide things like that and— Oh, you're joking! Well, I don't believe he would do it! I've read his books and they're *good.*"

"Have you got any of Graham's stuff around?" Tony asked hastily. "I don't think I ever read any."

"I shouldn't take time out," said Marian, a little sulkily, "but—"

She put down the sealer and shooed Tony off the trunk he'd been sitting on. A considerable quantity of wool socks and underwear turned up before she hit the right level. She handed over a conventional onionskin export edition. Tony read at random:

These are the words of the man who rules over the twenty-five million souls that hold the lifeline between America's frontier on the Yang-Tse Kian River and her allies in the Middle East: "Please convey to the people of your country my highest esteem and warmest assurances that the long peace between our nations shall never be broken without cause by me." The significance of this—

Tony handed the book back. "I don't think I've been missing much," he said.

Marian was still digging through the trunk, fascinated at the forgotten things she was turning up. It was surprising how little used were most of the items they had found essential to include in their limited baggage when they left Earth.

"Here's something," she laughed. "I used to read it back on Earth, and I thought it would be so useful here."

She held out an onionskin pamphlet titled in red: *The Wonders of Mars,* by Red Sand Jim Granata, Interplanetary Pioneer.

Nick took the book from her and riffled through the pages with a reminiscent smile. "It's terrible, Tony," he said. "Get these chapter headings: 'Mining for Emeralds,' 'Trapped in a Sandstorm' –Red Sand Jim should wish the air on Earth was as clear as the heart of a Martian sandstorm—'Besieged by Dwarfs in the Rimrock Hills.'"

"*What?*" demanded the doctor, incredulously.

"'Besieged by Dwarfs in the Rimrock Hills.' If you don't believe me, look. The dwarfs, it says here, were a constant menace to intrepid interplanetary pioneers like Red Sand Jim because they killed people and stole their babies and things like that. They didn't often see one—"

"Naturally."

"Naturally, Doctor, naturally. But they were little people who didn't wear shoes or clothes it says here—*which* reminds me." He closed the book. "I was out at the caves yesterday—took a ride with one of the prospectors. We've never really looked into the caves, and I had nothing better to do while you were teaching me safety precautions, so I wandered around some, and found kids' footprints in the entrance to one of them."

"They take the goats out there to graze sometimes," Tony said.

"That's not it. Looks like they've been going barefoot, and I don't think they ought to be allowed—"

"They certainly shouldn't!" Marian was indignant. "Why, they could *hurt* themselves. And they shouldn't be allowed in those caves either."

"They're not," Tony said grimly. "They have strict orders to stay away from the caves. But I never thought they'd be screwy enough to try going barefoot. I'll have to tell them about it."

"Tell them good," Nick urged him. "There's a lot of rock out there, and a lot of dangerous surface salts."

"I wish I knew some way to make it stick," the doctor said, worriedly. "Once those kids get a notion in their heads—if they still hang around the caves after listening to old man Learoyd's horror stories—I don't know."

"Don't take it so hard." Nick couldn't stay serious long. "Maybe it wasn't the kids. Could be it's dwarfs."

"Ve-ry funny. I'll pass the word to the mothers that there shouldn't be any barefoot-boy stuff on Mars. I've got enough trouble without frost-bitten toes, lacerations, and mineral poisoning."

"You better hope they're dwarf prints, Tony. That'd be easier to handle than teaching our pack of kids."

"Look who's talking! I'll thank you to line up that vote on an e.e.g. test for marcaine now while I dig up my medical references. Also"—he got up briskly—"if there's more trouble coming, I better take care of myself while I can. Lunch'll be all gone if I don't get there soon."

CHAPTER SIX

FORTY YEARS in the life of a planet is nothing at all, especially when the planet is ancient Mars. It had been that long since the first Earth rocket had crashed at the southern apex of *Syrtis Major*—and remained there, a shining, rustless memorial with only the broad fractures in its fuel tanks to tell its story to those who came after.

Forty years, almost, since the first too-hopeful colonists followed, three thousand doomed souls. Their Earth-bred bodies, less durable than the flimsiest of their constructions, were already rotted to the skeletons when a belated relief ship came with the supplies without which they had starved to death.

Forty years, now, of slow growth but rapid change, during which a barren world had played host to, successively, a handful of explorers; a few score prospectors and wanderers-at-large; a thousand or so latter-day homesteaders, with their lean, silent women; and finally—after OxEn—the new industrial colonies, none of them more than five years old.

The explorers had disappeared: gone back to Earth to lecture and write, or blended completely into the Martian scene; the prospectors and frontiersmen, most of them, had died; but the colonists, determined to stay on, drew fresh blood continually from the lifeline at Marsport—the quarterly rockets from Earth.

Sun Lake City Colony, alone among those who had come to Mars, wanted nothing more than to cut, once and forever, that vital tie with Earth. But it was too soon, still too soon; the Colony was not yet strong enough to live, if the umbilical cord was severed.

And the colonists knew it. After lunch they gathered in the Lab, every last man, woman, and child. Tony rose from the black box of the electroencephalograph to count heads.

"We're one over," he told Nick. "Polly's in the hospital, Joan's home, Hank's at Mars Machine Tool or on his way back. Tad's on radio shack. Who's the spare?"

"Learoyd," said Nick. "And I've got Tad messaging Machine Tool to confirm Hank's whereabouts for the last four days."

"Okay. I'll get Tad later."

A whiskery man who looked as though he was pushing 90 stormed up to the doctor.

"It ain't your business whether I take a sniff of marcaine now and again and it ain't for you to say I stole any hundred kilos if you do find I use it once in a while. Bunch of greeners!"

"Calm down, Learoyd," sighed the doctor.

"Greener!" taunted the old-timer. "Call yourself Marsmen!"

"You can call us anything you want, Learoyd," said the doctor. "Only we've got to straighten this thing out. When did you last take marcaine? It won't—"

"You don't even know where you are!" quavered the old man. "Lake-us Sole-us, my eye! You're right on the edge of Ryan's Plain and you don't even know it. He was here first and he had a right to name it! Old Jim Ryan—"

Patiently Tony tried to explain: "Brenner says somebody stole the hundred kilos of marcaine two days ago. It could have been any of us. You were around, so we've got to be able to tell Commissioner Bell—"

"Another greener—a politician greener. The Law on Mars!" Learoyd's voice was heavily satirical. "When there was twenty, thirty of us, we didn't need no law; we didn't go around thieving! We got here ahead of you all, you and the farmers, too. What for did you have to come crowding in?"

"*When* did you take that last belt of marcaine?"

The old pork-and-beaner sighed brokenly. "It was more'n two years ago. I ain't got money for marcaine. I ain't a panhandler and I do a good job hauling for you, don't I?"

"Sure, Learoyd."

"Then why do you have to come bothering me? We was here first!" He collapsed into the chair by the black box, grieving for the past of the red planet, before this damn OxEn, when Marsworthy lungs were a man's passport to adventure where no man had ever been before, where a mountain range was your mountain range and nobody else's, where Jim Ryan died in the middle of great, flat, spreading Ryan's Plain, starved to death out there when his half track broke down.

Learoyd chuckled, not feeling the electrodes they were putting to his head. He'd got off a good one—five years on Mars and these ten greeners landed. They wanted to be heroes, the little greeners, but he told them. He sure told them.

"Call yourselves Marsmen? In six months half of you'll be dead. And the other half'll wish they was."

Jim Granata was in that bunch—a sly one, pumping him, making notes, making sketches, but he wasn't a Marsman. He went back to Earth and made him a pot full of money with books and—what did they call it?—Granata's Combined Interplanetary Shows. Little Jim, he called himself Red Sand Jim Granata, but he was never a Marsman.

The Marsmen came first. Sam Welch surveyed Royal Range, the Palisades. Amby McCoy—he got killed by eating Mars plants; they found him with his food run out, curled up with the agony of poisoning. A thousand dollars a day they got then, when a thousand dollars was a thousand.

It was in '07 he told off those greeners, twenty-eight years ago. Only one rocket every couple years then, and sometimes they didn't get through. Jim Granata, he never set foot on Mars after '18 with his money and all; he wasn't a Marsman. They were here first. Nobody could take that away from them.

Sam Welch, Amby McCoy, Jim Ryan. Why not die too? Learoyd wondered bitterly. A thousand dollars a day they paid him when a thousand dollars was a thousand, and look at him now. Where had it gone? Why was he living by hauling dirt for the greeners when he had been here first? His lip trembled and he wiped his mouth.

Somebody was shaking his shoulder and saying, "That's all, Learoyd. You're in the clear. Nothing to worry about."

The old man slouched through the crowd and out of the Lab, shaking his head and muttering what sounded like curses.

Tony hadn't been very far from hoping that Learoyd would turn out to be the thief. The law would have to go easy on him and it would clean up the Colony's problem.

Colonist after colonist seated himself in the chair and cleared himself by revealing marcaine-negative brainwaves to the e.e.g. Tony didn't dare to think of what it meant. The last of them, the boy from the radio shack, was relieved to take his turn.

"That's the lot," Tony reported to Nick when young Tad, too, was cleared by the machine, and had gone back to his job.

Cantrella refused to share the doctor's gloom. "It's just what we needed," he insisted, smacking his fist into his palm. "Face it, man. There isn't any marcaine thief. Bell thinks he can run us off Mars by cutting off our import-export. *Let* them cut us off! We'll barter for OxEn. We'll damn well do without the Earthside enzymes and immunizers. We'll get tough with Mars, lick it on its own ground! We'll have to eventually; why not right now?"

"I don't know, Nick. I think you're going too fast," Tony demurred. "Look at old Learoyd—he's *us,* only a little worse."

"The pork-and-beaners imported their food, clothes, fuel, and look at them!" Nick insisted. "They failed. They didn't strike roots. They didn't adapt!"

"I don't know, Nick," the doctor repeated unhappily. "I've got to go see Polly and the baby now."

Tony lugged the e.e.g. back to his hospital-shack and found Anna holding the hand of a white, trembling, terrified Polly. Polly's other arm was around the baby, clutching the red-faced little thing as if it were on the edge of a precipice.

Without a word he took the child, snapped on his stethoscope and sounded its heart, which was normal. In spite of the red-faced creature's squirming, the minute oxygen mask was in place.

Baffled, he replaced the baby and demanded of the women, "What's wrong?"

"I have to work," said Anna abruptly. She patted Polly's hand and slipped out.

"I saw something," Polly whispered. Her eyes were crazy.

Tony sat on the side of the bed and picked up the hand Anna had been holding. It was cold.

"What did you see, Polly?" he asked kindly. "Spots on the baby? A rash?"

She disengaged her hand and pointed at the window in line with the bed and two meters from its foot.

"I saw a dwarf! It wanted to steal my baby." She clutched the child again, not taking her eyes off the window.

Normally Tony would have been amused and not shown it. Under the strain of the day, he fought down a violent anger. The little idiot!

At a time when the whole Colony was in real and deadly peril, she was making no effort to distinguish between a dream and reality.

"You must have drowsed off," he said, not as harshly as he felt. "It was just a nightmare. With your history, of *course* you're afraid that somehow you'll lose this baby too. You've heard all this pork-and-beaner and homesteader nonsense about funny-looking dwarfs, so in your dream your fear took that form. That's all there is to it."

Polly shook her head. "Gladys was staying with me," she recited monotonously, "and she had to go to that test in the Lab and she said she'd send somebody who'd been tested as soon as she got there. Just when I heard the door close, this face came up outside the window. It was an elflike face. It had big thin ears and big eyes, with thin eyebrows, and it was bald and leathery.

"It looked at me and then it looked at my baby. I screamed and screamed but it just looked at my baby. It wanted to steal my baby! And then it got down below the window sill just before Anna came in. Even after she put my baby here with me, I couldn't stop shaking."

Anger was getting the better of him. "Do you realize that your story is perfectly ridiculous if you insist on claiming it really happened, but perfectly logical if you admit it was a dream?"

She began to cry and hug the baby. "I saw it! I saw it! I'm afraid!"

Tony relaxed; tears were the best medicine for her tension. To help them along, he rose and got her a sedative and a glass of water.

"Take this," he said, putting the capsule to her mouth.

"I don't want to go to sleep!" she sniffled. But she swallowed it and in a minute or two felt under her pillow for a handkerchief.

When she had wiped her eyes and blown her nose, the doctor said quietly, "I can *prove* it was a dream. The dwarfs or whatever are just the kind of thing the pork-and-beaners and the homesteaders would invent to scare themselves with. And the myth got exploited on TV, of course. But there can't be any because there isn't any animal life on Mars.

"We've been exploring this planet up, down, and sideways for forty years now. We found a weed you can make dope out of; we found you can make liquor out of Mars plants; we found a lot of ores and minerals. But not one trace of animal life. Think of it, Polly—forty years and *nobody has found any animal life on Mars.*"

She reasoned, a little fuzzy with the sedative, "Maybe these funny little *things* could stay out of people's way. If they're smart they could."

"That's right. But what did they evolve from in that case? You know that if you have a higher form of life, it evolved from a lower form. Where are all the lower forms of life that evolved into dwarfs? There aren't any. Not so much as one puny little amoeba. So if there's no place they could have come from, there are no dwarfs."

Her face relaxed a little, and Tony talked on doggedly. "You got a bad scare and no mistake. But you scared yourself, like the homesteaders that started this nonsense." A sudden notion struck him. He put it in the urgent file, and went on. "You were afraid your bad luck would catch up with you and take your baby away. The vividness doesn't mean anything—you probably saw a scary picture in the papers of a baby-stealing Martian and stored it in your memory, and out it popped at the right time."

Polly cracked a sleepy smile and said, "I'm sorry," and closed her eyes.

She'll be all right, thought Tony, *and it's a good thing it turned up to remind me of the homesteaders—Thaler? Toller?*

Whoever they were, the old couple on the wretched "farm" to the south. Toller, that was right. He hadn't seen them for a year, but he was going to see them today.

Anna was in the other, residential, half of the shack. "I think I talked her out of it," he said. "You'll stay here?"

"Yes. Where are you off for?" He was lugging the e.e.g. out again.

"That old couple, the Tollers. I wouldn't put the marcaine theft past them and they're close enough to our general area. Before the last dozen Sun Lakers arrived, I had enough time on my hands to run out and see how they were coming along. If I just tell them it's time for another checkup, I'm pretty sure I can persuade them to give me a brainwave reading. That may break the case."

He strapped the black box to his bicycle and set off...

The Tollers were a different type from old Learoyd, and driven to Mars by a different urge. Learoyd had fancied himself an explorer and adventurer who would make a sudden strike and, after a suitably romantic life of adventure, retire to his wealth.

The Tollers laid the longer, slow-maturing plans of peasants: *In two years, when I have saved up seven schillings three groschen I will buy Bauer's bull calf, which will service the cows of the village; Fritz by then will be big enough to take care of the work. Zimmerman, the drunkard, will go into debt to me for service of his cows and pledge his south strip, so Fritz need not marry his Eva. Schumacher's Gretel has a hairlip but there's no escaping it—his west pasture adjoins mine...*

It hadn't worked out for the Tollers—the steady, upward trend of land values, the slow improvement of the soil, the dozen sons and daughters to work it, the growing village, town, city—

All that happened was they had scratched out a living, had one son, and gone a little dotty from hardship. Both had Marsworthy lungs. If she had not, Mrs. Toller would, like hundreds of other wives, have lived as matter-of-factly in an oxygen mask as her many-times-removed great-grandmother had lived in a sunbonnet.

The husband, by now, was stone blind. Data from him and hundreds of others had helped to work out the protective shots against ultraviolet damage to the eyes, a tiny piece in the mosaic of research that had made real colonization at all possible.

Tony knocked on the door of the hut and went in, carrying the black box. Mrs. Toller was sitting in the dark, crammed little room's only chair. Toller was in bed.

"Why, it's Doctor Tony, Theron!" the old lady explained to her husband. Not bad, thought Tony, since he hadn't been able to remember *their* names in a flash.

"Say hello to Doctor Tony, Theron. He brought us the mail!"

Mail? "No, Mrs. Toller—" he began.

The old man started out of a light doze and demanded, "Did the boy write? Read me what he wrote."

"I didn't bring any mail," said Tony. "The rocket isn't due for two weeks."

"Junior will write in two weeks, Theron," she told her husband. "These are our letters to *him,*" she said, producing three spacemailers from her bodice.

Tony started to protest, thought better of it, and glanced at them. All three were identical.

Our Dear Son,

How are you getting along? We are all well and hope you are well. We miss you here on the farm and hope that some day you will come back with a nice girl because one day it will all be yours when we are gone and it is a nice property in a growing section. Some day it will be all built up. Please write and tell us how you are getting along. We hope you are well.

Your Loving Parents

On the other side, the envelope side of spacemail blanks, Tony saw canceled fifty-dollar stamps and the address to *Theron Pogue Toller, Junior, R.F.D. Six, Texarkana, Texas, U.S.A., Earth.* The return address was *Mr. and Mrs. T. P. Toller, c/o Sun Lake City Colony, Mars.* Stamped heavily on each was a large, red notice: DIRECTORY SEARCHED, ADDRESSEE UNKNOWN, RETURNED TO SENDER.

The old man croaked, "Did the boy write?"

"I've come to give you a physical checkup," said Tony loudly, oppressed by the squalid walls and the senile dementia they housed.

"Isn't that nice of Doctor Tony, Theron?" asked Mrs. Toller, tucking the letters back into her dress. But the old man had fallen asleep again.

Tony clipped the electrodes on and joggled Toller awake for a reading. Marcaine-negative.

"We came in such a beautiful rocket ship," rambled Mrs. Toller as he put the e.e.g. on her. "It was quite an adventure, wasn't it, Theron? We were so young, only twenty-three and twenty-four, and we sold our place in Missouri. It was such a lovely rocket we came in, a little one, not like the ones today, but this was before Mars got built up. We had quite a fright when one of the steering jets went bad while Mars was ahead, just like a big moon and the poor crewmen had to go outside in their suits. It was quite an adventure, wasn't it, Theron?"

"I often wonder, Doctor Tony, whether Junior has ever been back to the old place in Missouri. We had him our first year here, you know; he's fourteen. He wanted to see the Earth, didn't he, Theron? He wanted to stay with relatives on Earth. So when he was twelve we went all the way to Marsport to see him off. It was quite an adventure wasn't it, Theron? And he sent us his address *right* away—" Marcaine-negative brainwave.

He was too sickened to stay, and the birdlike chatter of Mrs. Toller never stopped as he said good-by and wheeled off to Sun Lake.

Their horrible deterioration during the past year to senility in the mid-thirties answered Nick Cantrella's plan to establish the Colony immediately as self-sustaining,

Life on Mars without even the minimum of supplies, immunization, and adaptation shots was out of the question. If they asked his medical advice, his answer would have to be: "If we are forbidden Earth supplies we must go back to Earth."

Tony groped in his pocket for his pipe, and clenched it between his teeth. *All right then,* he thought, *go back to Earth—go back and get yourself a decent cup of coffee in the morning. Go back—*

Back to what? To a clinic in an industrial town where he could give slapdash timeclocked attention to the most obvious ills of men, women, and children whose fears and deprivations began in the womb and ended only in the grave?

Back to the office, maybe? An office like the one he'd had, briefly, in the penthouse of a New York apartment building. Take your patients one at a time, give them plenty of attention, they're easy to cure if you understand them—the ulcers and piles and false pregnancies, the thousand-and-one diseases of the body that grew out of the mind—fear.

Go back? He bit hard on his empty pipe. It would be consoling to stand again on Earth, and fill his pipe and light it, puff clouds of smoke—while he waited for the crowded, psychotic planet to blow itself up and put an end to man once and for all.

Chapter Seven

HANK RADCLIFF shook Tony awake a little before dawn. "I got the stuff, Doc." He grinned. "Just came in on foot from Pittco. The half-track broke down twenty miles out of Mars Machine on the way back, and I bummed a ride on a Pittco plane headed this way. The half-track's still at Rolling Mills and—"

The doctor shook his head groggily and thought of giving Hank hell for the abrupt awakening. But it was hard to stay mad at him, and Tony would have been roused by his alarm clock for the Lab check in a quarter-hour anyway. Did the Lab check matter? Did the medication for Joan matter? No. They were all heading back for Earth before long.

"Make me some coffee," he growled. "One minute by the clock."

He stretched, rolled out, shucked his pajama tops, and gave himself a sponge bath with a cup of water that would mean one less cup of coffee for him today. Some mornings he just couldn't stand the feel or stink of methyl alcohol.

Shivering, he gulped the coffee and pulled on pants, parka, and sand boots. "Let's see the stuff," he said. "Did Benoway give you a letter or note for me?"

"Oh, sure. I almost forgot." Hank handed over an ampoule and an onionskin. The note from the Mars Machine Tool physician said:

Dear Hellman:

Here is the T7-43 Kelsey you requested by radio message. Re your note by messenger; sorry to tell you symptoms completely unfamiliar to me. Sounds like one of the cases any company doc would ship back to Earth as soon as possible. The T7-43 has worked wonders in heat burns here and have seen no side reactions. Please let me know how it comes out.

In haste,
A. Benoway, M.D.

Tony grunted and beckoned Hank after him as he picked up his physician's bag and went into the bitter morning cold.

"Did you say you *walked* from Pittco?" he asked Hank, suddenly waking up.

"Sure," said the youngster genially. "It's good exercise. Look, Doc, I don't want to get out of line, but I couldn't help noticing that you're building up kind of a bay window yourself. Now it's my experience that those things are easier *not* to put on than to take off—"

"Shh," said Tony as they stopped at the Radcliff shack. They slipped in and Tony filled a needle with the new Kelsey drug. "Stay in the background until I get this over with and motion you in, Hank."

He awakened the girl.

"Here's the new stuff, Joan," he said. "Ready?"

She smiled weakly and nodded. He shot the stuff into her arm and said, "Here's your reward for not yelling." Hank duly stepped forward, switching on a light in her eyes that did Tony's heart good…

Breakfast was fried green Mars beans and "coffee"—bearable, perhaps, under ideal conditions, but completely inedible in the gloomy atmosphere around the big table this morning. Tony gulped down the hot liquid and determinedly pushed away his beans, ignoring the pointed looks of more righteous colonists, who cleaned their plates stubbornly under any circumstances.

The Lab radiation checked out okay; no trouble there at least this morning. After a meticulous cleanup, he visited Nick Cantrella in the hole-in-the-wall office at the back of the Lab.

"How's it look, now you've had a night's sleep on it?" Nick demanded. "You still want to throw in the sponge? Or are you beginning to see that we can lick this damn planet if we only try?"

"I can't see it," Tony admitted. Soberly he told the other man about his visit to the Tollers. "And look at Old Man Learoyd," he added. "He can't be much past sixty and that's stretching it. I know he came here when he was twenty-one; at least, that's what he says—so how old can he be? But I gave that man a physical checkup a few months back, and, Nick, he not only *looks* like an ill-preserved octogenarian, but if I didn't know otherwise, I'd stake my medical reputation on his being close to ninety."

Nick whistled. "As bad as that?"

"What do you expect? Chronic vitamin deficiencies, mineral deficiencies, not enough water, never-ending fatigue from never-ending work—you pay high for trying to live off the country. More than it's worth."

Half to himself, Nick said, "Six months. We lose our commercial contacts, we pay forfeits that eat up our cash reserve—what if we just go to the buyers and tell them what happened?"

Tony started to answer, but Nick answered himself:

"It won't work. They won't dare place another order with us because they'd be afraid it'd just happen all over again. And we haven't got the funds to sweat it out until they forget. Tony, *we're washed up!*"

"There's still a search."

"Hell, you know none of our people took the stuff."

"Let's have a council meeting. I want a search."

Nick, Tony, Gracey, and Mimi Jonathan held one of their irregular conclaves in the doctor's hut.

"I suppose," grunted Gracey, "that when you find there isn't any marcaine in our trunks, you'll tear the Lab apart looking for it."

"If we have to, we may," said Tony, poker-faced, but sickened at the memory of what isolation from the life-giving flow of materials from Earth had done to the Tollers. "I've had some nasty jobs before this." He thought of how he had lanced the swollen ego of Mrs. Beyles, the neurotic, and how she must hate him for it—an ugly thought.

By mid-morning, Mimi had the shakedown under way. Tony settled himself in the radio shack, firing message after message to Commission headquarters at Marsport, trying to get through to Lieutenant Nealey. The operator at Pittco who relayed from Marsport telefaxed the same reply to the first four messages: UNAVAILABLE WILL RELAY MESSAGE END CORPORAL MORRISON COMMISSION MESSAGE CENTER.

On the fifth try, Nealey still had not been reached—but Bell had.

This time the reply was: LIEUTENANT NEALY UNAVAILABLE MY ORDERS. UNDER NO CIRCUMSTANCES GROUND TRACING DEVICE M-27 LENT FOR PRIVATE USE. REMINDER LIMITED MARS MESSAGE FACILITIES TAXED YOUR FRIVOLOUS REQUESTS. REQUIRE CEASE IMMEDIATELY END HAMILTON BELL, COMMISSIONER P.A.C.

Gladys Porosky, the operator on duty, piped indignantly, "He can't do that, can he, Doctor Tony? The relay league's a private arrangement between the colonies, isn't it?"

Tony shrugged helplessly, knowing that Gladys was right and that Bell's petulant arrogance was a long stretch of his administrative powers—but due process was far away on Earth, for those who had the time and taste for litigation and the cash reserves to stick it out.

Gracey joined him in the hut long enough to say bitterly, "Come and see the loot we accumulated."

Tony went out to stare unhappily at the petty contraband turned up by the humiliating search: some comic books smuggled in from Marsport, heaven knew how, by a couple of the youngsters; some dirty pictures in the trunk of a young, unmarried chemist; an unauthorized .32 pistol in the mattress of a notably nervous woman colonist; a few bottles and boxes of patent medicine on which the doctor frowned; a minute quantity of real Earthside coffee kept to be brewed and drunk in selfish solitude.

By mid-afternoon this much was certain—any marcaine hidden in the Colony was not in a private home.

The Lab would have to be searched next.

It was like going into a new world, to escape from the doomed, determined optimism of the search squad and council members, back to the cheerful radiance that inhabited the hospital. Tony stood in the doorway, studying the family group across the room—father and mother thoroughly absorbed in each other and in the tiny occupant of the hospital bassinet.

It was still hard to believe the delivery had gone so well. Tony wondered again, as he had so often in the preceding months, what could possibly have gone wrong with all the previous attempts, before they came to Mars.

"He's awake again!" Polly hadn't quite made up her mind whether to be proud or worried. "He slept for a little while after you left, but then he started crying and woke himself up. You should have seen how mad he was—his face was so red!"

"He's quiet enough now!" Tony went over and stared down thoughtfully at the small circle of face, half obscured by the oxygen mask. Certainly there was no sign of ill health. The baby was a glowing pink color, and his still-wrinkled limbs were flailing the air with astonishing energy. But a newborn baby should sleep; this one shouldn't be awake so much.

"It's possible he's hungry," the doctor decided. "Hasn't he cried at all since he woke up?"

"Oh, a little, every now and then, but if you turn him over, he stops."

Tony went over and scrubbed his hands in the alcohol basin, then came back and surveyed the baby again. "I think we'll try feeding," he decided. "I've been waiting for him to yell for it, but let's see. Maybe that's what he wants."

"But—" Jim flushed and stopped.

His wife broke into delighted laughter. "He means my milk isn't in yet," Polly said to the doctor; and then to Jim: "Silly! He has to learn how to nurse first. He doesn't need any *food* yet. And the other stuff is there—what do you call it?"

"Colostrum," Tony told her. He removed the baby from the crib, checked the mask to make sure it was firmly in place, then lowered the infant to his mother's waiting arms.

"Just be sure," he warned her, "that the mask doesn't slip off his nose. There's enough area around his mouth exposed so he can feed and breathe at the same time."

The baby nuzzled against her for a moment, then spluttered furiously, turned a rich crimson, and spewed back a mouthful of thin fluid. Hastily Dr. Tony removed the infant, patted and held him until the choking fit stopped, and restored him to his basket.

Polly and Jim were both talking at once.

"Hold on!" said the doctor. "It's not the end of the world. Lots of babies don't know how to feed properly at first. He'll probably learn by the time your milk comes. Anyhow, he'll learn when he needs it. Babies don't stay hungry. It's like the oxy mask—he breathes through his nose instead of his mouth because the air is better. We don't have to cover up his mouth to make him do it. When he needs some food he'll learn what his mouth is for—fast."

"But, Doc, are you sure there's nothing wrong with him? Are you *sure?*"

"Jim, in my business, I'm never sure of anything," Tony said mildly. "Only I've never yet seen a baby that didn't find some way to eat when it wanted food. If your pride and joy won't take the breast, we'll get Anna to whip up some bottles for him. It's as simple as that."

Or not so simple—

George and Harriet Bergen's eight-month-old Loretta, conceived on Earth but born at Sun Lake, was still feeding from the breast. Loretta would be weaned not to milk but to the standard Colony diet plus vitamin concentrates when the time came. It was what the older children ate; they had forgotten what milk tasted like.

There were milch-goats, of course, and some day there would be milk for everybody in the Colony to drink. But to make that possible it was necessary now to allocate all the milk produced by the herd to the nourishment of more goats, to build up the stock.

It was hard enough to keep the herd growing even with the best of care. Yaks, at first, had seemed like a better bet for acclimatization to the Martian atmosphere, but they were too big to ship full-grown, and so far no young animals had survived the trip. So the Colony had brought over three pairs of tough kids, and bred them as rapidly as possible. Half the newborn kids still died, but the surviving half needed every bit of milk there was. Still, if necessary, a kid would have to be sacrificed, and the milk diverted to the baby.

Tony pulled himself out of the useless speculation with a start of dismay. There was no sense planning too far ahead now; Bell might solve this problem for them, too.

"Anything else you want to know before you go home?" he asked. "Have any trouble with the mask?"

"Anna checked us out on that," Jim told him. "It seems to be simple enough."

"Where is she?"

"She went home," Polly put in. "She said she had a headache, and when Jim came in she showed us about the mask again, and then went—"

"Hi, Tony. Can I see you a minute?" Marian Cantrella stuck her head through the outside door to the hospital. Tony turned and went out with her.

"Is she ready to go?" Marian wanted to know.

"Since this morning, really. But the damn search—How's their place? Did anybody get it back in order?"

"I just came from there," Marian said. "We've got it all fixed up and the new room's all done. The walls are still a little damp. Does that matter?"

"It'll dry overnight," Tony reflected. "They can keep the baby in the room with them till then."

"Right." She started away, and Tony was about to open the door when she turned back. "Oh, I almost forgot. Is it all right for Hank to take Joan out to watch? I was talking to her before, and she felt so left out of everything."

"I guess so." He thought it over and added, "Only if she's carried, though. Maybe Hank can fix up a tote truck from the Lab for her to ride on. I don't want her to use up what strength she has."

"I'll fix it," Marian promised. "I think it would mean a lot to her." Her golden curls shook brightly around her head as she ran off down the street.

Tony went back into the hospital. "Guess it's time to get you folks out of here," he told the Kandros. "Place is too cluttered up. I might need this space for someone who's *sick.*"

Polly smiled up at him from the chair where she had been sitting for the last hour. "I don't know what I can wear," she worried happily. "The things I came in would fall right off me, and I can't very well go out this way. Jim, you better—"

"Jim," Tony interrupted, "you better get some sense into that wife of yours. You'll go *just* the way you are," he told Polly, "and you'll get right into bed when you get there, too. You've been up long enough for one day."

While Jim helped her with her sandboots and parka, Tony wrapped the baby for his first trip outdoors. They were ready quickly, but Marian had been even quicker. When they opened the front door they were confronted by a crowd of familiar faces. It seemed as if all of Sun Lake City Colony's eleven dozen residents had crowded into the street in front of the doctor's house. They were determined, apparently, that whatever happened next week, the Kandros' homecoming would not be spoiled today.

"I suppose you all want to see the baby? All right," Tony told them, "but remember, he's still too young for much social life. I don't want you to crowd around. If you'll all spread out down the street from here to the Kandros' place, everybody can get a look."

Together Tony and Jim eased Polly into the rubber-tired hand truck that did double duty as a hospital stretcher. They placed the baby in her arms and adjusted the small portable tank for the oxy mask at her feet. Then they started slowly down the long curved street, stopping every few yards along the way for someone who wanted to shake Jim's hand, pat Polly on the shoulder, and peer curiously at the few square inches of the baby's face that were exposed to the weather.

The doctor fretted at the continual delays; he didn't want Polly or the baby to stay out too long. But after the first few times, he found he could speed things up by saying meaningfully, "Let's let them get *home* now." As the small party progressed down the street, they collected a trailing crowd. Everyone was determined to be in on the big surprise.

Polly and Jim didn't let them down either. The moment of dazed surprise when they saw the still-wet walls of the new room jutting out from their house was all that could be asked. Equally satisfying were the expressions on their faces when they opened their door and looked in at the array of gifts.

Tony gave them time to take it all in, then insisted that the door be closed and Polly and the baby be allowed to settle down. While he was unwrapping the baby, he heard them in whispered consultation, and a moment later the door opened again. Jim left it very slightly ajar behind him as he stepped out, so they could hear what went on.

"Wait a minute, folks," Tony heard him call. A slight hesitation, and then Jim's voice again: "Polly and I—well, we want to thank you, and I don't know just how to go about it. I can't really say I'm surprised, because it's exactly the kind of thing a man might know you folks would do. Polly and I, when we came here—well, we'd never had much to do with politics or anything like that. We joined up because we wanted to get away mostly.

"We—I guess you all know how long we've been waiting for this kid. When he didn't come, back there on Earth, we felt like we had no roots anywhere, and we just—wanted to get away, that's all. When we signed up we figured it sounded good. A bunch of people all out to help each other and work together, and the way the Statute says, extend the frontiers of man by mutual endeavor. It made us feel more like we belonged, more like a *family*, than just working for some Mars Company would have been.

"It wasn't until after we got here that we began to find out what it was all about, and I guess you know we liked it. Building up this place, everybody working together—it just couldn't ever get done that way back on Earth.

"And then this other thing happened, and the doc said it looked like it was going to work out all right this time.

"We started thinking then, and this is what I've been working up to. Maybe it's silly, but we figure it's something about Mars that made it work, or something about the Colony. And now the baby's here, I hope none of you will mind, but we'd like to name him Sun Lake City Colony Kandro—"

Jim stopped abruptly, and for a too-long moment there was only the grim silence of the crowd, the same bitter thought in every mind.

Then he went on: "Maybe you folks think that's not a very good idea right now. I don't know. If you don't like it, we won't do it. But the way we feel, Polly and me—well, we know things look bad right now, but they're going to have an awful hard time, the Planetary Affairs Commission or anybody else, getting *us* off Mars."

"You're damned well right, Jim!" shouted Nick Cantrella. He faced the crowd with his fists hanging alertly. "Anybody think the kid shouldn't be called Sun Lake City Colony Kandro?"

The harsh silence broke in a roar of confidence that lifted Tony's chin, even though he knew there was no justification for it.

CHAPTER EIGHT

Inside, the baby was wailing lustily again. From her position on the couch, Polly raised a commanding arm. "Turn him over, Jim. He'll probably stop crying if you put him on his tummy."

Tony watched while the new father slid his hand under his son's back with exquisite caution that belied his proud air of assurance. Turning to hide his smile, the doctor began piling hospital equipment on the hand-truck, to take back with him when he went.

"Look! Tony, look! Look at Sunny!"

"Sunny, is it?" The doctor turned around slowly. "So he's lost all his dignity already. I was wondering how you were going to get around that tongue-twister of a name. Well, what do you know?"

He watched the baby struggle briefly, then rear back and lift his head upright. He had to admit there was a cause for the pride in Polly's voice when a baby not yet two days old could do that.

"Well," the doctor teased, "he's Sun Lake City Colony Kandro, after all. You ask anybody in town if that doesn't make a difference. I won't be surprised if he walks next week, and starts doing long division the first of the month. Who knows, he might learn how to eat pretty soon!"

He realized abruptly he'd made a mistake. Neither parent was ready to joke about that.

"Doc," Jim asked hesitantly, "you're pretty sure there's nothing *wrong?*"

"I told you before," Tony said shortly, "I'm not sure of a blessed thing. If you can see any single reason to believe there's anything wrong with that baby, I wish you'd tell me, because I can't, but—this is Mars. I can't make promises, and I'll make damned few flat statements. You can go along with me and trust me, or—" There was no alternative, and his brief irritation was already worn out. "You can *not* trust me and go along with me. We have to feel our way, that's all. Now," he said briskly, "you're all checked out on the mask? No trouble with it?"

"No, it's all right. I'm sorry, Doc—"

"Got enough tanks?" Tony interrupted.

"You gave us enough to go from here to Jupiter," Polly put in. "Listen, Tony, please don't think we—"

"What I think," Tony told her, "is that you're good parents, naturally concerned about your child, and that I had no business blowing off. Now let's forget it."

"No," Jim said firmly. "I think you ought to know how we—I mean there's no question in anyone's mind about trusting you. Hell, how do I go about saying this? What I want to tell you is—"

"He wants to say," said Polly from the bed, "that we both very grateful for what you've done. It's a happiness we thought we'd never know."

"That's it," said Jim.

"He's your baby," said Dr. Tony. "Do a good job with him." He pushed the hand-truck to the door and waited for Jim to come and help him ease it through. "Oh, by the way," he added, smiling, "I'll fill out the birth certificate tonight, now that I know the name, if you'll come over and—"

"Doc!"

It was Hank Radcliff, running down the street breathless and distraught.

"Doc, come quick—Joan's dying!"

Tony grabbed his black bag and raced down the street with Hank plowing along beside him.

"What happened?"

"When I took her out in the tote truck," Hank panted "before she could walk to the street, she toppled right over—"

"Walk? You let her *walk?"*

"But she told me you said it was all right!" The youngster seemed close to tears.

"Joan told you that?" They slowed in front of the Radcliff hut. Tony wiped the anger off his face and went in.

Joan was on the bunk in a parka; the doctor stripped it off and applied his stethoscope. He had adrenalin into her heart in thirty seconds and then sat grim-faced, at the edge of the bunk, not taking the black disk from her chest.

"Get that coffee," he snapped at Hank without turning. "The stuff they found in the shakedown."

Hank raced out.

After long minutes, Tony exhaled heavily and put away the stethoscope. She'd pulled through once more.

The girl lifted her parchmentlike eyelids and looked at him dully. "I feel better now," she whispered. "I guess I fainted."

"You don't have to talk." Tony sat again on the edge of the bed.

She was silent for a minute, lying back with her eyes closed. He picked up her bird's claw of a hand; the pulse was racing now.

"Doctor Tony?" she asked.

"I'm right here. Don't try to talk. Go to sleep."

"Is Hank here?"

"He'll be back in a minute."

"I want to tell you something, Doctor Tony. It wasn't his fault. I didn't tell him the truth. I told him you said it was all right for me to walk."

"You knew better than that."

"Yes. Yes, I did. I know you'll have to send me back to Earth—"

"Never mind about that, Joan."

"I do, Doctor Tony. Not for me; for Hank. That's why I did it. I'd go back for the Colony because it isn't fair of me to take up all your time, but what about Hank? If I went back, he'd have to go back, too. He couldn't stay here in the Colony if I were on Earth—alive."

"What are you talking about?" demanded the doctor, though he knew with terrible certainty what she meant--what she had tried to do. "Of course he's going back with you. He loves you. Don't you love him?"

She smiled a little and said softly without urgency, "Yes, I love him." And then, again hysterically: "But this is what he's wanted all his life. He doesn't feel the way I do about the Colony, the wonderful way we're all working together for everybody. With him it's Mars, ever since he was a little boy. He's in the Colony and he works hard and everybody likes him, but it would be enough for him to be a prospector like old Learoyd. Ever since he was a little boy he used to dream about it. You know how he's always going out into the desert—

"Tell him he doesn't have to go back with me! Tell him I'll be all right. Talk to the shareholders. Make them let him stay. It would break his heart to send him back."

Tony didn't dare excite her by telling her that they might all be sent back, that the Colony was a failure. Even if they pulled through by a miracle, Hank couldn't stay.

They called it the "M or M" rule—"married or marriageable." Far from the lunacies of the jam-packed Earth, they had meant to build with children and allowed no place for new immigrant women past childbearing—or for Hank in love with a woman returned to Earth. It didn't matter now, he thought.

Wearily he lied: "They wouldn't make him go back if he didn't want to. But he'd want to go himself."

She sighed and closed her eyes. It seemed a long time before he was sure she was asleep.

Hank was waiting in the living-room with the coffee.

"She'll be all right for a while," Tony told him. "She's asleep now, I think." He looked at the open doorway and added, "Come outside a minute."

Sitting on the tote truck, he said, "Give her one cup of coffee each day as long as it lasts. After any meal. It'll make her feel better. God, I wish I knew what else we could do. That stuff from Benoway didn't have any effect. I'm sorry I sent you all the way out there."

"That's all right, Doc. There was a chance. And I like seeing the country."

"You certainly do. You should have been one of the pork-and-beaners."

"Hell, Doc, I like it fine here in the Colony!"

Liked it, yes. It was on Mars. *Tell him or not?* wondered Tony. *Young man, your wife tried to commit suicide so you could be free to stay on this planet. And what do you think of that?*

The hell with it. What he didn't know wouldn't hurt him, upset him, make him feel guilty—

"Doc, do you think we *will* have to go back?" Hank's voice was more than strained, it was desperate.

Tony stared. "It looks that way right now, Hank. But we have three weeks. Something—anything—may happen. I'm not giving up hope."

But the young man's face was tortured as Tony left him...

Joan Radcliff had wanted death and been cheated of it by adrenalin. Sunny Kandro wanted life, which meant his mother's breast, but some savage irony was cheating him, too. Newly born, five pounds of reflexes depending on the key suckling reflex that somehow was scrambled.

Sunny lay awake without crying, didn't seem to need sleep, could lift his head—all right, put that down to lighter gravity, even though the Bergens' little Loretta hadn't done it. Sunny had a wonderful color, a powerful nursing instinct—but he choked and gagged at the breast. Without fuel the machine of reflexes would run down and stop...

It didn't make sense to Tony. He had guiltily half-lied to the Kandros when he told them many babies didn't know how to nurse at first. That was the truth; the lie was that *this baby knew how,* but choked all the same. A feeding problem, they would have blandly called it on Earth, where there still were millions of cows, sterile hospitals, relays of trained nurses for intravenous nourishment regimes. Here a feeding problem was a feeding *problem.*

Any one of the wealthier industrial colonies would automatically have taken Earth-import powdered milk from its stores, but Sun Lake couldn't afford it, didn't have any. And what was more, Sun Lake wouldn't get powdered milk if Commissioner Bell made good on his threat.

If Sunny died, it would be worse than the unnamed little boy the Connollys had lost, and he had left a scar on the doctor's mind that time would never heal. Tony could still see the agonized blue face and the butterfly gasping for air—a preemie, but he never should have cleared Mrs. Connolly, seven months gone, until they'd had oxygen cylinders and masks and a tent for emergencies.

The Connollys had shipped back to Earth on the next rocket after the tragedy.

The father had cursed him insanely, damned him for a killer because he hadn't foreseen the need of oxy gear for their baby two months before it was due. OxEn they had, but OxEn made no change in the lungs of the baby. He'd given it intravenously, orally, in every solvent he could lay his hands on during the desperate hours before the improvised mask fed the last trickle of oxygen from the single tank into the lungs of the infant.

Tony forced his face into a smile as he passed a couple—Flexner and his girl Verna. Behind the smile he was thinking that it would be harder to bear a muter reproach from the patient Kandros than Connolly's raging curses.

Tony dragged the loaded hand-truck into the middle of his living-room and left it there. He could put the stuff away later; it was getting late now, and he had yet to make his afternoon radiation inspection at the Lab. There was a package on the table; he took time to pick it up and read: *For Doctor Tony from Jim and Polly Kandro—with much thanks.*

For a moment he held it, weighing it in his hand. No, he decided, he'd open it later, when there was time to relax and appreciate the sentiment that lay behind it. The gift itself would be—would *have* to be— meaningless.

There was no way for any colonist to purchase or procure anything at all from the outside. Except for the very few personal treasures that were somehow squeezed into the rigid weight limit on baggage when they came out, all plastic chairs and sinks, blankets, and windows were uniformly functional and durable. But they *were* uniform, and they were also scarce. Each household contained the same irreducible minimum; Lab space and work hours were too precious to be used for the production of local consumption items.

Tony closed his door behind him and set out for the Lab once more. *Dull, monotonous, primitive, uncomfortable,* he raged inwardly. *Every home, inside and out, just the same!*

Why had they come to Mars? For a better, saner way of life, to retrieve some of the dignity of men, to escape from the complexities and inequities and fear pressures of Earth. And what were they doing? Building a new life, with hard work and suffering, on the precise pattern of the old. There wasn't a person in the Colony who wouldn't do better back on Earth.

He found the Lab in an uproar. All work had stopped, so the grim hunt for the marcaine could go on. Nick had already begun an inventory.

"Make this an extra-good check, Doc," Tony was told in the office before he started out. "We'll be handling a lot of stuff that hasn't been used in a long time. And getting into all the corners too."

"Are the checkout tubes racked yet?" Tony asked.

"Right. We issued new ones to the men on the inspection squad."

"I'll do them first," the doctor decided, and went into the cleanup room where the wall racks were already lined with the tubes for that day. Usually they were checked in the following morning's inspection; but today the plant had closed down early for all practical purposes.

The tubes checked clean all down the line.

Tony selected a fresh tube from the opposite wall and went on out through the shipping-room to the workrooms. He didn't need armor for the afternoon inspection. The technicians had been in there working, and if their tubes were all clean there couldn't be any deadly hot stuff. The purpose of the late-day check was to catch reactions that were just starting up, and that might make trouble overnight. In the morning it was different. Anything that had been chaining for twelve or more hours could be vicious.

Back in the office, when he was finished, Tony reported a clean check-through. "What," he asked, "are you going to do about the shipment crates?"

"Leave them till last," Mimi Jonathan told him. "If anything turns up in the workrooms or storage bins, we'll have to open up the shipment crates one at a time. Doc, do you think—?"

She stopped, looked down a moment and then back at Tony, with a wry smile. "That's silly, isn't it? I don't know why I expect you to know more about it than I do. Oh, listen—they want you to stick around and monitor if they do have to open the crates. I'll let you know when it gets that far."

"Okay." Tony smiled back at her. "Try to give me more than five minutes notice, will you? I wish we had either a full-time radiological man or another doctor."

"How about Harve?" she suggested. "Could he fill in for you? We didn't want to assign him without your okay—he hasn't done any monitoring on his own yet, has, he?"

"No," Tony said thoughtfully. "Not yet. But this won't be anything more than standing by with a counter and keeping his eyes open. I don't see why not; he knows the routine as well as I do by now. I'd leave it up to him," the doctor decided. "If he feels ready to take it on, it'll be a big help to me."

"I'll ask him," Mimi promised...

This afternoon the familiar splendors of the Martian scene evoked no glowing certainties in Tony's mind. He walked back from the Lab in the early twilight, his eyes fixed on the far hills, his thoughts roaming bitterly beyond, to the other side of the range.

Tony had been to the new town, just once, to help out when a too hastily built furnace exploded. The injuries had been more than Pittco's green young doctor could handle all at once. The doctor's inexperience, like the faulty furnace, was typical. The whole place was temporary, until it showed a profit for Pittco. When it did, solid structures would replace the jerry-built shacks; an efficient company administration would put an end to the anarchic social organization.

But for now the town was just a sprawling collection of ramshackle buildings, constructed of a dozen different inadequate materials, whatever was available in Marsport when a new house was needed. There was no thought of the future on the other side of the hill, no worry about permanence, no eye to consequence.

If the camp went bust, the population would move on to one of the newer locations—and move again when that collapsed. If, on the other hand, the town survived, the population would move on anyhow. A new crop of workers would be imported from Earth, a tamer, quieter crew, to do routine work in an organized company town, at considerably lower pay. And the boom-town adventurers would go, to find higher wages and a freer life somewhere else.

They struck no roots there, and they wanted none. Of all the widely scattered human settlements on Mars, the Sun Lake Colony alone believed that man could and would some day flourish naturally on the alien soil.

Tony Hellman had a religion: it was the earnest hope that the day would come before he died, that he would live to see them cut the cord with Earth. Training and instinct both cried out against the new danger of abortion to the embryo civilization.

Tony was a good doctor; in Springfield or Jackson City or Hartford— anywhere on Earth—he could have written his own ticket. Instead, he had chosen to throw in his lot with a batch of wide-eyed idealists; had, indeed, jumped at the chance.

It was largely Tony's eagerness to emigrate that was responsible for the Colony's "M-or-M" ruling. The Sun Lake Society couldn't afford to turn Dr. Hellman down; they knew just how slim the possibility was of getting another doctor as good. So, after much deliberation, the bylaws were carefully revised, and the words "or marriageable" inserted after the word "married" in the list of qualifications.

The modification had resulted in a flood of new and highly desirable members. Skilled workers were inclined to be more footloose and adventurous before they were married, before they had settled into responsible, well-paid jobs on Earth. Bea Juarez, pilot of the Colony's ship, *Lazy Girl,* was one of the new acquisitions; so was Harvey Stillman, the chief radioman.

Anna Willendorf was another member who had come in after the revised "M-or-M" ruling, one whose skill was almost as much appreciated as Tony's for a different reason. Plastics, produced in the Lab, could be, and were used for almost every item of furniture or furnishings in the Colony; but for some chemical processes, glassware was still a must. And now that giant machines existed on Earth to turn out almost every conceivable glass utensil, glassblowers were far between, good ones almost non-existent. Without Anna's specialized talent, the Colony would have had to pay fabulous prices for the transport of bulkily packaged glassware from Earth.

Anna was one of the very few unmarried members of the colony who refused to participate in the communal meals. Laziness, or embarrassment, or both, served to drag in the others, like Tony, who might have preferred to remain aloof. Anna simply ignored the questions and remarks.

On rare occasions, however, she relented to the extent of "inviting" the doctor to dine with her—combining their rations, and preparing a meal for him in her own one-room hut. Then, for an hour, she would play hostess to him, an hour that restored, for both of them, the longed-for feeling of gracious, civilized living.

"One for all and all for one." "Mutual endeavor." "Collective self-sufficiency." The whole thing, Tony. thought angrily, was an anachronism; more than that, an impossibility. No sane man could believe in it—unless he came from Earth and had nothing to see to believe in.

For tonight, at least, he was free of it. Anna was at the door when he reached it, holding it open for him. She watched him set down his bag as though he were unloading the troubles of the Universe.

"You need a drink," she decided.

He grinned sourly at her. "Some nice, refreshing, vitamin-packed, Grade-A, synthesized orange juice, maybe?"

She disappeared behind the drape that hid her kitchen section. Not many of them bothered to separate the kitchen from the living-room; perhaps, Tony thought, that was what gave her room such a special look. A moment later, she was out again, with two long-stemmed fragile glasses in her hands.

She handed one to Tony, and awe and wonder crossed his face as he sipped. He looked his question at her over the rim of the glass.

"I shouldn't have spoiled your surprise, really." She smiled at him. "The Kandros. They wouldn't prepare anything for the baby, but they must have ordered these from Earth when Polly was just—let's see— three months along, to have had them here in time."

"Real wine," Tony marveled, and sipped again. *"Aged* wine. How did they get it? How could they afford—?"

"They couldn't, of course," she reminded him, "but they have relatives on Earth. You know they're not the only ones who left some cash behind, 'just in case'?"

The doctor looked up sharply, and found a faint smile flickering on her lips. "How do you know?" he demanded. "Where do you find out these things?"

"What do they call it—feminine intuition?" She shrugged and moved toward the kitchen again. "Which also tells me that supper will be a desiccated mess if I don't serve it right now."

She had set the table as usual in front of the big window. Tony took his place and looked out through the eerie twilight across the endless expanse of *Lacus Solis.* The ocean bed was like a vast black velvet now, studded with a million tiny, glinting jewels.

The doctor stared out until Anna returned with a steaming dish. Dinner performed its usual magic. Tony *had* been really hungry. Tilting his chair against the wall, with his empty pipe in his mouth, he found that things were getting back into proportion.

"Anyhow," he said, "we still have time." They had been talking about Bell's threat of quarantine.

Anna, very seriously, demanded, "Do you think Bell can run us out?"

He waved a little too expansively. "Prob'ly not. Any number of other possibilities. Somebody at Pittco might have taken the stuff; they're close enough. Nope—" He hauled up. "Ed Nealey wouldn't make a mistake like that. He was working the Bloodhound and there's a boy who'll do any job the right way. Don't worry about it, though. It's two weeks to rocket landing, another week to Shipment Day—something'll turn up. We'll send O'Donnell to Marsport. If there's a legal angle he'll find it. Maybe he can scare Bell into backing down. Bell's supposed to be a small-timer. He wouldn't want any real trouble."

Anna got up abruptly and filled his empty glass.

"Hey, you take some too!" Tony insisted.

She made a show of draining the last few drops into her own glass; the rims touched as they drank.

"You're a strange girl, Anna," said Tony. "I mean you're not like the other women here. Joan. Bea. Polly. Verna."

"No," she said. "Not very much like Bea."

Tony didn't know whether she was angry or amused and decided he didn't care. "I don't know why I don't marry you."

"Two reasons." Anna smiled. "One, you're not sure you want to. Two, you're not at all sure I do."

The sudden banging on the door was like an explosion in the quiet room. Harve Stillman didn't wait for any answer; he burst in. He was white-faced and shaken.

"Doc!"

Tony jumped up and reached for his bag. "What is it? Joan? The baby? An accident at the Lab?"

"Flash from Marsport. The rocket's coming in." The radio man stopped to catch his breath. "They're coming inside radio range now. Estimated time of arrival, four a.m."

"Tomorrow?" Anna gasped.

Harve nodded and Tony put down his bag with mechanical precision in the center of the table.

Tomorrow! Three weeks had been little enough time to find the marcaine and the thief and get rid of Bell's strangling cordon. Now, with the rocket in ahead of schedule, two of those weeks were yanked out from under them!

CHAPTER NINE

TONY GOT ONLY four hours' sleep before Tad Campbell came banging on his door at 3:15 a.m. The boy's enthusiasm was more than Tony could face; it would be easier to carry his own equipment than to answer questions while he was dressing. He sent Tad to wait at the plane and put some "coffee" on to brew, then did a last quick check on his portable health lab, making sure that there was nothing overlooked in the hasty preparations after the news about the Earth ship.

Gulping down the hot brew, he reviewed the instructions he had given Anna: feedings for Sunny Kandro; bacitracin for Dorothy; ointment and dressings for Joan, another injection if she needed it; and under no circumstances sedative for Mrs. Beyles.

He couldn't think of anything predictable he had failed to provide for. He folded the lab to make a large carrying-case and lugged his burden up the gentle slope that led to the landing field where *Lazy Girl,* the Colony's transport plane, waited.

Bea Juarez was warming the icy motors with a blowtorch. *Lazy Girl's* motors were absurdly small; their shafts spun on zero-friction air-bearings. Air-bearings dated from the guided missiles of 1950, but their expensively precise machining ruled them out for Earth. Shipping space to Mars was high enough to override the high manufacturing cost. Air-bearing motors were small and light; therefore virtually everything on Mars that turned or slid turned and slid on molecules of gas instead of oily films.

The bearings improved the appearance not only of machinery but of mechanics. Bea looked tired, cold, and unhappy; but she lacked the grease-smeared dinginess that would have marked her on Earth. The girl nodded to him, ran a hand over the moisture condensing on the metallic surface, and applied the torch to a new spot.

She shook her head doubtfully. "Don't blame me if she falls apart in mid-air after we take off. I put her together with spit overnight, Tony. She was scattered all over the field for a hundred-hour check. You'd think they'd let you know—" she grumbled, then broke off and grinned. "What the hell, if we blow up halfway between here and there, we don't have to worry about marcaine any more! Climb aboard, Doc." She snapped off the torch. "Hey, Tad! The doc needs a hand with his contraption."

Tony felt a twinge of conscience as Tad hopped out of the plane and ran to take the big box. It must have been a blow to the boy, to be deprived of carrying the heavy equipment from the hospital.

"How's it going?" Tony asked genially. "You seem to be getting along fine without your tail bone."

"Okay," the boy grunted.

He eased the box into the cabin, pulled it out of the way, and reached down a condescending hand to help Tony. "It don't seem to matter," he added, when the doctor was inside. "You'd never know it wasn't there."

Tad was the recent victim of an unhappily humorous accident. Butted in the seat by an angry goat, he'd had his coccyx severely fractured, and the doctor had had to remove the caudal vertebra.

Tony padded a couple of spare parkas into a comfortable couch on the cabin floor and stretched out. The plane had no seats. Coming back, they'd sit on the bare floor, and the parkas would have another use. The ship was unheated and the newcomers weren't likely to have warm clothes unpacked.

Lazy Girl was short on comfort and speed, cannibalized on Mars from the scrapped remains of obsolete models discarded by wealthier colonies. Tony, who didn't fly himself, had been told that she handled easily and flew an immense pay-load without complaining.

Tad had built himself a luxurious nest of parkas. He pulled the last one up around his shivering shoulders, leaned back, and examined the interior of the plane with a good imitation of a practiced appraisal.

"Nice job," he pronounced finally. "You don't get them like this back on Earth."

"You sure don't," Bea agreed ironically from the pilot's seat. "Hold on to your hat. Here we go!"

Say what you liked about Mars, about the Colony, about the poor old relic of a plane, Tony thought, when you took a look at the kids you began to understand what it was all about. A year ago, Tad had been a thoroughly obnoxious brat. But how could he be anything else on Earth?

They were all that way. You got born into a hate-thy-neighbor, envy-thy-neighbor, murder-thy-neighbor culture. In your infancy your overworked and underfed mother's breast was always withdrawn too soon and you were filled again and again, day after day, with blind and squalling rage. You were a toddler and you snatched at another one's bit of candy; you were hungry and you hated him; you fought him. You learned big boys' games—Killakraut, Wackawop, Nigger inna Grave-yard, Chinks an' Good Guys, Stermation Camp, Loot the City. The odds were you were hungry, always hungry.

Naked dictatorship and leader-worship, oligarchy and dollar-worship; sometimes one was worse, sometimes the other. The forms didn't matter; the facts did. Too many mouths, not enough topsoil. Middle classes with their relatively stable, relatively sane families were growing smaller and being ground out of existence as still more black dirt washed into the ocean and still more hungry mouths were born and prices went higher and higher—how long, in God's name, could it go on? How long before it blew up, and not figuratively speaking either?

The Panamerican World Federation, first with the most, refused to tolerate the production of mass-destruction weapons anywhere else in the world. Long calloused to foreign mutterings, the Western colossus would at irregular intervals fire off a guided missile on the advice of one of its swarm of intelligence agents. In Tartary or France or Zanzibar, then, an innocent-looking structure would go up in a smoke mush-room. But they never stopped trying, and some day Tartary, France, or Zanzibar would launch a missile of its own and it would mean nothing less than the end of the world in fire and plague as the rocket trails laced continents together and the bombers rained botulism, radiocobalt, and flasks of tritium with bikinis in their cores.

The damned, poverty-ridden, swarming Earth! Short of food, short of soil, short of water, short of metals—short of everything except vicious, universal resentments and aggressions bred by the other shortages.

That's what they were running from, the new arrivals he was going to meet today. He hoped there wouldn't be any more communicable disease carriers to quarantine at Marsport and fire back on the return trip without even a look around. There were supposed to be six medical examinations between the first application filed at the Sun Lake Society office in New York, and embarkation. But things must have gotten appreciably worse on Earth since—he started a little at the thought— "since his time." It seemed that now anybody could be reached. They used to say everybody had his price. Maybe it was true. He'd never had a chance to turn down a really big bribe, so he couldn't say. But if six boards of doctors could all be fixed, everybody's price must have taken a drastic slump.

Tad, sound asleep, rolled onto his stomach and humped up his behind, scene of the history-making operation, in a brief reversion to infancy.

"How come the rocket's getting in early?" Bea called back. "I didn't even have time to ask Harve about it last night, with the *Girl* spread out all over the field."

"Something about the throat liner. They have a new remote-control servicing apparatus on Earth," Tony said. "Gets the liner out and cleaned and in faster. We save two weeks on each trip, and get an extra trip—what is it?—every two years?"

"Year and a half," Bea corrected. She was silent a moment, then snorted, "Rockets!"

"At least," Tony dead-panned, "rockets give you a smooth ride. Fat chance of getting any sleep in this pile—"

"The *Girl* never gave you a rough trip in her life!" she interrupted angrily. She pulled on the stick and swung the *Girl* into a down wind.

The doctor drowsily studied her, silhouetted against the stars through the windshield. She was attached to the old crate—ought to find herself a husband. It had looked like her and Flexner for a while, but then the chemist had paired off with Verna Blau. As the motor warmed up, Bea unzipped her parka and shrugged out of it. Definitely, Tony decided, the best shape in Sun Lake. Trim, fined-down, athletic, but no doubt at all, from this angle, that the figure was feminine—even under the bulky sweater she still wore.

He lay back on his improvised couch and reflected on how pleasant it would be to stand behind her and run his hands down over her shoulders—infinitely pleasant just to stand behind her while she flew the ship. Pleasant but impractical. Play hell with her Estimated Time of

Arrival at Marsport, for one thing, and, to take a longer view, he probably would end up by marrying her—her and *Lazy Girl:* the two went together.

Tony stirred uncomfortably. While he was thinking idly goatish thoughts about Bea, Anna had turned up in his mind, with a half-smile on her face. It was typical, he thought, puzzled; Anna never intruded until the moment you wanted her—*if* you wanted her, he added unhappily, giving the verb a new meaning. Anna's smile was a tingling mystery; her dark eyes were wells of warmth in which a man could lose himself; but after all these months, he wasn't sure of their color. And even when she crept into his mind, it was only from the neck up that he visualized her.

That wasn't the way he saw Bea. Tony shook himself, stretched out, and let his eyes linger on the girl in the pilot's seat until he fell asleep…

The sun was up when Bea eased the freighter in among more planes than they had ever seen before on Arrival Day. They recognized the elegant staff-carrier from Sun Lake's neighbor, Pittco Three, but didn't know the other twelve that were parked.

"Swell ride, Bea," said the doctor. "Now what is *this* dress parade all about?…Oh, sure. Douglas Graham is going to do a Gunther on Mars. These should be the big-shots from the commercial colonies."

"Is he going to bother Sun Lake?"

"Nick thinks he might zip through at the end of his tour, if he has time." He hopped to the ground, Tad following with the boxed lab. "You've got the shopping list, Bea?" the doctor asked. "I have to go over to the Ad Building. Don't think I'll have time for anything else. Can you get all the stuff?"

"Sure," she said easily. "We're not buying much this time."

Tony ignored the bitter significance of the remark. "We'll see you later, then. I hope this red-carpet business for Graham doesn't slow things up too much. I'd like to get back before lunch."

Tad was fidgeting next to him, waiting for a chance to break in.

A year ago, the boy had spent two days in Marsport, when he arrived with his family and the other founding members of the Colony. Then he had nothing more than a pitying sneer for the village of 600 people; now it was a place of wonder.

"Dr. Tony," he asked eagerly, "can we go to the Arcade?"

"We can go *through* it," Tony decided.

The Arcade was Aladdin's cave to Tad. To the Planetary Affairs Commission, which rented out booth space in the ramshackle building, it was a source of revenue. To Tony it was the stronghold of the irrepressible small retailer, who found his way even to Mars with articles he could buy cheap and sell dear—a reminder of the extent to which Mars was already taking over the social and economic patterns of Earth.

Booths at the Arcade did not display radiation counters, hand tools, welders, rope, radio, aluminum I-beams, airplane parts, or half-tracks.

Those you bought at the P.A.C. Stores, which were reliable, conservative, and dull.

At the Arcade there was one booth which sold nothing but coffee in the cup: *Martian* $2.00; *Earthside* $15.00 *(with sugar* $25.00*).* Tony knew the privateer who ran this concession might be ruined by another arrival aboard today's rocket, landing in paper-light clothes with his garment and personal luggage allowance taken up by bricks of Earthside coffee and sugar, burning to undercut the highwayman who had beaten him to the happy hunting grounds of Mars.

At another booth Tad's jaw dropped with perplexity. "Dr. Tony, what are those?" he asked.

"Underwear, Tad, for women."

"But don't they get *cold* in those things?"

"Well, they would if they went out and worked like our women. But—well, for instance in Pittco, over the Rimrock Hills from us, there are some ladies who only work indoors, where it's heated."

"All heated? Not just beam heat on the beds and things?"

"I'm afraid I don't really know. Say! Look at those boots there—aren't they something?"

"Boy!" The boots were mirror-shiny zipper jobs. "What I wouldn't give for a pair of those! Put 'em on when new kids come in, and then watch them try to walk around in Earth sandals, and get a load of that sand."

Here on Mars, the price put the boots infinitely far out of reach for a boy like Tad, even if Sun Lake's policies did not prevent the purchase of such an item. Some supervisor in an industrial colony, Tony thought, would eventually acquire them as illusion of escape from the sands of Mars.

And that reminded him. He turned to Tad.

"By the way, what do you know about kids going barefoot around the colony? When did that start?"

"Barefoot?" Tad looked outraged. "What do you think we are—dopes?"

"I think," Tony answered dryly, "that anybody strolling around the Rimrock caves without boots on is about as much of a jackass as he can be."

"In the *caves?*" This time Tony thought he detected a note of more honest horror. All the kids went barefoot sometimes in the experimental fields; everybody knew about it and pretended not to. The kids were pretty careful about not stepping on marked planted rows, and the fields had been processed to remove native poison-salts from the soil.

"Listen, Dr. Tony," Tad said earnestly, "if any of the kids are doing that, I'll put a stop to it! They ought to know better! *You* remember that time you had to fix my hand, before the—uh—other thing, when I just thought I'd pick up a piece of rock and it practically sliced my finger off! They shouldn't be walking barefoot around there."

"I remember." Tony smiled. " 'Sliced your finger off' is a slight exaggeration, but I wouldn't like to have to handle a mess of feet like that. If you know who's doing it, you tell them I said to cut it out—or they may not be walking at all after awhile."

"I'll let them know." Tad walked along silently, ignoring the bright displays as they passed, and Tony seized the chance to direct their footsteps out of the Arcade. "Dr. Tony," the boy said finally, "you didn't mean for me to tell you who it was in case I knew, did you?"

"Lord, no!" The doctor *had* been hoping to find out. But he realized now what an error he'd almost made. A year ago, Tad had been as miserable a little snitch and tale-bearer as Earth could produce. "I just want it stopped, that's all."

"Okay, then." Tad's face relaxed into a friendly grin. "It will be."

We've got to keep going, the doctor thought. For himself, for the other adults, it didn't matter so much. But for the kids—

Tony had absolutely no respect for Nowton, the P.A.C. medical officer, because Nowton was stupid. Fortunately Nowton was so stupid that he didn't realize this and greeted the Sun Lake medic joyfully.

"Hear you been up to tricks, boy! Why didn't you come to me instead? I got ways to get marcaine!"

"Glad to hear it, and I'll bet you do. While we were stealing that marcaine, we also had a baby. Got a form?"

"Corporal!" yelled Nowton. "Birth form!" A noncom produced a piece of official paper and Tony filled it in, checking weight and other data with notes in his pocket.

"That hot pilot of yours still around?" asked Nowton.

"Bea Juarez? Sure. Interested? Just tell her that her plane's a disgusting old wreck and you'll get her a new one. She always falls for that line."

"No kidding?"

"Who'd kid you, Nowton? Say, is Ed Nealey anywhere?"

"In the signal room. Where's Juarez, did you say?"

"I'll see you, Nowton." Tony hurried off.

He found the lieutenant reading a medical journal which had passed through his own hands months earlier, on its way around the joint subscription club of which both men were members. The club made it possible for them, in common with twenty-odd fellow members on Mars, to keep up with technical and scientific publications without paying ruinous amounts in interplanetary postage.

"Hello, Ed."

Nealey put out his hand. "I didn't know whether you'd still be talking to me, Tony."

"Hell, you don't give the orders. You have to play it the way Bell calls it. Ed, off the record—you're pretty sure it was one of our people?"

"All I'm sure of, it wasn't a phony. To qualify with the Bloodhound on Earth, we had to follow made trails—where they dragged bags of aniseed over the spoor. You can tell the difference. This one faded and wobbled like the real thing. And we lost it not more than a couple of miles out of your place, headed straight your way. Tony, have you *searched*?"

"Some. We're not done yet." The doctor lowered his voice. "What's the matter with Commissioner Bell, Ed? Does he have anything special against us?"

The lieutenant jerked his chin a little at a Pfc sitting with earphones on his head, reading a comic book, and led the doctor into the corridor.

"God, what a post!" he said. "Tony, all I know is that Bell's a lost soul outside the Insurantist Party's inner circle. He had fifteen years of being looked up to as the Grand Old Man of the Mexicaliforniarizonian Insurantists, and now he's been booted to Mars. He'd do anything, I believe, to get back into the party. And don't forget that Brenner's been a heavy contributor to the Insurantist campaign funds during the last three elections. You know I'm professional military and I'm not supposed to and don't want to have anything to do with politics—"

Commissioner Bell came stumping down the corridor. "Lieutenant Nealey," he interrupted.

Nealey came to as casual an attitude of attention as his years of drilling would allow.

"Surely you have better things to do with your time than palavering with persons suspected of harboring criminals."

"Dr. Hellman is my friend, sir!"

"Very interesting. I suggest you go on about your duties and pick your friends more discriminatingly."

"Whatever you say, *sir!*" With slow deliberation, the lieutenant turned and shook Tony's hand. "I'm on duty now," he said tightly. "I'll see you around. So long, kid." He put his hand on Tad's shoulder, wheeled about smartly, and turned back into the signal room.

"Come on, Tad," said the doctor. "We're all done here. We might as well get out to the rocket field."

Chapter Ten

THEY WERE APPROACHING the rocket field and what was, for Mars, an immense crowd—some five hundred people behind a broad white deadline marked on the tamped dirt of the field. It was an odd-looking crowd because it was not jammed into the smallest possible space, body to body, Earth-fashion. The people stood separately, like forest trees, with a good square meter around each of them. It was a Mars crowd, made up of people with lots of room. Tony stopped well away from the fringe of the group.

"This looks like a good spot," he decided. "Put the box down there; we can start setting things up."

"Doctor Hellman—hello!" A tall man, fully dressed in Earthside business clothes, strolled over. Tony had seen him only once before, when he had appeared at the Lab with Bell to make his monstrous accusation of theft. But Hugo Brenner was not an easy man to forget.

"Hello," Tony said shortly, and turned back to his box.

"Thought you might be here today." Brenner ignored the doctor's movement away from him and went on smoothly: "I want to tell you how sorry I am about what happened. Frankly, if I'd known the trail would lead to your place, I might have thought twice before I called copper—but you understand, it's not the first time. I've let it go before. This time they took so much I couldn't very well overlook it."

"I understand perfectly," Tony assured him. "We disapprove of theft at Sun Lake too."

"Well, I'm glad to hear you don't take it personally, Doctor. As a matter of fact, I'm almost glad it happened. I've heard a lot about you and the kind of job you've been doing over there. I wish we could have met under more pleasant circum—"

"It's very kind of you to say so," Tony interrupted, deliberately misunderstanding. "I didn't think a man in your position would be much impressed by what we're doing at Sun Lake."

Brenner smiled. "I think Sun Lake is a very interesting experiment," he said in a monotone that clearly expressed his lack of interest. "What I had in mind—"

"Of course, Mr. Brenner." Whatever the drug man had to say to him personally, the doctor did not wish to hear it. "We realize your only interest is in the recovery of your stolen goods. We're doing our best to find the thief—*if* he really is a member of our Colony, that is."

"Please, Doctor, don't put words in my mouth. Naturally I'm interested in recovering my goods, but I'm not worried about it. I'm quite sure your people will turn up the guilty party." Again his voice carried a flat lack of conviction.

"Commissioner Bell has seen to it that we turn up *a* guilty party," Tony retorted.

"I think the Commissioner was unnecessarily harsh." Hugo Brenner shrugged it off. "If it had been up to me—Well, that's Bell's job; I suppose he has to handle it his own way. Let's quit beating around the bush, Doctor. I came over here to offer you a job, not to talk—"

"No."

"Suppose you listen to my offer first."

"*No!*"

"All right, then. Name your own terms. I'll meet your price. I need a doctor. A good one."

"I don't want to work for you at any price."

Brenner's mouth turned up at the corners. Obviously he enjoyed the game, and equally obviously he thought he was going to win.

"Let me mention a figure." He moved closer. "One million dollars a year."

Well, thought the doctor, now he had a clearer idea of what his own price was; now he knew it wasn't a million dollars. Ten times what he made in a peak year on Earth. He looked full into Brenner's smirking face, and knew something else: he hadn't been so clear-through boiling mad in a long time; and he was fed up with diplomacy. Deliberately, he raised his voice: "Didn't you hear me before, Brenner? Or, didn't you understand?"

He found it was gratifying to notice people turning his way, edging in to listen.

"Let me make myself absolutely clear," he went on loudly. "I don't want to work for you. I don't like the business you're in. I know what you need a doctor for, and so does everyone else on Mars. If your boys over at Hop Heaven can't keep their noses out of your marcaine, that's not my worry! I don't want to be resident physician in a narcotics factory. Stay away from me!"

The smirk had left Brenner's face; it was ugly, contorted, and much too close. Tony realized, too late, that Brenner's fist was even closer. Abruptly he stopped feeling like a hero and began to feel like a fool.

Then, quite suddenly, Brenner's fist was no longer approaching, and Brenner was flat on the ground. Tony tried to figure out what had happened. It didn't make sense. He became aware of a ring of grinning congratulatory faces surrounding him, and of Tad next to him, giggling gleefully. He called to the boy curtly, turned on his heel, and walked back the few steps to his portable lab.

Nobody helped Brenner to his feet. He must have got up by himself, because when Tony looked back, out of the corner of his eye, Brenner was gone.

A short man bustled up. "I heard that, Dr. Hellman. I didn't see you hit him, but I heard you tell him off." He pumped Tony's hand delightedly.

"Hello, Chabrier." *That makes two of us,* Tony thought. *I didn't see myself hit him either.* "Look, I know it's no use asking you not to talk about it, but go easy, will you? Don't blow it up too much when you tell it."

"It needs no amplification. You slap his face in challenge. He reaches for a weapon. You knock him unconscious with a single blow! You tell him: 'Hugo Brenner, there is not gold enough—' "

"Knock off, will you?" begged the doctor. "He wanted me to work over at his place by Syrtis Major—Brenner Pharmaceuticals Corporation, whatever he calls it. You know all his people get a marcaine craving from the stuff that leaks out of his lousy machinery. He wanted me there to keep giving his boys cures. I said no and he offered me a lot of money and I got sore. I shot off my mouth. He started to sock me and—"

And what? Tony still hadn't figured that out. He turned back to the box, still only half set up.

Chabrier said thoughtfully, "So you know that much, eh? Then you know it's nothing new, this business of missing marcaine?"

Tony abruptly turned back to him, no longer uninterested. "Brenner said something about previous thefts. What's it all about?"

"Only what you said yourself." Chabrier shrugged. "What did he offer you? Three hundred thousand? Four?" He paused, and when Tony made no reply, went on: "You can get better than that. It would be cheaper than junking his plant and building a new one."

"I know I can get better than that," the doctor said impassively. "What do you know about the missing marcaine, Chabrier?"

"Nothing all of Marsport doesn't know. Was it in the neighborhood of half a million? That would be much less than the freight rates for new machines. He's used to freight being only a small part of his overhead. He ships a concentrated, product." Chabrier chuckled happily. "How it must hurt when he thinks of importing plate and tubes and even, God forbid, *castings*. I tell you, a man doesn't *know* what freight can mean until he's handled liquor. Bulk is bad. Even just running the bulk liquor into the glass-lined tanks of the rocket ships is bad. It means that Mars ships water to Earth! *Actually!* But the foolish laws say we cannot dehydrate, let the water be added on Earth, and still label it Mars liquor."

"Please," said Tony wryly. "Please, Chabrier!"

The man shrugged. "So we take a *little* of the water out—fifty per cent, say. Water is water, they pour it on Earth, nobody knows, nobody cares. Bulk shipment is still bad, very bad. But bottles! Dr. Hellman, there is no known way of dehydrating a glass bottle. We ship them in, we fill them, we ship them back. They break, people steal them here and aboard ship, and at the Earth rocket port. All so the label can say *Bottled on Mars!*"

"Muffle your sobs, Chabrier. I happen to know that people pay for Mars liquor and pay a great deal for bottled-on-Mars. At least, you're legal, and I understand you make good stuff."

"I drink it myself," said Chabrier righteously.

"To save the freight on Earthside rye?" Tony grinned, then asked seriously, "Listen, Chabrier, if you know anything about this marcaine business that we don't, for God's sake, spill it! We—I don't have to tell you how hard this thing is hitting us out at Sun Lake. *What* does all of Marsport know?"

"Was it perhaps seven-fifty?" the other man asked blandly.

Fair exchange, Tony decided. "A million," he said.

"*So?* This I do not understand! Why so much for a doctor, if he is to have a new plant?" Chabrier shook his head, shrugged, and went on more briskly: "I have told you already, if you understand: Brenner needs a new plant. His machines are no good. They leak. His men inhale the micron dust, they get the craving, and they start to steal the product. Soon they are no good for the work, and he sends them back to Earth. You see today how many new men he brings in? Then one day there is more marcaine missing. He—"

"One minute, Chabrier." Tony turned and signaled Tad to take a break, then moved off a few steps, and motioned to the other man to follow him. "You think it's a frameup?" he demanded in a low, intense voice.

"You would have me speak against our Commissioner Bell?" Chabrier asked with only the faintest trace of sarcasm showing. "Such a thing I will not do, but I beg of you to consider, if Sun Lake Colony should be bankrupt, their Laboratory must be sold at auction by the Commissioner, and such a plant would suit Mr. Brenner very well indeed. They say here in Marsport the machinery in this Laboratory is adaptable to many kinds of production. They say it is good, tight, well-built equipment, it will not leak. Till now it seemed quite clear." The little man shook his head doubtfully. "Now I do not know. A plant? Yes. A doctor? Yes. But *both*... and he offered a million! This I do *not* understand, unless he plans to work both plants. There is a rumor which has some currency today—"

The deep bass booming of the warning horn cut him off. People began edging away from the center of the field, terminating conversations, rejoining their own groups.

"You will excuse me now? I must go," Chabrier said, when the horn died down enough to permit conversation again. "I have my place reserved, but they will not hold it."

"Place?" Tony, still trying to catch up with the implications of the other man's news, didn't follow the quick shift. "What for? Oh, are you after Douglas Graham, too?"

"Of course. I understand he is—let us say, a drinker. If I can reach him before any of those other vultures—who knows? Maybe a whole chapter on Mars liquor!" He seized Tony's hand in a quick grasp of friendship. "Good luck, Doctor Hellman," he said, and. dashed off, running ludicrously on his short legs to rejoin his own party before the landing.

Tony searched the sky; the rocket was not yet in sight. He got back to work, swiftly now, setting up his equipment. Chabrier had mentioned a rumor. Never mind, there was enough to think about.

The whole thing planned beforehand, to ruin Sun Lake. *Maybe.* Chabrier was notorious as a gossip and petty troublemaker. A frameup. *Maybe.* And how could they find out? Who was responsible? Who was innocent? Nealey, Nowton; Bell and Brenner; Chabrier with his fluid chatter and his shrewd little eyes. Nealey at least was a decent, competent man...*Maybe.* But how could you tell? How could you single them out?

Parasites! he thought bitterly, the cheerful Chabrier as much as the arrogant Brenner. Mars liquor brought fantastic prices because it was distilled from mashes of Martian plants containing carbohydrates, instead of being distilled from mashes of Earth plants containing carbohydrates. And the friendly, plump little man got plumper on the profits culled from Earth's neurotic needs. It wasn't really much of an improvement on Brenner's marcaine business. A minor difference in moral values, but all of them were parasites as long as they didn't devote their time to the terrible problem of freeing Mars from the shadow of Earth's dominance.

And what about our Lab? Unquestionably, it was better to concentrate radioactive methylene blue for the treatment of cancerous kidneys than it was to concentrate alkaloids for Earthside gow-heads, but that, too, was only a difference in moral values. Parasites, all...

"The rocket!" yelled Tad.

CHAPTER ELEVEN

IT LOOKED like a bit of the sun at first; that was its braking blasts seen from under. The monster settled swiftly, roaring and flaring in a teasing mathematical progression of successively shorter blasts more closely spaced. When you could see its silvery bulk in profile it was going *pop-pop-pop-pop-pop,* like a machine gun. It settled with a dying splutter and stood on the field some two hundred meters from the crowd like a remembered skyscraper.

Trucks raced out to meet it. Inside, the doctor knew, crewmen were walking around capstans that fitted over and unscrewed ten kilogram hex-nuts. The trucks slowed and crawled between the fins on which the rocket stood, directly under its exhaust nozzle. Drivers cut and filled to precise positions; then platforms jacked up from the crane trucks to receive the rim of the rocket's throat. Men climbed the jacks to fasten them.

The captain must have radioed from inside the ship; the last of the first hex-nuts was off. Motor away! Slowly the platforms descended, taking the reaction engine with them. The crane trucks crawled off, two ants sharing an enormous burden.

The crew inside was busy again, dismantling fuel tanks, while the trucks moved to the inspection and repair shed off the field. A boom lifted off the motor, and the drivers scuttled back to receive the first installment of the fuel tanks, the second, the third, and the last.

"Now do the people come out?" asked Tad.

"If the rocket hasn't got any more plumbing, they do," Tony told him. "Yes—here we go." Down between the fins descended a simple elevator, the cargo hoist letting down a swaying railed platform on a cable. It was jammed with people. The waiting port officer waved them toward the Administration Building. The crowd, which had overflowed gently past the broad white line on the field, drifted that way, too.

"Stanchions! Get stanchions out!" the port officer yelled. Two field workers broke out posts and a rope that railed the crowd from the successive hoist-loads of people herded into the Administration Building for processing. There was a big murmur at the third load—*Graham!* The doctor was too far back to get a good look at the great man.

The loudspeaker on top of the building began to talk in a brassy rasp:

"Brenner Pharmaceuticals. Baroda, Schwartz, Hopkins, W. Smith, Avery for Brenner Pharmaceuticals," it said. Brenner ducked under the rope to meet five men issuing from the building. He led them off the field, talking earnestly and with gestures.

"Pittco! Miss Kearns for Pittco Three!"

A pretty girl stepped through the door and looked about helplessly. A squat woman strode through the crowd, took the girl by the arm, and led her off.

Radiominerals Corporation got six replacements; Distillery Mars got a chemist and two laborers; Metro Films got a cameraman who would stay and a pair of actors who would be filmed against authentic backgrounds and leave next week with the prints. A squad of soldiers headed by a corporal appeared and some of the field workers let out a cheer; they were next for rotation. Brenner got two more men; Kelly's Coffee Bar got Mrs. Kelly, bulging with bricks of coffee and sugar.

"Sun Lake Colony," said the loudspeaker. "W. Jenkins, A. Jenkins, R. Jenkins, L. Jenkins, for Sun Lake."

"Watch the box," Tony called to Tad as he strode off.

He picked up the identification and authorization slips waiting for him at the front desk inside, and examined them curiously. Good, he thought, a family with kids. The loudspeaker was now running continuously. Two more for Chabrier, three engineers for Pittco Headquarters in Marsport.

A uniformed stewardess came up to him.

"Dr. Hellman? From Sun Lake?" Her voice was professionally melodious. He nodded. "These are Mr. and Mrs. Jenkins." She turned to the family group behind her. "And Bobby and Louise Jenkins," she added, smiling.

The kids were about seven and four years old respectively. Tony smiled down at them, shook hands with their parents, and presented his authorizations to the stewardess.

"—Prentiss, Skelly, and Zaretsky for Sun Lake," the loudspeaker called.

"Excuse me, I'll be right back," Tony said and headed back to the desk.

They gave him more authorization slips. He riffled through the papers quickly as he headed back to find the Jenkinses and wait for the newcomers. All different names. Only one family, the rest singles. Too bad.

He hunted through his pockets and found two packets of peanuts, mutated beyond recognition into chewy objects with a flavor something like grape pop.

By the time Bobby and Lou had overcome their shyness enough to accept the gifts, another stewardess was bringing up the rest of the group destined for Sun Lake.

"Dr. Hellman?" Her voice was as much like the first stewardess's as her uniform, but according to ancient custom this one was a blonde and the other a brunette. "Miss Skelly, Miss Dantuono, Mr. Graham, Mr. Prentiss, Mr. Bond, Mr. Zaretsky," she said and vanished.

Tony nodded and shook hands all around.

"Let's get out of here," he said. "It's quieter outside and I have to give you all a physical checkup, so—"

"Again?" one of the men groaned. "We just had one on board."

"I think I've had a million different shots since I started all this," one of the girls put in. What was her name? Dantuono? "Do we get more needles?"

"I'm afraid so. We have to be careful, you know. Let's get out of here," Tony said again. He offered his hands to the children, and they started moving.

By the time they reached Tad and the box that held the portable health lab the crowd was already thinning out.

"We'll get right to it," the doctor addressed his group. "I'm sorry I can't examine you indoors under more comfortable circumstances, but I have to make a quick check before we can even let you on board the ship. It won't take long if we start right away."

"Doesn't the port have facilities for this sort of thing?" someone asked.

"Sure. They've got a beautiful setup right inside the Ad Building. Anybody can use it. Sun Lake can't afford the price."

He called them up one at a time, starting with the Jenkinses, parents and then the children, so the kids wouldn't have too much time to get apprehensive about the needles. His trained reflexes went through the business of blood and sputum tests, eye-ear-nose-and-throat, fluoroscopy, and nervous-and-mental, while he concentrated on getting acquainted.

Names began to attach themselves to faces. He finished with the two single girls, and started on the men. The big, red-faced one was Zaretsky; skinny little bookkeeper type was Prentiss. The talkative one was Graham.

"First name?" Tony was filling in the reports while the samples went through analysis.

"Douglas."

"Drop-in or shares?"

"Drop-in, I guess. On Earth we call it the working press."

"Press?" Tony looked up sharply. "*The* Douglas Graham?"

"The *This Is* man. Didn't you know I was coming out?" Tony hesitated, and Graham asked quickly, "Your place *is* open to the press, isn't it?"

"Oh, sure. We just—well, frankly, we didn't think you'd bother with us. Certainly didn't think you'd come to us first. We'd have rolled out the red carpet." He grinned and pointed to the array of planes at the other end of the field; for the first time, he became aware of the curious and envious stares their small group was receiving from passersby. "Everybody else did. I guess we were about the only outfit on Mars that didn't at least *hope* to bring you back home today." He turned his attention to the checkup form. "Age?"

From appearance and general condition, Tony would have given the journalist ten more years; it was a shock to find that they were both the same age. He finished without further comment and went on to the next and last, a lanky blond youth named Bond. By the time he was done, the analyses and reaction tests were complete.

The doctor checked them over carefully. "You're all right," he announced to the group at large. "We can get started now."

It was a slow trip. None of the newcomers were accustomed to the low gravity; they were wearing heavy training boots acquired on board the rocket. And all of them were determined to see everything that was to be seen in Marsport before they took off. Tony led them across the spaceport field, and down the main street of Marsport, a mighty boulevard whose total length was something under five hundred yards, the distance from the spaceport to the landing strip.

He answered eager questions about the ownership and management of the hotels and office buildings that lined the block adjacent to the spaceport. These were mostly privately owned and privately built, constructed of glass brick. The native product had a sparkling multicolored sheen that created a fine illusion of wealth and high fashion—even when you knew that no building made of the stuff could possibly stand more than ten years. The same slightly different chemical content of Martian potash that produced the lustrous coloration of the bricks made them particularly susceptible to the damaging effects of wind and sand. Glass brick construction was, by far, more costly than the rammed-earth buildings at Sun Lake, or the scrap-shanties that characterized the Pittco camp across the Rimrock Hills from the Colony; but it was still much less expensive than the Earth-import steel and alumalloy used wherever strength and durability were important.

The Administration Building of the Planetary Affairs Commission, which occupied one entire side of the center block, was sheathed in a muted green alumalloy; the P.A.C. Stores and official P.A.C. hotel, across the street, were respectively dull rose and dove gray. The doctor pointed out each building in turn to his wide-eyed group. The writer was as eager as any of the others, and asked as many questions. Tony was surprised; he had anticipated a bored sophistication.

Graham responded equally unpredictably to the series of interruptions they met with en route. Chabrier was first, even before they had left the spaceport. He dashed up to pump Tony's hand and babble that he was delighted to see him again, and how well Tony looked despite his drab sojourn in the so-dull Sun Lake where *nothing* ever happened.

"But this is Mr. Graham, isn't it?" he exclaimed in delight.

"Yeah," said the writer dryly.

"How fortunate! Distillery Mars, my concern, small but interesting, happens to be preparing a new run of Mars liquor, 120 proof—we should be so honored if you could make a point of sampling our little effort, shall we say this afternoon? I have *comfortable*"—a sidelong glance at Tony—"transportation here."

"Maybe later."

"To a connoisseur of your eminence, of course, we should think it a privilege to offer you an honorarium—"

"Maybe later, maybe not," grunted the writer.

"You will perhaps be pleased to accept a small sample of the product of Mars Distillery?" The little man held up a gaudily wrapped package. He pressed the gift into Graham's indifferent grasp, wrung Tony's hand warmly, said heartily, "We will look forward to see you soon," and departed.

Halliday of Mars Machine Tool was next. His manner was more that of a man inviting a guest to his country club, but he *did* mention that MMT would, of course, expect to provide for a writer's necessary expenses. Graham cut off Halliday's bluff assurances as curtly as he had stopped Chabrier's outpourings. It was like that all the way.

Everybody who was anybody on Mars was in town that day, and each of them managed to happen on the Sun Lake crowd somewhere along the road from the spaceport to the landing strip.

Those who had met Tony at any time in the past were all determined to stop him for a chat; then they noticed Graham, and extended a coincidental but warm invitation. Those who were unacquainted with Sun Lake's doctor were forced to be more direct, and the bribe was sometimes even more marked than Chabrier's or Halliday's offers.

Graham was cold and even nasty to them. But once he took Tony's arm and said, "Wait. I see an old friend." Commissioner Bell was up ahead, striding toward the Administration Building.

"Him?" asked Tony.

"Yeah. Hey, Commish!"

Bell stopped as if he had been shot. He turned slowly toward Graham and stood his ground as the writer approached. When he spoke, there was cold hatred in his voice. "Just the company I'd expect you to keep, Graham. Stay out of trouble. I'm the man in charge here, and don't think I'm afraid of you."

"You weren't the last time," said Graham. "That was your big mistake—Commish."

Bell walked away without another word.

"You shot his blood pressure up about 20 millimeters," said Tony. "What's it all about?"

"I claim a little credit for sending Bell to Mars, Doc. I caught him with his fingers in the till up to his shoulder, at a time when his political fences were down, if you don't mind a mixed metaphor. I couldn't get him jailed, but I'll bet up here he sometimes wishes I had."

A wild hope flared in Tony. The *This Is* man was, sporadically, known as a crusader. Perhaps Graham's annoyance at the crude plays for attention meant that an appeal could be made on the basis of decency and fair play…

By the time they reached the plane, Tad was already on the spot with the portable health lab stowed away, and Bea was warming up the motors.

"Hi!" She stuck her head out of the cockpit to grin at Tony. "Got everybody? Tad, hand out the parkas to these people. Tony, they tell me you're a hero—had it out with big, bad Brenner in real style!" She didn't quite say, "I never thought you had it in you."

"Things get around, don't they? Bea, this is Douglas Graham. He's coming out to have a look at Sun Lake for a book he's doing. This is Bea Juarez," he told the writer. "She's our pilot."

Graham surveyed Bea. "I hope everything in the Colony looks as good."

"We'll be extra-careful to show you only the best," she retorted. "Hey, Tad, get that mink-lined parka, will you? We've got a guest to impress."

Tony was delighted. If everyone else in the Colony could take the Great Man in stride so easily, he would be pleased and very much surprised.

Tad came running up with a parka. "What kind did you say you wanted? This is the only one left, except Dr. Tony's."

The three adults burst into laughter, and Tad retreated, red-faced.

Graham called him back. "I'm going to need that thing if the temperature in the cockpit doesn't go up."

"You're going to need it anyhow," Tony assured him. "There's a lot to be said for *Lazy Girl* here, but she's not one hundred per cent airtight."

"I get the idea," the journalist assured him. "You people don't throw heat around, do you?"

"Not heat or anything else," replied Tony. "You'll see, if you can stick it out."

"What the hell, I was a war correspondent in Asia!"

"This isn't a war. There isn't anything exciting to make up for the discomfort—except, say, when a baby gets born—"

"No? I take it there was something going on just a little while ago: What were you saying about the doctor being a hero?" he called forward to Bea.

She shrugged. "All I know is what I hear on the grapevine."

Tony heaved a mental sigh of relief—too soon.

"I was there." Tad had stuck right by them. "This man Mr. Brenner came over and asked Dr. Tony to come work for him, and he wouldn't and he tried to get him with a whole lot of money, but he still wouldn't and—"

"Hold on," Graham interrupted. "First thing you have to learn if you're going to be a reporter is to get your pronouns straight. This Brenner was doing the offering, and Doc was refusing; that right?"

"Sure. That was what I was saying—"

"Look, Tad, we were only kidding about impressing Mr. Graham," Tony said quickly. "You don't have to make a hero out of me. I just had a disagreement with someone," he said to Graham, "and they're trying to make a good story out of it."

"That's what I'm after," Graham came back, "a good story. Tell me everything that happened, Tad."

The boy looked doubtfully from the doctor to the guest and back again.

"All right," Tony gave in. "But let's not make a fifteen-round fight out of it, Tad. Tell it just the way it happened, if you've got to tell it."

"Just *exactly?*"

"Yes," the doctor said firmly, "just the way it happened."

"Okay." Tad was far from disappointed. If anything, he was gleeful. "So this Mr. Brenner wanted Dr. Tony to come work at his place, curing people from *drugs,* and he wouldn't, and Mr. Brenner kept pestering him till he got mad, and he said he didn't like him and wouldn't work for him no matter what—I mean, Dr. Tony said that to Mr. Brenner—and Mr. Brenner got *real* mad, and started to swing at him, and—"

"Well, don't stop *now!*" Graham said. "Who won?"

"Well—then Mr. Brenner started swinging and—I stuck my foot out and tripped him, and Mr. Chabrier came over right away and said how wonderful it was the way Dr. Tony had socked Mr. Brenner, and I guess that's what everybody thought." He looked up at Tony's astonished face, and finished defensively: "Well, you *said* to tell it just the way it happened."

CHAPTER TWELVE

TONY FASTENED the hood of his parka more tightly around his head, as the chill air of flight crept into the cabin. Graham, beside him, was full of flip comment and curiosity, to which ordinary decency, let alone special diplomacy, demanded reply. But Tony shifted position and let his eyelids drop.

There was no mental eye to close and so thrust out the revised memory of the ridiculous incident with Brenner, nor any mental ear that could turn off the resounding echo of Bea Juarez's hilarity.

You knew all along you never hit Brenner, didn't you? he asked himself angrily. *You could have figured it out for yourself—if you wanted to! All right, then, don't think about that.*

The new colonists—he ought to do something about them, something to dispel the tense, apprehensive silence in the cabin. A speech of welcome, something like that.

Thank them for coming? Welcome them to Sun Lake? With the threat that hung over them all, new members and old, any speech like that would be ridiculous. Later in the day, they would be asked to sign final papers, turning over, once and for all, the funds they had already placed in the hands of the trustees on Earth, and receiving their full shares in the Colony. Before then they would learn the worst; they would be told about the accusation that might doom the Colony. But how could he tell them now, before they had even seen Sun Lake, before they had glimpsed the spellbinding stretches of *Lacus Solis,* or had a chance to understand the promise implicit in the Lab's shining walls, or Joe Gracey's neatly laid out experimental fields?

And in front of the Gunther, too, how much could he say, how much did he dare to say? Graham could wreck their hopes with a word—or solve their problems as easily, if he chose. Graham had exposed the

Commissioner's corruptness once; he wasn't always just a Gunther; he was a part-time crusader. Possibly he would understand Sun Lake's desperate necessity—possibly?

"Oh, by the way," the writer was saying. "I've been wondering what kind of checkup you have on these people for security."

"Security?" For a minute the word didn't make sense; Tony realized suddenly that he hadn't even heard the word for a year; not, at least, with that sinister, special meaning.

"Don't you investigate the newcomers' backgrounds?"

"The Sun Lake Society—the recruiting office—checks on their employment records and their schooling to see that we don't get any romantic phonies masquerading as engineers and agronomists. That and plenty of health checks are all we need. The office wouldn't have time for more, anyway. It handles all the Earthside paperwork on our imports and exports, advertises, interviews, writes letters to the papers when that damn free-love story pops up again—" He gave Graham a look.

"All right," laughed the writer. "I'll make a mental note: Sun Lake doesn't believe in sex."

Tony was ruefully aware that a comeback was expected of him, but he substituted a feebly appreciative smile and leaned back, tiredly letting his eyelids drop again, in an effort to simulate sleep.

Through slitted eyes he studied the new arrivals. They were crouched on the cabin floor, bundled into their parkas, talking only occasionally. Even Tad, at the far end of the cabin with the Jenkins children, was low-voiced and restrained. Tony could see him pulling miraculous Martian treasures from his pockets for display, then pouncing on the few Earth items the new children had to show in return, cautiously pulled forth from supposedly empty pockets, and held for view in a half-cupped hand.

Near them, Bessie Jenkins, the mother of the two youngsters, sat half watching them, half talking to the mousier of the two single girls… Dantuono? Rose Dantuono, that was it. Anita Skelly, her vivid red hair concealed under the hood of her parka, was carrying on a conversation in monosyllables with Bob Prentiss; they seemed to be communicating a good deal more by hand pressure than by word of mouth.

He shifted his gaze to the other side of the cabin where the remaining three men sat: Arnold Jenkins, the lanky Bond, and young Zaretsky. They lined up in a silent row, leaning against the bulkhead, evidencing none of the interested enthusiasm one might have expected. His own depression, the doctor realized, was affecting everyone.

What could he say to them? Here they were, newly escaped from Earth, from a madhouse with a time bomb in the basement. It had cost each one of them more than he could estimate, in courage, in money, in work, to make the escape—and what could he promise them now?

With luck, with the help from Graham, with all the breaks, the best they could look forward to was the everyday life of the Colony: working like dogs; living like ants, because it was the only way to pull free of the doomed world from which they had fled. At worst, and the worst was imminent—back on the same rocket, or the next, or the one after that, back with all the others, destitute. Back to Earth, with no money, no job, no place to live, and no hope at all.

"Doc!" Bea yelled back into the cabin. "Radio!"

Tony got up and leaned over into the cockpit to accept the earphones Bea passed him.

"I can only spark a message back," she told him. "We didn't load the voice transmitter this trip."

He nodded. Through the phones a self-consciously important teen-age voice was saying, "Sun Lake to *Lazy Girl,* Dr. Hellman. Sun Lake to *Lazy Girl,* Dr. Hellman. Sun Lake—"

"*Lazy Girl* to Sun Lake, I read you, Hellman," he said and Bea's hand sputtered it out on the key.

"Sun Lake to *Lazy Girl,* I read you—uh—seventy-two at Pittco, can *Lazy Girl* sixteen Pittco, over."

"Dr. Tony to Jimmy Holloway," he dictated, "cut out the numbers game, Jimmy, and tell me what you want, over."

The teen-age voice was hurt. "Sun Lake to *Lazy Girl,* medical emergency at Pittco Camp, can *Lazy Girl* change course and land at Pittco, over."

"*Lazy Girl* to Sun Lake, wilco, Jimmy, but where's O'Reilly, over."

"Sun Lake to *Lazy Girl,* I don't know, Dr. Tony. They messaged us that O'Reilly wasn't due back from Marsport all day, over."

"*Lazy Girl* to Sun Lake, we'll take care of it, Jimmy, out." He passed the phone back to Bea. "Somebody's sick or hurt at Pittco. Drop me off there and I'll get back on one of their half-tracks."

"Right." Bea pulled out her map table.

The doctor went to the rear of the cabin where Tad had stowed the portable lab. He came back with a box of OxEn pills, and stood in the doorway between the cabin and the cockpit, facing the assembled group.

"These are the same pills you took on board the rocket this morning," he told them. "I don't think I have to warn you always to keep a few with you. Wherever you go, whatever you do, as long as you're on Mars, don't forget that it's literally as much as your life is worth if you don't take one of these *every twenty-four hours.*" They all knew that, of course; but there was no harm in impressing them with it again.

There was more he should say, but he didn't know what. He chose the next best alternative and sat down.

"What's cooking?" demanded Graham.

"Somebody sick or something at the Pittco outfit across the hills from our place. Their doctor's still in Marsport."

"Mind if I stick with you? I'd like to have a look at the place anyhow—when they're not ready for me."

Tony considered a moment, and decided he liked the idea. "Sure. Come along."

"I'd kind of like to see that girl who was for Pittco."

"You met her on the rocket?"

"I met her, all right, but she gave me a faster freeze than your girl pilot here. What is she anyhow—a lady engineer? All brains and no bounce?"

"Not exactly," Tony said. "I guess she figured she was on vacation. She's a new recruit for the company brothel. Those are the only women they've got at Pittco."

"Well, I'll be damned!" Graham was silent a moment, then added thoughtfully, "No *wonder* she wasn't interested!"

Lazy Girl touched down at Pittco near noon. The doctor and writer were met by Hackenberg, the mine boss, who drove out in a jeep as Bea zoomed her ship off over the hills to home.

"I think you're too late, Doc," he said.

"We'll see. Hack Hackenberg, Douglas Graham." They climbed in the jeep, rolled past the smokestacks of the refining plant, toward the huts of the settlement.

"Hell of a thing," grumbled Hackenberg: "Nobody's here. Madame Rose, Doc O'Reilly, Mr. Reynolds, all off at Marsport. God knows when they're coming back. Douglas Graham, did you say? You the reporter Mr. Reynolds was going to bring back? How'd you happen to come in with the doc?"

"I'm the reporter," Graham said, "but it's the first I knew about coming here with Reynolds. Did he tell you that?"

"Maybe he said he hoped you would. I don't know. I got my hands full as it is. I got a contract to be mine boss; everybody takes off and Big Ginny gets her chest busted up, the girls go nuts, and I take the rap. What a life!"

"Was there a brawl?" asked the doctor.

"Nobody told me—they yanked me out of B plant. They found Big Ginny over by the hills. She was all messed up—you know what I mean, Doc. They thought she was raped. Rape Big Ginny, for God's sake! It ain't reasonable!"

"They *moved* her?"

"They took her back to Rose's. I tell them and tell them to leave 'em lay, just get 'em warm, give plasma, and wait for a doctor. It don't do any good. First thing they think of whenever anybody gets smashed up is he don't look neat enough, so they yank him around to lie nice and straight and they yank him up so they can get a pillow under his head and then they haul him like a sack of meal to a bed. I hope to hell I never have a cave-in here with these dummies. Back in Jo'burg it happened to me. A timber fell and broke my leg nice and clean. By the time all my friends were through taking care of me and getting me comfortable, it was a compound complicated fracture with bone splinters from my ankles on up."

The jeep stopped in front of a large house, solidly constructed of the expensive native glass brick. Unlike most of the jerry-built shacks that housed the temporary workers in the camp, it was one of the few buildings put up by the Company itself, and few expenses had been spared.

The door opened hesitantly, and a girl peered out, then opened it all the way. "Hello, Hack. Is this the doctor?"

She was dressed in neither the standard tunic of most Marswomen nor the gaudy clothes of her sisterhood on Earth; instead she wore tailored house-pajamas of Earthside synvelvet. She might have been any business woman or middle-class housewife answering her door back on Earth.

"Hello, Mary." Hackenberg turned to Tony. "Doc Hellman, this is Mary Simms. She's in charge when Rose is out. Mary, this is Douglas Graham, the famous Gunther." He stressed the last word only slightly. "You've heard of him?"

"Oh, yes." She was distantly polite. "How do you do, Doctor? Won't you come in?"

"I'll have to take off now." Hackenberg shook Graham's hand vigorously. "Glad to have met you. I'll pick you up later, Doc." He waved and headed back for the jeep. Tony and Graham followed Mary Simms indoors and pulled off their parkas.

The whole house *was* heated, the doctor noticed.

The girl led them through a large and rather formal parlor and into a smaller sitting-room. She crossed the small room, and opened a door on the far side.

"In here, *Doctor,*" she said. Tony stepped into the small bedroom and heard Graham right behind him.

"How about me?" demanded the writer.

The girl's voice was icy. "Professional courtesy, I suppose; we *are* in the same business, aren't we? By all means, come in."

The doctor turned his smile in the other direction. A huge blonde lay on the bed between fresh sheets. She was in coma, or—

"Out!" Tony said firmly, and closed the door on both of them.

He lifted the sheet and swore under his breath. Big Ginny had been washed and dressed in a rosebud-trimmed pink niron nightgown. Few people with internal injuries could survive such first-aid. He opened his bag and began the examination.

He stepped into the parlor. Mary rose from her chair to question him, but Tony forestalled her. "She's dead." He added in a puzzled voice, "Her chest was beaten in. Who found her?"

"Two of the men. Shall I get them?"

"Please. And—was there anything they found near by?"

"Yes. I'll bring it." The girl went out.

"How about the rape?" Graham asked.

"She wasn't," Tony said.

He dropped into a chair and tried to think it out. The woman had been pregnant, and there were signs of a fresh try at abortion—the "rape." Was the father known? Had they tried to abort her? Had there been a scene and a fatal beating out there by the hills? How did you know who was the father of a child conceived in a place like this? And who else would have any reason for the violence?

Mary Simms came in and said, "I passed the word for the men." She moved coolly so that her body was between Graham and the doctor, and handed over something wrapped in a handkerchief. "They found this."

"Did you know she was six months pregnant?"

"Big Ginny?" she asked, amazed.

"Why not?"

"Why, I've seen her medical card, and she's been here two years. She was married a couple of times on Earth—" The girl was flustered.

"Well?"

"Well, it surprised me, that's all."

He went into the small bedroom and unwrapped the object she had given him. It was a stained scrap of stout copper wire, about twenty-five centimeters long. That confirmed his diagnosis: attempted self-abortion, clumsy and dangerous because of the woman's bulk and probably hazy knowledge of anatomy. But the innumerable blows on her chest and back didn't make sense...

Back in the parlor, two men in miners' leathers were waiting. The writer was questioning them idly about living conditions in the camp.

"I'm Dr. Hellman from Sun Lake," Tony said. "I want to ask you about finding Big Ginny."

"Hell, Doc," said one of the miners, "we just walked over that way and there she was. I said to Sam, 'It's Big Ginny! Jeez!' and he said, 'Some cheapskate musta hit her on the head,' and we tried to bring her around but she wouldn't come to, so we made her comfortable and we went and told Mary and then we went back on. shift."

"That's all there is to it," said the other miner. "But it wasn't one of our boys. You ask me, it was one of those Communist crackpots from over your place, all the time reading—it drives you nuts, did you know that? How is the old bag, Doc? Is she yelling for her money?"

"She's dead," the doctor said shortly. "Thanks for the information."

"You ask me," the miner repeated stoutly, "it's one of those Communists did it."

"Can you beat that?" the other one said softly. "What kind of guy would kill a dame like that?" They went out soberly.

"Those guys were a little too innocent," said Graham suddenly. "Didn't you think so?"

"I know what that's about," said Mary Simms. "They didn't mention why they happened to be out strolling on the desert. They're gow-heads. They were picking up some marcaine. They have a deal worked out with one of the people from Brenner's Hop Heaven. He steals the stuff from Brenner and leaves it under a rock for Sam and Oscar. They leave money."

"I knew something was sour about them," said Graham broodingly. "What do we do now, Tony?"

"I'm going to write a note to Dr. O'Reilly and see if I can get Hackenberg to drive us to Sun Lake." He sat down and took out his notebook and pen, found a blank page, and carefully recorded what he had seen, without adding any of his conclusions.

He signed his name, folded and handed the sheet to Mary Simms. "When you give the doctor this," he said, "please tell him I was sorry I couldn't stay to see him. We're having big times over at our place. Ten new colonists." He smiled. "Nine immigrants and a new baby."

"Boy or girl?" she asked, with sudden interest. "How is it—all right? Was it difficult?"

"A boy. Condition fair. Normal delivery."

"That's nice," she said, with a musing smile. Then she was all business again. "Thank you for coming, Doctor. I can make some coffee for you while you're waiting for Mr. Hackenberg. We have real coffee, you know."

"I didn't know," he told her. "I'll take two cups."

Dr. Tony filled Hackenberg in on the jeep ride to Sun Lake. The mine boss profanely said nothing like that had ever happened before and he'd get the no-good swamper that did it and swing him from the gantry if he had to beat up every leatherhead in camp. He told some grisly stories about how he had administered rough justice to native coal miners in Johannesburg.

" 'Course," he admitted, "you can't do that to Panamericans."

It was a good thing, thought Dr. Tony, that there wasn't any Martian animal life. An intelligent race capable of being sweated would really have got the works from Hackenberg, who could justify abominable cruelty to his brothers on the grounds that they'd been born in a different hemisphere of his own planet. God only knew what he would think justified by an extra eye or a set of tentacles.

Hackenberg took the wide swing through the gap in the hills and highballed the dozen miles to Sun Lake City. He came to a cowboy stop in front of the Lab and declined their hospitality.

"I have to get back before the big shots," he said. "Thanks, Doc. I'll see you around."

CHAPTER THIRTEEN

THE BIG MAIN HALL of the Lab was jammed with people, standing in earnest groups, strolling around, all talking at once. As the door slammed behind the doctor and the writer, the hubbub quieted, and seventy-odd pairs of eyes turned on the newcomers.

"Quite a delegation," Graham commented. "For me?"

"I don't know," Tony confessed. He searched the room, and saw Harve Stillman break away from a small group and head their way.

"Hi, Tony, did you bring a friend?"

He turned to find Mimi Jonathan at his elbow.

"Oh, Mimi, this is Douglas Graham. Did Bea tell you he was coming? Graham, Mimi Jonathan. Mi—Mrs. Jonathan is the Lab Administrator, in charge of making the wheels go round. And this is Harve Stillman. Harve used to be—"

"—a newspaperman himself," Graham finished.

"Nope." Harve grinned. "A radio teletype repairman with the I.P."

"What a switch!" Graham smiled back and shook the other man's hand.

Tony turned from them to ask Mimi urgently, "How's it going? Did you finish up with the Lab search yet?"

"Afraid so. It's the same as the huts. Nothing turned up," she said harshly. "We'll have to check the shipping crates."

"Lord!" breathed Tony.

"Maybe it won't be so bad," Stillman ventured. "I've just given this crowd a briefing on handling hot stuff. Mimi seems to think we can clear it up in a day or two if we all pitch in."

"Provided," Mimi added, "we all work just a little harder than possible. I'm sorry you had to come to us at such a busy time, Mr. Graham. I hope you won't mind if we don't fuss over you too much. You're welcome to wander around and ask all the questions you want. Everyone will be glad to help you."

"It will be a welcome change," he assured her.

Tony waited very impatiently through a few more minutes of polite talk. As soon as Harve engaged the writer's attention again, the doctor turned back to Mimi. "What's the plan?" he asked.

"Five crews to get out about a kilometer into the desert, a half-kilometer apart. Everybody else brings them crates one at a time, they open and search, repack before the next one comes in. No contamination from crates standing open. Through all this you and Harve run back and forth checking the handling crews and the tote crews to see that they don't get dangerous doses and remove and treat them if they do. We figure four days to finish the job."

"Harve, do you think you're good enough to monitor the unpacking sites?" Tony asked. "Contamination from the native radioactives would be as bad as getting our own radiophosphorus into our radiomethyline blue."

"I didn't want to go out and try it on my own. Do you think I can swing it?"

"Sure. Go pick us five of the coolest spots on Mars."

The technician headed for the racked counters.

"Doc, can you let me in on that cryptic business?" demanded Graham.

"In a minute," said Tony, his eyes wandering over the crowd. "Excuse me." He had spotted Anna and was starting her way when she turned, saw him, and approached.

"We tried another feeding with the Kandro baby," she began without a preamble, "but he didn't take to it—choked it up again like yesterday."

Tony took out his pipe and bit abstractedly on the scarred stem. "No difference? No change at all?"

"Not that I could see. Tony, what's *wrong* with that baby?"

The doctor shook his head unhappily. "I don't know," he admitted.

There was something damnably wrong with the Kandro baby, something he couldn't quite figure. There was a clue somewhere in the vividly remembered picture of the gasping, red-faced infant, choking and spluttering on a mouthful of milk. Should he have tried water instead of normal feeding to get those scrambled reflexes into order?

"Doc—" said Graham.

"I'll be with you in a minute."

Anna went on serenely: "No trouble with Joan. I gave her her regular shot and changed the bandages when Tad told me you'd be late. She seemed fairly comfortable."

"Good. Miscellaneous complaints?"

"Kroll in engineering had a headache. And there's Mrs. Beyles. Her husband came and asked if there was anything I could do—they had a quarrel and he thought she went into a fit. It was a temper tantrum; I know you said not to give her anything, but John was so upset I gave her sedation to quiet her." She turned to Graham. "Sorry to have to drag out our hospital horrors. I'm sure you understand."

"Oh," said Tony. "I'm sorry. Douglas Graham, Anna Willendorf. Excuse me a minute, will you?" Mimi was tapping her foot, waiting for an opening. He told her, "I better get the afternoon safety done right now, and I'm damned if I'm going to do it with the whole Colony lurching around the Lab. Get 'em out of here so I can go to work, will you?

Graham, I can answer questions while I go through the Lab looking for over-level radiation. If you want to come along, you're welcome."

He led the writer out of the office into the dressing-room, as Mimi began to break up the knots of non-Lab personnel who had shown up to thrash out the search plan and learn their own parts in it.

Tony helped Graham into the suit of protective armor. He didn't usually bother with it himself on the afternoon inspection, when other people were all over the Lab, unprotected.

The doctor started his meandering course through the Lab, with Graham in tow.

"I'm making the second of our twice-a-day safety checks for excess radioactivity. It happens that we've got to unpack all our material scheduled for export, examine it, and repack it in a hurry if we want to get credit to pay our bills."

"Just routine, I suppose?" asked Graham blandly.

"I think you gathered that it certainly isn't. The fact is, your friend, Commissioner Bell, has accused us of harboring a thief and his loot—a hundred kilos of marcaine. We've searched everybody and everything so far except the export crates; now we've got to search them."

"Why not tell the old windbag to go blow?"

"If we don't turn up the marcaine, he can seal us up for six months to conduct an inch-by-inch search."

"What's so dreadful about that?" Graham asked.

"We're geared to two ships in six months now instead of one ship a year. If we missed two shipments, both incoming and outgoing, we'd be ruined."

Graham grunted thoughtfully, and Tony waited—and waited—the grunt was all. He'd been half hoping the writer would volunteer to help—perhaps by picking up his anti-Bell crusade or by promising to see his powerful friends, or by exposing the sorry mess to the public. But Graham, apparently forgetting the Bell business entirely, pitched the doctor a ferocious series of questions that threatened to stretch out the inspection endlessly:

"What's in this box? Why isn't this conveyor shielded? Where's the stock room? What do you do here? Is it technical or trade-school stuff? Where did this soil come from? What did you pay for it? Tile on this floor, concrete on that—why? Who's in charge here? How many hours does he work? That many? Why? How many hours does *he* work?"

As Tony paraded solemnly back and forth with the counter, checking off items on his report, he pressed a little on the writer.

"This crate here," he said, "is a typical sale. Radiophosphorus for cancer research. It goes to the Leukemia Foundation in San Francisco. It's a traceless pure—better than nine-nines. We're in business because we can supply that kind of thing. On Earth they'd have to first make the traceless-pure phosphorus and then expose it to a reactor or a particle accelerator, and the extra step there usually means it gets contaminated and has to be refined again. Here we just produce phosphorus by the standard methods and it *is* radioactive because the whole planet's got it. Not enough to present a health problem any more than cosmic rays on Earth do, but damned convenient for Sun Lake."

"Some crate," commented the writer.

"Lead, air gaps, built-in counter with a loud alarm. It's the law. Normally, we have five per cent of our manpower working in the shipping department. Now we have to unpack and recrate all this stuff in less than four days."

"You people should have a lobby," suggested Graham. "If something like that was handicapping Pittco, they'd get rid of it quick. Are we just about through?"

"Just about," said Tony flatly. So much for that, he thought; at least he'd given the writer an eyeful of the safety precautions they observed, and made him sweat a little under the heavy suit at the same time.

In the cleanup room they stripped and showered, with Graham chortling suddenly, "O'Mally was a prophet! My first city editor—he said when I got rich I'd install hot and cold running Scotch in my bathroom!"

"Sorry we only have cold, and don't drink this stuff unless you want to go blind. It's methyl."

"Can't be worse than the stuff I used to guzzle in Philly," Graham said blandly, but he stepped out quickly enough and followed the doctor's advice about a lanolin rubdown afterward.

"Dinner time now," said Tony, buttoning on his tunic. "Mess hall's here in the Lab. Only building big enough."

"Synthetics?" asked Graham.

"No, that's not the Sun Lake idea. We want to get on an agricultural cycle as fast as we can. Sun Lake has to be able to live on vegetables that grow naturally, without any fertilization except our own waste products. Naturally we're strong on beans, kudzu, yams, goobers—any of the nitrogen-fixing plants that contain some natural protein. You'll see."

Graham saw, he tasted, he expectorated. Into the shocked silence of the half-dozen at the table, he muttered an embarrassed apology and manfully choked down almost half of his vegetable plate—Mars beans, barley, stewed, greens, and another kind of stewed greens.

To Tony he muttered when conversation had sprung up again, "But why do they taste like a hospital smells? Do they have to disinfect them or something?"

Joe Gracey overheard it from the other side of the table. "That's my department," he said. "No, it isn't disinfectant. What you and most other people don't realize is that we with our Lab are pikers compared with the lowliest cabbage in synthesizing chemicals. We taste the chemicals in our Earth plants and we accept them as the way they ought to taste.

These are unfamiliar because there are Mars plants modified so that their chemicals aren't poison to Earth animals, or Earth plants modified so that Mars soil isn't poison to them. We're still breeding on this barley, which is generating too much iodoform for me to be really happy. If I can knock one carbon out of the ring— But you don't care about that. Just be glad we didn't try out the latest generation of our cauliflower on you instead of our test mice. The cauliflower, I'm sorry to say, generates prussic acid."

"Stick with those mice!" said Graham with a greenish smile.

"Only guaranteed-Earth animals on Mars, including you," said Madge Cassidy, beside Graham. He watched her wonderingly as she finished her barley with apparent enjoyment.

"How was that again?"

"My mice. The only animals on Mars guaranteed non-mutated. We have them behind tons of concrete and lead with remote feeding. It'd be no joke if some of the natural Mars radioactivity or some of the stuff flying around the Lab mutated them so they'd gobble Mars food that was still poison to people."

"You mean I might go back to Earth and have a two-headed baby?"

"It's possible," said Madge, getting to work on variety number one of stewed greens. "Odds are somewhat higher than it happening from cosmic rays or industrial radioactivity on Earth. But mouse generations go by so fast that with them it's a risk we can't take. Some of the pork-and-beaners died very unpleasant deaths when they tried eating Mars plants as a last resort. It *was* the last resort, all right."

"But isn't *anything* on Mars good to eat?"

"A couple of items," Gracey told him. "Stuff that would probably be poisonous to any native animal life, if there were any. You find the same kind of thing on Earth—plants that don't seem to be good for anything in their native environment. My theory is that the ancestors of poison ivy and other such things aren't really Earth plants at all, but came to Earth, maybe as spores aboard meteorites. We need a broader explanation of the development of life than the current theories offer. We've grown a giant barley here, for instance, out of transplanted Earth stock: but it wouldn't be viable there. The gene was lethal on Earth. Here—"

He rattled on, to the accompaniment of Graham's nod of agreement, until Harve Stillman broke in: "Hey, there was a rumor through the radio relay today. You know about it, Mr. Graham?"

"Doug," the writer corrected.

"Okay." Harve smiled. "About marcaine—no, not about us," he added hastily. "About marcaine being forbidden in Tartary. The Cham pronounced a rescript or whatever it is, and according to the guys in Marsport that means the price goes up, and Brenner's business is dou-bled. Do you know anything about it, Doug?"

The newsman looked surprised. "It was all over the ship," he told them. "Everybody was talking about it. How come you don't get it till now? The radio op on board told me he spilled it in his first message to P.A.C."

"It's true then?" Gracey asked sharply.

"I wouldn't know. I'm only a reporter myself." He looked across to Tony. "Don't tell me Marsport wasn't buzzing with it. Brenner knew, didn't he?"

"No," the doctor said slowly. "I didn't hear anything about it there." But he had heard of a rumor; who was it? Chabrier! Of course, that was Chabrier's rumor: marcaine prices going up, production will double, Brenner needs a new plant, needs a doctor, too...

Tony stood up abruptly. "Excuse me. Gracey, are you finished? Want to come along?"

The agronomist rose quickly, and the two left together. On the way to collect Nick and go over to the Jonathans', Tony explained the situation rapidly to Gracey.

"I wanted to get the Council together tonight anyhow," he finished up, "to tell you about my idiotic brawl with Brenner. I don't know what kind of jam *that's* going to land us in. But this business ties in with what Chabrier told me. Rocket to Bell and Bell to Brenner, and the rest of us can get the news whenever the Commissioner gets around to it!"

"It makes a nasty picture," the agronomist agreed soberly. "Now what? Where do we go from here?"

"Damned if I know. Maybe one of the others can figure it." He knocked sharply on Nick's door.

Chapter Fourteen

"It doesn't matter," Mimi said firmly. "We still have to go through with the search."

"That's how I see it, too," Tony admitted. "We can't bring any accusations until we know our own slate is clean."

"If we could only get hold of the Bloodhound—"

"Bell refused."

"And that means no matter how carefully we search he can still come in afterward and claim it wasn't done properly."

"Could we rent one or buy it?" Gracey wanted to know.

"Government property only," Mimi told him. "O'Donnell checked on that the other day."

"Okay, so we have to do it without the Bloodhound." Nick jumped up and paced the length of the room restlessly. "I bet I could build one if we only had a little time…Well, we have to go ahead, that's all. Where does Graham come in?"

Tony realized they were waiting for an answer from him. "I don't know. He has no use for Bell, but he doesn't exactly rise to the bait when I throw it at him either. I think we better go slow and feel him out. He didn't seem to go for the blunt approach when Chabrier and the others tried it."

"Slow?" Nick stormed. "Man, we've got six days! Go *slow?*"

"As fast as we can," Gracey put in. "We still have to get the search finished. I think we have to do that before we ask Graham anything. He has to have some facts to work with."

"Right," Mimi agreed. "Now let's get our plans organized. If we start at dawn, maybe we can do the whole unpacking operation tomorrow…*then* we can hit Graham. Means we'll have to leave crates open and repack them later, but I don't see any alternative now. How long is Graham staying, Tony?"

"He said maybe three days."

"Okay, then that's how we've got to do it. Maybe by tomorrow night we'll know better how to get at the guy."

They spent a busy ten minutes outlining the plan of operations, and then the three men went out, leaving the details for Mimi to settle.

Tony walked down the settlement street slowly, trying to get his thoughts in order. It had been a long day—three-fifteen in the morning when Tad woke him, and now there was still work to do.

Stopping in at the hospital to collect his bag, he found Graham kibitzing idly with Harve in his living-room.

"Just waiting for you, Doc." Stillman stood up. "I have to get over to the radio shack. Tad's on the p.m. shift this week, but he fell asleep before supper, so I've got to take over tonight."

Tony surveyed his guest uncomfortably. "Anything you'd like?" he asked. "I have to go out and see a couple of patients. Won't be too long."

"Could I go along?" Graham asked. "I'd like to, if it's all right with you."

"Sure. I want you to see the baby I was talking about anyhow. My other patient is pretty sick; you may have to wait while I look in on her."

They stopped at the Radcliffs' first, but Joan was asleep and she usually got so little rest that Tony decided not to disturb her. Anna had said she'd had a fairly good day. He'd see her tomorrow.

"Where is this infant?" Graham asked as they walked down the Colony street.

"Here. This is the Kandros' place. Hello, Polly," Tony said as the door opened, even before he knocked. "I brought Mr. Graham along to visit. I hope you don't mind."

"I—no, of course not. How do you do? Come in, won't you?" Her manner was absurdly formal, and her appearance was alarming. Tony wondered when she had last slept. Her eyes were over-alert, her lips too tight, her neck and shoulders stiff with tension.

"How's Sunny?" He walked into the new room where the crib stood, and the others followed. He wished now that he hadn't brought Graham along.

"The same," Polly told him. "I just tried. You see?" The baby in its basket was sputtering feebly, its face flushed bright red. *We're going to lose that youngster,* thought the doctor grimly, *unless I start intravenous feeding, and soon.*

"Tell me something, please, Doctor," she burst out, ignoring the reporter's presence. "Could it be my fault? I'm anxious—I know that. Could that be why Sunny doesn't eat right?"

Tony considered. "Yes, to a degree, but it couldn't account for *all* the trouble. Are you really so tense? What's it all about?"

"You know how it was with us," she said evasively. "We tried so many times on Earth. And then here we thought at first it'd be like all the other times, but Tony, do you think—is Mars dangerous?"

He saw she'd changed her mind in mid-confession and substituted the inane question for whatever she had started to ask. He intended to get to the bottom of it.

Over the woman's shoulder, he looked meaningfully at Graham. The reporter obligingly drifted back to the living-room.

Tony lowered his voice and told the woman, "Of course Mars is dangerous. It's dangerous now; it was dangerous before you had Sunny. I'm a little surprised at you, Polly. Some women think that having a baby ought to change the world into a pink spun-candy heaven. It doesn't. You've had Sunny; he's a small animal and you love him and he needs your care, but Mars is still what it always was. The terrain's rugged and some of the people aren't what they ought to be. But—"

"Tell me about the murder," she said flatly.

"Oh, is *that* what you're jumpy about? I saw worse every night I rode the ambulance at Massachusetts General. What's that got to do with Sunny?"

"I don't know. I'm afraid. Tell me about it, Doctor. Please."

He wondered what vague notion of terror she had got stuck in her head.

"The girl who got killed was named Big Ginny, as you may have heard. If you'd been on the wagon with me in Boston, you'd know there's nothing unusual about it. Women like that often get beaten up, sometimes beaten to death by their customers. The customers are usually drunk, sometimes full of dope; they get the idea that they're being cheated and they slug the girl. Another call for the wagon."

"I heard," she said, "that she was beaten to death with a lot of light blows. No man would do that. And I heard that Nick Cantrella saw footprints by the caves—naked footprints. He thought they were children's."

"Whose do you think they were?" he asked, though he had a sickly feeling that he knew what she'd say.

Polly moaned, "It was Martian dwarfs! I told you I saw one and you didn't believe me! Now they've killed this woman and they're leaving footprints around and you still don't believe me! You think I'm crazy! You all think I'm crazy! They want my baby and you won't listen to me!"

Tony thought he knew what was going on in her head and he didn't like it. She had seen the attention of the Colony shift from her baby to the marcaine search, and was determined to bring it back, even if it had to be by a ridiculous ruse. She'd heard all the foolish stories about the mythical Martians; she'd had a vivid anxiety dream which, he reminded himself, she had finally admitted was only a dream—and now she was collecting "evidence" to build herself up as the interesting victim of a malignant persecution.

"We've been over all this before," he told her wearily. "You agreed that you didn't really see anything. And you agreed that there couldn't be any dwarfs because no animal life has ever been found on Mars—"

"Doctor," she broke in, "I've got to show you something." She reached into the baby's basket and drew out something that glinted darkly in her hand.

"Good Lord, what are you doing with a gun?" the doctor demanded.

There was no more conflict on her face or hesitancy in her voice. "You can say I'm crazy, Tony, but I'm afraid. I think there could be such things as Martians. And I'm going to be ready for them if they come." She looked at the little weapon tensely and then put it back under the pad in the crib.

Tony promptly drew it out. "Now listen, Polly, if you want to believe in dwarfs or ghosts or Santa Claus, that's your business. But you certainly should know better than to leave the gun near him. I'm going to give you a sedative, Polly, and maybe after a good—"

"No," she said. "No sedative. I'll be all right. But can I keep the gun?"

"If you know how to use it and keep the safety on and put it some place besides under Sunny's mattress, I don't see why not. But all the Martians you'll ever shoot with it you could stick in your eye and never notice."

"Like the old lady, maybe I don't believe in ghosts but I'm terribly afraid of them?" She tried to laugh and Tony managed a smile with her.

"Nothing wrong with blowing your top once in a while. Nothing at all. Women ought to bawl oftener."

She grinned weakly and said, "Maybe Sunny's going to eat better now."

"I hope so. I'll see you tomorrow, Polly."

As they walked down the street in a strained, embarrassed silence, Graham looked as if he wanted to ask something. He finally did: "By the way, Tony, do you know where I'm supposed to sleep? Or where I'd find my bag? It was on the plane."

"Might as well stay with me. And your baggage ought to be at the Campbells'. Tad Campbell was that young sprout who deflated my fight with Brenner."

The baggage, a sizable B-4 bag on which Graham must have paid a ruinous overweight charge, was at the Campbells'. After picking it up, the writer followed the doctor to his hospital-hut.

Tony snapped a heat beam on the two plastic chairs and took off his sandboots with a grunt. Graham rooted through his baggage, picked up Chabrier's gaudy package, and hefted it thoughtfully, then shook his head and dove in again. He came up grinning with another bottle.

"How about it, Doc?" he asked. "This is Earthside."

"It's been a long time," Tony sighed. "I'll get a couple of glasses."

The stuff went down like silken fire. It had been a very long time.

"What's about dwarfs?" the writer asked suddenly. "I couldn't help hearing part of that when I went out of the room."

Tony shook his head. "*Dwarfs!* As if we didn't have enough troubles here, without inventing Martian monsters."

"Well, what *about* them? All I've ever heard is that deep purple scene in Granata's interplanetary show. It's silly stuff, but nobody's handled it yet at all except Granata. Maybe I could use something; it's a beautiful story if there's anything at all to back it up. Does anybody claim a connection between fairy book dwarfs and the Martian variety?"

"Two ways. First of all, Mars dwarfs are just as much a fairy story as the Earthside kind. Second, somebody once suggested that the ones in the story books were the space-traveling ancestors of the present-day hallucinations."

"Could be," the Gunther reflected. "Could be."

"Could be a lot of rot," Tony said without heat. "Space travel requires at an absolute minimum the presence of animal life—or at least mobile, intelligent life. Show me so much as one perambulating vegetable on Mars, let alone a native animal life-form. Then it's likely I'll think about dwarfs some more."

"How about a declining race?" Graham speculated. "Suppose they *were* space travelers, on a high level of civilization—they might have killed off all lesser life-forms. You see it happening some on Earth, and back there it's just a matter of living-space. We don't have the problem the Martians had to face, of dwindling water and oxygen supplies. Probably got them in the end, and destroyed their civilization—except," he added, "for the ones who got to Earth. I understand from authorita-tive sources that the last expedition to Earth was led by a guy named Oberon." Graham chuckled and drank, then asked seriously, "Has any-body ever *seen* one, except Granata?"

"Hundreds of people," Tony said dryly. "Ask any one of the old pros-pectors who come into town hauling dirt. They've all seen 'em, lived with 'em; some even claim to have been at baby-feasts. You'll get all the stories you want out of any of the old geezers."

"What are they supposed to look like?" the writer insisted.

Tony sighed and surrendered, recognizing the same intense manner Graham had displayed in the Lab. The man was a reporter, after all. It was his business to ask questions. Tony gave him what he wanted, with additions, explanations, and embellishments.

Martian dwarfs: an intelligent life-form, either animal or mobile vegetable. About a meter and a half in height; big ears; skinny arms. Supposed to be the naked remnants of a once-proud Martian civiliza-tion. (Except that there were no other remnants to support the theory.) In the habit of kidnapping human children (except that there was no specific authenticated case of a baby's disappearance) and eating them (except that that seemed too pat and inevitable an idea-association with the kidnapping—the sort of additional embellishment that no good liar could resist).

"It's an old prospectors' yarn," Tony wound up. "The homestead-ers picked it up to frighten kids into sticking close to home. There are hundreds of people on Mars today who'll tell you they've seen them. But not only is there no native animal life of any kind on Mars today—so far as we can tell, there *never* has been. No ruins, no old cities, no signs of civilization, and not so much as one single desiccated dried-out scrap of anything resembling an animal fossil."

"That's strictly negative evidence," Graham pointed out. He emptied his glass and poured another drink for both of them. "But on the other side you have footprints, for instance, and eyewitness stories."

"If you're talking about the cataract-covered eyes of old Marsmen," Tony retorted, "don't call it evidence."

"It wouldn't be," Graham agreed, "except that there are so many of them. I'm beginning to think there's a story in it after all."

"'You mean you believe it?" the doctor demanded.

"Do I *look* crazy? I said it was a story."

"So you came 150 million kilometers on a rocket, and then four more hours across Mars in a beat-up old rattletrap of a plane," the doc-tor said bitterly. "You eat food that tastes like hospital disinfectant, and live in a mud hut, all so you can go back home and write a nice piece of fiction about dwarfs—a piece you could have dashed off without ever leaving Earth!"

"Not exactly," the Gunther said mildly. "I was only thinking of using them for one chapter. Local color, tales and legends—that kind of thing."

"'You could get plenty of stories back on Earth," Tony went on bitterly. "Stories worth writing. How about Paul Rosen's story? There's a *real* one for you."

"Rosen?" Graham leaned forward, interested again. "Seems to me I've heard the name before. Who was he?"

"Not was. Is. He's still alive; a cripple nobody knows."

"Tell me about Rosen."

"I'll tell you about Mars; it's the same story. You came to write a book about Mars, didn't you? Well, Mars—this Mars, without oxygen masks—is Rosen's work. Rosen's lungs. And you never heard of him… Rosen was the medical doctor aboard the relief ship, the one that found what was left of the first colony. He had a notion about the oxygen differential, was convinced that it wasn't responsible for the failure. He was wrong, of course, but he was right, too. To prove his point he took off his mask and found he didn't need it.

"His assistant tried it, and nearly died of anoxemia. That proved some people could take Mars straight and others couldn't. When the ship got back Rosen went to the biochem boys with his lungs. They told him a few c.c. wouldn't be enough to work with, so he volunteered for an operation. Most of his lung tissue was removed. He was crippled for life, but they tracked down the enzyme that made the difference and worked out a test."

"That I remember," said Graham., continuing to fill the glasses almost rhythmically. "Half the guys I met in Asia claimed they enlisted because they weren't Marsworthy and life wasn't worth living if they couldn't go to Mars."

"That was the beginning of it," Tony said. "The ones who passed the test began to come over. Thousand dollars a day prospecting, and always the chance of finding bonanzas. At first they were pork-and-beaners, but the Mars vegetation they brought back took us one step closer to fitting into the Martian ecology. The biochem boys came up with a one-shot hormone treatment to stimulate secretion of an enzyme from the lining of the pylorus. It's present in most people without the shot, but not enough to break down the Martian equivalent of carbohydrates into simple sugars which the human body can handle. You asked me before what all the shots you got on board the rocket ship were for. That's one of them. It means you can handle the Mars plants which don't contain compounds poisonous to Earth animals.

"The other shots you got were to protect you against all the rest of the things that killed off the first pork-and-beaners—fungi, ultra-violet damage to the eyes, dehydration, viruses. For every shot you got, half a dozen of the first explorers and prospectors were killed or crippled to find the cause and cure.

"Five years ago came the payoff. The biochem boys got what they'd been looking for ever since they first sliced up Rosen's trick lungs. They synthesized the enzyme, your little pink OxEn pill, and that did it. That's when the Sun Lake Society was founded; and the new rocket fuel two years ago made Sun Lake a reality. With OxEn and four trips a year, we can make out until we find a way to get along without Earth.

"Sun Lake is Mars, Graham; Sun Lake's all's going to be left when you crazy bastards back on Earth blow yourselves up. The other colonists here aren't Mars; they're part of Earth. When Earth goes, they go. Sun Lake's all's gonna be left…"

"Coupla catches," said Graham, trying to make a glass stay put so he could fill it. "Commish Bell and his eviction notice. And you still need OxEn. Can you make that in a Lab?"

"Not yet," Tony brooded. He had forgotten the lovely optimism that could be poured out of a bottle. "Guess I had enough to drink. I have a hell of a day ahead of me."

CHAPTER FIFTEEN

A HELL OF A DAY it was. It started, for one thing, with a hangover. Tony heaved himself out of bed, glad to find Graham still asleep. He didn't want any cheerful conversation just yet. He prescribed, dispensed, and self-administered some aspirin, used an extra cup of water for a second cup of "coffee," finally decided he was strong enough to face the reek of methyl alcohol, and got washed.

Mimi Jonathan was in charge at the Lab when he got there. Law or no law, he raced through the a.m. Lab check to get ahead on the awful job of monitoring the unpacking operation. He rode out on a bike to the five spots Stillman had selected for the inspection crews and found them reasonably low in radioactivity.

Sheets of plastic had been laid down for flooring and tent walls were going up, with little tunnels through which the crates could be passed without the handlers bringing in all the dust of Mars on their feet. Blowers were rigged to change the air between each inspection, and radiologically clean overalls would be passed in at the same time.

A little after dawn, the careful frenzy was in full swing. A crew in the shipping-room eased out crates and passed them to wrappers who covered them with plastic sheeting and heat-sealed them. Aboard skids, the crates were manhandled up the slight slope from the "canal" bed to the tents in the desert, unwrapped, passed in opened, searched, checked for chemical and radiological contamination, sealed and passed out again. Back at the Lab, they would be wrapped in lead sheets pending re-crating and stored separately in every workroom that could be spared.

Mimi was everywhere, ordering a speedup on the heat-sealing, or a slowdown on the bucket-brigade manhandling, routing crates to the station that would soonest be free, demanding more plastic sheeting, drafting a woman to wash more coveralls when a stand of them toppled over. The few Lab processes that couldn't be left alone were tended under the direction of Sam Flexner, by people from agro and administration, and by specialized workers like Anna Willendorf.

Tony and Harve Stillman moved constantly up and down the line, back to the Lab and out to the desert, checking persons, places, and materials. Before noon Tony had the bitter job of telling Mimi, "We've got to abandon the Number Two tent. It's warming up. Radioactivity's low on the site, but it's from something that chains with the plastic flooring, I don't know what. Another hour and radiation from the flooring will contaminate the crates."

The woman set her jaw and picked another crew from the line to set up a tent on another monitored site.

Somebody slipped in the Number Three tent, and Harve Stillman found some of the Leukemia Foundation's shipment of radiophosphorus had got from the inside of the crate to the outside—enough to warrant refusal by the rocket supercargo in the interests of the safety of the ship.

But never a trace of marcaine did the search crews find.

Lunch was at noon, carried about by Colony children. Gulping cool "coffee," Tony told Harve Stillman, "You'll have to take it alone for a while. I haven't visited my patients yet. I missed Joan Radcliff altogether yesterday. Send for me if there's anything you really can't handle." Tony started back toward the street of huts before a new emergency could delay him.

He stopped at his own house to pick up his medical bag and found Graham awake, at work in front of an old-fashioned portable typewriter. Another surprise from the Gunther; Tony had assumed the man worked with a dictatyper. Even in the Colony they had those.

Graham looked up pleasantly and nodded. "Somebody waiting for you in the other room, Tony." He motioned with his head toward the door that led to the hospital. "You going out again?"

The doctor nodded. "I don't know when I'll get back. You can walk around and ask questions wherever you find anybody. You understand the situation here—we can't let up on this marcaine business even for the press. I'll get around in time to pick you up for supper anyhow," Tony promised.

Tony went into the hospital, where Edgar Kroll was waiting for him.

"Sorry to bother you today, Doc," Kroll apologized. "I came over on the chance you'd be around right about now. Another one of those damned headaches; I couldn't get any work done at all this morning. Guess I'm just getting old."

"Old!" Tony snorted. "Man, even in Sun Lake you're not old at thirty-five! Not just because you need bifocals. You've stalled around long enough now." And heaven only knew what boudoir taunting from young Jeanne Kroll lay behind that, Tony thought, as he reached into the dispensary cabinet. "Here's some aspirin for now. If you come around tomorrow, I think I'll have time to refract you; I just can't manage it today. Take the afternoon off if the headache doesn't go away."

He got his black bag and walked down the street with Edgar, as far as the Kandros' place. At the door he bumped into Jim, just leaving for the Lab after lunch.

"Glad I saw you, Doc." The new father stood hesitantly in the doorway, waiting till Kroll was out of earshot, then burst out, "Listen, Tony, I didn't want to say anything in front of Polly, but—are you sure it's going to be all right? Sunny still isn't eating. Maybe it's cancer or something? I heard of something like that with one of our neighbor's kids back in Toledo—"

Just exactly the sort of thing that made Tony almost blind with rage. He liked the man; Jim Kandro was his comrade in the Colony, but—! With his pulse hammering, he made it clear to Jim in a few icy sentences that he had studied long, sacrificed much, and worked hard to learn what he could about medicine, and that when he wanted a snap diagnosis from a layman he would ask for one. Jim and Polly could yank him out of bed at three in the morning, they could make him minister to their natural anxieties, but they could *not* make him take such an insult.

He stalked into the house, ignoring Jim's protests and apologies both, and professional habit took over as he greeted Polly and examined her baby.

"About time for a feeding, isn't it?" he asked. "Is it going any better? Since last night, I mean? Want to try him now while I observe?"

"It's a little better, I guess." Polly smiled doubtfully and picked up the baby. She moved the plastic cup of the oxygen mask up a little over the small nose and put Sunny to her breast.

To Tony, it was plain that the infant was frantic with hunger. *Then why didn't it nurse properly?* Instead of closing over the nipple, Sunny's mouth pushed at it one-sidedly, first to the right, then to the left, any way but the proper way. For seconds at a time the baby did suck, then released the nipple, choking.

"He's doing a little better," said Polly. "He's doing *much* better!"

"That's fine," Tony agreed feebly. "I'll be on my way, then. Be sure to call me if there's anything."

He walked down the Colony street wishing a doctor could afford the luxury of shaking his head in bewilderment. Maybe it was all straightening out. But *what* could account for the infant's fantastic behavior? There's nothing so determined as a baby wanting to feed—but *something* was getting in the way of Sunny's instinct.

He hoped Polly realized that Sunny would feed sooner or later, that the choking reflex frustrating the sucking reflex would disappear before long. He hoped she would realize it; he hoped desperately that it would happen.

Joan Radcliff was next and this time he found her awake. She was no better and no worse; the enigmatic course of her nameless disease had leveled off. All he could do was talk a while, go through the pulse-taking and temperature-reading mumbo-jumbo, change the dressings on her sores, talk some more, and then go out.

Now Dorothy, the sinus case, and he was done with his more serious cases for today.

Tanya Beyles had a green sick card on her door, but he decided to ignore it. He was already past the house when she called his name, and he turned to find her beckoning from the opened door.

She had dressed up to beat the band—an absurdly tight tunic to show off her passable thirty-plus figure, carefully done hair, and the first lipstick he remembered seeing around in months.

"I don't have much time, today, Mrs. Beyles," he said carefully. "Could it wait till tomorrow?"

"Oh, please, Doctor," she begged, and launched into a typical hypochondriac résumé of symptoms, complete with medical terms inaccurately used. What it boiled down to was that a thorough examination was in order though there was nothing *nasty* wrong with her.

"Very well," he said. "If you'll come over to the hospital—next week, perhaps—when I have more time." With a chaperon, he added silently.

"Wouldn't it be just as easy here, and more private?" she ventured shyly, indicating the bedroom, where a heat lamp was already focused on the made bed.

"Dear God," he muttered, and found the professional restraint that had taken over while he was with Polly Kandro had now quite abandoned him. "Mrs. Beyles," he said, plainly, "you may not realize it, but we do have a sense of humor here, even if we don't share your ideas of fun. We've been able to laugh off your malicious gossiping and the lousy job you do in Agronomy; you do get some work done in Agro, and you don't eat too much to keep your shape, and I've hoped you'd straighten out. But if you start being seductive around Sun Lake—even if you start with me—you'll get shipped out so fast you won't—"

"Is that so?" she screamed. "Well, maybe you'd like to know that I can get all the love and respect I want around here and where you got the idea that I'm at all interested in you I can't imagine. I've heard of

doctors like you before and if you think you're going to get away with
it you're very much mistaken. And don't think I don't know all about
you and that Willendorf woman. I know things people would love to
hear..."

He walked off before she could say any more. God only knew what
they'd do with her—deport her, he supposed, and her sad sack of a
husband would have to go, too, and it would all be very messy and bad-
tempered. Maybe Bell and Graham and all the others were right, regard-
ing Sun Lakers as anywhere from mildly insane to fanatically obsessed.

Maybe anything at all, but he still had to go to see Dorothy and her
sinuses. The doctor's facial muscles fell into their accustomed neutrality
as he walked into the girl's bedroom and his mind automatically picked
up the threads of the bacitracin story where he had left off two days
before...

Half an hour later, he was back at the unpacking and search operation where he took over alone while Stillman, groggy with the strain,
the responsibility, and the plain hard work, took a short break. The two
of them divided the job then, moving steadily up and down the lines,
checking, rechecking endlessly until, as darkness closed down, they were
suddenly aware that there were no more crates.

Mimi Jonathan bitterly enumerated the results of the search: "About
1,500 man-hours shot to hell, three crates contaminated beyond salvage, nine salvageable for umpty-hundred more man-hours—and no
marcaine. Well, nobody can say now that we didn't try." She turned to
Tony. "Your move," she said.

"Graham?" The doctor stood up. "All I can do is try to get him on
our side. He's friendly anyhow; he asked me to have supper with him
out of his private stock of genuine synthetic Earthside protein."

"You don't sound too hopeful," Gracey ventured.

"I'm not. Did I tell you what his favorite story is so far? Martian
dwarfs!"

"You mean he's passing up a yarn like the killing at Pittco, and he
wants to write about that stuff?" Nick asked incredulously.

"You think he's going to step on Pittco's toes?" Tony retorted. "Not
that smart boy! Okay, I might as well get back and make my try." He
started across the darkening desert, and Nick fell into step beside him.
"Why don't you come along?" the doctor suggested. "Maybe you could
talk his language better than I do. You might get a decent meal out of
it, too."

"It's a thought. A good one. Only Marian's probably got supper all
ready by now. I better check in at home first. I don't know—would you
say it was official Council business?"

"That's between you and your hunger," the doctor told him. "What
do you want most—meat or Marian?"

"Damned if I know," Nick admitted, grinning.

"Doc!" It was Jim Kandro, running down the street toward them. "Hey, Tony! I just came from the hospital—looking all over—"

"What's up?"

"The baby! He's having convulsions."

"I'll go right over. Pick up my bag at the hospital, will you?"

Jim set off in one direction, and Tony in the other. "See you later," Nick called out to the doctor's rapidly retreating back.

At the Kandros', he found Polly, near-hysterical, with a struggling infant in her arms. Sunny was obviously in acute discomfort; the veins were standing out on his fuzzy scalp, he was struggling and straining feebly, his belly was distended and his cheeks puffed out uncomfortably.

"How's he been eating?" the doctor demanded scrubbing his hands.

"The way you saw before," said Polly. "Better and better, but just the way you saw before, wiggling and pushing so half the time he was sucking on nothing at all. He was crying and crying, so I fed him three or four times and each time he got more—"

She fell silent as Tony picked up the baby and patted and stroked it. It burped loudly. The alarming red color faded and the tense limbs relaxed. With a whimper Sunny collapsed on the doctor's shoulder and fell asleep before he was back in his crib.

"Here you are, Doc." Jim came in and looked from Polly's empty arms to the quiescent baby in the crib. "I guess you didn't need the bag. What was it?"

"Colic," Tony grinned. "Good, old-fashioned, Earthside colic."

"But you told me—" Jim turned accusingly on his wife.

"And I told Polly," Tony put in quickly. "It doesn't usually happen. Babies don't have to be burped on Mars—*most* of 'em, that is. The mask feeds richer air into a Mars baby's nose so he just naturally breathes through his nose *all* the time and doesn't swallow air and get colic when he feeds. But I guess Sunny had his heart set on a bellyache. Was he crying when he fed, Polly?"

"Why, yes, a little bit. Not really crying, a kind of whimper every now and then."

"That could explain it. Just be sure to bubble him after feeding. Thank the Lord he's nursing."

Sunny was going to be all right; for the first time, Tony really believed it. Somehow that changed the whole dismal picture.

Tony entered his own house and found Graham still sitting in front of his typewriter, not writing now, but reading through a pile of onionskin pages.

"Hi. I was waiting for you."

There was a knock on the door.

"Come in," Tony called out.

"Oh, am I busting in on something?" Nick asked innocently.

"No, of course not. Glad to see you, Doug, this is Nick Cantrella. I don't know if you met him before. He's in charge of maintenance and equipment at the Lab, and a member of our Council. Nick, you know who Doug Graham is."

"Uh-huh. My rival. My wife's only true love."

"And you should see his wife," Tony added.

"This gets more and more interesting. You're not married to that lady pilot by any chance?" Graham extended a greasy hand. "No? Too bad. Join us? We're eating some meat I brought along."

"Don't mind if I do. How's the baby, Tony? Anything really wrong?"

"Yes and no. Colic. Good old colic," the doctor gloated. "It shouldn't happen, but, by God, it's something I know how to cope with; I think the kid's going to be all right. Coffee's ready. Where's the food?"

They munched sandwiches, and had "coffee" which Graham pronounced a very slight improvement over his own efforts. The two Sun Lakers were more than happy with it; it was sweetened with gratings from a brick of sugar produced by the Gunther from his wonder-packed luggage. The same suitcase turned out to hold another bottle of Earthside liquor, and Graham poured drinks all around.

"It's a celebration," the writer insisted, when Tony, remembering his hangover, would have demurred. "I got a week's work done today. Whole first chapter—complete draft of the trip out and the impressions of Marsport!" He fanned out a sheaf of pages covered with single-spaced typing, and corked the bottle.

Nick took a long deep swallow, settled back blissfully on the bunk where he was sitting. "Marcaine," he said at last. "That could explain it."

"What?"

"I've been sitting here imagining I was eating meat and drinking whisky. Can you beat that?" He sipped more slowly this time, savoring the drink, and said determinedly to Graham, "You're just about up to Sun Lake in your notes then?"

"That's right," Graham said. In the silence that followed, he asked brightly, "Say, aren't you the guy who saw the dwarf tracks?"

"Who me? You're sure you weren't thinking of unicorns?"

"Do unicorns leave little footprints?"

"Oh, that. Yeah, I saw something out around the caves in the Rimrock Hills. That's where the kids take the goats to graze."

"Are they allowed to go barefooted around there?" Graham asked.

"Allowed!" Nick exploded. "You haven't been ten years old for quite a long time, have you? How much attention do you think they pay?"

Quite a bit, Tony thought, remembering his talk with Tad, but he didn't bring it up. Out loud he said, "I've got a theory about that. I've been thinking about it since last night, Doug. Maybe you can use it in your book. I'll tell you what I think. I think some kids who weren't supposed to do it went exploring in a cave, and one of them got lost. Then the rest wouldn't admit what happened, and all the search party could find was kid-sized footprints. So we have 'dwarfs'! And a couple of dozen retired prospectors back on Earth are coining money telling lies about them," he finished more sharply than he meant to.

"I guess that squelches me." Graham laughed boisterously, picked up his papers, and stood up. "I better be getting along. Have to find out about getting this stuff radioed out." He started for the door and almost collided with Anna coming in.

"Oh, I'm sorry. I forgot you had company, Tony. They kept me busy all day out at the Lab, and I thought maybe I could get some work done here this evening, but—" She smiled apologetically at Tony and Nick, then turned to Graham. "Were you going out?"

"Shouldn't I?"

"Of course not," said Tony. "Not when Anna's just come in. Stick around, and you'll see something."

"What does she do?" Graham asked. "Song and dance routine? Prestidigitation?"

Nick said from his perch on the wall bunk, "Graham, if you had an ounce of Earthside chivalry in your bloodstream, you'd uncork that bottle and offer the lady a drink."

"You're right. I'll even offer you one." Tony got another glass and the writer poured. Then he turned to Anna, and asked again. "Well, what *do* you do?"

"I'm a glassblower, that's all. Tony likes to watch it."

The doctor said testily, "Anna is also my assistant, if you recall—neither one is a full-time job, so she keeps her equipment here, and combines the two."

For a few minutes the four of them sat talking inconsequentially, the three Sun Lakers answering Graham's endless variety of questions. Finally, Anna got up.

"If I'm going to get any work done, I better get started." She opened the cupboards and began pulling out equipment.

Graham stood up, too. "Well—" He picked up his sheaf of papers. "Tony!"

All three men focused their attention on Anna, who stood facing them, her arms full of assorted junk.

"Tony," she said bluntly, "have you told Mr. Graham about our problem here? Don't you think he might be able to help?"

"Well!" Graham sat down again, and suddenly grinned. "Tell me, what can I do for dear old Sun Lake?"

"You can save our necks," Nick told him soberly. "At least I think you can, if you want to. You're going back on the rocket," he explained, "and that rocket won't have our shipment on it because—actually because—we *did not* steal some marcaine we're accused of stealing. It's not here, so we couldn't find it, and that means Bell will throw a cordon around us on Shipment Day. You know Bell from way back. You could raise such a stink about what he's doing to us—if you wanted to—that there'd be orders recalling him to Earth on the next rocket that comes in. You're big enough to do it. And we don't know any other way."

"You're very flattering," the writer said, "and also too damn brief. I already know that much. Suppose you fill me in on some of the details."

"Bell tramped in three days ago," the doctor began carefully, and went through the story, step by step, not omitting the information he had picked up in Marsport, and reminding Graham at the same time about the Cham's new regulations against marcaine.

"Brenner wants to get his hands on the Sun Lake Lab," Tony wound up. "You got Bell kicked out of a good job once for crooked dealing. You could do it again. Unless Bell's got religion, and I see no sign of it, Brenner could easily hire him to kick us off Mars and then see that Brenner Pharmaceutical got the assets of the busted Sun Lake Colony—including the Lab—in a rigged auction."

The writer pondered, and then told them slowly, "I think I can do something about it. It's a good story, anyhow. The least I can do is try."

Nick let out a wild *Wa-hoo!* and Tony slumped with relief. He looked back to Anna's workbench, smiling—but she was gone.

"Now that that's settled," said Graham. "I want a favor myself."

"Up to but not including my beautiful blond wife," promised Nick fervently.

"If it was women, I'd want that lady airplane pilot. But it isn't women. I still want to get this stuff filed to Marsport by your radio. I'm going to have a crowded schedule before takeoff and every minute I clip off in advance, like getting this stuff typed and microfilmed, will help."

"Sure, pal! Sure!" Nick stood up and shook the writer's hand earnestly. "I'll take you to the radio shack myself and give you the blanchest carte you ever saw!"

Chapter Sixteen

It's a li'l Mars baby,
It's a li'l Mars baby,
It's a li'l Mars baby,
Li'l Mars baby
All—our—own!

IT WAS MIDNIGHt, and Polly sang her song very softly, so as not to awaken Jim. Her hand, on the baby's back, caressed the tiny, clearly defined muscles, rigid now with concentration of effort. Her eyes filled with wonder as she watched Sunny nuzzle awkwardly, but successfully, against her breast.

He was eating! He was swallowing the milk, and not choking on it or spitting it back!

With a touch of awe at the thought that she was the only mother on Mars who had the privilege, she laid the baby over her shoulder and gently patted. Sunny bubbled and subsided. She laid him in the basket and sat watching him raptly. Jim rolled over and muttered, so she decided not to sing her song again. She was hungry, anyway. She touched her lips to the baby's forehead, straightened his mathematically straight blanket and went to the little pantry cupboard in the living-room.

A dish of left over navy beans would settle her for two or three more hours of sleep. She found a spoon and began to eat, happily. She cleaned the dish and licked the spoon, put them away, and started back for bed.

She was halfway to the bedroom door when it happened.

Everything went slower and slower and came to a stop. She was frozen to the floor, giggling—and she was also somewhere else, watching herself giggle. The reddish walls turned the most beautiful apple-green, her favorite color, and put forth vines and branches. They were apple-tree branches, and they began to bear apples that were baby's heads—severed baby's heads, dripping rich, delicious juice. The babies sang her song in a cheeping chorus, and she saw and heard herself giggle and sing with them, and pluck the heads from the branches, open her mouth

"Jim!" she shrieked, and it all collapsed.

Her husband stood in the doorway, looked at her and leaped to catch her.

"Get Dr. Tony," she gasped after she had vomited and he had carried her to a chair. "I think I'm going crazy. There were these— Get Dr. Tony, please, Jim!"

The thought of being left alone horrified her, but she clutched the chair arms, afraid to close her eyes while he was gone. She counted to more than a hundred, lost track, and was starting again when Jim and the doctor burst in. "Polly, what is it? What happened?"

"I don't know, Doctor, *I don't know!* It's all over now, but I don't know if it's going to come back. I *saw* things. I think…Tony, I think I'm crazy."

"You threw up," he reminded her. "Did you eat anything?"

"I was hungry after I nursed Sunny. I ate some beans—cold beans. And then it was horrible. It was like a nightmare, only I was watching myself—"

"This happened right after you ate the beans?" he demanded. "You didn't eat the beans earlier?"

"No, it was right after I fed Sunny, and then I ate, and then it happened. I was frozen to the floor and I watched myself. I was going to do something horrible. I was going to—" She couldn't say it; she remembered it too clearly.

"That's too quick for food poisoning," the doctor said. "You froze, you say. And you watched yourself. And there were hallucinations."

"Yes, like the worst nightmare in the world, yet I was awake."

"Stay with her, Jim. I've got to get something. Can you clean up in here?"

Jim clenched his wife's hand in his big, red fist and then began to mop.

Tony came back with a black box they all knew—the electroencephalograph.

"Look here, Tony," growled Kandro. "If you're thinking that Polly's a drug addict, you're crazy."

Tony ignored him and strapped the electrodes to the woman's head. Three times he took traces, and they were identical. Positive brainwaves.

"You were full of marcaine," he told her flatly. "Where did you get it?"

"Well, I *never*—" and "God damn it all, Doc—" the couple began simultaneously.

Tony relaxed. "I don't need a lie-detector," he said. "It must have been put on the beans. Lord knows how or why."

Polly asked incredulously, "You mean people go through that for *pleasure?*"

"You had the reaction of a well-balanced person. It's the neurotic who enjoys the stuff."

Polly shook her head dazedly.

"But what are we going to *do?*" demanded Jim.

"First thing is to get some bottles and nipples and goat's milk for you. Breast-feeding is out for at least the next week, Polly. There'd be marcaine in your milk. You don't want to wean Sunny now?"

"Oh, *no!*"

Tony smiled. "We'll have to get a breast pump made, too, to keep your supply going. But that can wait till morning."

"But—" protested Jim.

The doctor swung around to face him. "All right, what do *you* suggest we do?"

Jim thought and said hopelessly, "I don't know."

"Neither do I. I'm a doctor, not a detective. All I can do is write a formula for the baby, and get people moving right now turning out the stuff you need."

He stepped into the nursery for a moment to peer at Sunny, in the crib—a beautiful, healthy child. Tony wondered for a moment whether Polly's earlier fantasy about a menacing Martian had also been caused by her food being doped. There had been no nausea that time, but it might have been a smaller dose.

Time enough later to figure all that out; Sunny would be hungry again in a few hours.

"Jim," he directed, "you better beat it over to Anna Willendorf's and tell her we'll need bottles right away. And get some milk while you're out. If you move fast, we'll have time to boil it and make the first formula before Sunny wakes up again."

"Milk?" Jim said, dazed.

"Milk. From one of the goats. Don't you know how?"

"I've milked cows," Kandro said. "Couldn't be much different."

"One other thing," Tony called to Jim, who was already at the door. "Nipples. Get Bob Carmichael for that. I think he can figure out some way."

"Right." Jim closed the door behind him…

They had the milk boiling on the alky stove when Anna arrived with the first bottle. "The others are still cooling," she explained. "What can I do now, Polly?"

"I don't know. Nothing, I guess. The doctor's showing me how to make formula and I suppose that's all there is. It was awfully nice of you to get up to make the bottles. I feel terrible about making so much trouble, but I just—" She trailed off helplessly.

"It wasn't your fault," Anna told her, then asked the doctor, "Do you want me to take over with the formula?"

"There's no need to," Tony told her. "For that matter, you can go back to bed if you want to. There shouldn't be any more trouble tonight."

"I have to go back and get the other bottles later anyhow," she protested. She took over at the stove, showing Polly the procedures of sterilization and measuring involved in the baby's formula.

Jim came from a second trip to the Lab in time to boil up one of the new nipples and fill a bottle before Sunny woke. Polly, still shaken, but determined to behave normally, picked the baby up and changed him, warmed the bottle herself under Anna's watchful eye, and settled herself on a chair with baby and bottle.

Sunny sucked hungrily, wriggled, pushed his mouth sidewise, and then to the other side, sucking all the time. Milk spilled out the side of his mouth as he sucked without swallowing, and turned his reddening face from side to side, squirming desperately.

Tony, suddenly frightened, took a step forward. He could see the trouble clearly enough, but from above, looking down at the baby's face, Polly couldn't possibly see what was happening.

Sunny was trying to make use of the peculiar sidewise suckling he had developed at his mother's breast, but he couldn't wedge his small mouth around the comparatively firm plastic of the new nipple. Tony opened his mouth to speak; in a minute the baby would—

"*Stop it! You're choking—!*"

Polly's hand, holding the bottle shot away from the baby's mouth. Tony whirled to see Anna crumble to the floor, her mouth still open in the drawn-out shriek.

"Jim!" he shouted. "Quick! Take care of her!" Then he turned back again without waiting to see what Kandro did. He lifted the choking, convulsive infant out of Polly's limp arms, turned him upside down, and stroked the small stiff back vigorously. Within seconds, a thick curd of milk dribbled out of the baby's mouth, and the terrible gasping sounds turned into a low, monotonous wailing.

Tony put the baby back in his mother's arms, and turned briefly to look at Anna. Jim had lifted her onto the wall bunk. Tony checked quickly to make sure she hadn't hurt herself.

"Just fainted," he said, puzzled, and gave Kandro instructions to restore consciousness.

Sunny's wailing was turning into a hunger cry. The doctor picked him up again and wrapped him in one of the warm new blankets.

"Where are you taking Sunny?" asked Polly with shrill nervousness.

"To the hospital." He turned to Jim, still standing over the unconscious Anna. "Don't let her leave when she comes to, Jim. I'll be back later."

He went out, carrying the screaming baby in one arm and his black bag in the other.

The walk back to his own house was haunted. The ghost of a newborn baby went with him along the curving street in the dark, a ghost that gasped and choked as Sunny did, twisting in agony until it died again as it had already died a thousand thousand times for Tony; only the first time was the worst, the first baby born and the first one dead in Sun Lake, and he'd had to watch it all, the ghost of a baby that died for want of air...

He went in by the hospital door. He didn't want to see Graham.

Systematically he turned on the lights and assembled his instruments in the sterilizer, turned a heat lamp on the examination table, and stripped off the baby's clothes. This couldn't go on; there had to be an answer to Sunny's troubles, and he was going to find it now, tonight.

Tony examined the child with every instrument and technique in his repertory. He felt it, probed and thumped it, listened to its interior plumbing. He could find nothing that resembled organic trouble. And he could think of no rational explanation for a masked baby breathing through its mouth.

"It's got to be nasal," he said out loud. Three times he had used the otoscope, and three times he had found no obstruction. But—

Carefully Tony slipped the mask off Sunny's nose. He slipped it over the mouth instead, stifling its scream in mid-voice. At least, he thought grimly, the baby would *have* to breathe through the mask now if it wanted to keep on crying. The doctor began to probe delicately into one nostril, and Sunny promptly reacted with the unexpected. Impossible or not, he tried to draw a breath through his exposed nostrils, found an impediment, and began to choke again.

Tony withdrew the slender probe and stared at the gasping, red-faced infant. For just a moment, a clear and frightening picture of the other baby blotted out what was before his eyes—the ghost baby that had come up the street with them. Then he looked at Sunny again and everything began to fall into place.

Sunny was the wrong color.

He should have been blue and he wasn't. He was gasping for air, he couldn't breathe; he should have been oxygen starved. *And he was flushed a bright crimson!*

It wasn't lack of oxygen, then. It was impossible! But it was the only logical answer. Tony removed the mask from the baby's face with trembling hands.

He waited.

It took Sunny less than thirty seconds to do what Tony knew he couldn't do—and most certainly would do. Sunny gasped sharply for a moment. Then his breathing became even, his color turned a normal healthy pink, and he resumed his monotonous hunger cry.

Sunny didn't need an oxygen mask at all to survive on Mars, nor did he need OxEn.

The fact was scientifically paralyzing—the child was adapted not to the rich air of Earth, but the deadly thin atmosphere of Mars!

CHAPTER SEVENTEEN

"SUNNY!" POLLY ran to the table where Sunny still lay crying, wrapped in his blanket again, hungry, angry, and perfectly safe. "Doctor, what did you—how can he—?"

"He's fine," Tony assured her. "Just leave him alone. He's hungry, that's all."

Polly stared, fascinated by the naked-looking baby. "How *can* he breathe without a *mask?*"

"I don't know," Tony said bluntly, "but I tried it and it worked. I guess he's got naturally Marsworthy lungs. Seems to have been the only trouble he had."

"You mean—I thought Marsworthy lungs just meant you *could* breathe Mars air; people like that can breathe Earth air, too, can't they?"

Tony shrugged helplessly. He was licked and didn't care who knew it as long as Sunny was all right. For the time being, it was enough to know that the baby had been breathing through his mouth all along just because he *did* prefer Mars air. He got too much oxygen through the mask, so he didn't use his nose; a simple reversal of the theory on which the mask was based. When his source of Mars air was blocked—first by his mother's breast, and then, when he had learned to adapt to that, by the less flexible plastic nipple—he had to breathe the richer air through his nose, and he turned red, coughed, sputtered, and choked.

"I want to take him back now," said the doctor, "and try another feeding. Bet he'll eat right away." He picked up the baby, firmly refusing to surrender him to his mother, and led the way out of the hospital room and back to the Kandros' house.

Just before they left, Tony heard the steady clicking of Graham's typewriter in the other part of the house. He realized it had been going almost continuously. Obviously, the writer understood that an emergency was in progress, or else he was so busy himself that he didn't want to be bothered, either.

Jim was thunderstruck by his maskless Sunny. Anna seemed to have recovered from her faint. She was a little pale, but otherwise normal, moving about briskly, picking up scattered blankets and baby equipment.

"I tried to make her rest," Jim explained, "but she said she felt fine."

"You take it easy, Anna," the doctor told her.

"I'm perfectly all right," she insisted. "I can't imagine what made me do anything so foolish. I'm awfully sorry."

"Polly, I want *you* to go to bed right away. You've had enough tonight—this morning, rather. Jim, you can handle the baby, can't you? You want to change him and get him ready for his feeding?"

Jim stooped over his son at the wall bunk, his big hands fumbling a little with closures on the small garments. Tony sat down and leaned back, closing his eyes. The baby screamed steadily, demanding nourishment.

"Doc, I still don't get it. How did you figure it out?" Patiently, without opening his eyes, Tony repeated his explanation for Jim.

"I'll take your word for it," the man said finally, "but I'll be darned if I can understand it. Okay, Doc, I *guess* he's all fixed up."

Tony stood up. "Do you know how to fix a bottle? I'll show you."

"Here." Anna was at his elbow. "I thought you might want one."

The big man, looking absurdly cautious, put the bottle to Sonny's mouth. Then he looked up, a tremendous grin on his face and his eyes a little wet. "How do you like that?" he said softly. The little mouth and jaw were working away busily; Sunny was feeding as though he'd been doing it for months.

They watched while he took a whole three and a half ounces, and then fell asleep, breathing quietly and regularly.

"A Mars child," said Anna gently, looking down at Sunny. "Jim, you have a real Mars child."

"Looks that way," said Kandro, beaming.

"Jim," said the doctor, "somebody ought to stay up and keep an eye on Sunny tonight, but I'm beat. And Polly's got to get some sleep. Will you do it?"

"Sure, Doc," said the father, not taking his happy eyes off the child.

"You get your parka, Anna, and don't argue with the doctor," Tony said. "I'm going to take you home and see if I can find out what made you pull that swoon. Come on…"

"I do have a headache," she admitted when they reached her house. "Probably all I need is a little sleep. I haven't been living right." She tried a smile, but it didn't come off.

"None of us have," Tony reminded her. He studied her and decided against aspirin. He selected a strong sedative, and shot it into her arm. Within a minute she relaxed in a chair and exhaled long and gratefully: "Better," she said.

"Feel like talking?"

"I-I think I ought to sleep."

"Then just give me the bare facts." He ran his fingers over her head. "No blows. Was it a hangover?"

"Yes," she said defiantly.

"Very depraved. From the one drink you had with us?"

"From—from— Oh, hell!" That came from the heart, for Anna never swore.

"I've had enough mysteries for one night, Anna. Talk."

"Maybe I ought to," she said unwillingly. "Only a fool tells a lie to his doctor or the truth to his lawyer, and so on." She hesitated. "I've got a trick mind. All those people who think they're psychic—they are. I am, but more. It doesn't matter, does it?"

"Go on."

"I didn't know about it myself for a long time. It's not like mindreading; it's not that clear. I was always—oh, sensitive, but I didn't understand it at first, and then later on it seemed to get more and more pronounced. I—haven't told anyone about it before. Not anyone at all."

She looked at him appealingly. Tony reassured her, "You know you can trust me."

"All right, I began to realize what it was when I was about twenty. That's why I became, of all things, a glassblower. If you had to listen to the moods and emotions of people, you'd want a job far away from everything in a one-man department, too. That's why I came to Mars. It was too—too noisy on Earth."

"And that's why you're the best assistant I ever had, with or without an M.D. or R.N. on your name," said the doctor softly.

"You're easy to work with." She smiled. "Most of the time, that is. Sometimes, though, you get so *angry*—"

He thought back, remembering the times she'd been there before he had called, or had left quickly when she was in the way, handed him what he needed before he actually *thought* about it.

"Please don't get upset about it, Tony. I'd hate to have to stop working with you now. I don't know what you *think,* just what you—*feel,* I guess. There are a lot of people like that, really; you must have sensed it in me a long time back. It isn't really so very strange," she pleaded. "I'm just a little—a little more that way, that's all."

"I don't see why I should get upset about it." He tried to soothe her, and realized sickeningly that it was a useless effort. He literally could not conceal his feelings this time. He stopped trying. "You must realize how hard I try not to show I'm even angry. It is a little disconcerting to find out—I'll get used to it. Just give me time." He was thoughtful for a moment. "How does it work? Do you know?"

"Not really. I 'hear' people's feelings. And—people seem to be more aware of my moods than they are of other people's. I—well, the way I first became aware of it was when somebody tried to—assault me, back on Earth, in Chicago. I was very young then, not quite twenty. It was one of those awful deserted streets, and he ran faster than I could and caught up with me. Something sort of turned on—I don't know how to say it. I was sending instead of receiving, but sending my emotion—which, naturally, was a violent mixture of fear and disgust—each more strongly than—than people usually can. I'm afraid I'm not making myself clear."

"No wonder," he said heavily. "The language isn't built for experiences like that. Go on."

"He fell down and flopped on the sidewalk like a fish, and I ran on and got to a busy street without looking back. I read the papers, but there wasn't anything about it, so I suppose he was all right afterward."

She stopped talking and jumped up restlessly. For quite a while she stood staring out of her window, toward the dark reaches of *Lacus Solis.*

Finally she said in a strained voice, "Please, Tony, it's not really as bad as that sounded. I can't send all the time; I can't do it mostly." She turned back to face him, and added more naturally, "Usually, people aren't as—open—as he was. And I guess I have to be pretty worked up, too. I tried to send tonight, and I couldn't do it. I tried awfully hard. That's why I had that headache."

"Tonight?"

"I'll tell you about that in a minute. Right now I want—well, I told you I never told anyone about this before. It's important to me, Tony, *terribly* important, to make you understand. You're the first person I ever wanted to have understand it, and if you keep on being frightened or unhappy about it, I just don't know—"

She paused. "Let me tell you about it my way. I'll try to ignore whatever you feel while I'm telling it, and maybe when I'm done it will all be all right.

"When that happened in Chicago—what I told you about—I had a job in an office. There was a girl I had to work with who didn't like me. It was very unpleasant. Every day for a month I tried to turn that 'send-receive' switch and transmit a calm, happy feeling to her, but I never could make it work. No matter how hard I tried, I couldn't get anything over to her. I knew what she felt, but her emotions were closed to mine. She didn't want to feel anything from me, so she didn't. Do you understand that? It's important, because it's true; you can protect yourself from that part of it. You believe me, don't you, Tony?"

He didn't answer right away. He had to be absolutely certain in his own mind, because she would know. It would be far worse to tell her anything that wasn't true than to say nothing. Finally he got up and walked over to her, but he didn't dare speak.

"Tony," she said. "you're—oh, please don't be embarrassed and difficult about it, but you're so *good!* That's what I meant, you're easy to work with. Most people are petty and a lot of them are mean. The things they feel aren't nice; they're mostly bitchy. But you—even when you're angry, it's a big honest kind of anger. You don't want to hurt people, or get even, or take advantage of them. You're honest, and generous, and *good.* And now I've said too much!"

He shook his head. "No, you didn't. It's all right. It really is."

There were tears shining in her eyes. Standing over her, he reached mechanically for a tissue from his bag, tilted her head up, and wiped her eyes as if she were a child.

"Now tell me more," he said, "and don't worry about how I feel. What happened tonight? Tell me about the headache. And the fainting—was that part of it too? Of course! What an idiot I am! The baby was choking and scared, and you screamed. You screamed and said to stop it."

"Did I? I wasn't sure whether I thought it or said it. That was strange, the whole business. It was terrible, somebody who hurt awfully all over and couldn't breathe, and was going to—to burst if he couldn't, and that didn't seem to make sense—and terribly hungry, and terribly frustrated, and—I didn't know who it was, because it was so strong. Babies don't have such 'loud' feelings. I guess it was the reflex of fear of dying, except Sunny is very loud, anyhow. When he was being born—"

She shuddered involuntarily. "I was awfully glad you didn't think to ask me to stay in there with you. When you sent Jim out, I talked to him, and sort of—concentrated on 'listening' to him, and then, with the door closed, it was all right. Anyhow, you want to know about tonight. The baby topped it off. I didn't think that would have made me faint, by itself, but I was working in there, in the same room with Douglas Graham for an hour or more, and—"

"Graham!" Tony broke in. "Do you mean to say he *dared* to—"

"Why, Tony, I didn't know you cared!"

For the first time that evening, she laughed easily. Then, without giving him time to think about how his outburst had given him away, she added, "He didn't do anything. It was—it was about what he was writing, I *think*. I know what he was feeling. He was angry and disgusted and *contemptuous*. He hurt inside himself, and he felt the way people do when they hurt somebody else. And it seemed to be all tied up with the story he was writing. It was a story about the Colony, Tony, and I got worried and frightened. If only I could be sure. See, that's the trouble. I didn't know whether to tell somebody or not, and I tried and tried to 'send' to him, but he wasn't open at all, and the only thing that happened was that I got that headache."

"Then when you came over to the Kandros'," Tony finished for her, "and the baby had all that trouble, of course you couldn't take it. Tell me more about Graham. I understand that you're not sure; tell me what you *think*, and why."

"When Jim woke me up, we went back to your place together, and Graham was working there," she said. "He asked me what the excitement was all about and I told him. He listened, kept asking questions, got every little detail out of me, and all the time he was feeling that hurt and anger. Then I started to work and he began banging away on his typewriter. And those thoughts got stronger and stronger till they made me dizzy, and then I started trying to fight back, to send—and I couldn't. That's all there was to it."

"And you can't be certain what it was that he was feeling that way about?"

"How could I?"

"Well, then," he said, with a laugh of relief, "there's nothing at all to worry about. You made a natural enough mistake. Those feelings of his weren't directed *against* the Colony at all, Anna. Earlier tonight, after you left, Graham promised to help us. He was writing a story about the spot we're in, that's all, and I know that he felt all the things you've described, but not about us, about Bell."

"It could be." She seemed a little dazed. "It didn't feel that way, but, of course, it could." She sighed and leaned back in her chair. "Oh, Tony, I'm so glad I told you. I didn't know *what* to do, and I was sure it was something vicious he was writing about the Colony."

"Well, you can relax now. Maybe I'll let you go to bed." He took her hands and pulled her to her feet. "We'll work it out, even if I have to take a few new experiences in stride. Believe me, we'll work it out."

She looked up at him, smiling gently. "I think so, too, Tony."

He could have let her hands go, but he didn't. Instead, he flushed as he realized that even now she was aware of all his feelings. There were tears shining in her eyes again, and this time he couldn't reach for a tissue. He leaned down and kissed her damp eyelids.

A thousand thoughts raced through his mind. Earth, and Bell, and the Colony, now or forever or never. That time in the plane, thinking of Bea. Anna—Anna always there at his side, helping, understanding.

"Anna," he said. He had never liked the name. "Ansie." There had been a little girl, a very long time ago, when he was a child, and her name had been Ansie.

He released her other hand and cupped her upturned face in both of his. His head bent to hers, slowly and tenderly. There was no fierceness here, only the hint of growing passion.

When he lifted his lips from hers, he laughed and said quietly, "It saves words, doesn't it?"

"Yes." Her voice was small and husky. "Yes, it does—dear."

If his mind was "open," he might feel what she did. Cautiously and warily, he reached out to her, with his arms and with his mind. He needed no questions and no answers now.

"Ansie!" he whispered again, and lifted her slender body.

CHAPTER EIGHTEEN

TAD'S LEFT EAR itched; he let it. "Operator on duty will not remove headphones under any circumstances until relieved—" There was a good hour before Gladys Porosky would show up to take over.

"Mars Machine Tool to Sun Lake," crackled the headset suddenly. He glanced at the clock and tapped out the message time on the log sheet in the typewriter before him.

"Sun Lake to Mars Machine Tool, I read you, G.A.," he said importantly.

"Mars Machine Tool to Sun Lake, message. Brenner Pharmaceutical to Marsport. Via Mars Machine Tool, Sun Lake, Pittco Three. Request reserve two cubic meters cushioned cargo space outgoing rocket. Signed Brenner. Repeat, two cubic meters. Ack, please, G.A."

Tad said, "Sun Lake to Mars Machine Tool," and read back painstakingly from the log: "Message. Brenner Pharmaceutical to Marsport. Via Mars Machine Tool, Sun Lake, Pittco Three. Signed Brenner. Repeat, two cubic meters. Received okay. T. Campbell, Operator, end."

Tad's fingers were flying over the typewriter keyboard. Mimi and Nick would want to know how the rocket was filling up. The trick was to delay your estimated requirements to the last possible minute and then reserve a little more than you thought you'd need. Reserve too early and you might be stuck with space you couldn't fill but had to pay for. Reserve too late and there might be no room for your stuff until the next rocket.

"Mars Machine Tool to Sun Lake, end," said the headset. Tad started to raise Pittco's operator, the intermediate point between Sun Lake and Marsport, to boot the message on the last stage of its journey.

"Sun Lake to Pittco Three," he said into the mike. No answer. He went into "the buzz," droning, "Pittco Three, Pittco Three, Pittco Three, Sun Lake—"

"Pittco Three to Sun Lake, I read you," came at last, mushily, through the earphones. Tad was full of twelve-year-old scorn. Half a minute to ack, and then probably with a mouthful of sandwich! "Sun Lake to Pittco Three," he said. "Message. Brenner Pharmaceutical to Marsport. Via Mars Machine Tool, Sun Lake, Pittco Three. Request reserve two cubic meters cushioned cargo space outgoing rocket. Signed Brenner. Repeat, two cubic meters. Ack, please, G.A."

"Pittco to Sun Lake, message received. Charlie Dyer, Operator, out."

Tad fumed at the Pittco man's sloppiness and make-it-up-as-you-go procedure. Be a fine thing if everybody did that—messages would be garbled, short stopped, rocket-loading fouled up, people and cargoes miss their planes.

He tapped out on the log sheet: *Pittco Operator C. Dyer failed to follow procedure, omitted confirming repeat. T. Campbell.* He omitted Dyer's irksome use of "out" instead of "end" and the other irregularities, citing only the legally important error. That was just self-protection; if there were any errors in the final message, the weak spot on the relay could be identified. But Tad was uncomfortably certain that Dyer, if the report ever got back to him, would consider him an interfering brat.

He bet Mr. Graham's last message had got respectful handling from Pittco, in spite of the pain-in-the-neck Phillips Newscode it had been couched in. They all wanted Graham. Tad had received half a dozen messages for the writer extending the hospitality of this industrial colony or that. The man had good sense to stick with Sun Lake, the boy thought approvingly. There was this jam with the rocket and the commissioner, but the Sun Lakers were unquestionably the best bunch of people on Mars.

"Pittco to Sun Lake," said Dyer's voice in the earphones.

"Sun Lake to Pittco, I read you, G.A.," snapped Tad.

"Pittco Three to Pittco One, message. Via Sun Lake, Mars Machine Tool, Brenner Pharmaceutical, Distillery Mars, Rolling Mills. Your outgoing rocket cargo space requirements estimate needed here thirty-six hours. Reminder down-hold cushioned space requests minimum account new tariff schedule. Signed. Hackenburg for Reynolds. Repeat, thirty-six hours. Ack, please, G.A."

Huh! Dyer repeated numbers on *his* stuff, all right! Tad acked and booted the message on. The machine shop in the "canal" confluence would get it, then the drug factory in the highlands dotted with mar-caine weed, then the distillery among its tended fields of wiregrass, then the open hearth furnaces and rolling mills in the red taconite range, and at last Pittco One, in the heart of the silver and copper country.

He hoped he wouldn't have to handle any of Graham's long code jobs. Orders were to co-operate fully with the writer, but even Harve Stillman, who'd taken Graham's story on his rocket trip and Marsport, had run into trouble with it. Tad leafed through the material to the coded piece by Graham and shuddered.

It was okay, the boy supposed, for Earth, where you didn't want somebody tapping a PTM transmission beam and getting your news story, but why did the guy have to show off on Mars where the only way out was by rocket and you couldn't get scooped?

"Marsport 18 to Pittco Three," he heard faintly in the earphones. Automatically he ran his finger down the posted list of planes. Marsport 18 was a four-engine freighter belonging to the Marsport Hauling Company.

"Pittco Three to Marsport 18, I read you, G.A."

"Marsport 18 to Pittco, our estimated time of arrival is thirteen-fifty. Thirteen-fifty. We're bringing in your mail. End."

"Pittco to Marsport 18, O.K., E.T.A. is thirteen-fifty and I'll tell Mr. Hackenburg. End."

Mail, thought Tad enviously. All Sun Lake ever got was microfilmed reports from the New York office and business letters from customers. Aunt Minnie and Cousin Adelbert wouldn't write to you unless you wrote to them; and Sun Lake couldn't lay out cash for space-mail stamps.

Tad's ear itched. One thing he missed, he admitted to himself in a burst of candor, and he'd probably have to go on missing it. The Sun Lake Society of New York couldn't spontaneously mail him the latest *Captain Crusher Comix*.

He had read to tatters Volume CCXVII, Number 27, smuggled under his sweater from Earth. And to this day he hadn't figured out how the captain had escaped from the horrible jam he'd been in on Page 64. There had been a Venusian Crawlbush on his right, a Martian Dwarf on his left, a Rigelian Paramonster drifting down from above and a Plutonian Bloodmole burrowing up from below. Well, the writers of Captain Crusher knew their business, thought Tad, though they certainly didn't know much about Mars—the *real* Mars. Their hero never seemed to need OxEn or clothing any warmer than hose and cape when on a Martian adventure. And he was always stumbling over dwarfs and dead cities and lost civilizations.

Bunk, of course. Dwarfs, dead cities, and lost civilizations would make Mars a more interesting place for a kid. But when a person grows up, other things mattered more than excitement. Things like doing a good job and knowing it. Things like learning. Getting along. Probably, Tad thought uncomfortably, getting married some day.

"Mars Machine Tool to Sun Lake. Sun Lake, Sun Lake, Sun Lake, Mars Machine Tool, Sun Lake—"

"Sun Lake to Mars Machine Tool, I read you, G.A.," Tad snapped, peeved.

The operator might have waited just a second before he went in to the buzz.

"Mars Machine Tool to Sun Lake, message. Pittco One to Pittco Three. Via Rolling Mills, Distillery Mars, Brenner Pharmaceutical, Mars Machine Tool, Sun Lake. Outgoing rocket cargo space requirements are: ballast, thirty-two cubic meters; braced antishift, twelve point seventy-five cubic meters; glass-lined tank, fifteen cubic meters; cushioned, one point five cubic meters. Regret advise will require steerage space one passenger. F.Y.I., millwright's helper Chuck Kelly disabled by marcaine addiction."

The repeats followed and Tad briskly receipted. He raised Pittco Three and booted the message, grinning at a muffled "God damn it!" over the earphones as he droned out the bad news about Kelly. Steerage passenger space didn't come as high as cushioned cargo cubage; a steerage passenger was expected to grab a stanchion, hang on, and take his lumps during a rough landing; but it was high enough.

Sun Lake couldn't afford cushioned cubage, ever, and settled for braced antishift. Sometimes crates gave and split under the smashing accelerations, but the cash you had to lay out for cargo-protecting springs, hydraulic systems, and meticulous stowage by the supercargo himself wasn't there. It meant a disgruntled customer every once in a while, but the tariffs made you play it that way.

The door behind him opened and closed. "Gladys?" he asked. "You're early."

"It's me, sonny," said a man's voice—Graham's. "You mind filing a little copy for me?"

The newsman handed him a couple of onionskin pages. "Phillips Newscode," he said. "Think you can handle it?"

"I guess so," said Tad unhappily. "We're supposed to co-operate with you." Blankly he looked at the sheets and asked, "Why bother to code it, though?"

"It saves space, for one thing. You get about five words for one. 'GREENBAY,' for instance, means 'An excited crowd gathered at the scene.' 'THREEPLY' means 'In spite of his, or their, opposition.' And, for another thing, what's the point of my knowing the code if I never use it?" He grinned to show he was kidding.

Tad ignored the grin and remarked, "I thought that was it."

He entered the time in the log and said into the mike: "Sun Lake to Pittco Three." Pittco acked.

"Sun Lake to Pittco Three, long Phillips Newscode message. Sun Lake to Marsport. Via Pittco Three. Message: Microfilm following text and hold for arrival Douglas Graham Marsport and pickup at Administration Building. GREENBAY PROGRAHAM SUNLAKE STOP POSTTWO MARSEST BRIGHTEST ARGUABLEST MARSING DOPEBORT FELKIL UNME SUNLAKE HOCFO-CUS ETERS STOP SAPQUISFACT ERQUICK..."

Graham heard the last of the story go out and saw the kid note down the acknowledgment in the log.

"Good job," the Gunther said. "Thanks, fella."

Outside, the chilly night air fanned his face. It had been a dirty little trick to play on the boy. They'd give him hell when they found out, but the message had to clear and that Stillman knew a little Phillips—enough to wonder and ask questions.

Graham took a swig from his pocket flask and started down the street. He'd needed the drink, and he needed a long walk. It was surgery, he told himself, but surgery wasn't always pleasant for the surgeon. That doctor might be able to understand if he could only step back and see the thing in perspective. As it was, Tony obviously believed Mrs. Kandro's absurd story about somebody doping the beans.

The writer grinned sardonically. What a cesspool Mars must be if even these so-called idealists were so corrupted! Marcaine addiction by a brand-new mother, theft of a huge quantity of marcaine clearly traced to the Colony. The doctor would hate him and think him two-faced, which he was. It was part of the job. He was going to start an avalanche; a lot of people would hate him for it.

An impeccable, professional hatchet job on Sun Lake was the lever that would topple the boulder to start the avalanche. The public-relations boys of the industrials used to be newspapermen themselves, and they could pick their way through Phillips. The word would be passed like lightning. They'd learn, to their horror, that this wasn't going to be a cheerful travelog quickie like his last two or three; that Graham was out for blood. The coded dispatch would be talked over and worried over in most of Mars' administration buildings tonight. They would debate whether! he was going to put the blast on all the colonies. But they'd note that he pinned all the guilt so far on Sun Lake, not mentioning specifically that the abortion and the prostitution had occurred at Pittco.

So, by tomorrow morning, he'd let one of the industrials send a plane for him. He'd been playing hard to get for two days—long enough. He'd put on his jovial mask and they'd fall all over themselves dishing out the dirt on each other. He'd make it a point to pass through Brenner Pharmaceutical. Quasi-legal operators like Brenner always knew who was cutting corners. And Bell—what tills did he have his hand in?

Graham knew there wasn't another newsman alive who could swing it—the first real story to come out of Mars besides press handouts from the industrials. And the planet was rotten-ripe for it.

Once he'd been a green reporter, lucky enough to break the Bell scandal. He'd actually been sorry for the crook. There'd been a lot of changes since. It was funny what happened to you when you got into the upper brackets.

First you grabbed and grabbed. Women, a penthouse with a two-acre living-room, silk shirts "built" for you instead of the nylon all the paycheck stiffs wore, "beefsteaks" broiled over bootleg charcoal made of real wood from one of Earth's few thousand acres of remaining trees.

You grabbed and grabbed, and then you got sick of grabbing. You felt empty and blank and worked like hell to make yourself think you were happy. And then, if you were lucky, you found out who you were.

Graham had found out that he—the youngest one, underfed, the one the big boys ganged upon for snitching, the one the cop called a yellow little liar, the one nobody liked, the one who always got his head knuckled when they played Nigger Inna Graveyard—yes, he had power. It was the monstrous energy of Earth's swarming billions. If you could reach them, you could have them. You could slash down what was rotten and corrupt: a thieving banker, a bribed commissioner, a Mars Colony.

Under the jovial mask it hurt when they called you a sensationalist, said you were unanalytical, had no philosophy.

Graham stumbled and took a swig from his flask.

Who had to have a philosophy? What was wrong with exposing crackpots and crooks? The first real news story to come out of Mars would break up the Sun Lake Colony. Some good would go with the bad; the surgeon had no choice. That Kandro woman and her baby! The child belonged on Earth. And it would go there.

"Hey!" he said. Where the hell was the doctor anyway? Wandering in the desert, high as a kite on his expected triumph. His feet had led him down the Colony street, along the path to the airfield, past it, and a few kilometers toward the Rimrock Hills. He blamed it on the Mars gravity. Your legs didn't tire here, for one thing. The radio shack light was plain behind him; dimmer and off to the left of it shone the windows of the Lab, merged in one beacon.

The radio shack light went out and then on again. A moment later, so did the light from the Lab.

"Power interruption," he said. "Or I blinked."

It happened again, first the radio shack and then the Lab. And then it happened once more.

The writer took out his flask and gulped. "Who's out there?" he yelled. "I'm Graham!"

There wasn't any answer, but something came whistling out of the darkness at him, striking his parka and falling to the ground. He fumbled for it while still trying to peer through the night for whatever had passed between him and the lights of Sun Lake.

"What do you want?" he yelled into the darkness hysterically. "I'm Graham! The writer! Who are you?"

Something whizzed at him and hit his shoulder.

"Cut that out!" he shrieked, and began to run for the lights of Sun Lake. He had taken only a few steps when something caught at his leg and he floundered onto the ground. The next and last thing he felt was a paralyzing blow on the back of his head.

CHAPTER NINETEEN

TONY WOKE UP in time for breakfast, an achievement in itself. He'd had some hundred and fifty minutes of sleep after a long and hard day, and that interrupted by emergency, crisis, and triumph.

He washed without noticing the stench of the alcohol. He noted the time; good thing there was no Lab inspection to do this morning. He noticed the closed bedroom door; good thing he'd so hospitably given up his own bed to Graham, considering the unexpected turn of events the night before. He threw his parka over his shoulders and stepped out into the wan sunlight, oblivious to the lingering chill; good thing he—

Good thing he could still laugh at himself, he decided. What was the old saw about all the world loving a lover? Nothing to it—it was the lover who loved the whole world. *Love, lover, loving,* he rolled the words around in his mind, trying to tell himself that nothing had really changed. All the old problems were still there, and a new one, really, taken on.

But that wasn't so. Graham had spent half the night writing his promised story. Sunny Kandro was all right at last. And Anna—Ansie— a problem? He could remember thinking in the distant past, as long as two days ago, that such an involvement would present problems, but he couldn't for the life of him remember what they were supposed to have been.

He went in to breakfast, not trying to conceal his exuberance, and sat down between Harve Stillman and Joe Gracey.

"What's got into you?" Harve asked.

"Something *good* happen?" Gracey demanded.

Tony nodded. "The Kandro baby," he explained, using the first thing that popped into his head. "Jim woke me up last night. Polly was—was having trouble with the baby," he hastily amended the story.

He'd have to tell Gracey about the marcaine. There *was* a problem after all, but this wasn't the place for it; a Council meeting after breakfast maybe.

"You know we've been having feeding trouble all along," he explained. "I found the trouble last night. I don't understand it, but it works. I took Sunny's mask off."

"You *what?*"

"Took his mask off; he doesn't need it. Eats fine without it, too. Trouble was, he couldn't breathe through his mouth and eat at the same time."

"Well, I'll be— How do you figure it?"

"Hey, there's a story for the Gunther," Harve suggested. " 'Medical Miracle on Mars,' and all that stuff. Where is he anyhow?"

"Still sleeping, I guess. The bedroom door was closed."

"Did you talk to him last night?" Gracey asked.

Tony attacked his plate of fried beans, washed them down with a gulp of "coffee," and told the other man about Graham's promise. "He was up half the night writing, too. I heard him while I was examining the baby."

"Did he show it to you?"

"Not yet. He was asleep when I got back."

Harve pushed back his chair with a grunt of satisfaction. "I feel better already." He grinned. "First decent meal I've had in days. What's the program for today, Doc? You going to need me on radiological work?"

"I don't think so. I'll let you know if we do, after Joe and I get together with the others. Got time for a meeting after breakfast?" he asked the agronomist, and Gracey nodded.

"Okay, I'll be in the radio shack if you want me," Harve said. "The kids took over all day yesterday. Don't like to leave them too long on their own."

"Right. But I don't think we'll need you."

That marcaine business—how in all that was holy, the doctor wondered, did anybody get marcaine onto Polly's beans? After all the searching, in the middle of the hunt, who would do it? Why? And above all, *how?*

Maybe one of the others would have an angle on it…

"One thing I'm glad about," Gracey said soberly. "We *did* make a thorough search. Whatever happens from here on out, at least we've proved to our own satisfaction that nobody in Sun Lake stole the stuff."

"That's nice to know," Mimi agreed with considerably less feeling. "But frankly, I'd almost feel better if we *had* found it. I'd gladly turn the bum who took it over to Bell's tender mercies, if it was one of us. This way, we have to depend on Graham. You're *sure* he's with us?" She looked questioningly from the doctor to the electronics man.

"How sure can you get?" Nick shrugged. "He said so. Now we wait to see his story, that's all."

"I don't think we have to worry about that," Tony said. He couldn't tell them any more. He was sure himself, but how could he explain without giving away Anna's secret? "Look," he went on briskly, "there's something else we *do* have to think about. I told you about Sunny Kandro, Joe. There's more to it than what I said at breakfast."

Nick and Mimi both sat forward with new interest, as Tony repeated the news about the removal of Sunny's mask. He cut off their questions. "I didn't tell you how it started, though. Jim came to get me, not for the baby, but for Polly."

A sharp rap on the door stopped him. Harve Stillman walked in. His face was grim; he carried a familiar sheaf of onionskin pages in his hands.

"What's the matter, Harve?" Mimi demanded. "Aren't you supposed to be on the shift in the radio shack?"

"That's right. I walked out."

"No relief?" she snapped. "Are you sick?"

"I'm sick, all right. And it doesn't make any difference now whether the radio's manned or not." He slapped the onionskin onto the table, and threw down on top of it two sheets of closely written radio log paper. "There you are, folks, have a look. It's all down in black and white. That's the translation on the log sheets. The bastard filed it in Phillips, so Tad wouldn't know what he was sending. When I think what a sucker I was, letting him pump me about who knew newscode around here! Go on, read it."

Mimi picked up the sheets and glanced at the penciled text. Her face went white.

"Hey," Nick protested, "could you maybe let us in on it?"

"Certainly," she smiled bitterly. "This is the story written for us by D. Graham, your friend and mine: 'I was greeted by a frightened crowd on my arrival at Sun Lake, and no wonder. After two days in this community, I am able to reply to the heads-in-the-clouds idealists who claim that on Mars lies the hope of the human race. My reply is that on Mars I immediately came face-to-face with drunkenness, prostitution, narcotics, criminal abortion, and murder. It is not for me to say whether this means that Sun Lake Colony, an apparent center of these activities, should be shut down by law and its inmates deported to Earth. But I do know—' "

"That's crazy!'" Nick broke in. "I heard him say myself—" He stood up angrily.

Tony reached out a hand to restrain him. "He didn't promise a damn thing, Nick. We just heard it that way. He said he'd do a story, that's all."

"That's enough for me," Cantrella replied. "He promised, and he's by God going to keep his promise."

"Sit *down*, Nick," Mimi interrupted. "Beating Graham up isn't going to solve anything. Harve, you get back on duty, and buzz one of the kids to go over to Tony's and collect Graham. If he's asleep, tell them to wake him up. We'll go through the rest of this while we're waiting."

Harve slammed the door behind him, and Mimi turned to the others. "I'm sorry. I should have checked with you first. Every time something goes wrong, I start giving orders as if I owned the place. Here." She handed the sheets to Joe Gracey. "You look calm. You read it."

Joe took the papers and went on where she had stopped before.

"He can't do that!" Nick protested furiously, when Joe finished. "That story is full of lies! The murder wasn't here. Neither was most of the other stuff. How can he—"

"He *did*," Tony pointed out. "How much convincing do you need?"

"It's carefully worded," Gracey said. "Most of it isn't lies at all, just evasions and implications."

"We've got to assume he's smart enough to write a libel-proof story." Mimi had recovered her briskness. "There's one place I think he slipped, though. Can I see those sheets of Graham's again, Joe?"

Her eyes were shining when she looked again. "We've got him!" she said. "I'm sure of it! Let's call in O'Donnell and get his opinion on it. This stuff about Polly." She read aloud: " '...the young mother of a new-born baby, unable to feed her infant because of her hopeless addiction to marcaine. This reporter was present at a midnight emergency when the Colony's doctor was called to save the child from the ministrations of its hysterical mother...' Tony, you can testify to that!"

"I don't know," said the doctor painfully. "Sure, I realize Polly's not an addict, but—that's what I was starting to tell you when Harve came in. That's what Jim got me up for last night. Polly was sick, and there's no doubt that it was a dose of marcaine that was responsible."

"*What?*"

"*Polly?*"

"But she couldn't be the one. She was—"

"How did Graham find out about it?"

"We were both asleep when Kandro came in," he explained, "and the noise woke Graham too. I didn't see him again myself, but I heard him typing when I was in the hospital with the baby. And Ans—Anna told me she talked to him while she was making the bottles. She had no reason to hold back any information. I told her myself that he was writing a friendly story."

"Well, that fixes us, but good. Where did Polly get the stuff?" Nick demanded.

"I've been trying to figure that myself," Tony said. "I don't think *she* got it. Her reactions were not those of a marcaine user, and I'd swear she was shocked when I diagnosed it. The stuff was put there—and don't ask me who, or why, because I can't even begin to guess."

"Well, we've got our hands full," Mimi said thoughtfully. "Where do we start? It seems to me the same answer is going to settle two of our problems. Where did Polly's marcaine come from, and how are we ever going to get out of this impossible situation with Bell?"

"That's not all," Nick added grimly. "We can solve both of those, and still get booted off Mars when this story breaks."

"That's a separate matter. All I can do about it is try to talk to Graham—or prove to him that at least part of the story is libelous. Come in," Mimi called, in answer to a knock outside.

Gladys Porosky pushed the door open and announced breathlessly, "We can't find him. We looked all over and he's not any place."

"Graham?" Tony jumped to his feet. "He was asleep in my bedroom; I left him there. He has to be around."

Gladys shook her head. "We opened the door when he didn't answer, and he wasn't there. Then we scattered; all the kids have been looking. He's not at the Lab, or in the fields, and he's not in any of the houses. Nobody's seen him all morning."

"Thanks, Gladys," Mimi cut her short. "Will you try to find Jack O'Donnell for me? Ask him to come over here."

"Okay." She slammed out of the door, leaving a whirlwind of babble and excitement behind her.

"I suppose he's skipped," Tony said. "Probably messaged one of the industrial outfits in that damn code of his, and got picked up during the night. His bags are still at my place, though—I saw them this morning. That's funny."

"What's luggage to a guy who can write like that?" Gracey asked. "He can get all the luggage he wants by wiping out another plague spot like us."

O'Donnell came in, and they waited in tense silence while the ex-lawyer read through Harve's penciled translation. "Only possible libelous matter I see is about the marcaine-addict mother. What's all that?"

They told him, and he shook his head. "No more chance in a court of law than a snowball in hell," he said flatly.

"But I don't care *how* he worded it. The story's not true."

"How many stories are? If truth or justice made any difference in the Earth courts, I wouldn't be here. I loved the law. The way it looked in the books, that is. I guess I'll have to pass my bar examinations all over again. Mars is under the Pan State, but I suppose this constitutes interrupted residence anyway."

"Big fat chance you'll have of getting to take your bar exams after that smear," said Gracey. "I'm not kidding myself about getting to teach college again. If I can get some money together, I'm going to try commercial seaweeds."

"God help Sargasso Limited," said Nick Cantrella. "And God help Consolidated Electronic when I start my shop again in Denver. It took them three months to run me into bankruptcy last trip around, but I'll get them up to four this time. They can't stand much of that kind of punishment."

"Let's not jump to conclusions," Mimi said, with the quiver back in her determinedly businesslike voice. "Let's assume Graham's skipped and the story's going through. We might still be able to hang on if we can square ourselves with Bell."

"Bell and Graham have no use for each other," Tony said. "Maybe this will make Bell easier to deal with."

"That I doubt. Let's figure on the worst. Suppose we *can't* convince Bell. We'll have two possible courses of action. We can sell out fast. From what I understand of this situation, I'm sure that the Commissioner would find a legal loophole for us on the marcaine deal if we decided to sell to, for instance, Brenner. If we do that, we can pay off what money we owe on Earth, book passage for our members, and with luck, have a few dollars left over to divide between us." She smiled humorlessly. "You might even have a capital investment of five or ten dollars, Nick, to start working on Con-Electron."

"Good enough," he said. "It'll give me courage—if I can still find a bar with a five-buck beer, that is."

"That," Mimi went on, "would be the smart thing to do. But there's another way. We can hang on through the cordon, hoping to prove our point. It leaves us some hope, but it leaves us penniless, even if we manage to stick out the six months. Whatever cash or credit we have on hand we'll have to pay out for OxEn. Don't think Bell is going to let us have the stuff free. Meanwhile, our accounts payable keep coming due, and accumulating interest. There's a good chance that long before the six months are up we'll be forced into involuntary bankruptcy. That's how Pittco got Economy Metals last year. We'd then be shipped back to Earth as distress cases, with a prior lien on our future earnings, if any."

Mimi sat down and Tony studied her handsome face as if he were seeing it for the first time. She'd been way up in the auditing department of a vast insurance company once. It would be hard on her. But he wanted to yell and beat down doors when he thought of what it would mean to Anna, plunged into the screaming hell of Earth's emotional "noise" that she couldn't block out.

He tried to think like a schemer and, knowing that it wouldn't work, told himself: *You marry Anna, take Brenner's offer—it's still open; good doctors aren't that easy to come by on Mars—and you set her up in a decent home.* But the whole thing crumbled under its own weight. She wouldn't marry a doctor whose doctoring was to patch up marcaine factory hands when they sniffed too much of the stuff…

"Eh?" he asked. Somebody was talking to him.

"Sell now, or hang on?" Mimi patiently repeated.

"I want to think about it," he told her.

The others felt the same way. It wasn't a thing you could make up your mind about in a few minutes, not after the years and years of always thinking one way: Colony survival. To have to decide now which way to kill the Colony…

Tony headed out to the Lab, racking his brains for an answer. But halfway there, he found to his chagrin that he wasn't serious at all. He was striding along freely in the clean air and light gravity, to the rhythmic mental chant: Ansie—Anna—Ann—Ansie—

Chapter Twenty

Joan Radcliff lay almost peacefully, drugging herself against the pain in her limbs and head by a familiar reverie of which she never tired. She saw Sun Lake Colony at some vague time in the future, a City of God, glowing against the transfigured Martian desert, spiring into the Martian air, with angelic beings vaguely recognizable in some way as the original colonists.

Her Hank, the bold explorer, with a bare-chested, archaic, sword-girt look; Doctor Tony, calm and wise and very old, soothing ills with miraculous lotions and calming troubled minds with dignified counsel; Mimi Jonathan, revered and able, disposing of this and that with sharp, just terseness; Anna Willendorf mothering hundreds serenely; brave Jim and Polly Kandro and their wonderful child, the hope of them all.

She wasn't there herself, but it was all right because she had done something wonderful for them. They all paused and lowered their voices when they thought of her. She, the sick and despised, had in the end surprised and awed them all by doing something wonderful for them, and they paid her memory homage.

Nagging reality, never entirely silent, jeered at her that she was a useless husk draining the Colony's priceless food and water, giving nothing in return. She shifted on the bed.

Pains shot through her joints and her heart labored. *You're as good as they are,* whispered the tempter; *you're better than they are. How many of them could stand the pain and not murmur, never think of anything but the good of the Colony? But I'm not,* she raged back. *I'm not. I shouldn't have got sick; I can't work now; they have to nurse me. But you didn't drink any water until Tony made you,* said the tempter. *Wasn't that more than any of them would do? Won't they be sorry when you're dead and they find out how you suffered?*

She tried to fix her tormented mind on her Hank, but he had a sullen, accusing stare. She was tying him down; if they sent her back to Earth, he'd have to go too. They wouldn't let him stay in the Colony.

She wished Anna hadn't left, and swallowed the thought painfully. Anna's time belonged to the Colony and not to her. It was nasty of her to want Anna to stay with her so much. She straightened one puffy leg and felt a lance of pain shoot from toes to groin; she bared her clenched teeth but didn't let a whimper escape her.

Anna had propped her up in bed before, so she could look out the window. Now she turned her head slowly and looked out.

I see through the window, she told herself. *I see across the Colony street to a corner of the Kandros' hut with a little of their streetside window showing. I see Polly Kandro cleaning the inside of the window, but she doesn't see me. Now she's coming out and cleaning the outside of the window. Now she turns and sees me and waves and I smile. Now she takes her cloth and goes around her hut to clean the back window and I can't see her any more.*

And now something glides down the Colony street with Sunny Kandro in its thin brown arms.

And now Polly runs around her hut again, her face white as chalk, tries faintly to call me, wave to me, and falls down out of sight.

Joan knew what she ought to do, and she tried. The intercom button had been put in so she had only to move her hand a few inches. She reached out for the button, and held her finger on it, but there was no answering click. It was a few seconds and maybe minutes, and the thing that had stolen Polly's baby was gone down the other end of the street.

The sick girl sat up agonizingly and thought: *I can do something now. They won't be able to say I was foolish because if I wait any longer I won't be able to catch up; it will be too far away. There's nobody else to do it except Polly, and she fainted. It has to be done right away. I can't wait for them to answer and then come from the Lab.*

Poor Polly, she thought as her heart thudded and faltered. *We must help one another.*

She shaded her eyes against the late morning sun and looked up and past the Colony street through the clear Mars air. There was a moving dot passing the airfield now, and she started after it, one step, two steps, three steps, as the City of God reformed in her mind and her eyes never left the moving dot...

Earth would be gone, a dead thing swimming in the deeps of space, a grave example for children. See? You must not hate, you must not fear, you must always help or that will happen to us. You must be kind and like people; you mustn't make weapons because you never know where making weapons will end.

And the children would ask curiously what it was like, and their elders would tell them it was crowded and dirty, that nobody ever had enough to eat, that people poured poison into the air and pretended it didn't matter. That it wasn't like Sun Lake, their spacious, clean, sweet-smelling home, that there wouldn't have been any Sun Lake if not for the great pioneers like Joan Radcliff who suffered and died for them.

She wept convulsively at the pain in her limbs as she stumped across the desert rocks. They sliced her bare feet but she dared not look down ahead of her for fear of losing that fleeing dot she followed.

I have done what I could, she thought. *Hank, you are free.* She fell forward and dragged her sprawled right arm, along the ground so that it pointed to the moving dot and the Rimrock Hills beyond it...

Somebody grabbed Tony by the arm and motioned to his helmet. He stared a moment, uncomprehending, then switched on the helmet radio.

"What's up?"

"Joan—Joan Radcliff!" It was one of Mimi's young assistants in the Lab office. "She picked up the intercom and buzzed it. When I answered it, it went dead."

"I'll be right out." The doctor made it on the double, in spite of the hampering suit, out of the shipping room and into the shower. He would have given a year of his own life to be able to speed up the decontamination process this one time, but he'd been near the open crates. It wouldn't help Joan if he exposed himself, and her, too, to radiation disease.

He ran the distance from the Lab to the street of houses. He was still running when he approached the Kandros' hut, and almost missed seeing Polly's limp figure in the road. Thoroughly bewildered, he picked her up and looked around for help. There was no one in sight.

A moment's indecision, and then, quickly, he carried Polly toward the Radcliff hut and deposited her gently on the wall bunk in the living-room. Pulse and respiration okay; she would keep. He headed for Joan's bedroom.

The doctor wasted a scant second staring at the empty bed; to him it seemed an endless time that had gone by. He pressed the intercom button, and waited through another eternity till the Lab answered.

Whatever had happened, whatever mysterious force had removed Joan from her bed and left Polly unconscious in the street, this, he realized, must have been the ultimate agony for Joan—to lie in this bed, in dreadful haste, to press this button and wait and wait until it was too late...

"That's you, Doc? What's up?"

"Trouble. Get Jim Kandro out here. To the Radcliffs'! And get Anna. Send her to Kandros'. There's no one with the baby. Is Mimi there? Put her on."

"Tony?" The Lab administrator's crisp voice was reassuring; he could leave part of the problem, at least, in her competent hands.

"There's trouble here, Mim—don't know what, but Polly's fainted and Joan's disappeared."

"I'll be right there." She hung up. Tony retreated one step toward the living-room, had an afterthought, and went back to the intercom.

"Get Cantrella here, too," he told the Lab office. "Tell him to bring along the e.e.g. setup. Fast."

Polly didn't look too bad. Marcaine again? He'd know soon.

Jim Kandro burst in, panting and terrified. His wide eyes went from his wife to the doctor, and a single miserable word came from him. "*Again?*"

"I don't know. She fainted. Take her home, then look at Sunny. Anna's on her way over to help you."

Jim left with his burden in his arms, and Tony returned to the sick girl's bedroom. There was no trace, no clue, nothing he could find.

A heartbroken shout from across the street sent him running out of the house, over to the Kandros'.

The living-room was empty.

In the bedroom, Polly lay alone, still unconscious. He found Kandro in the new nursery, squatting on the door beside the baby's empty crib, rocking in misery.

CHAPTER TWENTY-ONE

"They ought to get the test finished in a few minutes, but if you're ready, you might as well start now. It's a hundred to one chance against its being anything but cave dirt." Joe Gracey crumbled between skinny, sensitive fingers a bit of soil taken from the nursery floor.

"As soon as we get the transceiver," Mimi said. "Harve's bringing it over now."

Anna appeared in the doorway.

"She's conscious now." Tony went back into the bedroom. "Polly?"

Her eyelids fluttered open and closed. Her pulse was stronger, but she wasn't really ready to talk. He had to try. Without a stimulant, if possible.

"What happened, Polly?" he asked.

"What's the use?" she said feebly. "What's the use? We tried and tried on Earth, and I just got sick, and we had Sunny here, and now they've taken him. It isn't any good!"

"Who's taken him, Polly?"

"I went out to clean the windows. I cleaned the front window and then I went around to clean the back window. When I looked in Sunny was gone. That's all. They took him. They just took him."

"*Who* took him, Polly?"

"I don't know. Martians. Dwarfs. We tried and tried on Earth—"

"Shock," Tony muttered. "There will be a reaction. She shouldn't be left alone."

"I'll stay," Anna offered.

"No, not you. We'll need you along with us."

"I'd rather not," she said.

"Ansie," he pleaded, biting back his angry disappointment.

"I shouldn't have told you," she said dully. "I should never have told anybody. All right, I'll go."

He smiled and gripped her arm. "Of course you will. You would have anyway."

"No," she said. "I wouldn't."

"Then maybe it's a good thing you told me." His voice was stern, but his hand pulled her closer to him.

Polly twisted on the bed and sobbed. Anna pulled away. "Maybe." She bit her lip, looked up at him. "Only *please* don't be angry at me. I can't stand it, if you keep getting angry at me." She turned and fled.

Tony went back to the bed, erasing Anna and her problems from his mind with practiced determination. Polly was trembling uncontrollably. There was no more information to be had from her. He gave her a sedative and went out to join the others.

Harve had arrived with the transceiver in his hand. On Anna's suggestion, a rush call was sent out for Hank Radcliff to stay with Polly. He didn't know about Joan; they decided not to tell him about it.

"We need a man here with her," the doctor explained briefly. "The baby's disappeared, and we're going out now and try to track it. Polly might want to get up and follow. *You keep her in bed.*"

"Sure, Doc."

"Nick Cantrella will be over with some equipment. Tell him to test Polly."

They left the house, Mimi and Anna and the doctor, Jim Kandro, Harve Stillman, and Joe Gracey.

"Look at that." Gracey was bending over in the road, pointing to the barely discernible mark of a bare toe. Here in the bottom of the old "canal" bed, where the settlement was built, the land retained a trace of moisture, enough to hold an impression for a while.

Only part of a toe, but it pointed a direction.

They headed up the street, past the huts toward the landing field.

"Hey, Joe!" Someone was pounding up the hill after them, shouting. It was one of the men from the Agro Lab.

"That test—it's from the hills, all right, most likely from inside a cave, but hill dirt. That all you wanted?"

"Right. Thanks."

"They told me you wanted the word fast," the man said curiously. "Glad I caught you."

"Glad you did," Gracey agreed mildly. "Thanks again."

He turned his back on the man. "Let's go."

They topped the slight rise that marked the farthest, extent of the old river bed's inundations, and faced a featureless expanse of level desert land, broken only by *Lazy Girl*, chocked on the landing field at their left, and the hills in the distance. No other human being was in sight. It was hopeless to look for footprints here, in the constantly shifting dust.

"The hills?" Mimi said.

Tony looked at Anna; she shrugged almost imperceptibly.

"Might as well," he agreed.

They moved forward, Kandro striding ahead with his hands knotted into bony fists, his eyes set on the hills, unaware of the ground under his feet or of the people with him. It was Harve who found the print they had known was impossible—not really a footprint, but a spot of moisture, fast evaporating, still retaining a semblance of the shape of a human foot.

A little farther on there was another; they were going the right way. Tony stopped for a minute at one of the damp spots, poked a finger curiously into the ground. Grit and salt, as he had expected.

She couldn't have lived through it. He didn't know how she got as far as she did, but even if her heart held out, she must have sweated her life away to have left those damp indicators in the thirsty soil.

Only a little farther and the ground began to be littered with the refuse of the Rimrock Hills—here and there a sliver of stone, a drift of mineral salts. Gradually the dust gave way to sharp rock and hard-packed saltpans. And the footprints of sweat gave way to footprints of blood.

Mimi drew in her breath between her teeth at the thought of the sick girl stumbling barefoot over the slicing, razor-edged stones.

"I see her," Kandro whispered, still striding ahead.

They raced a kilometer over the jagged rock and planed-off salt crust to the girl's body. She lay prone, with her right arm flung up and pointing to the Rimrock Hills.

Tony peeled back her eyelid and reached for the pulse. He turned to his bag, and Anna—blessed Anna—was already getting out the hypodermic syringe.

"Adrenalin?"

He nodded. Swiftly and efficiently she prepared the hypo and handed it to him. He bent over the girl busily, then sat back to wait.

He glanced at Anna and straightened up quickly. "What is it?"

Her face was withdrawn and intense, her head held back like an animal scenting the wind. She scanned the broken waste and pointed a hesitant finger. "Out there—it's *that* way—moving a little."

Kandro was on his way before she stopped speaking.

Stillman shaded his eyes and peered. "A rock in the heat haze," he pronounced finally. "Nothing alive."

Tony saw Anna shake her head in a small involuntary disagreement.

They stood and waited in a tense small circle until Jim reached the spot. He looked down and they saw him hesitate, then move on with the same determined stride. Gracey lit out after him. Mimi murmured approval. There was no telling what Kandro might do in his present mood.

The barely audible noise from the ground, and Tony was on his knees beside Joan. Her eyes went wide open, shining with an inner glory that was unholy in the dirtstreaked, bloodstained dead white of her face. She smiled as a child might smile, with perfect inner composure; she was pleased with herself.

"Joan," the doctor said, "can you talk?"

"Yes, of course." But she couldn't. She only mouthed the words.

"Does it hurt any place?"

She shook her head, or started to, but when she had turned it to one side she lacked the strength to bring it back. "No." This time she forced a little air through to sound the word.

She was dying and he knew it. If it were only the heart, he might have been able to save her. But her body had been punished too much; it had given up. The water and the air that kept it alive were spent. Her body was a dead husk in which, for a moment, abetted by the little quantity of adrenalin, her heart and brain refused to die.

He had to decide. They needed what information she might have. She needed every bit of energy she had, to live out what minutes were left. The minutes didn't matter he told himself.

He knew, even as he made up his mind, that this, like the ghost baby, would haunt him all his life. If he was wrong, if she had any chance to live, he was committing murder. But another life hung in the balance too.

"Listen to me, Joan." He put his mouth close to her face. "Just say yes or no. Did you see somebody take the Kandros' baby?"

"Yes." She smiled up at him beatifically.

"Do you know who it was?"

"Yes—no—I saw—"

"Don't try to talk. You saw the kidnaper clearly?"

"Yes."

"Then it was someone you don't know?"

"No—yes—"

"I'll ask it differently. Was it a stranger?"

"Yes." She looked doubtful.

"Anyone from the Colony?"

"No."

"A man?"

"No—maybe."

"A woman?"

"No."

"Someone from Pittco?"

She didn't answer. Her eyes were staring at her arm. The doctor had rolled her over, and the arm was at her side, stretched out. She let out a weird cry of fury and frustration. Tony watched and listened, puzzled, till Anna bent over.

"It's all right, Joan," she said softly. "You showed us. We saw the way it pointed. Jim is going that way now."

The girl's eyes relaxed, and once again the dreadful light of joy shone from them.

"Love me," she said distinctly. "I helped finally. Tony—"

He bent over. She was trailing off again, less breath with each word. She might have minutes left, or seconds.

"Nobody—believed—me—or—them—it was—"

She stopped, gasping, and the quiet smile of content gave way to a twisted grin of amusement. "Dwarf," she said, and no more.

Tony closed her eyes and looked up to Anna's serene face. He saw that they were alone with the body of the dead girl.

"Where—?" He got to his feet, carefully dulling sensation, refusing to feel anything.

"Over there." She pointed to where two figures stooped over something on the ground. Farther off, Kandro's tall figure, still resolutely facing toward the hills, was being restrained by a smaller man—Joe Gracey? That meant it was Mimi and Harve close by.

"They found something?"

"Somebody," she corrected, and couldn't control a small shudder.

Tony started forward. "You better stay with Joan," he said with difficulty, hating to admit any weakness in her. "I'll call you if—if we need you for anything."

"Thank you." She was more honest about it than he could be...

They saw him coming twenty meters off.

"It's Graham," Mimi called.

"The lying bastard steals babies too!" Harve spat out in disgust.

"He looks bad," Mimi said quietly. "We didn't touch him. We were waiting for you."

"Good." The doctor bent down and felt along the torso for broken bones. Carefully he rolled the writer over.

Graham's puffed eyes opened. Through broken lips with dried blood crusted on them he rasped jeeringly, "Come back to finish the job? God-damned cowards. Sneak up on a man. God-damned cowards!"

"None of our people did this to you," Tony said steadily. His hands ran over the writer's battered head and neck. The left clavicle was fractured, his nose was broken, his left eardrum had been ruptured by blows.

"Let's get him back to the hospital," he said. "Harve, tell the radio shack to raise Marsport. Get Bell. Tell him we need that Bloodhound. Tell him I will not take no for an answer."

CHAPTER TWENTY-TWO

IN AWKWARD SILENCE the little procession walked along the Colony street, Kandro and Stillman together, carrying the writer, and Tony bearing the dead girl in his arms. The news had gotten around. Lab work seemed once again to have stopped completely.

They escaped the heartsick stares of the colonists only when they entered Tony's hut-and-hospital. He deposited Joan there, on his own bed. It was still rumpled from Graham's brief occupancy the night before. They settled the writer on the hospital table. With Anna's help, he removed the torn and bloody clothing from Graham's body.

"If you don't need us for anything, Tony, I think we better get going," Mimi said. "We ought to stop in and see Polly."

"Sure. Go ahead—oh, wait a minute." Jim Kandro turned from his fixed spot in the doorway to listen.

Tony beckoned the black-haired Lab administrator to the other side of the room.

"Mimi," he said in an undertone, "you ought to know that Polly has a gun. I'm not sure whether Jim knows it or not. You might want it if you're going out again. Anyhow, somebody ought to get it out of there."

She nodded. "Where is it?"

"Used to be in the baby's crib, but I think I talked her out of that. Don't know now."

"Okay. I'll find it. I think we better take it along. Oh— I'll send Hank back here."

He was thoughtful. "Anna." She looked up. Her face was set and miserable. "Are you going out with the search party?" he asked, an innocent question to the others who listened, with a world of agonizing significance for Anna.

"I—isn't Nick picking the people to go?"

"I thought you might *want* to go. If you're sticking around, you can handle Hank, can't you?"

"Oh, yes," she said eagerly. "I'd be much more useful that way, wouldn't I?"

He shrugged and tried to figure it out: she was perfectly willing to stay here in the hospital, to expose herself to Graham's physical pain and Hank's inevitable agony. But she was afraid to go out after the baby. Why?

Later, he decided, he could talk to her. He went briskly back to the table and began his examination of Graham. The writer was a mass of bruises from his chest up; he cursed feebly when the doctor felt for fractures. Tony set the collar bone and shot him full of sedation. "Your left eardrum is ruptured," he said coldly. "An operation can correct that on Earth."

"You bust 'em, somebody else fixes 'em," Graham muttered.

"Think what you want." He pushed the wheeled table over to the high bed Polly occupied just a few days earlier.

Graham groaned involuntarily as Tony shifted his shoulder. The doctor eased up. *What for?* he stormed at himself. *Why should I be gentle with the dirty sneak?* He glanced hastily at Anna and caught the half-smile on her face as she pulled the covers over the writer.

"I'm going into the other room, Graham," Tony said. "You can call me if you need me."

"Sure," Graham told him. "I'll call you soon as I feel ready for another beating. I love it."

Tony didn't answer. In the other room, he sat down and faced Anna intently. "Do you know whether any of our people could have done that to him?"

"They aren't haters," she said slowly. "If they were, they wouldn't be here. Somebody might fly into a rage and break his jaw, but methodical *punishment* like that—no."

"I'll tell you what it reminds me of. Big Ginny."

"She was killed."

"She was beaten up, though that wasn't what killed her."

"Does it have anything to do with Pittco?" Anna asked. "Why should they beat Graham? Why should they have beaten that woman?"

"I don't know." He managed a feeble grin. "You know that." He lowered his voice. "Can you 'hear' him?"

"He's in a lot of pain. Shock's worn off. And he hates us. God, he hates us. I'm glad he hasn't got a gun."

"He's got a by-line. That's just as good."

"Evidently that just occurred to him. Can he hear us in there? He's gloating now. It must be a fantasy about what he's going to do to us."

"Hell, we're through anyway. What difference does it make? All I want now is to find Sunny and get off this damned planet and give up trying. I'm sick of it."

"You're not even kidding yourself," she said gently. "How do you think you can fool me?"

"All *right,"* he said. "So you think my heart is breaking because Sun Lake's washed up. What good is it going to do me? Anna, will I be seeing you back on Earth? I want us to stay teamed up. When I go into practice—"

The woman winced and stood up. She closed the door to the hospital. "He was listening," she said. "He let out a blast of derision that rattled my skull when he heard you talk about going into practice on Earth."

Tony pulled her down beside him and held her quietly against his chest. "Ansie," he said once, softly, "my poor sweet Ansie." He kissed her hair and they sat very still until Hank knocked on the door.

Hank stared at his wife's body, refusing to believe what he saw.

"She didn't feel much," Tony tried to explain. "Just a bad moment maybe, when her heart gave out. She couldn't have felt anything, or she'd never have gotten so far."

"We were there at the end," Anna reminded the young man. "She was—she was very happy. She wanted to be useful more than anything else in the world. You know that, don't you? And in the end she was. She loved you very much, too. She didn't want you to be unhappy."

"What did she say?" Hank wouldn't tear his eyes from the bed. He stood and stared ceaselessly, as if another moment of looking would show him some fallacy, some error.

"She said—" Anna hesitated, then went on firmly: "She said, 'Tell Hank I want him to be happy all the time.' I heard her," she answered Tony's look of surprise. It wasn't much of a lie.

"Thank you. I—" He sat on the bed beside his wife, his hand caressing the face stained with blood and dust.

Tony turned and left the room. In the hospital, Graham was asleep or unconscious again. Tony went back to his own chair in the living-room.

There were so many hints, so many leads, so many parts of the picture. Somehow it all went together. He tried to concentrate, but his thoughts kept wandering, into the hospital where the writer lay beaten as Big Ginny had been beaten; into the bedroom, where Joan lay dead of—of Mars; where Anna was comforting the young man who would never realize, if he was lucky, that he had killed Joan himself as surely as if he had throttled her.

The last thing she said before she died! Tony snorted. The last thing she said, with that glorious light in her eyes, and a grin of delight on her face was "Dwarf!"

And there it was!

Within a few seconds' time everything raced through his mind, all the clues, the things that fitted together—Big Ginny, and Graham's story, Sunny and the mask and Joan's dying words. Everything!

He jumped up in furious excitement.

No, not everything, he realized. Not the marcaine. That didn't fit.

He paced the length of the room and turned to find Anna standing in the bedroom door.

"Did you call?" she asked. "What happened?"

He smiled. He went over and pushed the door closed behind her. "Ansie," he said, "you just don't know how lucky you are to have a big, strong, intelligent man like me. When are we going to get married?"

She shook her head.

"Not until you tell me what it's all about."

Chapter Twenty-Three

Refuse entertain request this date. Police powers this office extend only to intercolony matters. PAC does not repeat not authorize use of police equipment for intracolony affair.

Hamilton Bell
Planetary Affairs
Commisioner

Tony read through the formal message sheet, then the note attached to it:

That's the master's voice up there. The PAC radio up in Marsport told me, on the side, that the old man doesn't believe a word of your story. If the baby really is missing, he figures "that Markie Mamma did it in." Graham really fixed us. I hope you're taking good care of him. If you get him back in shape, I won't feel so bad about taking a crack at him myself. Harve.

The doctor smiled briefly, then asked Tad Campbell, who was waiting to take his answer back to the radio shack, "Did Mimi Jonathan see this?"

"No. It just came in. Harve wants to know what answer to send."

Cantrella and Gracey were out with the search party too, Tony realized. That left the decision squarely up to him.

He scribbled a note: *Harve, try this one on the commish: 'Request use PAC facilities to track vicious attacker of our guest, Douglas Graham.' That ought to get us every tin soldier on the planet; and old man Bell himself heading the parade. Graham as victim gives him an out, too; he can call it intercolony. Get hot. We need that bloodhound. Tony.*

When the boy was gone, Tony paced nervously around the living-room, started to heat water for "coffee," and decided he didn't want it.

There was an almost empty bottle of liquor on the floor near the table—Graham's. The doctor reached for it and drew back. It wasn't the right time or the right bottle.

He headed for the bedroom door, and remembered that Joan's body was still occupying the bed. He peered into the hospital; Graham was still sleeping. Nothing to do but sit and wait, and think it out all over again. It checked every time—but it couldn't be right.

He hadn't told Anna yet. When you came right down to it, the whole thing was too far-fetched; he wouldn't believe it himself if somebody else had proposed it. But it checked all the way every time.

He got up again and hunted through his meager stack of onionskin volumes and scientific journals. Nothing there, but Joe Gracey ought to know. When the search party came back— It was more than an hour since Tad had left. Why no reply from Harve?

Tony went to the front door, opened it, and peered up the street, out over the housetops to the landing field. Nothing in sight. He turned to go back in, and out of the corner of his eye saw them rounding the curve of the street.

Gracey, Mimi, Juarez, and then Kandro, taking each step reluctantly, his heart back in the hills, while Nick Cantrella and Sam Flexner, one on each side, urged him forward. Tony's heart sank; there was no mistaking defeat…

"I'm sure," Mimi said steadily, "we heard him cry. Just for a minute. Then it was as if someone had clapped a hand over his mouth. Tony, we can't wait. We've got to get him out right away."

"What about the other caves?"

"We tried them all around," Gracey said. "Five or six on each side and a couple up above. But every one of those fissures narrows down inside the hill the same way. We couldn't get through. I don't see how the kidnaper did, either."

"How about the other side?" Tony asked. "Someone could go around with a half-track and take a look."

"We thought of it," Mimi said sharply. "Nick got Pittco on the transreceiver. *Mister* Hackenburg was so sorry. *Mister* Reynolds was away, and he didn't have the authority himself to permit us to search on their ground. He was *so* sorry!"

She stood up abruptly and turned to the wall, not quite quickly enough. Tony saw her brush at her eyes before she turned back and said throatily, "Well, little men, what now? Where do we go from here?"

"We wait," Joe Gracey said helplessly. "We wait for Bell to answer us. We wait for Reynolds to get back. What else can we do?"

"Nothing, I guess. We left half a dozen men out there," Mimi told the doctor. "They're watching, and they have the transceiver. I guess Joe's right. We wait."

Silence, and Tony tried to find a way to say what he had to say. They couldn't just wait, not while he knew something to try. The baby might be all right, but maybe they would get there just one minute too late.

He turned to Gracey.

"Joe, what do you know about lethal genes?"

"Huh?" The agronomist looked up, dazed, shook his head, and repeated without surprise at the irrelevant question, "Lethal genes?" He stopped and considered, mentally tabulating his information. "Well, they're recessives that—"

"No, I know what they are," Tony stopped him. "I thought I heard you say something about them the other day. Didn't you say you thought you'd hit on some that were viable on Mars?"

Anna drifted in, with Hank at her heels, and they went straight through, into the room beyond where Joan still lay.

"Oh, yes," Gracey said. "Very interesting stuff. Come out to the Lab when you have the time and I'll show you. We—"

Mimi jumped up. "*What* are you gabbing about?" she demanded. "This is an emergency! We have to find some way to rescue that baby!"

"I'm sorry, Mimi." Gracey was bewildered. "What's wrong anyway? Tony asked a perfectly innocent question, and I answered him when we'd all agreed that we had nothing to do but sit around and wait. Why not use the time?"

Abruptly Tony made up his mind. It was up to him now. And to Anna. He got up and called her from the bedroom, led her outside, into the street in front of the house, where they were out of earshot of all the others.

"Well?" She smiled up at him. "Will you stop feeling sorry for me and tell me what you're sorry about?"

"In a minute. Anna, last night when we took the mask off Sunny— when you fainted—how did it feel?"

"I told you."

"Yes, you said it was very strong, stronger than you thought a baby could—feel. But was it just stronger or was there something *different?*"

"That's hard to say. I was—well, I was all worn out and upset. It might have been different, but I don't know how. I'm not even sure it was."

"It checks," he said to himself. "Listen, Ansie, there's a job to be done. A tough job. A job nobody can do but you. It may—hurt you. I don't know. I don't even know if it will work. It's a crazy theory I've got, so crazy I don't even want to explain it to you. But if I'm right, you're the only person who can do it." He stopped. "Anna, did you hear what Joan's last word really was? She said, 'Dwarf.' " He looked down into frightened dark eyes.

"Tony, there aren't any, are there?"

"You mean do I believe there are? No, I don't. But I do think there's *something.*"

"You want me to go out there and listen?"

"Yes. But that's only part of it. I wouldn't let you go alone; if you do go, I'll be with you—if that helps any. But I want to go into the cave where they heard the baby and see what we can find."

"No!" The cry was torn from her. "I didn't mean that," she caught herself. "It's just—oh, Tony, I'm *afraid.*"

"We've got to find out. Ansie, we've *got to find out.*"

"The Bloodhound?" she asked desperately. "Can't you track them with the Bloodhound?"

"Bell hasn't answered us. How long can we wait?"

She stood silent for a moment, then turned her face up to his, serenely quiet now and trusting.

"All right," she said at last. "All right, Tony, if you say it has to be done."

"I'll be there with you," he promised…

Mimi and Joe didn't understand, and Tony didn't try to explain. He simply repeated that he had an "idea"; he wanted to go, with Anna, to the cave where the baby's cry had been heard.

He left careful instructions about the care of Graham if he should awake, and about Hank, Polly, and Jim, all three of whom were too upset to be left to themselves.

A ten minutes' ride on the half-track and they were within the shadow of the Rimrocks. The drifting stench of Pittco's refineries on the other side began to reach them; then the ground became too rocky to go on. Tony stopped the machine and they got out. Farther up the face of the nearest hill they could make out the figures of the five who had remained on guard.

One of them came running—Flexner, the chemist. "They said on the transceiver you were coming," he told Anna and Tony. "What's your idea? We're going nuts sitting around waiting. Tad thought he heard Sunny cry again but nobody else did."

"I just wanted to see if I could turn up anything," Tony told him. "We're going into the cave."

Together they walked out of the sunlight into the seven-foot opening in the hard rock. One of the guards would have preceded them, but Anna firmly refused. A chalk mark on the wall, drawn by the others when they had left the cave, was guide enough.

They followed the white line on and down some fifty meters, then fifty more along a narrowing, left-handed branch, and then a hundred meters, left again and narrowing, to another fork. Both the branches were too small to squeeze through. The chalk line pointed into the right-hand cranny.

That was as far as they could go. They stood at the narrow opening, listening.

There was nothing to hear, no sound at all in the rock-walled stillness except their own breathing and the tiny rustling of their hands along rough alien stone.

They waited, Tony's eyes fixed on Anna's face. He tried to silence his thoughts as he could his voice, but doubts tore at him. He turned, finally, to the one certainty he knew, and concentrated on Anna and her alone; on his love for her, her love for him.

"I hear something," she whispered at last. "Fear—mostly fear, but eagerness, too. They are not afraid of us. I think they like us. They're afraid of—it's not clear—of people?"

She fell silent again, listening.

"People." She nodded her head emphatically. "They want to talk to us, Tony, but—I don't know." Her brow furrowed in concentration and she sat down suddenly on the hard rock floor, as though the physical exertion of standing was more than she could bear.

"Tony, go and tell the guards to go away," she said at last.

"No," he said firmly.

"Go ahead. Please. Hurry. They are trying—" Abruptly she stopped concentrating on the distance. "You spoiled it," she said bitterly. "You frightened them."

"How?"

"You didn't trust them. You thought they'd hurt me."

"Ansie, how *can* we trust them? How can I leave you here alone and send the guards away? Don't you see that I can't take that risk?"

"You made me come here," she said tiredly. "You said I was the one who could do the job. I'm trying to do it. Please go now and tell the guards to leave. Tell them to get out of range—down at the bottom of the hill, maybe as far away as the half-track. Please, Tony, do as I say."

"All right." But he was still hesitant. "Anna, who are they?"

"I—" The bitterness left her face. "Martian dwarfs. Animal life, thinking *things,*" she said.

"But what does that mean?"

"They're *different.*"

"Like Sunny?"

"Not exactly." She made a small useless gesture with her hands. "More—distinct. No, maybe you're right. I think they're like him, only older."

"How many are there?"

"Quite a few. Too many for me to count. One of them is doing all the—talking."

"Talking?" Yes, that was part of what had bothered him. "Ansie, how can you understand so clearly? You told me you can't do that. You didn't know what Graham was angry about. How do you know what they're afraid of?"

"Tony, I don't know how. I *can* understand, that's all, and I'm sure it's right, and I know they're not tricking us. Now please, please go and tell the guards."

He went.

Chapter Twenty-Four

"Keep him away from me!" Graham screamed.

Mimi raced through Tony's living-room into the hospital half of the hut.

It was Hank, standing rigidly still, glaring at the writer. "You don't understand about Mars," Hank was saying in a hard monotone. "You never saw the Rimrocks when there was just enough light to tell them from the sky, or walked a hundred miles in the desert watching the colors change every minute."

"Mrs. Johnson, get him out of here. He's crazy."

Mimi took Hank by the arm. "I'm not crazy," he said. "Those boomers at Pittco, this writer here, Bell and his soldiers, Brenner and his factory, they're crazy. They're trying to cheapen Mars."

Hysteria, thought Mimi. She'd coped with enough cases of it when she'd bossed girls at desks, as far as the eye could see, on the 76th floor of the American Insurance Groups Building.

"Radcliff!" she said.

There was a savage whip-crack in her voice.

He turned to her, startled. "I wasn't going to hurt him," he said confusedly.

Get him to cry. Break him. Until then, there's no knowing what will happen. "Your poor wife's lying in there," she said with measured nastiness, "and you find time to brawl with a sick man."

"I didn't mean anything like that," he protested.

Still unbroken. "Get into the bedroom," she said. "Sit there. That's the least you can do."

He walked heavily into the room where his wife's body lay and she heard him drop into a plastic chair.

"Thanks, Mrs. Johnson," said Graham painfully. "He was spoiling for a fight."

"Mrs. Jonathan," she corrected. "And I don't want your thanks."

She turned and rattled through drawers of medications, hoping she'd find something she could give Hank. She didn't know what to use or how much. She slapped the drawer shut and was angry with Tony and Anna for not being there when she needed them.

She stalked into the bedroom and stared at Hank without showing any pity. He was looking dully at the wall, a spot over the bed on which Joan's broken body lay. No shakes, no tears, unbroken still. But she couldn't bring herself to lash him further and precipitate the emotional crisis.

She went back into Tony's living-room and threw herself into a chair. She'd hear if anything happened. Mrs. J., the terror of auditing, Old Eagle-Eye, and a few less complimentary things when the girls were talking in the old Earth days, between the booths in one of the 76th-floor johns. Efficiency bonuses year after year, even bad years, and that meant you *were* an old witch. She must be out of practice, or getting soft, she decided harshly, if she couldn't handle an absurdly simple little thing like this.

We ought to have Tony train somebody besides Anna, she thought. *There's Harve, but he only knows radio-health.* And then she remembered that it didn't matter; Sun Lake wouldn't last that long…

She heard a plane coming in at the landing field and wondered whose. She got up and had a drink of water from the wall canteen, and then, defiantly, another, because it didn't matter now. She felt like taking on the world for Sun Lake. Joan must have felt like that. Their water supply was scanty, but it was water—not the polluted fluid of Earth, chlorinated to the last potable degree.

The intercom in the bedroom buzzed. She walked in and picked it up, glanced at Hank, still numbly staring.

"Hello, Mimi." It was Harve. "Answer from Bell. Quote: 'Re assault on Douglas Graham I and detail of guards will take action this matter. Request use PAC facilities denied. Hamilton Bell' et cetera., What do you figure he'll do—try and pin the Graham slugging on us too?"

"I don't know," she said. "It doesn't matter. What plane was that?"

"Brenner's. The bastards didn't even check in with us. Just sat right down on the field."

"He might as well. He'll own it soon enough."

She heard Harve clear his throat embarrassedly. "Well, I guess that's all."

"Good-by," she agreed, hanging up. She shouldn't have said that; she was supposed to pretend that while there was life there was hope.

"Hank?" she asked gently and inquiringly.

He looked up. "I'm all right, thanks."

He wasn't, but there was nothing she could do. She looked through the door to the hospital. Graham seemed to be dozing. She sat down in the living-room again.

Brenner came in without knocking. "They told me you were here, Mrs. Jonathan. I wonder if we could go to your office in the Lab. I want to talk business."

"I'm staying here," she said shortly. "If you want to talk here, I'll listen."

Brenner shrugged and sat down. "Do we have privacy?"

"There's a boy in the next room going crazy with grief over his dead wife—and over the prospect of leaving Mars. And there's a badly beaten man sleeping in the hospital quarters."

The drug manufacturer lowered his voice. "Relative privacy," he said. "Mrs. Jonathan, you have the only business head in the Colony." He opened his briefcase on the table and edged the corner of a sheaf of bills from one of its pockets. The top one was a thousand dollars. He didn't look at it, but riffled the sheaf with his thumb. They were all thousands, and there were over one hundred of them.

"It's going to be very hard on some of the colonists, I'm afraid," he said conversationally.

"You have no idea."

"It needn't be that hard on all of them." His thumb flipped the big bills. "Your colony is facing an impossible situation, Mrs. Jonathan. Let's not mince words; it's a matter of bankruptcy and forced sale. I'm in a position to offer you a chance to retreat in good order, with some money in your pockets."

"That's very kind of you, Mr. Brenner. I'm not sure I understand."

"Please," he smiled, "let's not be coy. I'm being perfectly candid with you. If it comes to a forced sale, I intend to bid as high as necessary; I need this property. But I'm not a man who believes in leaving things to chance. Why shouldn't you sell out to me now? It would save yourselves the humiliation of bankruptcy, and I believe everyone concerned would benefit financially."

"You realize I'm not in a position to close any deals, Mr. Brenner?" she asked.

"Yes, of course. You have a council in charge here, don't you? And you're a member. You could plead my case with them."

"I suppose I could."

"All right." He smiled again, and his thumb continued to riffle the pile of bills. "Then I have to plead it first with you. Why should you stay on Mars? In the hope that 'something' will turn up? Believe me, it will not. Your commercial standing will be gone. Nobody would dream of extending credit to the people who were six months behind on their deliveries. *Nothing will turn up,* Mrs. Jonathan."

"What if the stolen marcaine turns up?"

"Then, of course—" He smiled and shrugged.

Mimi read a momentary alarm in his face. For the first time since the crisis she entertained the thought that it was not a frameup.

She pressed harder. "What if we're just waiting to hand Bell the hundred kilos and the thief?"

Brenner turned inscrutable again. "Then something else will happen. And if the Colony survives that, something else again." He quickly denied the implication of sabotage by adding, "You have a fundamentally untenable financial situation here. Insufficient reserves, foggy motives—what businessman can trust you when he knows that your Lab production workers might walk out one fine day and stay out? They aren't bound by salaries but by idealism."

"It's kept us going."

"Until now. Come, Mrs. Jonathan, I said I wanted an advocate in the Council. You have a business head. You know that if you *do* produce my marcaine and the thief, Mr. Graham's little story—which I read with great interest—will be another bad bump to get over. There will be more."

He meant two things: more bumps, and more sheafs of thousand-dollar bills for her if she took the bribe.

"Are you offering to buy the Colony, Mr. Brenner? Would you care to name a price?"

"What are you asking?" he countered.

Oh, no, she thought, *you're not getting away with that.*

"All right, we'll play it your way," she said. "Name two prices. You want to buy my services, too, don't you?"

"Whatever gives you that notion? I'm not trying to bribe you, Mrs. Jonathan." He picked up the sheaf of bills and placed them in front of her. "There's a hundred thousand—*for a down payment,* whenever you say. My price for the Colony only," he added distinctly, "is exactly five million."

"Plus your down payment?" she asked, amused.

"That's right."

"That would just about pay all our fares back to Earth. We'll smash the Lab to bits before we let you get it for any such price."

"You'll rot in prison if you do," Brenner said easily. "There's an injunction on file at Marsport signed by Commissioner Bell restraining you from any such foolishness. An act of contempt would mean imprisonment for all of you. I mean *all.*"

"No such paper has been served on us."

"The Commissioner assured me it had been served. I don't doubt his word. Not many people, including appeals judges would doubt his word either."

"It'll have to be put into form by the Council and voted on by the entire Colony," she said painfully. "You wanted an advance. Take your money back; I'm not for sale. But I *will* plead your case if you'll make it ten million. God knows, it's still a bargain. There's absolutely no depreciation on the Lab to be figured. It's better now than it ever was. Maintenance has always been top-level. Better than anything you'll ever be able to find in industry."

"Five million and five hundred thousand was my offer. I'm not the Croesus uninformed people take me for. I have my expenses on the marcaine distribution end, you know…"

In the meantime, Tony was sweating out the time. Eight minutes creeping along the chalk line in the dark—he'd left the light with Anna. Five minutes scrabbling over the boulders at the cave opening on the face of the hill. Twelve long minutes talking the guards into leaving, and a painful tortured eternity—maybe another twelve minutes reentering the cave and tracing the chalk line by the dim light borrowed from Tad.

Tony was sweating ice by the time the radiance from Anna's light came into view. He rounded the last curve in the winging passage, and something jumped up from the floor and stood, tense and watchful as the doctor.

Anna, seated on the cold floor, laughed softly, melodiously. She was all right. Tony relaxed a little and instantly felt—something, a gentle stroking, a tentative touch, not on his head but *in* it. No menace, no danger. Friendship.

The doctor stared across the cavern: leathery brown skin, barrel chest, big ears, skinny arms and legs; the height of a small man or a large boy; and—a telepath.

The friendly touch on his mind persisted through his quick distaste, his exultation, his eagerness.

"Anna," very softly, "is it all right to talk?"

"Not too loud. His ears are sensitive."

"Who is he? Are there more? *Does he have Sunny?* Ask him that, Anna—ask him!"

"A Martian 'human.' A dwarf." She laughed again, joyously. "There are four more down there, inside, with Sunny."

"Is he all right?"

"Yes. They took him to help him, not to do any harm. He needed something, but I can't find out what."

The strange little being squatted again on the floor beside Anna. Tony approached slowly and sat down next to them.

He felt goose flesh and memories of old nursery-book horrors, but nothing happened. He forced himself to ask Anna, "What kind of thing?"

"Something to eat, I think. Something like the first sip of water when you're thirsty, and as necessary as salt, and—*good.* Maybe like a vitamin, but it tastes wonderful."

Tony ran through a mental catalogue of biochemicals. But that was foolish; how could you tell what would taste good to anything as alien as a Martian?

"Have you tried sign language?" he asked Anna.

"Where do you start?" She shrugged. "You'd have to build up a whole set of symbols before you could get anything across… Tony, I'm sure we can get the baby back if we just understand what it is he needs."

The doctor reached over, hesitated, and forced himself to tap the weird thing lightly on the shoulder. When he had the creature's attention, he whispered to Anna, "Tell him we're trying to find out what it is." He pointed to his own eyes. "Show us," he said to the creature, and tried to project the thought, the image of seeing, as hard as he could.

They kept repeating it with every possible combination of thought and act: Then, suddenly, the Martian dwarf jumped and dashed off, down the tunnel.

"Did he get the idea?" demanded Tony. "Is he coming back?"

"It's all right," smiled Anna. "He understood."

Silence in the eerie place was almost unbearable.

"Don't worry so, Tony," Anna said. "If you want to know, he almost scared the wits out of me, too. I was sitting, trying to look down the little opening, and still—talking—to the ones down there, and he came up behind me. I was concentrating on them so I didn't hear him, either way."

Tony sat back thoughtfully. It was all true then; his crazy theory was right—there were actually "men" on Mars, a form of life so highly developed that it was telepathic, and with no lower life-forms to have evolved from. He wondered if he had hit the right explanation, too, but there *was* no other explanation.

The little fellow was back, carrying something, a box. Large letters in black on the side read:

DANGER
SEALED MARCAINE CONTAINER
Do Not Open Without Authorization
BRENNER PHARMACEUTICAL CO.

CHAPTER TWENTY-FIVE

TONY HELPED ANNA dismount from the half-track, with her valuable burden in her arms. She jounced Sunny happily, and cooed down at the pink face. The doctor didn't jounce his own burden; he lifted it down even more carefully than he had helped Anna. The marcaine box was tightly wrapped in his shirt and hers. They were counting on the several layers of cloth to trap escaping dust and protect them from marcaine jags, but the doctor still wasn't taking any chances on stirring up the contents of the half-full box.

They cut across the bare land in back of the row of houses, heading toward the curved street near the Kandros'.

"Tony," Anna asked anxiously again, "*how* are we possibly going to explain it?"

"I told you I don't know." He was only a little irritable. They had the baby; they had the marcaine. "We'll have to talk to Mimi and Joe and Nick, and probably the others too. We'll see how it goes—"

"No, I don't *mean* that," she stopped him. "I mean to Polly. And Jim. Jim isn't going to like it unless he hears the whole story, and I don't know if we ought to—"

"Like it or not," Tony said briskly, "Kandro'll do what I tell him to. We'll have to tell them it's marcaine; I don't dare risk mislabeling the stuff. You'll have to blow some ampoules for it, I guess, and, I'll figure out some way of wetting it down and getting it into the capsules. But you're right," he added, "if you mean we shouldn't say any more than we have to just now."

They stepped onto the packed dirt of the street and cut across to the Kandros'.

Joe Gracey was sitting alone in the living-room.

"Praise God," he said quietly, and called, *"Polly! Jim!"*

The couple appeared, red-eyed, at the nursery door, saw their baby, and flew to him.

Tony said, "You can feed him in a minute. Now listen carefully. This young man of yours, you know, is special in some ways. He can take the Mars air and like it. It turns out that there's something else he needs—something that's good for him and bad for other people, just like the Mars air. It's marcaine."

Polly's face went white. Jim began a guffaw of unbelief that turned into a frown. He asked carefully, "How can that be, Doc? What *is* this all about? And who took him? We have a right to know."

Anna came to Tony's rescue. "You're not going to know right now," she said tartly. "If you think that's hard on you, it's just too bad. You've got your baby back; now leave the doctor alone until he's ready to tell you more."

Jim opened his mouth and shut it again. Polly asked only, "Doctor, are you sure?"

"I'm sure. And it *won't* have anything like the effect on Sunny that it had on you. But it's real marcaine, all right, and he's got to have it or die."

"Like OxEn?" asked Kandro. "It's only fair in a way—"

Tony ignored him. "I guess you're going to have to wean the baby after all, Polly," he said. "You can't keep taking marcaine for Sunny's sake. But for now, I guess you might as well nurse him. Your milk still has marcaine in it."

Kandro was still adjusting himself to the idea. "Sunny doesn't need OxEn, so he's got to take something else?"

"Yes," Tony said; "like OxEn—" He broke off, and Anna spun toward him, her eyes wide. The doctor forced his face into calm lines. "I want to have a talk with Joe now. And Nick Cantrella. Anna, will you see if you can get Nick on the intercom? Ask him to come over here right away. I've got an idea."

In the living-room, he told Gracey: "You won't have to keep an eye on them any more, Joe. But watch *me*—*I* feel like Alexander, Napoleon, Eisenhower, and the Great Cham all rolled into one."

"You're certainly grinning like a lunatic," the agronomist agreed critically. "What's on your mind?"

"Wait a minute…Did you get him?" Tony asked as Anna came into the room.

"He's coming," she nodded. "Tony, what *is* it?"

"I'll tell you both, soon," he promised. "Let's wait for Nick, so I won't have to repeat it." He paced restlessly around the room, thinking it through again. It ought to work; it ought to!

When Cantrella arrived, he turned on the two men. "Listen, both of you!" He tried not to sound too eager. "If I handed you a piece of living tissue with a percentage of oxygen enzyme—and I don't mean traces, I mean a *percentage*—where would we stand in respect to—" He halted the cautious, complicated phraseology. "Hell, what I mean is, could we manufacture OxEn?"

"The living virus?" Gracey asked. "Not crystallized OxEn processed for absorption?"

"The living virus."

"We'd be a damn sight better than halfway along the processing that the Kelsey people do in Louisville. They grow the first culture from the Rosen batch, then they cull out all the competing enzymes, then they grow what's left and cull, for hundreds of stages, to get a percentage of the living virus to grow a pure culture they can crop and start crystallizing."

"How about it, Nick?" Tony demanded. "Could the Lab swing a job of crystallizing a crop from that and processing it for absorption?"

"Sure," said Nick. "That's the easy part. I've been reading up on it since we talked about it before."

"Look here," Gracey exploded, "where do you think you're going to get your living virus from? You have to keep getting it, you know. It always mutates under normal radiation sooner or later, and you have to start over again."

"That's my end of the deal. I have a hunch I can get it. Thanks, both of you." He went into the nursery and told Polly calmly, "I'm taking your youngster away again—just for a few minutes, though. I want to check his lungs in the hospital. Anna?" She was already taking the baby from Polly's arms. Tony picked up the wrapped marcaine-box and started out.

"Hey, Doc, what goes on?" Gracey demanded.

He brushed past Nick and the puzzled agronomist. "Tell you later," he called back.

On the street, Anna turned a worried face up to his. "Tony, what are you *doing?* You can't operate on a five-day-old baby…can you?" she finished, less certainly. "You seem so—so happy and *sure* of yourself."

"I am," he said shortly, and then relented enough to add, "The 'operation,' if you want to call it that, won't hurt him." But he wouldn't say any more.

Mimi and Brenner were in Tony's living-room. The woman said hopelessly, "Hello, Tony. Mr. Brenner's made an offer— Oh! It's Sunny!"

"Hello, Mimi," said Tony.

"The youngster, eh?" Brenner said genially. "I've heard about him."

With a brusque "Excuse me" to the drug manufacturer, Tony said to Anna in an undertone, "Rig the op table, sterilites on. Get out the portable biopsy constant-temperature bath and set the thermostats to Sunny's blood temperature. And call me."

She nodded and went into the hospital with the baby. Tony dropped his bundle into his trunk and began to scrub up.

"What's been going on, Mimi?" he asked.

"Mr. Brenner's offered five million, five hundred thousand dollars for Sun Lake's assets. I said the Council would put it in formal shape and call a vote."

The descent from his peak of inspiration was sickening. Nothing had changed, then, Tony thought.

"Ready," Anna said at his side. He followed her silently into the hospital, slipped into his gloves, and said, "Sterilize the Byers curette, third extension, and lubricate. Sterilize a small oral speculum." He spoke quietly. Graham was asleep in the bed across the room.

Anna didn't move. "Anesthesia?" she asked.

"None. We don't know their body-chemistry well enough."

"No, Tony. Please, no!"

He felt only a chill determination that he was going to salvage some of the wreckage of Sun Lake, determination and more confidence than he knew he should feel. Anna turned, selected the instruments, and slipped them into the sterilizer. The doctor stepped on the pedal that turned on the op lights.

Anna put the speculum into his hand and he clamped open Sunny's mouth. The prompt wail of protest turned to a strangled cry as the sinuous shaft of the Byers curette slid down the trachea into the left bronchus. One steady hand guided the instrument, while the other manipulated the controls from a bulb at its base.

"Hold him," Tony growled as Anna's hands weakened and the woman swayed. Bronchus, bronchia, bronchile, probing, and withdrawing at resistances—and there it was. A pressure on the central control that

uncovered the razor-sharp little spoon at the tip of the flexible shaft and covered it again, and then all flexure controls off and out. It had taken less than five seconds, and one more to deposit the shred of lung tissue in the biopsy constant-temperature nutrient bath.

Hank was at the door. Anna, leaning feebly against the table, straightened to tell him, "Go and lie down, Hank. It's all right."

"Keep him away from me," warned Graham from the bed. "He was going to jump me before."

"I just wanted to see the baby," Hank said apologetically.

Tony turned to the intercom, buzzing the Kandros'. "Come on over," he told them "You can have your baby back for keeps now. Is Gracey still there? Joe? I think I've got that tissue specimen for you. How fast can you get a test?"

"For God's sake, Tony, where did you get it?" Gracey was demanding on the other end.

"From a Martian dwarf." He couldn't resist it. "That's what I said. Lung tissue of a native Martian."

He hung up. Minutes went by...

"It *is* true! There are 'beings' here, aren't there?"

Tony turned to find the Kandros standing by the examination table. Polly already had her baby in her arms.

Jim patted her shoulder. "He doesn't really mean it, Polly. Do you, Doc?"

Graham was grinning openly.

Tony turned from one to the other, not answering.

There was a commotion in the living-room and Brenner burst in, carrying a familiar box. "He just dived for it, Tony," Mimi said. "He said it was—"

"Careful!" said the doctor. "You'll spray marcaine all over the place. Put it down, man!"

Brenner did, and unwrapped it with practiced precision. "My stuff, Doctor," he said. "Think I don't know my own crates? Mrs. Jonathan, my price for your assets has just dropped to two and one-half million. And I am now in a position to prosecute. I hope none of you will make difficulties."

Jim Kandro said, "I don't know what this is all about, but we need that stuff for Sunny."

"You don't *believe* that, do you?" the drug maker asked scornfully.

"I don't know what to believe," said Kandro. "But he's—different. And it makes sense. He doesn't have to take OxEn, but he has to take something else. You better leave it for us, Mr. Brenner."

The drug-maker looked at Jim wisely. "It's okay, Mac," he decided. "If you've got the habit and you can't kick it, why don't you come to work for me? I can use you. And you don't have to take so much. The micron dust in the air takes your edge off—"

"That's not it," said Kandro. "Why don't you listen to me? We need that stuff for Sunny. The doctor says so and he ought to know. It's medicine, like vitamins. You wouldn't keep vitamins from a little baby, would you?"

Graham snickered.

Kandro turned and lectured angrily: "You stay out of this. There hasn't been anything but trouble since you got here. Now you could at least keep from braying while a man's trying to reason with somebody. You may be smart and a big writer, but you don't have any manners at all if you can't keep quiet at a time like this."

He turned to Brenner. "You know we don't have any money here, or I'd offer you what we had. I guess the box is yours, and nobody has a claim to it except you. But Polly and I can get permission from the Council to go and work out whatever the box would cost. Couldn't we, Tony? Mimi? The rest would let us, wouldn't they?"

"I'm sorry, Mac," the drug maker said. "I wish I could make you understand, but if I can't, that doesn't matter. This box is going with me. It's evidence in a crime."

"Mr. Brenner," Jim Kandro said thickly, "I can't let you out of here with that box. We need it for Sunny. I told you and told you. Now give it here." He put out one big hand.

"How about it, Mrs. Jonathan?" Brenner seemed to be ignoring the big man's menacing advance. "Two and a half million? It's a very reasonable price, all things considered. Your new father here would be glad to take it."

"I'll take it, all right," growled Jim. "Hand it over. Right now." He was a scant four feet from the drug maker; Brenner's eyes were still fixed mockingly on Mimi Jonathan.

Kandro took one more step forward and Anna cried faintly, "No!"

Brenner stepped back and there was a large pistol in his hand. "This," he told them, "is *fully* automatic. It keeps firing as long as I hold the trigger down. I can spray the room with it. Now for the last time listen, all of you. I'm going, and I'm taking my box with me. If you try to stop me, I have a perfect right to use this gun. You know better than I do what fingerprints the authorities will find on the box. You're caught red-handed and I won't have any trouble proving it to my man Bell."

Mimi Jonathan said clearly, "So you're going to throw us off Mars, Mr. Brenner?"

"If necessary," he said, not following.

"You mean you're going to kick us out and we'll never see Mars again? And all the sacrifices we've made here will be a joke?"

He didn't get what she was driving at. "Yes," he said irritably. "You're quite right—"

He was cut off by Hank, broken at last under the goading. The youngster sprang, raving, at Brenner, bowling him over as the pistol roared in a gush of bullets that ripped Hank's body. But even in death Hank kept his fingers on Brenner's throat.

And then there was a silence into which Sunny Kandro shrieked his fear. Mimi leaned against the wall and shut her eyes. She wanted to vomit. She heard Tony's awed whisper: "...smashed his trachea...broke his neck...belly shot clean out..." She shuddered, and hoped and feared she'd carry this guilt alone to the grave.

CHAPTER TWENTY-SIX

"COME ON, POLLY. You come out here." Kandro led his wife, still carrying Sunny, out to the living-room.

Faces were peering through the hospital window and they heard Nick Cantrella shouting, "Let me through, dammit! Clear away from that door!" And he was in, latching the door from the street. He snapped the curtains shut with an angry yank. "What in God's name happened? I was coming for that tissue culture and now this—"

"Don't worry about it," said Graham dryly arid with effort from the bed. "Just a little useful murder. Hank Radcliff, hero of the Colony, gives his life to save the world from Brenner." He swore in awed delight. "*What* a story! 'The Killing of Hugo Brenner'—an eyewitness account by Douglas Graham! Didn't Brenner know who I was?"

Mimi started. "I guess not," she realized. "I never told him."

"You're plenty beat up," Tony pointed out. "He wouldn't have recognized you. Hey, Nick, let's get those bodies out of here."

"Beat up is right," Graham chortled, "and it was worth it! Thank *you,* my friends, whichever one of you—or how many was it?—did that job on me. I thank you from the bottom of my poor old Gunther's heart. Just to be able to lie here and listen to all that!"

"I don't know who did it last time." Nick took one menacing step toward the bed. "But, by God, if you're starting on another of your yarns, I know who's going to—"

"Nick, wait a minute. You don't know what he heard."

"Hey, Cantrella, I need a hand here."

"I *know* who did it." Anna had to shout to make herself heard above Mimi and Tony, both talking at once. In the sudden silence, she said, "Didn't I tell you, Tony? I guess it was while you were away that I found out. *They* did it. I think he was planning to hurt the baby. Or they thought he was."

"*They?*" the writer asked contemptuously. "Dwarf-things again? You're a good second-guesser, Miss Willendorf, but you missed out this time. The only designs I ever had on the Kandro kid were to get him back to Earth where he could be properly cared for—instead of getting marcaine dosed out to him to cover up for Mamma."

"Listen, you lying crimp." Nick continued his arrested advance on Graham. "If you think you're safe to turn out more of that kind of stuff just because you're laid up in bed, you better start thinking all over again. I've got no compunctions about kicking a rat when he's down."

"Nick! Stop it!" Swift and sure and deadly sharp, Mimi's voice came across the room like a harpoon. Give him a chance! You didn't hear what *he* heard—what Brenner said. I don't see how anybody could get a story against Sun Lake out of it."

"Thank you kindly, ma'm." Graham grinned painfully. "Good to know somebody around here is still sane. Don't tell me you go for this dwarf nonsense too!"

"I—don't know," she said. "If I'd heard it from anybody but Tony and Anna, I wouldn't believe a word of it. But they *did* get the baby back."

"Back from where?"

Tony realized for the first time that Graham didn't even know about Sunny's kidnapping. And the others for that matter, still didn't know what had happened in the cave.

"Listen," he said. "If you'll all take it easy for a few minutes, Anna and I have a lot to tell you. But first…Nick, help me move them to the living-room floor. Anna, get blankets to cover them."

"Wait a minute." She went into the living-room. "All right," she called back a moment later, and Tony and Nick together carried what was left of Hank through the door. "I wanted to get the Kandros out first," Anna explained, locking the front door again.

They laid out Brenner's body next to Hank's, and covered them both with blankets. The two men started back to the hospital, but Anna laid her hand on Tony's arm to stop him.

"Could I see you a minute?"

"Of course." He let Nick go ahead, then asked, worried, "Ansie, darling, what's the matter?"

She closed the door. "Tony, we can't tell them," she said. "Not now."

"Why not? They've got to know."

"Don't you *see?* We shouldn't have talked as much as we did. We shouldn't have said or done anything in front of Graham, but he doesn't believe it yet. If we convince him—Tony, the dwarfs are terrified of people. They've kept away from people all along. For a reason. Don't you *see?*" she asked urgently. "Think what would happen to them. Think! I got just a flash of Graham's mind when I said *they* did it, before he decided to be skeptical. It was brutal. They'd be exterminated."

He did see it. She was right. He thought of Hackenburg over at Pittco, and the little Martian "men" being worked in the mines—"native labor." He thought of what an Earth power would give to have telepaths in its military intelligence. He thought of the horror and hatred people would feel for the "mind-reading monsters." He thought of them in zoos, on dissecting-tables…

He thought of Sun Lake, still facing a charge of theft; of the difference it would make in Graham's story if he knew it *wasn't* Sun Lakers who attacked him. He thought of what the existence of the strange new race of 'men' would mean to medical and biochemical research. And he made up his mind.

Anna looked away with anger in her eyes, hopelessness in the set of her shoulders.

"*Why?*" she begged. "They're— Oh, Tony, they're *decent!* Not like most people."

"Because *we* know about them, that's why. Because you can't—you just *can't* keep a secret like that. Because—it means too much to men, to all men, to mankind, or whatever part of it survives the end of Earth. Anna, Sun Lake may not be the answer to our future—the dwarfs may be. Have you thought of that? They need us, they need to learn some of the things our civilization has to offer—and we need them. That piece of tissue I took from Sunny's lungs may mean the end of dependence on Earth for OxEn, and that's just one first thing. There's no knowing how much we can learn, how they can help us to adapt, what new knowledge will come out of the contact. We *can't* keep it to ourselves. That's all there is to it."

"There's no use arguing, is there?"

"I'm afraid not," he said as gently as he could. He opened the door. "Are you coming back?"

She hesitated, then followed…

"That's it," Tony wound up the narrative of their visit to the cave, and then repeated, this time to Graham:

"That's it. But I think you ought to know that Anna was trying to persuade me not to tell this story in front of you, to let you go on not believing in these dwarfs. She was afraid of what people would do to them once it became known. I'm afraid too. What you write will have a lot to do with it." He paused. "What *are* you going to write?"

"I'm damned if I know!" Graham tried to lift his head, and decided against it. "It's either the most ingenious yarn I've ever heard—it covers every single accusation against you people, from marcaine theft to mayhem on my person—or it's the biggest story in the world. And I'm damned if I know which!"

He relapsed into a thoughtful silence, broken suddenly by the roar of a large plane. An instant later there was the noise of a second, and then a third. One at a time they came closer, and died out.

"That would be Bell." Mimi stood up wearily. "I don't mind saying I'm confused. What do we do now?"

"He's coming," Tony reminded her, "to help Mr. Graham. Perhaps we should leave it up to our guest to tell the Commissioner whatever he sees fit."

The writer was silent, stony-faced.

"There's a slight matter of a couple of stiffs in the living-room," Nick reminded them. "The Commish might want to know about them. Strictly intercolony stuff."

"You know," Graham broke in suddenly, "if I were dumb enough to believe your story about Martian dwarfmen—and if your little experiment with the kid's lungs works—Sun Lake could get to be quite a place."

"How do you mean?" Gracey asked.

"The way Mr. Brenner had it figured, your Lab is practically made to order for marcaine manufacture. And I gather you think you can turn out OxEn too, if that lung tissue is good. If there's anything behind all this dwarf talk—well, you've got a deal that looks worth a trillion. You can supply OxEn to all of Mars at what price? It wouldn't cost you anything compared to Earth-import." He looked around the circle of astonished faces.

"Don't tell me none of you even *thought* of that? Not even *you?*" he appealed to Mimi.

She shook her head. "That's not the Sun Lake idea," she said stiffly. "We wouldn't be interested."

Anna smiled, very slightly, and there was a violent banging at the front door.

Tony went slowly through the living-room. The door was beginning to shake under the blows.

"Cut that out and I'll open it!" he yelled. There was silence as he swung the door open. A sergeant of the guards, three others, and Bell, who was well in the rear. He must have heard there'd been shooting.

"What's been going on?" the Commissioner began. He sniffed the air and his eyes traveled to the covered bodies. "Graham? If it is, we might have a murder arrest. His dispatch gave you people plenty of motive."

"No. Brenner," Tony said shortly. "And a young man named Hank Radcliff."

Bell, starting for the figures, recoiled. "Sergeant," he said, and gestured. The non-com gingerly drew back the blankets, exposing the drug maker's face. The Commissioner stared for a long moment and said hoarsely, "Cover it, Sergeant." He turned to Tony. "What happened?"

"We have a disinterested witness," said the doctor. "Douglas Graham. He saw the whole thing."

Tony led the way into the hospital. The sergeant followed, then the Commissioner. Graham said from his bed, "Visiting a dead friend?"

Bell snapped, "It's an intercolony crime. Murder. Obviously I can't take the word of anybody who's a member of this community. Did you witness the killing?"

"I was a witness, all right," said Graham. "Best damn witness you ever saw. Billions of readers hang on my every word." He made an effort and raised himself on one elbow. "Remember the chummy sessions we used to have in Washington, Bell?"

On the Commissioner's forehead sweat formed.

"Here's the story of the killing," said Graham. "Brenner pulled his gun on the man named Kandro during a little dispute. He threatened to kill Kandro, went into some detail about how fully automatic that gun was and—let me think—his exact words were 'spray the room.' With a babe in arms present. Think of it, Bell! Not even you would have done a thing like that; not even in the old days. The Radcliff kid jumped Brenner and took all the slugs in his belly. I guess they were dumdums, because the gun looked to me like a .38 and none of them went through. Only the Radcliff boy squashed Brenner's neck before he knew he was dead. Reminded me of a time once in Asia—"

Bell cut him off. "Did Brenner die right away? Did he say anything before he died?"

"Deathbed confession? Delirious rambling? No."

The Commissioner relaxed perceptibly.

"But," said the newsman, "he talked quite a bit *before* he pulled the gun. He didn't recognize me with my battered face and I didn't introduce myself. He thought it was a bunch of Sun Lakers in here and that nobody would believe a word they said about him. Brenner talked quite a bit."

"Sergeant!" Bell broke in. "I won't be needing you for a while. Wait for me in the other room. And see to it that nobody touches those bodies!"

The door closed behind the non-com, and Graham laughed. "Maybe you do know, eh, Commish? Maybe you know Brenner liked to refer to you as 'my man Bell'?"

The Commissioner's eyes ran unhappily around the room. "You people," he said. "Get out. All of you. Leave us alone—so I can take a statement."

"No," said Graham, "they stay here. I'm not a strong man these days, but Brenner talked quite a bit. I wouldn't want anything to stop me from getting the story to an eagerly waiting world."

Bell looked around hopelessly. Tony saw Nick's face twist into a knowing, malevolent grin; like the others, he made an effort to imitate it.

"What do you want, Graham?" asked the Commissioner. "What are you trying to get at?"

"Not a thing," the writer said blandly. "By the way, in my statement on the killing, should I include what Brenner had to say about you? He mentioned some financial matters, too. Would they be relevant?"

Tony tried to remember what financial matters Brenner had discussed, aside from the price he offered for the Colony. None—but Graham was a shrewd bluffer.

The Commissioner made a last effort to pull himself together. "You can't intimidate me, Graham," he rasped. "And don't think I can't be tough if you force my hand. I'm in the clear. I don't care what Brenner said; I haven't done a thing."

"*Yet,*" said the writer succinctly. "Your part was to come later, wasn't it?"

Bell's face seemed to collapse.

"Still think you can get tough?" Graham jeered. "Try it, and I guarantee that you'll be hauled back to Earth on the next rocket, to be tried for malfeasance, exceeding your authority, accepting bribes, and violating the narcotics code. I can also guarantee that you will be convicted and imprisoned for the rest of your life. Don't try to bluff me, you tinhorn sport. I've been bluffed by experts."

The Commissioner began shrilly, "I won't stand for—" and cracked. "For God's sake, Graham, be reasonable! What have I ever done to you? What do you want? Tell me what you want!"

The writer fell back on the bed. "Nothing right now, thanks. If I think of anything, I'll let you know."

The Commissioner started to speak, and couldn't. Tony saw the veins of tension stand out. He saw, too, how Anna's lip was curling in disgust.

Graham seemed amused. "There *is* one thing, Commish. An inter-colony matter under your jurisdiction, I believe. Will you remove those carcasses on your way out? You'd be surprised how sensitive I am about such things."

He closed his eyes and waited till the door was shut behind the departing guest. When he opened them again, all the self-assurance was gone out of them.

"Doc," he moaned, "give me a shot. When I got up on my elbow something tore. God, it hurts!"

While Tony took care of him Joe Gracey said, "It was a grand performance, Mr. Graham. Thank you for what you did."

"I can undo it," the reporter said flatly, "or I can use it any way I want to. If you people have been lying to me—" He sighed with relief. "Thanks, Doc. That's a help. Now if you want anything out of *my* man Bell—show me one of your Martian dwarf-men!"

CHAPTER TWENTY-SEVEN

GRAHAM'S CHALLENGE fell into a silent room. Everyone waited for Tony to speak; Tony waited for Anna.

"I don't see why not," she said at last. "I guess they'd do it." She looked despairingly at Tony. "Is this the *only* way?" she pleaded.

"It's the only way you're going to beat that marcaine theft rap," Graham answered for him.

"All right. I'll go out there in the morning. I think I can talk them in to it."

"If you don't mind, Miss Willendorf. I'd rather it was right now. In twelve hours, your hot-shot engineer here could probably *build* a robot dwarf."

"I can try," she said. "But I can't promise. Not even for tomorrow. I only think I can talk one of them into coming here. I don't know how they'll feel about it."

Graham grinned. "That's about how I figured it," he said. "Thanks, folks. It was a good show while it lasted."

"We're going," Tony said grimly. "And we'll bring you back a native Martian."

"Still not good enough," the writer said. "If you go, I go with you. You mind if I'm just a little suspicious?"

"It's ten kilometers to the Rimrocks," Tony told him. "Most of it by half-tracks, the rest by stretcher for you."

"All right," the writer said. "When do we start?"

Tony looked questioningly at Anna, who nodded. "Right now," the doctor said, "or any time you're ready." He opened a cabinet and fished out a patent-syringe ampoule. "This should make it easier." He started to open the package.

"No, thanks," Graham said. "I want to see what I see—if anything." His eyes went swiftly from one face to another, studying them for reactions.

"If you can take it, I can," the doctor told him. But he dropped the package in his pocket before they left.

In the rattling half-track, with Anna driving and Tony in the truck body beside Graham, the writer said through clenched teeth, "God help you if you tell me these creatures aren't biting tonight. It's a damn-fool notion anyway. You've been telling me they are born of Earth people. Why aren't there any born on Earth?"

"It's because of what the geneticists call a lethal gene. Polly and Jim, for instance. Each one of them had a certain lethal gene in his heredity. Either of them could have married somebody without the lethal gene and had ordinary babies, on Earth or on Mars, because the gene is a recessive. On Earth, when Polly's lethal gene and Jim's lethal gene matched, it was fatal to their offspring. They never came to term; the gene produced a fetus which couldn't survive the womb on Earth. I don't know what factors are involved in that failure—cosmic rays, the gravity, or what. But on Mars the fetus comes to term and is—a mutant.

"A Martian. They don't just *accept* Mars air like an Earthman with Marsworthy lungs. They can't *stand* Earth air. And they need a daily ration of marcaine to grow and live. That's who stole Brenner's marcaine. That's why they slipped marcaine into Polly Kandro's food. They wanted her to pass it to Sunny in her milk. When we put Sunny on the bottle, they stole him so they could give him marcaine. They surrendered him on our promise to see that he got it."

"And that's a perfect cover-story for a dope-addict mamma," scoffed the writer. "How many of these mutants are there supposed to be?"

"A couple of hundred. I suppose about half of them are first generation. There must have been a very few in the beginning, children of homesteaders abandoned on a desert ranch when their parents died, who crawled out and lived off the country, chewing marcaine out of the weed. And they must have 'stolen' other Martian babies from other homesteaders when they grew."

Graham swore against the pain. "The Kandro kid looks as normal as any other baby. How are the mutants supposed to know he isn't? Does he give them a password?"

Tony explained wearily: "They are telepathic. It explains a lot of things—why they're only seen by people they want to see them, why they could steal Brenner's marcaine and not get caught. They can hear people coming—their thoughts, that is. That's why they beat up Big Ginny; she was aborting a Martian baby. Why they beat the hell out of you. Why they sensibly keep away from most Earth people."

"Except Red Sand Jim Granata, eh?"

"Granata was a liar. He probably never saw one in his life. He heard all the dwarf yarns and used them to put on good commercial shows."

Anna maneuvered the half-track around a spur of rock picked out by the headlights and ground the vehicle to a stop. "It's too rugged from here on," she said. "We'll have to carry him the rest of the way."

"You warm enough? Another blanket?" asked Tony.

"You're really going through with this, aren't you?" said the writer. "I'm crazy to play along, but *if*—*if* this is a story and I get beaten on it— Oh, hell, yes, I'm warm enough. Stretcher ought to be easier going than this tin can."

Anna led, with Graham swaying between them on a shoulder-suspended litter that left the bearers' hands free. The writer's weight was not much of a burden in this gravity. Both she and Tony used torches to pick their way among the scree that had dribbled for millennia, one stone at a time, down the weathering Rimrocks. They smelled the acrid fumes of Pittco across the hills, fouling the night air, and Graham began to cough.

"Anna?" asked the doctor.

She knew what he meant, and said shortly, "Not yet."

Another hundred meters and Tony felt her begin to pull off to the right. Her "homing" led them to the foot of the mesa-like hills a few meters from a cave mouth. They headed in.

"Quite soon," said Anna, and then: "We can put him down."

"Be very quiet," Tony told the writer. He himself felt the faint, eerie "touch" of a mutant in his mind. "They're very sensitive to—"

"Gargh!" shrieked Graham as a weird little fellow stepped into the beam from Anna's light. It clapped its hands over its ears and fled.

"Now see what you did!" raged Anna in an angry whisper. "Their ears—you almost deafened him."

"Get him back!" The writer's voice was tremulous.

"I don't know if I can," Anna said coldly. "He doesn't have to take orders from you *or* me. All I can do is try."

"You'd better. It scared the hell out of me, I admit, but so did the fakes in Granata's Interplanetary Show."

"Man, didn't you *feel* it?" asked Tony incredulously.

"What?" asked Graham.

"Please be quiet, both of you!"

They waited a long time in the cold corridor before the thing reappeared, stepping warily into the circle of light.

Suddenly Anna laughed. "He wants to know why you want to pull his ears off. He sees you thinking of pulling his ears and the ears coming off and he's as puzzled as he can be."

"Shrewd guess," said Graham. "Do I get to pull them?"

"No. If you have any questions, tell me, and I'll try to ask him."

"I think it's a fake. Come out from behind those whiskers, whoever you are. Stillman? Gracey? No, you're too short. I'll bet you're that little punk Tad Campbell from the radio shack."

"This isn't getting us anywhere," said Tony. "Graham, if you think of a person or a scene or something, the little fellow will get it telepathically, give it to Anna, and she'll say what it is."

"Fair enough," said the writer. "I don't know what it's supposed to prove, but it's some kind of test. I'm thinking."

A moment later Anna said evenly, "If you weren't beaten up already, I'd slap your face off."

"I'm sorry," said Graham hastily. "I was only kidding. I didn't really think it would—but it did, didn't it?" With mounting excitement he said, "Ask him who he is, who his people were, whether he's married, how old he is—"

Anna held up her hand. "That's enough to start. I can't think of any way to ask him his name. His parents—homesteaders—a shack and a goat—a kitchen garden-tall people, the man wears thick glasses— Tony! It's the ToIlers!"

"That's impossible," he said. "Their son's on Earth. He never answers their letters," the doctor remembered. "They keep writing, and—how old was he when he left?"

"I don't know," she answered a moment later. "He doesn't understand the question."

"I felt it," said the writer, suddenly, in a frightened voice. "Like a thing touching you inside your head. Is that him?"

"That's him. Just don't fight it."

After a long silence Graham said quietly, "Hell, he's all right. They're all-right people, aren't they?"

"Do you want to ask him any more questions?" asked Anna.

"A million of them. But not right now. Can I come back again?" asked the writer slowly and heavily. "When I'm in better shape?" He waited for Anna's nod, then said, "Will you say thanks to him and get me to the 'track?"

"Pain worse?" asked Tony.

"No, I don't think so. Hell, I don't know. As a matter of fact, I'm just worn out."

The small mutant glided from the circle of light. " 'Bye, fella," said Graham, and then grinned weakly. "He said good-bye back at me!"

Gracey and Nick and half a dozen of the biochem lab boys were waiting for them at the hospital when they got back. Joe must have been watching out of the window, because he ran out to meet them.

It was late, and the lights were already out in most of the double row of rust-brown huts. But Joe Gracey, the quiet one, the gentle ex-professor, possessor of eternal calm and detachment, came flying down the dim street, shouting, "Doc! Tony! *We've got it!*"

"Sh-h…" Tony nodded toward the dozing man on the shoulder litter, but Graham was already opening his eyes.

"What's up?" he asked mushily. "What's all excitement?"

"Nothing at all," the doctor tried to tell him. "We're back in the Colony. And you're going to bed. Hold on just a minute, will you, Joe?" He knew how Gracey felt; it was hard enough to restrain his own jubilance and keep his voice in neutral register. But Graham had had enough for one night, and Tony had to get his patient back to the hospital bed before he could take time to listen even to such news as Gracey bore.

Joe helped them get the writer comfortably settled, and waited impatiently while the doctor made a quick check for any possible damage done by the trip. Finally Anna pulled up the covers, and the three of them started out.

"Oh, Doctor—" Tony turned to find Graham up again on one elbow, wide-eyed and not a bit sleepy. "I was just wondering if I could have my typewriter." Before Tony could answer, the elbow collapsed and Graham smiled ruefully. "I guess not. I couldn't work it. You don't have anything as luxurious as an Earthside dictatyper in the place, do you?"

"Sure," Tony told him. "We've got one in the Lab office. You get some rest now, and we'll set it up for you here in the morning."

"I'm okay," Graham insisted. "There's something I'd like to get on paper right away. I won't be able to sleep anyhow if I don't get it done."

"You'll sleep," the doctor said. "I can give you a shot."

"No." Graham was determined. "If you can't get the dictatyper out here now, how about some pencil and paper? I *think* I still know how to use them."

"I'll see what we can do. Anna, will you come with me?"

Tony led her, not to the living-room where the others were waiting, but into the bedroom. "How about it?" he asked in a whisper. "How's he feeling?"

"It's a funny mixture, Tony," she said, "but I think it's all right. He's not nearly as excited as he was before. He's eager, but calm and—well, it's hard to express, but *honest,* too."

"Right." He tightened his hand swiftly on her shoulder and smiled down at her small, earnest face. "A man could get too used to this," he said. "How do you suppose I got along before I knew about you?"

He strode into the living-room and consulted briefly with Nick, after which two of the men from the biochem section tramped out to the Lab and brought back the machine for Graham to use.

Through the living-room door, Tony heard the writer's voice droning on, dictating, and the soft tapping of the machine. But what was going on in the hospital didn't seem important.

The thing that mattered was the tiny pinch of pink powder Nick and Joe had been waiting to show him.

"Tony," said Nick, exultantly, "look at this stuff! It's damn near oral-administration OxEn. Took it through twelve stages of concentration and we'll take it through exactly three more to completion when Anna blows some hyvac cells for us. I tried and all I got was blistered fingers."

"It works?" asked Tony.

"It's beautiful," said Gracey. "The Kelsey people must have fifty contaminants they don't even suspect are there. Now I want to know where that sample tissue came from and where you're going to get more. And what did you mean about dwarfs?"

"Didn't Nick tell you?" Tony looked from the puzzled face to the startled one, and chortled appreciatively. "You mean you've been working together on this thing all evening and you never—?"

"He didn't ask," Cantrella said defensively. "Anyhow, we weren't working together. We weren't even in the same Lab."

"Okay," Tony grinned, "here goes again. You gave me the idea originally, Joe. As much as any one person or thing did. You were talking the other day about lethal genes. Remember, I tried to ask you about it this afternoon?"

"When Mimi blew up? Sure."

"That's when it hit me. I got that lung tissue from Sunny Kandro, Joe. After we brought him home. He's a mutant—the result of a Mars-viable gene that's lethal on Earth."

"And there are more of them?" Gracey leaned forward excitedly. "Are they co-operative? Will they answer questions? And submit to examination? When can I see one?"

"They're co-operative," Anna said, smiling. "The reason you haven't seen one yet is that they can't stand humans—too unco-operative to suit them. Examinations? I don't see why not, if your intentions are honorable. They're telepaths, so they'd know you didn't mean to harm them."

"Telepaths!" Gracey breathed the word as Nick exclaimed it. "What other changes—" the agronomist started to ask, then said instead, "No sense you telling me. I *will* see one? Soon?"

Anna nodded. "Why not?"

"How about new tissue then?" Joe asked her. "Can we get it when we need it? You know how this stuff works? The old culture keeps mutating, and you have to start it over again. We can't keep taking slices out of Sunny all the time."

"I don't know," she had to admit. "I don't know if they'd understand what for, or why you're doing it."

"I don't think we'll have any trouble," Tony put in. "Nick, our Lab is equipped to turn out marcaine, isn't it?"

"Well, hell—yes, of course, but what for?"

"Marcaine and OxEn both? Do we have the facilities for it?"

"Sure. Processing the OxEn won't take up much."

"Then I'm sure we can get our lung-scrapings," the doctor said. "What do you say, Ansie? Will they do it? After all, you're the expert on these mutants."

"They like us," she said thoughtfully. "They trust us, too. They need marcaine. Yes, I think they'd do it."

"Doc!" It was Graham, calling from inside. Tony opened the door. "There anything left in that bottle of mine?"

"Hasn't been touched."

"Pour me a shot, will you? A good, long one. I'm not in such hot shape. And pass the bottle around."

Tony filled a glass generously. "Take it and go to sleep," he ordered. "You're going to feel worse tomorrow."

"Thanks. That's what I call a bedside manner."

Graham grinned and tossed off the drink with a happy shudder. "I've got some copy here," he said. "Can Stillman get it out tonight?"

Tony took the typed paper from the dictating machine and paused a moment, irresolutely.

Graham laughed sleepily. "It's in the clear," he said. "No code. And you can read it if you like. Two messages and Take One of the biggest running story of the century."

"Thanks," said Tony. "Good night." He closed the door firmly behind him.

"Story from Graham," he said to the group. He buzzed Harve.

"Read it!" said Nick. "And if that lying rat pulls another—"

Tony gathered courage at last to run his eyes over the copy, and gasped with relief. " 'Message to Marsport communications," he read. " 'Kill all copy previously sent for upcoming substitutes. Douglas Graham.' And 'Message to Commissioner Hamilton Bell, Marsport, Administration. As interested lay observer strongly urge you withdraw intended application of Title Fifteen search cordon to Sun Lake Colony. Personal investigation convinces me theft allegations unfounded, Title Fifteen application grave injustice which my duty expose fullest before public and official circles on return Earth. Appreciate you message me acknowledgment. Douglas Graham.' "

Nick's yell of triumph hit the roof. "What are we waiting for?" he demanded. "Where's Mimi? We have packing to do!"

"What's the matter with him?" asked Harve Stillman, coming in.

Tony was reading the last of the messages to himself. Anna told him, "You like that one best of all. What's in it?"

He looked up with a grin across his face. "I'm sorry," he said. "This is how it starts: 'Marsport communications, sub following for previous copy, which kill. By Douglas Graham. With mutants, lead to come.' Harve, what does that mean?"

The ex-wire-serviceman snapped, "It's additional copy on a story about the dwarfs—the first part isn't ready to go yet. What's he *say*, Tony?"

The doctor read happily: " 'The administrative problems raised by this staggering discovery are not great. It is fortunate that Dr. Hellman and Miss Willendorf, co-discoverers of the Martians, are persons of unquestioned integrity, profoundly interested in protecting the new race from exploitation. I intend to urge the appointment of one of them as special Commissioner for the P.A.C. to take charge of mutant welfare and safety. There must be no repetition of the tragedies that marked Earthly colonial expansion when greedy and shortsighted—' "

"Damn, that's great," muttered the radio man. "Let me file it."

The doctor, with the grin still on his face, handed over the copy and Harve raced out.

Joe Gracey said, "Well, I certainly hope whichever one of you turns out to be Commissioner is going to give us Lab men a decent chance at research on the mutants. I was thinking—I could probably work out a test for the lethal gene, or Martian gene, better call it. Spermatozoa from a male, a polar body or an ovum from a female and we'd be able to tell—"

"No!" said Anna hysterically.

The others were shocked into silence.

"I'll take you home, Ansie," said Tony.

He took her arm and they walked out into the icy night down the Colony street.

"Ansie, I've been sort of taking things for granted. I should ask you once, for the record." He stopped walking and faced her. "Will you marry me?"

"Oh, *Tony!* How *can* we? I thought—for just a little while after I told you about me, I thought perhaps we could, that life could be the way it is for other people. But now this. How *can* we?"

"What are you afraid of?"

"Afraid? I'm afraid of our children, afraid of this planet! I was never afraid before. I was hurt and bewildered when I knew too much about people, but—Tony, don't you *see?* To have a baby like Polly's, to have it grow up a stranger, an alien creature, to have it leave me and go to its—its *own* people—"

He took her hand and began walking again, searching for the words he needed.

"Ansie," he began, "I think we will be married. If you want it as much as I do, we surely will be. And we'll have children. And more than that, the hope of all the race will lie in our children, Anna. Ours and the children of the other people here. And the children of the mutants. Don't forget that.

"They look different. They even think differently, and nobody knows more about that than you. But they're as human as we are. Maybe more so.

"We've made a beginning here at Sun Lake tonight. We've cut the big knot, the knot that kept us tied to Earth. Our mutants helped us do that, and maybe they can help us lick this planet in all the ways that still remain. Maybe they can help us cure the next Joan Radcliff. Maybe they can keep us from going blind when the protective shots from Earth stop coming through."

"But maybe they can't."

"Ansie, if our children should be mutants, we'd not only have to face it, accept it without fear—we'd have to be glad. Mutants are the children of Mars, natural human children of Mars. We don't know yet whether *we* can live here; but we *know they can.*"

"They're gentle. They're honest and decent and rational. They trust each other, not because of blind loves and precedents, as we do, but because they know each other as Earth humans never can. If blind hates and precedents end life on Earth, Ansie, we can go on at Sun Lake. And we can go on that much better for knowing that even our failure, if we fail, won't be the end."

He stopped at the door and looked down at her, searching for the understanding that had to be there. If Anna failed, what other woman would comprehend?

"I'll ask you this time," she said soberly. "Tony, will you marry me?"

Shadow on the Hearth

VEDA

Veda was sick that day. She woke up at seven, as always, but her joints ached, and even a cup of hot tea did not ease the queasy feeling. She waited till almost eight, so as not to wake anyone, then wrapped herself from collarbone to bony ankles in an ancient blanket bathrobe and made a labored descent to the telephone in the hall. She felt her way along the windowless stairwell, feverishly angry at the landlady's refusal to light the landing during the day.

Ordinarily Veda was inclined to be, as she put it herself, "tolerant to a fault," so the poisonous black hatred for Mrs. Kovan shocked her and confirmed her judgment in staying home that day. She called the Mitchell home, and the Missus answered right away.

Mrs. Mitchell was sincere in her sympathy. Her voice sounded sleepy and warm, and Veda could hear one of the kids yelling from another room. It made her feel bad about staying out.

"Now don't you touch the washin', Missus," she said plaintively. "I kin manage that fine tomorrer."

"Don't be silly, Veda. You take care of yourself, and don't worry about anything. And don't suffocate yourself in that room of yours, hear me?"

Veda hung up and climbed back to her room, smiling in spite of the dark landings and the ache in her joints. Missus Mitchell was a fine woman, but she had a lot of foolish notions. Veda inspected the windows and weatherstripping in her room and stuffed an old stocking in the only crack she could find.

She brewed more tea in the curtained kitchenette and pulled the extra comforter over her bed. Then she checked the bolt on the door. She never could get to sleep in a public rooming house without making sure her door was locked shut.

Sealed off from the world, she took two pills from an old green bottle and pulled another stocking—a woolen one—over her head to cover her ears. Finally she climbed in under the double comforter to sweat out the poisons. She had no way of knowing she had just saved a life.

CHAPTER ONE

GLADYS MITCHELL left the phone and could not repress a small sigh. In the dining room Ginny was clamoring for breakfast. Upstairs Jon was loudly demanding some clean socks. Veda, she reflected, was a good worker and a fine person; but she did have her ailments, and there was no way out of it.

"Barbie," Gladys called over the noise, "see what Ginny wants, will you?" She passed the hall mirror and frowned into it; there ought to be some way to turn the thing off in the morning. She called up to Jon and told him where to find the socks, then listened to his footsteps as he followed her instructions. Ginny had stopped yelling, but that was not necessarily good. Gladys walked swiftly into the dining room and found the five-year-old contentedly stuffing herself with hot oatmeal.

Barbara came through the swinging door from the kitchen. She set down her own oatmeal and gave Gladys a cup of steaming coffee. "Everything was ready on the stove, so I just dished it out." She was defiant about it. At fifteen, she knew she ought to hate housework.

Touched, Gladys squeezed her daughter's arm and sipped gratefully from the hot cup. She thought of Veda, alone in the dark little boarding-house room, and she looked from her two daughters to Tom's picture on the lowboy—a freckle-faced boy grinning out of an open-necked khaki shirt, his R.O.T.C. cap pushed back on his head, the world in his hands. He had sent it home from school two months before, proud testimonial to his homemade photo enlarger. Her eyes wandered on to the window and the big maple tree outside. Then Jon came in and dropped a kiss on the top of her head before he crossed to the other end of the table.

He surveyed the uneven edges of his grapefruit and asked with the first mouthful, "Veda out again?" He picked up his paper. "Maybe you ought to get someone else, Glad?"

He hid his smile behind the raised newspaper as three feminine voices answered immediately and firmly. He knew how they felt about Veda.

"I ought to do the wash," Gladys was thinking out loud, "but there's that luncheon today…"

"Oh, Mother! Isn't the laundry done yet? I've got to have those things for tonight."

Gladys surveyed her older daughter absently. "What's tonight?"

"The class! I don't see how you can forget it every time. And I gave you the jackets a week ago…"

"You gave them to me Monday night," Gladys pointed out. "We only do laundry once a week around here, you know."

"I can iron 'em myself when I get back from school," Barbie pleaded, "but they've got to be starched and everything—they have to be washed this morning, Mom."

She still calls me "Mom" when she wants something, Gladys noted with amused satisfaction. "Mother" had come into use some months back as part of Barbara's campaign to convince the whole family, and primarily herself, that she was now fully mature.

"Are we taking in wash now?" Jon looked up from his paper.

"Oh, Daddy, I told you all about it. It's the white jackets for the baby sitters, and I got them at a sale, and they were all dirty. I'd never have got the kids to use them if they weren't so cheap."

"I don't know which is worse," Jon grumbled contentedly. "First it was Tom trying to blow the house up with a basement lab, and now you've got us running rings around a batch of baby sitters. Who started that club anyhow? And why in the name of all that's holy do baby sitters need white jackets?"

"I did," Barbie said defiantly. "And I already collected the money for the jackets, so I don't see what good it does to argue about that. I've just got to have them, that's all."

"Well, I ought to do the laundry anyhow. I think I can manage if you drive them to school…" Gladys looked inquiringly at her husband. "You could take the car right into town. Barbie'll have to come straight home from school anyhow, so she could bring Ginny home on the bus."

"Okay." Jon nodded and went back to his paper. The headlines jumped at him, bearing threats of war and disaster; in the shaded room the warnings were ludicrous. He half heard Ginny babbling something about a loose tooth and Barbara assuring her that she would have to wait at least another year. The news the paper spoke of existed in another world, not in his home. Gladys never even read the front page; maybe she had the right idea. He gulped his coffee and called to the girls to hurry up if they were going with him.

"Mommy…Mommy, I can't find Pallo." Ginny stood in the center of the living room, fighting back tears and waiting, apparently, for the favorite horse to detach itself from the surroundings and walk up to her.

Gladys rescued the battered blue plush pony from behind the armchair. "If you'd ever remember where you put things—*any* of you!"

She pressed the toy into her daughter's arms, wiped away a lonely tear track, kissed the dry cheek, and propelled the child gently toward the door.

Jon's hat and briefcase waited, as always, on the hall table, but she forestalled the inevitable question and held them ready for him as he strode through the dining room, shrugging into his jacket and straightening his tie.

"Busybody!" He grinned at her, planting a quick kiss to stop her retort. By the time she caught her breath and opened her mouth he was out the front door, racing Ginny to the gate. Barbara, sedate with a new ladylike pace she had read about in a magazine the week before, trailed after them. Gladys watched from the open window, torn by her older daughter's desperate reaching for maturity, and warmed again with tenderness as Jon slowed to let Ginny reach the car first.

"I won, Daddy—I'm the leader, I won, I won!" Then the car door slammed to shut out their voices.

She ought to get the laundry started, first thing, if she was going to make that luncheon. The bedrooms could wait, but, surveying the damage wreaked by the family tornado on its way out, she decided she'd have to tidy up downstairs first.

In the living room she made do with a swift straightening up: a pile of things to be taken upstairs later and put away—Ginny's toys…Jon's necktie, pulled off last night…Barbie's "Sit-Kit," designed to take a baby sitter through any emergency, small or large, just finished last night and brought down for display, and, of course, never put away again. The dust rag and broom took care of the more conspicuous spots; she could vacuum later, or if she missed it altogether today it wouldn't matter so much. The room looked clean, whether it really was or not. The dining room was littered with the breakfast dishes, last night's newspapers, some of Barbie's schoolbooks. The girl was getting more careless every day. She was so busy telling other people how to take care of other people's babies and get along in other people's houses that she didn't even have time to pick up after herself any more. That would have to stop. It had seemed like a good thing when Barbara first organized the baby sitters' club, but even a good thing could be carried too far.

Gladys piled things up and put them away—dirty dishes in the kitchen, pencils and papers in the desk drawer; the knitting she was trying—for the fourth time—to learn, she stuffed regretfully into the sideboard. There wouldn't be any time for that today.

Washing up the breakfast dishes, she opened the casement window over the sink. She could never look out this way, across the clean green sweep of the broad back yards, hers and her neighbor's, without a sharp contrasting memory of crowded dim-lit flats and furnished rooms in the city. There had been a time when Tom and Barbie were young, and before they were born, when Jon was not "Mitchell Associates, Consultants in Civil Engineering," but a junior partner in a small struggling firm; when every penny that wasn't spent for necessities went into clean shirts and ties for Jon, or into the bank, to build the dreams that had since come true…this house among them. Now, looking up over the breakfast dishes, she could see out across the lawns, where the bread wagon was working its way along between the double row of houses. The unnamed road was too pretty, with its white gravel set against green lawns, to be called an alley. She could see the Grahams' three-year-old boy playing across the way, digging a hole smack in the middle of the early garden his father had been planting. How was Annie Graham going to explain *that* one tonight? And if she kept on explaining things away to Todd, Sr., what was going to become of the child anyway?

Impatiently she cut off the train of thought and moved her eyes past the play pen in the next yard, letting them linger on the baby buggy out back of the Turners'. Peggy had finally had the baby she wanted; after three years of trying, and four solid months flat on her back, she'd done it. Now with little Meg already six weeks old, Peggy wasn't out of bed yet, and so far there was no sign that she would be. But with Jim back from the most recent of his "business trips," things should be easier for Peggy…

Annoyed at herself again, Gladys bent sternly over the dishes; other people's troubles were easy to think about, she told herself, when you had none of your own. Everything's almost too good. That was superstitious and silly, she knew, but she couldn't help it. How long could things go on, getting better all the time?

Scouring the last pot, she thought she heard her name called. Across the yard her next-door neighbor, Edie Crowell, was clipping the hedge against the budding of the first spring leaves, a tall graceful figure in tailored slacks, floppy hat, and worn gardening gloves, perfectly in place in the well-planned flower garden back of the big white colonial house.

"Good morning," Edie called across. Her polished voice carried clearly across the grass and arrived pleasant and well modulated, as if she were carrying on a tea-table conversation. By comparison, Gladys' own hearty hail always sounded to her like a fishwife's cry. But she couldn't go out; she wasn't dressed yet. She waved a reply to the greeting and Edie promptly left her hedge and started over.

Groaning inwardly and apologizing out loud for the wrapper she still wore, Gladys opened the kitchen door and stood talking to her neighbor on the back porch.

"I was just wondering," Edie explained, "if you'd mind terribly going to the luncheon alone. I'll be there of course, but Phil didn't get back last night, and I have to go to the bank this morning. I could come back, of course, but…well, the bank is so close to the Cortlands'…of course if you can get away early enough, you could come along with me…"

Gladys explained rapidly about Veda and the laundry. It was going to be hard to get ready on time, let alone early.

Edie listened sympathetically, but of course she couldn't really understand. "You won't be late, will you? I've *reserved* a place for you."

Gladys was stung by the implied rebuke. She had an errant impulse to leave the laundry after all. The luncheon was something she'd been looking forward to for days—actually for months, but the invitation had not been forthcoming until two weeks ago. The luncheon was a monthly affair held at a different woman's home every time, and the circle was limited. It was the first chance she had had to meet any of the Crowells' friends, and if she were late today, it might be the last.

But she couldn't let Barbie down. And Ginny really needed some clean socks. And Jon's field trip—was it tomorrow or Wednesday? He didn't have any clean khakis. If it was tomorrow, then they had to be done today. If she had to do that much she might just as well do all of it. Defiantly she thought that she had done more than that in a day's work before—with two small babies on her hands and no washing machine.

Just a shade too sweetly she promised Edie that she'd be on time, and dashed off to answer the ringing of the telephone. Somebody wanted to speak to Miss Barbara Mitchell. Gladys took the woman's name and telephone number, jotted them down, and explained that the sitting service's hours were before eight-thirty and after three-thirty. Miss Mitchell, she said, would call back.

She finished up in the kitchen without any more dawdling and started downstairs. Of course this had to be the morning that she would get a splinter groping along the rough board for the cellar light. The switch was just too far out of reach, and the stairs too precarious to manage in the dark. Jon had promised a hundred times to fix the switch—but now she had to take time out to remove the splinter and patch up her finger.

By the time she got down to the laundry she was saving seconds. She sorted things out swiftly, stuffed the first washing of white things into the machine, and let it run while she went back upstairs to tear through the bedrooms, whirling sheets, blankets, duster, and broom in a tornado of determined energy. Still, when she passed through the kitchen again on her way back downstairs, the toy clock on the wall told her it was after ten-thirty. She pulled towels and underwear out of the machine, and filled it again with light-colored wash clothes, compromising with conscience by deciding to leave the flatwork for Veda to do when she got a chance. But by the time the first load was in the drier she realized there just weren't enough corners to cut. She couldn't bathe, dress, and get to the other side of town by twelve-thirty. She shouldn't have tried to do it all; she could have done Barbie's things, and Jon's, and let the rest go. But now she had started it, she couldn't very well leave it. And after the exchange with Edie this morning she would rather not go than risk being late.

It would be the better part of courtesy to let Edie know right away. She went upstairs to call but the Crowells' phone didn't answer. Of course—Edie was at the bank. Mrs. Cortland, luncheon hostess for the day, was formal and distant on the telephone. Apparently household emergencies did not come under the heading of acceptable excuses for these affairs.

With the polite phrases still lingering in her head, Gladys went back to the laundry and made a furious attack on the pieces that had to be done by hand. About to put the last load into the machine, she was suddenly ravenously hungry and went up to the kitchen for a sandwich. The phone rang again, but she ignored it. She didn't want to talk to Edie Crowell or to any of Barbie's babies' mothers. Dutifully swallowing a hated glass of milk, she tried to convince herself that she didn't really care about joining the Crowells' social circle. She finished eating, but stayed in her chair an extra moment to watch the painted porcelain figures parade out of the Swiss chalet on the toy clock, announcing that noon had come.

Even in the bitterness of the solitary lunch the clock made her feel good. She had had one like it in her room when she was a little girl, and had always wanted another. But Jon wouldn't have it; he said they were always breaking down and that there weren't any watchmakers any more who could repair the delicate old mechanisms. He held out firmly, until the day Mitchell Associates got its first big commission—and then he never even told her the news till almost a week later, when he came home bearing a mysterious package which had to be unwrapped before he would tell his big secret. It was the clock, the one she had watched in a store window for months, afraid it would be sold before she could persuade Jon—and just as the outside had been carefully worked over, all the bright colors restored and the chipped spots repaired, so the insides had been taken out bodily and replaced with a new electric mechanism.

Gladys went back to work with renewed energy, only a part of it from the food she had eaten. But, piling the last load of heavy-duty clothing into the machine, she worked more slowly than she had in the morning, overcome by a nostalgia that brought its own solace to banish the memory of cultivated, condescending tones. Jon's last remaining set of G.I. khakis, reserved for basement and garden work, were a humble contrast to the new field outfit that went in right afterward. And they brought back grim pictures of the washbasin in a rooming house near Fort Bragg; Ginny's utilitarian overalls brought on a surge of memories even more remote, from the time before the war, when the depression had lifted to become merely a "recession"—a series of Manhattan walkups, each with its identical small dark kitchen, each with the same stained double-duty sink, where Tom's and Barbie's well-worn corduroys had got their weekly scrubbings.

A factory whistle screamed in the distance and broke into her thoughts, setting her hands to flying faster and her head to clearing. One o'clock already? She stopped a moment, altogether, to listen more closely. It couldn't be a factory whistle; the sound had fitted perfectly into her memories, but it had no place in lower Westchester. Even as she listened the sound died away, too short-lived for a factory call. And the timbre of it was different. In spite of its shrillness it could almost have been mistaken for thunder, if the brilliant sunshine streaming through the high window hadn't just then redoubled in its intensity, bathing the whitewashed cellar walls with a deluge of red-gold light. She shook her head and tried to dismiss the whole thing, but for some reason the sound, dead now in reality, lived on inside her head, eerie and almost frightening. Then, as if to fit her change of mood, the small window darkened and the reassuring brightness of the sun disappeared. Maybe it had been thunder after all, a freak electric storm, too early in the year.

Gladys snapped the light switch, and the glaring overhead bulb cleared away all kinds of shadows. She pulled fresh, sweet-smelling clothes out of the machine and sorted them rapidly for the drier, for the mangle, for starching.

Upstairs the phone was ringing, but she ignored it. One more inquiry about a baby sitter would be one too many. She stayed at the ironing board, trying to work out the strange mood that had descended on her. She had made up her mind to be through with this before the children came home. Veda would have been done long ago. The pile of flatwork, neglected in the corner, reproached her.

When she finished, finally, she was damp and disheveled, but triumphant; she still had more than half an hour to rest and change her clothes before the children got home. While she washed, upstairs, the phone started in again. She dropped her towel to run and catch it, but got there just in time to hear the receiver on the other end click down in disappointment. And going back up, her tired feet and pounding heart protested and she had to take the stairs at a careful pace. Whatever she had been able to do ten years ago, she was out of practice now.

A little after three, she stood on the porch in a clean dress, washed and combed, and convinced that powder and lipstick hid the tired lines in her face. Her eyes were fixed on the corner where the streetcar stopped, watching to see the big girl and the little one get off together. Intent on the distance, she was startled when a car horn honked at the front gate. Ginny and Barbara tumbled out of opposite doors—the baby landing on the sidewalk, and Barbie forgetting to be sedate as she ran around from the street side.

Gladys recognized the car; it was that nice new teacher who sometimes passed the house on her way home. She started down the walk, thinking, I ought to ask Miss Pollock in for a cup of tea—she's been so nice.

But before she could reach the gate Ginny piled on her, arms and legs flailing and small red lips puckered for a welcome kiss. By the time they were disentangled the motor was starting up again and Gladys caught only a few words over the noise of the starter, something Miss Pollock was saying about "awfully good of you."

Barbie was pouring out eager conversation. "Miss Pollock thought it was so sensible of you not to call. All the other mothers did and she said to thank you specially." Dazed, Gladys realized that she never had spoken the invitation aloud and that the teacher's polite thanks referred to something else entirely.

"Well, why would I call…?"

"I don't *know!* Everybody did, though. *All* the mothers."

"I know, I know!" Ginny was dancing up and down. Gladys put her hand on the baby's bright hair, trying to quiet her a minute. But she was too tired to think about it, and Ginny would not be quieted. "I *do* know, Mommy. Listen to me." She stopped jumping and tugged at Gladys' skirt. "Please listen, Mommy."

"All right, baby." Gladys gave up trying to straighten out the conversational mix-up. "You tell me all about *everything* that happened, Ginny."

"It was raining!"

Barbie gave a snort of disgust and stalked away, her shoulders set in studied contempt of Ginny's baby stories and of people who listened to them. "Maybe I can find out something on the radio," she flung over her shoulder, "if nobody else around here even *cares* when something important is happening."

"I don't know how important it is," Gladys called after her, "but there's a message for you on the phone pad. And I wish you'd tell those people what hours you're home. I'm getting tired of playing secretary for you."

Ginny was tugging at her impatiently. "Mommy, it was raining on *one* side of the street," she reported ecstatically. "First there was a funny noise like thunder, only different, and then the sun was shining bright like a sunset, sort of, and then it was dark all of a sudden, only the cloud was far away, and then after a while it began to really rain, only it was raining across the street and not in the yard." She frowned. "Only Pallo wanted to know if it was really raining, and Teacher wouldn't let me out to see. It was all foggy on our side, but it was *raining* across the street."

Gladys struggled with a long-buried memory—herself as a little girl, discovering that it didn't always rain every place at the same time. Maybe there had been some sort of freak storm after all. It was early in the year for an electric storm, but that could explain why people were calling the school. Maybe some lightning had struck near by. She laughed again and scooped Ginny up in her arms. "Since when," she asked, "does the sun shine bright at sunset? Do you know what sunset is?"

Ginny managed to look very unconcerned. "Oh sure," she said, "yeah."

"Yes," Gladys corrected automatically. "I don't know where you pick these things up." Ginny squirmed in her arms and Gladys felt something cold and damp pushed against her. "What in the world…? *How* did you get that horse so wet?" She let the child down and followed her through the open door.

"She won't even let go of him long enough to get washed." Standing at the phone, Barbie covered the mouthpiece with her hand to offer the comment.

"Well, give it to me now," Gladys told the little girl. "I'll put it up on the shelf in the kitchen till it's dry."

Looking excessively guilty, Ginny thumped up the stairs to her room. Listening, Gladys marveled again at the persistence of the phrase about the "pitter-patter" of little feet.

"That's funny." Barbie put the phone down with a puzzled air. "I dialed twice and I can't get her."

"Maybe the lines are down somewhere," Gladys suggested.

"I don't know—but something's certainly going on. I'll let you know what I find out," Barbie offered generously, and followed Ginny up the stairs.

Gladys started toward the kitchen, thinking of the roast that had to be put on, refusing to think about how tired she was after a half day's honest work.

She was shelling peas when Barbie called from upstairs.

There are all sorts of noises children make—some to be ignored, some to be thought about, some to be tended to, and one in particular that must have immediate unhesitating attention. Gladys dropped the peas and took the stairs on the run.

Barbara's door was open and the girl sat huddled near her midget radio set, listening, not only with her ears, but with dilated eyes and out-stretched hands; her whole body was curiously intent. She didn't turn as Gladys came in but one hand motioned rapidly, "Come here," while her lips pursed in a half-aspirated "sh-h."

Gladys knew, of course. She had lived through the one war already; no one who had would ever forget that pose of horrified fascination in front of a radio. She crossed the rag rug, every color in it distinctly visible, every pattern of light and shadow in the room sharp and clear, every step a century long, before she was within hearing range of the radio. She stood immobile next to the girl on the bed as the impossible words hurled themselves at her.

"…one-fifteen P.M., Eastern Standard Time, this afternoon. It is almost certain that equal damage was sustained throughout the country. The cities outside the radius of two hundred miles, roughly, have not yet been heard from. Transcontinental wires are down and radiations appear to be interfering with radio communications in all directions." Static crackled out of the set with every word. Listening was torture to the ears as to the mind.

"Flash! We have just received our first report, since the bombing, from Washington, D.C. The Capitol was hit by at least one bomb at about one-thirty today. The larger part of the governmental area has—" The voice cut off abruptly, replaced by a chattering flow of noisy interference. "For security reasons," the same voice, sounding less assured, returned, "it is necessary to condense the report from Washington, D.C. It is estimated that only one bomb exploded there."

"We repeat—we repeat, please don't leave your homes. If you are in a dangerous area you will receive orders for evacuation. Do not leave your homes. If you are near a bombed-out area you are safe only indoors. DO NOT LEAVE YOUR HOMES.

"So far as we can determine, no damage has been done except in areas in and around the major cities. We do not yet know who the aggressor was. We do not…"

The bland professional voice edged upward, strident and shrill, through the last half-dozen words, and broke at last into a raucous scream of laughter. The radio went dead.

Another voice cut in. "You have just heard a report from Washington, D.C., received by teletype from a relay station in the outskirts of Philadelphia. For those who have just tuned in, we repeat: several atomic bombs of unknown origin landed in and near the harbor of New York City this afternoon. The first explosion occurred at about 1:15 P.M., Eastern Standard Time, and was followed by others over a period estimated to be approximately one half hour. It is known that no bombs were dropped after two o'clock. Eyewitnesses state that the first bomb exploded underwater at the mouth of the East River, affecting harbor shipping in New York and Brooklyn, and substantially damaging a large part of the lower tip of Manhattan Island. There is no official statement as yet…"

The words were clipped, staccato, rigidly controlled, shooting out of the little radio with penetrating, meaningless malevolence. "Although the attack was focused on Manhattan, bombs are known to have been dropped in outlying boroughs, and one at least in New Jersey. First reports from reconnaissance planes indicated that Manhattan itself is almost completely destroyed from the Battery up as far as Ninety-Sixth Street, with only a narrow strip of land west of Ninth Avenue, along the Hudson, apparently intact. This damage appears to be the result of two air-exploded bombs, both of which were aimed at targets on the East Side. But everywhere, except at the target centers of the explosions, some buildings are still standing, and it is believed that survivors will be found all over the bombed area."

…except at target centers. Gladys remembered a description, read and shuddered over, and set aside, she had thought, even from memory…the description of an atomic bomb landing at Twentieth Street and Third Avenue…The El, Gramercy Park, the courthouse, the high school, City College, flattened, melted into a compound featureless surface, the buildings that had not gone up into thin air at the instant of the explosion, reduced by inconceivable heat to a glassy expanse of poisoned wasteland.

The words kept coming, swarming at her out of the radio, sting-ing, biting, bitter. The words kept coming, but Gladys no longer heard them. She knew she should be listening—there were things she had to know—for the children, for herself, for Jon.

Jon was in the city all day!

Somewhere inside her she heard the beginnings of a scream and then her ears heard it, and it was Barbara, not herself at all. There was no time to think about Jon now. The incredible words were attacking Barbie too. There was no time for thinking at all; Gladys' reflexes acted for her. Rocking back and forth, she cradled the girl's head on her breast, pat-ting the wild curls—crooning a little, calming, soothing. And when that didn't work she pulled the girl's face up and slapped her sharply.

Shock succeeded panic. Barbara fell back limply, long enough for Gladys to tell her in swift harsh tones, "We have Ginny to think of. You'll have to help me. Barbie, stop it!"

The sound that would have been a scream came out as a sob, quiet, dull, and hopeless. And now there was another noise, a familiar one among the symphony of stranger sensations. The thump of small sturdy shoes on the stairs and the rattle of dangling roller skates brought Bar-bara jumping to her feet.

"I'll get her. She can't go *out!*" Horror came to a climax and broke loose in the last word.

She was halfway to the door when her mother called after her curtly, "No!"

"Ginny!" she called, breathing deep, searching for inner calm and for ordinary unfrightening words. "Virginia! Did you dust your room yet?"

Downstairs reluctant footsteps lagged.

"Virginia!" Just a note of sharpness—and this time the feet turned back.

"I was just getting the dust rag, Mommy." Ginny appeared at the foot of the stairs, guilty innocence in every line of her face, skates nowhere in evidence, and a large gray cloth in her hand. The scene had played itself out this way a hundred times before, and it had always been funny. Now it wound to a close like an old worn out film. The two who stood at the top of the stairs watched with tortured senses the inevitable ending of the stalled sequence.

From behind, Gladys heard an outpouring of breath, a jerky sign of finished fear. She waited in silence till Ginny had passed them and gone shamefaced into her room, then turned to the older girl. "Barbie, you'll have to get her playing something inside. Don't scare her. Don't tell her she *can't* go out. Just keep her interested in something in *here.*" She turned again, started for the stairs.

"I can't," Barbara said hopelessly. "I can't. I don't know what…"

"Of course you can." Gladys didn't even look back. "You have to." Halfway down, she paused and called back. "I've got to do some phoning. Turn off your radio, Barbie, and I'll listen in downstairs. Remember what I said." Without waiting far a reply, she went on down, drawn by an instinctive need too strong to resist. She picked up the phone and had to wipe sudden futile tears from her eyes before she could dial.

"What num-ber are you call-ing?"

"ATlas 9-4200. Mitchell Associates." Her voice was still clear, some-how untouched by the fear that clutched at her throat.

"I am sor-ry. That number has been discon-nected...due to emer-gency. "

"Thank you." The receiver dropped from her hand, and she mar-veled at the bored everyday efficiency of the operator. Perhaps she had been overfrightened. Maybe it was her own dread that had crept into the radio announcers' voices.

She switched on the radio, loud, and tuned it down again immedi-ately, keeping the rush of words locked up in the room with her, not letting them get out to do their damage upstairs.

"Do *not* leave your homes. Stay indoors." It was the same man she had heard in Barbie's room, and even that small familiarity was welcome. "The governor has arrived at Emergency Headquarters in White Plains and will speak to you over this station at four-fifteen. The time is now three fifty-three. The governor's message will be heard in exactly twenty-two minutes. Stay at home and keep your radio tuned in. Citizens are requested not to use their telephones for personal conversations. All lines still up are needed for rescue work and emergency squads. All persons with medical or safety control training are asked to report to Emergency Headquarters immediately by telephone. Just call or dial the operator and ask for the nearest E.H.Q. All others will please refrain from use of the telephone. I repeat, keep your radio tuned in, and do not use your telephone. The governor will deliver his message in twenty minutes at four-fifteen, Eastern Standard Time. Stay tuned to this station."

Three fifty-five! This, all of this, in half an hour. It was already after three when she had stood on the front porch and watched for the chil-dren. And now—not yet four o'clock!

CHAPTER TWO

SOMEWHERE A SIREN was shrieking, off in the distance. It had been going on for a long time, sustained shrill background to the crazy words that spewed from the ceaseless, coughing static of the radio. Now as she lis-tened it began to die, fading away until its shattering impact ceased to fall on bruised nerves, until its caustic cry was heard in memory alone. Memory held another siren, that was not a siren, that was thunder. That was not thunder; it was the warning scream of slaughter in the skies. And now again the sound, the dying sound, like a factory steam whistle left to blow itself out.

The smell of scorched metal roused her from nightmare. She ran through the dining room, and the swinging door to the kitchen flapped open and shut, open and shut, as she turned off the flame under the kettle, dry now and empty, blackened on the bottom and in one wide streak up the side. Sitting forlornly on the spout, the silenced robin returned her stare with one accusing eye.

Robins, Gladys thought, are supposed to say, "Cheer-up!" It seemed very funny. Laughing, she reached for the insulated handle, dropped it again as it burned her fingers. The sudden pain cleared her head. She folded a pot holder around the handle and carried the pot over to the sink. The hiss and sizzle of cold water hitting the bottom, spattering up against the dry-hot sides, was familiar, reassuring. She saw the peas still standing on the worktable, half shelled, and thought with a grateful start, we still have to eat.

She tackled the small task with a furious release of pent-up energy, her fingers working with accustomed speed and knowledge through the pile of unshelled pods; she finished just as the toy clock struck four. In fifteen minutes the governor would speak. She shook the peas loose in the colander, but her hand, halfway to the tap, stopped in mid-air.

The water—was the water all right?

The phone pealed urgently, and Jon's face swam before her, his voice sounded in her ears. She started running for the front of the house, but the pounding of her heart made her slow down. You couldn't keep on running, no matter what kind of emergency it was.

"Jon!" she breathed. There was no answer, only the tense silence of a telephone where someone waits to speak. "Jon," she cried again, "Jon, where are—"

"This is Telephone Central," a mechanical voice broke in, "calling to check your wire. Thank you for an-swer-ing."

"But what...who...?"

"This is Telephone Central," the voice said again, "calling to check your wire. Thank you for an-swer-ing."

"Operator!" Gladys demanded. "Operator, you cut into my—"

"This is Telephone Central," it began to repeat. They couldn't hear her at all. It was a one-way connection.

Gladys didn't believe it. She stood there, jiggling the hook futilely, until the phone went dead, buzzing monotonously in her ear.

She dropped the receiver back on the cradle, then picked it up again and dialed the operator with a swift angry circle of her finger. Nothing happened; no inquiring voice, not even the comforting delay of a ring on the other end.

Angry at herself now, she hung up and tried again. This time she waited for the dial tone. Now at least it rang—on and on, endlessly. She was ready to give up for the last time when the operator's precision-machined voice finally asked what she wanted.

"Emergency Headquarters, please." Miraculously the operator made the connection without questioning her need.

Then there was a man's voice at the other end, bored, weary, but human. Gladys tried to stay cool and rational, but the man's voice was too close to kindness and her purpose thawed. Horrified, she heard herself babbling about water, and her husband in the city, her son, and the bombs, until he interrupted sharply.

"This is a priority wire, lady. What do you want?"

One at a time, she told herself firmly, one thing at a time.

"My husband," she said quickly, "my husband is in the city. How can I find out—"

"You'll be notified if we get anything," he broke in. "It'll all be on the radio when the governor talks. You listen in to that."

A dozen urgent unanswered questions circled dizzily in Gladys' mind. She was terrified that the man would hang up. "My son," she threw at him hastily. "He's at school. He's away at Texas Tech."

"An engineering student?" The voice sounded faintly interested.

"Yes," Gladys breathed hopefully.

"All technical students are being mobilized into the Army," he said.

Gladys gasped and recovered. "But he can't—I mean he's only seventeen—"

"All technical students are being mobilized," the man insisted. Gladys didn't believe it; it was absurd. "But there must be some way I can find out—"

"The Army will notify you."

"The school's in Lubbock," Gladys said hopefully. "Do you know anything…?"

"I'm sorry, lady. That's all I can tell you." The phone clicked again and buzzed while she stood there holding it to her ear until finally another of the mechanical voices cut in.

"Num-ber, please?"

Gladys couldn't think. One immediate question filled her mind now. "The water," she implored. "I've got to know about the water. Is it all right? Can I use it?"

"I am sor-ry. We do not have that information at this exchange. You will be noti-fied by the prop-per author-rities."

A definite click at the other end broke the connection. Gladys put the receiver down slowly. Jon…Tom…what did she know that she hadn't known before? The water…"all technical students"…"proper authorities"…Phrases swam around in her head and suddenly achieved meaning.

She had to remind herself again not to run up the stairs unnecessarily. "Barbie," she called, and waited to hear the door of Ginny's room opened. "Barbie, you know where Tom's old schoolbooks are?"

A vague affirmative floated down the stairs.

"You go look and bring me down everything on physics. Right away."

"Mom, there's *two shelves* full of physics!"

"Well, you know what I want," Gladys said impatiently.

"I don't see how I'm to know what you want if you don't..." The injured tones drifted down the stairs.

"For heaven's sake, Barbara, just use your judgment for once." No answer, but footsteps marched down the hall. *She called me Mom again!* Gladys thought suddenly. *I have to be careful...I have to watch myself.*

The kettle began to whistle. Gladys couldn't remember why she had put it on again, but now she got down a big canning jar and filled it, running boiling water over the top and sealing it tight. She put it out on the window sill and filled the kettle once more. At least they would have drinking water if they needed it.

The clock said four-ten. Barbara pushed the door open, hugging a toppling stack of books to her bosom. "I hope these are right," she said stiffly.

"I'm sure you chose better than I could," Gladys assured her. "Maybe you can find what I want. Do I have to boil the water or anything like that? Maybe I should have read up more before...but I don't know; I never could believe, really..."

"It wouldn't do any good," Barbara said knowingly. "Even gas masks don't help." But she was trailing a finger down contents pages, riffling open the most promising book. "Maybe some of the stories in those magazines he used to read would tell you more. Really, Mother"—she was upholding Tom's seven-year-old family argument—"they had some pretty good stuff in them...anyhow Tom said they did."

"We wouldn't know what to look for," Gladys told her. "We couldn't go through all the magazines. Anyhow, he was afraid I'd throw them out and he put them down in the cellar in a wooden crate. I don't even know which one it is."

"Mother," Barbara broke in suddenly, "who called up before?"

"They were just checking to find out if the phone was working." Gladys took a deep breath. *How much can I tell her? How much should she know?* After that panicky quarter hour at the radio upstairs it was hard to decide.

"But I called Emergency Headquarters and they said they didn't think Tom's school had been bombed. They said the Army would notify us; they're drafting all the technical students."

"Did they give you his address? Did they know what part of the Army he's in?"

Gladys shook her head. "They're supposed to notify us." She couldn't understand the easy excitement of this reaction.

"Here's something," Barbara was saying. "It tells about safety measures at Oak Ridge——" She stopped short at the look of dismay on her mother's face, and then comprehension flooded over her. "Oh, Mother, everybody knows we're the strongest country in the whole world—we've got a"—she struggled with the words, trying to get them straight—"a stockpile of bombs and bases and planes and missiles, and——" She stopped. "Tom told me," she confided. "He always knew it would happen, but you never let him talk about it, and he was always wishing it would wait till he was old enough and now he's *in* it, don't you see? I'll bet he's so excited he can hardly——"

She stopped short, vaguely aware that she had said something wrong. "But, Mother, don't you see there's nothing to worry about? It's not like fighting in the old days. Tom won't have to go to the front or anything. He's a technician, and he'll work at the base, and—well, the danger is only in the big cities, and—well, they *must* have the radio or telegraph or something working all over the country already, or they wouldn't have known about Tom's school. Mom! *Where's Daddy?*"

With numbed lips Gladys framed the lie. "He's all right, honey. I'm sure he wasn't hurt, only they won't let him out of the—the danger zone, until everybody's checked. I don't understand, but the governor is——" Her eyes flew to the clock. "It's started already. Make sure Ginny's all right, will you, Babs? And then come down if you can." She flung it over her shoulder, already on the way to the radio.

The speaker was giving forth a low authoritative rumble, none of it distinguishable as words, but the sum total of it clearly the governor's speech. She turned it up too far, and a bombardment of words filled the room.

"The Army is fully mobilized and there is nothing further to fear. There will be no more attacks. A screen of radar shields every inch of our borders, from below sea level to the far reaches of the stratosphere. Nothing can get through. We are living inside a great dome of safety, our whole nation protected by the radar sweep from bases prepared long ago."

But they didn't work. It didn't work before. Gladys tried to understand.

"Our entire energies now must be directed to rescue work in the bombed areas, and to safety measures in nearby zones. When I have finished, the emergency radiologist for the entire area will speak to you. For full information about safety measures, be sure to keep your radio tuned in. Several important announcements will be made by the radiologist. In closing, I want to comment on the remarkable courage—the heroism—displayed by all of you in this national emergency. In times of great crisis the true mettle of a people emerges; and I may say, without fear of exaggeration…"

For a moment she was aware of Barbie at her shoulder.

"The governor?" the girl asked, awed. Gladys nodded, motioning for silence. The governor—and he was only a tired man, trying to cover his own confusion with words.

Still, it was the words that mattered. She listened obediently, attentively. Barbie went off toward the stairs, lingering over each footstep to hear as much as she could.

"...sustained so great an attack with such single-minded determination to carry on in the face of danger—never has any country on earth had better cause for pride in its fearless and co-operative citizenry."

More words—no courage, no confidence, no hope—only the voice of a weary salesman, suavely peddling unwanted wares.

"For reasons of security, it is impossible for me to tell you more at the present time, about the extent of the damage incurred, or our plans for retaliation. But you may carry on with your duties to home and country, assured that the enemy shall not go unpunished! At this moment plans that have lived only on paper for many years are grinding slowly but surely into action.

"Our enemies shall learn now to fear the eagle in its nest.

"Thank you, my friends. Courage and patience are all we need to win."

Gladys heard the last words with a sinking sensation of bewilderment. The man had said nothing, nothing at all. Nothing about the city, about the people trapped there...nothing but words...

"That was Governor Cauldwell, speaking from Emergency Headquarters. Please do not turn your radio off. In one minute you will hear the district radiologist. While waiting, please supply yourself with writing equipment. You will hear information of vital importance. Get paper and pen or pencil now. The radiologist will be on the air in forty seconds."

"I'll get it, Mom." Gladys didn't know Barbara had come back until she spoke.

"Thanks, baby." She took the pad and pencil and looked up into her daughter's excited face. "I don't know what I'd do without you. I really—"

She stopped. The radio was clearing its throat and the announcer's voice had come through again.

"Here you are, ladies and gentlemen. The man who holds our safety—yours and mine—in his hands throughout this emergency—District Radiologist Harold F. Hennessy, speaking from Emergency Headquarters. Will you come in, please, Dr. Hennessy?"

A second's silence, broken only by the incessant low-pitched barking of the static—then one more voice in the welter of voices.

"One hour and fifteen minutes ago you heard the first radio report of the bombing of New York City. You know now that our whole country has been attacked and severe damage has been inflicted in many major cities.

"For security reasons I cannot tell you the exact extent of the damage, but I can tell you that communications are being restored and that a national government will shortly be in operation.

"For the rest of you—you already know that the island of Manhattan, where the largest damage was inflicted, has been completely closed off. Washington Heights, where radioactivity is below danger level, including the entire area from 125th Street to the river, has been transformed into a gigantic emergency headquarters, field hospital, and Army base. Scores of radiologists are at work there, testing conditions to provide for the safety of suburban areas. Rescue squads are penetrating from the hospital base there to the lower part of the island, inspecting every building, subway, sewer, or shelter of any kind still standing where survivors may be holding out.

"At the present time fires are still burning in many parts of the city, but most of the larger buildings are still standing, and many of these are fireproof. Outside the areas of direct hit, many survivors are expected."

The words were stern; there was no attempt to allay fear, but like the dentist who says, "This will hurt a little, but it won't take long," Hennessy renewed courage by the simple admission that things were bad. The knowledge, new to Gladys, that the national government had broken down, seemed credible and bearable, as long as something was being done.

"Another hospital base is now being established in the Pelham Bay section of the Bronx, to care for victims of the bomb burst in the lower riverside area of the East Bronx. Similar smaller bases will be set up as rapidly as possible in the outskirts of Brooklyn and Queens, and hospitals are already treating emergency cases in some suburban areas.

"No one at present is being allowed to leave the areas of heavy contamination except by way of the hospital bases and decontamination centers. A cordon of police and National Guardsmen is being thrown across Westchester County at New Rochelle and across Queens County at Jamaica. Similar patrols are being established by the local governments in New Jersey. We are anxious to release survivors as quickly as possible, but it is essential to prevent exposed individuals from leaving the area without a thorough examination. Special equipment and training are required to detect the presence of atomic radiations and many survivors within the danger zone may be unaware of their own condition.

"Remember—trained personnel are now at work directing rescue squads. Operations are being carried out in accordance with well-integrated plans developed and improved over many years. Unorganized attempts at assistance or escape can only result in panic and confusion. Our object is to move everyone as quickly as possible out of contaminated areas and away from any danger of infection.

"For the time being your first concern must be your own safety. Radioactive rain, resulting from the underwater explosion, as well as dust, smoke, and wind, may endanger large areas around New York City. The entire area of Greater New York, including Staten Island; Westchester County as far north as Pleasantville; the lower part of Fairfield County, including Ridgefield and Wilton, in Connecticut; all of Suffolk County in Long Island; and all parts of New Jersey along the Hudson from upper Middlesex County to the New York State line; and in Rockland County in New York State, as far north as New City—

"If you live inside this district you will receive a visit within the next few hours from an emergency squad truck. Members of emergency squads will be prepared to answer your questions and to handle immediate difficulties.

"If you live outside the limits I have described you are requested to stay near your homes and hold yourselves ready to assist Emergency Headquarters. Your help is desperately needed in the danger zones.

"Further information and instructions for all will be broadcast over a local station in your vicinity. Please listen carefully and write down the information that is given you. But before you turn your dial, one last word of encouragement. We have been damaged but not destroyed. Local governments are functioning. Trains are running in most sectors. Local wire and telephone services are in operation. Emergency Headquarters are operating in the vicinity of every bombed area. Amateur radio operators are already filling in nationwide gaps in communication. Everything that can humanly be done to save lives and prevent further disaster is being done."

Abruptly the voice stopped and it was hard to tell whether the sound that followed was a snort of disgust or just more static.

"In order to conserve power and to prevent this information from reaching the enemy, this broadcast will be continued over a low-power short-range station. Please tune your radio now to 980—that is number 980 on your radio—number 980—please tune your radio to number 980..."

Gladys got up stiffly and handed the pad and pencil to Barbara. "Will you listen carefully, Barbie? I want to take a look at Ginny—she's too quiet." Barbara nodded raptly, already turning the dial, intent on finding the station.

"I'm *not* too quiet." It was a high-pitched indignant voice, immediately behind Gladys' elbow. Perched on Jon's big lounging chair, legs straddling the fat armrest, Ginny rested one foot defiantly on the forbidden upholstery. A tense smile tried to deny round frightened eyes in her white face—a shockingly mature face from which curved baby contours had vanished in an hour's time. Gladys scooped the little girl into her arms, feeling the nervous resistance of thin wiry muscles. Ginny's head burrowed into her shoulder.

"I don't *like* that man, Mommy. Turn him off." The words were muffled, and Gladys could feel the moist mouth moving against her throat. She sat down in the big chair, cradling Ginny in her lap.

"I can't turn him off, baby. We have to listen and find out something. See how Barbie's going to write it down!"

Ginny obstinately buried her eyes against her mother's face. "I don't want to look. I want to turn him off."

"Why, honey? Why don't you like the man?"

"He won't let my daddy come home. Turn him off and make him let my daddy come home!" At last the tears came. Gladys didn't try to stop the convulsive sobs. She held Ginny on her lap quietly, soothed her with firm hands and wordless comforting sounds.

Barbie looked up from the radio, annoyed, gesturing from Ginny to the loudspeaker, and Gladys stood up, stumbling a little with the weight of the child in her arms. In the kitchen they could sit together in the big old rocker until the shock wore off and Ginny quieted down.

CHAPTER THREE

THE SOBS CAME fewer and further between, until finally Ginny picked up her head and stared at her mother out of great doleful eyes. Gladys reached for a paper napkin to wipe away the tears, but Ginny pushed her hand away and began rubbing at her own eyes with crayon-stained fists. The final effect made it easy for Gladys to laugh, and when she carried Ginny over to the mirror the little girl joined in.

But the question had not been forgotten.

"*Why* won't that man let Daddy come home?"

Gladys wondered how long Ginny had been in there listening, and how much she had understood. It was a continuous source of astonishment to her, the ability of small children to comprehend anything frightening or misleading, while presenting a blank reflecting surface to all useful forms of knowledge.

"Well," she began, "there was a big explosion in the city today, and everybody has to be extra careful for a little while."

"Did Daddy get hurt?"

"I don't think so. Daddy had to go way uptown to see a man today, and the accident was all the way downtown."

"Well, why won't they let him come home?"

Well, why don't they? I don't know. "I guess they need all the strong men to help the people who are hurt, darling."

That was inspired; Gladys wished she could satisfy herself as easily. The little girl broke her stiff stance and ran to wipe her eyes formally on the kitchen towel.

"Can I go out and play now?" she demanded. Gladys glanced dubiously at the clock.

"It's too late, Ginny." She didn't wait to find out if the act was convincing. "Did you finish your drawing?"

"I'm tired of it."

"What did you make?" Gladys repressed a sigh. "May I see it?"

The little girl was thoughtful. "I guess I'll have to finish it first." She started toward the door and then stopped and went back to the sink. The water glass was standing where it always did, well within reach for Ginny and her smaller-sized friends. It took Gladys a moment to realize what was happening.

"No, honey." She snatched the glass from her daughter's hand and got the sealed jar of water. "Drink this instead."

But her own fear was in her voice, in her face, in the way she took the glass.

"I don't want to. What is it?" Ginny responded promptly.

"Water."

"Why can't I drink the other water?"

"Just because."

Ginny recognized the note of finality. She took the glass and pouted. "It's warm."

"I'll put an ice cube in."

"I don't want an ice cube." She was dangerously close to tears again. "I just want a drink of water."

To save her life, Gladys couldn't think what to do next; then the door burst open, and Barbara came in, waving the pencil and pad with wild excitement.

"I've got it all, Mom. They're starting to repeat it now, but they said to keep the radio on and they said if there are any flashes they'll ring a gong or something so people will come back and listen."

Gladys took the pad and glanced at the penciled scrawl. Barbara had recently been affecting a sophisticated backhand penmanship, but today she seemed to be growing rapidly back toward childhood in every way.

"The emergency trucks are starting around now," Barbie was rattling on. "And they're going to give us equipment and sheets of information and everything—"

"Hold on a minute." Gladys turned to Ginny, so absorbed in her big sister's report that she was sipping the warm water without a murmur. "Aren't you going to show me your picture?"

"For heaven's sake, Mother," Barbie broke in, "don't you want to hear—"

Gladys quelled her with a look.

"For 'evan's sake, Mommy," Ginny imitated her sister.

Gladys smiled and added a firm push on the small behind to a one-word dismissal. "Scoot!" It was emphatic.

With enormous dignity Ginny put down the glass of warm water and walked slowly out of the kitchen. Gladys held up a warning hand until the footsteps had passed the dining room.

"Now"—she turned to Barbara—"tell me first, did they say anything about the water?"

Barbie shook her head impatiently. "No, they didn't say anything about things like that. They said we should ask the emergency truck people about anything that worried us. All they said was the trucks would come around and we should stay indoors and not go out till after the trucks come—and they want blood donations, but I don't think from us—and there's information you're supposed to have ready for the trucks when they come."

"What do they want to know?"

"You have to write everything about Daddy—his name and description and everything. Everyone who has anybody in the city is supposed to do that. A whole description so they can identify him in case—"

She stopped, and cast a worried look at her mother, but Gladys seemed calm.

"Well, anyhow, they want a description and they said be sure and write it clearly. Then you have to do another sheet for us—one for each, I mean. You're supposed to write down our names and ages and put the address on, and then put down where we were during the day. Every place anybody went, and what time it was. You have to do a separate sheet for each one and put them on the bottles—"

"Bottles? What did they say about bottles? What for?"

"Oh, that's for the urin-urinas—" She took the scribbled note sheets from Gladys' hand and skimmed through them till she found the word. "Urinalysis," she pronounced triumphantly. "They want everybody to give them a sample. You're supposed to sterilize bottles and put it in, and then put the paper with the information about each person on the bottle. I mean—well, when I say it," she finished defensively, "it sounds all confused, but it isn't, really."

"Are you sure you got that straight? What would they want the samples *for?*"

"I don't know. I don't know *what* they want them for, but that's what they said." Barbie's tone was aggrieved. She handed the papers back to her mother and pointed to the spot she had been studying. With the verbal report to help her, Gladys found it easier to make out what Barbie had written. Apparently that *was* what they wanted.

"I think I understand," she murmured. But she didn't. "What's this?"

"Oh—that's about the phone. They kept saying not to use it for anything except emergencies."

"Thanks, dear," Gladys said absently. "You did a fine job." She checked through the pages again, then pulled her chair up to the table and tore a fresh piece of paper off the pad.

"Mom…"

Gladys was having trouble with the sheet. Her eyes didn't seem to focus right when she had to put down the necessary statistics. She tried to brush aside Barbie's intruding voice and concentrate on the pencil and paper.

"Mom, I guess it's all right to drink fruit juice or something out of the refrigerator, isn't it?"

"Yes, of course." The refrigerator door slammed and she heard the noise of pouring absurdly loud, as if whatever had gone wrong with her eyes was making her ears work better.

She didn't hear the footsteps, though, because the sudden touch on her arm made her jump.

"Mom—would you like me to do it for you?" The shy politeness in her daughter's voice almost pushed Gladys over the edge into tears, shameful and revealing. She managed to smile an equally polite and almost as shy "Thanks" and pushed the pad across the table.

She sat there until things came back into focus again and then she continued to sit, watching Barbara fill the sheet with a meticulously legible description of her father.

They understand so much, she kept thinking. You don't know it until something happens, but they're so grown up inside.

She got up and went over to the bright-colored Tyrolean plaque on the wall that held a tiny pad of paper for marketing lists. The top sheet bore notations from another world: "soap flakes," "soda," "call cleaner." She tucked the slip of paper in an apron pocket and began jotting down on a fresh sheet the things she wanted to remember for the emergency squad.

In the front room the phone came to strident life again.

Barbara looked up, but Gladys was already through the door. This time she didn't let herself think at all about what it might be; but still her hand hung hesitantly over the receiver. When she finally brought the phone to her ear she had no chance even to say hello.

"Gladys?" a voice demanded. For a moment she couldn't identify it and then the voice rushed on. "This is Edie Crowell."

Of course, Gladys thought. But what's wrong with her voice?

"Hi," she said with forced brightness. "Are we allowed to use the phone now?"

"I don't know—we're not supposed to, but I couldn't stand it any more. Phil was on his regular route up in Peekskill when it happened and they called me up and said he was drafted for rescue work. I'm here all alone and I keep thinking about him and—I tell you, I'm going crazy, Glad!"

Why, she's hysterical. Gladys could see the Crowells' big white house through the hall window. It had a lot of rooms for a worried woman to rattle around in.

"It must be awfully lonely," Gladys said, trying to get used to this sudden rush of pity for Edie Crowell. "But listen, Edie, is it all right to use the phone now? Didn't they say something about leaving the wires clear?"

"Gladys, you're inhuman!" Edith shrieked. "I only called to find out if I could come over. I just can't stay here any more by myself."

"Well, we're not supposed to go out." Gladys hesitated. "Why don't you wait for the emergency truck to come around and maybe they'll say it's all right. You know we'd be glad to have you here. Oh, Edie," she burst out, *"why* won't they let them out of the city?"

"Let them out?" The voice rose to a shrill crescendo of panic. "You want them to let people out to spread radiation disease everywhere? Every living soul in the city is as good as dead. *Let them out?*" She was practically screaming now. "What I want to know is why do they waste more lives sending rescue squads *in?*"

Gladys' head was very light. It was spinning around, trying to get up enough momentum to free itself from the lead weight of her body. She groped for the chair, telling herself that Edith was half crazed with worry, that she didn't know what she was talking about.

"But," she said feebly, "they said on the radio—"

"Lies!" Edie stormed. "They haven't told us the truth all these years, do you think they'll tell it now? They said it couldn't happen, didn't they? All that nonsense about radar screens!"

"Edith!" Gladys broke in against the current of mania. "Stop it! You've got to stop it! Right now! They're *not* lying to us. I don't know what happened before, but this is real, this time. Jon's in the city, and he was there all day, and at least they're doing something to try and get him out. The other time, in Japan, they saved a lot of people."

"Japan!" Edith raved. "That was nothing. They didn't even—"

"Edie, you shut up—shut up! Shut up!" She repeated it savagely, so deep in her throat it came out like a whisper. "I won't listen. I'm going to hang up."

Ginny was coming down the stairs, carrying her picture in one hand. Gladys kept her voice low, turned her head so the child couldn't hear.

"You stay off the phone, do you hear me? If Jon and Phil can stand it in the city, you can stand it there by yourself!" She slammed the receiver down viciously, not trying to control the surge of anger. It seemed to make her stronger, helped her throw off the permeating weariness.

"What's the matter, Mommy? Why are you mad?" Ginny had come up behind her.

"Because I was talking to a very, very silly woman." Cleansed by fury, she found she could even be gay now. She admired the drawing enthusiastically and saw the child relax before her eyes, as her own manner returned to normal. "Go on now." She shooed Ginny into the kitchen before her. "We're all going to make supper together, and you can help. How're you doing, Babsy?"

"Mother, I've *asked* you…" Barbara said coldly, straightening up over her work.

"I'm sorry, darling." The baby name, forbidden for almost two years now, had popped out irrepressibly at the sight of the young shoulders hunched over the kitchen table, the tightly clenched pencil laboriously covering fresh paper. It was just so that a younger Barbara had sat over her homework at the same table, night after night, in the last of the city apartments.

Gladys laughed, and saw it was wrong, then couldn't stop herself. "I'm sorry, but you looked so…so…" There was no way to explain. "Well, I'm sorry!"

Unassuaged, Barbara held up three finished sheets of paper. "These are done, if you want to look at them," she said stiffly.

"If you think they're all right I won't bother," Gladys answered hastily. "I want to get those bottles ready, and get started on supper—see if we can get done before the truck gets here. You'll make the salad, Barbie, and Ginny can set the table." But she couldn't help adding, "Just be sure you've got down everything about the times you and Ginny went outdoors during the day. I didn't go out at all."

"That's what I'm *trying* to do." Barbara was still on her dignity. "If you think Virginia can spare a moment before she starts setting the table, maybe I can do this one right."

Gladys kept herself very busy pulling mason jars off the top shelf, until she could stop smiling. Then she climbed down and commanded Ginny to answer her sister's questions. She got out the big pot that had once sterilized the babies' bottles and filled it with water for boiling.

The roast was still standing on the table where she had left it hours before. There wouldn't be time to cook that now. She put it back in the refrigerator and got out some of the cube steaks she kept for Jon's midnight raids. Outside the sun was beginning to set and she turned on the lights. The steaks sputtering on the broiler and the children's voices in the lamplit room brought life suddenly back to a familiar, livable plane.

She issued brisk orders, and the two girls obeyed swiftly, happy to seize on a pattern of behavior that they knew. It was a victory when Barbara so far forgot the world outside that she squabbled briefly with Ginny over the proper placement of the forks.

It all went quickly—too quickly, because when they were done the three of them had to sit down around the kitchen table, as they always did, when Jon stayed in the city too late to come home for supper.

CHAPTER FOUR

THE MOOD that had sustained them through the bustling preparations for dinner fell rapidly away. Nobody mentioned Jon; but not wanting to mention him, they didn't talk at all. Once tires screeched on the street out in front, sending Barbara and Ginny both dashing to the door.

Gladys heard the door open, and fear shot through her, raised her out of her chair and after them to bang it closed again. She turned on them with flaming sudden anger.

"Barbara, you ought to be ashamed of yourself! You knew better than that! Ginny, next time you leave the table you're going straight up to bed!" Shame reddened in the older girl's face, and a tremulous underlip shaped itself into a pout on the five-year-old's. Without a word Barbara turned on her heel and started back to the kitchen. Ginny just stood still, facing her mother. Her small red lip curled outward as if it wanted to wrap itself around her chin, and the visible reaction, finally, transformed itself into a vocal one.

"I want my daddy," she sobbed. "I hate you. I hate you and I want my daddy!"

Impulsively Gladys bent down to the child, now seated squarely on the floor, and tried to fold the stubborn baby flesh in her arms.

I want him too. Oh, Ginny, if you knew how I want him!

The words were in her mouth, in the tears that lay ready behind her eyes, in the lump of loneliness growing in her breast, but she didn't say them. The child was frightened enough already. She satisfied her own yearning arms with a quick hug.

"I want my daddy!" Ginny shook off the embrace.

Gladys straightened up stiffly. "Well, you'll have to be a big girl and wait till he comes home." The words were pathetic in their weakness, but they were all she could offer.

"I won't. I want my daddy. I'll run away and find him." The little girl did not move to make good her threat, but the words stopped Gladys, already halfway through the room. She went back and locked the door and windows, bolted them, too, firm against small hands…and proof against invaders from outside. It should have been done anyhow.

"I hate you! I hate you! I hate you!" The words of controlled rebellion faltered as she went out. By the time she reached the kitchen she could already hear the first sobs shaking the little girl in a convulsive release of violent emotion.

Barbie stood at the table, looking down silently at her half-eaten supper. "Aren't you going to do anything?" the girl demanded.

"No. Sit down and eat your supper. She'll come in when she's ready." Every impulse urged Gladys to go back, but she knew that any other day

Ginny's squalling would leave her unperturbed. Special sympathy now would only get the child more upset. She couldn't be placated; she just had to cry it out.

"But, Mother, you can't just..."

"I said, sit down and eat your supper," Gladys repeated slowly. "I thought you were old enough to know better, Barbara."

Blushing again, and miserably aware that she had started the whole thing by running to the door, Barbara pulled back her chair, the legs scraping against the linoleum in a long-drawn-out screech that set off their nerves to skittering frenzy again. Doggedly Gladys attacked lukewarm peas and potatoes.

The crying stopped. There was no sound in the house except the determined scraping of Gladys' fork across her plate. Barbara sat with downcast eyes, staring at her plate.

"Mother, I...I don't feel so well. May I be excused?" The formality of the request left Gladys no alternative.

"Certainly, Barbara," she said coldly. "Perhaps you'd better go upstairs and lie down?"

"I think I'd better." Barbie robbed her of the victory, accepting the proposal as willingly as though it were not a command.

"I don't feel good either." The swinging door edged noiselessly open to permit the entry of a small red nose, tight white lips, and a stray lock of soft brown hair. Ginny herself stayed hidden behind the door.

More relieved than she wanted to admit, Gladys unashamedly reversed her tactics. "Well," she announced blithely, "that fixes us all up, because I feel perfectly rotten. Let's throw out all this junk and have some good hot tea."

The red nose snuffled once rapidly, and the waving strand of brown hair advanced through the door, followed by a transformed child. *"Tea?"* she asked. "Really, truly, *tea?*"

"Really truly, goopy." Barbara relaxed immediately. "I'll fix it, Mother." She got up, with plates in each hand, in a flurry of activity. Gladys would cheerfully have traded places with her daughter, but she forced herself to sit still and wait while Ginny made a casual sidewise advance to the table. Finally one small hand came to rest on her knee. Then with a sudden scramble the little girl was on her lap, hugging her in a passionate frenzy of reformation, nestling and nuzzling against her until, communion achieved, the small head came bolt upright again. Then red-streaked eyes watched anxiously, still not entirely convinced, as Barbara poured steaming water over tea leaves and brought the covered pot to the table.

"Tea!" In her own seat at last, Ginny cuddled the warm cup in both hands and took a great noisy sip of the milky stuff. "Tea!" she marveled, and Barbara smiled at her mother again.

It was a hiatus in the storm, a valley of safety where they were safe and peaceful together for ten minutes that night. Later Gladys remembered it, relived every one of those minutes in the warm, bright kitchen, with both her girls trusting her, secure, mysteriously confident in her power to fix things, somehow.

Then Barbara was pushing her chair abruptly back and reaching for one of the jars Gladys had ready. She shouted something through the flying door. "...while I can." And it was strange enough behavior for a grown girl. But emotional ups and downs could do these things, as Gladys suddenly realized with painful acuteness. Apparently the youngest one was alone in her freedom from reaction to too great tension.

Gladys gave Ginny a smaller bottle and sent her after her sister, to the upstairs bathroom, no less amused than she was astonished that for once her own urgency was more compelling than her young daughter's. Barbara could take care of the little one. She herself needed a moment alone to mend her defenses.

She left the dishes for the time being, half aware that they would be a welcome task later, and when she was done labeling her own jar she went into the living room. There was music coming over the radio, and upstairs the sounds of footsteps and running water. Gladys moved about straightening things from long habit-putting the room to rights for the evening, switching on lights.

It was all so normal, so usual, so like every other day. Against her will she was drawn to the window, where street lights should be casting shadows from the spring-greened maples. But out there it was dark and only the cloud-cased moon sent an occasional wavering shape or shadow around the street.

The noises upstairs were not normal or usual. Barbara wasn't getting ready for a date; Ginny wasn't undressing for bed. They were busy filling mysterious jars for strange men to take away. She realized that the noise of combat and persuasion had died away upstairs. The girls were taking a long time for a simple job. Maybe she'd better go up.

Gladys stood at the foot of the stairs, and familiar sounds and shadows grouped themselves into a pattern. The light was on in Ginny's room. A low rhythmic murmur revealed itself as Barbara's voice when it rose to a dramatic word or phrase. Barbara was reading aloud to Ginny.

One light went out, and footsteps measured the length of the hall, toe-steps, really, cautious and quiet, walking away from the room of a child just fallen asleep. The bathroom door closed, shutting out the remaining light. Gladys hesitated on the first step. She wanted to go upstairs, to tuck Ginny in, to see what Barbara was doing. But she had an obscure feeling that something important was happening, something she shouldn't interfere with. Something that had started in the kitchen, at dinner…or before that, upstairs, in front of the little radio. Something that had made Barbie offer to write the report about Jon, had made her put Ginny to bed without being told.

Whatever it was, it belonged to Barbara. Gladys went back to the living room and sat down, made herself stay there till the girl came into view on the bottom steps.

She was holding the two glass jars, big and little, carefully balanced in her hands.

"Ginny's in bed." She went straight across the living room toward the kitchen, carrying the jars. "I told her you'd come and look in on her later." She disappeared into the dining room and reappeared a moment later, carrying all three jars on a kitchen tray. She took the tray out to the hall table and stood there, wrapping each one carefully in its labeling sheet.

"It'll be all ready when they come." She was elaborately explanatory, as if she knew her mother would never otherwise understand why she had bothered.

*But I do…I do…*Only there was no way to say it, no gesture she knew how to make.

Impulsively she went over to the china closet in the corner and opened the cupboard in the bottom where they kept the rarely used liquor. Jon wasn't much of a drinker. She pulled out a couple of bottles and held them up, studying the labels.

"I'm going to have a drink," she announced, and now the whole thing seemed silly. Was this a symbol for maturity? She tried to sound natural. "Would you like something, Barbie? A little wine or"—she couldn't help hesitating—"perhaps some brandy?"

"Moth-*er!*" Barbara was clearly shocked.

Gladys held up the bottle. "Well," she asked a little sharply, "do you want it or don't you?" She watched the struggle of conscience and curiosity on her daughter's face. Barbie's new-found maturity might be fundamental, but it had not yet begun to affect her superficial reactions and attitudes.

"We could make some eggnog." Gladys proposed a compromise. "It might settle your stomach a little." She started toward the kitchen, but Barbara jumped up to intercept her. She wondered if she had the same look of foolish guilt on her own face.

"I'll do it, Mother. Francie's mother taught us how, once." She grinned then. "I guess I never told you about that."

The bright smile twinkled familiarly until the girl vanished through the dining-room door. Gladys turned the radio up louder, wondering how many other things she would learn about her children in the days ahead.

"…rioting and panic in some sectors." The brutal words from the loudspeaker drove everything else out of her head. "However, Emergency Headquarters in all districts are carrying on a determined effort to maintain order. If you have not yet been visited by an emergency squad truck, please do not become alarmed. There has been no trouble in this section and emergency measures are proceeding as scheduled. All of you will have been visited by trained squadmen before midnight tonight. Stay indoors. Do not use the telephone unnecessarily. Assistance is coming to you.

"We repeat our news broadcast. Amateur radio communication lines are now operating throughout the country. The amount of damage done to major cities is still unknown, but government is functioning from secure headquarters, and the Army is already mobilized for retaliation."

Gladys listened dutifully, knowing these things should concern her. But they never said anything about the city, about survivors, about evacuation...*about Jon!*

Her attention wandered back to the radio. "There have been reports of rioting and panic in some sectors, however..." The announcer was repeating what she had heard before.

"Do not become alarmed," he said.

Gladys caught a glimpse of her own face in the mirror over the mantel, and the long lines of haggard middle age shocked her. It seemed frivolous, in the face of the fear that hung about them, to go upstairs for powder and lipstick. But she had to go up and look at Ginny anyhow, and she felt dirty, spoiled. She could at least wash her face.

The bright light in the bathroom hurt her eyes—gleaming polished porcelain and paint. The evening mess was all cleaned up; Barbara was certainly going through a change. Tenderness rushed over her again, and compassion, for the girl who was too young to grow up so much. Gladys doused her face in cold water and pulled a stiff-bristled brush through her hair. Combing it, she took a good long look in the mirror and added fresh powder and lipstick after all. Then she stopped in her room long enough to remove the confining girdle, stockings and shoes, and padded downstairs again in soft furred slippers, cherry red to match the warm wool robe Jon had given her for Christmas.

Barbara had the foaming pitcher already set down on the coffee table and was reaching for two of the hand-painted glasses from the top shelf of the china closet. Formally, like a child's tea party, Gladys poured the drinks. Then she curled up on the sofa and let tiredness claim her. Gradually warmth penetrated downward and spread out inside her. She could feel the tension in all her muscles flowing away; now there was nothing to do but wait. She sipped at the drink, and the glass in her hand grew heavy, until she put it down on the end table, unfinished, and remembered to pick it up for another sip only with difficulty. Nothing to do but wait...

THE CITY

There was no way out of it; he'd have to go all the way uptown to see McMahon before he could close the Kellogg deal. He grabbed a cab, irritated at the unlooked-for expense; irritated at himself for not bothering to get the car, for not even thinking of the subway; irritated at all the shouldering, shoving people who—like himself—didn't have sense enough to get out before it was too late.

Out of what? Too late for what? He didn't know. He thought of the headlines in the morning paper, but that was foolish. You didn't take those things seriously, personally. It was just—too many people, not enough time. There used to be more time.

He paid off the driver, and as soon as he walked into McMahon's dining room he realized what was wrong with him. He was hungry, that was all. He accepted a cup of coffee and watched the old hypochondriac finish off lunch enough for twelve healthy men.

Mack was surprisingly reasonable. They got everything cleared up in a few minutes, except the paragraph he'd known there would be trouble about. He could get out and get a meal soon. Then they saw it.

The big window across the room faced east; at first all they saw was a darkening of the sun, a funny color in the sky. They went over to the window, and there it was, blossoming out in the sky away downtown, so beautiful you forgot to be scared...or else you were so scared it wasn't like any fear you could recognize.

They watched the big cloud form in the sky over the bay: white, then tan, muddy, and at last a swirling pinkish mass. They began to believe it, really, when the swirling stopped and the climbing column of steam turned back on itself and became a pounding pillar of rain, falling out of the giant cloud like a trick shot in a movie.

They didn't say anything, except just Mack's one word, "Well!" Then they turned and headed for the door, walking, not running, because that was the way McMahon was, But he noticed Mack had forgotten to limp. He edged past the older man, being polite but determined about it. Then he flung himself down the staircase, leaping, running, taking two, three steps at a time. He was on the second landing when the blast shook him.

The house shuddered, but it stood. He kept going down, more carefully now. Another blast, and he could hear windows breaking, but not the sound of the bombs. He felt the blast; he didn't hear it. Then there was one he heard, different, close by.

A gas tank going up, a real old-fashioned explosion; he had time to recognize it before a flying beam found his head.

He couldn't have been out long, because it was still light when he dug himself out. Up the block three different fires were burning. Clouds hung over the city in every direction, but they weren't using that trick movie shot any more. The clouds were gray, good old honest gray, no rosy linings...or was it glasses? Did you use smoked glasses to make the color show? He couldn't remember. Someone was running down the street, passing him.

"Mister!" he shouted. "Mister, I'm lost!" He began running, too, running after the other man, trying to catch him and find out how to get home.

Chapter Five

"Wake up, Mother." It was Barbara bending over her, shaking her shoulder. "Mother, please don't go back to sleep." The face was pale and drawn, sharply in focus now.

"What is it?" Immediately Gladys was wide awake. Then, as Barbara relaxed, she realized there was no immediate crisis. "I must have dozed off."

The girl nodded her head. "I wanted to let you sleep, but I guess the eggnog...and all that stuff on the radio...I don't feel so good, I've got kind of a headache and—"

"Of course, baby." This was easy. Among all the strange new things these words came automatically. "You go upstairs and take an aspirin and get into bed." It was wonderful not to have to *think* what to say. "If you can't get to sleep, call me."

She managed an encouraging smile, and Barbara responded with a watery imitation of her own grin.

"I'm sorry," the girl fumbled. "I don't like to walk out on you..."

"Go on," Gladys told her. "Shoo! Get to bed."

The old formula was still good. Barbie turned obediently and went up the stairs.

Gladys glanced at her watch. It was only a little after nine. She hadn't slept long, and she was stiff all over, but she felt better. She walked around the room, getting the kinks out of her joints.

She could hear Barbara splashing in the bathroom. Once a door opened, and once she thought she heard Ginny's voice pleading outside the bathroom, then the click of the latch and the two voices raised a little in minor altercation, quiet now and then arguing again. After a while there were footsteps going down the hall, and finally Barbara returning to her room alone.

Gladys turned the radio up a little louder and sat down in the big armchair where Jon listened to the baseball game, Saturday afternoons. Her fingers rubbed the worn upholstery, wandered of their own accord to the table that held his pipes and tobacco, riffled the pages of the big, bright-colored merchandising magazine in the rack underneath. Frightened by the longing that crept up on her, she tried to concentrate on the radio.

"Evacuation is already beginning in some sections. Please do not call Emergency Headquarters for information. If you are to be evacuated, you will receive instructions…"

Something was thumping at the door. It was heavy, authoritative, but strange. She hesitated, trying to make it out, and it came again, imperatively. She went to the front window that gave a clear view of the porch and pulled back the drape.

She had forgotten to turn on the porch light, and the street lamps were off. In the moonlight only the bulky outline of a man was dimly visible. Another bang on the door: Gladys almost ran to unbolt it, opened it hastily, and stepped back a pace in sudden panic.

The visitors took her reaction for invitation. They stepped inside and closed the door behind them. Not until then did either one of them lift the visor set into the helmet top of the bulky one-piece suit that covered each completely, shoes, hands, head, and all.

The simple act of revealing their faces changed them from fictional monsters to human beings. Gladys breathed again, and recognized one of the men, with surprise, as Peggy Turner's husband, Jim. The man with him was young and serious-looking.

"This here is Dr. Spinelli, Miz Mitchell," Turner introduced him. "He's an intern over at the new V. A. Hospital."

Gladys tried to acknowledge the introduction with a smile but her mouth was still stiff from the moment of fear.

"Sorry if I gave you a turn, Miz Mitchell," the big man apologized, "but I knew you had kids here, so I thought it would be better to knock instead of ringing the bell. I know it makes a funny sound with these gloves on."

"Oh, it wasn't that. It was just—well, you look so strange."

"You should hear the kids, some places we go," he broke in, grinning. "They think we're Martians or something. Some of 'em never quit bawlin' till we go." He laughed, a big-sounding masculine laugh that made her worries seem silly.

"Do you…" She hesitated. "Is it dangerous outside? Is that why you have to wear *them?*" she blurted out defiantly.

"Now don't you get yourself upset, Miz Mitchell," he reassured her. "We got to wear these things because we go out so much in different neighborhoods. Some places could be dangerous, and we never know till we get there. But this street right here, you could go out for a pleasure walk and never get hurt."

Dr. Spinelli cleared his throat uncomfortably. Gladys turned to him, questioning, and he said hastily, "Mr. Turner's absolutely right, Mrs. Mitchell. But just the same, you better not try it." He produced an apologetic smile. "This neighborhood's been perfectly safe all along as far as we know, but there are still clouds of hot stuff blowing around. You shouldn't go outdoors until you get word it's all right—maybe sometime tomorrow."

Jim Turner bent on the younger man a glance of amusement that brought a slow flush up over the bony features. Gladys remembered the urine samples and reached for the tray.

"Do you take these now?" she asked, too brightly, breaking the silence.

The young doctor accepted them eagerly. "I'll take them right out to the truck," he said. "I have to ask you a few questions later, but I can get these checked meanwhile."

She noticed that he stowed the jars away carefully in a big pouch pocket built into one side of his suit, and fastened the zipper securely before he opened the door.

Turner followed her into the living room. "Don't let the young feller worry you, Miz Mitchell," he repeated. "He's a nice kid, but he's fresh out of school—all he knows is out of books, and he thinks that's all there is to know. We got to wear these outfits just because we're out so much," he insisted. "No real danger anyplace around here now, but you know how it is—a little bit here and a little bit there…"

He opened up the bulging pouch on his own suit, exposing a sheaf of rough white paper, and counted off several sheets. "Now this'll tell you more about everything than I could do myself," he said. "You can study it up after we're gone, and then if there's anything still bothering you, we'll be around again tomorrow, and I can explain it to you."

Gladys took the papers from him. They were numbered in sequence, as if they were meant to be fastened together as a booklet. On top of the first page it said in big block letters:

Vital Facts for Civilians—Atomic War —Radiation Effects—Evacuation

Underneath, everything was in close black type, blurred slightly from rapid mimeographing. She tore her eyes from the page, trying to get her thoughts together, to remember all the things she had to ask. Turner was saying something, but she didn't listen. She had written everything down someplace. Of course, it was all in her apron pocket, upstairs.

"Listen," she said, "some things have got me worried." There was one special thing that couldn't wait till morning. What was it? Then she remembered. "Is there anything in here about the water?"

"Water?" He didn't understand.

"Is it all right?" she persisted. "Do we have to boil it or anything?"

"Nothing to worry about there." He seemed very confident. "The water's okay. They've got a gang of Geigers on it all the time. Anything went wrong, they'd cut off the supply."

He saw her mouth open for a horrified protest. "I mean, just the supply from the local reservoir," he amended quickly. "There's some way they can bring the water straight through and by-pass this reservoir altogether. Might be without for a couple of hours, but no more than that. Boiling wouldn't help anyhow," he added. "You can't get hot stuff out that way. You just relax and take it as easy as you can. I'll be around again on the truck, and when you read through those papers you'll see we didn't leave much out."

"But how…who's doing it all?" For the first time Gladys was curious. "Who's running everything? Who put these out?" She rustled the papers in her hand.

"Oh, we've been getting ready for this a long time." He smiled knowingly. "Our country wasn't so dumb."

"I know," she said impatiently, "the bombs and planes and all that. You can't read a newspaper without knowing about those things," she added bitterly. "But I didn't know about anything else—the trucks you're using, and those—diving-suit things you wear—"

"Well, nobody else knew either," he assured her. "Nobody who wasn't in it. When you want to win you got to keep a poker face and play it close to the vest. And any time the government let out any information about what we were doing some scientist would start yelling about warmongers, or some Reds would have a demonstration."

"Well, when did *you*…?" Then she realized: Of course—the "business trips"! She sat down on the, edge of the sofa, thinking, and looked up at Turner with a new respect. *I wonder if Peggy knew?*

"I was in the Reserves," he said, "and I guess I had the right kind of background or record. They sort of eased me in slow. They had to be pretty careful about picking people who could keep their mouths shut. Now," he changed the subject firmly, "let's see, is there anything else you got to know? They're gonna be wanting blood donations, but I don't think they'll take 'em from folks this close to the city. Not till after the lab boys get them samples checked, anyhow."

When she wanted to know what the blood was for he pointed again to the papers he'd given her.

"It's all in there—in that part about radiation disease," he said. "You read that good, and you'll know practically as much about it as I do. Now there's one other thing I got to tell you, about evacuation. If—"

A muffled pounding at the door interrupted him. This time Gladys flew to open it. The young doctor came in and went straight into the living room, waiting until Gladys had closed the door again before he raised his visor and nodded curtly to Turner.

"Looks okay. The Geiger doesn't show anything," he told Gladys. A peculiar feeling of antagonism between the two men seemed to fill the room. It was upsetting; she almost didn't hear the question the doctor was asking.

"I'm sorry." She tried to cover up the wave of irrational resentment. "I'm afraid I didn't…"

"Just a routine question," he explained. "Has anyone in your family been ill any time during the evening?"

"Well, none of us felt too good." She didn't know whether it counted, really, but she started to tell him about the incident at supper. The doorbell buzzed sharply. Turner waved her to go on and answered it himself.

He was back almost immediately, explaining, "They need me there." There was an edge of triumph in his voice that Gladys didn't understand. But he couldn't go yet; there were too many things she still had to know.

"Will you be back?"

His visor was already halfway down, but he opened it again and turned back to her.

"I think I told you just about everything," he said. He was reassuring again, but impatient too. Whatever was waiting for him outside, he wanted to get to it.

Why, he likes this! Gladys thought suddenly. He's having fun!

"Anything special on your mind?" He was waiting, restlessly polite.

"About the water," she said urgently, remembering her fear. "I know you said it was all right, but…" She felt foolish, pressing the matter, but she had to ask. "Didn't I hear something about germs that could be put in the water supply? Wouldn't boiling help that?"

"They're checking that too," he told her impatiently. "You don't have to go looking for extra work, Miz Mitchell. You'll have plenty to do, just following instructions. If there's anything dangerous, we'll let you know. Now…" His voice was warm and genial again, reassuring her. "If that's all that was on your mind…"

He wouldn't wait any longer.

"No!" she exploded. "No, that's not all! There are a million things on my mind. I want to know why my husband can't come home, and what to do for my children, and where my son is, and whether my house is safe. How long is this whole impossible thing going to go on? How long do I have to wait to find out if my husband's alive or dead?" The involuntary violence of the declaration left her startled and ashamed. She sat down again weakly. "I'm sorry." Her voice was dull. "I know you can't tell me any of those things."

He made the faintest motion toward the door. "There's nothing else, then?"

"No," she agreed, "there isn't anything else."

The doctor was nice. He waited until the door was closed and said, as if nothing had happened, "You all felt better after the tea, though?" He smiled for the first time, really, a smile that used his whole face. It was unexpectedly sweet, and totally disarming.

"Yes…oh yes." She wanted to thank him, but she didn't know how. It was hard to concentrate on the story. She heard the motor start up outside and was suddenly panic-stricken. He was going away; she knew he wouldn't come back. He thought she was just another hysterical woman.

The doctor was asking her to go on. Of course—they couldn't go without him! But she could see he was worried too. She told him about Barbie feeling bad again after the eggnog.

"That doesn't sound so bad," he told her. "I think everybody in the country must have lost his appetite tonight." He smiled again, that surprisingly charming smile in his long, sober face. "Of course we won't know anything for sure until we get real lab analyses on all the samples, but so far there is no reason to believe that your children were exposed to anything. Your girls' symptoms don't sound too serious—you *would* know if either of them had been really sick? I mean real nausea with vomiting."

"Good Lord, yes!" She found it was possible to laugh. "I'd have had to clean it up."

"Well, I guess that takes care of everything." He paced restlessly to the window and tried to look out. Then he stood still, his head cocked to one side. What was he listening for? "Look," he said suddenly, "there's one question of yours that I can answer." He stopped, hesitated, and then explained, "I don't think I'm supposed to tell you. I'd rather Turner didn't walk in on it…But you shouldn't count too much on your husband getting back here soon. There's some talk about evacuating this whole section—and I know they've stopped sending patients through to the hospital here. It's the same thing I told you before: we won't really know how safe this neighborhood is until after the analyses are finished at the lab."

"You mean you don't even know yet whether it's all right out there?" She stared at the soft drapes closed across the windows, as if she could see through to the unknown danger.

"Oh, I'm sorry—I didn't mean to make you think *that*. We know it's okay right now. What we have to find out is whether it was all right all day—and whether it'll still be all right tomorrow."

"But the bombs were miles away! How could there be any danger around here?" she demanded.

"It's not that simple," he explained. "There's dust and smoke from the city—God knows what a freak wind could do. And with the underwater bombs, there's the rain—and then we don't even know yet what kind of bombs they used. I mean what they had in them—there are different kinds of fission materials, you know. They need different treatment. And we don't even know how the damn things came over—excuse me, Mrs. Mitchell. I get—"

"Don't be silly." She wanted him to go on. "I'm a big girl."

"Well, we don't know whether they were bombs or guided missiles. Our radar didn't catch any airplanes overhead, and that looks bad. The war heads could have been on self-propelled missiles with atomic engines, and that would mean—"

Gladys made a helpless gesture of protest. "I'd like to explain it all, Mrs. Mitchell," he wound up ruefully, "but I'm afraid it would take too long, if you don't understand that part. You'll just have to take my word for it. Until we know more about the nature of the bombs we have to double-check everybody and everything anywhere near a bombed area. And these urinalyses will give us a safe check—at least as long as the lab equipment holds out."

"I guess I should have read more about it before," Gladys said diffidently. "I…well, I just couldn't believe it. I never really believed any nation would *use* it this way."

"*We* did," he said harshly. "We used it in 1945. In Japan. Why wouldn't somebody else use it on us? God knows—" He stopped himself. "I'm sorry," he said shortly. "After all, it isn't *your* fault. I'm just blowing off steam."

"Well, it was your turn," Gladys smiled. "I blew my top a while back."

He looked bewildered and then remembered. "That was nothing! You should see some of the women we run into. I think it was probably just because you've been behaving so well that I forgot *I* was supposed to be helping *you*. Anyhow," he resumed briskly—and Gladys thought suddenly, He's so young!—"the thing to remember about radiation disease is that it can be treated and cured just like any other disease…just so we catch it early enough."

"What do you mean? How early?"

He didn't answer right away; he was listening again. Faintly, now, Gladys heard the motor starting up again, but far away, as if it were down at the other end of the block.

"I'll explain that later," he said hastily. "They'll be back in a minute now, and there's one other thing I wanted to tell you. *Please* don't let it alarm you—but that wasn't a bad idea you had about the water—just to make extra sure. We don't know whether they're going to try any bacteriological—"

The ringing of the telephone aggravated an already heightened imagination.

"Hello," she breathed into the mouthpiece, hope and fear fighting for possession of the syllables.

"Oh, Gladys, I'm so glad you're still up. Did that squad truck get to your house yet?"

Edie Crowell again. "They're here now." Gladys was annoyed. "I mean, the doctor is. Do you need him?"

"How could I possibly know whether I need him? They won't tell us anything, so we have no way of knowing if there's anything wrong. I just thought I heard a motor outside, and I wondered if the truck was getting near the house yet." A stifled sob came over the line. "Gladys, can't you understand? I'm here all alone, and I keep hearing about these rioters and looters and maniacs out in the streets—"

"What on earth are you talking about?" Fear tightened in her throat again. "What's *wrong* with you, Edie?" She was dimly aware of the doctor crossing the room to answer another muffled thumping at the door.

"Well, Betsy called me up and told me all about it," Edith rushed on defensively. "She got the information because she works for the *Telegraph*. There are all kinds of people wandering around who escaped from the city, and they're crazy because they know they're going to die, and they're breaking into people's houses, and drinking, and attacking women, too. And I'm all—"

Oh, my God! Helplessly Gladys moved the receiver a little further from her ear to protect herself from the penetrating shrillness. Finally, unable to listen any longer or even to find words to end the conversation, she dropped it unceremoniously back on the hook. The doctor had returned, bringing Turner with him. Flushed and frightened, she repeated what Edith had told her.

"We better get over there," Dr. Spinelli said wearily.

Turner nodded agreement. "I know that one. Thinks she owns the whole town. Give her something to knock her out, Doc, or she'll be making trouble all night." He turned to Gladys. "You'll be all right, Miz Mitchell," he promised. "Just don't get panicky. If you have any trouble, remember I'll be around again tomorrow."

He laid a gauntleted hand on her shoulder, and she knew it was meant to be reassuring. But something in the touch of the heavy glove sent chills chasing down her spine. She was glad when he wheeled his bulk around, pulled his visor smartly down, and headed for the door.

A soldier off to the wars! It was funny, until she realized that was just exactly what he was.

CHAPTER SIX

SHE WAS STILL shivering. Her hands were icy, and the teapot on the table offered no warmth when she touched it. She picked it up and carried it back to the kitchen. It was while she sat waiting for the fresh water to boil that she realized neither of them had answered her question about the things Edie said on the phone. She remembered the doctor's shrug and Turner's impatience to be gone—but they had never once said whether it was true.

She tried to fight down panic, telling herself she was as bad as Edie Crowell, that she couldn't afford to give in to the fears and vapors that a childless woman could have. Still the thought persisted, and even as she sipped at the comfort of hot tea in a brightly lit room she couldn't throw off the newly aroused fear—the age-old fear—of wild men lurking in the dark. Every noise outside was a skulking footstep, and every familiar creak in the house a stealthy intruder.

Hastily she picked up the teapot, and took it into the living room, where the radio was producing music. She listened incredulously to the pulsing rhythm of a song she had danced to with Jon—when was it? A week ago? Four days? In another lifetime? Standing there alone, in the middle of the room, she could feel his arms around her, and the still firm length of his body against hers, their legs moving together, his head bent toward her, so she could see the gray that was beginning to touch the edges of his hair—and the urgent pressure of his hand on her back that made her forget the gray.

The music changed, drifted into an old, old song, played without words, taunting her memory. The yearning conviction of Jon's nearness left her, but, eyes still closed, she managed to keep him in the room. He was in his leather jacket, the old brown suede; he had taken the trash can outside and a gust of cool night air came in before he locked the back door again. He was bent over his desk, plowing grimly through a piled-up stack of papers. On the ash tray at his hand a cigarette burned monotonously, offering up incense at midnight to the gods of success. He was down on his back on the floor, mock wrestling with Ginny, scrambling and rolling around, his uneven white teeth parted in a shout of good will toward the world. He was, best remembered of all, standing legs akimbo in the bedroom, his hair still damp from the shower. The fresh white, lightly starched shirt bloused out smartly as he buckled his belt flat across his narrow waist and hips. The smell of talc and shaving lotion was so real, the billowing white shirt so crisp and right, that Gladys knew, suddenly and surely, that Jon was there with her; this whole thing, this impossible afternoon and evening, was a nightmare, a sick dream, and in a moment her husband's hand would be on her shoulder; his voice would be bantering, refusing to take serious stock in woman's ills, but just the same he would ask her, "Tea make you feel better, honey?"

On the radio the announcer's voice broke in over the fading strains of the music.

"Until there is further news we will continue our selections of favorite songs. Stay tuned in to this station; we will interrupt this program to announce any new developments. Next we have an old favorite—'Stardust.' Stay tuned in." The music began again. The haunting, nostalgic strain. The song of her own adolescence. This was no nightmare. Jon wasn't in the kitchen. He might never be in the kitchen again.

The songs changed, and every now and then the announcer spoke for a few extra minutes between selections, with news designed to be reassuring. "Our radar screen has now been pronounced impenetrable by Army experts," they kept saying, and, "Survivors have been found on the island of Manhattan, even on the narrow strip of land west of the main explosion."

She picked up the sheaf of rough-paper mimeographed sheets Turner had given her and tried to read. She put aside the one on radiation sickness and found one labeled "General Instructions and Information."

BLOOD DONATIONS—required of all citizens not resident in danger zones or in areas immediately adjoining danger zones. Well, she had given blood before; if they came for it she could do that much.

DANGER ZONES—those where the bomb blast had been visible and those that had been swept by radioactivity following the blasts. Well, this was neither…and then she remembered that moment in the laundry, the instant of brilliant, blinding sunlight, and then the cloud and darkness. Was that the bomb blast? What time had that been? Was that what they meant by "visible"? But if it were, surely, she'd have known sooner than she did. The neighborhood would have been alive with talk and fear and rumor.

"It must have been something awfully important," Barbara had said. "Everybody called up; all the mothers." And the phone kept ringing— the phone at home. She'd never answered; she thought they were all for Barbie. And that nice young teacher: "…so good of you," Miss Pollock had said. Because she hadn't called up, of course.

She riffled unenthusiastically through the sheets. She knew she should read them through and she didn't want to. She was too tired; it was too easy to get scared. On the radio, music and announcements repeated themselves, old songs, a generation old; old news, an hour, almost a day old. The sheets of information that she didn't want were a blur of black and white, turning gray. The cherry-red robe held her warm as if, being a present from Jon, it still held the feel of his arms in its fiber.

His arms, and his mouth…

How silly, she thought drowsily. How silly to feel this way now: a respectable old married woman wanting her husband as she had wanted him almost twenty years before, feeling the same desperate urgency for him. She stroked the soft wool of the robe and shrugged down inside the collar, rubbing chin and cheek on the comfort of it.

Resolutely she picked up the sheet about radiation sickness. She stumbled through a prefatory paragraph. It was nothing to become alarmed about, the pamphlet assured her; it was no mystery; it could be cured. Adequate supplies of blood for transfusions were already being collected. "Injections of toluidine blue restore the ray-impaired ability of the blood to clot. Phenyldrazine is an antidote for anemia…Urinalysis will readily detect the presence of more dangerous and faster-working fission products. Alpha emitters such as plutonium…"

She skipped the introduction, wondering why every effort they made to reassure her, with radio announcements and music, scientific phrases and soothing words, did nothing but frighten her all over again. There…" SYMPTOMS. After first general malaise and period of apparent good health, victim will be subject to a variety of symptoms. Hair may fall out; itching, burning, or skin discomforts, including boils and blisters, skin hemorrhages, etc., may develop. Weakness…nausea…"

The sheet dropped from her hands. Out of the jumble of unfamiliar words and phrases the only thing that made sense was the sudden memory of dinner, of Barbara, picking at her plate. "I…I don't feel so well." And Ginny, repeating, "I don't feel so good." Barbara, rushing so suddenly from the kitchen…

That was nonsense; the doctor knew all about that, and he said it was all right. The doctor would have known.

She picked up the sheet again and held onto that thought. He would have told her. She stood up restlessly. Her watch said twelve forty-seven. That was impossible; it must be later than that. On the way through the dining room the big oak clock said twelve forty-eight. They couldn't both be that far wrong.

The music on the radio gave way again to the announcer's molasses tones. "All residents of lower Westchester County are urged to be prepared for evacuation," he said, and it didn't make sense. *This* was lower Westchester. She listened as he repeated it and went on. "Spotty danger zones have been located, along the banks of the Hudson, and in the Larchmont-New Rochelle area. Residents of these areas are already being evacuated. Please do not become alarmed. If your neighborhood is in a danger zone you have already been informed. However, *all* residents in the lower part of the county are urged to be prepared for an evacuation order any time in the next few days. For further information, please read your instruction sheet carefully." Gladys found the mimeographed pages on the sofa where she had thrown them down. She searched through the close-typed pages.

EVACUATION. There it was. "If you receive a warning to prepare for evacuation, by radio or telephone, do not become alarmed. The measure is taken to protect you. It does not necessarily mean that you are in a danger zone or that you have been exposed to dangerous radiations. Many people who have not been exposed will be evacuated for their own future safety. Wherever possible, the plan is to evacuate all persons within a ten-mile radius of any known danger zones. DO NOT MISTAKE *warning* for an *evacuation order*. Orders for evacuation can come *only* from Emergency Headquarters. The radio or telephone warning will come first.

"If you receive an *evacuation order,* after the warning, you will still have time to prepare your family and possessions. If you do receive such an *order,* study the suggestions below carefully, and start preparing immediately. Remember, no one will be allowed to take more than he can carry himself. Take only those things that you are certain you will *need.* If there are valuables in your home, which you are forced to leave behind, give a list to your squadman to be filed at Emergency Head-quarters. Small items of jewelry and similar valuables may be given to the squadman, if well wrapped and clearly labeled..."

Gladys put the sheet down. All kinds of people wandering around, Edie Crowell had said, crazy, drinking, housebreaking...You could think about your home and possessions, you could plan on hiding things, on saving and packing. People had done that before; that was what war meant. It was the other part you couldn't think about: strange deadly radiations, silent, invisible killers.

The announcer finished repeating his message, and some idiot in the broadcasting station started playing cowboy songs. Gladys turned the radio down as low as she dared and set about making up a list of all the things they'd need. Ginny wouldn't be able to carry anything—not much at least. She'd want a toy, probably Pallo, and she might be able to handle a small suitcase, the tiny one she used playing around the house. Barbie was strong; she could take a big bag. And another big one for herself. She thought of substituting two smaller cases, to make balancing easier, but she'd have to keep a hand free, with Ginny along. The things to go in: pajamas, bathrobe, slippers, toothbrush, hairbrushes and combs...She stopped herself. This was the wrong kind of thinking. One brush and comb could do for all of them. Towels? A couple if there was room. She thought of stories of the last great war in Europe, and added: soap, toilet paper.

Blankets? No. She could wear her fur coat, and Barbie the heavy camel's hair, in spite of the warm weather. They could sleep under them if they had to, and Ginny could use the bathrobes. One set of decent clothes for each of them, dress, stockings, slip, everything, but they'd better wear slacks and shirts traveling. She tried to remember where she'd put the blue corduroys.

Upstairs, in the attic, maybe, something creaked, and the wind blew the branches of the old elm against the house. *Thud, rattle, thud, rattle*—the branches of the elm, and a loose window rattling.

Gladys sat bolt upright. Her watch said one-twenty. She ducked around swiftly, to the peeping window, but there was no one on the porch. *Thud, rattle.* Not a man knocking. No one banging at the door. Just the tree and a window, nothing more. She was glad now that she had locked up everything downstairs, when Ginny had her tantrum.

But that was only downstairs.

She started at the top, in the attic. She had to force herself to open the trap door and reach for the light string, then go prying around with the flashlight, into all the dark corners where an invader could hide. She checked the small windows, made sure they were locked.

It was easier when the attic was done. On the second floor there was the familiar big bedroom, Tom's room, and the guest room. Carefully she locked the only window that was open.

She hesitated to use the overhead light in Ginny's room, but if she left a shadow unexplored she'd worry all night. Resolutely she switched it on and scanned the room, then turned it quickly off again, as Ginny started burrowing under the covers to escape the light.

Under the gentler beam of the flashlight the child slept in her favorite position, knees drawn up under her, arms sheltering her head. Her breathing was even and regular. Her cheek, when Gladys touched it, was warm with sleep, and nothing more. Most assuredly her hair was not falling out, nor was her soft baby skin marred with angry rough blotches.

In Barbie's big back room, only recently converted from bright-colored washables to adolescent chintz and frills, it was perfectly safe to keep the light on. Nothing short of mayhem could ordinarily wake Barbara before she had slept her fill—and at that, it would have to be a noisy kind of mayhem. Now pink-pajamaed limbs sprawled out in every possible direction from the tangled knot of bedclothes; wavy dark hair tumbled over the wrinkled pillow slip; the gently curved young breast rose and fell evenly.

Gladys went over and dropped a kiss lightly on her daughter's untroubled forehead. She made a futile attempt at straightening out the blankets, but gave up when Barbara stirred restively. She turned to go, and a sleep-soaked, half-aspirated word followed her. "Mommy?"

"Yes, baby," she whispered. "I'm sorry I woke you. Go back to sleep."

"Is Daddy home yet?"

"Not yet, darling. Go back to sleep." Now that the girl was half roused anyhow, Gladys bent again to smooth the blankets. Automatically Barbara lifted a leg to let the sheet be unwrapped.

"I *wish* Daddy would come home," she said.

"I know, baby. I do too. He will." She sat on the edge of the bed, stroking the girl's head, knowing she wasn't really awake. Barbara had been known to carry on conversations for as long as half an hour in the middle of the night, and never remember a word of it in the morning. She whispered, low enough so Barbara wouldn't hear if she was asleep, "Do you feel all right now, Barbie?"

"Sure." There was healthy irritation in the answer. "There's nothing wrong with me. You go to bed, Mom." She turned over, away from the stroking fingers, and was immediately asleep.

Bed? Gladys thought. Why not? She had never gone to bed before, until Jon was home, but tonight—tonight it would be silly to wait up for him. She thought of the bed, cold and empty and alone. Not alone as it was when Jon was working late downstairs, nor as it was when on a rare Sunday morning he crept out to let her sleep, and fixed breakfast to bring up to her later. But now a different kind of alone, something she'd never thought about without a shudder that drove the thought away—alone, perhaps, and cold for the rest of her life. No.

She might curl up on the couch in the living room. Then if the phone rang, or if anything at all happened..." People wandering... crazy...home-breaking, drinking...attacking..." If anything at all happened, she would be there, ready, and not in her empty bed.

She had to do something. She would never stay awake if she didn't find something to do. She couldn't go down there to the empty living room and the terrifying radio.

She opened up the big upstairs closet, the one she'd been meaning to clean out for years, and began exploring for things they might need.

There was Jon's camping stuff, unused since he had given up fishing in favor of golf. The nested pans and utensils would be useful. And maybe the knapsack. She slid the straps over her shoulders and stifled a giggle, remembering her one dismal attempt to tramp through the woods alongside her new husband with one of these things on her back. Maybe Barbie could use it; she was a more athletic type.

Then, with half the things on her list collected, and as many more that weren't on the list at all, weariness fell on her like a smothering blanket. The wind must have started up again, because she could hear the tree and the window once more. *Thud, rattle...thud, rattle.* She wasn't imagining it. *Thud. Rattle. Thud.* She glanced again at her watch. Almost four! Well, she could try to wake Barbie, in another hour. But somebody had to stay up.

Down in the living room she found the cold teapot and took it back to the kitchen, then decided on coffee instead.

The electric clock said three fifty-six. Outside there was a gray hint of dawn approaching—not enough to make any real light, just enough to make the shadows seem darker. She sat at the gleaming white-topped table, struggling to keep awake until the robin on the kettle whistled for her, and once more the noises and imagined footsteps assailed her. The rattle and thump of the wind sounded for all the world like someone trying to force the door. The porch creaked, and she was sure someone was out there, but she wouldn't look. Again it creaked, and still she wouldn't look—but she did.

There was a man outside the glass panes of the door. She shut her eyes to blot out the image. When she opened them again the man was still there. He knocked on the doorframe—*thud;* he shook the doorknob—*rattle.* Gladys couldn't understand why she was no longer afraid. *Thud…rattle; thud…rattle.*

Hope sped through her mind and was gone almost before it came; Jon had a key. And the squadmen used the front door. A neighbor? Edie Crowell, driven at last to leave home in spite of all the warnings? No, the shadowy bulk was definitely masculine. Of course, it was the hat; there was no mistaking the outlines of a man's hat.

Thud, rattle. He was at it again. Fascinated, Gladys sat at the table and watched the door shake. She couldn't think of anything to do about it. The noise stopped, and the man, whoever he was, moved off a little.

He's going away, Gladys thought, almost disappointed.

The robin began to emit a low preparatory whistle, and she reached for a pot holder and pulled the little bird off its perch at the end of the spout. She kept watching the door. A vague shape moved outside; the man hadn't gone away after all. He seemed to bend down, and then something slithered through the crack between the threshold and the door. A piece of paper lay on the floor, small, close-lined, with three ripped round holes to show where it had been torn out of a loose-leaf memo book. She took a single step forward to pick it up, then instinctive caution stopped her from exposing herself in front of the glass pane in the door.

The pot holder was still clenched in her hand. Inspired, she picked up the kettleful of boiling water and approached the door, slowly, from the side, until she could reach out one foot and slide the paper closer to her. She bent over to pick it up, convinced with every move that she was about to drench herself with scalding water. But when she straightened up again, shakily, she had kettle and paper both clutched safe.

She remembered to back away to a safe angle before she put the kettle down and pinned her attention on the note. The scrawl was hasty and barely legible, the characters small and crabbed, reminiscent of nothing so much as notes taken in college lecture halls, quick small letters written rapidly in an ill-lit room. It was oddly reassuring; you couldn't picture a fear-crazed housebreaker forming such dry, concise letters. She read, with difficulty, "Please let me in. Have something important to tell you. Explain everything—too much to write. Don't worry—am not dangerous."

Almost, she opened the door; it was completely convincing in its terse simplicity. *Maybe he had a message from Jon!* She started toward the door, and halfway there thought better of it. She got a sheet from the marketing pad and scribbled on it hurriedly, "Who are you?"

Then she was stopped. She couldn't slip it back under the door. The crack was too narrow. Pushing anything through would take careful maneuvering, and while she was bent down at the threshold the man could break the glass pane over her head, or push the whole door in on her. If he *was* dangerous it would almost be safer to let him in than to take that chance.

The window over the sink opened out on the back porch. Still watching the door, she opened the right-hand casement a half inch and let the paper flutter down, then banged the window hard to attract his attention, and locked it securely.

It worked. Footsteps creaked on the porch, and the shadow disappeared from the doorway. She couldn't see anything out of the window. He must be reaching from the side as she had, not taking chances either. Looking into the well-lighted kitchen, he had probably seen the hot-water kettle in her hand. She crossed over to the door and waited there until the shape reappeared on the other side of the glass pane, and then disappeared again briefly, bending down to slide the same paper back under. Edging it over with her foot, she got well out of range before she stooped to pick it up. She was beginning to feel very silly, balancing the kettle all this time, but she held onto it, grimly reminding herself that it was better to be foolishly careful than just plain foolish.

"Dr. Levy—teacher at Burl's—yr. daughter Barbara my math class," she deciphered under the smudges made by the sole of her slipper.

Dr. Levy…The name was familiar, but she couldn't recall Barbie talking about him. Who was it? Where did she remember it from?

She stood there, staring at the note. I've got to decide what to do, she thought. Right now! She saw another sheet from the same memo book come through under the door and, less cautious this time, retrieved it more rapidly.

"Please let me in," it said briefly. "Can't stay here. Getting light. Will be caught."

If she didn't let him in he'd go away. And she didn't want him to go away. It was as simple as that. She didn't give herself a chance to reconsider. The door key was in the lock; she turned it quickly and opened the door enough to let him slip through, but she kept the kettle ready.

The man paid no attention to the steaming water. "Turn out the light," he commanded, and turned his back on both Gladys and her improvised weapon. A thrill of alarm went through her as she saw him lock the door.

His face was shadowed by stubble and streaked with dust. The rough tweed suit, baggy on his thin frame, might have been good once; now the pants were spattered with mud and grime, and one sleeve was ripped halfway up.

Terror-stricken, Gladys watched his right hand slide inside his jacket to the spot below the shoulder where she knew—from the movies—a holster could hang. Her hand, on the kettle, tensed and drew back.

"For God's sake, woman," he said again, "turn the light out! And put that pot down before you hurt somebody."

Jon, oh, Jon, she prayed, I need you! She stood there, holding the kettle she knew she wouldn't use, and watched him back away to the far corner of the kitchen, out of range of door and windows.

"Look, if you won't turn the light out, isn't there some other room where people can't see in so easily?" At last his hand was coming out from under the jacket.

Jon…Jon, come home!

Incongruously the man brought forth a spectacle case from which he removed a spotless pair of glasses, and placed them tenderly on the bridge of his nose.

In spite of his rough urgency, his voice was modulated, his speech educated, his words rational.

I'm a fool, she thought. He's crazy. I'm being such a fool. But she put the kettle down and motioned silently to the swinging door.

Chapter Seven

"Mrs. Mitchell, I came to warn you…about your children. You better sit down," he interjected, "and listen carefully. I can't stay long."

It was like something out of a bad play—the man, dirty, torn, and battered, standing in that cheerful room. Gladys tried to remember whether Barbie ever had, really, mentioned his name.

"Of course," she murmured, "go on."

At first the words and phrases kept jumbling together in her mind, full of things she didn't understand, and, like the information sheets and the radio, filling her with formless fears.

After a while the fear took form. She knew what he was going to say. She felt herself beginning to shiver.

"I wish you'd sit down," he interrupted himself again. She shook her head stubbornly, but he wasn't waiting anyhow. "Possibly I am wrong," he said. "I pray God that I am. But I think your daughter was exposed to radiation today, perhaps to a dangerous extent."

He's crazy, she told herself again…certainly half crazed with worry and fatigue. He must have been out all night; that would explain the stubble and grime, and the wild shining eyes.

"I'm sorry, Mr. Levy." She was very cool, fire in her head and ice in her voice. "I'm sure you're trying to tell me something, but I guess I'm too tired to follow it very well. What radiations do you mean? I didn't know there was a bomb near here. I'm afraid I really know so little about all this…" She looked across at him, hopefully, politely.

"You're too tired!" Scorn wiped the weariness out of his voice. "My dear woman, don't you realize…? No, of course you wouldn't. You and all the others! You—"

When he spoke again his eyes were still wild, but not his voice. "That doesn't matter; you don't have to understand—just listen. I have good reason to believe that the school was in a danger zone. The bomb, as you put it, must have passed directly overhead. Certainly there was radioactive rain in this vicinity."

"But it said over and over on the radio," she objected reasonably, "that the government would notify us if we lived in a danger zone. Are you sure?"

"Yes, I'm sure!" he snapped. "Why in God's name do you think I came here? I'm sorry, Mrs. Mitchell, but I've met this same thing everywhere tonight—people who didn't understand before and refuse to believe now." He took a step forward, too close to her. Her first quick fear gave way to a fantastic notion that he was about to shake a finger in her face.

"Now listen, will you? They couldn't have told you if they don't know yet themselves." Who? she wondered, and tried not to let her thoughts stray; she really ought to listen. "I just happened to be there, but I don't have all the facts either. I don't know how wide a range it covered…"

What? What covered what?

"And I don't know how penetrating it was. Not everybody in the dangerous area was necessarily affected. People who were indoors, for instance—I think your little one was—"

"Well, weren't *you* indoors, Mr. Levy?" The more he spoke, the less convincing he was.

"No! The bombs fell in the city between one-fifteen and one-thirty. It just happens that during the one o'clock hour I took a group of ninth-graders out to Belsen's—the aircraft plant. About fifteen minutes' walk from the school. We got back just about two, and it was starting to rain. That's when I noticed your little one—she's in the kindergarten group, isn't she?" He didn't wait for her to answer, didn't give her a chance to stop him. "They were outside playing in the yard when we came back, but they were hustled indoors as soon as the rain started. I think they were inside at the other crucial time, but you should check on that. At any rate I'm certain they weren't exposed to the rain, because I distinctly recall what an unholy fuss they made about going in. It wasn't actually raining in the yard, you see, just across the street. But there was fog around the school."

"Yes, I know all about that," Gladys stopped him.

"You do?"

Why was he so startled? "Please go on," she said clearly. "I can't imagine that you came here to tell me my little girl didn't catch cold in the rain."

"*Catch cold?*" His face was carefully devoid of expression, his manner infuriatingly patient, as if she were a particularly dull small child. "Look, I want you to sit down now and listen carefully; once all the way through, while I explain it. Go on," he repeated grimly, "you better sit down."

Gladys became conscious of her hand gripping the chair in front of her. With complete astonishment she stared at the whitened knuckles, as if they belonged to someone else, saw the fingernails biting into the rough fabric of the chair.

"If *you* will," she bargained.

"All right." Impatiently he started to sit down on the sofa in back of him and became painfully aware of the mud caked on his clothes.

"Don't worry about it." But she was pleased and surprised at his hesitation.

He took a deep breath. "I was outside at a time when I believe there were bombs overhead," he began. "Your daughter Barbara was with me. We were also, for a very short time, exposed to rain that may have been radioactive. At one of those times Barbara received radiations that may have been serious enough to make her sick. I've been—"

"Mr. Levy!" Gladys caught her breath between her teeth. "Do you know what you're saying?" He was too controlled; that was a kind of hysteria too. "Can you prove any of it?"

"God damn it, yes! Yes, I have proof—the best proof there is! I know *I* was exposed because I've tested myself. And I was about to tell you that two of the other children I saw tonight have already shown symptoms of radiation disease. *Now* do you understand?"

She was rooted to the chair, her legs and arms, like her throat, paralyzed with disaster.

Oh, Jon, come and help me!

The man's face went through a total transformation from fury to abject apology. "I *am* sorry, Mrs. Mitchell," he said. "I shouldn't have told you that way…"

"Don't." She found her voice at last. "*No*, don't touch me!" He drew back his hand; it had almost reached her shoulder. He's crazy! He is!

"No, I'm not crazy." His laugh was tired and bitter. She must have said it out loud. "You want me to go away," he said. "Well, I have to go. I've spent too much time here already. There are other people…Maybe Barbara escaped." He started toward the dining-room door. "If she hasn't shown any symptoms yet…"

"Of course she hasn't!" But now that he was going, a million doubts had to be pushed aside. "Don't you think I'd have done something about it before now? The doctor was here, you know. He said there was nothing wrong with her:"

"The doctor?" He stopped and looked back.

"Of course. On that squad truck they have." Then she remembered. "And what's more, he did a urinalysis, and *that* was all right."

"Urinalysis? You mean you got a report already?"

"Right away, while the truck was here." She felt smug. They're all right. They're both all right. Now he'll see they are.

"The truck? Why, the fools!" he exploded. "They're actually letting people believe...Look, Mrs. Mitchell, did they say they made an *analysis* in the truck? How long did it take?"

"Not long." She simply would not answer any more questions. You said you were going, she thought fiercely. Now get out of here! "They didn't say what they did. They just said the checkup was all right." Then she remembered. "They said they were taking samples to a laboratory for analysis, but they checked it, and it was all right." He had to believe her.

"They must have Geiger-checked it. Well, that helps. Look, are you *sure* Barbara hasn't been sick?"

"Of course I'm sure."

"Have you asked her?"

"I don't need to ask her. It wasn't anything but nerves."

He *had* to believe her. Hopefully she looked up at his impatient brown eyes, but there was no comfort there. Jon would have soothed her, would have taken the burden on his own broad shoulders. Jon's eyes were gray. Why did this man have brown eyes? Why didn't he *help* instead of making things worse?

"I hope you're right," he said. "At any rate, if I haven't convinced you of any danger by now, I never will." He started for the door again. Thank God, thank God, he's going. "You will do as you like, of course," he finished. "But if I were you I'd wake Barbara up and ask her—right now."

But she was all right when I looked at her. She was sleeping all right. Maybe she'd just had a touch. Maybe she was over it already. Maybe...

He was going. Maybe...

"Wait!" she cried, suddenly frantic. "Wait, please don't go." What would I do if she had it? "I'll wake her right now; it won't take long." She walked faster. "Please," she said again, and saw he was standing there, waiting.

Even with the overhead light shining in her eyes, Barbara didn't want to wake up. "Umm-hmm," she said emphatically, and pulled the crumpled heap of bedding off her legs, over her head.

Just like her father!

"Wake up, Barbie. Barbie, you've got to wake up and tell me something."

"Ummh? What?" She sat up, abruptly and startlingly awake, shedding the blankets and blinking. "What is it, Mother? *Has anything happened?*"

"No, honey. Nothing's happened. Only there's something I have to know. Listen, Barbie, last night—"

"What time is it? Did Daddy come home yet?"

"A quarter past five. Listen, Barbie, last night, when you didn't feel well, did you…" She was taken aback at the awkwardness of the question. Why, it was insulting! "Did you throw up or anything last night?"

"Well, gosh, I just felt a little sick, that's all." Barbara flopped back on the bed and pulled the sheet disgustedly over her head.

"You're sure that's all?"

From under the sheet she muffled, "Sure."

Gladys stood up dizzily, smoothed the sheet, straightened the cover. "I'm sorry I woke you, Babsy, but someone came from the school and got me all worried. You can go back to sleep."

"From school?" Sleepy but curious. "Who?"

"A Mr. Levy. He says he's your math teacher."

"Doc Levy? Is he still here?" Barbara sat bolt upright, ignoring the bright light. "Why did he want to…Is he on the emergency squad?"

"No. Should he be?" *Doc Levy!* Now she knew where she'd heard the name. Not from Barbie at all, but from Tom—incessantly, for two years, before he went away.

"He knows everything about atom bombs," Barbara told her. "He was at Oak Ridge and everything." She was struggling with the zipper on her bathrobe. "Only he got black-listed or something on account of refusing to do war work, and making a lot of speeches and being on committees, so he had to go be a teacher. It's supposed to be a secret. If he's not on a squad or anything, what did he come for, Mom?"

"He just came by himself. It was really awfully nice of him, I guess, but he nearly scared the wits out of me." Going down the stairs, she kept throwing words carelessly over her shoulder, chattering with relief. "He thought you'd been exposed to something, and he made me wake you up to find out how sick you were last night."

Barefoot, Barbie padded noiselessly behind her; Gladys couldn't know when one silent foot stopped suddenly and hovered over the stair tread, in the middle of a step. Nor could she hear the quick frightened intake of breath.

"It was awfully nice of him to come, but I did get scared…You didn't really have to get up, you know. He has to leave right away. Dr. Levy…"

She came around the turn of the stairs, through the hall, into the living room. "Here's Barbara herself. You can ask her anything you want to. I'm sure you'll see she's all right!" She was gay in her victory.

"I'm so glad." He'd been sitting on the sofa. Now he got up, tossed aside the sheaf of mimeographed sheets he'd been studying. Gladys' last doubts about him vanished at the sincerity of his smile.

"I don't need to tell you how worried I was. I've been called an alarmist before," he admitted ruefully. "Unfortunately I *wasn't* wrong that time. Anyhow, these sheets…" He pointed to the instructions and information Gladys had struggled with the night before. "I didn't see them before. Is everybody getting them? They seem quite complete—"

His sentence broke off sharply. Gladys turned to see what he was staring at, and Barbie stepped through from the hall, white-faced and shaken.

"Barbie, Barbie, baby!" Gladys didn't have to think; she knew. And there was nothing she could do. She took the girl's two hands and held them in her own, trying to re-enact a miracle, to pass life and health through her own flesh into her daughter. But…

"Oh, Babsy darling, why didn't you tell me? Why?"

The hands in hers trembled violently, and for just a moment her shoulders shook convulsively. Then, before it went too far to stop, Barbara stiffened, straightened, and lifted her head.

"I didn't want to"—she had to stop and steady her voice—"to worry you. I didn't know it mattered." She shook off Gladys' protests and braced herself to meet the teacher's eyes. "Doc, is it very bad if I did throw up?"

"I don't know, Barbara. There just isn't any way to know." There were pain and regret in his words, but no pity, no pity at all.

Barbara sat down in her father's big armchair. Her fingers stroked the worn armrest; her back was ramrod-stiff. "But if I am," she demanded, "what's the *worst* thing? Will I—do people die from it?"

There was nothing to mark the impact of those words but Gladys' involuntary gasp. Barbara's voice, like the teacher's, was painstakingly impersonal. Only the little pauses, the trouble finding words, betrayed either of them.

"You'd have a good chance, Barbara. More than good. It's not like Hiroshima. We…They know how to handle it now. And they seem to have things pretty well in hand."

"But—people *do* die from it, don't they?"

"Sometimes." He answered the question as bluntly, this time, as it had been put.

It's not natural! Gladys tried to interrupt. "Don't you think—"

"Just a minute. I think you ought to phone these people and tell them…" He picked up the sheet headed "Radiation Disease." "Here, you've read this." He let his indictment of her negligence come at her askance. "Tell them that your daughter's symptoms check with this description. And that you're calling *as instructed.*"

She held the sheet, reading, as the night before: "Malaise…nausea… vomiting…"

"But I saw this. And I didn't know…" Her eyes dropped to the next paragraph.

"Do not be mislead if the patient appears to recover perfect health after the initial attack. Many cases of stomach disorder will prove to be superficial, but *all* should be reported. The serial number at the top of this sheet is your family's identification. Use it when you make your report. *Do not delay!*

Dr. Levy moved restlessly. "You'll be able to take care of everything now, Mrs. Mitchell, and you'll be having these Emergency Headquarters people here. I'm not exactly…popular…with them."

She tried to phrase an objection to his leaving, and found herself saying instead, "Well, if you really *have* to go…"

Astonishingly Barbie had rushed up to him and was clinging to his arm. "Please, Dr. Levy," she begged, "you don't have to let her chase you away."

"Barbara!" He took his arm sternly away. "Your mother's quite correct. I do have to go."

"But you don't realize—Mom's been up all night and she—" Anguished, the girl paused, then turned around to face Gladys. "I'm sorry, Mother, but it's true!" She turned back to the teacher. "She just doesn't want to believe that there is anything wrong with me. *Please* don't go!"

"Naturally your mother's upset," he answered. "She wants to be alone with you for a while, and it will probably be good for both of you. If you're not scared she won't be."

Gladys felt fury burning within her and didn't know whom to be angry at. She turned swiftly to the telephone.

CHAPTER EIGHT

THE OPERATOR didn't seem to *want* to understand her. Gladys talked urgently into the phone, pouring out her troubles to a half-dozen unidentified switchboards, until someone finally connected her with the clerk at the Emergency Headquarters laboratory.

All the time she was aware of muted conversation, of footsteps coming and going, in the room behind her. She spoke into the mouthpiece, reading off the serial number from the top of the sheet, repeating the exact symptoms as Barbara had told them to her.

"She began to feel ill about five-thirty, became acutely nauseous, thought she was going to vomit, but didn't. Later on, she says, she was sick—about nine o'clock." Why, that was…No wonder she didn't tell me, Gladys thought, she must have thought the eggnog did it!

"Yes, they checked it on the truck. They *said* it was all right." And I heard her in the bathroom, and I never knew! "Slept well…feels all right this morning…Barbara Mitchell…B-a-r-b-a-r-a Mitchell, M-i-t-c-h-e-l-l, 2036…that's right…Have you any idea how long it will take? I see…*Please,* if you can…Thank you.

"They're going to do the analysis," she said to the room at large. "They said it might take several hours. They didn't seem to think it was too serious, Dr. Levy. They said—"

He wasn't there. Barbara alone sat in the center of the big chair, slender, fragile, and erect. She didn't look like a girl condemned to…

Stop it! Gladys screamed at herself.

"Where…?" she asked out loud.

"He's gone." Barbara licked her lips to ease the numbness out of them. "Did they say anything else?"

"No. They just said they'd notify our squadman and call us back if they could. Maybe…" She couldn't stand by any longer, without offering the child some hope. "Maybe it's a false alarm, honey. Maybe you're all right. It could have been the eggnog, you know. It really could. They said it was kind of late for you to get sick. That teacher can't be sure, you know. You *feel* all right, don't you?"

Under the flood of sympathy Barbie's dam of tears broke. Gladys soothed and patted, feeling sanity return with the grip of the tense young fingers. She had to keep going; Barbie still needed her.

"There, baby," she whispered, "you go ahead and cry. You'll feel better afterwards. Don't you believe for a minute that man knows everything. He's been wandering around like a maniac all night, and if he was really so sure he'd be in the hospital himself, wouldn't he? There, baby…"

Her voice went on in its soothing, monotonous reassurance, even after Barbie had pulled away.

"Hospital?" She sniffled and groped in her pocket for a handkerchief. "Why should *he* be in the hospital?"

"Didn't he tell you? That's why he was going around to all the houses. He says he got it while he was taking a walk with some of you in the afternoon."

Barbie's eyes, dry now and wide, were fascinated. "But how does he *know?*"

"He doesn't!" Gladys insisted. "He just thinks so, and he's beep going around scaring everyone half to death."

The word seemed to linger on her lips, tasting bad, feeling wrong. *Death.* It bounced around the room, hurled itself back at her.

"But I mean, is *he* sure? Does he really think he has it?"

"He *thinks* so."

"Oh, Mom, you shouldn't have let him go out! We should have asked him to stay here—"

"He wouldn't have stayed, baby. There were other people he wanted to see."

"No, there weren't." Barbara shook her head. "He said it was too late to go anyplace else—it was too light out. He said he was going to try and get back to his room. But—"

"Look, Barbie," Gladys interrupted briskly, "if he was going home, then that's the best thing he could have done. I don't know why he didn't go to the hospital anyway if he thought he was sick. He didn't have to go around all night telling people—he could have told the squad."

"But he couldn't! He's on a list of—well, he didn't tell me much, but I know he couldn't go to Emergency Headquarters because they would have arrested him. Didn't he tell you?"

Gladys shook her head. There *was* something wrong with the man! It was better to have him out of the house.

"He tried to call Emergency Headquarters first," Barbie said, "but as soon as they heard his name they started stalling around, and...I told you about that blacklist he was on for making speeches and everything...and they wouldn't listen when he tried to tell them about us kids. They just said to wait where he was, and they sent some men out to arrest him. Well, anyway," she consoled herself, "I told him to come back if he needed someplace to stay. I'm glad I did that much."

"Why should you do anything?"

"Well, he might have saved my life, that's all!"

"Oh, darling..."

Barbara broke away from her mother's hand and stalked dramatically to the window. She pulled back the drape and stood there, staring out into the empty street. Her blue-robed back faced the room with a passive defiance that Gladys could not penetrate.

The phone was ringing. It would wake Ginny up.

She picked up the receiver and cut off a ring in the middle. She could hold it like that, keep her hand firm over the earphone, never hear what they wanted to tell her.

She raised the receiver to her ear. "Hello." The flat word was no greeting, but an acknowledgment of the expected disaster.

"Gladys!" Somebody was shrieking at her, somebody alive, personal, not the controlled inhumanity of an official dealing out death. A woman.

"Hello, Edie." Recognition was curious; it was like waking up. "How are you? I mean, Edie, have you heard anything?"

"*Heard* anything?" The harsh laughter hurt her ears. "How could I hear anything? They won't let us find out. They won't tell us anything. They've got hillbilly songs on the radio now!"

"What do you mean, Edie?" Nothing about Jon; nothing about the city. The excitement drained out of her, left her too tired to talk. "What did you call for?"

"Because I'm a damn fool!" Edie snapped. "Because I thought you could—" She broke off, stifling something that sounded like a sob. "I don't know why," she finished dully. "There's nothing you can do. I'm sorry. I shouldn't have..." Gladys had to strain to hear; the words seemed to crumble away before they reached her.

"Well, maybe I *can* do something. What's wrong? You've got to tell me what's wrong first." She felt a perverse gratitude to Edie, for being so weak, weaker than she was.

"There's nothing you can do."

"Well, what's the matter?"

"No. They wouldn't do anything, and there's nothing you can do. I'm sick, that's all, and they wouldn't believe me. I told them I was sick, and they didn't care. They just went away."

"But, Edie, if they *said* you're all right…?"

"What do they care? How do they know how sick I was? I read all about it in those papers they left, and I was right, I tell you I was right! I was sick, Gladys. I never get sick, and I was so sick. They could have— Glad, they gave me a sedative. My God, I was sick all over the house and they gave me a pill to quiet my nerves."

"Did you take it?" The doctor said Edie was all right. The doctor said Barbie was all right. The doctor knew.

"No, I didn't take it. Go to sleep and die in your sleep, and make it easy for them! They just don't want to bother. My God, Gladys, my hair! I'll lose my hair. Do you realize it says—"

"Look, Edie, you take that pill they gave you." Gladys tried to sound sympathetic, but it came out cold and stern instead. "You'll be all right."

A muttering sound in the living room behind her made her sharply aware of Barbie's presence. Barbara could hear everything she said. Edie was talking again, but Gladys didn't listen to it. "You take that pill!" she said again, fiercely. She heard the receiver on the other end banged down, a furious impotent gesture of defiance. Edie would be all right. She had to be. The doctor said so.

"What do you want, Barbie?" She turned back to the living room, but it wasn't Barbie who was talking. The muttering sound came from the radio, the first news report of the morning.

"Reprisals are being made. There is little or no further danger of attack. Our radar screen is now constantly in operation and all large centers are under the protection of military government. Many saboteurs have been apprehended, and any still at liberty will no longer be able to operate under new military restrictions. The type of missile used by the enemy is worthless without the co-operation of an agent at the point of attack. If all citizens co-operate with the emergency government, there is no further danger of enemy attack. Stay tuned to this station for further news in twenty minutes. Meanwhile, some recorded music…"

Impatiently Barbie turned the radio down. "They didn't say anything at all," she complained angrily. "Nothing but a lot of stuff about rioting and panics. It's quiet enough here, heaven knows!" She went back to the window.

"Barbie." Gladys' voice tugged at her back. "Barbie, did they say anything about the city—anything at all about what's happening there?"

"No. Nothing new."

"What about the panics? What kind of rioting?" She didn't really want to know, but, whatever happened, she couldn't let the silence grow between them again.

"It's nothing important," Barbie said impatiently. "Fires and stuff, just the same thing they said last night. Oh," she remembered something, "if we see any strangers wandering around we're supposed to report them to Emergency Headquarters right away, and not let them into the house, whatever happens, because some of them are looting and robbing and stuff like that."

She stopped suddenly. "Dr. Levy!" she said, aghast. "They said the squadmen had been instructed to shoot if necessary. Oh, Mom, we shouldn't have let him go!"

Gladys held back her anger. "He'll probably come back," she offered, "if it turns out to be too hard to get where he wanted to go."

"He didn't *have* anyplace to go," Barbie insisted.

She was not going to argue about the man. Maybe after she had some coffee she could do something about Barbie. She went back to the kitchen and waited once again for the water to boil. But now the sun was beginning to stream through the window. The white enamel was shining and familiar, and the porch was empty. All outdoors was empty of any sound. There was nobody outside this morning—no one emptying a garbage can or trying to start a recalcitrant car, no dogs whining at back doors for admittance, no babies being put out for the first morning sun.

The robin let out a soft preparatory whistle, and Gladys got up wearily and poured the steaming water into the coffeepot. She let it drip and went back to the window to stare out into the silence.

It was so quiet. Not even birds…*No birds!*

She looked out now, eagerly scouring the trees and telegraph poles with her eyes. Then she saw them on the ground, right in back of the house—three sparrows on their backs with toothpick legs turned pleading to the sky; another across the lawn; a few more farther away. Those that hadn't died had gone. Where?

"Daddy, where's Daddy?" The swinging doors slammed against the wall under the impact of flying small fists and feet. Ginny stood breathless in the middle of the room, her pajama pants hiked above her waist to free her legs, the top dangling from her other hand to the floor. "Where's Daddy? I heard him talking. Where is he?"

"That wasn't Daddy, darling. Daddy didn't come home yet. That was a man who came to tell us Daddy was all right," she improvised. "He said Daddy will come home as soon as he can."

Ginny shook her head, "No," she said firmly. "That was my daddy. He came home. I heard him last night, and he never came up to say goo' night. I want my breakfast." She backed to a chair and sat down next to the kitchen table.

Gladys poured a cup of coffee. "I know what," she said. "We'll have a special Sunday breakfast."

"With French toast?"

"Yes. And all the trimmings."

Ginny was thinking. "We can't have a Sunday breakfast because it's Tuesday, because I went to school yesterday, and I didn't go to school the day before."

"Well, we'll pretend it's Sunday. Barbie!" she called into the front room.

"But if we pretend it's Sunday, then I don't have to go to school."

Gladys hid her relief behind her coffee cup—one less item to explain. "Right. Barbie!" she called again. "Don't you want your breakfast?"

No reply. Gladys shoved her cup regretfully away. She started for the door and found her younger daughter trailing, puppylike, behind her.

"Sit down, Ginny. I'll be right back."

"I want my breakfast."

"I said I'll be right back."

"I want my breakfast *now.*"

There was nothing to do about it. Gladys scooped a can of frozen orange juice out of the freezer, opened it, and mixed it with absent ease, then set the glass in front of her pouting daughter and said sternly, "You sit right there until I come back. And finish that juice."

Barbie was prepared for her. "I'm not hungry," she said as soon as Gladys walked in.

"I don't care whether you're hungry or not. We're going to have breakfast, and a decent breakfast, too," Gladys told her. "If you don't want to eat you don't have to, but you do have to sit there and behave yourself."

With the whole world shaking around her, Gladys was still firm in one faith—the effects of the smell of French toast on her children's appetites and tempers. All she had to do was get Barbie *in* there.

"Listen, Barbie," she said quietly, "Ginny heard voices down here before, and she thought it was Daddy. I told her it was a man who came to tell us Daddy was all right. You've got to help me, Barbie," she pleaded desperately. "I know how you must be feeling, but there's nothing we can do till we find out, one way or the other. There's no reason to get Ginny upset until we're sure. If I have to have trouble with her right now I just don't know what I'll do."

There was no answer still, but when she turned back to the kitchen Barbie followed her. And when she looked she found the girl's face fixed in a determined pattern of good humor. She set herself to getting breakfast with a concentration of energy that drove all thought of the children from her mind for a few minutes.

But when she sat down she discovered that Barbara was confining her facsimile of conversation to the little girl. On the infrequent occasions when Gladys forced attention to herself she could evoke nothing but a furious glare. The silence outside was a constant oppressive lack in the background. Sooner or later Ginny was going to look out the window and see the birds. She couldn't put off explaining things to the little girl much longer. She'd have to find some way.

Against the general silence the one small noise was an uproar. The children began to jump up, then hesitated, remembering what had happened the night before. But this time Gladys was no less curious than they. All three of them rushed to the front room and stared out of the windows, watching the truck grind to a halt in front of the house.

"It's Daddy coming home!"

Gladys knew why the truck was there; so did Barbie. Across the little girl's head they stared at each other, while Gladys hunted dumbly for the words she felt she ought to find.

"But they said it would take hours…"

Barbie's protest was so much an echo of her own futile will to resist—with a choked cry, half of pity, half of relief, she threw out her arms to her daughter. And with a headlong rush of escape Barbara's contorted face came to rest on her mother's shoulder.

"It isn't my daddy—it's a lady in pants and she's got a washing machine. Mommy, she's got two of them and they can walk."

It was impossible to sustain the drama of the moment in the face of Ginny's announcement. Barbie had to look too.

"There are not washing machines, silly!" she told Ginny. "They're diving suits. But, Mother, why?…Oh!" The explanation dawned on her.

Chapter Nine

"Mother, it's Veda! Ginny! Ginny, hurry, it's Veda! They've brought her home."

She struggled with bolts and latches and flung the door open just as Gladys came up from behind.

Coming up the front steps, flanked by the massive suits of the squadron, was Veda indeed—but a strange, unfamiliar Veda. Her face was pale, her eyes swollen, and she was covered from head to foot in a rough, flapping suit of men's overalls. Her tightly braided hair had come undone on one side and dangled in stiff iron-gray waves on her shoulder. The overall shirt, several sizes too large for her, was tucked bulkily inside the sagging denim bib. On her feet she wore nothing but a pair of cheap straw scuffs.

Gladys pulled Barbie back from the door as the strange trio approached. But she forgot about Ginny, who launched herself at Veda with a violent sidewise attack that seriously upset the dignity of the squadman on the left and made him lose his hold on Veda's arm. Gladys thought he was going to be knocked off his feet, and wondered hysterically if they could get up by themselves when they fell in those suits. But nothing catastrophic happened. Veda disentangled herself from the child and the men both, the door shut, and they were all standing in an ill-assorted circle in the small front hall. There was a jumble of talk from the two children, mixed with indignant voicings from Veda and an attempt at explanation from one of the men. Gladys couldn't understand anything. She shook her head impatiently and motioned toward the living room.

They trooped in together, but when Veda tried to cross to the other side of the room one of the men took her firmly by the arm again.

Gladys turned on him indignantly. "Would you mind explaining—" she began, and then interrupted herself. "Will you *please* be quiet"—she turned on the children sharply—"so I can hear what's going on?"

In the lull the man spoke up. "You Mrs. Mitchell?" Gladys nodded. "Sorry to bust in on you like this," he said, "but this woman here says she works for you and we have to get some information about her. Now if you'll just answer a few questions we won't take much time."

"I'll be happy to answer your questions"—Gladys was still indignant—"as soon as your friend takes his hands off my maid."

"She does work for you, then? I'm sorry, lady, but we can't let her go. She might be dangerous."

Dangerous? Veda? "I've never *heard* anything so ridiculous!" Gladys told him heatedly. "If you expect to find out anything at all from me you'll let her sit down decently right now." For the first time since the whole mess started she had found someone on whom she could righteously vent some of her wrath.

"Listen, lady"—the man who had been holding Veda's arm spoke for the first time—"this woman talked us into coming over here to corroborate her story. If you don't feel like co-operatin'—"

Gladys ignored him. "Now, Veda." She took the offensive. "You sit down, and if they bother you any more I'll report them immediately."

"Mrs. Mitchell." It was the first man again, and he seemed to be trying not to laugh. "You probably don't realize that what you're doing is obstructing the path of justice. This woman is a suspected saboteur."

"Suspected *what?*"

"That's what I said. You got a radio; you know how the bombs came over. Well, every one of them bombs had a radar beacon set to bring it in to its target, and every one of them beacons was set by an enemy agent. We have to find the people who did it, and find 'em fast. Now do you want to help, or don't you?"

"All right," Gladys sighed. But she still protested weakly. "Only I don't see why he has to hang onto her arm like that."

"First of all, what's her name?" The man overrode her objection smoothly. He took a notebook out of the zippered pocket in his suit and dug for a pencil.

"Veda Klopak."

"Age?"

Gladys saw a look of alarm chase across Veda's face and heard Barbie, behind her, snickering. Veda had been an official thirty-nine ever since she came to work for them. Some rapid mental figuring produced a doubtful answer. "I don't know for sure, but I think about fifty-six or -seven." Veda stopped shaking her head and looked relieved.

The squadman hadn't missed Veda's vigorous negatives or Barbara's snicker, either. He was smiling when he said, "That checks close enough. Address?"

"I'd have to look it up," Gladys said. "I know it's in the East Bronx, but I don't remember the number since the last time she moved."

"Know how long she's been there?"

"Oh yes." Gladys thought back quickly. "It was just after Christmas she moved in…" The year Tom broke his arm…that was the year before we got the washing machine…"Four years ago," she finished triumphantly.

"You don't know the present address?"

"I have it written down someplace. I don't know exactly where." Gladys was increasingly flustered. This wasn't a joke or a silly misunderstanding. They were *serious!*

Barbie was tugging at her sleeve, but she waved the girl aside and looked frantically for the telephone pad.

"Mother—"

"Just a minute, darling…"

"But, Mother, here—"

"Barbie, I *said* wait a minute. I'm busy. Where in the world did I…?" The pad was nowhere near the telephone.

"But, Mother…Mom…are you looking for the pad?"

Gladys whirled around. "For heaven's sake! I've been looking all over for that. Where—"

"Well, I've been trying to give it to you."

Gladys riffled through the pages, trying to hide her confusion. Everything that happened this morning seemed to make her feel more foolish. And now she couldn't find the street number in the book.

"I have the phone number here," she said finally, avoiding the amused eyes of the man with the notebook. "I don't know *where* I've put the address, but I know I have it someplace. I can look in my bag upstairs; sometimes I just keep things in there on scraps of paper, I—"

"No need to do that. The phone number's enough. We can check it against the address we have."

"Well, I'd be glad to run up and find it for you," she assured him. It would be a pleasure to get out of that room for a moment, to have a chance to make sure her hair was combed, and to get hold of herself again. She took a step back.

"It don't look so good, lady." The other man, the one who had been holding onto Veda all along, spoke up again. "You bein' so anxious to get out of this here room. Mebbe you just better stick around here. My buddy told you the phone number was good enough."

Gladys found the number in the pad again and discovered that her fingers were trembling. The man's hard eyes and set face, his expressionless voice, and even his choice of words were all straight out of a grade-B gangster picture. But he was real. It was all real.

"Why don't you ladies just sit down and make yourselves comfortable?" the man with the notebook asked. "No need to get all bothered. All we want to do is ask a few questions."

"Sure, go ahead," his companion offered dryly, clearly excepting Veda, by his tone of voice as well as by his continued tight grasp on her am. "Make yourselves comfortable. I can see this is going to take some time."

It did. Endlessly Gladys repeated vital statistics about Veda, her household, herself, and events over the fifteen years during which Veda had worked for her.

But they were never satisfied. Over and over they went back and forth, covering the same ground from different directions, shooting an occasional question at Barbara, and even one or two, that she could answer, at Ginny, trusting more to the children's lack of dissimulation than to Gladys' greater knowledge.

She told them about old Mr. Klopak, whom she still firmly believed had been the last real carpenter alive, about how Veda had come to work for her, part time, when Tommy was two, and Barbie just born, and old Mr. Klopak, repairing Tommy's old baby furniture for them, mentioned that his daughter was out of a job. Then Barbie got to play-pen age just as the recession struck, and Veda worked elsewhere for a couple of years. When Jon began making money in the early war years Veda had come back to them, and in one way or another had been with them ever since.

After her father died she had thought about coming to live with them, but never could make up her mind to do it. She had her own ways, and she was set in them; she knew they didn't fit into Gladys' household. Finally she had found a boardinghouse in the Bronx where she could sleep and fix herself an early breakfast, and keep her own things the way she liked them to be.

"I'll tell you, ma'am," he said finally, "we found this woman under suspicious circumstances. The whole neighborhood where she lived got a big dose of hot rain—"

Barbie sat up on the edge of her chair and opened her mouth to question him, but he went right on without giving her a chance.

"Everybody else around there—you understand, everybody for at least five blocks either way—is either dead right now or pretty sick. This one never got a drop on her. She had herself all wrapped up and shut in that room, like she had a pretty good idea what was going to happen. That don't look so good—especially when you know that there had to be somebody around there to set that gimmick in place in the river."

"I don't know anything about the gimmick you're talking about," Gladys protested for what seemed the hundredth time. "But I've already told you that's what Veda always does when she's sick. I've argued with her about it for years, but she's been doing it ever since I've known her. Besides which"—wearily she tried to hit a lighter note—"she couldn't possibly be an enemy agent. She just works too hard. She wouldn't have the time."

She won a feeble smile from the friendlier of the two men, but nothing could prevail over the stony mask of the other. The questioning was resumed, and now they wanted to know in detail everything Gladys could tell them about Veda's personal and medical idiosyncrasies.

But in the end they were satisfied; they had to be. And even then it seemed to Gladys that they were reluctant to give up a suspect.

"We'll leave the woman in your custody, Missus," Flinty Eyes said finally. He loosened his grasp on Veda's tortured arm. She stood there, rubbing the spot he'd been holding, angrily silent.

"But that means she stays here. You don't let her out of this house for any reason whatsoever, without clearance from the Security Office," he added. "I can't say I'm sure about her yet, but we can't waste time on cases like this one. Right now we got to prove, and double-prove, every accusation we make. Things get a little worse, they're going to realize security is more important than jury trials."

"Things get *worse?*" Gladys gasped. "But it said on the radio—you—the squadman in the truck told me—things *can't* get worse."

"The radio isn't telling everything," the other man put in. "But you'll be okay as long as you're telling the truth. Things'll be a lot better when they give our office some leeway—better than if it gets to the vigilante point, anyways."

"You just keep a close watch on her," his partner said. "We might be coming back to check. Can't say for sure."

Once more Gladys felt herself burning with a passion of indignation, but this time she contained it. There was no purpose in flaring up now, when they were ready to go.

At the door the friendlier of the two paused. "You can call us through the Emergency Headquarters if you need us, Mrs. Mitchell. Just ask for Security." His smile did not include Veda.

For a long time, it seemed, they stood there, after the final closing of the door, mother and daughters staring at the rumpled, ruffled woman whom they had known so long and so well, and were now really seeing for the first time.

At last Veda broke the silence.

"Coffee's boilin'," she said, sniffing.

CHAPTER TEN

GLADYS' HAND leaped to her mouth. "I had it on to stay hot," she breathed. "I'll—"

She had to stop talking. She had to blink back tears and it was hard to keep her mouth straight. Her voice promised to quaver babyishly if she said another word.

She couldn't let the children see this; she couldn't act this way in front of Veda. She couldn't understand it either. Veda was back, and she wasn't alone any more, and here she was ready to cry because her coffee was spoiled.

She made a muffled noise that she hoped they would interpret as an apology or explanation, and dashed for the kitchen. She stood there, over the stove, staring down into the muddy remains of the steaming fresh pot of an hour ago—the pot she had started to make when Dr. Levy came creaking and rattling the boards of the back porch, and finished making when he left.

She filled the kettle once more and took the coffeepot over to the sink, letting hot water flow into it. She picked up the plastic robin that went on the kettle spout. Cheer up! she thought hysterically. Cheer up! Cheer up!

Veda came through the swinging door and brushed past her, the ridiculous overalls flapping as she walked. Almost at the door of the little back room, she turned back to the sink and deliberately turned off the hot-water faucet.

"I was rinsing that pot!" Gladys said too sharply, and immediately regretted it. There was no sense taking out her feelings on Veda.

"Thought you might be wanting to save yer hot water." Veda's stony assurance was so normal it was incredible. "There's no tellin' how long you'll have it," she finished patiently, as if explaining matters to a small child.

"No telling…? Yes, of course." Gladys looked curiously at the other woman. "Veda, how are things…outside?"

"Purty bad," she said laconically. "If you don't mind, Missus Mitchell, I'd like to kinder change my things, an' we kin talk afterwards."

"Oh—is there anything you need? I don't know if my things would fit…"

"Thank you jest the same, Missus Mitchell, but I got everything I need. Lucky thing I allus kept some things here."

"Well, go ahead." Gladys smiled. She surveyed the cold food and scattered dishes on the table. "I'll start some more breakfast. You must be hungry too."

"I could use a bite to eat." She disappeared into the back room.

It was a shock, on this strange morning, to see Veda emerge, ten minutes later, looking exactly as always: cotton house dress, white apron, shiny black shoes, gray cotton stockings, smooth hair severely pinned back in a braided bun—no different from a thousand other mornings.

Gladys became acutely conscious, once more, of her own disheveled appearance, remembering the unbelievable moment when the man had interpreted her desire to escape upstairs as part of a deep-dyed plot. And now Veda wouldn't let her escape. She started off with a vague murmur about washing up, and Veda reminded her tartly that there was a sink right in front of her.

"Who you fixin' up fer?" she demanded pointedly. "You sit right down an' have some of that fresh coffee. Plenty of time fer primpin' all the rest of your life. You look about beat right now, an' you need a little coffee in you more'n you need a comb."

Gladys lacked the will to disagree. She rinsed her face in clear cold water and sat down once again at the white-enameled table, letting Veda take over at the stove.

"I don't know how you do it," she said plaintively, watching the older woman move briskly around the room. "You must have had a worse night than I did."

"I dunno." She cleared off dirty plates swiftly and replaced them with clean settings. "Look like you been up all night, an' you must of had a hard day yestidday, with me not in." She set bacon to sizzling on the stove, cracked an egg in the white bowl. "You want more French toast, I guess? I'll mix up a little cinnamon sugar. The little one goes crazy for it. All I did was sleep all day," she went on, "right up until them men come an' dragged me out of bed, an' that wasn't till the middle of the night. Had myself three days' sleep before that happened."

"Dragged you out of bed?"

Barbie was standing at the door, holding it open, and Gladys saw Ginny's head peeking out around her. Both children were clearly enthralled by the picture of the two heavily suited men invading that prim boardinghouse bedroom and *dragging* her out. Gladys thought she saw the older woman's face crimson, too, but Veda was turned away.

"Some people are never happy without they're asking questions," Veda told the wall. "Good way to get into trouble, too," she informed the frying pan. Finally, turning to Barbie, she finished, "I'll tell you everything you want to know. Wasn't for your mother, and you too, the Lord knows where I'd be now. But I ain't goin' to tell it more'n once, so you better wait till I got my breakfast on the table, an' then I'll tell you once and fer all." She slid the spatula under a piece of egg-puffed bread and flopped it over to expose a thick golden crust. "Once I finish up, I ain't answerin' *no more questions*. That clear?"

"Um-humh." Barbie knew when to mollify Veda. "Okay. Only you have to really tell us the whole story."

"She'll tell you," Gladys said firmly, "just exactly as much as she wants to, not one word more. Is *that* clear?" She was watching Ginny, who was standing there soaking it all in, wondering how much the little girl had already understood, how much she would understand of Veda's story, how much Veda would say in front of her.

While she wondered Ginny found her tongue. "Did my daddy save you from the accident in the city?" she demanded.

"Your daddy?" Veda turned around, surprised, then shocked. "You mean your daddy never come—" She caught herself, then finished the sentence. "He never come after me at all, he didn't. Can you imagine him savin' other people and never thinking about poor old Veda?"

"Mr. Mitchell ain't home yet, then?" Veda chose her words carefully, and Gladys was grateful, but she couldn't play up. Not now, not any more. Later maybe. All she could do was sit there and think about the dead birds in the grass, about the squadmen's heavy suits and Veda's airtight room. And Jon, Jon who was in the city...still in the city.

"No," she said, "no, no, he didn't come home yet. No, he—"

"Missus Mitchell." She felt Veda's hand firm on her elbow; the coffee cup in her other hand was shaking. "Missus Mitchell, you must be jest about wore out. Think you kids'd have more sense an' consideration fer your mother..." She directed a scathing, unwarranted attack on the children, transforming their uncomfortable wonder promptly to outraged defense. "Poor woman's been up all this time, all wore out, and never one of you had sense enough to know she'd need some rest. Come on now." She took Gladys' arm and steered her toward the door.

"But I don't want to—"

"You stop that now, Missus Mitchell. You sound jest like Ginny. You got to get some sleep."

"I can't..." Somehow they were in the living room. She *couldn't* go to bed. Something she had to find out. About Barbie. She pulled her arm loose from Veda's guiding grasp and headed for the couch. "I'll just rest awhile in here," she said as firmly as she could. "I'll be fine right here."

Veda tried to make her get up, but she wouldn't. After a while the other woman relented and even brought her her half-finished coffee. She had to stay up; she *had* to.

Regretfully she put the empty coffee cup down. She wanted more, but the kitchen was an endless number of steps away. She shrugged down in the corner of the sofa, inside the red wool robe, away from the invading chill in the air, away from loneliness and fear, inside the warm wool present from Jon.

She wanted more coffee, and she wanted a blanket, but it was too much effort to get up for either. She had started shivering, and now it was increasing. She called out, but something was wrong with her voice. She tried again and this time it worked, but a burst of laughter from the kitchen drowned out her efforts. She felt infinitely sorry for herself.

"Oh, Jon, I need you," she whispered out loud. "Jon darling, please come home. Come home quick. I can't stand any more." Tears welled up in her eyes, and she dabbed them furiously away. They were all laughing in there. Everybody else was all right; they had slept and rested, and she alone had lived through every minute of this horrible night. Barbie was all right too. She couldn't imagine, now, what had possessed her to let that crazy teacher in. She hoped someone caught him before he got into any real trouble. With her own daughter safe, she felt sorry for him. She hoped he wasn't really sick and would be all right.

She got up to get the blanket from the chest in the corner, and the tears still standing in her eyes made it hard for her to see; she stopped where she was and wiped them away, glancing guiltily toward the door, relieved to find nobody had witnessed her foolish scene.

She heard the radio droning on, turned down low. It was right in front of her. Once more she brushed away the tears, until she could see the dial, and made it a little louder, to catch the evasive words that had been tickling her ears since she sat down on the sofa.

They were reading off a list of names. She sank down in Jon's big chair near the radio and tucked the blanket around her shoulders, and under her feet. Warmth flowed over her. The names stopped on the radio, and the announcer repeated what she had not quite heard before.

"We will continue to deliver personal messages of importance on this station, and to give out lists of survivors and casualties. Keep tuned to this station, and keep listening. There will be no more telephone messages to relatives of survivors and casualties. If you live in middle Westchester and are waiting for news of someone in your home, you will receive it on this station. Keep listening.

"Mrs. Hanson Delaney, of 104 Bracklane Street, to her son, John Delaney. Mrs. Delaney is safe at her sister's home on West Hope Street.

"Bob Bellowes, to his wife, Nita Bellowes. Mr. Bellowes is an emergency squadman and is safe and at work but unable to come home.

"Message to Mrs. Lydia Johnson. Your two daughters, Jenny and Ruth, are in the Emergency Hospital in this area, being treated for radiation disease symptoms.

"To Mrs. R. L. Petronelli. Your son, Peter, is in the hospital in this area, being treated for radiation disease.

"To Mrs. Harlan Frame, of Purchase Street. Your sister, Amy, and her daughter, Gladys, are in the hospital, being treated for radiation disease and shock.

"To Mrs. Emory Bar…We interrupt these messages for the latest list of survivors from this area, rescued in the city. All of the following persons have been checked into an emergency station and will be evacuated as soon as their condition is diagnosed.

"Please listen carefully. Someone you know may be among the persons found. John Damien, 1413 Broad Street; Alexander Emory, 105 Haimes Street; Cynthia Evy, 1214 St. Clare Avenue; Michael Foucek, 479 North…"

Gladys listened curiously as the names, foreign and familiar, harsh and melodious, individual and indistinguishable, rolled out of the radio in a steady procession. From time to time a thrill of compassion or of sympathetic joy would move her, when the name of a friend or neighbor penetrated the gray haze in which she was wrapped, inside the warm blanket in the soft chair.

The butcher's son (in the city buying meat?) was reported safe at a checking-out station. Old Mrs. Cross, down the street, was dead of a heart attack, found in the street by a rescue truck. Tim Claragh, who was Peggy Turner's cousin, was doing rescue work in the city. "Watch out for looters and rioters. Refugees have gotten through part of the barricade around the city. Admit no strangers. There will be music for fifteen minutes…"

They never said Jon's name. They never said anything.

Jon! Jon! It was like a knife, cutting the soft protective haze, cutting away the fog and fuzziness too. She struggled out of the suffocating blanket, reached over, and twirled the dial frantically. All she could get was static. She managed to climb out of the chair and crouched, shivering, in front of the radio.

"Mother!" The surprise in Barbie's voice was fresh and almost amused; then immediately it was terrified. "Mom! What is it? What's the matter, Mom?"

"Nothing." Gladys was irritated. She must look ridiculous.

She stood up, trying to do it easily and gracefully, almost lost her balance, and had to grab the arm of Jon's big chair for support. She saw Barbie's face, drawn into a tense peak of fear.

"Mom, what is it? What did they say, what did it say on the radio now?"

"Nothing. I'm all ri—" Then the sense of the girl's question penetrated. "Nothing, it's nothing at all. They were reading things off, and I lost the station. I was trying—"

"Lost the station?" Barbie was incredulous. "But you couldn't! They—"

"Well, I'm sorry." Even to herself, Gladys sounded peevish, but she couldn't think how to do anything about it. "I'm sorry, but I couldn't help it. They started playing music, and I tried to get another station, and then I couldn't find anything at all." It was all so perfectly simple.

"But you couldn't lose it," Barbie repeated too patiently, "because it's the only one we can get. All you can get on the others is static."

Well, I know that, all right, Gladys thought. She looked across the vast space to the sofa, thinking how many footsteps it would, take to get there, and that she would have to let go of the chair arm to do it.

"What made you think…?"

"I don't know," she answered shortly. Why didn't Barbie leave her alone? "I guess I'm just too tired to think." She couldn't remember now why she had wanted to keep hearing names. Somebody wasn't going to call up. She sat down again in the chair. "It's chilly in here, isn't it?" she asked, marveling at how her voice had cleared up. It was normal and distinct now.

"Mom…Mom, are you all right? Mom, you're not—" Barbie was terrified about something. Her voice sounded pulled out, tight, like a rubber band about to snap. "You're not…sick?"

"Don't be silly!" Gladys didn't want to be annoyed. She laughed, but it didn't sound right.

"But, Mom, it's not cold in here at all It's warm, and…you seem so funny. Mom, you're not sick, are you?"

Someone was tugging determinedly at her arm—Veda.

"C'mon, you're goin' upstairs, and wash your face and go to bed."

Resisting, her fingers tightened on Jon's chair, and she remembered, her fingers remembered for her, what her dazed mind refused to hold.

Personal information no longer by telephone. They would not call. They'd never call. It would be on the radio. They would tell her about Jon on the radio.

"Somebody will have to listen all the time…"

Veda tugged again, and Gladys stopped trying to explain or protest. She'd told them now; she'd remembered. Obediently, childishly, she let herself be led up the stairs.

"Come on now," Veda urged her. "You wash your face, and we'll get you into bed."

She floated through the bathroom door and kept on floating. She was in bed, but she remembered she was in the bathroom. No, in bed. Floating.

He was walking toward her and he kept coming, very slowly coming on, but he never got any closer; she couldn't see him clearly, although the light was very bright, red and bright, but she saw a shape, not his shape, and still she knew who it was; he was coming on all the time, walking toward her, and if she waited long enough, if she could keep her eyes on him, on the shape that had to be him, everything would be all right.

She was floating, but he was coming, Jon was coming. It was hard for him, and she didn't understand why, until the clouds cleared away. The red light was on everything, and she saw the treadmill in between shredded wisps of pink marshmallow-fluff clouds. He was walking on the treadmill and trying as hard as he could not to let it pull him backward.

CHAPTER ELEVEN

THE CRIES GOT CLOSER, ringing in her ear, and the treadmill let out a wailing screech as it disappeared from sight. Gladys sat up in bed, still holding the twisted damp sheet in her hand.

"There now, Missus Mitchell, you're awake all right now." Veda tugged the sheet gently away from her perspiring hands and smoothed it out. She started to lie back again, but Veda plumped out the pillows and put one in back of the other for a support, then fitted the breakfast tray neatly over her knees.

"Now *there,*" she said again, and lifted the coffeepot to pour it where the beckoning aroma would rise right under her nose. "You drink that an' you'll feel fine."

Gladys picked up the coffee cup and had to put it down on the tray again to steady it. She tried both hands next time. The cup was hot, but it felt good.

"You could of used a little more sleep, but that telephone never stopped ringin', and I heard you thrashin' around up here. Can't hardly seem that kind of sleep would do you much good."

The telephone kept ringing. Then part of the dream wasn't a dream. Jon...that part wasn't a dream either. Barbie!

"Who called?" She remembered too much now, she could tell just where the dream began and ended.

"Yer friend, Missus Crowell. She's been callin' all day. Seems mighty worried—"

"Who else?" She had no mind for Edie Crowell's worries now.

"Wasn't nobody else."

"Not even the laboratory? Didn't they call up? About Barbie?"

"Nope. Ain't nobody called about Barbie."

"What time is it?"

"Must be close on four o'clock. It was more'n half past three when I was in the kitchen."

So late! She didn't feel as if she'd slept that long.

"Did the truck come?"

Veda looked puzzled.

"Didn't they come yet?" Gladys asked again. "The squad truck, with the doctor?"

"Oh, them! With that Mr. Turner from across the way? They come… let's see…aroun' noontime. Ginny was takin' a nap. She was so cranky, with all the goings on this mornin', I fixed her lunch early—she didn't hardly eat a thing at that—an' it was right after I got her into bed that Mr. Turner come in."

"Did they have any news—about Barbie? Did they tell you anything?"

"Couldn't rightly say, Missus. The doctor, he talked to Barbie some, and Mr. Turner, he jest wanted to talk to you and there wasn't nobody else good enough."

"They didn't say anything about the analysis?"

Veda just looked blank. I never told her, Gladys realized. All that time, when she was so tired, she had been trying to remember something, something she had to tell Veda. She had remembered something, but it wasn't the right thing. I never told her about Barbie!

"Didn't Barbie tell you?"

"Mom!" A shout of joy vibrated through the house, and Barbara came pounding up the stairs and skidded to a halt just inside the door. "Mom, it was on the radio. Just now! About Tom!"

Gladys sat up so suddenly she almost spilled her coffee. "What?"

"He's all right!" Barbie had caught her breath. "He's in the Army. It didn't say where, but it gave a serial number. I wrote it down." She waved a scrap of paper triumphantly under her mother's nose. "Oh, Mom, he's all right!"

"Thank God!" It wasn't just something to say, a symbol of relief. It was a deeply religious thanksgiving. She put the coffee down on the bed table and let Barbie wrap her in an exuberant embrace.

"Mummmmmmmy—y." Barbie disentangled herself and dropped the scrap of paper on the blanket. "Here, you keep this. I'll go take care of Ginny. I got so excited, I forgot she was sleeping." She was gone almost as swiftly as she had come.

"Is Ginny just getting up? When did she go to sleep?" Her mouth put the question, but her ears hardly heard the reply, because of the whirling thoughts in her mind.

"She was all wore out. Jest couldn't keep up with ever'thing goin' on."

Thank God, thank God! He's safe! Gladys answered Veda with a smile, but inside she prayed. Tom's safe; now Barbie. Please, God. Please… She couldn't remember praying for years and years, not really praying. She went to church and said the words, but this feeling, this—believing…Tom was all right. God could hear her prayers. Barbie, and…She stopped the thought, half formed. Maybe it was silly, but she thought God had enough to do, watching out for the children; she would have to worry out the part about Jon by herself. Prayers and thanks and fears swirled around in her mind, pushing Jon out, with only an instant's terrified half memory of seeing him disappear, once before, into shapeless, formless terror, on a road that moved forever away.

Veda was saying something. She wiped her hands on the sticky sheet and made herself think of Tom, nothing else. Thank God, *thank God.* She smiled brilliantly at Veda. Everybody'll be all right.

"Excuse me, Missus Mitchell, I don't mean to ask questions…but all this time you been so worried about Tom wanting to go in the Army. An' now he's gone an' done it, you're practically crying from joy."

"But he's alive, Veda! Of course I don't want him in the Army. He's all right, don't you understand?" Gladys stared at the other woman incredulously. It was so silly to have to explain. "He's all right," she repeated. "He didn't get *hurt!*"

Veda's mouth opened, but no word came out. "You mean," she said finally, "it's…*all over?* It's every place?"

"You didn't *know?*"

"All I knew was here in New York. You mean there was bombs all over? In all the cities?"

Rapidly Gladys filled in all she had heard the day before, most of it news to Veda, who had known only of the disasters in the city.

"Didn't Barbara tell you anything?" Gladys demanded.

"Didn't have much chance for talking," Veda explained. "Barbie jest hung onto that radio all day, except when she was tellin' stories to Ginny in the morning, and a little while in the afternoon when the doctor come." Veda smiled. "She sure enough told me ever' time they got some new rules out for what we had to do, but I guess she wore out her voice jest tellin' me that. She was kind of mad at me—I wouldn't tell nothin' about what happened to me, not till you got up. Seemed like you was kind of worried about that before you went to sleep." She smiled again. "So I jest told the kids I wasn't goin' to tell that story more'n once, and it'd have to wait till you got up. Guess she was kind of gettin' even. Anyways, I was too busy to do much talkin'." She explained that she had spent the day trying to do everything she could to prepare for emergencies. She had washed all the dirty linens, except those on Gladys' bed, and boiled as much water as she could get into the available jars.

Her voice went on, reciting a narrative of the day's activities, but Gladys was only half listening. Barbie had never even told Veda about herself! She interrupted Veda's report to explain about Barbie. "And the laboratory never called?" she asked.

"Ain't nobody called but Missus Crowell."

"Did she want anything special? She kept calling last night. First she wanted to come over, and then she was afraid to."

"Says she's sick," Veda answered laconically. "I kind of thought I might run over and take a look at her, but I ain't had time up till now. You think…?"

"Sick?" Gladys demanded. "What kind of sick? *What's the matter with her?*"

"Couldn't make out. Didn't know she was such a *perticular* friend"— Veda clearly did not approve of Edie Crowell—"or I'd of found out more'n I did."

"She's not such a particular friend." Gladys pushed the tray away and reached for her robe. "I told you she kept calling up yesterday and…" She faltered. And what? If she has it, that doesn't mean Barbie does. "And I feel kind of responsible if she is sick," she finished weakly. "I kept telling her she was imagining it all; I kept telling her she didn't have it. *What's* the matter with her?"

"Told you, I couldn't make out, she kept talkin' so much. Nothin' serious, I don't think, but soon's you get up, mebbe I'll jest run over there an' see fer myself."

"Is it all right to go out?"

"Long as you stay near yer own house. They got some kind of curfew goin', though. Nobody allowed out after eight o'clock. Barbie kin tell you better. She heard it on the radio. When she told me, I thought we could mebbe lay in some supplies, and I went down to Monnassey's, but they got a big sign printed up, 'No Business.' Said it was under the pertection of the Emergency Headquarters."

Gladys shrugged into her robe, feeling again the familiar comfort of the soft wool. It was silly, having it mean so much to her, but in some way it had come almost to replace Jon in her mind. She pulled it tight around her waist and knotted the belt. She was fully awake now; there were things she had to think about.

"How can we get food?" she asked briskly. "There must be some way."

"The sign didn't say. Seems like Mr. Turner would know, but he jest couldn't be bothered talkin' to me."

"Did he say when they were coming back? Why didn't you wake me up?"

"You needed your sleep," Veda insisted.

"You don't think he had anything important to tell me, do you?" Gladys controlled her irritation with Veda. Veda was probably right. She had needed the sleep.

"No'm, I don't," Veda said sharply. It was too respectful. Gladys waited, knowing there was more coming.

"Tell you, Missus Mitchell, this ain't none of my business, an' I know I oughter likely as not keep my mouth shut, but…I don't like that Mr. Turner. I jest plain don't like the way he was askin' fer you, or the way he couldn't talk to nobody else. Never did think much, though I ain't one to gossip, the way he treats that nice wife of his. I hear plenty," she added as Gladys, surprised, started to protest, "that ain't talked about except in the kitchen, an' I ain't passed it all on to you neither. Like I said, it's none o' my business, but it wouldn't hurt you to keep an eye on him."

"Veda," Gladys protested, "I don't know what kind of talk you've heard—" It was surprising enough to have her admit she had ever listened to idle gossip; in Veda's book, loose talk and aimless questioning were cardinal sins. "But I don't think you should say things like that about Mr. Turner. He's been very nice and—"

"That's jest what I'm talkin' about."

"He's been very nice," Gladys repeated firmly, "and you have to remember that those other men might have told him…might have said something to him…well…" Why did I ever get into this? "Well, they *could* have said something about you being under suspicion." She saw hurt bewilderment on Veda's face. "After all," she added hastily, "just because you and I know that you didn't do anything, that doesn't mean *they* believe it. And what's more," she beat a hasty retreat to the original subject, "I suppose it's all those trips of his you were thinking of. Well, they weren't as mysterious as they seemed. He was—"

"No'm," Veda broke in again. "Mebbe I listened to some talk I shouldn't of, but I got some sense. What I'm talkin' about ain't what happened when he *wasn't* there—"

"Mommy!"

A flying wedge of five-year-old burst through the door and clambered into her arms, dripping large wet kisses all the way.

"Mommy…" Ginny voiced her grievance promptly. "They didn't let me go out *all day!*"

"Didn't they? I know what." Gladys freed herself from the smothering embrace. "I know something you can do—something you like."

"What is it, Mommy?" Ginny tagged after her to the closet. "What can I do? Can I go outside, Mommy? I'm tired of stories."

"Oh, something much better than that," Gladys teased. "Something that's much more fun."

"What is it? Please tell me. Please, Mommy, please."

"Well…" There it was, last year's dinner gown; and the black sandals that were beginning to be too worn. She reached for a box on the shelf and found a filmy silk scarf with only two or three little holes in it. Another box produced an elegant sequined bag, shiny with silver and purple. And sequins to pick up all over the house, too!

"Well…" she temporized, not letting Ginny look past her. There— the big hat with the long pink feather.

"There." She turned and dumped the glamorous pile at Ginny's feet. "*That's* what!"

Ginny was, briefly, speechless. But she recovered before Gladys could get out into the bathroom, in time to ask, "Can I put on lipstick too? And *powder?*"

"And," Gladys finished for her, nodding, "perfume too—the little blue bottle, and don't use more than half of it!" Going into the bathroom, she wondered if the last bit of humor might have been too subtle, and almost went back. Oh, it doesn't matter! she decided recklessly.

Rinsing her face, Veda's worried words came back to her, and she chuckled at herself in the mirror, enjoying the picture of Gladys Mitchell, settled mother of three, being wickedly pursued by Jim Turner— beefy face, bedrock convictions and all. Veda really thinks things like that happen! She tried to imagine herself cowering before an amorous airtight suit. "No, no, a thousand times…"

The muffled ringing of the phone downstairs interrupted her private melodrama. She pushed the door open and saw Veda, loaded down with dirty linens, presumably from her own bed, going by on her way to the stairs.

"That woman again!" she tossed over her shoulder to Gladys. "I'll jest bet it's that woman again…" She disappeared down the staircase, still muttering.

Gladys took the time to dry her face and run a comb through her hair, glad now that she had finally had it cut short. She glanced quickly in the mirror, surprised to find that her face was still the same as it had been when she started down to answer Veda's phone call just—thirty-six hours ago. A day and a half…two days and a night since Jon had kissed her good-bye.

She was downstairs while Veda was still waiting for a connection to be made.

"It's some switchboard operator." She handed over the phone happily enough. "She said, 'Wait a minnit,' and then nothin' happened at all."

"Hello?" Gladys spoke sharply into unresponsive silence; but the phone wasn't dead. "Don't you know who it was? What kind of operator was it?"

Veda only shook her head.

"Hello, is this 1439 Maple Avenue?"

"Yes." Gladys hastily uncovered the mouthpiece. "Yes, who is this, please?"

"Emergency Headquarters lab," the young man's voice said concisely. "We got a report here on an analysis from your house. You want to take the report?"

"Yes, please." Gladys pulled open the little drawer in the table, rummaged for a pencil, and found the back of an envelope to write on. "Go ahead."

"We performed an analysis on Sample No. 2036C, on request of Mrs. Gladys Mitchell, and of James Turner, squadman for the area," he reeled off monotonously. "Sample was of fifteen-year-old girl, briefly exposed to radioactive rain, reported ill..." Briefly exposed to radioactive rain...radioactive...active rain...radioactive rain...The words kept ringing in her ears. "...quantity of alpha emitters present in the sample, probably residual plutonium, apparently inhaled or swallowed. Insufficient evidence—"

"Excuse me." Gladys struggled for breath to form the words. "Could you repeat that, please? please, I'm sorry, but I didn't get all—"

"Okay. Try and get it this time." He didn't mind showing his irritation. "Analysis showed a small quantity of alpha emitters present in the sample, probably residual..."

Small quantity! She allowed herself the space of the words she'd already heard to savor that, knowing it probably didn't matter, that a little was likely as bad as a lot, but holding on, while she could, to the idea that Barbie might, after all, be all right.

"...ficient evidence of lethal or dangerous dose. No hospitalization required." She had to hold onto the table for support, dropping the pencil from her free hand, as her tensed body went limp with relief. She almost missed the rest. "Blood count will be necessary for final diagnosis. Please request the medical assistant on your squad truck to take blood counts as indicated, and submit to lab."

"But...I don't understand." This last threat was meaningless, absurd. He'd just said Barbie was all right. "What are the blood counts for? Why—"

"You got all that information handed out to you in mimeographed sheets," he told her acridly. "Don't *any* of you take the trouble to read 'em?"

"I'm sorry," she appeased; he had to answer one more question. "I should have seen that, I guess, but could you just tell me, please, whether this means that she's...*sick*...or not?"

"It means I don't know. It looks like not; but she still could be. If you don't understand what it says on that sheet you've got, the doctor will explain it to you when he comes around. I can't give courses in radiation disease over the telephone. I wouldn't even have called, except that your squadman specially asked me to. He'll explain everything to you."

The phone clicked emphatically at the other end.

"It's okay, Mom." Barbie's voice, so close by, startled her out of all relation to its timid tones. "I read up all about it, and Dr. Spinelli—that young doctor in the truck," she reminded Gladys anxiously, "explained it all to me; probably we won't know anything till tomorrow—" She stopped, alarmed by the horrified look on her mother's face.

"You read...?" Gladys began, then realized the more urgent part of what her daughter had said. "*What* did Dr. Spinelli explain to you?"

"About radiation sickness." Defiance tinged the hesitation in her voice; she had known Gladys wouldn't like this. "When he took the blood count he told me just what I should—"

"*Took* the blood count?" Gladys demanded. "But they just called now to tell me he should take it. What made him…?"

"I told him, that's why," Barbara retorted. "I told him all about being sick last night, and how I didn't tell you when I should have, and how you called Emergency Headquarters when you found out, but we hadn't heard anything, and I couldn't find the information sheets they kept talking about on the radio, and I asked him how come we didn't have any, and he said he was sure we did, but anyhow, he gave me another one about radiation disease, and told me just what would happen to me if I was sick, what they'd do at the hospital and everything." She stopped, out of breath, and watched for her mother's reaction.

Gladys stood still, silent. She remembered seeing the sheets on the sofa in those hectic sleepy moments in the morning, and hiding them. She remembered how they had frightened her when she read them. If Barbie had read…"hair may fall out…itching, burning, skin discomforts…" That's what it said on that sheet. "…hemorrhages…boils, blisters…"

Maybe Barbie thought she knew a lot more than she really did; the doctor couldn't have told her too much. In any case it was ridiculous to get angry now.

"Well!" She searched for, and found, a small smile. "So you're an expert on radiation disease, are you?" She managed to turn it from sarcasm to a friendly joke in mid-sentence. "Come and tell me about it while I get something to eat."

She could smell bacon on the stove in the kitchen, and found her anger and bewilderment both melting under the sudden attack of ravenous hunger.

She almost made it, but not quite. The pounding on the front door was both loud and urgent.

Gladys turned, took one step forward. But they can't! They can't be here already!

That was foolish. It didn't even sound like the way the squadman knocked. It could be—it could be *good!*

The pounding didn't stop even at the noise of the bolt shooting out, not until the door was actually opened. Even then the woman at the door had her hand raised to knock again, and almost fell against Gladys before she grabbed the doorpost and managed to stop the swing of her own momentum.

"Tried to call," she said. "Tried and tried. Couldn't call, so I came." A caricature of a smile said clearly, Wasn't that clever of me?

She withdrew her hand from the doorpost and steadied herself on high-heeled gray satin mules. "*May* I come in?" she enunciated elegantly.

"Edie! My God!" Gladys stared, uncomprehending, at the mud on the little satin slippers, at the dusty train of flowing gray chiffon gown, at the stains that chased down the front. "For God's sake, come in!" Automatically, now, she locked and bolted the door before she turned around to find Edie wavering unsteadily, right behind her in the hall. In the living room Barbie and Veda both stood watching.

Edie stayed where she was, waiting—for what Gladys didn't know; but she seized the opportunity.

"Edie!" She slipped in between the visitor and her family, and breathed one quick horrified question. "Are you...sick? Is it the *disease?*"

"Of course it is!" Edie answered shrilly.

She's got to keep quiet! Gladys took Edie's arm, tried to lead her toward the stairs, away from the living room. Don't let her say anything else, not yet! She'd find some way to explain it to Barbie.

"I told you I was. I told you and told you, and I told them, and nobody would believe me." Still that elegant painstaking enunciation of each syllable. "Nobody!" She sat down abruptly on the bottom step, almost tripping on the hem of the long gown as she turned. "Nobody!" Then she covered her face with her hands and proceeded to cry, in stagy, articulated bursts of sound. It was the first time Gladys had ever heard anybody really cry, "Boo-hoo."

At just that moment a strange vision appeared on the stairs over Edie's head. Small feet in wobbling high-heeled shoes came first, reaching uncertainly for placement on the treads; voluminous wine velvet folds of skirt swayed precariously above the bare ankles, and finally small, clenched fists came into sight, struggling to hold the bunched velvet fabric high above the shaky footing. Eventually Ginny was completely visible, all the way to the tip most peak of the plumed hat.

She was so preoccupied with the problem of the descent that she almost tripped over the woman on the stairs. But as soon as she became aware of the obstruction she forgot all about her fabulous finery. Dropping one whole fistful of velvet, she pointed an inquiring index finger and opened her mouth wide.

"*Who?*"

Gladys turned appealingly to Veda, who had made no move throughout the scene, but stood grimly sniffing and disapproving. Now, apparently determined to misunderstand, she did nothing about the children. Instead she took a step forward.

"You leave that one to me, Missus Mitchell," she said almost menacingly. "I know what to do fer the likes of her."

Gladys turned to the child on the stairs. "Will you stop staring your eyes out?" she demanded. "It's none of your business. Barbie!" Inspiration hit her. "Run downstairs and get some clean linens. I want to put Mrs. Crowell to bed. And take Ginny with you," she added as the older girl started off reluctantly.

"Veda." Gladys turned back to the maid angrily. "For heaven's sake, she's—"

"She's nothin' but stupid drunk," Veda finished for her.

CHAPTER TWELVE

"MOMMY…will Miss Crole die?" Ginny perched on a favorite chair by the kitchen table, munching a cracker and waving her feathered hat in front of the window.

"Why, baby, don't be silly!" Gladys dumped the contents of a can of soup into a pot and measured out a canful of boiled water from a pitcher on the table. *I've got to stop jumping every time one of them says anything. I ought to be used to it by now.* She put the pot down on the stove, sniffing. The reek of alcohol still seemed to cling to her nose, but through it there was a faint odor of gas.

"But, Mommy, will she be dead—like the birdies?"

"Like the…?" *Oh! She had forgotten, forgotten all about that.* "No," she said sensibly. "Of course not. She just isn't feeling well. She'll be all right."

"Will they take her away to the hospital?"

"No, I don't think so. I don't think she's really very sick."

"Did she throw up?" Ginny climbed down and moved closer to her mother. "She smelled funny, like she threw up."

The stove wouldn't light either. That accounted for the smell; the pilot was out. Gladys reached for a match, struck it, and had trouble getting the flame to light. She kept hunting for the right answer to Ginny's questions and struggling with the stove at the same time.

"Did she throw up like Barbie?"

Gladys forgot all about the stove. "What do you mean, like Barbie?" She put down the blackened match and reached for the little girl's face, turned it up so their eyes met. "What do *you* know about Barbie being sick?"

"She threw up—threw up," the little girl corrected herself hastily. "In the middle of the night." Any time after dark was the middle of the night to Ginny. "I had to go to the bathroom, to make Number One," she added, explicit as always, "and she wouldn't let me come in, and I said I'd holler, because I never wet my pants any more, do I? I knowed you didn't want me to wet my pants, and I told Barbie I'd holler so she let me in." It was all coming out fast now, in a virtuous rush of confession. "And I looked and looked to see what made such a funny smell, it was like part of the smell on Miss Crole. Is she going to the hospital and die like the birdies?"

"Of course not." She couldn't stop to consider niceties of the answer now. "Why didn't you call me when you woke up? Why didn't you tell me Barbie was sick? How do you know she was?"

"She didn't clean up good. I looked and looked and then I saw some on the floor, and she made me cross my heart an' hope to die, but I could tell you now, because she told herself, didn't she, Mommy? Mommy, how do you *know* Miss Crole isn't going to be dead?"

"I *don't* know it," Gladys had to admit. "I don't know anything like that, but I don't see any reason why she should be. She isn't even very sick." Thoughtfully Gladys turned back to the stove. The soup still sat, lumpy and solid, in the lukewarm water; underneath the pot the flame was weak and blue. She reached to turn the burner up and found it was already turned all the way. That didn't make sense. She turned it off and tried lighting another one. Somewhere she could remember a gas stove that acted that way. Of course, the one in the Quonset hut, where they used bottled gas. Whenever the pressure got low…

"Mommy."

"Just a minute, baby." Worried now, she tried the other burners. They were all the same. She lit the pilot again, watched to see that it stayed lit, and turned on the weak flame under the soup again. It would just take a little longer, that was all. But why should the pressure be so low?

"Mommy, please…"

She recognized urgency, but she could still smell gas from the pilot. Should she open a window? Maybe just for a little while. If people could go out now it must be all right.

"Mommy, you won't answer me!"

"Of course I will, dear." She patted the small head abstractedly and pushed the window casement out a little. "What is it?" The pilot flame sputtered in the small breeze.

"Mommy, will *Barbie* be dead?"

"Will *what?*" Instinctively she bent down and wrapped her arms around her baby. "You silly, silly girl." The child was shaking, now that the question was out at last. "Who's been putting ideas like that in my girl's head?"

"Nobody," she said. "I thought it for myself. Mommy, are you sure, Mommy? Even if they take her away to the hospital?"

"Who said she was going to the hospital?" Gladys was furious. She tried not to show her anger, aware that the child would take it as directed against herself. But she *had* to know.

"Nobody," Ginny insisted. "Nobody said so, only I know. If you throw up you have to go away to the hospital. They were all talking about it, all the people, the funny men and Barbie and Veda, they was all talking about it."

"When?" She could straighten out Ginny's ideas later. Right now she had to find out who'd been talking to the child.

"Well, I couldn't sleep," Ginny said defensively, " 'cause they made so much noise. It wasn't my fault if I couldn't go to sleep." In a minute she'd start crying.

"No, baby," Gladys said wearily, "it wasn't your fault. Was it nap time?"

The child nodded dumbly.

"And you were listening? You were up on the stairs?"

She shook her head. "No, I wasn't. I just had to go to the bathroom, I had to make *Number Two!*" It was triumphant.

"It must have taken you a long time to get there," Gladys commented dryly. Well, that was that, and nothing anyone could do about it. But they'd all have to be more careful what they said and where they said it. She let Ginny go and stood up again. The room still smelled of gas, but she'd have to close the window or the tiny flame would never stay on. There ought to be some way to disconnect the pilot. She sighed and closed the window. The soup was just beginning to steam a little bit, not yet simmering. She stirred it automatically, her mind on Ginny, who sat now, contentedly chewing on her cracker. How much did the child understand? Or misunderstand?

Steady, solid footsteps approaching. The swinging door opened to let Veda in, her arms piled with towels, a basin, and soiled linens.

"Finished changin' all the beds while I was at it." She headed for the cellar door. "Thought I might's well get these washed while we still got water."

That's what's doing it, Gladys thought, that kind of talk. But she couldn't say anything then, not with Ginny right in the room.

"Got yer flame on?" Veda maneuvered the basin onto the table and stood still, sniffing. "Mighty smell o' gas in here."

Don't you think I can smell? Gladys dropped the spoon into the soup and had to get the tongs to fish it out. "I know it!" She tried not to snap. It was silly to be so upset. "The pilot was out," she explained, stirring furiously. Veda shrugged and declined to quarrel. She started for the door.

"Is Mrs. Crowell feeling better now?" Gladys asked meaningfully.

"She's one sick lady." Veda refused to understand or co-operate.

"There'll be questions." Gladys inclined her head ever so slightly in the direction of her daughter.

"And I've got answers!" Gladys lifted one eyebrow inquiringly. "Never saw the time yet the truth wasn't good enough," Veda said sharply.

Gladys was fuming inwardly, but there was nothing she could say, not in front of Ginny. Veda stood still, waiting for a reply. When she got none she sniffed audibly and started once again for the cellar door. With both hands full, she had to struggle to open it. Gladys made no offer to help, but stayed at the stove, monotonously stirring her soup.

Then the door came flying open, and she forgot the whole ridiculous quarrel.

She had presence of mind enough to turn off the flame on the stove first, before a spark could catch. Then, even while she was thinking, realizing that the gas escaping from the pilot light couldn't possibly have smelled so much, she shrilled at her daughter.

"Ginny! Get out of here! Upstairs quick! Tell Barbie!" She pulled at the catch on the casement, flinging both windows wide open.

Ginny didn't stop to ask questions. Only four or five times in her memory had her mother screamed at her that way. She ran.

Gladys turned from the window to see Veda pulling open the door to the porch, a trail of dirty linen marking her rush from the cellar door. She got to the window over the table, the one that always stuck. Without waiting to find if it would open this time, she banged the frame heavily, with a pot picked up on the way. It rattled satisfactorily loose, and she heaved it violently upward.

Together they headed for the swinging door. Gladys was almost through the dining room to the front, where the living-room door could be closed tight against the foul-smelling poison, when she saw Veda stop and go to one of the dining-room windows.

I wouldn't have thought of that! She went back to the other one herself. She remembered she had been angry with Veda about something, but the memory itself didn't last long enough for her to do or say anything about it.

They slammed the living-room door behind them, and it became possible to think about what had happened.

"Mom!" Barbie called from upstairs. "What happened? What's the matter?" Her voice was small and scared. Behind it they could hear Ginny whimpering quietly.

"Gas," Gladys called up. "The cellar's full of gas."

"Should we come down?" Ginny had stopped crying. The explanation would carry no meaning to her, Gladys realized, but Barbie understood.

"You might as well come down," she decided. "We've got the door shut. You'll be just as safe here." The radio was making too much noise. She went over to turn it down.

"Don't," Barbie called from the foot of the stairs. "Don't turn it off, Mother."

"Well, we're not listening to it. I can't think with all that noise."

"They're reading the names again," Barbara insisted. "If you just leave it on low we'll hear it, if they say any name we know. I was reading before, and I heard it every time they said anything that mattered."

"Well…" She let it go; there was no time to argue. Now they had to do something, quickly. Why, the house could explode! The whole house!

She almost dropped the receiver, trying to pick the phone up too quickly. She had to wait forever for a dial tone, but this time she didn't try to dial. She whirled around the red 0 for the operator, and waited again while it rang five, six, eight, nine times, before a tired voice answered.

She didn't have to think what to do: Jon had told her over and over. "I want the Fire Department," she said.

"Lady," the operator said with a bright interest that overcame her weariness, "are you nuts?"

"Am I…? No!" Gladys said indignantly. "I want the Fire—"

"Mother—Mom." Barbie was shaking her head vigorously. "Mom, there *isn't* any Fire Department. They're all in the cit—"

"I'm sorry. Give me Emergency Headquarters," Gladys told the operator. Jon had told her, over and over, what to do if anything like that ever happened, so she wouldn't have to stop and think, so she could act right away. And now she hadn't stopped to think. In a curious way she was almost angry at Jon.

"Hello!" It was the switchboard again, and she couldn't think whom to ask for, so she explained her trouble to the bored young man who answered.

"Just a minute, lady."

She got another connection, an older, deeper masculine voice, and repeated her story.

"Address?" he asked brusquely.

Thank God! They're actually going to do something! She told it to him and listened to paper rustling in the silence that followed.

"No trouble in that neighborhood, lady," he said at last.

"But there's trouble right here!" she exploded. "I'm right in the house, and I *know* there's—"

"Yeah, I know, you just told me. But we can't send a repair truck out for just one house. I mean the mains are okay."

"That's nice to know! What am I supposed to do?"

"Wait till your squad truck comes. They'll help you if they can."

"But the house could explode! We—anything could happen!"

"You said you opened up the windows, didn't you? The house won't explode. Just watch out for fire and you'll be okay. Did you turn off your electric equipment?"

"No, I didn't. I opened all the windows I could, and shut off the gas from the rest of the house, before we all passed out, that's what I did. Maybe you don't understand. I've got *a cellar full of gas.* Am I just supposed to stay here, with my children, and just let it keep leaking?"

"You could try and fix it," he suggested. "Or you could go stay with a neighbor. Don't take it out on me, lady. There's nothing I can do. Your squadman'll have to fix it." It was decisive.

"Thank you!" Gladys said bitterly, and hung up.

"What did he say, Mom?"

"Nothing. He said we should fix it. Or go to the neighbors'."

"Why don't we?" Barbie liked the idea. "We could all go over to the Crowells'—and take Mrs. Crowell along. We could all stay there till we got somebody to fix it."

"Well...I don't know." Gladys tried to think.

"Then, if anything happened"—Barbie was increasingly excited—"you know, if the house blew up or something, we'd all be okay."

"No! We'll try fixing it first. If that doesn't work we'll have to get out. But I'm not leaving this house till I know I have to." Her mind was made up now. If the house blew up! And even if it didn't, everything would be ruined by gas.

"I'm going down and see what I can do," she announced. "I'll get the windows open, anyhow. And the cellar door. That should clear it out enough so I can look around."

"Daddy was always saying something about the valve," Barbie suggested. "And we could break the windows, couldn't we? From outside? That's what the Fire Department does. That's why they have those axes. Then you wouldn't have to go down till—"

"I don't know that's such a good idea," Veda broke in. "They been warning us all day on the radio about these crazy folks running around, an' the curfew and all. We wouldn't be able to lock up..."

Gladys didn't give anybody, including herself, any more time to think about it. Whatever was done had to be done fast.

She ran up the stairs to her room, shed the red wool robe, and went out to the hall closet for the slacks she had piled there the night before.

She found a work shirt of Jon's, much too big; but, buttoned up, and tucked into the slacks, it covered her all over. In the bathroom she soaked a big towel in cold water. That's what they do, isn't it? She tried to remember, to think of stories, movies, newsreels where people had to fight gas. All she could remember was wet towels over your face.

CHAPTER THIRTEEN

OF COURSE THERE WOULDN'T BE anything to see. She kept telling herself that. She held the sopping towel close against her face. Through it the air had a laundry smell and nothing else. And the haze she had expected wasn't there.

She went straight across and through the furnace room to the outside cellar door. At the nearest window Veda's legs were clearly visible out in the grass. There was nothing to it, she kept reminding herself. Just push back the bolt, and after that the rest is simple.

It was an ordinary slanted double door at the top of a small flight of stairs. She strained at the bolt overhead until the muscles in her arm ached, clear to the shoulder, but she couldn't budge it. She tried to remember whether it had been opened since they had painted. But whitewash didn't make things stick, did it? She didn't know.

She needed both hands, she found. Maybe she could release one by tying the towel around her face. She stopped pulling at the stubborn bolt and fumbled behind her head with the bulky ends of the heavy towel. It wouldn't knot, and cold drops began trickling down her spine. Veda rapped on the window, bending down to give her a worried, questioning look, but she shook her head.

The whole thing was ridiculous. Even through the towel she'd smell gas if it was so bad she really needed the towel. She wriggled to dislodge a clammy rivulet playing waterfall down her spine, and impulsively ripped the towel from her face, tossed it on the window sill, and used both hands to pull back hard on the bolt.

She must have been holding her breath at first, because she didn't notice anything right away; but, using all her strength on the door, she took a deep breath and got it all at once.

Choking and gasping, she grabbed for the towel again and bunched it up against her face till she couldn't breathe at all. Veda was rapping at the window again. She shook her head, which made her feel dizzy. She stopped and concentrated on getting the towel straightened out. This time she paid no attention to the chill trickles under her collar. She knotted the towel firmly behind her head, covering her whole face up to her eyes.

Her head began to clear. The dizziness was going away, but the faint sour odor remained; it seemed to be right in the towel now. Grimly she reached up again. *Why* wouldn't it open? They'd never had any trouble with it before. Some light would help, but she didn't dare turn one on. "Don't use your electric equipment," the man had said.

She ran her fingers all around the bolt, trying to make them see for her.

There was, of course, a safety catch. She felt her face flush warmly under the damp towel. She turned the small knob on the bolt, out of the locked position. When she pulled on it this time she almost fell over backward, it opened so easily.

The towel seemed to be soaked in gas instead of water. She pushed the double doors open and stumbled up the stairs.

She sat down on the grass in the sun and didn't ever want to get up again. But the job wasn't finished yet.

"Are you all done? Did you fix it already?" Barbie danced around her with questions.

She shrugged the girl away and started up to the bathroom. Then she thought better of it and explained to Barbie what she wanted: a fresh towel, soaked through, but only in the middle.

"…and leave the ends dry, so I can tie it."

Barbie got back almost too soon. Gladys' back and shoulders ached all over, and she was still drawing in great gulps of air.

She didn't want to go down there again; she didn't want to. She had to force herself to go down the stairs, one step at a time, without thinking about anything but the necessity for getting to the bottom.

She went to the first window along the wall and carefully turned the latch first. It stuck, just a little, but it wasn't too hard to do. Then suddenly it was all very easy again. Just one window at a time, take it easy, don't get panicky.

It was done. She went up and dropped into a chair to rest while she waited for the air to clear. She hadn't done much, but it seemed as if she'd been down there for hours. She got a fresh towel and the biggest wrench she could find in Jon's toolbox.

He had said something about a valve. Which valve? She didn't see anything that looked like a valve. The meter was smooth-surfaced. Whatever was supposed to turn the gas on and off must be inside, but how did you get to it? She remembered seeing the man do it once—or was that the electric meter? *That* one opened up; she could see the little door on it. She hit the front of the meter box with the wrench. Nothing happened, except that she dented the smooth metal front. She was surprised that she could hit so hard.

The towel was beginning to smell of gas.

Up above the meter the pipe turned, and at the elbow a thick screw jutted out. It wasn't a valve; she knew what a valve looked like. But maybe it did something. She reached up and tried to turn it with her fingers, but it was set firmly in place. Maybe she could knock it loose with the wrench.

It couldn't do any harm anyway. She hit it once, a glancing blow, and thought it moved a little. She hit at it again. It *had* moved—just enough to show it could. But hitting wasn't the right way.

She got a box to stand on and looked at it more closely. It stuck out of the pipe about an inch, and wasn't more than a half inch through, probably less. The part in the pipe was smoothly round, except for the thread of the screw, and she could just see the edge of that, where it met the pipe. But the end near her wasn't round; it was squared off, and she remembered that was the kind of thing they used a tire wrench on. She tried the wrench she had, but it was too big; it wouldn't grasp the screw at all.

She'd have to go back upstairs and find something else. The towel was soaked with gas now.

She couldn't come back again; she just couldn't.

On top of the oil burner she found an ordinary small pliers and grabbed it up. She was beginning to be dizzy again. She should have gone back upstairs for a new towel.

She got the jaws of the pliers around the square end of the screw, but every time she tried to turn it, it slipped off. Only she had felt it move; she knew she had. It must be what Jon had meant by a valve.

She held the jaws onto the screw with her fingers and pulled down hard with her other hand. It moved. Just a little.

She hung on, straining down. The smell kept getting stronger, and she had to get out of there. With every bit of strength she had left she pulled down on the pliers handles.

This time, when it gave, she was expecting the reaction, but she had been pulling too hard. She couldn't stop herself, and for a moment her arms waved wildly, then she was on the floor, and the towel had slipped out of place.

She heard Barbie calling from upstairs, and Veda from outside. The box had made a lot of noise. She couldn't answer them; the towel was off her mouth, but she was afraid to open it. She got her arms out from under her and yanked the towel back over her face. It didn't seem to do any good at all any more. Gas was in her nostrils and her throat. Strangely enough, she wasn't dizzy any more, but her eyes were tearing and they smarted. She set the box back in place. She seemed to be moving very slowly, but everything was getting done, quicker than she expected, too. She didn't quite understand it, but she supposed it was all right. She knew she had to turn that screw some more. It had been in one way, now she had to get it all the way the other way.

She had to stop and remember which way she had turned it. This time it responded easily. She kept turning until the whole length of the round part had disappeared inside the hole in the pipe. When she couldn't make it go in any more at all she got down off the box and went upstairs. She felt very calm in spite of the awful smell. She was surprised to find she was sobbing.

CHAPTER FOURTEEN

SHE WAS STILL DIZZY. She sipped once more at the whisky, but it tasted awful. Ginny was crying monotonously on Veda's lap. Barbie squatted in front of the radio. Gladys lay still on the sofa, wanting to get off and remove the dirty slacks, wondering if there would be grease stains on the pale green upholstery.

She tried to lift her head, but it made her feel woozy again. The radio was forcing itself on her consciousness. She didn't want to hear it.

"Do you know where the hot plate is?" she asked Veda. "I don't remember seeing it around."

"That little one from the Silex is right in the kitchen cabinet." Veda kept on rocking Ginny, answering Gladys without changing the tone of voice she used to soothe the little girl.

"I mean the big one, the two-burner."

"Ain't seen that one in a long time."

"Daddy took it to the office once," Barbie contributed over her shoulder. "Did he bring it back?"

"Don't know as he did," Veda said thoughtfully. "We got the electric broiler, though, could work like a hot plate upside down."

"The waffle iron?" Barbie threw in.

How can she listen to two things at the same time? Gladys was having trouble focusing her attention on one conversation.

"There's a Sterno stove in Mr. Mitchell's camping kit," she told Veda.

"I dunno. We might need the Sterno stove worse later on."

"For heaven's sake, Veda!" Gladys protested. "How much worse can it *get?*"

"Waffles." The word had penetrated slowly into Ginny's sleep sodden head. "I want waffles for supper."

Veda looked questioning, and Gladys shrugged.

"Might's well," the maid said. "Waffles on the iron, an' coffee in the Silex, an' we ain't got no problems at all."

"Are we *really* gonna have waffles?" Ginny sat bolt upright. "Right now?"

"As soon as we can get in the kitchen," Gladys promised.

"I'll go see." Barbie jumped up restlessly, but she didn't have to do any more than open the door. The smell made her slam it shut again.

Ginny surveyed her suspiciously. "I want waffles *now.*"

"Well, you can't get them *now,* so quit being a baby about it." Barbie was feeling intoxicated with adventure and a whiff of gas. Ginny, feeling only sleepy and hungry, promptly burst into a fresh flow of tears.

"Come here, baby." Gladys found she could sit up now, and she stretched her arms. Still crying, Ginny made her way across the room to her mother, stumbling on the hem of the velvet gown she still wore. Safe on Gladys' lap, she defied the world.

"Am *not* a baby!"

Barbie opened her mouth and closed it as promptly when she saw Gladys' emphatic headshake. Her challenge having gone unanswered, Ginny gathered courage for another sally. "I'm hungry," she said firmly. "Want my waffles."

"Shush." Gladys patted the defiant shoulder absently, ignoring the repeated demand.

"I want my—"

"Oh, shush up, Ginny." Barbara, still listening with one ear to the radio, turned it up so they could all hear.

"…special police are constantly patrolling the area. There is no danger, except through carelessness. Keep your doors and windows locked and admit *no unauthorized strangers* to your homes after curfew hour. These precautions are concerned *only* with protection from acts of larceny and violence. There is no foundation in fact for any rumors you may have heard to the effect that these gangs of lawbreakers are made up of contaminated refugees from within the city limits. It is virtually impossible for anyone to leave the city area now, except by way of the decontamination stations.

"Evacuees from the city are not entering the Westchester residential area. They are being sent directly to evacuation camps upstate, on special trains already in operation.

"This station will continue to announce the names of persons released from the city through decontamination centers…"

Veda snorted with rich contempt but refrained from any comment. Gladys was grateful. Whatever Veda had seen in the city, Gladys didn't want it discussed just then.

"Mommy, what's commamminashun?"

"Contamination," she corrected automatically. "It's—well, it's being hurt. The people who were hurt by the accident in the city are contaminated—"

"Mother!" Barbie was shocked. "That's no—"

"Barbara! I am perfectly capable of answering Ginny's questions. You pay attention to the radio, and let me—"

"Listen!" Barbara had already returned her attention to the radio.

"…still need homes for a number of children whose parents are in the city, or whose homes have been broken up as an indirect result of the attack. Adequate supplies for the care of the children will be issued to you. If you have an extra bed in your house, and any adult capable of providing supervision for a small child, please get in touch with Emergency Welfare Headquarters *now*. Pick up the telephone and ask for Emergency Welfare. The operator will connect you.

"We have just received a new list of evacuated persons from the Washington Heights Headquarters. The following persons…"

"Mom—Mother, we've *got* to take some of them."

"Take some children, take some children!" Ginny chanted gleefully.

"We got room, anyhow," Veda pointed out. "Can't say I'd want to depend on them food supplies they're promising—but we could make do with what we got."

"We've got plenty!" Barbara insisted. "We can manage. You said yourself," she appealed to Gladys, "that it couldn't very well get any worse. We'll be able to get food, even if they *don't* bring it along."

"That's enough," Gladys said flatly. "I'll have to think about it."

"Children, children, gonna take some children," Ginny chanted.

"See?" Gladys demanded. "We'll talk about it later."

"But, Mother—"

"I said *later!*" She saw the bright red color suffuse her daughter's face and added quickly, "Do you want to take a look now, Barbie, and see how the kitchen is?"

Wordlessly the girl got up.

"You set still, Missus Mitchell." Veda got up stiffly. "I'll bring the makin's right in here. Save a lot of fuss and trouble." She nodded toward the little girl, curled up on her mother's lap, hypnotizing herself with a barely audible chant, "Children, children, gonna take the children…"

Gladys smiled thankfully and let Veda follow Barbara out to the kitchen.

The radio chattered on. Names and addresses, this one evacuated, that one hospitalized, another safe at a friend's home. Three dead in the city, one rescued, a whole family found alive under a burned building. The names went endlessly on, and they meant nothing. Ginny's chant turned into a quiet sleepy murmuring. It was beginning to get dark outside. Gladys wondered what time it was, and thought of turning on a light, but the gloaming was too restful. She wouldn't listen, she *wouldn't*…

"Mrs. Tod Graham, and son, Tod Graham, Jr., three years old, of 1482 Orchard Boulevard, found trapped in burning building in midtown Manhattan…"

Mrs. Tod Graham! Annie!

"Mrs. Graham is being treated for shock and burns at the hospital base in Washington Heights. Tod, Jr., is being treated for radiation and minor injuries…"

But they were home. I saw Tod in the garden. With difficulty she brought that morning back to her mind, remembered Annie's chagrin at not being invited to that luncheon, the luncheon Gladys herself hadn't gone to. Annie had said she always had lunch in town on Mondays, anyhow, with her husband.

"…now repeat a list of the identified casualties in the city today. Please listen carefully. There may be no way of notifying the friends and relatives of these persons except by radio announcements. Dead: John Anderson, Main Street, White Plains; Hilda Allderdick, 42 Green Lane, Henley; Anthony Ameranto, 2205 Hartley…"

Now she couldn't stop listening. Every name, every syllable, penetrated her senses. She didn't feel Ginny's weight on her lap; she didn't know whether it was dark or light in the room. She just listened.

"…friends and relatives may not be notified…today's casualties…" Annie Graham…hospital base…Jon!

She was only dimly aware of it when Veda and Barbara came back in, arms loaded with food and equipment.

"…Alden Gramercy, Hope Street, Tappan…"

Veda snapped on the big lamp on the reading table.

"…R. Jardiniere, Marley Avenue, Plainstown…"

They got through the list. Somehow, finally, they finished reading the roll call of the slaughtered.

"…hospitalized for today. For the sake of speed we will read only the names and not the addresses of these persons : Avery Abbott, James Abbott, Kenneth Abbott…"

She realized she could stop listening. It was alphabetical. She didn't have to listen any more until the M's.

"Barbie, you forgot the syrup." Veda looked up from the bowl where she was mixing waffle flour and milk. Barbara ran out to the kitchen and came back with the syrup, already opened.

"Smells okay," she announced.

"Better leave me have a taste before we use it," Veda offered.

Barbie immersed a finger delicately in the sticky stuff.

"I said *me,* not you. Now give that here."

"It's fine," Barbara insisted, licking off her little finger with evident relish.

"You give that here," Veda said angrily. "Got no more sense than that little one. Done everything you wanted all your life, an' now we got real trouble you can't stop. Well, believe you me, you'll be learning to do what yer' told the next few days. Like to see you act that way jest once with that young doctor 't was here sticking needles in you."

"Veda!" Barbara's face blanched at the reminder, and Gladys got angrily to her feet, easing Ginny, now asleep, onto the couch.

"Lissen, Missus Mitchell." The maid stopped stirring and turned to her purposefully. "I think we could use some plain talkin' around here. You keep tryin' to make out nothin's the matter, when we all know there's plenty that's the matter. Every which way I turn somebody's trying to keep something back from the next person. And some of the lies I heard on that radio! They got no business—"

"What lies, Veda?" Barbie broke in excitedly. "What did they say on the radio that—"

"Keep quiet, Barbara. Don't interrupt. I don't know what you think you heard on the radio that wasn't so, Veda, but I'm sure the people up there know more about what's going on than you do."

"Mebbe so—an' mebbe there's plenty they ain't tellin'. I keep tryin' to do like you want—an' don't think," she added stiffly, "that I ain't grateful fer you helpin' me out when them men came draggin' me in here. I ain't fergot that, nor I won't. But it jest ain't in my nature to keep coverin' things up that ought to be aired out."

"Well, *I'd* be grateful," Gladys retorted, "if you'd leave it to me to decide what needs airing and what doesn't. Barbie," she added as she saw the girl prepare to speak again, "Veda was perfectly right about your being too careless, and about how important it is for you to do what you're told right now. There's probably nothing to worry about any more, but until Daddy comes home I'd rather be a little extra careful. When he gets here he'll know what we should do."

"You goin' to keep right on—" Veda clamped her mouth on the words and vented her feelings on the waffle batter. Barbie went sulkily over to the radio and squatted down again in front of it.

"…Andreas Popoulisk, June Quest, B. K. Quiller, Lionel Quist…"

They've passed it, she thought. They went right by M, and I wasn't listening.

She cleared her throat. "Barbie," she called quietly, "Barbie."

The face that turned to her was still sullen. "What do you want?"

"Please keep your voice down. I want to know…were you listening? I mean, when they read the names."

The girl motioned impatiently toward the radio.

"I know, they're reading them now, but…" *Why* wouldn't she understand? "When they read the M's, was…Daddy's name there?" Barbara shook her head. "No *what?* You weren't listening or the name wasn't there?"

"I was listening," Barbara said briefly, and turned her attention back to the radio.

Gladys forced herself to stay calm. There was no sense in letting the quarrel enlarge itself. She walked back across the room, to where Veda had established the temporary kitchen on the hall table.

"What can I do?" she asked, trying to sound as if nothing had happened.

"Everything's done." Veda pointed to the indicator on the waffle iron. "One of 'em'll be ready for Ginny in a minute."

Gladys went back again across the room and roused the little girl. "Waffles!" she announced as soon as Ginny had one eye open. That brought the other one wide open right away.

"Come on, we'll get washed up." She led the little girl up the stairs, past the enticing odor that was beginning to bubble out of the top of the waffle iron. When they got down again Veda was pouring fresh batter, and Barbie was already settled with a plate and cup.

"Waffles?" Ginny called from halfway down. "And cocoa too." Veda answered her.

"That was a good idea." Gladys smiled at the other woman. "Thought I'd try an' save the milk. That hot chocolate you got, it's got powdered milk already in. Seems to me like we could keep what fresh we got for the mornin'."

They got Ginny settled next to her sister, with a syrup-laden waffle and a cup of steaming cocoa.

"Now that's hot," Veda warned. "Don't you try an' drink it too fast." She went back to the waffle iron and brought out a crisp new one. "There's fer you, Missus Mitchell."

"You take it," Gladys urged her. "I'll wait for the next one."

"Now you ain't had a thing to eat since you woke up," Veda protested. "You take this one. I'll have another one ready in a jiffy."

"We'll split it," Gladys decided, and cut it down the middle as she spoke. She moved one half to an empty plate and found a cup of coffee waiting for her. Veda poured a second cup for herself.

"Good thing you got used to drinking it black when you was on your diet," Veda said, almost with a smile. "We got to hang onto our milk now."

And suddenly it was all right. The quarreling and confusion were over. She sat down next to the children, and Veda came to join them a moment later, with a fresh waffle to divide among them.

"I'll watch the next one." Barbie had already finished her first and refused any part of the reinforcements. She felt the change in the atmosphere too. Passing in back of Gladys, on her way to the improvised kitchen in the hall, she stooped suddenly to hug her mother, for no reason at all. Then she turned on another light. There was music on the radio again. Ginny looked up and smiled a sticky, syrup-encased smile at the world in general.

"This is fun, Mommy," she announced. "Why doesn't Daddy come home?"

THE RESCUE

"I'm lost," he said. "I've got to get home." They couldn't hear him; they wouldn't listen. It was like a dream, trying to say something and never getting it out.

It was a dream. He remembered, in the dream, that he'd had them before, times when he had to talk about it or bust, and there was nobody to talk to. Nobody wanted to talk about it. Nobody wanted to think about it. Then he'd go to bed and dream. Great pink clouds and searing fires exploding. He'd wake up in a sweat and reach out to touch her. He'd feel her breathing evenly under his hand, and see the shadow of the trees outside, and everything would be all right.

"Just tell me how to get home," he said in the dream. "I'm all right. I'm lost, that's all. Listen, bud, how do I get home from here?"

They kept dragging him along, pulling him when he didn't walk. They wore suits like divers, but more like asbestos than rubber, and they had helmets closed over their faces. They couldn't answer him; they couldn't talk through the helmets. Maybe they couldn't hear him either.

They pushed him into a big truck and shut the door behind him. There were a lot of other men inside, standing up, and sitting on the floor. Some were lying down, stretched out on the floor. One of them looked dead, maybe only unconscious. Some of the men were talking, and some were swearing. A lot of them had burns or cuts. There was blood on everything, and a bad smell. Somebody was crying.

A little light came through the truck from a pane of glass set in front, near the driver's cab. He edged his way through the crowd to the pane of glass and began tapping on it. A man on the seat turned around and shook a fist at him, but he kept tapping, patiently, till the man turned around again.

"I've got to get home," he said then. "Let me out. I have to go home."

CHAPTER FIFTEEN

IT WAS ALREADY DARK when Gladys left Ginny asleep upstairs. She came down to find Barbie lying flat on her stomach in front of the radio, intent on the pages of a heavy volume she had found in Tom's room. From time to time she flipped a page with one languid finger, moving no other muscle except her bare calf, which waved with pendulum regularity in the air. She abandoned the book long enough to greet her mother with the news that the fifteen-minute curfew warning had just been announced.

"I guess we better get the door and windows closed in the cellar," Gladys decided. "I hope it's all right down there now."

Veda came in, drying her hands on her apron. "Kitchen's okay," she said. "I was washing up, an' I shet up ever'thing in there. Got the door down to the cellar open, an' it smells like it'd be all right to go down."

"Well, I guess I might as well get it over with."

After that she could go up and change. She wondered why she hadn't thought of it before she came down, and decided it was just as well. She hadn't looked in a mirror since she'd got out of bed; out of long habit she raised her hand to her hair, trying to smooth it into place, but it was too tangled; it felt gritty and nasty under her fingers.

"I could go down, Missus Mitchell," Veda offered. "Don't matter if I get a bit dusty, this bein' a work dress."

"Don't be silly. I'm all dirty anyway."

She left Veda at the head of the cellar steps and groped for the light switch. He never did fix it! she thought, and went cautiously down the stairs, planting each foot in the precise center of the narrow tread, sniffing at every step for traces of gas.

She put foot at last on solid cement flooring and flipped another switch, flooding the whitewashed laundry room with light. That wasn't very smart, she thought. Suppose there was still some gas…

But she didn't smell anything, and nothing had happened when she used the light. It must be all right.

The door that led through to the meter, in the furnace room, was closed. She was sure she'd left it open. The latch was rusty, and she had to struggle with it. They never used that door. *I'd remember if I'd closed it,* she thought.

She stopped fighting the latch and stood still a minute to drive the tenseness from her muscles. She tried to think back to the last time she left the cellar, but all she could remember was the wonderful moment when the outside door opened and she stumbled up the stairs to breathe sweet air again. The rest was a blur.

Suppose she had closed it then? It was almost worse that way. The door was tight; it would keep out the gas. If she hadn't really got it turned off before, if it was still leaking, then when she opened the door, there'd be that sickening smell again.

Oh, Jon! Jon wasn't there. He was in the city, and he couldn't help her. In the city! It was a shock to realize she could think that much now, think it in so many words, without trying to deny it.

She put her hand firmly on the latch and pushed down. Something made a scuttling noise, and instinctively she stepped back.

I told him there were mice down here, she thought angrily, and then forgot to be afraid. She tried once more and ignored the noise when it came again. Maybe it was something the latch did. Anyhow, it was silly to be scared by a fleeing mouse. She shoved the door open before she had a chance to become frightened again.

Bracing herself against the doorframe, she reached her arm around to the light switch.

Scraping, scuttling noise, and something fell loudly. No mouse did that!

"Who's there?" she called, knowing it was the wrong thing to do, standing there in the lighted doorway.

"Me—it's just me, Mrs. Mitchell."

A man's voice…a stranger…but he knew her name! With the light at her back, she couldn't see more than a few feet in front of her. From every object in the room, small or large, a deepening shadow stretched to inky gloom in the far corners. Over all, her own shadow bulked. She tried to find him by his voice, but muted echoes spread the sound too much.

A dark shape detached itself from the looming black furnace and turned gradually into the figure of a man. She wanted to scream, to run, but, without knowing why, she knew she had to stay quiet.

He was close now, and she couldn't see his face. There was nothing familiar about him.

"Who are you?" The panic-sharp whisper bounced back at her from the echoing walls.

"Don't be alarmed, Mrs. Mitchell, it's just me—Garson Levy."

Of course! The voice had awakened recognition, even before she could fit a name to it.

"What are you doing here? How did you—" That was silly. It was perfectly obvious how he had got in. "I was just coming down to lock everything up," she finished.

"I'm terribly sorry." Gladys was startled to see her own distress honestly mirrored on his face. "I didn't mean to frighten you. I shouldn't have broken in this way, but I had to get in someplace during the curfew patrol."

"I better get things closed up here before someone else gets the same idea," Gladys said dryly. She walked over to the nearest window and slammed it down.

Silently he went to the next one and closed it himself. When the door was closed and bolted and all the windows locked, he turned to her again.

"I can leave now if you prefer, Mrs. Mitchell," he said stiffly. "I'm afraid I rather took advantage of Barbara's offer. But I hope you understand that I didn't expect to stay here."

"Barbara's offer?" she broke in.

"Yes, to come ba—oh, I see. Of course I thought you knew. I *am* sorry." He hesitated. "I can go right away, but if you don't mind too much, I'd like to wait until the patrol is over. It's just another twenty minutes or so—and for your sake as well as mine it's better if I'm not caught leaving here."

"Well, why on earth did you come out again?" Gladys asked irritably. "If you keep wandering around when you're not supposed to you're bound to get caught sooner or later."

"I didn't have much choice. My landlady was under strict orders to notify the Security Office when I came in. She gave me a bed in her own apartment instead, and got some clothes from my room, but she could hardly keep me there."

"You mean you don't have anyplace to stay?"

"I'm afraid not," he admitted.

It was hard to stay angry at him. If he hadn't come to warn them about Barbie...

If he hadn't come the urinalysis would have told them anyhow—a little later. Perhaps too late.

She studied the man in front of her. Nothing extraordinary about him. Nothing, that is, except the fact that he was in her cellar. He didn't look like a madman, or a hero either. He looked like a scholarly middle-aged man who never remembered to have his suit pressed.

He ran his hand nervously through the thick gray waves of his hair and she saw why he always had a slightly wild look.

"What are you going to do when you leave here?" She tried to be stern. "Where are you going to go?"

He shrugged. "Try to find a place to stay…try to get some papers… try to get into the hospital." He dismissed the subject. "Have you heard anything about Barbara yet?"

"They're taking a blood test," she told him briefly. "They called up about the analysis and said she was exposed, but they didn't seem to know whether she's sick yet. Why shouldn't you be able to get into the hospital?"

"A matter of identity. When they found out who I was they decided they'd rather have me in jail. I'm dangerous," he added bitterly. "Because I kept saying this was going to happen. Worse yet, I tried to prevent it. That makes me a public enemy."

"Well, surely they won't refuse to take care of you!"

"Maybe not," he agreed. "But, frankly, I don't care to make the experiment. From my earlier experiences, I think they're shooting first and asking questions afterwards."

Gladys remembered the men who had brought Veda in that morning. The one with the notebook might ask questions. The other one—there was no way to tell what the other one would do.

Suddenly she wanted to help him. But she *couldn't* keep him in the house.

"Are you…hungry?" she asked inadequately. "If there's anything at all I can do for you before you go…?" She was ashamed, but she couldn't help it.

Surprisingly, he smiled. "That's very kind of you, Mrs. Mitchell, but I had something to eat just before I left…home."

"Well, if there's anything at all…" Anything, anything, she promised him silently. Anything except staying here.

"There's really nothing." He glanced at his watch. "I can leave in a few minutes now. Tell me about Barbara."

"They have to wait and make two tests before they can tell."

Levy nodded. "Did they say anything else about the urinalysis?"

"They said there was some alpha emitter present," she quoted carefully, "but it didn't seem to be a sufficient quantity to make her sick." A question came to her mind. "But if it takes two blood counts, how could *you* tell right away? Is there some other way?"

"I don't know for sure how sick I am," he explained. "But I could tell I'd been exposed to heavy radiation because I know what my normal blood count is. And I also know I haven't been exposed recently to any other diseases or infections that would cause a drop in the white-cell count—flu or a strep infection, for instance. The doctor doesn't—"

"Missus Mitchell!" The call, shrill and imperative, came from far away. Veda was in the living room, Gladys thought, and then heard the approaching footsteps. "Missus Mitchell!"

"Get back there." She pointed to the far corner of the furnace room, where she had found him. "Hurry, please. Where she can't see you."

She turned and ran for the stairs. Hot and breathless, she met Veda at the kitchen door.

"What is it?"

"That Mr. Turner jest come in, an' the doctor with him. Mr. Turner's about ready to take a fit, he's that hot on talkin' to you."

What am I going to do? Veda in the kitchen, Edith Crowell sleeping upstairs, and now the squadmen in the living room—with a hunted man hiding in the basement!

"Somethin' wrong, Missus Mitchell? You run up here like the devil was after you, an' now you can't catch yer breath to walk in there."

"Oh…one of the windows," she improvised. "I couldn't get it closed, and I got mad at it." She smiled. "Then I got scared when I heard you call. You sounded so *urgent.* I didn't know what—" She had to think of something to do; she had to think fast.

"It ain't me that's so urgent," Veda retorted. "Only I don't think that Mr. Turner'll last the day if he don't see you soon. You better go on in. I'll fix the window."

"I guess I better." But she didn't move. She stood solidly where she was, blocking the doorway and the stairs.

"Barbie!" she called wildly. She couldn't think of anything better; this would have to do. Barbie wanted to help the man. Here was her chance. "Barbara!"

"Mom, it's the squad truck," the answer floated back. "Mr. Turner and Dr. Spinelli. They're waiting for you."

"I'll be right out. Come here a minute, will you?" Veda was watching her with a puzzled frown. "Barbie can fix the window," she explained hastily. "I don't want her around when I talk to the doctor." *That's* true enough, Lord knows.

She ignored Veda's silent stare of disapproval. One thing at a time.

"Barbie, there's a window down there I couldn't shut. Will you see what you can do?"

"But, Mom, I *told* you—they're here, and they want another blood sample."

"I'll go see Mr. Turner." Gladys overrode her protests. "That window's got to be closed."

"But I have to give Pete some more blood—I mean Dr. Spinelli." The slip tended to spoil the patiently tolerant quality of her explanation, but it didn't stop her. "Veda can—"

"*Pete* can wait a minute. You go fix that window," Gladys said firmly. "I want to talk to your Dr. Spinelli too."

"Oh, Mom, I wish you'd stop worrying so much." Barbara was sure she understood now. "He doesn't know anything yet. He would have told me if he did," There was a tinge of pride in her assurance, just enough to bring Gladys' earlier irritation at the doctor back into focus.

He would, would he? I'm going to have a few words with that young man, she promised herself. "I'll worry just as much as I want to," she told her daughter blithely. In spite of all its dangers, there was a certain relish in the situation.

"As a matter of fact that's not what I was worried about. Perhaps you'll understand when you're older." A few minutes older, I mean. "Can't you manage the window by yourself?" She was being deliberately provoking, making it essential for the girl to do the job herself. But she had to give some sort of warning too. How, in front of Veda?

"Be careful," she called as Barbie started angrily down the stairs. "I think there are"—the word popped into her mouth of its own accord—*"mice* down there."

CHAPTER SIXTEEN

"HELLO." The two men waited for her in the living room, ominous in their heavy suits, their faces shadowed by the raised visors of their helmets. "I was just downstairs, closing the cellar windows."

She couldn't keep her hands quiet. Nervously she straightened lamps and ash trays, patted cushions into place.

Neither of them said anything. Even Jim Turner's hail-fellow was missing.

What's wrong? She stopped bustling and turned to face them. Fear gave way to amusement and then to acute self-consciousness, as she realized why they were staring. I never did go up and change! She yearned for a mirror and was glad she couldn't see one. Aggressively she turned to the doctor.

"I don't suppose you have any news yet about my daughter?"

She was pleased to hear her voice stay steady, not too intense, not too worried.

"Not really," he said. "If she were sick enough for the first count to show anything the analysis would have looked worse than it did. I want to take another sample now. We should have a definite answer for you tomorrow."

"Well then…" It wasn't so easy to keep her voice steady this time. "The first sample wasn't too encouraging?"

"In a sense it was," he hedged. "But I'd rather not raise your hopes—or hers either—until we know more. I hope Barbara's not getting panicky. I explained it all to her this morning, and I think she understands."

"Well, as long as *she* understands…"

He didn't miss the edge in her voice. "I hope she didn't get too worried by what I told her," he said unhappily. "She seemed to take it all right, didn't get flustered by the needle or anything, and then she began asking questions. You weren't around"—he was floundering now—"and the lady who was there—I think Barbie called her Veda—" Barbie! Barbie and Pete. Gladys raised mental eyebrows and lost her grip on the mood of irritation.

He felt the change and gathered assurance. "She said you were sleeping and she thought you shouldn't be awakened. I didn't want to wait to take the sample, and I just explained as much as I thought Barbara could understand."

Turner was getting impatient. "That's okay, *Doc*," he said, and turned to Gladys. "I told him to go ahead, soon as the kid told us her story." The subject was closed now; he made that clear. She had lost the initiative as soon as she stopped being angry, and the squadman was taking over.

"Where'd the kid go to?" he asked. "We got to be running along in a minute. Just finished curfew patrol, and we have to check in at headquarters. I figured it would speed things up some for you if we took another sample back to the lab on our way."

"Barbie's just finishing up in the cellar," Gladys said quickly. "I'll get her right away."

"Don't you bother. *Doc*'ll find her," Turner insisted. "I want to talk to you a minute. They wouldn't wake you up when I was here before. You stay up all night?"

"No—that is, yes." She edged toward the door, staying in front of Spinelli.

"Oh, Doctor, I wanted to tell you—"

"Yes?"

"I'm worried about Ginny," she blurted out. "Veda said she didn't eat any lunch, and she seems so listless—it's probably just nerves—being shut in and no one to play with, but…I don't know. Maybe I'm just getting jittery now?"

"It doesn't hurt to be a little extra careful. I could take a blood count now," he said doubtfully, "but there's no sense bothering her unless we have something definite to go on. Suppose I check with the lab on her urinalysis?" he suggested. "Then we'll know whether there's anything to worry about."

"Thank you. I'll go get Barbie now," she said breathlessly. "I'll be right back."

"Ain't that just like a woman!" Turner's laugh boomed good-naturedly. "Up all night, slept all day, and now I bet she's worried how her kitchen looks. You sit down an' take it easy, Miz Mitchell." He took her arm and led her to a chair.

"Go on, *Doc.*" He threw the words over his shoulder impatiently. "You can find the kid, can't you?" He settled Gladys in the chair and turned to face the younger man. "You'll be using the kitchen to take that sample, won't you?" he asked meaningfully. The doctor nodded, but still hesitated, standing irresolute in the dining-room door.

Gladys had a sudden horrified memory of the moment that morning when the Security man thought she had some nefarious reason for wanting to go upstairs. Was that why Jim Turner made her stay here now? Were they suspicious? Had anyone seen that man come in?

"Barbie!" she called.

There was no answer. And under the pressure of Turner's will the doctor started slowly through the door. She *had* to warn Barbara…

"Veda!" It was a risk, but less than the other. "Veda, will you tell Barbie the doctor wants her?"

It was all she could do. She had to pay attention to Turner now.

"How come your cellar windows were open?" he asked. Was it interest or suspicion? There was no way to tell.

Belatedly she explained about the gas and about what she had done. "I don't know if that was the best thing to do," she wound up, "but maybe you could take a look at it later on? Next time you come. I know you're in a hurry now."

"I guess we could take time to look at it right now," the big man decided.

"It could wait," she said doubtfully, trying to sound as if she didn't care. Why did *everything* have to lead to the cellar?

"I'm not so busy I can't do that much for a neighbor," he said, waving aside her protests. "I'll just take a look. Might be you shouldn't stay here. And I don't know if I'll have a chance to get back tonight. I was wondering," he chuckled, eying her greasy slacks again as she stood up, "what you got yourself up in that rig for. You look like you could be Barbie's sister instead of her ma."

"I'll have to wear it more often." She produced a smile and raised her arm again in the futile habitual gesture, patting and pushing with her fingers at the tangled waves of her hair. Turner stood still, staring at her, and she didn't know why she was blushing.

She couldn't see, as the big squadman did, how the motion of her arm accentuated the curve of her body inside Jon's big work shirt; or how the loose shirt, tucked tightly into her slacks, flared out above the waist; she didn't know how the rough clothes and rolled-up sleeves, the grease stain on her leg, the smudges on her arms, created an absurd and delightful effect of femininity on masquerade—or how the uninvited color, flooding up under her clear skin, heightened the contrast of her clothing.

She saw only the dust on her hands after she had touched her hair, and felt the steady eyes of her neighbor's husband staring at her. And she knew it was not suspicion that made him so anxious to help.

She took a step forward, for the first time with assurance. She could hear Barbie and the doctor in the kitchen. Surely any danger was past. Barbie must have gotten the man out.

Turner stepped forward as she did, brushing close to her, too close, before either of them could check the momentum of the stride. Even as he stopped and balanced himself, waiting for her to go ahead, something far below the conscious level of her mind leaped up in frenzy.

Jon, oh, Jon! Come home!

With heavy footsteps following at her heels, she went into the kitchen, forced the cry of need from her mind. She had known Jim Turner for years, and there were more real things to worry about right now. Veda had started it, Veda with her silly talk in the bedroom, when she was only half awake. A man had brushed against her—not, she told herself, purposely. He had stopped as soon as he could. That was that. Forget it.

But the self-assurance she had gained in the moment at the doorway didn't leave her. Going through the kitchen, she questioned Barbie casually.

"It's okay, Mom, I got it fixed."

Gladys went on to the stairs with no show of hesitation. She was again acutely aware of Turner's bulk right behind her, and just before the light flashed on, she had an instant's fright as to what it might reveal. But both fears passed, and after only the hastiest eye-sweeping, she led the way into the furnace room.

The squadman sniffed the air and went over to study the meter.

"How'd you know what to do?" he asked. "I couldn't hardly do it better myself."

"You mean I did the right thing?" Approval tasted very sweet after the day's frustrations. "I was just guessing," she told him.

"Well, you guessed good. You got nothing to worry about."

"But what about getting it turned *on* again? Would it be safe?"

"That depends. Did you find out where the leak is?"

"No." She couldn't see how it would matter, but she told him about the pilot light on the stove.

"Out, was it?" He pulled at his lip thoughtfully. "I'll tell you," he said finally. "They haven't got it on the radio yet, because they don't want to get people worried, but there ain't going to be any gas pretty soon. As long as you got it turned off, you might just as well leave it that way."

"No gas? But what happened?"

"The way I heard it, they had an explosion in one of the mains, that cut off the—"

"Explosion!" she broke in. "I didn't know anything was hit near here. When did it happen?"

"Now don't go getting worried," he said hastily. "No bombs up here in our neck of the woods. It was some kind of accident they had, that's all. The real trouble is manpower. They just can't make repairs and keep the gas going. Pressure's pretty low already. How're you fixed for something to cook on? I could get you—"

"We have a hot plate we've been using," she told him quickly. "We can manage with that all right. But our hot-water heater is gas too," she remembered.

"Well now," he sympathized, "that could make it kind of tough on you, but one thing, it won't be for long. That's what I wanted to see you about. It's classified stuff, really, but I know you can keep your mouth shut. Thing is, we're making plans right now for evacuation—cleaning out this whole section."

"There *were* bombs!" she breathed.

"Now, Gladys, I *told* you there weren't. It's supplies and manpower where the trouble is. Food's too hard to bring in. And we can't use the men we got to fix gas mains and things like that, when we need every one of them to work in the city. Matter of fact, phone service might be out, too, pretty soon."

She shook her head doubtfully, and remembered that Dr. Levy had said something about bombs directly overhead, What connection was there?

"Now don't you worry about it," he said, misreading her troubled expression. "Things won't get too bad. It looks like the move'll start Thursday—Friday at the latest. There's plenty of food till then. An' I can see to it," he promised, "that you folks get onto the first train out."

"But…" She stopped. But I don't want to go. That would be a silly thing to say. It wasn't a matter of what she wanted.

"I can get you settled up at the camp too," he added. "We're taking over the Navy base up at Sampson. Beautiful country up there. I think I can work it for you to get into the staff quarters. Find something to put you in charge of, and that would give you a priority for the train seats too. That way, you won't be too crowded, and you won't have to wait around down here if things get bad."

"But—" she began again. "That's very kind of you, but there's really no need to take all that trouble. We'll manage."

"A man ought to at least look out for his friends!" Turner broke in indignantly. "It's no trouble anyhow. All I have to do is put in your name for some kind of supervisor's job, and the rest'll take care of itself."

"But there's nothing I can do," she protested. "I don't have any kind of training."

"You just leave that part of it up to me." He smiled and winked. "I'll figure something out."

I won't go. I won't. She almost said it out loud.

"Now, you understand," he reminded her, "you got to keep this to yourself. Even the boys on the truck don't know about it yet. We'll put out a warning on the radio pretty soon, but even then you better not say I told you. This is strictly confidential. Meanwhile," he went on, "you're better off not to bother with the gas or anything."

She couldn't listen any more. She thought she'd smother if she didn't get out of there, but he kept talking, rambling on about preparations and baggage limits, offering warnings and reassurances, to which she replied with forced monosyllables.

I won't go. I won't!

"Wouldn't hurt to get these windows boarded up, either," he was saying. He had gone over to look at the locks. "That maid of yours could do it for you. You got some lumber?"

She nodded, and he came back and looked down to see, for the first time, the horror in her face.

"Now, Gladys," he urged, "you got to be sensible. It's only a couple more days, and there's probably no danger at all. But if you board up the windows, then you're *sure*. No sense asking for trouble."

"You mean those gangs they've been talking about?"

"Well, what'd you think I meant?"

She shook her head. Everything was too confusing.

"Now you come on upstairs," he said. "There's nothing to get so scared about. Come on."

She nodded gratefully. That was what she wanted, to get out of the cellar, up to where the other people were, to where she could breathe again. When he reached out his hand to pat her shoulder reassuringly she turned swiftly, before he could feel the shudder his touch evoked. She ran all the way upstairs.

CHAPTER SEVENTEEN

VEDA WAS IN THE KITCHEN, cleaning up, but Gladys didn't stop there. The heavy footsteps were too close behind her, and she swept through to the living room where Barbie and the doctor were waiting. Blessedly the footsteps paused in their pursuit. She dropped into the big armchair and pressed her fingers hard against the rubbed nap of the upholstery. She was safe.

Muted conversation from the kitchen. She smiled a little, thinking he must be telling Veda about those windows, wanting to make sure it got done without frightening her any more. Then he came in, and through the hasty good-byes she used weariness as a defense, stayed in her chair, and let them go without a word.

Then Veda came in, stared at her curiously, and called Barbie out to the kitchen. She heard again the snatches of a quiet conversation, and then her daughter's careless feet on the cellar stairs. Then for a few long minutes there was absolute peace, and nothing to think about, time for her tortured mind to rest.

Too soon, Barbie was back again, dancing around the room with a suppressed excitement Gladys couldn't understand. Pete, she remembered. Barbie and Pete. Maybe it wasn't so funny. Maybe she should take it more seriously.

"Mom!" Barbie saw her eyes were open now. "Mom, I'm going down the cellar to fix the windows. Do you want to come down?"

"I can't, darling. I'm too tired."

"But, Mom, I'm going *down the cellar!*"

"Well, you've been there before!" She didn't want to sound cross. She smiled. "Very recently." It was something they shared. "I'm worn out, Babsy. You go down." She closed her eyes again, but Barbara didn't go.

Instead the girl came over and took both her hands, pulling a little, playfully.

"Please come down with me, Mom. You don't have to do anything."

Gladys opened her eyes in astonishment. Why should it mean so much?

"Please, Mom, it's…" She lowered her voice to almost a whisper. "It's Doc!" she said.

For a moment it didn't make sense, then Barbie added, "Doc Levy!"

Gladys was instantly fully awake. "What about him?" she demanded.

"He wants to talk to you."

"Where is he?"

"In the cellar, of course," Barbie said impatiently.

"Did he come *back?* When?"

"Come back?" The girl was bewildered. "He never *went* anywhere."

"But when I sent you down—before they first came—didn't you *warn* him?" That was impossible too. "He wasn't there when I went down with Mr. Turner," she finished.

"Oh, wasn't he?" Barbara was clearly delighted with the effect she was producing. "Of course I warned him," she teased, and added more soberly, "That's what he wanted to do—go away. But he didn't even know where he was going, and the truck was right in front of the house, so—"

"You mean he's still down there?"

"Sure!" Barbie totally misunderstood her mother's horrified intonation. "Now will you come down?"

"I certainly will!" Grimly Gladys followed her daughter through the dining room and into the kitchen. When she got down to the bottom of the cellar steps the air was already crackling with questions and confusion.

"But you told me you didn't have any place to—"

"Just a minute, Barbara," the teacher interposed. He turned to Gladys. "I'm sorry, Mrs. Mitchell. I'm afraid I didn't make things quite clear enough to Barbara. I shouldn't have come in at all, I suppose, but I really thought it would be all right—"

"Well, it *was* all right," Barbie insisted.

"It just happened to be," he said wearily. "Or rather, your mother made it so. But she can't keep on hiding me from Mr. Turner indefinitely. This time he was in a hurry. Next time he might not be."

"Well, next time you won't be in the cellar."

"Barbara, *will* you stop arguing? Dr. Levy knows what he wants to do."

The girl stared at her incredulously. "Well, don't you *want* him to—"

"You heard what your mother said, Barbara!" His tone was sharp. Gladys saw hurt succeed surprise on her daughter's face. "I'm sorry I chose such a bad time for my—visit, Mrs. Mitchell," he went on. "I didn't mean to endanger you, or even to cause a family upset." He was, oddly, being suavely polite, here in the basement, with his clothes dirty, a hammer dangling from his hand and the police after him.

"I really meant to leave as soon as the patrol was over, but Barbara convinced me it was unwise to go out while the truck was parked in front of the house. Then when she came down again..." He smiled a little sheepishly and waved the hammer in his hand to indicate the one boarded-up window. "Maybe I just took the first excuse I could find to stay a while longer, but—"

"Mother, he did *everything*," Barbie insisted. "All I did was hand him nails. I *tried* to do it myself, but everything kept going wrong."

The man's apologetic smile broke into a grin that gave his broad face, under the thatch of gray hair, a look of impish merriment. "I'm afraid Barbara's quite right," he said. "I couldn't stand watching the way she held that hammer, and I started out just to show her how. Then it seemed the least I could do, to pay for my keep, as it were, was to stay and finish the job. But"—he was serious again—"when I realized you didn't know I was still here I sent her up to get you."

Well, what am I supposed to say now? Gladys wondered. How could he take it all so casually, make jokes, and find cause for laughter? His own life was forfeit, and he was endangering theirs every minute he stayed. Get out of my house! her mind screamed at him, but she couldn't say it out loud.

"I see," she managed. "That was very thoughtful of you."

"Well, what are you going to do, Mother?" Barbara demanded coldly. "Are you going to make him go away after all he—"

"I think," he smiled ruefully, ignoring the girl, "I'd better go now. But there was another reason I wanted to talk to you, Mrs. Mitchell. I took a grand tour of your gas pipes while Barbara was upstairs, and I think I found your trouble. I don't know if you'll want to bother with it now, but it's just possible you could get it going again."

"Why, that would be wonderful! Is it safe, you think?"

"If I've diagnosed it right, it is." He walked over to the hot water heater. "I have a hunch all your trouble was in here. Of course it could be in the pipes," he added, "but I just don't think so."

"What could the heater have to do with it?" Gladys wanted to know.

"I think that's where the gas was escaping from. It occurred to me when you mentioned the pilot light went out. From what Mr. Turner said—"

"You heard all that?" Gladys interrupted. *"Where were you?"*

"Oh, I never told you!" Barbara seized the opening. "I ought to make you guess!" Delightedly she stretched out the moment. "You'd never think of it. He was in the clothes drier!"

"And a very dry, clean drier, too," he put in. "I'm afraid I *did* overhear most of your conversation—or rather," he smiled, "Mr. Turner's."

Gladys flushed, remembering the nature of Turner's conversation. But Dr. Levy went on without giving her a chance to be embarrassed.

"From what he said about trouble in the mains, and from the way you described your trouble with the stove upstairs, I think that when the pilot light went out, upstairs, the one down here in the heater must have done the same. Only the big flame in the heater was on at the time, and that stayed open. It shouldn't," he added. "These gadgets are supposed to be foolproof. But something didn't work when it should have, and as soon as the gas came through again it began pouring out of the burner. If I'm right, then it's perfectly safe to turn the gas on again, just so the heater's off first."

He walked over to the meter and examined Gladys' handiwork.

"Will it go on again?" she asked. "Frankly, I don't know just what I did to it."

"You did the right thing anyhow. And a thorough job, too," he told her. "What did you use to turn it off?"

"There was a pliers." She looked around, trying to remember what she'd done with it.

He was back at the heater, fooling with handles and knobs. "That should do it," he said finally. "This thing's off tight now. You can turn on the gas any time. All you have to do is screw that valve out—the one you closed before—but you better check up carefully after you turn it on, and make sure I'm right. If you come down every half hour or so you'll be able to notice the smell long before there's any danger, just in case there really is a leak somewhere."

"I don't know…" Gladys hesitated. "I'd—isn't there any other way to tell?"

"No safe way," he said, "unless you're sure you know what you're doing. You'd have to crawl all over the place to follow the pipes."

"Well," she said doubtfully, "we'll see. But thank you, anyhow. It was very kind of you."

"Of course," Barbara said coldly, "it wouldn't occur to you that Doc—oh, never mind," she finished helplessly.

Gladys looked wearily from her daughter to the teacher. The man ran his hand through his hair, brushed off the dusty sleeves of his jacket, and straightened his tie.

"I—" It was his turn now to be embarrassed. "In spite of my perhaps ill-placed humor before, Mrs. Mitchell, I hope you realize I wasn't really looking for an—excuse. I've stayed too long already."

"You've been...very kind," Gladys repeated inadequately. There must be something she could say or do, something that would help. "I'm afraid," she said weakly, "I haven't exactly—well, I certainly haven't thanked you for all you've done."

"Please, Mrs. Mitchell," he said uncomfortably, "that's not necessary. Believe me, I realize just how difficult it's been."

"The only difficult thing anybody's done," Barbara said bitterly, "was your coming here last night to warn us."

Gladys felt miserably ashamed of her own fears. She was tired and mixed up, torn between pity for the man and terror of having him in the house. And things would only be more complicated if she admitted to herself that she was beginning to like him. What Barbara wanted wasn't really so unreasonable. What if he did stay a little longer? Turner certainly wouldn't be back again soon.

In the end it was her weariness that won.

"It might be a good idea if you took a look outside, Barbara," Dr. Levy said. "I'd hate to add any more to my sins by involving you people now."

Wordlessly the girl started for the stairs, but Gladys put out a hand to stop her.

"Dr. Levy." She turned to the man and gave him a pleading look, begging him to understand just what she meant. "I want you to know," she began cautiously, "that I really do appreciate all you've done. I'm awfully tired, and I'm not sure I'm being very clear, but if—well, if you would like to stay awhile, I'm sure it would be a big help to us. I..." She tried to make it easier. "I know I could never manage the gas myself," she added.

She was grateful when Barbara took it upon herself to override his protests, leaving her to escape to the comfort of Jon's big chair upstairs. She could rest now, without quarrels or exertions. She didn't have to think about windows or gas; she didn't have to argue with Barbie.

There was music on the radio again. She closed her eyes, trying to bring Jon back into the room, as she had tried the night before. But he wouldn't come; she couldn't imagine him there at all. He was gone.

In the last war there had been a day when, suddenly, she couldn't remember what he looked like. She had stared at his picture and the face on it had been a stranger's. But that was after months of separation. This was just...not even...two days.

Veda came in, and Gladys opened her eyes in greeting, then closed them again when she saw nothing was required of her. Veda picked out a magazine and sat down on the sofa. She must be tired too.

Everything was extraordinarily peaceful. Music on the radio, down low, pages turning once in a while, Ginny asleep upstairs. *Edie Crowell is asleep up there too.* Ginny asleep. Barbie, boarding up windows…a stranger hiding in the cellar…She wouldn't think of those things. A man fixing the gas, she corrected herself. Turner couldn't fix it, she thought, but Jim Turner was one more person she didn't want to think about.

She wouldn't answer the phone either. She'd just let it ring. But it made too much noise.

"Missus Mitchell!" She was supposed to get up now. Veda had answered it.

"I don't want to talk to anybody."

"Yes, you do. You come talk now,"

It was something good. *It was good news!* She ran to the phone and took it from Veda's extended hand.

"Yes?"

"This is Peter Spinelli, Mrs. Mitchell. I had a minute before we left headquarters, so I thought I'd let you know. Barbie's all right."

CHAPTER EIGHTEEN

"But how could they know so *soon?*" Barbie left a thoroughly embraced Veda brushing off cellar dust and spun back to her mother. "I thought it took hours!"

"He said it didn't take long to make the count—just waiting for them to get around to it. But Dr. Peter Spinelli, for some unknown reason, wanted to find out about Miss Barbara Mitchell right away, so he went right in and did it himself."

She did not add that Squadman James Turner had been so concerned about Mrs. Gladys Mitchell that he had procured the difficult lab pass that made the quick test possible. Watching Barbie's glee, she dismissed the disquieting obligation. Time enough to think of that later. She felt as if she had just awakened from a long, long sleep—far more refreshed than when she had actually got out of bed, five hours earlier.

"Hey, I've got to finish those windows! It's getting late." Barbara stopped prancing. "Come with me, Mom. Keep me company."

"All right," Gladys agreed.

"Missus Mitchell." Veda restored her magazine to its precise spot in the rack. "If there's nothin' special you want me for, I think mebbe I'll get to bed now." She covered a yawn. "Looks like there ain't no call fer me to set up no more."

"Do you mean to say you were staying up just on account of me?" Gladys asked indignantly. "You shouldn't have."

"Yer' feelin' pretty chipper now," Veda stopped her, "but you didn't look so hot a ways back. Anyways, Mr. Turner, he give me strict orders to look out fer you. I jest didn't dare do nothin' else."

The remark brought a general laugh, but made Gladys acutely aware of another worry she had deferred. Something would have to be done about Jim Turner.

The music on the radio ended with a noisy flourish, and a man's voice announced the ten o'clock news. For the first time since the speeches the afternoon before, Gladys found she really wanted to hear a broadcast all the way through.

"Let's go downstairs after the news is over," she suggested. The two of them settled down together in front of the radio, and Barbie accepted the decision willingly.

To Gladys' surprise, most of the news was encouraging. No further attempts at bombing attacks had been made. Retaliation was already in effect. Then the startling, unexpected information that all action against the enemy was by means of remote-control aircraft; land forces would be used only for mopping up.

Tom was safe! Whatever they had him doing at address unknown, he was not landing in enemy territory or fighting the dread sort of man-to-man battle they'd had in the last war.

There were reports of communication hookups to all parts of the country, of trains and rails repaired for evacuation purposes, of supplies being brought into big-city areas.

The national news was followed by a series of brief reports on local matters. There was something about the explosion in the gas main that Turner had mentioned; and there was also a report about the preparation of the Navy base for use as an evacuation camp. There were new hospitals opened up, railroad lines put in use, telephone services repaired.

The broadcast ended with a repetition of the request for temporary homes for homeless children.

Impulsively Gladys got up and went to the phone. When she came back, after the now familiar struggle with operators and switchboards, she felt obscurely pleased, even while she reckoned up the new difficulties the decision would bring upon her. But now that she knew Barbie was all right the whole thing seemed much easier. It might, in fact, give Barbara something to do when boredom and confinement began to tell on them all. And certainly it would be wonderful for Ginny. All in all, it might save more trouble than it made.

They started reading off the long lists of victims and survivors found in the city, and Gladys let her thoughts drift away. The news all sounded so good, she reflected, things seemed to be improving every hour. Then it occurred to her that nothing had been said about the imminent failure of the gas supply or about the possible discontinuance of telephone service. The news of the evacuation camp's preparation did not include any mention of the projected mass evacuation. It wasn't all quite as good as it sounded after all; maybe the other part, the big news about the whole country, was weeded out the same way.

"Mother?" Gladys raised her eyes from the tufted carpet and looked at Barbie inquiringly.

"I just wanted to tell you, I think it was awfully nice of you to change your mind about those kids—and about Doc Levy."

"I didn't exactly change my mind about him," Gladys told her. "It bothers me, just having him in the house. Maybe I'd feel better if I knew what it was that he did that makes him have to hide, but—well, I just don't like the whole thing!"

"But you *said*—"

"I know what I said. I said that if he wanted to stay awhile it would be a big help to us. It was perfectly true, and I don't see what else I could have said at that point. I know he's done a lot for us, but frankly I'll be a lot happier when he's gone."

"You mean you're still going to make him go? You're not going to let him stay here?"

"Suppose *you* tell me where we'd keep him—if not in the clothes drier? And how we'd keep Ginny from finding out? Or Veda?"

"He could stay up in the attic," Barbie insisted. "You know how Tom and I used to play up there when we were kids? There's plenty of room for a man to hide behind those boards, too, if he had to."

When we were kids! Staring at her daughter in mingled shock and amusement, Gladys almost missed the rest of what Barbie said.

"Anyhow," the girl finished, "I don't see why they shouldn't know."

"Barbie, you know Ginny would never be able to keep quiet about it. Even if we could make her understand it was a secret she couldn't keep it. And now," she added as inspiration struck her, "with those children coming—well, it's just impossible."

"And what about *Veda?*" The question did not come from Barbie.

Fully dressed, and not looking the least bit sleepy, Veda was firmly planted in the dining-room door, arms folded on her chest, eyes flashing.

"How long…?" Gladys started.

"Not long enough," she said. "I don't yet know his name or what he's doing down there."

"Have you *seen* him?"

"Yes, I seen him. Crawlin' all over the floor down there like an animal. This one," she said, pointing a long arm accusingly at Barbie, "tryin' to tell me she fixed that gas up her own self. *You're* right smart at keepin' things to yerself," she accused Gladys. "But if Miss Snippity here wants to know your secrets, my advice is, don't tell her. She can't keep 'em."

One baleful glare stopped Barbara's retort before it got fairly started. "Now, lissen, Missus Mitchell, I ain't forgettin' you did me a favor this mornin'. But I've had to do some fancy remindin' myself the last couple of hours. Mebbe you think what them fellers said about me is true, an' so I'll put up with anything. Well, it ain't true. I never did a thing in my life I'd be afraid to admit out loud, an' up till right now I thought the same about you. But if it's got so you'd set your own daughter to lyin'—"

"Veda!" Gladys protested. "I know perfectly well you haven't done anything wrong. And neither have I. You ought to realize that."

"Well, I'm right glad to hear you say so. But just don't you mind, I want to have my say out this once. If you folks kin make up yer minds to let me know what's goin' on around here, and if it don't seem wrong to me, that's one thing. But if you can't see fit to tell me what that man is doin' here I don't see nothin' for it but to get out—even if it means I got to call up the Security men an'—"

"Veda!" Barbara, appalled, forgot to be cowed. "You wouldn't *tell* them! You wouldn't tell about Dr. Levy?"

"No'm." Veda directed her answer to Gladys, seeing the same question in her eyes. "No'm, I wouldn't. I told you I ain't forgot about this mornin' and ain't like to. Only I jest can't stay here unless we get things straightened up. I'm sorry, Missus Mitchell, but it ain't *jest* that man. I tried to talk to you before and didn't get nowhere. But it ain't in me to keep on—"

"Of course you're going to stay, Veda." Gladys had finally recovered her self-possession. "You know we wouldn't let you go. Now sit down, will you, and give me a chance to tell you about it?"

Reluctantly the maid crossed the room and sat down. She listened, stiffly at first, while Gladys went over the whole story, some parts of which Barbara, too, was hearing for the first time. In the course of the tale Veda's indignation died away, but by the time it was done she was afire once more.

"You mean to set there an' tell me you let that man stay down in that cellar all this time," she demanded fiercely, "and him sick, too?" She got up and headed briskly for the kitchen.

After that Gladys felt she had lost all ability to be surprised. If she were still capable of it, nothing could have been stranger than the immediate warmth of the friendship between Veda and Garson Levy.

The woman, almost uneducated, opinionated, practical, and warmly emotional; the man, well informed, scientific, precise of speech and mannerism, a little too erudite, almost pedantic—it seemed there could hardly be two people with less in common.

Gladys sat and marveled, while the teacher weeded out his vocabulary, choosing words Veda would be sure to understand, taking care not to offend her, drawing her out. He wanted to know everything that had happened to her, what she'd seen and heard in the city and in the decontamination center.

It took a long time for the whole story to come out. Some of it they heard while Levy tested the kitchen range, and some while Veda filled all the remaining empty containers with boiling water. The teacher kept her talking while he devised airtight seals for jars and pitchers that had no tops, and longer still while they all sat drinking coffee and cocoa in the living room.

Veda told them how she had turned away the first people who tried to rouse her—two of the roomers who had taken it upon themselves to get everyone out of the house. She even told, with a deprecatory smile, how she stood cowering in a corner of the room, wrapped in her bathrobe, angrily convinced that her fellow tenants were drunk and violent in the middle of the afternoon.

She had steadfastly refused to open the door, and apparently the neighbors' interest in her welfare had not extended to knocking it down. She went back to bed with a firm resolution to have a long talk with the landlady, and went promptly back to sleep. The steady downpour of radioactive rain all that afternoon did not disturb her. It was after two o'clock in the morning when an official rescue crew came through the building, broke down the door, and dragged her out of bed and out of the house, with barely time to get her bathrobe on.

The rain was over by then and the street was bright with fires, raging in defiance of the lingering wetness. She didn't see much outside, however, because she was led directly from the house door to a big closed truck only a few feet away.

She shared the interior of the truck for more than an hour with the few other female survivors rescued in that neighborhood. She was the second one in, and when the truck started rolling steadily westward there were nine altogether—three cripples, one idiot, two drunks, two senile old ladies, and herself. As near as she could make out, everyone who was conscious and capable, as well as most of those who weren't, had fled the poisoned streets long ago.

The nine of them were unloaded in front of a big stone building that might have been a college, a library, or a museum, and taken through a little side entrance to a series of small rooms where they were subjected to indignities which Veda passed over without detail. These Gladys shrewdly guessed to be connected with a change of clothing and an assembly-line medical examination.

They had then been led through a series of rooms where unfamiliar machines, big and little, quiet and noisy, were aimed at her.

Levy explained that these must have been the testing devices for radiations and fission products. He seemed impressed at the number and size Veda reported, but Gladys was inclined to discount some of it. She was familiar with Veda's impressionability where machinery was concerned.

In any case she had been separated from her truck companions immediately afterward. Something was said about a hospital, so she assumed that was where the others were taken. She herself, it seemed, was in excellent health—considerably better than she had ever thought. She was taken to another large building, located within the same roped-off area of several city blocks. This one was easily identifiable as a public school.

The entire place, Dr. Levy said, was undoubtedly the Washington Heights Decontamination Center.

In the school she was taken to a brightly lit room where several men questioned her, over and over again, about her reasons for sealing her room. In endless embarrassed succession she repeated the same answers to the same questions, until eventually one of them decided on the trip to the Mitchells' to check on her story.

It was almost midnight by the time Veda finished. Then, when Levy found out how long she'd been without sleep, he did something Gladys would have sworn to be impossible, and persuaded her to go off to bed, leaving the dishes for him to do.

Barbara was half asleep, too, but reluctant to leave a gathering where she had acquired such a wealth of information. Gladys let her stay up for the twelve o'clock news, then sent the girl off to bed. She herself went up to the attic to fix a cot for Dr. Levy. There was no longer any question that he had become a semi-permanent guest.

When she had finished she called down to let him know it was ready, but she didn't go back to the living room.

For all his redeeming traits, she still found the teacher hard to talk to. Perhaps it was because, even now, she felt so strongly the indefinite menace that his presence in the house implied, perhaps because everything connected with him continued to be so unrealistically melodramatic. She wanted to know more about him—a great deal more—but she could not bring herself to go down and question him.

She opened up the hall closet again and began working through a pile she had started the night before, reflecting uncomfortably on the fact that while he was drawing out Veda's story Levy had told little or nothing of his own.

She dug down among the old work clothes and camping things, refusing to think about the extra baggage she would be allowed if she took Jim Turner's offer. She was going to *have* to do something about that.

Ruefully she wondered which man was more of a problem. Then, underneath Tom's old tennis racket, she found Jon's *Camper's Manual* and opened it curiously.

CHAPTER NINETEEN

THE CRASH CAUGHT HER in the middle of the chapter on first aid. She dropped the book and flew downstairs before she could think about it and get too frightened to go down at all. It was not loud enough to be an explosion; it was too loud to be furniture or a lamp. There was a battering sound to it and, mixed with it, the tinkling shatter of glass. Everything was all right in the living room, but Dr. Levy was nowhere in sight.

Gladys went back to the kitchen and pushed open the swinging door into darkness.

"Close it!" That was Dr. Levy. "For God's sake, shut the door. Don't let the light in." He was shouting in a whisper, if that were possible. He seemed to be across the room, down near the floor, and moving around. It felt as if she stood in the lighted doorway forever, but she realized that she must have acted quickly to close it when she heard his grunted "Good."

"Get down," he ordered, still whispering, and she obeyed. On the other side of the room the door to Veda's bedroom creaked cautiously open, but no light showed through.

"It's all right, Veda," Gladys called. "We're out here." Another thundering crash at the kitchen door and the little glass that was left in the panes fell tinkling to the floor. It's all right...what made her say a thing like that?

"What's the matter? What's happening?" Veda's voice was a hoarse whisper.

"Come over here," Levy told Gladys. He was moving around again. "And keep low. Stay down as close to the floor as you can."

Something hit the door again, and the whole room shook.

Veda came up next to Gladys. "Is it that gang they was talking about on the radio?"

Gladys nodded, then realized it was too dark for Veda to see her. "Yes."

She felt something being put into her hand. "Give it to Veda," Levy said. Dutifully she passed on the heavy iron skillet. He kept handing her things. Another skillet, a carving knife, the iron and, ludicrously, a rolling pin—anything he could lay his hands on that could possibly be a weapon.

"Pile them up in front of you."

Gladys did as she was told, simply because she knew nothing better to do.

"I'm going over behind the door on the other side," Levy whispered. He was kneeling down right in back of them, so they could both hear.

"You stay here together and when the door comes down throw the lighter things first, as fast as you can, and as much as you can. If there aren't many of them the confusion might be enough to stop them. If that doesn't work, use the heavier things, but you haven't got many of those, so don't waste them. If you do have to use them, aim to hit."

He started crawling across the floor, rattling some unknown kitchen utensils behind him. A few feet away he stopped.

"Just try not to hit me," he pleaded, and continued his slow progress across the floor.

It had been a long time since the last crash. Were they reconsidering the plan of attack? Or going away? Or gathering strength for the final blow?

"Dr. Levy!" It was absolutely quiet outside, and even her whisper sounded loud.

"Yes?"

"What do we do with the knives?"

"Nothing more than you can help," he said tersely. "If they get in, you may need them."

He had barely finished making his way to his self-appointed station on the far side of the door when the crash came, louder and more violent than any before. It hit the door and continued hitting it, until the frame, boards and all, shook, shivered, and fell.

Gladys' rolling pin flew from her hand toward the first shape that loomed in the doorway. By a miracle of bad aim, it went straight by him to bring forth a yell of pain from someone right in back. A moment later Levy brought a heavy skillet down on the foot of the man in front, putting him out of the battle completely.

Later on Gladys remembered those two opening incidents clearly, but the rest was a chaos of flying fists and kitchenware, from which only an occasional incident stood out. The first flurry of flying objects from Gladys and Veda caused a hesitation in the ranks that made it clear the intruders had not expected resistance. But they rallied quickly and surged into the room. One of them had a flashlight.

"Oh, it's just a couple of dames," he shouted, and the others rushed through. The swath of light had completely missed Levy, crouching beside the door. The teacher stood up, raised his arms over his head, reached forward, and brought down the pot in his hands-upside down. He snatched the light easily, while its former owner struggled out of the tight-fitting helmet he had acquired. Gladys was aware of herself springing up from the floor with a skillet in one hand and a carving fork in the other; afterward, also, she remembered Veda breathing heavily, jumping forward and, later, shouting. She knew that she hit out blindly in front of her, over and over again. And she knew that after a while the noise and movement stopped, and the intruders were gone—all but one.

Someone turned the light on then, and she was standing in the middle of what had been a clean, orderly kitchen, looking down at a motionless body on the floor in front of her, memorizing it.

Dr. Levy was moving the kitchen table in front of the broken door. Veda held the door in place until the table was set to brace it.

The man had blond hair, beginning to go bald at the temples. He was very thin and his suit had been light gray when it was clean.

Levy said something about wood and went off down the cellar stairs.

There was a clean cut on the man's forehead, not a very big one. Just a little bit of blood trickling off into the blond hair. It didn't seem like enough to kill a…

"Missus Mitchell, stop that now, Missus Mitchell! It ain't goin' to do no good, havin' you stand over him like that. You go on and sit down."

The words broke the spell. "I don't have to sit down," Gladys said. "What are you doing?" Then she looked. "Fixing the door?"

"Doc Levy went after some wood so we kin nail it shut. Seems to me we ought to shut up all the windows on this floor, same as in the cellar."

Gladys nodded and bent down to pick up a pot, feeling herself unpleasantly close to the body she didn't want to think about. Not looking to that side at all, she crossed the room and began picking up scattered utensils near the door. Everything was lightly spattered with blood and mud and sprinkled with splinters of wood and bits of plaster. She straightened up and let Veda take the armful of utensils from her, her eyes searching for the spot the plaster had come from. She found it finally, clear across the room, near Veda's door, where someone had aimed wild with a food chopper.

She walked over and picked up the chopper, trying to remember whether it had been hers, wondering if she had reached such a pitch of excitement that she could have thrown it unawares. The worst thing was being unable to remember. She didn't know what she had done in those minutes. She didn't know whether she had used a knife. She raised her fingers to the hole in the wall, exploring its contours curiously, feeling what the chopper would have done if it had hit the man.

The teacher came back, loaded down with pieces of board, a hammer, and nails. He dumped everything on the kitchen table in front of the door and went back again to survey the man on the floor.

"We'll have to do something about him."

Gladys and Veda looked to each other and to the two men. "We can't just leave him there," Gladys stated foolishly. "The children will be coming down in the morning."

"Well, we could start by bringing him to," Levy proposed. "Do you have any ammonia in the house?"

"Bring him to?"

"You mean he's not…?"

Both women spoke at once with a swift return of vitality. It was Levy's turn now to look from one face to another, uncomprehending.

"I mean," he said when he finally understood, "that he's quite enough alive so that you'd better have something ready to tie him up with before you get the ammonia."

Veda produced a quantity of rope from a hidden hoard, and Levy put aside the problem of nailing up the door while he secured the knots around the unconscious body. When he was certain the man was safely tied he picked up the hammer and nails and started for the door again. He climbed up on the table and got the board into position while Veda fished out the bottle of ammonia from the back of the cleaning closet. Gladys went over to hold the board in place for him, but he changed his mind just as he was about to start.

"Wait a minute," he called to Veda, who was already bending over the prostrate form. "You can put that down," he told Gladys. She lowered the board onto the flat surface of the table, and watched, puzzled, as he bent over the blond man and moved the ropes so that the hands no longer covered the suit pockets. Neatly he turned the pockets inside out, one after another, turning up a grand miscellany of items from brass knuckles to half a sandwich.

Speechless, Gladys continued to watch as he stood up, triumphantly holding a battered wallet, and went systematically through the contents of the billfold.

Veda was anything but speechless. "Now, listen here, she said indignantly, "you kin go too far. There's some a man shouldn't do."

Levy smiled more than ever like an imp and, ignoring the money in the wallet, slid a small white card out of a cellophane pocket.

"Veda," he said sternly, "you're too suspicious. You should have more faith in human nature."

She didn't want to be joked with. "I know what's right," she said stubbornly, "and I know what's wrong, and what you're doin' ain't right."

"What do you think, Mrs. Mitchell?" The teacher turned to her. "Are you voting against me too?"

"Why, I don't know." She watched him fold the wallet closed, still holding the little white card in his other hand, and at last she realized what it was. "No," she smiled, "but you might introduce us."

"I see by the little card," he said, "that my name is Albert Carney. I live at 5813 Grand Concourse, in the Bronx. I have served two years of compulsory military training and am a member of the Reserve Army Corps."

That was when Veda stopped looking stonily disapproving and understood what he was doing.

"And furthermore," he finished, reading the draft card, "I have had a very sad life."

"I'll bite," Gladys smiled. "Why have you had a sad life, Mr. Bones?"

"Bones?" he asked. "Bones, indeed! In my heydey I used to be referred to as skin-and! The reason why I have had such a sad life is that I am only"—he had to check the card again—"only thirty-two years old, and *most* prematurely gray."

In the reaction to the strain, all three of them went off in shouts of raucous laughter. They laughed till it hurt, till all the strain and tension were gone out of them. Then they set to work boarding up the door, meanwhile considering what to do with their victim.

Gladys didn't want to keep him in the house, for the children to find in the morning. Veda objected strenuously to the risks involved in reviving and releasing him. They thought of just putting him out on the porch, out of sight, and calling Emergency Headquarters to pick him up, but it was a heartless procedure, and one by one they found excuses not to do it.

"Seems to me, with Doc here in the house, we're a sight better off not askin' any extra cops inside," Veda added.

"We could untie him," Levy proposed, "and put him outside. Then when he comes to, he'll be free."

The last thing Gladys remembered of that incredible night was Levy-Carney leaning out of the dining-room window, cautiously lowering an unconscious man into the soft earth of the flower bed below.

CHAPTER TWENTY

"…SIMPLIFIED SYSTEM OF DISTRIBUTION. Your neighborhood food stores are now open, under the supervision of emergency squadmen. Supplies are being distributed to the stores by emergency squad trucks. No money is necessary to receive…"

The announcer's voice rushed up the stairs to greet her with the day's new problems—the third day of the third war of her life. Gladys didn't want problems. She wanted breakfast. Even more, she wanted to go back to bed.

"…birth certificates if possible. Driver's licenses or Social Security cards will also be acceptable. But remember, you must have absolute proof of the number of persons in your household."

Edie Crowell sat on the living-room sofa, desultorily turning the pages of a magazine. She was wrapped unbecomingly in Gladys' old pink nylon robe. When she looked up to nod, her face was unnaturally pallid. Her general appearance finished the job the radio announcer had started, and removed the last vestige of relaxation left over from the long night's sleep.

"Good morning," Gladys said quickly, and turned to the radio as an excuse to postpone further conversation.

"…may be some delay, but there is enough for all. Remember, others are also waiting for supplies. This concludes our eleven o'clock news broadcast. We will continue to…"

"Hello!" Edie stood up, stretching, and dispersing some of the gloom settled around her. "I thought you were never going to get up!" She smiled and looked more like herself.

Memory came into focus, and the events of the day before lined themselves up for Gladys' inspection. A wave of relief swept her as she realized that Edith had, incredibly, slept through all the excitement of the night.

"I slept so late yesterday, I couldn't get to sleep last night," Gladys lied happily. "You must have been up early. What's been happening around here?"

"Nothing," Edith laughed. "Nothing at all. It's the most *peaceful* morning I've had in ages! I haven't seen a living soul since breakfast. If I had anything to put on I'd have gone home, but I understand my dress isn't exactly…" She let it drift off.

"It's not in very good shape," Gladys admitted, "but Veda could have got you something of mine. I don't know why—"

"I'm afraid your Veda doesn't exactly approve of me." Edith began to look better as animation returned to her. "I was given to understand it would be perfectly all right for me to wear your robe home"—she plucked at the worn pink material humorously—"provided I did it quickly. I decided to be a difficult guest instead, and wait around till you got up, in hopes of a better offer."

"Oh, of course. Anything you want. I'm sorry about Veda. I hope she wasn't—unpleasant?" But Gladys couldn't help smiling; she was too familiar with Veda's uncompromising attitude toward alcohol.

"She wasn't." It was a relief to see Edie's answering smile. "She was just…uninterested. So I kept out of her way, and she left me alone. Anyhow, I think I agree with her. When this mess is over I'm going to join the anti-liquor league. Or at least a temperance society. I had enough of it yesterday to last the rest of my life!"

At least she'd mentioned it first. "Don't be silly," Gladys said weakly, and was saved from having to think of anything else to say.

"That you out there, Missus Mitchell?" Veda emerged from the dining room. "You comin' in to eat now? Ought to get yer breakfast before lunchtime." She smiled, pointedly ignoring the other woman.

"Have you eaten yet?" Gladys hesitated, looking from one to the other.

"Hours ago," Edith told her.

"You're sure? You won't join me?"

Veda shifted her weight impatiently. "I got the coffee heatin'," she told no one in particular. "Mebbe I better go turn it off." She turned on her heel and marched off.

"Well, if you're sure?" Gladys apologized to her guest. "I am awfully hungry." The swinging door wafted the smell of bacon from the kitchen. "I'll get you something to wear as soon as I'm done. Veda seems to have everything all ready," she fumbled.

"That's perfectly all right. You go ahead. I don't want to put you out."

Why can't I send her up to get it for herself? Somehow that was impossible. Irritated at Edie and at herself, Gladys started for the door.

"Oh, by the way, Glad." The other woman's voice called her back. "I'm sorry—I don't want to keep you. But I was wondering if you had any cigarettes around? I know you don't smoke much, but your husband does, doesn't he?"

"They're in the drawer," Gladys broke in.

It was hopeless. No matter how firmly she made up her mind, she couldn't keep from playing hostess for Edie. To her intense chagrin, Gladys found herself recrossing the room, opening the drawer in Jon's desk, and bringing forth a fresh pack of cigarettes. She hunted for matches and found them pushed away in the back.

"Thank you. I'm sorry to be such a nuisance, but you don't have to worry about me now. I've been sitting around all morning, dreaming about a cigarette, but I didn't see any, and I didn't want to go hunting through your things. That's half the reason why I wanted to get home." She held up the full pack, smiling. "This makes me feel positively luxurious."

In the kitchen Gladys found her place already set. She sat down at the white table and felt the sun streaming in the window over her shoulder.

"Where are the kids?" she asked.

"Up the attic. I could call them," Veda offered, "only I thought mebbe you'd want to eat yer meal in peace, without them to bother."

"You couldn't have had a better thought," Gladys agreed. She had planned to send Barbie for the dress, but it could wait. Right now she was hungry. When had she last eaten a decent meal? Not Tuesday. Monday, supper was spoiled; she'd had a sandwich for lunch. That was a long time.

It didn't matter if Edie Crowell spent a few more minutes in the house. Just concentrate on the table, the sun, the smell of the bacon, and the tall glass of orange juice that was waiting for her. Time enough for problems later.

She picked up the juice and took a long drink. It was canned. Veda smiled at the face she made.

"None of the frozen left," she explained. "Ain't done a big marketing since last week. That's jest as good for you," she added. "You drink it up."

"I don't want to," Gladys pouted, in imitation of her youngest daughter. "*Will* you stop taking such good care of me, Veda? Ever since I got a little gas into my system yesterday you've been acting as if I was likely to fall apart."

"Well, you sound more like yerself now," Veda admitted. "I was thinkin', if you kin manage all right with lunch for the kids, it would mebbe be a smart idea fer me to get down to Monnassey's, right away, an' try to get up at the front of the line."

"I think I can probably muddle through," Gladys smiled at her. "But don't stay away too long," she warned. "I could easily melt."

She finished the juice and worked her way happily through pancakes and bacon, while Veda got ready to go. By the time she got to her coffee Gladys was beginning to feel prepared to face some of her problems.

"Is Mr.—Carney upstairs?" she asked.

"No, he went out a couple hours ago. Said he'd likely be back around three. Said he had to get some things fer himself an' pick up some parts for the kerosene stove."

Gladys looked up, startled. "What on earth is he going to do with that?"

"He got a plan figured out to rig up that kerosene stove underneath the hot-water burner where the gas went out. Says he kin fix it so's we'll have runnin' hot water again. He's a right handy man around a house, Missus Mitchell," Veda said with satisfaction. "Never would've thought it of a teacher like that."

Dr. Levy, Gladys reflected, was getting to be a household prop. She wished she could resolve her mixed feelings about the man. Mr. Fix-it...in a fix!

"Did *she* see him?" Gladys nodded toward the living room.

Veda shook her head. "He told Barbie to watch out fer when she went in her room, an' then went out."

"And Ginny? Did she see him?"

"Couldn't help that. That's why I thought mebbe it was jest as good if she stayed up the attic till yer friend goes home. I told 'er he was a friend o' mine, jest in case."

Gladys looked doubtful. "We'll have to try and think of something to keep her from talking about him."

"Don't really matter too much," Veda pointed out. "If he kin go out, he kin come here. Jest so she don't know he's sleepin' here."

"That's true." Gladys sipped thoughtfully at her coffee.

"I'm about ready to go now, Missus Mitchell. I got lunch all fixed on the stove there. All you got to do is warm it up. I think they said on the radio I got to take some kind of identification with me. You know where I kin find something?"

Gladys got up and started for the living room.

"I didn't mean fer you to get up."

"Well, I am up. Will you stop babying me, Veda?" It didn't seem funny any more.

Barbie was in the living room, talking to Edith Crowell and looking superbly secretive. I'll have to speak to her about that, Gladys thought, and remembered about the dress.

"Barbie, could you take Mrs. Crowell up to my room and help her pick out something to wear?" Veda could feel bad or disapprove or just ignore it. "Take whatever you want, Edie. We can offer you a complete assortment. Barbara knows where everything is."

Veda said pointedly, "Mebbe Barbie would know where—"

"Where what?" Barbara turned back from the stairs.

"I came in to get the birth certificates," Gladys explained shortly. "I'm sure I can find them."

"For heaven's sake, Mother, don't you ever remember where you put anything? They're in the bottom drawer in Daddy's desk. That's where they always were."

There was no use hoping Barbie was wrong. Gladys had long ago stopped trying to compete with her daughter's memory. Rebelliously she went to the drawer and found all the family birth certificates in a neat pile, probably put away by Jon, not, as Barbie said, by herself. She was sure she would have tucked them in a cookbook, or in a vanity drawer, for easier reference.

She bolted the door after Veda and went back to her rapidly cooling coffee. Ginny came running down a few minutes later, demanding to know why no one had told her her mother was up: She seemed in better spirits than she had been the day before, and certainly her appetite had returned. Not until she had stuffed down the last mouthful of dessert did she stop to ask the burning question.

"When are the children coming?"

"Soon, I think." She'd completely forgotten about that. They had told her twelve o'clock on the phone, but it was after twelve already. Better not to be too definite about it with Ginny.

"How soon?"

"They'll probably be here when you wake up from your nap," Gladys told her.

"I don't want a nap."

"Of course you do. You want to be wide awake to play with the children, don't you?"

"No, I don't." Ginny shook her head vigorously. "I'll be asleep when they come."

"Maybe I'll wake you up."

"Maybe, if what?"

"Maybe, if you go to sleep *right away.*" It was half promise, half threat. In any case it was adequate inducement. Meekly Ginny let herself be led upstairs, washed and de-shoed, and put to bed.

And then there was nothing to do. It was astonishing how a house that had always kept two women busy now seemed to take care of itself. She thought of getting lunch for the others, but Barbara came down and fixed a sandwich for herself, and Gladys didn't know whether Edith would want to eat before she left. She had another cup of coffee while Barbara ate her quick lunch, and the dishes were being cleaned when they heard the gauntlet-muffled knock of authority on the front door.

Gladys left Barbie in the kitchen and flew to open it.

But instead of the appealing small faces she had expected, she found only the impersonal surface of Jim Turner's squad suit. By the time he came in, and the doctor behind him, she had covered her disappointment, and greeted them cheerfully.

"I didn't have a chance to thank you last night, but I'm sure you know how much it meant to us to get the news so soon." She turned to Spinelli. "I'm afraid I didn't thank you properly either. I was so excited and I wanted to tell Barbie."

"There's nothing to thank me for. I wanted to find out too. By the way, I brought you some more good news. We got the check on Ginny's urinalysis today—nothing in that one at all. It's perfectly all right. Yours hasn't come through yet, but I don't see how there could be anything wrong there."

Gladys laughed. "I suppose I'm not supposed to thank you now either. I know," she forestalled him, " 'I didn't do anything.' Well, I have to thank somebody, and it might as well be you."

Jim Turner took a step forward impatiently. "Well now, that's all cleared up, how are you making out with your other troubles? Didn't have any more trouble with the gas, did you? I could take a better look at it now, if it's still leaking. Would have come back last night if I could, but they kept me busy up at headquarters almost all evening. Can't get anything done up there without six conferences first."

He sounded very important. Gladys asked demurely, "Don't you ever get any rest? They keep you so busy."

"Well, we've got a big job to do," he responded happily. "There'll be plenty of time to take it easy afterward. There's something big in the air right now," he added meaningfully. Gladys refused to let him catch her eye. "You'll be hearing about it pretty soon on your radio, I guess, but the only thing released so far is, the regular squad routes are breaking up. Now that it's okay to go out, you're supposed to file some kind of notice at your neighborhood food store, if you have any troubles. Then the squadman comes around later on to check up."

"Oh, then you won't be making regular visits any more?" She tried to sound unhappy about it.

"Now, Gladys," he reassured her promptly, "I'm not so busy I can't stop by here once in a while. I told you I'd look out for you, didn't I?"

Barbara was directing frantic questioning looks at the young doctor. Gladys, watching her, almost missed her cue to murmur an appropriate, "Thank you," and missed entirely Turner's sudden look of astonishment.

"Well, I'll be God damned!" she heard him say. "Pardon me, ma'am, but we been looking for that lady all over town since last night." He was staring over Gladys' head and into the hall. "How long've you been here?" he demanded.

Gladys turned to see Edie Crowell looking spruce, if startled. Combed and washed, dressed in Gladys' new spring suit and Barbie's freshly cleaned brown and white pumps, she seemed prepared to face down any quantity of Jim Turners.

"She came over yesterday," Gladys explained quickly. "She didn't want to stay all alone in that big house, so I asked her over here." She laughed inwardly as Edith nodded a stiff assent.

"You mean to say she was here all the time last night and you never said a word?"

"Let's see, I don't know whether she came before you did or not…yes, I guess she must have. You came after curfew, didn't you? I guess I just didn't think about it. I had so much on my mind."

"I went to bed early," Edith added. "I didn't have a wink of sleep the night before."

"Well, we were just about ready to bust your door down this time, Miz Crowell. You could've let us know."

"I wasn't aware that I had to keep you informed."

"You mean you never heard anything? I told them to put it on the radio. Now, Miz Crowell"—he turned suddenly exceedingly solicitous—"just don't you get all wrought up."

"I'm sure we don't have to worry about how Mrs. Crowell takes the news." The interruption by the young doctor was startling. Gladys realized it was the first time, since she had seen the two together, that young Spinelli had taken the initiative from the older man.

"Of course you really knew it all along, Mrs. Crowell," he added. "It's a good thing you persuaded me to take that blood count. We realized you were right as soon as we checked it."

Gladys forgot to be surprised by the news, she was so flabbergasted by the combination of blatant flattery and forthright brutality in the doctor's brief speech.

Jim Turner was shocked and disapproving, both. "Now, Miz Crowell," he picked up where he had been interrupted, "there's no need to get all wrought up."

"I am not the least bit likely"—this time Edith didn't let him finish—"to become, as you put it, wrought up." She turned to Gladys with
just a hint of her old arrogance. "I told you all along," she accused. "But
you didn't believe me; none of you believed me."

"You don't have to worry about a thing," the squadman repeated
doggedly, and Gladys thought, I have never seen anyone less worried
in my life! "They'll take fine care of you up at the hospital. Won't they,
Doc?" Turner appealed to the younger man.

"They tell me our hospital is one of the best equipped in the country
for this kind of thing," Spinelli told her.

"I'm perfectly well aware that the hospital is well equipped, young
man." Edith was completely herself again. "I've certainly done my share
to make it so, and I assume that since everyone in authority seemed to
know this was going to happen"—she turned to the big squadman with
a look that made clear her opinion of him and of the authority he represented—"*some* of the funds raised for the hospital were used to purchase
the necessary equipment."

It didn't make sense. Monday night Edie Crowell had had screaming
mimis on the telephone because she was afraid of just this thing. Yesterday she had walked into the house dead drunk and ready to pass out
because she wasn't able to face the worry. Even this morning, before she
got the news, she had been a little subdued. Now that she knew for sure,
she was entirely restored.

"If there's nothing else you have to tell me," Edith addressed Jim
Turner coldly, "perhaps I'd better go on home and get ready to go. When
do you suppose they'll be ready to take me to the hospital?"

"Well, if you're in such a hurry to get in there"—he was very obviously annoyed—"we can take you along to headquarters in the truck
right now. They'll send you along with the next load."

"Do they ship us by freight or parcel post, Mr. Turner?" Her voice
was venomously saccharine. "I should tell you, by the way, that I intend
to see to it the proper people are notified of the dangerous delay I suffered." She turned to the young doctor and went smoothly on. "I want
you to know that I am aware it was not *your* fault."

Without waiting for a reply from either of the men, she turned her
attention to Gladys. "I wish I knew some way to thank you properly.
I do realize that I must have inconvenienced all of you, and"—impulsively she took Gladys' hand—"I think I ought to thank Veda before I
go, too. In her own way, she was good to me also."

"She's not back yet." Gladys was still too dazed to attempt any more
complicated reply.

She followed Edith to the door, bolted it behind her, and returned
to the living room.

"Well, I'll be God damned! Excuse me, ma'am." That was Turner, of
course. "I just can't figure that woman out." He shook his head in heavy

bewilderment. "Listen, before I forget. Did you say something about your maid not being *back* yet? Did you let her go out?"

"Why, yes, she went down to the store when we heard the announcement on the radio." Out of the corner of her eye Gladys saw the doctor incline his head ever so slightly toward the far corner of the room. Barbie began drifting slowly over there.

"Well now, you know you shouldn't have done that, Gladys. I can understand it's hard for you to believe she could've done anything, but you got to remember she's still under suspicion. You know they told you she wasn't allowed out without a clearance from Security."

"How did *you* know about that?"

"That's my job around here. I'm responsible for the safety of this whole neighborhood. It's only natural I'd get reports on anybody under suspicion. Matter of fact, if it was anyone else I'd feel like I had to take some action right now, but being it's you," he smiled beneficently, "I'll just pretend I never heard a thing. Only you got to remember after this, she can't go anywheres out of the house without a clearance. You can get it from the Security Office, or from me, either one."

The whole thing was fantastic. "Well then, why don't you give me a clearance now? That would take care of the whole nonsensical business."

"I can't do that." He looked horrified. "You got to understand, she needs a special written pass to go out anyplace. Right now she could get picked up any minute by a Security officer. Now, I'm sure you're going to be more careful about that." He looked around and found that Barbara and the young doctor were clear across the room, out of earshot. Lowering his voice, he went on, "You remember what I told you yesterday? About the evacuation?"

"Yes." She nodded. "I've thought a lot about it, Mr. Turner, but I haven't made up my mind—"

"Just call me Jim," he said. "No need to be formal now. We've been neighbors all these years. It's high time we got to know each other a little. Now, what I wanted to tell you…I've got everything just about lined up. Turned out to be easier than I figured, because I'm gonna be in charge of that train myself—"

"But, Mr. Turner," she broke in, aware of the other two drifting back toward them. She had to make him understand quickly.

"I told you you should call me Jim."

It was useless. He just wouldn't listen, and now Barbie and the doctor were right next to them.

"You bear in mind what I told you," Turner admonished cheerfully, "and don't start worrying again. Just let me take care of everything. "

"Mother."

Gladys looked questioningly at her daughter, but Turner said, "You tell your ma after we go, Barbie. We got to get moving now if we're gonna get Miz Crowell back to headquarters in time for the next truck."

"I only wanted to ask," Barbara said stiffly, "whether you knew anything about those children."

"Oh, that's right." Gladys turned back to the man. "We called up last night and offered to take two of those homeless children they've been talking about on the radio. They were supposed to come at noon, and we were wondering if anything was wrong."

"Oh, now, I don't think that's such a good idea, Gladys. They sent me in a form to check off whether your house was okay. Of course I know it would be nice for the kids here, but you got to remember what I told you before. It wouldn't make things any easier to have a couple of extra kids here."

"Maybe. not," she said firmly, "but I do want to have them. Did you—check off the form yet?"

"Haven't really had a minute to do it so far today," he admitted.

"That must be what held it up, then," Gladys persisted. "Do you think you'd have a chance to take care of it when you get back to headquarters? I would like to have them here for supper, so I can get them settled."

"I'll fix it up the best way I can," he promised. "Come on, Doc." He turned a good-natured smile on Spinelli. "Say good-bye to the girl. We got to go."

Barbara's angry blush was clearly visible, but the young doctor was unperturbed. He walked back the few steps' distance to Barbara, took her hand, and said, "Good-bye, girl. We got to go."

Delightedly Gladys watched him pat Barbara's shoulder in sober imitation of Turner's reassuring gesture. He seemed to have some perspective on the whole crazy business that she wished she could share. She was still smiling when she closed the door after him.

"I don't like that man!"

"Why, Babsy, what's the—"

"He's got you doing it too!" Barbara burst out miserably, her voice trembling on the brink of a sob. "First he treats me like a baby, and then he has to make a nasty crack—"

"Oh, *him!*" Gladys put her hand on Barbara's shoulder. "I was thinking about Dr. Spinelli. He certainly handled Edie Crowell. I didn't know he had it in him. He seemed so—diffident." She laughed. "Maybe that's how he handles *me.*"

There was no more fortunate choice of subject where Barbie was concerned. She forgot her resentment immediately in contemplation of the young doctor's many virtues. "Wasn't that terrific, the way he figured her out? It all sounded crazy at first—I couldn't understand how she could take it that way. It was easy enough to understand afterwards, but Pete had it all figured out beforehand."

"Well," Gladys smiled, "it's really not too difficult to figure out that Edith Crowell likes to have her own way. But I should think it would take a certain amount of courage to take advantage of the fact the way he did. 'Of course, you knew it all along, Mrs. Crowell!' That's my idea of bravery under fire. You better watch out for that young man, Barbara," she teased. "If he could talk Edie into thinking radiation sickness was her very own idea, I hate to think of the effect he must have on the younger generation of females."

"Oh, don't be silly, Mother. He's old!" she disclaimed him completely. Barbara was obviously delighted at the thought that Peter Spinelli might sometime try to talk her into anything at all. "Anyhow"—she cast loyalty to the winds—"I don't think it was *just* what he said that made Mrs. Crowell change so much. I was thinking about that when she was telling Mr. Turner off, and I remember how I felt—before."

Gladys looked at her curiously. The girl was dead serious now.

"It seems to me," she went on, "that it wouldn't be nearly as bad to *know* you had it as to worry about whether you did or not. It's like—well, like the jokes they always make about going to the dentist. When you get there and something's being done, it's not nearly as bad as when you're thinking about it before you go. I think," she finished with an air of ultimate discovery, "the worst thing in the whole world is not knowing—about something important, I mean—or, well, I'm getting all mixed up, but you know what I mean, don't you?"

"You sound just like your father," Gladys laughed. "I mean your father with two drinks in him at a cocktail party. He gets very serious about the state of the world. Once he made a half-hour speech on the subject of ignorance."

"Well, I hope Daddy likes it when you laugh at *him,*" Barbara cried, and ran from the room. But at the foot of the stairs she turned back to aim a bombshell at her mother. "I suppose you're not interested either that Pete told me she's probably going to *die!*"

CHAPTER TWENTY-ONE

SHE KNEW where it had happened. She knew where Edie had been at the critical time.

If Veda hadn't been sick…

If Barbie hadn't insisted on the laundry…

If Edie hadn't refused to understand the difficulty…

If I had gone to the luncheon…!

It was silly to think about it. She hadn't gone, and there were other, far more pressing problems. Jim Turner and Garson Levy, Barbie, Veda, Edie Crowell, the Security officers, and the evacuation. And those children. Ginny was going to be impossible if the children didn't come.

If Jon were here… That was silly too. All the ifs were silly. Jon wasn't there. For more than two days Jon hadn't been there. The other time, the other war, it was different. Then she wrote him cheerful, encouraging letters, telling him all the little troubles that came up each day, the little things he customarily solved, that she had to learn to cope with. But these were not little problems now, nor were they the kind that anyone customarily solved.

What would Jon do?

That was the old formula, the way it had worked in the last war. She'd ask herself and get the answer. Now there was no answer. If Jon never came back…

Another if!

She had longed for a few minutes of solitude, for time to think. Now it was a relief when she heard Ginny, waking, call her upstairs. She ran up, afraid Barbie might get there first. Then she would have nothing to do again.

Ginny was grumpy. "You said they'd be here when I woke up. You said they would."

"Well, darling, I can't help it if they're late."

"Yes, you can, too." Ginny was definitely being unreasonable.

"Come on," Gladys said as gaily as she could. "We'll put your shoes on and go downstairs and see what there is to play with."

"Well, I don't want to play by myself. There isn't anything to play with."

"I'll play with you. Where's your other foot? Did it get lost?" She tried an old game, casting her eyes around the room, searching for the other foot, which had supposedly vanished.

"Can't find it," Ginny announced. "It isn't anyplace. I'll have to hop all day."

"That would be a terrible, terrible tragedy, wouldn't it? I'll tell you what we'll do. I'll just pretend to put the shoe on and when you find the foot the shoe will be on it already."

Ginny didn't co-operate, but she did submit, and the shoe was laced on the missing foot.

"I don't want to play with you either," she decided. "You're no fun. Why *didn't* the children come yet?"

"I don't know." But she was afraid she did. "Maybe they found their own homes again," she said hopefully. "Wouldn't that be nice?"

"No, it wouldn't."

Gladys gave up. "Let's go down and have some cocoa," she suggested brightly.

"Don't want cocoa. I want the children. I don't want them to find their own homes. I want them to come here."

Downstairs the front door banged.

"Come on, we'll go see what Veda brought home." Ginny followed her silently, not wanting to admit any interest in Veda's activities or in anything at all except the coming of the other children. But when they came in sight of the hall she objected violently.

"You said it was Veda."

"Well, I thought it was Veda," Gladys said wearily. "Hello, Mr. Carney. I didn't think you'd get back so soon."

"It was simpler than I expected. There are a lot of people outside with bundles from the stores, so my bundle wasn't terribly conspicuous." He pulled up an ancient shopping bag from the hall table and displayed it proudly. "Doesn't it look convincing?" He started up the stairs.

"Didn't you bring me anything?" Ginny was incredulous.

"What sort of cad do you take me for?" he asked, outraged. "Of course I brought you something. But you can't have it yet. If you come up to my very private room in about half an hour I shall make a formal presentation."

"You mean you'll give it to me?"

"You understand me perfectly," he told her, "but remember, you have to wait half an hour."

Out in the kitchen Ginny studied the toy clock soberly, and finally made up her mind to ask for help.

"Will you tell me when a half an hour is?" she demanded suspiciously. "Will you tell me right?"

"Of course I'll tell you right. What's got into you?"

"Well, you didn't tell me right about the children."

Again! "Do you want cocoa or juice?"

"Don't want anything." Then, after a moment's reflection, "Cocoa."

The stove didn't light. For just an instant Gladys had a nightmare sensation that all this had happened before. Then her mind separated the sequence of events in an orderly manner. This was simply the gas failure Turner had predicted.

She tried the other burners to make sure and, with the memory of the last time still entirely too clear, couldn't resist opening the cellar door just a crack.

There was no smell of gas. It was all right. She got out the hotplate again and fixed the cocoa for Ginny.

"Well, why don't they call up if they're late? You told Barbie people should always call up if they're going to be late."

"Maybe they're someplace where they can't call."

"You mean they really and truly don't have any homes? They're not anyplace at all except outside?"

"That's not exactly what I mean. They're staying at a place like a school, but if they were on their way here they couldn't call up. Anyhow, nobody's supposed to use the phone except if they really have to."

"Why not?"

"Well, because—because it said on the radio that we shouldn't."

"Why?"

This could go on forever if she let it. "Just because," she said firmly. "I don't know why. It just said we shouldn't, so we don't."

For fifteen minutes after that she managed by dint of concentrated effort to keep Ginny from mentioning the children again. Then at last it was time to send her upstairs.

Barbara came down with her when she returned to display the promised present—a big, brightly painted toy car which looked oddly familiar to Gladys.

"Mr. Carney bought it home for me," Ginny announced proudly. "It really runs. Look." She began winding busily.

"Brought, darling, not bought."

She kept trying to remember why the car looked so familiar. Then it came back to her, and she waited to see what would happen when Ginny tried to make it go. To her surprise the car worked perfectly—but she could have sworn it was the same one that had been given to Tom at Christmas the first year they moved in there. He was—she stopped to think—ten years old at the time, and his first act after sending it on a trial spin around the room was to find a quiet corner where he could take it apart. Jon had firmly refused to fix it for him, informing him that when he took things apart it was smarter to be sure beforehand that he knew how to put them together again. The car had gone up to the attic, and by the time Tom knew how to fix it he was no longer interested in toy cars. Gladys wondered whether the car had already been fixed when Dr. Levy answered Ginny's question on the stairs.

"Did you show it to Pallo yet?"

"I forgot!"

That was Barbie, trying to get rid of Ginny. What next? Gladys wondered. She was determined not to have any more bickering with the girl.

" 'Scuse me, Mommy, I'll come back. Only I forgot to show Pallo my car, and he'll feel bad."

"Mother!" Barbie could hardly wait till the little girl was gone before she burst out with her news. "You ought to see the things he brought back! He's got a Geiger counter, a little one that they used to make for prospectors, and—"

"Isn't that interesting!" No quarrel, thank goodness. Maybe she could get an answer to the question in her mind. "Barbie, do you know when Dr. Levy fixed that car? Was it after he told Ginny he had something? Or did he have it already?"

"I don't know. I guess maybe he was fooling around with it while I was looking at his stuff. He's got everything, Mother! He said he packed it all up at the school before he left on Monday. And he's got a gadget… Oh, he wants some boiling water. That's what he sent me down for."

She got a pot from the closet and filled it. "You know, he's got everything he needs to—"

"You better use the hot plate," Gladys told her. "The stove isn't working any more. I guess the gas really is all gone now."

"Mother, I wish you wouldn't keep interrupting me. I've been trying to tell you about all the things he brought, and you just won't listen!"

"All right," Gladys said wearily. "You just pretend I didn't interrupt you, and go ahead and use the stove instead."

"I didn't mean that. Anyhow, you could have waited just a minute." She plugged in the electric plate and put the water on. "I don't understand you, Mother. Aren't you even *interested*?"

"Of course I'm interested, darling. But I've got so many things to think about right now—and you know I don't know anything about Geiger counters and all that technical part of it. Now look." She did want to make friends with Barbie again. "Suppose you fix his cup of tea, or whatever you're making, and take it up, and then when you come down you can tell me all about it. We can—"

"His cup of tea! I'm boiling this water for— Oh, never mind! You don't understand. You don't know much about these technical things," she parroted.

"Barbie, I'm sorry if I hurt your feelings."

"You didn't hurt *my* feelings."

"I—" She didn't know what else to say. She fell silent, and the silence lasted till Barbie went upstairs with the boiling water.

After that the girl just kept out of sight. She didn't even come down when Veda returned, laden with provisions, news, and worries.

"Never saw such a time!" She went through to the kitchen to get rid of her bundles and Gladys went with her.

"People thought it was hard to get food in the last war," Veda said. "But there never was anything like this before. I had to stand in line near three hours before I got inside that store and then I tried to tell about them kids that are coming, but that squadman wouldn't listen to nobody. He said I had proof fer five people, and five people was all I was goin' to get food for. Never even thought to ask was all five home. He took a look to see all the names was different, an' told Mr. Monnassey to give me fer five."

"You didn't have to tell him your name?" Gladys asked.

"No'm, I never did." She put down her bundles and found a seat on one of the white-painted kitchen chairs. "I'll get that stuff put away in a minute," she promised. "Jest want to catch my breath. That was real heavy carryin' home."

"You sit still," Gladys told her. "I'll put it away." She began unloading shopping bags, talking at the same time, telling Veda about all that had happened while she was gone. She skimmed over Turner's references to Veda as lightly as possible.

"The whole thing's a lot of nonsense," she insisted, "but I guess for the time being I better not make any outside trips. Meanwhile we'll get this clearance he was talking about." Then she went into the story about Edie Crowell and drew it out for is fullest effect.

"But don't forget," she wound up, "that if I'd listened to you I'd be just as bad off as Mrs. Crowell right now."

"And what do you think you mean by that?" Veda demanded.

" 'Now don't you worry about the washin', Missus Mitchell,' " Gladys mimicked. " 'I kin take care of that fine tomorrer.' "

Veda laughed with embarrassment. "I kin remember something else, too, proves you were tryin' jest as hard to get me sick."

"What did I do?"

"I kin remember clear as day, hearin' you say, 'Don't you suffocate yourself in that room of yours, Veda.' Mebbe I saved your life an' mebbe not—but I sure took care o' my own."

They were both laughing when Ginny came back with her car to show off to Veda.

Gladys finished putting things away while the toy was being admired.

"I don't see what you're worried about," she told Veda. "Seems to me you've got all the food we can eat in a week."

"I jest wish I knew fer sure would they bring some along with them kids," Veda said. "I don't see how we'll make out if they don't."

It was a tactical error. Ginny, reminded, wanted to know once more why the children didn't call up if they were late.

"They're supposed to call," she insisted stubbornly. "They *are*!"

"All right." Gladys surrendered at last. "I shouldn't do it, but I'll call up. Only remember this, Virginia Mitchell. After I call I don't want to hear it talked about any more. Whatever they tell us is final. That clear?"

Ginny nodded happily. But the bargain proved more difficult to keep than Gladys had expected.

She picked up the receiver, but no dial tone came through, and when she jiggled the hook nothing happened either. Forcing herself to a patience she did not feel, she hung up, let it stay down a moment, and tried again.

Ten minutes of trying convinced her. She put the phone down and turned around to find Barbara on the stairs in back of her.

"The phone too?"

Gladys nodded and turned tiredly to Ginny. "I'm sorry, darling," she said. "I can't call up. It isn't working."

Unexpectedly there was no fuss. With the sudden sympathy that little children sometimes show for adult troubles, Ginny offered her best reassurance.

"That's all right, Mommy," she promised. "They'll come."

Barbara laughed. "Time for the news," she said. "Let's all go in the living room and see what good news they have on the radio *now.*"

"Come on, Ginny," Veda snorted. "We don't want to hear no news, good *or* bad. You an' me are goin' to go in the kitchen an' make some supper for these folks."

Gladys followed her older daughter slowly into the living room.

"Don't tell me you think those kids are still coming?" Barbara demanded bitterly. "Didn't Mr. Turner promise to fix it for you?"

"I told him I wanted them," Gladys answered sharply. "I don't see what more I could do."

"I don't know." Barbara turned the radio up, and news of hospitals, trains, and armies filled the room. "I don't know," she repeated miserably, "but you should have been able to do something."

The radio intruded: "…since the official evacuation warning was issued for lower and middle Westchester. There is no cause for alarm because of the warning. You are not in danger from any kind of radiations. All danger zones within this area have already been evacuated. The new decision is due to scarcity of food supplies and imminent failure of utilities.

"Please remember, this is an evacuation *warning*. An evacuation *order* may come at any time within the next forty-eight hours. You will be assigned to an evacuation train by your neighborhood squadman. There is no other way to get a seat. There is no quicker way to leave.

"We have just received a list of persons rescued…"

"They can't *make* us go, can they, Mother?"

Gladys turned unhappily to her daughter. "No," she said, "not exactly, but they can make it awfully uncomfortable to stay here." How much can I tell her? Jim Turner had said not to tell anyone, but now it was on the radio.

"Well, we could manage," Barbie said stubbornly.

"I don't want to go either," Gladys told her. "But…" *gas…phone… electric power…water…* "I'm afraid it's not going to be up to us." Never mind what he said. Barbie had a right to know. "Mr. Turner told me—"

"Oh, you and your Mr. Turner!" Barbara faced her mother furiously. "You'll do anything *he* says, won't you? Well, I'm not going," she announced. "You can decide for Ginny and yourself, but I won't be going."

"You'll be doing what you're told to do, young woman." Gladys was exasperated. "What do you mean, you won't be going?"

"I mean I'm staying here. I'm—going to go to work in the hospital."

"You're *what?*"

"They said on the radio they need volunteer workers," she defended herself.

"Barbara, for heaven's sake." Gladys controlled her temper with an effort. "What makes you think they're taking children of fifteen to work in the hospital?"

"I'm not a child, and anyway, you only have to be seventeen to volunteer. Lots of people think I'm older than I am, and I can do just as much as anybody seventeen years old can do. I can tell them I'm seventeen, and I bet Pete'll back me up."

"Barbie! What kind of romantic nonsense are you building up? Dr. Spinelli's been nice to you—all right, that's how a good doctor has to be. It's obvious that he likes you too—he went to a good deal of trouble last night for your sake. But he's not a boy you can wrap around your finger. And he's not very likely to lie to the hospital authorities, just to help you get into trouble!"

"I happen to know he will. I asked him."

"Do you mean to say you asked him before you said anything to me?" Gladys was getting very annoyed. "Well, I still don't believe he'd do it. You're not going to work in any hospital full of people with radiation disease and heaven knows how many things you could catch. You just aren't going to do it. You may think you're not a child any more, but you'll find the people at the hospital will agree with *me*."

"And you can't understand why I talked to him first!" Barbie retorted bitterly. "At least he *listened* to me. All right, have it your way. I'll just stay here and play with Ginny, like a nice girl—"

"Wait a minute, Babsy," Gladys pleaded. "Don't get—"

"That's another thing!" The girl was working herself up to a fury. "I've told you over and over and over I don't want to be called Babsy. If you don't want to call me Barbie you could at least call me by my right name, instead of a baby nickname. You just don't ever want me to grow up! You want me to be a baby all my life! That's why you never tell me anything; you're afraid I'll know as much as you do!"

"Bab-Barbie," she corrected herself hastily, "listen, darling, there's nothing to get all upset about *now*. You're all right, and Tom seems to be. The bombing's all over. Everything will get better now. You'll see, and…" There was one thing she couldn't promise, one reassurance she dare not give. She compromised with, "And we'll hear something about Daddy soon. I'm sure we will. Is that what was bothering you?"

"No, it isn't!" the girl contradicted. "See, you're doing the same thing again right now. You try to make me think everything's all right when I know it isn't. I just wish you'd stop trying to hide things from me. You did the same thing with the information sheets you didn't want me to read, and when you tried to tell me Doc Levy was crazy…And please don't try to shut me up by telling me Daddy's coming home. I'm too old for lullabies, Mother. You know he can't come home even if he is all right. Yes, Pete told me that too. *He* doesn't think I'm a kid who can't understand anything!"

"Oh, for heaven's sake, Barbara!" Gladys stopped trying to control her growing irritation. "Perhaps it hasn't occurred to you that if I've tried to spare you at all it was because I knew you were just on the verge of hysteria. And the way you're acting now proves it. You get a little information, *some* of which is *partly* correct, and look what happens!"

Barbie's head shot up and her eyes widened at the preposterous charge. "I am not hysteri—Mom! *Listen!*"

"…aple Avenue, Purchase Village, being treated for shock and minor injuries. Bliss Mizzen, Central Street, Yonkers, held for observation in…"

"They said Mitchell!" Barbie broke the dazed concentration. "They said Mitchell! They did! I didn't hear the first part, but I know they said Mitchell. Oh, Mom, it's Daddy! Daddy's all right!"

THE ESCAPE

He was lying down, and the cots stretched in a row out of sight in front of his eyes. He was on a cot too. It hurt when he turned his head, but there weren't as many cots in the other direction. He could see the door. Somebody would have to come through the door sooner or later.

He discovered his hands, and began exploring his body. He had no clothes. There was a sheet over him and he wasn't cold, but he couldn't get home without clothes. There was a bandage on his head. That made sense; it hurt so much when he turned it.

A man got off the cot next to him, and he realized he could get up too. He sat up and waited for the dizziness to go away. Then he stood up. He was naked. Down the row of cots he saw that the other man was naked too. Nobody seemed to care.

He followed the other man and went through the door. An old man was sitting right outside. The man who got up first had turned to the right. He looked both ways, and the old man told him, "Down that way," pointing to the right.

He followed again, and the other man went through a door marked "Men." He went in, too, but when he came out he kept on down the corridor. He found another door, and tried it, but it was another room full of cots. After a while, trying doors, he found a closet with overalls and shirts in it. He still needed shoes.

He went down some stairs, and some more, and he was in a cellar. He found some boots and put them on his bare feet. There was a little door that led out into the street. He walked a long time, carefully reading the street numbers to make sure he was going the right way.

190…191…192…that was right. That was the way home. He had to get home.

CHAPTER TWENTY-TWO

"WAKE UP, MOMMY. Please, Mommy, wake up."

"Hello, baby." Gladys edged over in the bed and patted the empty space beside her, hoping Ginny would lie down and snuggle up, but the hands kept tugging at her.

"All right, I'm awake." Obstinately she refused to open her eyes. "I'm awake. Now just let me rest a minute."

"You'll go back to sleep," the child accused.

"No, I won't. I'm wide awake."

"Open up your eyes. If you're awake, why don't you open up your eyes?" Ginny demanded triumphantly. "You are not either awake," she concluded.

Face it, Gladys told herself, and tried letting a little light into one eye. The sun wasn't too bright. It must be early. She let her eye open far enough to include a vision of her daughter's ink-stained hand tugging at the blanket.

"What happened to you?" she demanded. "And, anyhow, who told you you could wake me up?"

Ginny studied her mother's face and decided she wasn't really angry. "Barbie let me use her fountain pen," she confided. "Veda said I should wake you up. Somebody's knocking at the door." Ginny read the curiosity on her mother's face for disbelief. "She did, too, say so."

"I'm sure she did, baby." Gladys pulled back the covers and sat up gingerly. To her own surprise, she felt fine. Then she remembered...Jon was all right! "Who is it? Did she tell you? What do they want? Is it Mr. Turner?"

"They want to come in. Who's Mr. Turner?"

"You know perfectly well who Mr. Turner is. He lives right next door, and he has a little baby."

"A brand-new baby?"

"That's right." She stood up and wrapped the cherry robe snugly around her. It was eight o'clock. She'd slept for eleven hours. She felt fine.

"Listen," she told the little girl. "I want you to do something for me. I want you to go downstairs and ask Veda who it is and what they want, and then come right back up without stopping and knock on the bathroom door and tell me what she said. Can you remember all that?"

"Sure." Ginny was disdainful. "That's easy. I can remember lots more."

"Well, you don't have to remember any more. Just remember that much and don't forget to come back up right away."

Gladys headed for the empty bathroom. She washed quickly, wondering who it was. She was brushing her hair when Ginny knocked.

"Veda don't know what he wants," she yelled.

"Doesn't," Gladys corrected automatically.

"Wasn't what?"

"I said doesn't."

"I can't hear you, Mommy. What did you say?"

Impatiently Gladys went to the door. "Never mind what I said. What did Veda say?"

"I told you. She doesn't know what he wants."

"Well, who is it?"

"Mr. Turner," Ginny replied. "Just like you said."

"All right. Thank you, baby." Gladys went back for a last once over in front of the mirror. "Will you tell him I'm coming right down?"

"Mommy's coming right down," Ginny obligingly shouted down the stairs. Hastily Gladys pulled her robe tight around her and ran down.

"Well now, you're looking a little more chipper today," Turner boomed.

"Oh, did you hear the announcement?"

"Now, there've been a whole lot of announcements, Gladys. Just which one did you have in mind?"

"I guess you didn't, or you'd know," she said. "About Jon! He's all right! They had it on the list of people admitted to the Washington Heights Hospital last night. They said he was suffering from shock and minor injuries, and they never mentioned radiation disease at all."

"Well, that's sure good news," he said, but it seemed to Gladys his tone was just a little less hearty than usual. "I guess you won't feel so bad about leaving," he added, "now that you know your hubby's in good hands."

"Leaving?" She had actually forgotten about it. "Oh yes, I wanted to ask you about that. Does an evacuation order mean that we *have* to go? I mean, what happens if I decide I want to stay?"

"What happens," he told her, "is, I talk you out of it. Understand, headquarters ain't going to force anybody to go. Folks that want to stick around without food or gas or electricity, and maybe without water, are welcome to do so. That many less to take care of at the camps. But as far as you folks are concerned, headquarters has nothing to do with it. I'm not going to let you stay here. I told you I'd watch out for you, and as a matter of fact that's just what I came by to tell you now."

He moved closer and lowered his voice. "This is strictly on the q.t., Gladys, but they already got it fixed up that the first train is leaving tomorrow morning. It's a special for staff and families. I got seats for you and your girls, and I'm working on a fancy title for you now. So you just hold tight and get your things packed up. You got nothing to worry about at all."

Her impulse was to refuse, outright. She remembered laughing in the bathroom at the notion of telling Jim Turner, "No, no, a thousand times no." She might yet have to do it. But he had said without gas or electricity or maybe water... She tried a less direct approach.

"For me and the *girls?* What about Veda?" she demanded. "You know I can't go and leave her here."

"Looks like she'll just have to go to the detention camp. Now don't get all upset, Gladys. I told you yesterday about that, and I checked up on it for you since then. They won't give her a clearance to go with you, and that's that. You'll have plenty help up there, don't you worry."

"I'm not worried about *help!*" Politic or not, she had passed the point of self-control. "I'm worried about Veda! And what's more, I'm not leaving without her. I don't want to leave anyhow. I think we'll just make out as best we can until Jon gets home."

"Now, Gladys," he pleaded. "You got to calm down. Why don't you just sit down and take it easy a minute? I got everything all arranged, you know. You can't just stay here. I already told you that. And you got to get over thinking your hubby'll come back here. You'll get to see him a lot sooner at Sampson," he promised. "You just leave it up to me."

How could she stay angry when she wanted to laugh? He was trying to soothe her and, perversely, succeeding because of the very clumsiness of his attempts.

"And you'll fix it?" she asked. She remembered something else and found she could still be angry after all. "Just like you fixed it about those children?"

"Now, how'd you know what I did about that?"

"That's easy. They didn't come."

"It's too bad," he said. "I know your girl was pestering you about that, but you got to see I had to decide according to what was best for everybody concerned."

"I'm afraid I don't see what it was you had to decide," she said stiffly. "I thought you said the form just asked you whether my house was adequate?"

"You sure do remember every little thing," he chuckled. "But you can't blame a man for doing his best. After all, if they were here now we'd have to be figuring on them going along with you when—"

"You mean *if,*" she broke in. "I'm not at all sure I'm going anywhere."

"Well, one thing I can tell you for sure," he laughed. "You couldn't keep them kids here after an evacuation order. Now look, Gladys, I got to be getting on. Just stopped in to let you know things were comin' along all right, but I guess I kind of barged in on you too early. You get yourself some breakfast, and things'll look brighter to you."

It was infuriating, being treated like a spoiled baby. But what could she say?

"Kind of gloomy in here, too, with your windows all boarded up," he added. "It was a smart thing to do, though," he approved, moving toward the door. "I'll come back later if I get a chance," he promised, "but I couldn't say for sure. I wouldn't of come so early if I was sure I could make it later on."

It seemed as if he would never go, as though he would stay there at the door and ramble on forever. But at last she pushed the bolt to behind him and turned back to the dim interior of the living room.

The boards did make the place gloomy, she thought. She'd forgotten all about them until Turner noticed. Maybe that did account for some of her rapid depression and trigger temper. She'd been feeling so *good* when she got up.

She found Veda, Barbie, and Ginny all in the kitchen.

They all had breakfast together, and then Gladys escaped upstairs to the incredible luxury of a real bath with hot water out of the tap. Gar Levy had worked on his kerosene burner the evening before, while she and Barbie did the first-floor windows.

Now she could lie in the tub, and for a little while at least think about inconsequentials. Amused, she caught herself in the act of shifting her attitude toward the teacher. He had been Dr. Levy, and then Doc to all the others. And now she found herself getting used to a first-name basis by her old expedient of thinking both names together. It was foolish, perhaps, to resent Jim Turner's calling her "Gladys," and still be amused when she caught her subconscious mind scheming to have Garson Levy do the same thing. But Turner...

No problems in the bathtub, she told herself firmly, and concentrated on Jon's chagrin when he came home and found all the wood for the new garage on the living-room windows, and the things that had happened to the plaster in the process!

But no bath lasts forever. She had to get out, finally, and get dressed.

In the bedrooms, at least, there were no boards, and the sun was bright through the sheer curtains. She decided she could stay upstairs most of the day.

Gar Levy came by her open door and waved a greeting. His tie was knotted, and his hair was freshly combed.

"Are you going out again?" she asked, smiling. "You're getting to be pretty sure of yourself, aren't you?"

"Frankly," he told her, "I tremble and quake every time I have to take a step on the other side of that door. But it looks like I'll have to go this time. And if I'm lucky I won't be back—at least not until this mess is over and I can come to thank you with a box of candy, or some such small consideration, for saving my life."

"Oh, stop it! What do you mean, if you're lucky? Haven't you found the accommodations satisfactory?"

"Very much so. When you decide to take in permanent boarders, put me first on the list. I'm headed for the hospital, which I don't expect to be nearly so pleasant."

"The *hospital*? I thought you said you'd treated yourself with something. And Barbie told me about all that stuff you brought home yesterday—"

"That was mostly equipment to find out if I was getting better or worse. I found out," he finished with a wry smile, "so today I'm going to see if I can get into the hospital under my nom de plume."

"I hate to see you go," Gladys said slowly. "You've gotten to be almost part of the family. If there's—I don't know what—but if there's anything at all we can do…"

"As a matter of fact, there is." He smiled. "I haven't wanted to bring it up before, but just before I go—I've been wondering whether you've had any news at all about Tom. I've always been very fond of him—"

"No more than he was of you." She told him about the only news they'd had, on the radio, and he seemed almost as happy as she herself had been. "You know," she added, "when you first came in that morning, I couldn't place you at all. I didn't know whether you were a—well, a maniac or what. The name was vaguely familiar, but it just didn't connect. Not until Barbie woke up and said *Doc* Levy. *That* name I'd heard—approximately every third sentence, for a year or so, from Tom."

"I never thought I'd be glad to hear Tom was in the Army," he said thoughtfully. "We used to have long talks about Life and Science in the afternoons, and I think I spent more time trying to talk him out of joining up than I did teaching him anything."

Gladys was startled. Tom had never admitted to her that the beloved Dr. Levy shared her feelings about the Army. But of course he did. That's what he was in trouble about.

"Look, Gar—" She hesitated, not knowing just how to put it. "I don't know exactly why it's necessary for you to go. You realize how little I understand about all this. But I know you feel rest is important, and it occurs to me," she smiled, "that you haven't had much here. If it's any reason like that—I mean if there's anything we can do that would make it unnecessary for you to go—you know we'd be glad to have you stay, all of us. When you first came I—"

"When I first came," he said for her, "you were most sensibly disturbed about the danger I represented. But once you made up your mind to let me stay, and realized I wasn't going to politely refuse, you did everything you could to make me comfortable. If there were any more you could do I might very well feel it was asking too much—but as it happens, there isn't. You don't have the equipment, and the hospital does. So, much as I prefer the company of your family to that of a lot of overtired, disagreeable nurses, I'm going to do everything I can to get in there. But don't be *too* surprised if you find me sneaking back into the clothes drier tonight. I don't know how it will turn out."

"Well…just be sure you do come back, if you want to."

"I've already made sure I had an excuse. I didn't leave my gloves, but my Geiger counter. Barbara hid all my stuff away in what she assures me is a safe place upstairs. You're not supposed to have things like that around, you know—it's all been commandeered. See?" The gentle grin broke across his broad face. "I may take my charming presence away, but I leave my menace with you. I hope I don't have to add that if you think it advisable you are perfectly free to dispose of the stuff at any time."

"You know," she laughed, "every time I forget you're a teacher, and decide to treat you just like other people, you come out with a sentence like that. 'If you think it advisable,' " she mimicked. "I wish I could talk you into staying."

"Not a chance. Anyhow"—he took her hand between both of his— "what do you suppose your husband would say if he came home and found you were keeping a man in the attic?"

"At my age?" She smiled. "He'd be right proud of me."

"Not after he saw the man, he wouldn't. At least, not unless I get to that hospital soon and persuade them to patch me up a little. Good-bye, Gladys, and…'thank you' is pretty inadequate. I'll try to find something better for when I come back."

She walked downstairs with him and waited while he said good-bye to Veda. He had already taken his leave of the two girls upstairs, and asked them to stay up there till he was gone. He did not, he explained, want to have to warn them about loud good-byes.

Gladys thought to step out, before he left, and make sure there was no patrol truck in sight. Then he slipped out of the house, and possibly out of her life, very quietly, and with much less drama than anything he had done before.

Chapter Twenty-Three

The house felt strangely empty when he was gone. Gladys remembered how glad she would have been to see the last of him only two days ago, and thought, *Now there's no man in the house again.*

Knowing where that kind of thought could lead, she banished it by plunging into a fury of housework.

"We better use the hot water while we've got it," she told Veda. "Lord knows if we can keep that stove going by ourselves."

The two of them washed, scrubbed, and cleaned, with Ginny's dubious assistance, while Barbie took her turn at the bathtub. Then Gladys sent Veda off for her share of their greatest luxury—hot water—and found it was already time for lunch. She scouted the contents of the refrigerator and found, next to the roast she had planned for Monday, a lone lamb chop which would do nicely for Ginny.

Moving around the kitchen, pulling things out, rearranging them, she felt busy and useful and almost happy. Then, from force of habit, she tried to turn on the gas range, and the happy illusion vanished when she had to take her pan over to the hot plate instead.

She sat with Ginny at the table while the little girl ate—or, more accurately, refused to eat—her lunch. Inactivity and confinement were beginning to tell on her. Maybe I could just take her for a walk, Gladys thought. Really, there was no reason not to. But she hesitated, and decided not to say anything yet.

Spurning her vegetables, Ginny bit ferociously into the chop. But after an experimental chew she returned the bite promptly to the plate.

"Ginny, I've told you about that, over and over again!"

"But itsh got stonesh in it," Ginny complained, and they both realized what had happened. "Mommy, my tooth!"

"Let me see," Gladys demanded.

Small fingers plowed through the mess on the plate and came up with ivory. Then Ginny opened her mouth proudly and pulled back her lip to show the hole. "I 'old 'oo…" She discovered that talking with her mouth open was even more difficult. "I *told* you it was loosh."

"I guess you did."

"And you didn't believe me. I told you, didn't I? You wouldn't even feel it." She was learning to negotiate the air hole.

But I did feel it. It was puzzling, till she realized that wasn't the one she had, after all, felt. She must have misunderstood when Ginny pointed it out.

The loss of a tooth at the age of five and not quite a half is a memorable occasion, but not one conducive to hearty eating. When Ginny refused to stay at the table any longer Gladys had to scrape a half-filled plate of food into the garbage pail.

Clutching the precious tooth in her hand, Ginny went off for her nap, and Gladys had her own lunch, together with Barbara, in the darkened kitchen. She wanted to get upstairs again, where the sun still came through the windows, but the inexhaustible radio stopped her on her way through the living room.

"The news for today in the lower Westchester area. All residents are requested to discontinue any unnecessary use of electric power. Electricity must be conserved. You are being asked to use electric power in your house for none but essential purposes. In those areas where the gas supply has failed, cooking by electricity will be permitted. You may continue to use your radio, but broadcasts will no longer be continuous. News broadcasts will be made once an hour on the hour, and you are requested to turn your set off when the broadcast is concluded, and leave it off until the following hour.

"There are to be no electric lights used during daylight hours. Heating devices of any kind are not to be used unless authorized in writing by an emergency squadman. I repeat: if you wish to use special heating devices, or any kind of special electric equipment, you must obtain written authorization from your squadman. This restriction applies also to electric irons, mixers, toasters, and similar household equipment. A squadman or emergency policeman may visit your home at any time to check on the equipment in use. Please understand that this action is necessary in order to conserve power during the emergency. Violations reported by inspectors will be severely penalized.

"Emergency Headquarters for the lower Westchester area reports that plans for evacuation are now being completed. An evacuation order is expected momentarily, and it is reported that the first special train to the Civilian Evacuation Camp, at the Sampson Navy Base, will leave sometime tomorrow.

"Your squadman will notify you when you are to be evacuated, and you will receive notice in ample time to prepare to leave your homes. You are urged, however, to consult your information sheets now and plan your preparations ahead of time. If you cooperate with Emergency Headquarters the evacuation can be conducted in a safe and orderly manner.

"News has been received here from Denver, Colorado, by way of amateur radio relay stations, to the effect that…"

"I guess it's no use asking how you feel about it," Barbie said. "This morning I thought for a little while maybe you'd decide to stay here, but if the news yesterday made you want to go…"

"I don't know, darling."

Barbara looked at her with quick surprise. "You mean you're not sure? You *might…*"

"That's right. Jim Turner was here this morning," she began.

"I saw him. I didn't want to talk to him."

"Neither did I. He said we can't get a clearance for Veda to go with us. He also…I just don't know, Barbie, I don't know what to do."

She got up, paced around the room, and came back to where her daughter still sat on the floor. "Things are going to be bad here. I don't see how we can stay. And I don't see how we can go."

"Maybe…" Barbara stood up to face her. "Maybe it would be better to go—for you and Ginny. Mother!" Excitement flared in her eyes. "Mother, I'll bet Veda could go to work in the hospital! Then you wouldn't have to worry about me, if she was there. That would take care of everything."

"Not quite," Gladys said. "Barbie, please don't make me quarrel with you. I don't want to. But as far as the hospital is concerned, that's out, for you. I don't want to hear it discussed again. For Veda, it might not be such a bad idea. I don't know. I just *don't know.*"

She turned and clenched her fists, fighting against weariness and fear. When she turned back Barbara was walking silently away. Maybe that was better, better than quarreling anyway. What you didn't say you didn't have to explain away.

She went to find Ginny. The little girl had to have a bath. She had to be ready, in case…

I don't know. How can I know what to do?

Ginny had gotten over her cranky spell of the day before. She seemed to have accepted solitude and had taken over the attic, since that morning, as her own domain.

Gladys found her there and whisked her through a tub, then buttoned the shiny-clean child into a freshly starched frock.

"And when," she demanded, looking the little girl over, "did you last brush your hair?"

"I don't know." Ginny refused to take it seriously until she saw her mother pick up the brush and comb. "Not the comb," she said firmly. "Just the brush."

"The brush," Gladys repeated, *"and* the comb. The way it is, you'll have birds building nests in your hair soon."

"Can't," Ginny pointed out with cheerful logic. "All the birds went away." She smiled hopefully at her mother, decided the argument hadn't worked, and set her face again in firm resistance. "No comb," she said stubbornly.

"Well, we'll see." Gladys began pulling gently with her fingers to separate the tangled mat in back before she brushed it. "For heaven's sake, hold still, Ginny."

"But you're pulling."

"I am not pulling. *Will* you stay still?"

"Ouch!" Ginny jerked her head to the side, away from Gladys' probing fingers. Gladys couldn't let go in time.

"I'm sorry, baby," she started to say, "but I have to—" Then she stopped. Ginny had jerked her head away. Ginny's head was no longer in her hands, but Ginny's hair was.

Gladys stared with speechless fascination at the mat of hair between her fingers. Her eyes followed the wisps of hair out in all directions from the central tangle. Down here—the ends; up there—the roots.

"Ginny!" she cried. "Baby!"

Ginny promptly burst into tears. "I'm sorry, Mommy. I'm sorry. I didn't do it on purpose. I couldn't help it, 'cause it hurt."

"Oh no, baby. No, that's all right. Ginny darling, stop crying. Please stop crying," Gladys begged. "Stop crying and tell me something. It's very important."

But the little girl didn't, or couldn't, stop. She put her head on her mother's lap and let the tears flow.

"There, baby, there." Gladys started to pat the shaking head and hastily moved her hand down to the shuddering small shoulders.

She had to get control of herself before she could stop Ginny, she knew that. "There, baby, it's all right. There's nothing to cry about."

Slowly the sobs diminished and the tears dried up. Bit by bit the child grew calmer. Finally Gladys picked her up and settled the little girl on her lap.

"Now listen, baby." She tried to talk quietly. "I want to know just what happened. Whatever it was, it's going to be all right, but I do have to know. Listen carefully now. You remember when Barbie got sick?"

Ginny nodded her head.

"You do remember? And you remember how she told you not to tell me? Remember how you promised?"

Again Ginny nodded.

"And then you remember afterwards it was all right to tell?"

"Uh-huh."

"Well, now I want you to tell me whether you were sick too. Even if it wasn't all right to tell me before, it's all right now. You have to understand that. But if you were sick I've got to know."

She must have let too much urgency creep into her voice. She got no answer, but only a fresh flood of tears and protests.

"I'm a good girl, Mommy. I'm a good girl. I didn't do nothin' bad."

"You're sure you didn't throw up? Are you *sure* you didn't?"

"Mommy, don't make me go away. Don't let them take me away like Mrs. Crowell. Please, Mommy, I don't want to go away. I'm a good girl. I didn't do nothing—anything—bad!"

There was no use trying to find out any more. "All right, baby." Gladys gave up. "You go show Barbie how pretty you look."

"You mean I don't have to get my hair brushed?" Immediately the tears gave way to a bright smile.

"No, darling." The words were hard to pronounce. "You don't have to get your hair brushed. You go ahead and play."

She waited until Ginny had vanished into Barbara's room, and then headed straight for the telephone. She must have stood there, holding the unresponsive receiver to her ear for several minutes, before she remembered that there would be no answer. The phone was still dead.

She found Veda in the kitchen, cooking supper.

"That child kin make more noise'n any ten men I ever heard," Veda commented as Gladys walked in. "She was screamin' so's you could hear 'er a block away."

"Veda," Gladys blurted out, "I think Ginny's—sick. I think she has *it*."

The spoon dropped into the stew.

"You ain't—you—now, there just ain't no *way* she could've got it," Veda protested. "She's been safe in this house fer days."

"I know. I know that," Gladys said. "But..." She didn't know how to start.

"What's that you got in your hand?" Veda asked. And Gladys realized that she was still holding the matted strands of hair clenched in her fist. She opened the fingers to let Veda see. Then, bit by bit, she got the story out—everything that had happened, how Ginny had acted, and all her own fears and worries.

"We don't know nothin' fer sure," Veda said doubtfully when she had finished.

"I tried to call up," Gladys told her. "I forgot the phone wasn't working." Helplessly they stood there and looked at each other.

"We're supposed to go to Monnassey's," Gladys remembered at last, "and file a complaint."

"I'll go right now." Veda began taking her apron off. "An' I got an idea, too. Mebbe if I jest stop by Mrs. Turner's house she'd have some idea where Mr. Turner an' that doctor would be, an' I could fetch them."

"That's a good idea. You stay here, Veda. I'll go."

But Veda wouldn't hear of it. "You start running around askin' questions, you're goin' to go crazy," Veda told her. "I tell you what. You jest settle down here an' fish that spoon out of the stew an' finish makin' supper. That'll give you a little somethin' to do, with out you goin' to talk to people. I'll go right over there an' be back in a minute." She had her coat, and she was already out of the kitchen.

Gladys retrieved the spoon and set to work, stirring the stew. When Veda came back to say that Monnassey's was closed, and there was no one at home at the Turners', Gladys received the information without surprise or apparent disappointment. She accepted, with equal lack of enthusiasm, Veda's offer to go out and look for the truck itself. There was nothing she could do, nothing—until the doctor came.

The front door banged behind Veda, and Gladys still stood at the hot plate, stirring as if her sanity depended on it.

Chapter Twenty-Four

Six o'clock, and Veda not yet back.

She didn't come. The truck didn't come; the doctor didn't come.

There wasn't enough to do. Supper was all ready, and too easy to serve. The children ate well. Ginny's appetite had returned, and she was being determinedly angelic. She was out from under the spotlight and wanted to stay that way. Barbie insisted on doing the dishes. There was no way to keep busy.

Seven o'clock.

She would have to put Ginny to bed. It was getting late, and sleep could be important.

She did everything slowly, stalling for time, trying to convince herself that Veda would be there any minute with the doctor. But in the end she had to tuck Ginny in with the blue plush Pallo, kiss her, and turn out the light, just like any other night.

Seven-thirty, and she sat with Barbie in the living room again, in front of the radio, waiting.

"I wonder what's taking Veda so long?"

Gladys looked up from the little crystal circle on her wrist with its graceful mocking hands.

"She hasn't got much time before curfew. You wouldn't think the stores would stay open so late."

"The stores?" Of course, Barbie would have wondered about Veda's absence. Or had Veda told her that? The girl was waiting for an answer. What was it she had started to say? The stores? That gave it away, of course.

She looked down again, trying to think, and the hands of her watch were glittering spears, piercing her reserve. She hadn't wanted to say anything to Barbie, not till she knew for sure. But she couldn't keep it to herself any longer..

Barbara heard the story out with a combination of horror and suppressed excitement.

"Look, Mom," she burst out as soon as Gladys was finished, "I bet *I* could get her to tell me what happened. When I got sick she found out, and I made her promise not to tell. If I promised her I bet she'd believe me."

Gladys wished she'd thought of it before. It just might work. "It's too late," she pointed out to Barbara. "She ought to be asleep now. I don't think we should wake her up."

"I'll go see if she's really asleep. I won't get her upset. I can handle that kid."

"Sit *down,* Barbie! I said no, didn't I?"

"Well, don't you want to know?" she demanded.

"What I don't want is to wake her up. She has to have rest."

"Well, but that's—" Barbara looked pleadingly at her mother. "You should have told me before anyway," she complained. "Then I could have talked to her before she went to bed." Barbie went back to her seat on the floor and picked up her book with a great display of concentration on the printed page. Gladys made no effort to reopen the conversation. She just sat, now, waiting.

The radio announced the fifteen-minute curfew warning and, still in silence, the two of them made the rounds, checking windows and doors. That didn't take long enough either; everything was all right, closed, tight, secure; danger was locked out and fear sealed in. She didn't hear a truck pull up, but at the first knock she flew to the door.

"Doctor!"

"Thought I'd never make it." Garson Levy pushed the door closed behind him and leaned against it, resting a minute. "Got held up by a patrol truck a few blocks away." He was breathing hard. "They start questioning people just before curfew, and then they let you go just in time to be picked up by another one for being out late." He straightened up and walked toward the living room, peeling off his dusty jacket and smoothing his wild hair as he went. Then the tension in the house caught at him.

"What did you say?" He turned back to Gladys. "Before, at the door? What's wrong?"

"Ginny. She's got—I mean I think   her hair—" The words kept getting mixed up in her throat. "Her hair came out. I was brushing it, and it came out in my hand, and I think she's—"

"Has the doctor been here?"

Gladys shook her head. "Veda went out. The phone isn't working, and Veda went to find the truck. That was hours ago, and she isn't back yet. I don't know *what* to do."

"Where's Ginny now?"

"In bed. You said, I think you said once, that sleep would help. She didn't act sick or anything; she felt fine except for the fuss when it happened. I was brushing her hair, and some of it came out, and she started crying when I asked her if she threw up. It came out right in my hand."

"Is she asleep?" He wasted no time on sympathy.

"I think so. I don't know. Why?"

"I could take a blood count while we're waiting," he suggested. "It wouldn't prove anything of course. But if it's gone that far already... I don't know. I don't see how it could. But we might find out something."

Gone so far? She remembered the doctor saying "...if we catch it early enough..." but he had never told her how early that was.

"Did you say you can take a blood count yourself? Don't you need all those things, the little tubes and—"

"I told you, Mom." Barbie had been waiting for a chance to get into the conversation. "I told you he brought all those things home yesterday: the Geiger counter and blood-count gadget and all that stuff. You just never listen to anything I say."

"But don't you have to be a doctor?" Gladys looked from one to the other with growing comprehension. "You mean anybody can take a blood count?"

"Not anybody, but anyone with a little training in lab work can do it easily." Levy loosened his tie and ran his fingers restlessly through his unruly hair. "It's just a matter of equipment, and I have everything here already. That's how I've been keeping track of myself. You remember when I asked you for the boiling water last night, don't you? That was for sterilizing the stuff. There's nothing difficult about doing it," he repeated. "If you put some water on to boil now, we could have some kind of result in less than an hour, I think."

"I don't think Mother would want you to wake Ginny up," Barbie put in primly, still nursing her grievance.

"Barbara, I don't believe you were asked—"

"Oh, Barbara! I'm glad you reminded me," he said briskly, treating Gladys' anger and her daughter's petulance with equal indifference. "There's one big thing somebody's got to do right away: the patrol trucks are still out now. If you go out and watch, maybe you can stop one and ask the patrolman to get a message to the doctor. That should be about the quickest way to get him here. They call in to headquarters at regular intervals, I think."

"But Veda—" Gladys stopped herself and turned to her daughter. "Would you start the water first, please, Barbie? I want to go up and see if Ginny is sleeping."

Gladys ran up the stairs after the teacher and caught up to him in the hall.

"Veda went out to look for the truck," she told him. "I don't know why it's taking her so long, but what good do you think it would do for Barbie to send the same message?"

"I don't know if it would do any good at all," he answered. "But I do think Barbara ought to have something to do, and it just might help."

"Do you really think it's safe for her to go out?" Gladys demanded.

"I really couldn't say," he retorted. "Is she easily damaged by fresh air?" Gladys flushed with anger and saw his face relent immediately. "I'm sorry," he said. "I shouldn't be sarcastic right now, but that was pretty silly. If it's all right for me to go out, and for Veda, why wouldn't it be all right for Barbara?"

"I don't know," Gladys admitted. "I just feel as if nobody should go out unless it's necessary. That's what they keep saying on the radio anyhow," she added stubbornly.

"You're right, of course, up to a point. But what I said before was not strictly true, as long as we're splitting hairs. Has it occurred to you that something might have happened to Veda? The curfew patrol is remarkably efficient, and I expect she is on her way to some sort of trouble right now, for violating the curfew. Stopping a patrol truck might be our last chance to get a message to the doctor until the squad truck comes around—whenever that may be."

There was no possible answer to his array of arguments. Gladys simply absorbed the succession of shocks and reminded herself that it didn't pay to challenge this man. Every time she backed him into a corner he turned around and bit her with some new unpleasant information.

"Before you wake Ginny up," he said, "there's one thing I wanted to tell you. I didn't think of it when I first offered to make the blood count, but the only good it will do is to let you know the worst—if it is the worst—a little sooner. All this kind of equipment has been commandeered, you know. It's illegal to have any of the stuff in your house. You won't be able to tell the doctor that a blood count was already made, and it won't save any time in his diagnosis. About the only concrete thing you can hope to get out of it is a personal knowledge of just how urgent it is to get the doctor here. Do you still want to do it?"

"I think so." She stared at the closed door to Ginny's room. "Suppose I go see how easy it is to wake her up? If she's sleeping soundly, maybe we oughtn't to bother."

"That sounds sensible," he agreed. "I'll get the things together meanwhile, just in case."

Gladys crossed the darkened threshold into Ginny's room and groped for the chain to the soft night light

A gentle glow diffused the room, just as a cheerful high voice announced that Ginny was, after all, wide awake.

"Hello, Mommy. Did you come to tuck me in again?"

"No, baby. Doc—Mr. Carney just came home, and he wanted to say hello to you, so I came to see if you were asleep yet."

Ginny puzzled over that "Why?" she demanded finally.

"Why *what?*"

"Why does Mr. Carney want to say hello when I'm s'posed to be *asleep?*" The young voice was prim and virtuous.

"Well, he—" She's not afraid of needles. Did she see the doctor take the blood from Barbie? Gladys wondered. "He wants to play a kind of game with you." She saw her daughter's startled disbelief and realized her own nervousness wasn't helping matters any. "He wants to take a kind of test."

"When I'm s'posed to be *asleep?*" Ginny asked again incredulously. Virtue was rapidly turning to suspicion.

"Well, it's kind of important. And he didn't get home before."

Ginny sat bolt upright, hugging faithful Pallo tight against her cheek. "I don't want to. I want to go to sleep." Oh dear! Now what? "I'm sleepy. Turn my light out." The child suited the histrionics to the words and lay down again, burrowing under her blanket.

What in the world...?

"Mom!" A door banged loudly, downstairs. Barbara's voice was breathless and excited. "Mother! Mom, c'mere!"

"I'll be right back, baby." She dropped a kiss on the tiny patch of Ginny's forehead that still showed above the covers. The patch promptly disappeared, and something emerged from under the covers about turning the light out, but Gladys didn't stop to listen.

"The truck's outside, Mom," Barbie greeted her on the stairs. The front door was wide open. "They wouldn't listen to me, but I told them I'd get my mother."

"All right, I'll talk to them."

"I'll go take care of Ginny."

"You better leave her alone. She's all upset." *I hope Gar doesn't get down there before I get back. I hope…* There was no use thinking about it. "You stay here," she called again, to Barbie, and went out the door.

The big squadman stood at the porch steps, his visor down, his foot rocking impatiently on the flagstone. It was as close as he could come to impatient tapping in the heavy shoes. At the back entrance to the truck another man looked out curiously, visor open for a clearer view. Gladys didn't recognize him at a distance.

"Come in," she told the squadman impatiently. "Isn't the doctor with you?" She had to stop to catch her breath. Her voice wasn't working right again.

"Sorry, ma'am, I can't come in. We're on patrol."

"Oh!" She was startled. Standing above him on the porch, she hadn't been able to see his face, shielded as it was by the raised visor. But his voice was that of a total stranger. "I thought you were—"

"If you want your regular squadman, he'll be around later on," he said. "They're changing off the regular schedule, so I can't say just when—but you watch out for him; he'll be here."

"Wait a minute. Please wait!" He was going away. He didn't understand.

"Lady, I can't wait. I've got a job to do."

"But my *daughter—please!* Listen to me!"

He didn't stop, but he started and half turned back. It was all the time she needed. "I can't wait for the regular squadman," she told him quickly. "I have to get a message to the doctor right away. We sent somebody out to find the truck, to get the doctor, but that was five o'clock and she's not back yet. All I want to do is let the doctor know."

At last he was showing some interest. Gladys stopped to catch her breath and he filled in the pause with a swift question of his own. "Still out? What's her name?" She told him Veda's name and, on demand, produced a brief description. "If we pick her up now, we'll know who she is," he explained, tucking away the notebook in which he had scribbled the information.

"But I need a *doctor!*" Gladys protested. "That's what I stopped you for."

"Who's the doctor on duty here?"

"Dr. Spinelli, Peter Spinelli. He's an intern at the new Veterans' Hospital. The squadman is Jim T—"

"Hey, Spinelli's the kid on duty this evening at headquarters, ain't he?" That was from the man in the back of the truck. For the first time Gladys realized how loud she must have been talking.

"Yeah, I think so. I'll leave a call for him when I check in."

"Please let him know as soon as you can," she pleaded, knowing it was useless. The man just didn't care. "It's my little girl," she explained again. "Her hair—"

"I'll tell him, but your kid ain't the only sick one, you know:" He had lost all interest.

There had to be some way. "Do you know Jim Turner?" she asked, trying to keep him there until she could find something that would work. Unexpectedly Turner's name had an immediate effect.

"You a friend of his?" the man asked.

"Well…yes."

He caught her hesitation. "He's your squadman, uh? Not a personal friend?"

"No, that is, yes." She forced confidence into her voice. "He's the squadman here, but he's an old friend too. He said if anything went wrong to be sure and let him know right away. If you—"

"Well, look, Miss—Mrs.—I mean, I'm only trying to do my duty. I'm not supposed to handle anything but violations on curfew patrol, but I said I'd get the doctor for you, didn't I? Look." He fished out the notebook again. "Maybe you better give me more details. What's the kid's name? Age? He'll know who she is, won't he?" He wrote rapidly. "I'll leave a call for the doctor, like I said, but he's on duty right now, I know. Can't say when he'll get here. Mr. Turner could probably get him quicker for you. Tell you what, suppose *I* call Mr. Turner for you, how's that?"

"That's not—Yes, of course, that's a good idea." It dawned on her just in time that the man was trying to keep her from calling Turner. It didn't make sense. If she had a phone working she wouldn't have had to stop him in the first place. But she kept herself from asking questions or saying anything more that might modify his incomprehensible change of attitude.

She watched him fill in the house number in his little book and turn back to his truck.

Why should Jim Turner's name have such a startling effect? It certainly wasn't a matter of personal liking. The man's attitude had been one of respect or…

The full significance of the patrolman's change of mind finally struck her. He'd been afraid. Was it possible that Turner was actually as important in the new scheme of things as he would have her believe?

She wished there had been some way to keep the patrolman from calling Turner.

She almost wished she had never mentioned Turner's name. But if it meant getting the doctor sooner…

"What did he say? Didn't they have a doctor? Are they going to get Pete—Dr. Spinelli?" Barbara flew down the stairs toward her.

"What? Oh." She pulled her thoughts away from the mystery of Jim Turner's name. "He's going to call the doctor and Mr. Turner both. They're just the curfew patrol truck. They don't have a doctor with them, but they said Dr. Spinelli's on duty at headquarters, and they'll call him."

"Well, what do they have to call Mr. Turner for?"

"I don't know." *I wish I did.* She started up the stairs.

"Mom."

"What? Oh, is the water ready yet, Barbie?"

"I was just coming down to start some more. He's got some on the hot plate upstairs for sterilizing things. I thought I'd make some tea or coffee or something, and Doc didn't eat anything yet, so I figured I'd heat up the stew. There's still some left."

"That's fine." She's really such a good girl. Gladys reached out and squeezed her daughter's arm with sudden tenderness. It was terrible to be so young and not able to do anything, when the world turned upside down like this. "I…" There just weren't any *right* words. "I don't know what I'd do without you, Barbie," she finished lamely.

"Mom, listen."

Gladys stopped, her foot already on the first step. Barbara hadn't moved toward the kitchen at all.

"Listen, Mom, don't go up."

"What do you mean, don't go up? For heaven's sake, why not? After all, Ginny hardly even knows him and—of course I'm going up." Impatiently she shook off the girl's hand.

"Well, listen, Mom. It's just—well, you know how Ginny's always better at the doctor's if you don't go into the room with her. Little kids just are that way. You told me that yourself, and I know it's true. Anyhow, you're all—well, you're all nervous and everything. Don't get mad at me again, Mother, please. Only I think it's better if you don't, honest."

Gladys could only stare at the girl, amazed.

"Besides, she isn't upset, and anyhow, he's in there with her already, and—*please* don't be mad at me, Mom—but I was sitting with her awhile, before Doc Levy came down, while he was getting his stuff together, so I asked her about—you know—if she was sick."

Gladys took her foot off the stairs and followed her daughter through the living room.

"What—what did she say?" That was silly; she knew the answer. *"When* was it?"

"Well, that's what I don't understand. She says it was Tuesday, when you were sleeping. It must have been when she was taking her nap—come to think of it, she didn't feel so good at lunchtime—but that's practically impossible because Pete said it's always within a few hours after exposure. It was about eight hours for me and they said that seemed like a long time. Tuesday afternoon would make it a whole day, or even the morning would be an awful long time."

"Are you sure she didn't go outside Tuesday morning?"

"I was with her myself practically every minute," Barbie insisted, "and anyhow, the door was locked up on top. She can't open that. I *know* she wasn't out."

"Well, she must have been. I don't know how, but she must have been."

"Well, there's another thing too. Listen, Mom, Doc says sometimes it's much quicker with little kids, and if her hair is coming out so soon, in just a couple of days, that would mean she would have had to be sick just about right away. So maybe—maybe it's something else. Maybe she hasn't really got it."

Gladys looked away from the pleading eyes and shook her head. "No." There was no way out of it. "She's got it. I knew you didn't, and I know she does." She could feel the matted strands of hair again, as if she still held them in her hand. She wiped the damp palm against her apron.

"I promised," Barbie said suddenly. "I promised not to tell." She turned and pushed through the dining-room door, letting it slam behind her. Gladys started after her and stopped. Leave her alone, leave her alone. She has to be alone.

She started again for Ginny's room. Out of old habit she stopped at the bottom step to listen. There wasn't a sound from upstairs, no voices, no footsteps. He must have the door closed. Except for the ceaseless, senseless chatter of the radio, the whole house was silent, deadly silent. What is he doing up there? Gladys went back into the living room, made herself sit down, forced herself to stay there, to sit and wait.

CHAPTER TWENTY-FIVE

GAILY CARVED IN THE KITCHEN, oak-framed black on the dining-room wall, tiny gilded stripes in the watch on her wrist, with unremitting patience the hands completed and renewed their circles. And still they didn't come. No sign, no word, from Veda, from Turner, from the doctor.

Alone in her room again, Ginny cried a little bit in sleepy protest, then fell asleep in the middle of a sob.

Downstairs Gladys heard the news without surprise when Garson Levy explained that the blood count made it certain Ginny was sick, and almost as certain what the nature of her illness was. The white-blood-cell count was drastically low, and checked too well with the symptoms they already knew. Gladys tightened her grip on the arms of Jon's big chair and thanked him quietly.

"Of course, I'm not sure. I can't be sure. Another count…"

"Yes, of course." Gladys cut him off. She was sure; she didn't need another count.

When is the doctor coming?

Levy went back upstairs, to dismantle his makeshift laboratory and put his things back in the attic hideaway. Barbara went quietly out to the kitchen to get the warmed-up supper she had fixed for him. Gladys sat alone, studying the unchanging pace of the little gold hands on her wrist.

Afterward, when the dishes were put away and there was nothing to do again, they gathered in the living room and tried to talk. But every subject led, by a devious route of its own, to the one thing Gladys could not, would not, talk about.

Unworried and unhurried, the little hands on the watch, the big ones on the clocks moved steadily past nine and ten and toward eleven. Somewhere in those rounds of time Jim Turner came. They all heard the car in front of the house, and the sound pulled Gladys blindly from her chair, drew her unthinking to the door. It was Barbie who remembered and made her stop and wait, to let Levy get out of sight upstairs before she opened the door.

And then it was only the squadman. The doctor wasn't with him, and he knew nothing about Veda. He had come straight to the house when he got the patrolman's message, and knew only that there was trouble at the Mitchell house.

Gladys listened impatiently to his explanations, and once again she told the story of Ginny's hair. But now it was maddening when he tried to reassure her, when he urged her to wait for the blood count before she worried too much, when he stood there *talking* instead of doing something, and she couldn't tell him a blood count had already been made.

And when she told him about Veda his only answer was a knowing shrug. "She couldn't get very far. The boys have probably picked her up already. I'll let you know if she turns up at headquarters, but I don't think they'll let her go again. Don't make much difference. I'll get the doctor for you, and I already told you she'd probably be pulled in before evacuation anyhow."

The door closed behind him, and there was another chilling thought to add to the sum of fear in the household. She asked Dr. Levy, but he could not, or would not, add anything to what Gladys knew about the Security Office. She felt as he talked that there was much he was not saying, and that none of it was good, but she did not press him. She knew already that if anything in his own experience would help, however unpleasant it might be, he would tell. If he was holding back, it was because he saw no useful purpose in adding to her fears.

When the desultory conversation died out entirely Barbie suggested cards. But Gladys couldn't keep her mind on three-handed bridge, and she broke away to find a corner where she could bend unseeing over a magazine and not have to talk. She was grateful when the others went off upstairs and left her to nurse her worries alone. Barbara explained that they'd be within earshot, but far enough so she could open the door without waiting, and she nodded in reply, never raising her eyes from the blurred page on her lap.

Once in a while she looked at her watch, but time went on forever, and the hands barely moved. She knew it was after midnight, though, when a car pulled up again in front of the house.

"Oh, thank God, thank God you're here!" Gladys was almost as relieved at the sight of Veda's familiar face as she was at the doctor. "You're all right?" she asked Veda. "What happened to you? We were so worried." Without waiting for an answer she turned to Spinelli. "She's upstairs, Doctor, do you want to see her right away? They told you, didn't they—about Ginny?"

He nodded. "I'll go right up. As soon as I can get this thing off." He was fumbling with the heavy helmet of his suit.

"Can I help?" Barbie came down the stairs, across the hall, and reached up shyly but efficiently to unfasten the metal closing that held the helmet to the suit.

"Thank you." He let her take the heavy headpiece. "Is she sleeping?" he asked Gladys.

"She was last time I looked. I don't understand it; she seems so healthy."

He nodded. "That can happen. Just a minute, will you? Barbie, will you take care of Veda while we go up? She's had a bad time tonight. She ought to go straight to bed."

"What...?" Startled, Gladys saw Barbara help Veda out of the chair near the door. "What happened? Is it serious?" She saw Veda try to protest and then give in weakly. "What happened to her, Doctor?"

"The Security Office," he said briefly. "I'll tell you about it later. Or Veda will. It's not serious—she just needs a good rest. You go ahead." He turned to the maid, standing in the doorway, leaning on Barbie's arm. "Get into bed before I put you in myself."

She smiled weakly. "I was jest thinking," she pleaded, "I'd ruther wait till there's some word about Ginny. I couldn't rest good not knowin'."

"I'll come in and tell you," Barbara promised. "Come on, you heard what the doctor said."

Veda shook her head. "I'd a sight ruther lay down in here awhile, if Missus Mitchell don't mind. Then I'd know fer sure."

"Of course I don't mind."

"Well, I do." The doctor was firm. "You get her into bed right now, Barbie. And don't take any back talk. I'd have been here an hour ago," he told Gladys when they were gone, "if I'd left her there. Those boys had it all figured out she was a dangerous enemy agent."

He started up the stairs as he talked, taking two steps at a time, so Gladys had to run to keep up and hear what he was saying.

"They picked her up after curfew, without identification, and she kept asking for me. She told them who she was, and when they checked they found out she was supposed to have a clearance to be out at all. Of course they didn't believe a word she said about why she was out, and—"

They were at Ginny's door. He stopped and lowered his voice to finish the story. "They never thought of finding out who I was. They just took it for granted she was lying. She was getting a pretty rugged third degree—polite American variety—bright lights and lots of questions, for about two hours, till Turner's call came in, and I was paged on the speaker system. When they realized I was right in the building, they called me in to identify her. Then it took me about an hour, after I verified her story, to get them to release her. They just couldn't stand the idea of giving up a suspect."

"Is she—will she be all right?" Gladys asked.

"Sure. They didn't hurt her. I told you it was the polite type. But she's beat. She ought to take it easy tomorrow too."

"I'll see to it," she promised.

"Okay." He grinned at her. "Now I've got that out of my system and said enough to be damn near court-martialed, suppose we take a look at the kid."

Gladys led the way. She switched on the overhead light, and they saw Ginny curled peacefully around her friend Pallo, nuzzling the worn fuzziness of his plush hide.

"Wake up, baby." Gladys nudged the small shoulder and leaned over to drop a kiss on the flushed cheek. "Wake up. You have to wake up now. You've got some company."

Ginny transferred her embrace from the blue horse and twined her arms sleepily around Gladys' neck to pull herself up. Then she looked over her mother's shoulder and her eyes flew open.

"Hello." She seemed to find it perfectly natural that the doctor should be standing by her bed. "I know who you are," she announced. "You're Pete. You was talking to Babsy. I remember you."

Gladys saw the rare, sweet smile spread across his face, and immediately everything seemed easier and less fearsome.

"That's very clever of you," he told Ginny gravely. "This time I came to talk to *you.*"

Ginny promptly released her strangle hold on her mother and patted the side of her bed invitingly.

"Sit down," she offered.

"That's a nice horse you've got," he complimented her. "You know your mother thinks you're sick?"

Ginny nodded. "Only I ain't. Amn't," she assured him.

"You feel pretty good?" he asked.

"Sure I feel good. What's that for?" She was pointing to the long zipper on the back flap pocket that held his medical equipment. He pulled it open and let her peer in at the jumbled assortment of tubes and jars and implements. "See?" he said. "All the things you need to be a doctor with."

"You gonna stick a needle in me and make me bleed like before?"

"I never did it to you before, though," he said. "Just Barbie. I only do that to big girls and you were too little before."

"I'm big enough now," she assured him. "Because Mr. Car—"

"Ginny's used to needles," Gladys broke in hastily. "She's had all kinds of shots at the doctor's."

The doctor didn't seem to notice anything. "All right," he said. "If you'll get me some alcohol we can start right in and do it just the same way I did for Barbie."

"With the funny thing you squeeze?" Ginny asked. "Like a horn, only no noise?"

"You've got the idea." He turned to Gladys. "If you don't mind…"

She did mind. There was no telling what Ginny might say while she was out of the room. But there was nothing else to do.

"No, of course not. I'll be right back."

She fairly flew to the bathroom and back, but when she got there Spinelli met her at the door and took the bottle from her hands. "Thank you," he said politely. "This won't take long." Then he stepped back into the room and very firmly shut the door in her face.

Angry and worried both, still she lacked the courage to open the door and go in. He was the doctor. She stood where she was and tried to distinguish words from the murmur of voices that came through the wall, until at last he opened the door to admit her.

"That's a good girl you've got there, Mrs. Mitchell," he said. "She did everything just right." He was holding a thin tube of pinkish liquid corked at either end. It didn't look much like blood to Gladys.

"Look, Mommy." Ginny was wide awake and cheerful. "Look what Dr. Pete gave me." She waved a wooden tongue depressor gleefully in the air. "Look."

"I see, baby. That's very nice." Gladys walked past the doctor, afraid to look at him. Over her shoulder she asked him, "Can she go back to sleep now?"

"She might as well."

"I don't want to go back to sleep. I'm all woke up."

"Well now, it's the middle of the night, Ginny. You have to go back to sleep." Gladys tried to make her lie down, without success.

"Don't want to go back to sleep. Want to get up."

"Don't be silly, darling, you can't get up now. I told you it's the middle of the night." She couldn't quite keep an edge of sharpness out of her voice. She *had* to talk to the doctor.

Spinelli left the room while she tried futilely to quiet the child. When he came back Barbie was with him.

"Barbie's going to read to you till you fall asleep, Ginny," he said firmly.

She was perfectly willing to make a good bargain. "Will you read the *whole* mouse book?"

"Every single word of it," Barbara promised.

But when Gladys faced the young doctor out in the hall he was no longer smiling. His face was once again as she had first seen it, long and bony and too sober.

"Who is Mr. Carney, Mrs. Mitchell?" He came straight to the point.

"Mr. Carney?" Gladys was prepared. "Why do you ask?" She turned her back on him and started walking down the hall. "Don't you think we'd be more comfortable in the living room?"

"I don't really care. If you don't mind, Mrs. Mitchell, I'd like to discuss it right now. It's important. Who is Mr. Carney?"

It was silly even to try, because she knew it couldn't work, but she tried to make it sound convincing. "He's a friend of Veda's," she lied. "He's—Ginny is crazy about him. He was over here yesterday."

"What would make Ginny say he took a blood sample from her?"

"I don't know. I guess he heard some talk about Barbie, so maybe he pretended to give Ginny a blood test. He's always playing make-believe games with her." She looked straight into his eyes and tried to fill her own with innocence. "That's the only thing I can think of that would account for it."

The doctor shook his head. "It's hard to believe your little girl could know as much as she does, unless she's really had a sample taken before," he said stubbornly.

"But, Doctor," Gladys objected, "you must realize I'd tell you if she had. Why should I try to keep it from you?"

"Because you know as well as I do that any man with the knowledge and equipment to take a blood count had no business being here. Now who *is* Mr. Carney? Where is he?"

"I told you," Gladys said slowly. "He's a friend. A friend of Veda's."

"Where is he? I want to see him."

"Well…he's not here now. I don't know where he lives."

"Look here, Mrs. Mitchell!" It was hard to believe he could be so angry. He had been so even-tempered all the time. "I'm willing to concede that you must have some good reason for lying to me. It would have to be a pretty darn good reason to weigh in the balance with your daughter's life. Or perhaps if you understood fully that the previous blood count could make all the difference in the world, you'd change your story."

Ginny's life?

Ginny, lying in the room behind the closed door, listening to a story and dying as she listened. Dying, dying, dying every minute.

She thought of Garson Levy, coming through the night to warn her about Barbara's danger, fighting off invaders in the darkened kitchen, repairing the terrifying gas leak, boarding up the windows, fixing a toy for Ginny, bringing courage and hope back into the house.

"I don't want to turn anybody in to the Security Office, Mrs. Mitchell. After the way I blew my top before, I should think you'd realize that. All I want is to find out the results of that last blood count. Anyhow"—he smiled a little grimly—"you've got nothing to worry about. Any friend of Mr. Turner's is a friend of the Security Office. I don't care who your mystery man is or what he's done; I just want to avoid any further wait in diagnosing Ginny's case."

Any further wait…They had waited to hear about Barbie. She had waited for the doctor to come. She knew the poisonous fear of waiting. She knew it too well.

She couldn't wait any more; she could do anything but wait. She looked up. The good-natured young man wasn't smiling; his face was set and determined. He saw surrender in her eyes and pounced on it.

"If you won't tell me, the only thing I can do is take her in to the hospital right away. I'll just have to assume it's as bad as it looks."

There was no way out.

"I…" *Forgive me, please forgive me.* She breathed a silent prayer, whether to God or Garson Levy, she didn't know. "I…" It was harder to do because she knew he would forgive her—Doc Levy would. She wet her dry lips.

"It's all right, Gladys." The door to the attic stairs stood open, and the teacher took a step forward to join them. She hadn't heard it open; how long had he been there? "You're Dr. Spinelli?" He turned to the younger man courteously and extended his hand. "Mrs. Mitchell and her daughter have both told me a great deal about you. I'm sorry I had no chance to speak to you before, but there were circumstances…" As if there were nothing to explain, as if it were the most common, everyday sort of meeting. "I'm Albert Carney. You want to see the results on the little girl's blood count, don't you?"

CHAPTER TWENTY-SIX

"OH, THERE you are."

Gladys scrambled to her feet as the doctor pushed through the swinging door.

"How is—can you tell—I mean, do you know anything yet?"

"Not really. I just came down to ask you—" His eyes took in the bubbling pot on the hot plate. "Oh—I see you knew what we'd need."

"What?" She followed his glance, and understood. "No," she admitted. "I should have, I guess, but I was just boiling it to keep. Really," she added, "just to have something to do. Are you going to make the blood count right here?"

"It seems like the best thing—certainly a lot quicker than taking it back to the lab. Levy's got everything I need. He's setting it up in the bathroom now. I was going to help, but that water's almost ready; I might as well wait here for it."

"What did you say?"

"When?"

"Just now—about Mr. Carn—"

"Oh, that." Amused, he leaned against the kitchen cabinet, where he could watch the water, and told her, "I knew him as soon as I got a good look at him. Well, what's so surprising about that?" he demanded. "After all, I was a high school senior, and a science major in Year One of the atom bomb. And I was a college freshman the year Gar Levy was making big noises in the papers with his Survival Kit. I heard him talk several times, and I gave money to his committees. I even managed to get introduced to him at a dinner once. He didn't remember me, of course, but I'd know him anywhere."

The water was boiling. He felt the pot handle gingerly, and Gladys handed him two pot holders, one for each side.

"I could hardly forget him," Spinelli added, "seeing that the money I gave and the petitions I signed were largely responsible for making me a doctor. I had planned on biochemistry," he explained, "in connection with radiation therapy. Unfortunately the work you can do in that field is negligible unless you can pass a loyalty check. I got turned down for an atomic scholarship because of my—ah—unfavorable associations, Gar Levy among others."

He lifted the pot, tested the weight of the scalding water, and began walking carefully toward the door. "At any rate you don't have to worry about my turning him in, believe me. Thanks."

Gladys was holding the swinging door open for him to go through with the steaming pot. She moved ahead to open the other door, into the living room. He paused a minute before he went through and showered her with the warmth of his singular smile. "And thanks again," he said. "Not for the doors. It—means a lot to me, knowing that somebody took him in. He's important."

He went through the door and on to the stairs. Gladys almost followed him, and then remembered that she hadn't turned the hot plate off.

Back in the kitchen she decided to put another pot on, instead of turning the stove off. She found a jar that would hold the boiled water, in case the doctor didn't need it, and left the problem of sealing the jar, which had no top, to the inventiveness of her *important* guest. Barbara's teacher…Tom's teacher…Doctor…Doc…Gar Levy…

She left the water heating up and went up to look in at Ginny. But as she passed the bathroom the young doctor called to her through the half-open door.

"Mrs. Mitchell?"

"Yes?" She peered in and saw a strange-looking machine plugged in to the outlet Jon had installed for his electric razor. The sink was full of little tubes and rubber pieces and needles and glass slides. Spinelli had his sleeve rolled up and was busy sticking one of the little needled tubes into his own arm.

"He wants to check the accuracy of the counter," Levy explained, answering the question in her eyes. "Take his own count first, and check it against what it should be. These things are delicate and they can get out of adjustment pretty easily—and I had no way of checking it."

The doctor's hand relaxed on the little rubber bulb, and he pulled the needle neatly from his arm, swabbed the puncture, and corked the tube, almost with one gesture.

"I just wanted to suggest"—he turned to Gladys—"maybe it would be just as well if Ginny didn't go to sleep right away. I won't know till I finish this, but it might be best to take her to the hospital tonight. Look, don't—well, it's silly to say, don't get upset. But if Levy's count is right, then the quicker we do something, the better off she'll be."

"Yes…yes, of course." She ought to do something. She shouldn't just stand there. She watched him doing swift, competent things with tubes and liquids and slides, but she didn't really see anything. "Yes, I was just going in there anyhow."

The hospital?

He used a walkie-talkie on a squad truck to call headquarters when he was done.

Wisely, Gladys allowed Barbara to dress the child. She herself was strung to a high pitch of nervousness that would have infected Ginny immediately. It gave her a chance, too, for a few minutes alone with the young doctor.

"Do you want to come along?" he asked. "It won't be very pleasant for you, but maybe you'd rather?"

All she could do was nod. There was something she wanted to ask, but she had to wait for her voice to come back.

"How bad is it, Doctor?" Why did they always make you ask? Why couldn't they just tell you? "How did it happen?"

"I don't know. How it happened, that is. When we get her to the hospital the diagnosis might give us a clue. There are all kinds of radiation disease, Mrs. Mitchell, and they've got instruments there that will show just what she's got. Then we can guess how she got it."

"But how bad is it? You're in such a hurry to get her there…"

"Well, it's hard to answer that. The disease has obviously taken a rapid course… But that can happen with children. In an adult the hair falling out so soon might indicate something serious. In a child—there's no telling. I'd really rather not say anything until we see what the testing machines say. How bad it is depends partly on the type of radiation too. I don't want to give you any false hopes, Mrs. Mitchell, but the fact that she's feeling all right is encouraging. The white-cell count I got must be pretty recent."

Gladys waited for him to go on and then closed her mouth on another question. He'd tell her when he had something to tell. There was no reason to torment him with futile questions.

"Thanks." It sounded bitter. She summoned up a ghost of a smile to show she didn't mean it. "I guess I better wash my face if I'm going. Will she—need anything along with her? Clothes or a toothbrush or anything?"

"No." He was thoughtful. "Well, maybe you better take along a pair of pajamas, just in case, but I don't think we'll be there more than an hour or two."

"You mean…?" She couldn't believe it. "You mean we don't have to *leave* her there? You mean she's coming *home?*"

"Oh, I'm sorry! I thought—didn't Levy tell you? About the hospital?"

"Oh, I never even asked him. I forgot all about it. I was so worried about Ginny."

"I haven't been at the hospital since it happened, myself," he told her. "But if things are anywhere near as bad in the children's section as he says they are in the rest of the place, I think she'll be better off here at home. We can draw supplies from the pharmacy there and bring them back to the house for treatments."

"Then she can stay with me? I can take care of her myself?" Now she could think about Doc Levy. "Is that why he came back? I never even asked him," she repeated. "What's he going to do? Did he get a—treatment, or anything?"

"He got a diagnosis. He couldn't be treated without waiting till it was too late to come back today, and he didn't want to stay there. He says his case isn't too serious—a medium dose of gamma, so he's probably just as well off here. I'm going to bring back some stuff for him, too, if I can."

"What's gamma? What does that mean?"

"Oh. Well, as far as treatment is concerned, it means what he needs is rest, and if he could get some blood, that would help too, but—Oh, hello," he broke off. "Ginny's all ready. You better get started, Mrs. Mitchell, if you want to wash up."

Barbie was bringing Ginny, dressed in her best, down the stairs, and Gladys passed them on the run, going up.

"Don't *we* look pretty?" She saw that Barbie was dressed too.

Levy was in the bathroom, clearing away equipment.

"Oh, Gar…" She paused on the flight to her room. "I—Dr. Spinelli was just telling me about you, about this afternoon. I never even asked you before. I just couldn't think about anything but Ginny, and—"

"Of course not." He dismissed the subject. "You want to get in here? Are they waiting for you?"

"I'll go change my dress while you finish. The car's not here yet." She had to hurry. "I seem to owe you a whole new set of thanks, Gar. I don't think I've even realized, half the time, how much you were doing. You just keep…stepping in, when we need you. But—"

"Has it occurred to you that you very likely saved my life when you took me in here?"

"I? That's nonsense! What I wanted to say was, Dr. Spinelli says he's going to try and bring back some stuff for you. I don't know just what it is, but he also said what you need most is rest. All this time you've been doing everything for us, and I just wanted you to know that it won't be that way any more. If there's anything any of us can do—"

"You may get your chance, but I'm not that sick yet." It was the first time she had seen him really embarrassed. "Now go ahead and get dressed. I'll be out of here in a minute."

But when she got downstairs there was a new problem to face. Barbara had made up her mind she was going along. For just a moment Gladys hesitated. Then she remembered the mysterious "conditions" Spinelli had referred to. *"It won't be pleasant."* And things had been too bad there for Levy to stay.

"No," she said firmly, and the battle was joined. That was how Ginny heard the word "hospital" and found out where she was going.

"I don't want to go to the hospital."

"But, baby, you're not going to stay."

"I don't want to go to the hospital. I won't go to the hospital."

She sat down on the floor, spread her hands flat on the rug as if she could cling to the hairs of the nap, and repeated her defiance.

"Darling," Gladys explained patiently, "we're going to take a ride there with the doctor and come right back. We're not—"

But Ginny had found a single sentence that perfectly expressed her feelings, and stuck to it. She stopped repeating it only to try the effects of an occasional sob. They tried ignoring her, and for a while it seemed as if it was going to work. Ginny was tired, after all, and within a few minutes she had almost fallen asleep, had actually dozed off, only to come awake, screaming and kicking, when Gladys tried to pick her up. The noise brought Veda out of her room, bundled in a bathrobe, pale and frightened.

She tried her hand, too, but her "No nonsense!" attitude had no more effect on Ginny than Gladys' explanations or Barbie's promises. Eventually, under the doctor's stern injunctions, she went back to bed, leaving Ginny still in possession of the floor.

"Not gonna go. Not gonna go."

In the ensuing hour the little girl was alternately coaxed, threatened, ignored, patted, pacified, and pulled at. But when the car came she still clearly had no intention of going anywhere.

Spinelli solved the problem then by simply wading in and picking her up, bodily. With his heavy suit on, he could afford to ignore nails, teeth, and shoes. He dumped her unceremoniously in the car, and Gladys followed meekly. Barbie had lost all interest in arguing. She watched them go and made no effort to push her plea again.

Chapter Twenty-Seven

NIGHTMARE RODE WITH THEM through the empty streets in the speeding car. Every familiar pattern of the suburban night was gone. There were no late cars coming back from town, no lonely men out walking in the night, no hastily dressed women pulling on the leashes of their dogs.

Throughout the five-mile drive there was nothing to stop the car, hardly anything to slow it down. The headlights pushed a golden fan ahead, to underscore the darkness all around, picking out blind street lamps and dead traffic lights in their glare. The only signs of life they passed were squad cars and trucks parked here and there on neighborhood patrols. And when they hit the highway, even the trucks were gone.

The noise of the motor made a roaring world of its own inside the car, and the only other sound in the night was the steady wailing of the terrified child.

It was a nightmare from which they woke only to face the white-lighted horror of the hospital. And this horror was not a dream; this was such reality as Gladys had never known before. The sight, the sound, and above all, the smell, of pain and fear, not hidden discreetly behind closed doors, not closed away in back of neatly folded screens, not quieted by starched, white, rubber-soled nurses, not, in any way, the civilized sadness of a hospital.

This was pain on parade, fear on exhibition. All doors stood open, so tired nurses and doctors could hoard what energy they had. Basins and bedpans stood by the beds; no one had time to fetch and carry. Inside each room the floor was crowded with cots, begged, borrowed, improvised from stretchers and wooden blocks. And in the heart of the building, away from the traffic of the outside doors, mattresses lined the floor along the corridor walls. They passed a wagon piled high with dirty dishes outside a ward; a little farther on, an attendant in rumpled khaki coveralls was serving tea to corridor patients. Each one in turn held up a cup or glass, or a small basin, to be filled from a soup ladle out of the bucket she wheeled along.

A young man with a bandage on his head got up and walked along beside her, picking up the cups of those too weak to sit. After a little way the attendant spoke to him, shaking her head, and he went back to lie down on his mattress. There was a small crimson spot on his bandage. A middle-aged woman with one arm in a sling took his place. She wore a torn sweater over the cotton operating gown the hospital had given her. The flapping of the gown on her legs annoyed her, and she draped it to one side with her good arm, then looped the long end over her sling to keep it out of the way.

They reached the children's section by walking through endless corridors and climbing interminable stairs. The elevators were not running; whether for lack of power or personnel, they did not know.

Here bigger rooms and smaller beds made overcrowding less of a problem. The rooms were lined with rows of cots which Gladys recognized as standard nursery school equipment. Different-colored canvas and different types of legs marked their varied origins. She pointed out to Ginny the familiar square green legs and the yellow canvas of the cots at Burl's, but the little girl wouldn't look.

Again Gladys tried to explain to her that she would not have to stay. Ginny only shook her head wisely, refusing to be fooled. She had long ago stopped crying, but ever since they entered the harshly lit white corridors she had been using her own legs and her mother's eyes to walk with. Her two hands clung fiercely to Gladys' skirt, and her head was turned in toward its folds. She would look up only when they were ascending the stairs, where the lights were dimmer, and there were no frightening rows of cots and mattresses.

Now, when her mother's interest in the cots informed her they had reached the children's section, she still refused to show any interest in her surroundings. But when the doctor, looking down at the disheveled curls, remarked kindly, "We're almost there—just around the corner," she responded immediately.

With a howl of protest she flung herself away from Gladys and ran back to the head of the stairs. Too tired and confused to attempt an escape by descent, she seized the doorknob and clung with all her might.

"I won't go!" she shrieked, and the noise echoed down the corridor. "I won't! I won't go!"

"Ginny!" Gladys swept down the corridor after the child. "Ginny, you ab-so-lute-ly-have-to-keep-quiet! There are children sleeping—sick children. Now you behave yourself. If you don't want to get well, *they do.* Now stop it, once and for all!"

To her complete surprise, the shrieking stopped. Gladys seized the opportunity. "Get your hands off that knob," she commanded, "and walk down this corridor like a lady. I'm sick and tired of your nonsense."

Meekly the child did as she was told. And belatedly Gladys understood. Every effort they had made, in the house and on the way, had been with the consciousness of Ginny's trouble in their minds. Now for the first time she had gotten angry enough to forget to be sorry for the little girl—and Ginny had promptly stopped being sorry for herself.

They went around the bend in the corridor, down to a little room labeled "Dispensary."

"If you wait right here"—Spinelli pointed to a bench—"I'll be right out." He knocked on the door and entered without waiting for a reply. Gladys and Ginny sat down on the bench in silence and stayed that way. Determinedly Gladys controlled an impulse to pet the little girl, to apologize to her. Her hand kept trying to move that way, and she kept pulling it back. But the effort was worthwhile. After minutes of utter silence a little voice whispered, "Mommy?"

"Yes?" She tried to make it sound still annoyed.

"Mommy, will I really not have to stay? Can I *really* go home again?"

"Of course you can, Ginny. I told you so over and over again."

"Mommy." The little voice was honeyed with an appeal Gladys recognized only too well. Ginny had learned the art of successful apology early, but Gladys never had been able to resist the sweet contriteness of the tone. She looked down and allowed herself a very small smile.

"What?"

"Mommy, I'm sorry. I'm sorry I was bad."

"All right, baby." She squeezed the small hand that wriggled into hers. "Now forget it and behave yourself." The poor tyke. *She's too little. It isn't fair!*

Promptly Ginny dropped her head in her mother's lap, and the tears began to flow afresh, more quietly this time, but no less fluently.

"Ginny, I said *stop it*!"

"Will you come in now?" A nurse, this one in crumpled white, opened the dispensary door.

Gladys stood up and prayed that Ginny would follow without more emotion. When she looked she found the cheeks still wet, but the eyes were dry and, miraculously, alert.

"What's that?"

"That's a very smart machine," the nurse told her. "It knows all about everybody who sits in that chair, and we're going to sit you in that chair, and then we'll know all about you without asking you anything at all."

Gladys braced herself for the resistance and watched her daughter walk over, examine the chair, and announce happily, "You don't have to sit me in it. I can sit in it myself." She scrambled up promptly, and the nurse moved to a switch on the wall and threw a lever. Nothing happened but a gentle humming. Then lights began to flash on the machine. The nurse watched closely, at the same time guiding a piece of tape through a gadget near her side, with one hand, and with the other moving a small lever. Curiously Gladys followed the connections to the lever with her eye and finally located a small glass-tipped tube on the big machine that kept moving in response to the nurse's motions.

Abruptly the nurse switched it off, pulled out the tape, and studied it briefly.

"Pete."

Dr. Spinelli came through a door in the side wall, and the small incident shook Gladys more than anything else. You read about floods and earthquakes and emergencies. You heard of overcrowded hospitals, saw newsreels of corridors like the one outside, but one of the unchangeable things in life, somehow, was that a nurse never, never called a doctor by anything but his title in front of a patient. It was such a little thing, but it told so much more than the soiled uniform, the linenless mattresses, the dirty dishes; or the tired lines on the nurse's face. Gladys remembered the woman's unhurried patience, explaining the machine to Ginny, and marveled at it.

"I think the photoindicator would be a good idea." She showed the doctor the tape, and he examined the little punches on it carefully. "Oh, you haven't used these much, have you? There's a chart someplace." She found it under a pile of discarded tape, a heavy cardboard intricately diagrammed; she fitted the tape across it precisely and handed it back to him. This time he looked it over swiftly and nodded.

"Looks that way. Come on, Ginny, we're going to take some pictures of you." He picked up his helmet and the nurse helped him fasten it back onto his suit.

Docilely the child jumped down from the chair, cast one dubious glance at Gladys, and took a step forward.

"Like at the dentist?" She didn't like the idea of the helmet.

"Same general idea, only more so." He had the visor working now.

She decided in favor of it, and followed him through another door in the opposite wall. Gladys started to get up, but the nurse motioned her back.

"Sorry," she said briefly, "you can't go in there."

"But *why?* What are they going to do?"

"Just another test." She explained no more.

Gladys went back to her seat. *She didn't have to say it that way!* She watched angrily while the nurse looked around, decided there was nothing that had to be done immediately, and sat down. Scientifically and deliberately the woman relaxed in the straight white chair, shifting her position to rest each weary muscle separately, and closing her eyes for a brief, blessed moment of escape from the white light overhead. Gladys' protest died unspoken. *"Pete,"* she remembered, and marveled again at the sustained cheerfulness with which the nurse had treated Ginny. She had to let go sometime.

"I *am* sorry."

She hadn't meant to say it out loud. The nurse's eyes opened to regard her with embarrassing surprise. Then the eyes softened and warmed, and she saw that the woman understood what had impelled the remark. They smiled at each other, and Gladys had an impulse to thank her for being so nice to Ginny, but she left it unsaid. It wasn't necessary.

The girl closed her eyes again, and Gladys sat there, studying her. *"Pete,"* she thought again, and tried to imagine the nurse, fresh and untired, dressed up, out on a date with the strange young man who was so sober and so unexpectedly warm. She smiled inside now, thinking how Barbie's new-found love would have flared into jealousy.

The door opened, and Ginny came out, chattering and blinking at the strong light. Gladys caught a glimpse of a screen and a bulky machine in a darkened room, and then the door was closed again.

"If you'll wait just a few minutes," Spinelli told Gladys, "I'll collect the stuff we need." The nurse came to help him with the helmet, but he shook his head.

"Never mind, Jan." He was scribbling something on a pad of paper. "I won't be here much longer." He tore off the page he'd written on. "Could you do me a favor? Put this through to Supply for me?"

She took the sheet, glanced at it, and looked up, puzzled.

"I wouldn't ask you," he apologized, "but I've got to talk to old man Kallen before I go, and I have to get out fast." He looked significantly at Ginny, and Gladys began herding the child toward the door.

"That's okay. But all this…" Gladys had the door almost closed; the nurse must have thought she couldn't hear. "What are you putting over, Pete? I don't get it."

"Tell you later, kid. It's important, that's all." Gladys was too curious to feel guilty about eavesdropping. "They *need* this stuff." The nurse wasn't convinced. "What the hell do you think *I* want it for?" There was silence for a second, a kind of whispering silence, and then Spinelli's voice again. "For God's sake, keep it under your hat. That's what I have to see the old man about. Now be a good girl and see how fast you can make them move down there."

"Right." All the tiredness had gone out of her voice. Gladys heard footsteps and moved unhurriedly away from the door toward the bench, once more aware of what Ginny was telling her.

"Mommy, he said they were my *bones,* but they didn't look like bones. It was all dark, and shadows…"

Gladys tried to keep her mind on Ginny's prattle, but she kept thinking about the conversation she had overheard. What was it all about? What was wrong with the supplies he wanted? Why did he have to talk to "the old man"? Who was that?

Peter Spinelli was so young, so terribly young, to carry the responsibility that had been suddenly thrust upon him. For just a moment Gladys felt panic, wondering if he knew what he was doing, whether Ginny was safe in his care.

But what can I do? What else can I possibly do? If she only knew more about it…You could tell when a doctor was no good if your child had measles or pimples or a rash. You knew something about those things. But how could you tell now? What was he planning anyhow?

"Lady, do ya know where the toilet is? I gotta go to the toilet, an' I can't find it."

The little boy's voice reached her first. When she saw him she was shocked into silence. She could only shake her head, to show she didn't know. Ginny was equally silent—until the child stretched his hand out from under the rolled-up sleeve of the man's shirt he was wearing.

"Pretty," he said. "So pretty," and reached for the furry muff that dangled from Ginny's coat sleeve.

"Mommy!" It was a whisper, and it was a scream. "Don't let him touch me. Don't, don't! Mommy!"

Bandages covered the boy's arm; but on the active hands they couldn't stay in place. Blood and pus ran from a visible open sore; inside his sleeve the bandage was stained with the accumulation from others unseen. His hair wasn't shaved off, she realized then. There just wasn't any. And there was something wrong with his face, something that made him look as much younger than his four years as the bald pate made him look older. She placed it at last. No eyebrows. None at all.

Ginny was drawing in close to her, shrinking away from the child's touch.

"Are you her mama?" He ignored Ginny. "She's a baby. She acts like a baby. You seen my mama any place?"

"I am not a baby. You're dirty. Go away."

"Shush, Ginny. Would you like me to find the nurse for you?" she appealed to the little boy.

"No, I want my mama. Do you know where the toilet is? I gotta go real bad."

"You wait a minute," she told him. "I'll get the nurse."

"I don't want any old nurse. I want—"

"Don't go away. Mommy, don't *go away!*"

"I—" She didn't want to leave Ginny alone with the little boy, not with that open sore, not with…

She sat down again. The door opened, and the doctor came out. "Hey! What're you doing out of bed?" He surveyed the child.

"Which room are you in? Where's your bed?"

But the little boy was no longer there. He paused just long enough to take in the bulky suit the doctor wore and skittered away down the corridor for dear life.

Around the corner he stopped and peered back, showing only enough of himself to be able to see.

"Can't catch me," he shouted defiantly. "Bogeyman can't catch me!" Then he was off again.

When they went down the stairs the nurse was following the youngster's path of flight down the hall. Ginny was sobbing uncontrollably, and they made no effort to stop her. They had to wait again, down in the main hall, while Spinelli collected an armload of apparatus, the things he had asked the nurse to order for him. Then they were outside, and the empty dark that had been so frightening before was a blessed relief.

CHAPTER TWENTY-EIGHT

THE DOOR FLEW OPEN while they were still coming up the walk in front of the house, and a breathless Barbie ran out to meet them. As soon as they were inside, with the door shut behind them, Gar Levy appeared on the stairs and came down to join them. "How'd it go?"

"About what we thought," Spinelli told him briefly. "I got everything we needed."

So that was it, Gladys thought. Something for him.

"You find the trouble?" Levy asked.

"Um-hmh." He nodded, and didn't explain. Mystery upon mystery. Why did they have to talk in code? Maybe when Ginny wasn't there...

She hung up coats in the hall closet and turned to find the doctor stripping out of his big suit again, with Barbie's help.

"Can I sit on your lap?" Ginny approached the older man.

"That's what I've got one for," he admitted. "How did you like your trip?"

She shook her head vigorously, made what she fancied to be a horrible face, and confessed, "They took pictures. It was dark. He said it was a picture of my bones. But it was all dark. It didn't look like bones." She snuggled into the warmth of his lap, and he looked up at Spinelli questioningly. The doctor answered with a nod, and Levy pursed his lips.

I wish I knew what was going on!

"It was nice riding in the car." Ginny sat up now. "It went fast— wheeee—all the way home."

"You must be all tired out."

"Nope." She snuggled down again with a sigh of contentment. "Your lap is almost as nice as my daddy's. Do you know my daddy? Where is he?"

"Doctor," Gladys asked hastily, "should she go to bed now, or... what?"

"Not just yet," he said thoughtfully. "I think we better take agglutinization samples first," he told Levy, "and we can arrange everything else while they wait." The older man nodded agreement. "For transfusions," Spinelli explained to Gladys, "to test blood types."

Transfusions!

"Is there anything I should do?"

"I don't think so. We'll need boiling water of course."

"What for?" Ginny had been following the conversation as well as she could. Now she was suspicious.

"To wash things in," Gar told her. "You wouldn't want to take any medicine from a dirty spoon, would you?"

"I don't want to take any medicine."

She's so tired, Gladys thought. This was going to be a struggle. But the teacher was laughing, as if the child had said something outrageously funny, and Ginny, finally convinced, joined him. The subject of medicine was, temporarily at least, disposed of.

"I'll start the water," Barbie offered. "Would you like me to make some coffee, too, Mother?"

"Why, yes, I guess we could use it." Gladys quelled her own restlessness and let the girl go out alone. Barbie wanted to be efficient and helpful while the doctor was around to see it. There would be plenty for her to do later, Gladys realized.

Barbara was back to keep Ginny entertained, too, while the men set up their bathroom laboratory again. Surprisingly quickly the young doctor was coming around with alcohol, cotton, and hypodermic needle, collecting neat little samples of blood from each of them. Barbie proudly announced that it wasn't necessary to take hers, because she knew her type, but Spinelli explained that that wouldn't help if they didn't know Ginny's.

"I'm AB," she told him gratuitously.

"Oh." He finished swabbing her arm but didn't stick the needle in. "Are you sure?"

"That's what the school doctor said when they tested us there."

"Well…" He hesitated. "We might as well take a sample anyway. In case you made a—Ginny's might be the same anyhow."

"What's wrong with AB?" She offered her arm. "Why wouldn't you take—"

"AB's pretty rare," he explained, "and it means you can't give blood to anybody except another AB. Do you know what your husband's type is, Mrs. Mitchell? If he was in the last war it must have been on his dog tag."

"B," she answered automatically, without having to think about it. She remembered the dog tag, she could see it around his neck. She hadn't thought about Jon for a long time. How long? Never mind how long. This was no time to start. She could see the metal chain, with the flat coin at the end, swinging forward when he leaned over the sink in the flat near the camp…*Stop it!*

The doctor started upstairs with his collection of tubes. "Oh, Mrs. Mitchell, I think you could get Ginny undressed now. Levy's fixing up some stuff for her. It ought to be ready any minute."

"What is it, Mommy? What's gonna be ready? What is it?"

"Just some things to keep you from getting sick. Let's go up and get into your pajamas, so you'll be all ready to go to bed afterwards."

"I'm not sick," Ginny insisted. "Not sleepy either." But she came along docilely. She was unnaturally quiet while Gladys took her clothes off, then, with her pajama half on, she suddenly twisted around to face her mother.

"Mommy?"

The child was terrified again.

"What is it, baby?"

"Is it—is the medicine—to keep me from being sick like that boy? So I won't get like him?"

She was glad enough to escape when Spinelli remembered they had no blood sample from Veda, and asked Gladys to wake her. She turned Ginny and Ginny's difficult questions over to Barbara and went downstairs to knock on the door of the little room.

Veda wouldn't wake up, and she finally had to try the door. Surprisingly it was unlocked. But where tapping had failed to waken her, the lightest footstep brought her bolt upright immediately.

"What is it, Missus Mitchell? Is Ginny bad?" She was reaching for the robe on the chair beside her when Gladys turned on the light, trying to wrap it around herself under the blanket.

"Ginny's all right, and you lie down," Gladys told her promptly. "Go on, now. The doctor said you weren't to get up." She stopped talking and refused to say any more until the woman put the robe away and lay back under the covers again. "Dr. Spinelli wants to take a sample of your blood," she explained. "He's taking them from all of us, to find out who can give transfusions to Ginny. But he said you're not to get out of bed. He's—"

"Transfusions?" Veda stared at her in horror. "Ginny didn't look near that sick. She take a turn for the worse?" She was reaching for the robe.

"Put that back and lie down. She's no worse than she was. That's just what they do for this kind of sickness. Please, Veda, the doctor specially said you shouldn't get up. You've got to take care of yourself. I can't have *you* sick too."

That did it. Veda lay back again, frowning. "But how's he goin' to take that sample? You jest now said he had to have some of my blood."

"Yes, I did." Gladys tried to sound firm. "But he's coming right down here as soon as I tell him you're ready, and you don't have to budge out of bed."

"No'm. I'd rather get up."

"Well, he ought to know what he's doing. He says you should stay in bed. Now for heaven's sake, Veda, don't be foolish. All you have to do is stick an arm out. I'm going to get him, and I want to find you right where you are when I get back." She turned and left before there could be any argument, but when she got back with the doctor she found Veda had struggled into the robe while she was gone. True enough, she was in bed, but sitting up, and bundled up to her ears. Gladys refrained from comment and wisely did not try to leave the room till the doctor was done. Then she let him go out first and did not close the door till she had given Veda a last warning about staying put.

"We don't need you for anything now, but we probably will tomorrow," she pointed out. "You go back to sleep. I can always come and get you if anything happens."

In the living room she found the doctor waiting for her. There was time now to ask some of the questions she'd been saving up.

"You see, we can't really treat the disease at all," he told her. "There's no way to deactivate an ionized cell. But if we treat the symptoms, just help the body through the worst of it, the damaged cells are eventually replaced, and the patient is all right again. There are several different drugs that are useful. I'm leaving some dramamine in case she gets nauseous again, and Gar has some other stuff."

He rattled off a series of things, most of which, she gathered, affected the blood in some way, and none of which were familiar, except one called toluidine. "That was on the information sheet, wasn't it?" she asked.

"That's right. Gar has all the stuff, and I've given him complete instructions. If I had more time I'd rather show you everything myself, but Gar's familiar with the techniques, and I think it's better to space the treatments—give each drug a little while to work before we shoot her full of a new one. She should get regular doses, and he has it all written down. You don't have to worry about that part of it at all right now."

"Will—will she be very sick? How long does it take?"

"It's hard to answer either one. They're really the same question. It'll take months before she's completely healed—before her hair grows back and her blood count is entirely normal. But how long it will take her to start recovering, or how sick she'll get…it's different with everybody. So far the disease seems to be taking a rapid course, and she hasn't shown much evidence of being affected by it. But when the blood count drops this way—well, we just don't know."

"You said, till her hair grows back. Is it—that is, will it all come out? Like that little boy, the one in the hospital?" She was being as foolish as Ginny.

"No telling." He smiled slightly. "If that was all we had to worry about…As a matter of fact," he went on briskly, "I'm not even trying to do anything about that. I'm worried about her teeth. The hair'll grow back by itself when she gets better. The teeth—I don't know. It doesn't matter about these first ones coming out, but I wish I knew what would happen to the second teeth. Well, a good dentist can worry about that later on. I don't know anything to do about it right now."

"You mean, that tooth that came out…That's part of it too?" She was so proud!

"Oh, didn't you know? I guess that wasn't on the information sheet. It's usually a much later symptom. Anyhow, the thing we have to concentrate on is the blood. That's where the greatest damage occurs, especially in the type of disease she's got."

"What type? What's the difference?" There's so much I don't know.

"That's a tough one," he said. "The diagnosis is inhalation of a fission product, with an alpha emitter lodged in the bones. In plain English, that means she breathed in some particles resulting from the explosion of the bomb, and that the particles were deposited inside her body, in her bone marrow. They're still there, and until they burn themselves out there's no way of getting rid of them. What complicates things is that we don't even know what isotope it is. It doesn't behave like anything I know. It might not even be a uranium derivative, although God knows what else…Anyhow, we'll be able to find that out later on.

"Meanwhile, at least we know what it's doing. An alpha emitter lodged in the bone destroys the marrow and stops production of blood cells. Later on we may have to worry about anemia; that's not serious yet, and we might be able to forestall it with liver extract. I'm leaving some of that too. But the white-cell count is dangerously low right now. The first thing for that is transfusion; after that the stuff I'm leaving will help too. I'll give one transfusion before I go, and they should be repeated regularly—say, every ten or twelve hours. You could give her one tomorrow morning, and another before bedtime, and after that it would be regularly twice a day. Got everything clear now?"

"Practically nothing," she admitted, "but I guess Dr. Levy can explain most of it later on, when there's more time."

He had already risen from his chair, impatient to get started.

"Wait a minute," she asked. "There's just one thing I've got to understand now. Do you mean I'm supposed to give her transfusions?"

Why should he look so surprised?

"Well, of course," he said, "some of them. Unless your type's not right. That's what I took the samples for. Levy can't give any, of course; he'll have to get some. I almost forgot I wanted to tell you about that too." He stopped edging toward the stairs and rested his weight against the edge of the table. "You and Barbie and Veda ought to take turns—if everybody's blood's all right, that is. You won't have to give much anyhow. I guess I made it sound like a lot when I said twice a day. After this first one it won't be more than about half a pint for Ginny each time. You could give that much yourself each time for a couple of days and not have it bother you. Unless..." A new thought struck him. "Unless there was some reason you thought you shouldn't—the time of month, or anything like that?"

"What? Oh no! I didn't mean...It wasn't giving the blood I was worried about, it was giving the *transfusion,* you know, *doing* it. Isn't it awfully delicate?"

His smile was warm again. "Don't worry about that. You have to be careful of course," he explained, "but it's not the major operation it used to be in young Dr. Kildare's day. I'll show you how to do it when I give Ginny hers. And I think I'd better give Gar some, too, before I go. Then, for him, the day after tomorrow would be soon enough for the next. That is, tomorrow, really—Saturday. It's Friday by now, isn't it?"

"I guess so." She hadn't looked at her watch since just before he came, around midnight. Now the hour hand was almost four.

"Look," he said, "Ginny ought to get some sleep. Let's finish up with her first, and fill in anything you want to know afterwards. I think the samples should be ready by now."

But when he had examined the samples he was less cheerful. Levy explained it to Gladys.

"Barbie was right. She is an AB, or it looks that way. And Ginny isn't. Anyhow, whatever the classifications are, we can't use Barbie's blood at all. But I wouldn't worry. You'll be able to give Ginny all she needs if Veda's doesn't turn out right."

"Mine is all right?"

"Yours is fine. There's really nothing to worry about. I was just thinking about Barbie, though. She's going to feel bad about this. She wants to help so much, and she's got this bee in her bonnet about going to the hospital to help out there."

"Has she been bothering you about that too?"

"It wasn't any bother. She has to talk about things. Then Veda's not in such good shape, and you'll need some rest. If Barbie can't give any blood herself, why don't you put her in charge of the sickroom? Let her do the transfusions and take charge of Ginny's shots and general care? I think it might make her feel more a part of things, and take a load off your shoulders at the same time."

"But—she can't manage all that."

"I thought she was doing some kind of child care. She had a baby sitters' club, didn't she? Something like that. She was forever asking about first aid and such in school. That's why she had her blood tested, I believe. She had some notion of being prepared for emergencies. Why shouldn't she be able to handle it?"

"Well, naturally she can help. But I don't think she ought to do anything as complicated as a blood transfusion. She just isn't old enough for that kind of responsibility!"

"I was thinking just the other way round," he urged. "Let her take the responsibility and *I'll* do the helping, if there's anything too difficult for her."

Gladys shook her head doubtfully.

"You ready now, Mrs. Mitchell?" the doctor asked. "We can give her the transfusion and let her go to sleep. Looks like you're elected as donor in chief."

"Think it over." Levy put in a last word.

"All right." She let herself be led away.

The transfusion itself turned out to be simpler than she had imagined possible. The doctor drained blood out of her arm exactly as he had done before for the sample, with the difference that he had her lie down beforehand, and that it flowed into a larger container, in which a small amount of some fluid had already been placed. When he had as much as he wanted he changed the needle and rubber tubing on the jar and took the apparatus into Ginny's room.

"Maybe you'd like to hold her on your lap, Mrs. Mitchell?"

Ginny let the doctor take her arm and wipe it off, and watched him suspiciously while he inserted the needle and taped it down. Explaining each step carefully, he flicked a valve, and the blood began, very slowly, to drain from the upended jar. Ginny squirmed a little and giggled.

"It tickles," she announced when the doctor checked the tape to make sure her squirming had not dislodged it.

Then it was done, and Ginny had only to be tucked into bed, with a scrap of adhesive on her arm, to show where life had flowed in. It seemed a much more serious matter that Pallo had mysteriously disappeared. Gladys hunted under the bed and all over the room, but the horse had vanished. Ginny called his name in vain, decided he had run away because she hadn't taken him along to the hospital, and dropped off promptly into a deep normal sleep.

"You mean that's all there is to it?" Gladys demanded when she was out in the hall again. "I was so worried about giving transfusions. It seemed so—technical."

"The only part that's even a little delicate is getting the needle in just right. And on a child that's easy, as long as you have small needles. The veins are so easy to see." The doctor was doing mysterious things again, with a little tube of blood, in the bathroom lab. He put it down and turned to Levy. "Looks like Veda's a type O, too, so you'll be okay. She ought to be able to spare some by Saturday afternoon, if she takes it easy till then. You don't think she'll have any objections, do you, Mrs. Mitchell? She was very anxious to give some to Ginny, I know, but yours is all right for Ginny, and Veda seems to be the only one who can give anything to Gar—except me, and I don't know when I'll be around."

"No, I'm sure she won't mind." Now it began to penetrate why he had been so upset about the failure of Barbie's sample. He'd been worried about Levy, not Ginny. She was so wrapped up in her own problem, she kept forgetting…

"I'm sure she won't," Gladys repeated. "She's—almost as devoted to him as we are."

"While we're on the subject of admiring me," Gar broke in, "remember what I was talking about before? I was trying to convince Gladys," he told Spinelli, "that we should make Barbie nurse in chief. I think she could handle the techniques all right, don't you?"

"That's a good idea." He kept working while he talked, sterilizing the jar he had used for Ginny's transfusion. "She can do it all right," he added easily. "Might get her mind off the hospital, too. This place is rapidly turning into a hospital annex anyway."

He was silent a moment, concentrating on the work in his hands. "You were right about conditions there," he went on to Levy. "But I don't know what else we could have expected, the way they were piling them in there the first few hours."

"Do you really think she can do it, Doctor?" Gladys asked. "She's so young. I'd hate to have anything go wrong."

"She's not that young. She's good with her hands. And she can certainly manage both patients. She's got this one"—he pointed to Levy—"wrapped around her manicured toenail." The two men smiled at each other, with an understanding that left Gladys out. How could they be so cheerful, at this hour of the morning, with horrors just past still in mind, and the future holding nothing but fear?

"Anyhow, we can find out," the doctor finished. "Let her practice on the boss over here, tonight, and I'll be around to see how she does."

"Anybody want that coffee?" Barbie's voice floated up the stairs.

"Do you need more proof?" The doctor grinned at Gladys. "The girl's not only competent—she's clairvoyant." He put the jar carefully into the boiling water.

"Not anybody!" he called down. "Everybody!"

Pursuit

He was very thirsty. He wasn't hungry any more, and his head had stopped hurting a long time ago, but he was afraid to drink from pools, and afraid to go into a house. He'd had a drink somewhere, but he didn't remember when. He was very thirsty.

It didn't matter, because he was almost home. He knew he could wait for a drink till he got there. The road he was on looked like home. It was pretty white gravel, and now that the sun was coming up the lawns were green on either side.

He had to find someplace to hide. It was getting too light, and now he'd come this far, he couldn't take chances. He was too tired to dodge, and being so thirsty made him dizzy. He didn't always see people coming soon enough.

He'd have to hide, and he didn't want to. He was so close now, he didn't want to wait another day to get home.

"Halt!"

His eyes searched the road ahead, the trees, the lawns, the houses. He needed someplace to hide, to dodge.

"Halt!"

There was someplace up ahead. He began running.

"Halt or I'll shoot!"

He couldn't stop running. A hot poker went through his shoulder. There was a terrifying loud noise, and he tripped and fell.

He lay still. A man's boot nudged him, but he didn't move. The man walked away and said something to another man. He didn't move for a long time, until he was sure the men were gone. Even then he was afraid to stand up. He crawled forward slowly, not caring about the dampness of the ground or the gravelly stones.

CHAPTER TWENTY-NINE

"WHAT ABOUT THOSE—sores?" Gladys asked.

"Well…"

In the pause while the doctor considered his answer they all heard distinctly the sound of the shot outside. It was no longer a novelty, nor even uncommon, but Gladys could not get used to it.

"I know they look awful." Peter Spinelli sipped his coffee and tried to ignore the interruption. "Gar is going to be a gruesome sight in another week or so, unless this stuff I'm giving him takes hold faster than it has any reason to. You were thinking about that kid in the hospital?"

Gladys nodded. All night her voice had been playing tricks on her; now she only used it when she had to.

"Well, if it's any comfort, Gar's won't look so bad, for the simple reason that they'll be properly cared for. You've treated pus sores before, haven't you? This is just more of them all at once. It's an inevitable result of the drop in the white-cell count. There just isn't any way for the body to fight off minor infections. As far as Ginny's concerned…I don't know. We haven't had too much experience with the kind of radiations she got, and if they haven't shown up yet…I just don't know."

He fell silent, and they all waited for him to go on.

"I keep saying that, don't I? 'I don't know.' I wish there was some other answer. You just fix your mind firmly on the fact that those repulsive red blotches are unimportant secondary symptoms. They only become important if they're not kept clean. In the hospital, without enough nurses, that's a problem—particularly with the youngsters, who don't keep their bandages in place and won't lie still. But here…You might have to lance one occasionally. Do you know how to do that?"

Gladys nodded again. "I think so," she added.

"Just like an ordinary boil," he told her. "Aside from that, just keep them clean—by which I mean antiseptically clean, not just free from dirt. And I think I brought some salve in with the other stuff, but I'm not sure."

"We have some penicillin ointment," Barbie put in, "from when I had acne." Even in the middle of the more important conversations, Gladys was startled at Barbara's casual reference to a forbidden topic—*and* in front of the attractive young doctor.

"That should be all right if it's still good," he said. "Or anything else you'd use for a pus pimple or a boil."

"You keep talking about boils." Gladys essayed a full sentence. "Do you think Job got irradiated in the whirlwind?"

The gale of laughter that greeted the small joke was out of all proportion. It must have covered the first knock on the door, because when it died down they heard a steady determined banging from in front.

"Ten past five," Barbie announced. "Who in the world?"

But Gladys knew. "It's Jim Turner," she told them. "He—"

It seemed very funny, and she had to control an impulse to giggle before she finished. "He has seats for us on the *priority* train this morning. He's going to be very annoyed that we can't come." She got up.

"I better get up to my castle in the air." Levy rose with her.

"You stay here, Mr. Carney," the doctor told him. "Let's see. Can you drive a car?"

"Haven't driven one for years, but I used to."

"All right, you're my driver, if anything comes up. You better go let him in, Mrs. Mitchell." The thumping had started again. "Keep him in front if you can. I'll join you if I can think of anything to say that might help. But frankly, I think you can handle Turner better than I can."

The trip to the front door was like walking in a dream. From time to time she would look around and discover she had traversed five or six feet after all; each time it was a fresh surprise.

The banging stopped while she was making the long passage through the front hall. She didn't quite dare to hope that he had gone away. When she opened the door he had his gloved fist raised to knock again.

"Well now, I'm glad to see *you*," he boomed. "Couldn't see a light on anywheres in the front of the house, and I didn't know if your kid was home sleeping or in the hospital or what. You look like they put you through the wringer tonight all right. What happened?"

One thing about Jim Turner, she thought, I don't have to talk. She didn't answer, and he went right on.

"They take her in to the hospital yet?" he asked.

Gladys shook her head.

"Well, I can see just to look at you it wasn't no false alarm. What did the kid say? I called in to him right after I saw you, around eleven. Told the clerk there to get him a relief and let him come right over here. You better sit down, Gladys. You look beat."

He took her arm and led her to the armchair, almost pushed her down into it.

"Now you take it easy," he said, "an' I'll get everything cleared up. But first you got to tell me what the Doc said. I been looking all over for him, but he never got back to headquarters tonight, so I don't know what happened at all."

"Ginny's sick," she said. "We took her to the hospital and found out what it is." Even that much was an effort.

"Well now, I know she's sick, Gladys, but you said just before she didn't go to the hospital."

"No, I meant they didn't—we brought her back."

"Now that don't make sense. You sure she's sick?"

She was too tired to be indignant. Bit by bit, in half sentences, and mostly in small corrections of his statements, she told him most of the story.

"I wish I knew where the kid got to," he said finally. "I don't know what he wanted to bring her back home for. Now we got to get a truck and take her in again. Maybe I can get a car; that would be quicker. That train goes at six-thirty. There ain't too much time."

"But I can't—"

"You can make it," he assured her. "I can get a car here in ten minutes, if I have to, and we can get her all settled at the hospital ill plenty of time. You could even go along if you want to, and get back in time. I'll tell the driver to stick with you."

"You don't understand," she said clearly. Now I have to tell him. Spinelli...no hospital...no train. She listed the things carefully in her mind.

"You're not worrying about your things, are you?" he asked. "If you're not packed up, don't give it another thought. We'll find you everything you need, and with the place boarded up like it is, you don't have to worry about anybody breaking in."

He was trying to anticipate everything. Why, he's being kind, she thought. It wasn't even fair to be so surprised. He'd been kind all along.

"No," she said firmly, out loud. "I'm tired, and I'm not—I guess I haven't been too clear. It's hard to talk," she explained, and added a smile, apologetically. "Just give me a minute and I'll get it straight," she promised.

He waited, and she went over her mental list again.

"Dr. Spinelli's here," she said, "if you want him. He's been with us all night. That's the first thing." She paused to form the next thought into words, and he filled in the silence.

"I kind of thought he'd be here when he wasn't at headquarters, but then I didn't see a car out front, so I figured he was gone."

"He sent the car away. He said he'd get another one when he was done." She remembered. How is he going to say Gar's his driver? He must have forgotten, too, about the car. Now she *had* to keep Turner out of the kitchen.

"I got a bone or two to pick with that young man," Turner said. "Where is he?"

"I don't know. Upstairs, I guess. Wait a minute. Please."

He had already risen. Now he paused. She pointed to his chair, and he sat down again reluctantly.

"Let me finish, please. I have to tell you. I'm not going. I'm going to stay here. I'm going to keep Ginny home and take care of her. She isn't going to the hospital."

"You can't do that," he explained patiently. "You just can't do it, Gladys. How're you gonna take care of a sick kid without gas or electric? What're you going to do for food? How do you even know the water'll keep running?"

"I don't know. I don't know anything, except I won't send her to that hospital!"

"Now, you're getting too excited, Gladys. You got to calm down. I can see how you wouldn't want to send your little girl away from you, but for her own sake, you got to think where she'll be best off. You can't take care of her—"

"Where she'll be best off?" At last her voice had come back. "I saw that hospital! If you think I'd let a child of mine—"

"Now, there's no call to yell at me, Gladys. I told you, you got to calm down. I know just as good as you that hospital's crowded, and things ain't all they might be. Maybe if you saw some of the other places you'd realize how good that one is. We had a good outfit in this district. We were all set up, and we kept things running smooth. But you got to understand it won't be that way after tomorrow. The only place around here that we're hanging onto is the hospital. They'll get supplies, and the folks there'll be taken care of."

"I am not going to send my child to that hospital!"

"Gladys, do you think I'd ask you to do anything I wouldn't do myself? I never told you, because I figured you got enough troubles of your own, but I had to send my own wife and baby there, on account of not having anybody to take care of them at home. They didn't even get exposed, but you know Peggy's been laid up a long time. She couldn't take care of herself, and whether I like it or not, she's better off at the hospital. That's true for your kid too."

"You sent Peggy…?" Gladys stared at him incredulously.

"That's right. Now you see what I mean."

"Have you *seen* that place?"

"I ain't had the chance to get up there, but I was figuring on going up before I transfer to the camp."

She didn't know what she might have said, or what she could have said, if Spinelli hadn't come in then. For a while she just sat still, not even really listening. The men were arguing about Veda, she realized, and about the hospital.

Then abruptly Turner announced that he had to go. "There's still time for you to make that train, Gladys," he told her, ignoring the doctor. "I can arrange for Ginny to get to the hospital, and you could come down and see her as soon as things get running a little smoother." He wasn't pleading or arguing. He just made the statement and waited for her answer.

Exhausted, she shook her head stubbornly and said nothing.

"You sure now? All right, then, I hope you don't mind me telling you a thing or two before I go. I think you're being a damn fool, if you'll pardon my saying so, to listen to this kid. Neither one of you has any idea what's going on in this country. You hear what it says on the radio, and you think everything's hunky-dory. Well, it ain't. Maybe you don't think much of the way we run that hospital," he told Spinelli, "but wait till we're not here, and see how the doctors do it!

"And if *you* think sending Peggy up there was so bad"—he turned back to Gladys—"wait till you get a taste of what it'll be like around here when there's no more controls and no more supplies." He headed briskly for the door. "When you come to your senses," he added, "maybe when you get some sleep"—he softened it a little—"there'll still be patrols around here till Saturday night. Any one of 'em can fix you up with seats on some other train."

He was gone.

The young doctor helped Gladys out of the deep chair. "In my professional opinion," he said gravely, "you need some more coffee."

Gratefully she accepted his arm and went back to the kitchen. She didn't want to talk about Jim Turner. She was glad when he returned to his instructions for Ginny's care, as if there had been no interruption.

"The most important thing is to keep her in bed—aside from the treatments, of course. In a way it would almost be better if she felt worse. Her body needs all the rest it can get. If you have to hold her down by main force, you do it. With three able-bodied adults in the house, that shouldn't be too hard."

"Four," Levy corrected with a meaningful look at Barbie.

"Three," the doctor repeated grimly. "It would be better for *you* if you felt worse too." He turned to Barbara thoughtfully. "A lot of this is going to be up to you," he told her. "Suppose for a start you see to it that the patients stay in bed—I mean both of them. Do you think you can keep your kid sister under your thumb, and the boss here too?"

"I'll try," she promised happily.

He studied her eager face and reached a decision. "Your mother is worn out," he added. "And Veda—well, I'll come back to that. But all in all, it kind of leaves you holding the bag for the next day or two. I'd like to show you how to give transfusions. Then you could take care of the most delicate jobs, until your mother and Veda are ready to help."

"I'm all right," Gladys started to protest, but her voice had stopped working right again, and she had to laugh herself at the feeble sound of the statement.

"Do you really think I can do it?" Barbara was starry-eyed.

"I *know* you can. It only depends on whether *you* believe it."

"I..." She hesitated. "I wouldn't want to take a chance on doing anything wrong."

"You won't have a chance," he assured her. "You can give one to Gar tonight, under my eagle eye. If it goes all right, and I don't see why not, he'll watch you do Ginny's tomorrow. If you feel shaky about it he can do it himself. But he ought to stay put as much as possible, not even exert himself that much. How about it? You want to try bleeding me now?"

"Come on." Levy pushed his chair back and got up, without giving the girl any time for doubts. "I need my pint of blood."

They were milling around, getting ready to go, but there was something else Gladys wanted to ask about.

"Wait a minute," she pleaded. They were quieter, waiting, and it was easier to get everything clear in her mind. I am so tired…"I was wondering, about what Jim Turner said," she told the doctor. "How *are* we going to manage? We've got food for a week, so we don't have to worry about that right away." She forced herself to keep talking coherently. "But he said the electricity and the water—what can we do without water?"

"I think that was mostly bluff," Spinelli said slowly. "They can't stop the water. It would be silly to bother, for one thing, and they'll have to keep it running for the hospital. The electricity might go, though. I don't know…"

"I could probably do something about that," Levy said. "We might have to use candles for light, but I have plenty of batteries in the lab at school, that would run any electric equipment you want to use. Or I could rig up something."

Mr. Fix-it! She smiled.

"*You,*" the doctor said again, "will stay in bed and do nothing. My God, man, what do you think you're made of? Impregnated lead? You can tell somebody else where the stuff is, how to get it, and what to do with it. Doctor's orders," he added brusquely. "Is there anything else on your mind?" he asked Gladys.

"Veda," she said. "What about Veda?"

"Oh yes…Look." He turned to the others. "You two go upstairs and get things started, will you? I want to talk to Mrs. Mitchell a minute anyhow. As far as Veda's concerned," he went on, "I told you she needs to take it easy a day or two, but there's no special care required. There is one thing that worries me, though. I have a hunch the Security officers are going to be here looking for her, either this morning or tomorrow when Turner gets back. He's—a little annoyed at the way I walked out with her. It wouldn't hurt to keep her out of sight until they move their office to the camp. Maybe Gar could share his hide-out with her whenever company comes. If you tell them she just walked out on you and disappeared they'll be very ready to believe it, you know."

She tried to smile. Her face was stiff and didn't want to bend.

"What I wanted to tell you," he went on, and she realized the others were gone, "was about Barbie. I hope you don't think I took too much on myself. It just seemed like the best thing to do." He took her arm and began propelling her through the door, toward the living room. She didn't have the energy to question him or to resist.

"After all," he was saying, "I'm supposed to be the doctor here. You know, a couple of days ago, I wouldn't have had the nerve to take over like that. The very idea of telling Gar Levy what to do!"

They were in the living room, and he steered her to the couch. "But these last few days—well, I'm not the only one. Barbie's been growing up too. You have to realize that. Wasn't there a quilt around here?" he broke off, looking for it.

"I'm not trying to make you go to bed," he explained, wrapping it around her legs, "because I know it wouldn't do any good. But if you don't get some rest you'll be on the sick list too."

Under his warmth she relaxed. What *was* it about that smile?

"Doctor," she asked dreamily, "why are you doing all this? You don't have to take so much trouble. There are other people…so many people…" She thought of the hospital, and a shudder ran through her.

"Why? I don't know." He smiled at the recurrent phrase, but he wasn't joking now. She tried to concentrate on what he said, because it mattered.

"Partly because you took Gar Levy in. Maybe mostly because of that. You don't know what that means to me. I've been going around with Turner from house to house, going back to headquarters, calming hysterics, taking urine samples, making blood tests, giving first aid—and all the time knowing it's come at last—the whole bloody mess is really here, and we've all just been sitting on our backsides all this time, letting it come. All of us except people like Turner, that is. *They* were ready—all set to pick up their big sticks and wave them around playing soldier."

He broke off sharply. "I shouldn't be talking this way," he said. "You're tired, and I've got work to do. Gar Levy is a special person to me, that's all. But even if it weren't for him I'd want to help you. That first evening, when we came in here—honestly, I can't remember anything you did or said that should have made any difference."

He half smiled. "That was four days ago. I'm not the same person now. I can't remember what happened. I do know that I'd had a bellyful of Turner by that time. He went out for a while, looking for someone they spotted in the trees, and all the time he was out I was listening for a shot—like the shot tonight. I know I blew my top, and gave you a lecture for no good reason, and you didn't get angry. I think I blew off because you didn't understand something I said, and I don't know why I should have expected you to. It was something…but it all happened too long ago. I don't know now what it was."

I know, she thought, I know what it was. But it would take too many words to explain.

"…playing soldier," she repeated, and hoped he would understand. "It wasn't funny," she remembered out loud. She wanted to make it clear to him that they had shared the same distaste, that she had been thinking the same thing.

"Mrs. Mitchell," he said suddenly, "this is a silly thing to ask now, but—would you mind telling me how old you are?"

"Thirty-seven." She looked at him quizzically.

He nodded, thoughtful again. "I'm just about halfway, you see—between you and Barbie," he said, as if it explained something. "You go to sleep now, if you can." He was brisk and medical again. "I'll wake you up before I go if there's anything at all to tell you." He took the stairs three steps at a time.

CHAPTER THIRTY

SHE MUST HAVE DOZED off right away, because she remembered he was still in sight going up, and when she looked again he was standing at the foot of the stairs. He had his suit on, and Barbie was holding out his helmet. He seemed to be putting Ginny's blue horse in his pocket. She saw him close the zipper, and Barbie handed him the helmet. They were talking all the time; at least they were moving their mouths, but she couldn't hear anything.

She came all the way awake, trying to decide when she had stopped dreaming. That was silly about the blue horse...

They were talking in low voices so as not to wake her.

"You did fine, Barbara," he said. "I know you won't believe it, but I couldn't have done any better."

She turned her face up eagerly to his smile. "Do you really think so? It'll be all right with Ginny too?"

"That's easier," he assured her. "Just be careful about sterilizing—ask Levy if you forget anything—and that's all there is to it."

"Will you—do you know when you'll be back?" She seemed to be standing on tiptoe, her whole body poised toward him, tense and completely worshipful.

He shook his head, keeping his eyes on her face. "I couldn't say. God knows what's going on back there. But I'll get back here, one way or another, before you people have to get out. I don't know just what I can do about it, but there are a lot of people who'd be willing to help Gar. Maybe they'll have some ideas."

Barbara nodded, looking up to him, waiting.

"He's pretty sick, Barbie—sicker than he says. Take good care of him."

Again she nodded, and silence hung between them. He fumbled with his helmet. "I have to go now. But I'll get back."

She didn't move.

"Pete," she said, and then with a rush, "oh, Pete, I'm so young!" His free hand cupped her chin and raised her face closer to his. Then, with the fierce swiftness of self-conscious youth, he bent his head and pressed his lips against hers.

She didn't touch him. Her hands stayed at her sides, but her mouth clung to him until he wrenched away.

"Cut it out! Oh, God, cut it out!" He didn't say it to her or to any-body. He said it to the world. Gladys knew that; she hoped Barbara knew it too.

Something went *burp* on the radio no one had remembered to turn off. Gladys managed a convincing start. Barbie covered the minute by running into the room to adjust the volume. The doctor had his helmet to keep him busy.

"Five thirty-seven A.M., Friday, May seventh," a hoarse voice intoned. "That is the historic moment. We have just received the official news from General Headquarters. The war is over! The enemy conceded at 5:37 A.M., Eastern Standard Time, just five minutes ago. Ladies and gentlemen, the national anthem!"

Gladys could hardly hear the scratchy record because Barbie was laughing so hard. She sat in the big armchair, helpless with laughter, until it was done. Spinelli went out in the middle, closing the door very quietly behind him.

When she was spent with laughter Barbara went over to turn the radio off. Then they heard the announcer's voice again.

"An important notice: all evacuation orders for suburban areas are temporarily suspended. There will be no evacuation trains leaving for suburban residents until further notice. The war is over, ladies and gen-tlemen. At five thirty-sev—" Barbie's hand closed on the switch.

"Hurray for the red, white, and blue!" she said. "Red for courage and white for purity and blue for Pallo."

Pallo? Then it wasn't a dream.

"What about Pallo?" Gladys sat up and shoved the blanket away.

"What about Pallo? You know perfectly—" Hysteria drained slowly out of her face. "Didn't anyone tell you?" she asked. "Doc found it with his little Geiger counter. Pallo's a Trojan horse, atomic style. He's hot—a one-man radioactive rodeo." A travesty of a smile crossed her face. "Ginny should have known better." The smile twisted. "She left him out in the *rain!*"

Gladys stood up uncertainly, rubbing her arm where it was stiff from sleeping on it.

"Pallo?" She tried the sound of the word, but that hadn't changed. "It was Pallo." She left it out in the rain…she brought it home and went to bed with it…

There was a clear picture in her mind—the worn blue horse and the pink and white girl safe on the pillow together, night after night. *Isn't anything safe? Not the rain or the house? Not even a little blue horse?*

"But the war's *over,"* she said out loud.

Would anything ever be safe again?

Heavy, pounding footsteps on the porch, heavy, pounding hand on the door. She crossed the room and pulled back the bolt, numb to all further shock.

Peter Spinelli pushed past her to the living-room sofa, carefully deposited the limp form he carried over his shoulder.

Gladys took one curious step forward.

"Keep away," Spinelli warned. "I think he's out of decontam. Barbie, go up and get Doc's Geiger." He closed his visor and turned back to the unconscious man, feeling through his heavy gloves for broken bones, aligning the flaccid limbs in more normal positions.

When Barbie came back with the counter he opened his visor to speak briefly again. "Better get some water boiling. He's been shot, I think."

Barbara ran off again, and Gladys watched from across the room while the doctor set up the small machine and angled it every way from the man's body.

"Okay," he said at last. "He's not hot anyway. Poor beggar looks like he's come a long way, though." He took off his gloves and helmet, set to work ripping off the bloodstained shirt. He studied the shoulder wound and grunted, "They just grazed him."

He began pulling things out of his pocket, instruments familiar and unfamiliar to Gladys. Briefly he vanished into the kitchen, to wash his hands and give Barbie the things that needed sterilizing.

Gladys stayed behind, staring with painful fascination at the man on the couch. Step by slow step she went closer, till she could see clearly. She found herself curiously unsurprised. Just once she rested her hand softly on the man's head and felt him stir in response. Then she heard the doctor returning, and retreated to where she would be out of the way.

She waited patiently while he finished his examination. He turned to her at last, relief clearly written on his face.

"I think he'll be all right. I'll clean out that wound as soon as Barbara brings the things, and I don't think there's anything else very serious. They just left him lying there," the young man said sourly. "Shot at him and drove off. They—" He stopped and looked questioningly at Gladys. "He'll need care. He's in bad shape, but he can pull through with care. Of course he might turn out to be another radiation case. The Geiger wouldn't show that. If he is, I'm afraid there's no hope…"

He's not. She knew that much at least.

"We'll take care of him," she told the doctor. *Shock and minor injuries,* the radio said. "We'll take very good care of him." Then she explained.

"It's Jon, you know. He came home."

THE LAST WORD

Many other people besides the editors helped produce this book.

Principal technical support was provided by Dave Grubbs. Deb Geisler, Mark Olson, and Geri Sullivan also provided technical support.

Proofreading was done by Bonnie Atwood, Anne Broomhead, Jim Burton, Gay Ellen Dennett, Dave Grubbs, Pam Fremon, Tony Lewis, Paula Lieberman, Mark Olson, Sharon Sbarsky, and Tim Szczesuil. Lis Carey and myself get the credit for typos missed.

Dave Grubbs did what we thought was the final copy checking but it turned out that we were slightly optimistic at that time.

Steven Silver suggested what proved to be the title for the book.

Tony Lewis provided the bar code.

Alice N. S. Lewis produced the dust jacket.

For those wondering about the omission of *The Tomorrow People* which had originally been planned to be included, space limits and a significant price increase for the book were the controlling factors.

NESFA Press is part of the New England Science Fiction Association,Inc. a non-profit literary and education organization. See www.nesfa.org for further details and a list of available books.

Rick Katze
Framingham MA
May, 2008

Superlative SF Available
from the NESFA Press